THE
UNCONQUERED

★

The
Uncon

BEN AMES WILLIAMS

quered

1953

HOUGHTON MIFFLIN COMPANY

BOSTON ·· The Riverside Press, Cambridge

BOOKS BY

Ben Ames Williams

SPLENDOR

THE STRUMPET SEA

THREAD OF SCARLET

COME SPRING

THE STRANGE WOMAN

TIME OF PEACE

AMATEURS AT WAR (*Editor*)

LEAVE HER TO HEAVEN

IT'S A FREE COUNTRY

HOUSE DIVIDED

FRATERNITY VILLAGE

A DIARY FROM DIXIE (*Editor*)

OWEN GLEN

THE UNCONQUERED

The Riverside Press

CAMBRIDGE · MASSACHUSETTS

PRINTED IN THE U. S. A.

Contents

Preface   *vii*

PART ONE — *The Copperhead*   I

PART TWO — *The Thug*   61

PART THREE — *The Scalawag*   215

PART FOUR — *The Carpetbagger*   349

PART FIVE — *The White League*   563

Postscript   685

Preface

★

Preface

WHEN I BEGAN to write *House Divided*, I proposed to present a picture of life in the South during the War of the Sixties; but I intended, too, to carry on the narrative through the early stages of Reconstruction, following General Longstreet to New Orleans and recording the beginning of military government in what had been the Confederate States.

With this purpose in mind, when in the first draft of *House Divided* I had finished the chapter covering the surrender at Appomattox, I wrote the next chapter through the eyes of Trav's daughter Lucy, who was then sixteen years old. She had spent the winter of 1864–65—in that early version of the novel—with friends in Washington, Georgia, and she was there when Jefferson Davis held there his last cabinet meeting, and when he was captured, not far away, a few days later. So, through her, I was able to witness and to report the last agonies of the Confederacy.

In due time, I explained, Trav and Big Mill went to fetch Lucy home to Chimneys, through a countryside overrun with paroled soldiers and Northern troops and murderous bushwhackers as ready to attack Southerners as Yankees. At Chimneys, she watched while her father contracted with the slaves there for their summer's work. I wrote on toward Christmas of 1865, intending to cover another two years.

But then I suddenly realized that with almost three thousand pages of manuscript in hand, I had gone far enough! If I wrote any more, no publisher would be able to put the whole thing between boards, and no one could read the weighty volume without suffering extreme fatigue.

So I lopped off the hundred pages or so which I had written to follow the Appomattox chapter, and wrote a new ending for the work. But Lucy, by that time no longer a child but a lovely young woman of sixteen, had occupied for a month or two so much of my attention that I wanted to know her better. Certainly she was old enough to have a beau, so I revised earlier passages and gave her young Tom Buford; but in a jealous hope that she would not learn to like him too well, I decided that he had lost several teeth by starvation in a Yankee prison camp. Also, I extended some of the scenes in which she had appeared, particularly a scene or two with General Longstreet, and she assumed identity and substance.

Thus when the book was done and she had gone out of my life forever, I missed her. I had last seen her the day Trav sent his family away from besieged Richmond. She sat with the others in the cart that bore them to the station, the panic-driven mob around them, her head high, her lovely countenance composed. But what happened to her thereafter? Did she marry Tom Buford in spite of his teeth? Did she face the hard years of Reconstruction as steadily as she faced that Richmond mob? Did she, like most Southern people, come to scorn General Longstreet's name?

There were so many unanswered questions; to learn the answers I found it necessary to follow her a little further through the years.

For help in the task of bringing this book to completion, I owe thanks to Thomas R. Hay, of Locust Valley, New York, who allowed me to draw freely on his life of Longstreet after the War years.* My thanks, too, to Miss Louise Guyol of New Orleans, who relieved me of much of the drudgery of reading the New Orleans newspapers of the day. While I was at work on *House Divided,* intending to carry that novel on into June, 1867, P. Victor Bernard of New Orleans had collected for me much of the correspondence leading to Longstreet's ostracism in the South. That now became indispensable. Robert Goree of Aberdeen, Mississippi, furnished manuscript letters written by his father, who was Longstreet's aide during the War and his friend afterward. These letters, transcribed and bound by the University of Louisiana Press, gave details of the General's overland journey to Mississippi after the War, and were made available by Dr. M. M. Wilkerson, the head of the Press, who also permitted my access to the then unpublished Hay manuscript.

An anecdote about Longstreet's service in Tennessee was supplied by Mrs. Helen Topping Miller of Arrowhill Farm, Talbott, Tennessee. F. R. Longstreet, of Gainesville, Georgia, and Mrs. Helen Dortch Longstreet, the General's widow, supplied details of Longstreet's life during the Reconstruction years, and other details came from the memories of the General among his Mississippi relatives.

Through the courtesy of the Board of Commissioners of the Port of New Orleans—and with particular thanks to Richard B. Swenson,

* *James Longstreet: The Soldier,* by D. B. Sanger; *The Politician,* by T. R. Hay.

Captain Adolf Konrad, Captain John A. Rucker of the *Good Neighbor,* and James E. Hubbard—I had an opportunity to see the river for twenty miles below New Orleans, and the river front of the fictitious Paradise plantation which is the locale for some scenes in the book. Mrs. Elinor Robinson Konrad presented me with a copy of the *Louisiana Historical Quarterly* containing useful material.

Mr. Samuel E. Wilson of New Orleans helped me study his copy of Robinson's Atlas, to decide where in New Orleans Trav and his family should make their home. The uptown, river corner of Prytania and Hestia Streets seemed particularly suitable because there is no Hestia Street in New Orleans. The name—Hestia was goddess of the hearth— was suggested by a passage in John Chase's delightful book, *Frenchmen, Desire, Good Children; and Other Streets of New Orleans.* I am indebted to that work for many sidelights on New Orleans history. Published in New Orleans by Robert L. Crager and Company, it tells more that is interesting about that remarkable city than any other volume I know.

For the monotonous labor of typing and retyping the manuscript, I am indebted to Mrs. Lorenz Muther, Jr., and to Mrs. Edwin D. Smith, both of Newton, Massachusetts. Mr. Legare H. B. Obear of the Library of Congress met every request. Mrs. Edward Hanson, of Macon, Mississippi, searched newspaper files to date General Longstreet's visits to Macon. Miss Marguerite Renshaw of the Howard-Tilton Memorial Library at Tulane repeatedly smoothed my path through material there, and Director John Hall Jacobs and the staff of the New Orleans Public Library made the task of reading old newspapers as easy as possible. Dean Pierce of Siler's bookstore in New Orleans found books badly needed for the work.

But despite the kindness of these individuals, the encouragement of my son Roger, and my own persistent efforts, without Mrs. Williams the book could not have been written.

B. A. W.

Searsmont, Maine
October 1, 1952

PART ONE

The Copperhead

★

I

THEY RODE at a footpace, side by side, threading a way among the scuppernongs, and Travis Currain studied the neglected vines, deciding what must be done to bring them back to full productivity. But Lucy's eyes were more often on her father. Trav was a heavily-shouldered man who seemed to stoop a little, yet without actually doing so; his countenance was mild and calm. He pulled up his horse to look at a great vine, ragged from neglect, that sprawled and looped away along its supporting poles, and when he spoke it was quietly, a deep contentment in his tone.

"We used to get over a hundred bushels of grapes off that one vine, in a good year, Lucy," he said. "Yes, and we will again, when we get it pruned and trained, and the deadwood cut out of it." His eyes swept all around. "Lots to be done, everywhere; enough to make a man sleep well of nights."

"You love it, don't you?" Not yet seventeen, Lucy wore the first warm bloom of young maturity. Her head was bare, her bonnet hanging by its strings, her cheek recklessly exposed to sun and wind. A wrap-around riding skirt of yellow nankeen protected her checked cotton dress. Her mare was a chestnut with gold in her coat and hot blood in her clean lines; she walked as though on tiptoe, tripping daintily, sheering away from every rustle of a leaf beside the way.

"I'm glad to be back, yes," Trav agreed. "I never took to soldiering." He had served through the War on General Longstreet's staff.

"I remember when we left here and moved to Great Oak. I knew you hated leaving."

"I went more to please your mother than anything else."

She looked at him with searching eyes, seemed about to speak, hesitated, then said affectionately: "I love it here as much as you do, riding with you every morning, watching you enjoy it, enjoying it with you."

"I expect you do," he agreed. "You take to it. Always did, even when you were little." They came up through the vineyard to the comb of the ridge and paused. Along the slopes below them the hands were transplanting tobacco seedlings, some stooping, some crawling on hands and knees. Tobacco was the most profitable crop Chimneys produced, but it made heavy demands. Even the soil of the seedbeds must be baked under great bonfires to destroy every weedseed and parasite. When Trav and James Fiddler, who had been overseer here before the War, returned after the surrender, they laid out the beds and planted the seeds, and while Trav went to Lynchburg and to Richmond to fetch his family, Mr. Fiddler stayed to oversee the preparation of as many acres of proper, sandy, well-drained soil as the people could tend.

Lucy nodded toward the workers, smiling. "I remember watching them working like that when I was little."

"Tobacco's a slow crop," Trav reflected. "It took two months to grow those seedlings, and now we'll have to cultivate the fields over and over, and hoe them, and do a lot of hand weeding, and pinch off the suckers and the extra buds. All that for another two months. Then we'll top them—"

"What's that?"

"Cut the tops off. It stops their going to seed. And along in October we'll start the harvest." His tone was abstracted, his words running with his slow thoughts. "And after the plants are hung to dry, and fire-cured, and fermented, it will take another two years to age them properly."

While they talked, their eyes swung from the stooped figures of the hands at work below them across the intervening ridges to the big house on the height two or three miles away. Chimneys had been built seventy-odd years before, built of huge bricks burned in a kiln on the place, built on a frame of oak timbers cut on these hills. Trav's grandfather Anthony Currain, who had been a friend of Lafayette and of Washington, added Chimneys to his other properties. The second Anthony Currain, Trav's father, sold it on terms to men who did not meet the terms, and Trav came from Great Oak, the home place near Williamsburg, to live here and restore the exhausted land. A year or two before the War, to please his wife—after coming to Chimneys he married Enid Albion—he had painted the brick walls white; so now the house shone bright in the early sun, and Lucy said softly:

"It's beautiful, isn't it. Why did you ever leave here, Papa?"

"Great Oak was run down." He spoke slowly, for though these things had happened just before the War, they seemed long ago. "Uncle Tony never was a farmer." As the eldest son, Tony—Anthony Currain the third—had made Great Oak his home. "But I'd brought

Chimneys back to bearing, so he and I changed places." He added: "During the War, Uncle Tony shifted Chimneys out of tobacco into corn, but here last December he moved to New Orleans and gave Chimneys back to me."

He spoke in deep content. The War had left most Southern men bankrupt, but Trav—though for the moment he was one of the proscribed—had not only some thousands of dollars in greenbacks, the profit of wartime transactions in tobacco, but also a house on Clay Street in Richmond which as soon as he received his pardon he could sell. President Johnson's amnesty proclamation excluded all general officers and public officials, and all men worth twenty thousand dollars who had voluntarily aided the Confederacy, and Trav fell into the latter category; so till his pardon came he was legally an outlaw, everything he owned liable to confiscation. But he was sure his pardon would not be long delayed, and though Chimneys would yield little for a year or two, he could wait.

From the slopes below them the Negroes began to drift away, and he lifted his reins. "We'd best get back to the house. The agent from the Freedmen's Bureau's coming this morning." The Bureau required planters to make contracts with their former slaves, and must approve those contracts and oversee the signing. This was the business of the day.

Lucy's eyes, as she kneed her mare to follow him, were bright with indignation. "What right have they to boss you around?"

"Well, they beat us. Remember? We're still—prisoners of war, so they can give the orders."

She looked at him in a puzzled wonder. "You don't seem to mind at all. Don't you ever think you'd like to go off to Mexico, or South America, or somewhere?"

"No." His tone was mild. "I know many have gone, or will go, but they're deserters. The South needs her men at home here now even more than she needed them on the battlefield. What I want is to put this good land to work again."

"You could do it better if the Yankees let you alone."

He nodded. "Yes, if they'd tell us what they want us to do with the nigras, and then let us do it, I think we'd get along."

"How long are they going to keep interfering?"

"Not very long, I'm sure. We just want—peace and quiet, and a chance to go back to work, and that's what Northern people want, too, so it won't be long."

"But—how long?"

"Oh, maybe the first of the year. General Schofield says there's no need of keeping Union soldiers here, and once they're gone, we'll be all right."

Her mare danced away from a swaying weed, and Lucy said: "Oh, Nellie, don't be absurd." And she added happily, "I love being here, Papa. I always felt like a visitor at Great Oak, or even in our own house in Richmond. I was born here, wasn't I?"

"Yes." His eyes dimmed with memories. "Yes. Mama was just a year older, when you were born, than you are now."

"Were you both awfully happy?"

"After we had you, yes. Before that, Mama was pretty miserable." His tone made her laugh. "Then she made you miserable, too!"

He smiled. "I was miserable for her sake, but mighty happy you were coming."

They turned into the wood along a foot trail which threaded the underlying thicket of dogwood and redbud, long since past their rich blooming. Trav led, and after a moment Lucy, behind him, asked in a strange voice, as though she were half frightened by her own question: "Papa—do you and Mama love each other?"

For an instant Trav forgot Lucy, forgot everything in lightning recollection. He remembered Enid forever querulously discontented with her surroundings here at Chimneys, forever haunted by fear of having another baby, yet forever forgetting that fear in sweet demanding ardors. He remembered a night after they had gone to live at Great Oak when she announced her intent to leave him, and he had felt at first a sort of shamed relief, and secretly welcomed her decision; but about that time something in him changed forever, and he crushed her into obedience and submission. Afterward, during the War years, when he was often away at the front for months on end, he could not control her every hour; so that which happened, since he knew the hunger in her which could never be long assuaged, did not much surprise him. In his first fury at the discovery that she had given herself to young Darrell, he might have killed her; but afterward he found excuses for her, and so forgave her, and knew again bright glowing hours.

All this, on Lucy's question, he remembered in an instant's time. "Why, of course, Lucy," he said, so quickly there had been no measurable interval between her question and his reply. "What makes you ask such a thing?"

"Well, you don't sleep together." Trav's room was on the first floor, in the front of the house; Enid's directly above his, and next to Lucy's.

"That's just because I keep your mother awake with my snoring."

"Oh, I know. And I know you're married, and married people are supposed to love each other. But—well, Mama gets awful mad at you, sometimes. For making us come back here to live, for instance. But we had to, really, didn't we? You didn't do it just to be mean to her?"

"Why should I want to be mean to Mama?"

"Oh, you're not! You never are! But lots of times she's mean to you, saying mean things, and the way she says them, and all." She said in sudden fierce tenderness: "Sometimes I just want to slap her!"

Trav frowned, deeply troubled. "You musn't feel that way about Mama, Lucy. Husbands and wives have little jokes together, jokes that no one else understands, and sometimes they sound like quarreling."

"It isn't jokes when Mama talks to Peter and me about how mean you are! She's got Peter so he hates you!"

"Oh, Pete and I get along." Yet as he spoke he knew this was not true; he and his son were forever at odds.

They emerged from the timber, and Lucy drew up beside him. "Children see a lot more than grownups realize, sometimes, Papa. And they understand a lot more, too. I remember how Mama used to hate it here, but when we went to Great Oak, she loved it whenever Uncle Faunt came, or Darrell."

Trav held his voice steady. "That was natural, Lucy. Mama's young and gay, and I'm—" He smiled. "I've always been old, and sort of settled down, even when I was a boy. So she and I don't always want— the same things."

She caught at his hand and pressed it against her cheek. "You're wonderful, and I love you ever so much," she assured him. "But I know Mama does like young men. When they're around, she acts sort of gentle and soft—and oh, as if butter wouldn't melt in her mouth. It's just sickening, Papa!"

He tried to laugh aside her words. "I've seen other people do that! You're always specially pretty when Garland Longstreet's around, or Tommy Buford."

Her color rose and she tossed her head. "Well, maybe I am, but Mama's old enough to behave herself!"

"People don't grow old as fast as you think, Lucy. Your mother was born young and she'll stay that way. She's no older than you, really." And fearing this might sound like a criticism he added hastily: "She's a fine woman."

Lucy reached forward with her crop to brush a fly off her mare's neck. "April doesn't think so! I can tell by her sniffs." April was the old Negro woman who had been Trav's nurse when he was a baby, who when they went to Great Oak made Lucy and Peter her charges, who now waited on Lucy's every need. "You know the way she sniffs when she's mad." Trav in a hard, swift anger decided to get rid of April, to sell her, but then he remembered that April was no longer his possession. All the men and women and children who had been his slaves, his property, now were free. That agent from the Freedman's Bureau was coming this morning to supervise his signing of a contract with the Negroes here on the place, and the thought was so absurd that he made a grim, half-mirthful sound. "There you go, thinking about something else," Lucy protested. "I hate it when you do that, start thinking, forget I'm here, go right away from me!" Her laughing eyes flashed to his. "I used to hate having you away so much, during the War."

"I won't need to be away now."

She nodded, and after a little she asked: "Why did Uncle Tony move to New Orleans?" Trav hesitated, and Lucy said teasingly: "Nobody has ever told me, so I suppose that's one of the things I'm too young to know."

"You remember Mr. Lenoir? He used to be one of our neighbors." She nodded and he said: "He was a Union man, and folks around here made it disagreeable for him, so after the Yankees occupied New Orleans in 'sixty-two, he moved down there. Uncle Tony liked him. Maybe that had something to do with it."

Lucy asked in a quizzical tone: "Was Sapphira really beautiful?" He swung toward her and she said hastily: "I know she used to take care of me when I was a baby, but I don't remember her; but Mama says you thought so, till she made you sell her. I know Uncle Tony bought her back and took her to New Orleans with him, and Mama says she wished you had enough gumption to do the same! Move to New Orleans, I mean, or anywhere away from here."

"Don't worry about Mama. She and I understand each other."

She laughed at him. "Well, you don't need to sound so solemn about it! Why are you so serious about everything?" They came to the branch and the horses dipped their muzzles.

"I suppose I've lots of things to be serious about."

"Oh, surely not on a fine morning like this!" Beyond the stream a cart track led up through laurel thickets heavy with bloom. A trumpet flower twined through the branches of the oak beside the stream, and a cardinal flashed down to the waterside to drink, and somewhere not far off a log-cock beat his loud tattoo. "It's no time to be serious!" She flung her mare through the ford. "I'll race you to the top of the ridge," she called, at once in a full run and away.

Trav touched Nig's flank and the big horse responded, bounding half across the ford; but at first Trav did not try to overtake the girl, curbing Nig, staying three or four rods behind, watching her in a fine content. He would have let her win, but Nig's hot blood fretted at restraint and Trav loosed him till he was on Lucy's heels, clods from her mare's hooves pelting back at them. Trav swerved then and sent Nig at a plunge through the thicket and thus cut off an angle of the cart track, emerging abreast of Lucy, holding even with her. For the last few rods they rode thus, full pitch, side by side, till at the crest of the ridge she lifted her hand and pulled up, and he too, and the horses, with flaring nostrils and tossing heads and heaving flanks, danced for a moment and then were quieter.

Lucy was flushed and happy, ordering her wind-blown hair. "Fun?" she demanded. "I love riding with you every morning this way, but you always just walk and walk and walk!" She reached across to stroke his horse's neck. "You liked it, Nig, didn't you." The big black tossed his head and blew.

"Time to be getting home," Trav reminded her.

"I know." But when Nig started forward, she checked her mare, and Trav turned back to face her. "Papa," she said quietly. "Want to do something—for me?"

"Of course. Anything."

"Well let's pretend, whenever we're alone, that I'm grown up. Can we? So we can really talk about everything, anything."

"Why, I thought we always did." He smiled.

"There, that's what I mean. Humoring me as you would a child."

He hesitated. "I don't know, Lucy. There are a lot of things in the world so ugly that I wish you need never know they exist. A lot of things to which I wish we could all shut our eyes."

"But we can't!"

"I'm not sure we can't."

She smiled, touched his arm. "You still think I'm your little baby, don't you?"

"When you have babies of your own, they'll always be babies, children, to you."

She leaned to kiss him. "Well, even if you won't let me grow up— I'm glad you're my father, anyway."

They had breakfasted at dawn, were abroad before full sun, now came slowly homeward in the still fresh coolness of early morning. They descended to the highway and followed it as far as the cart track that led up past the sawmill and through the quarter. The cabins there were all deserted, and Trav said: "Guess the people are already up at the house, waiting for the big doings. Will you watch the proceedings?"

"I certainly won't! I hope I never have to lay eyes on any old Yankee!"

He smiled. "Never's a long time. There are bound to be a lot of them around."

"Well if I ever do see one, I'll pretend I don't!"

There was no one in the smithy as they passed, no one near the poultry yards nor in the shoemaker's shop; but in the open space beside the house, they found the people gathered. James Fiddler came to greet Trav. The agent from the Freedmen's Bureau had not yet arrived, and the overseer explained: "He said he'd come here first off, but like as not he'll take his time, keep the hands loafing around all day." His tone was rather resigned than resentful. He looked toward the waiting Negroes, talking and laughing together in excited little groups. "It's a picnic for them. Look at 'em, talking big!"

Trav dismounted and the overseer took Nig's rein while Trav swung Lucy to the ground. He said affectionately: "Better put your bonnet on before Mama sees you, Honey, you're red as a rose! Specially your nose!"

"I like the sun, and the wind! Why must young ladies be pale?" Nevertheless she adjusted the bonnet, and they walked toward the house together, her hand contented on his arm. They entered by a side door at the ground level, and Trav turned into a room which once had been the kitchen and which he had made into his office. It was stone-floored, low-ceilinged, with half-timbered walls. His desk was here, and James Fiddler's, and shelves heavy with ledgers, and a letter press on a stout stand with a pile of letter books beside it. The deep hearth was still fitted with spit and crane, an oven in the thickness of the wall. Since the room, after a rain, was damp, the fireplace had regular use, and a pile of lightwood lay ready. In the corner behind the woodpile, a commode held pitcher and basin and towel, and Trav went to wash away the dust of his ride.

Lucy had paused in the doorway. "This is my favorite place in the whole house," she said, her eyes moving all around. "Yours, too, isn't it?"

He spluttered through his hands, groped for the towel. "This and the veranda." The westerly facing veranda looked across fertile bottom lands to where the south fork of the Yadkin set a bound, and to mountains beyond.

"Will you sign the contracts in here?"

"It's not big enough to hold all the hands. No, we'll carry a table out into the yard."

"Well, I shall stay in my room till it's over!" She crossed to kiss his cheek. "Thanks for a lovely ride. 'By."

The Currain family fortune, when the War began, was made up of securities, land, and slaves. Belle Vue, on the Northern Neck, was then the home of Faunt, the youngest son. During the War, Faunt rode with Mosby, and before the end he died. Trav was at Great Oak, Tony at Chimneys. Cinda, the older of the two sisters, had married Brett Dewain, and the Plains in South Carolina was her dowry; Tilda, the younger, married Redford Streean, of whom none of them approved, and received as her portion a sum of money and a house in Richmond.

Now the securities and the slaves were gone, but the lands remained. Belle Vue was abandoned, but Brett and Cinda were at the Plains. The big house at Great Oak burned in 1862, but Cinda's daughter Vesta and her young husband had built a cabin there, and as soon as Trav received his pardon he would deed the place to them. When Tony left Chimneys for New Orleans, he wrote Trav a derisive letter of relinquishment, so Trav counted Chimneys now his own. It was true that he had only Tony's letter as title, but when his pardon was granted, he would send to Tony for the proper instrument.

Two or three weeks after Appomattox, he came back to Chimneys and found James Fiddler already here. Since the place was off the beaten track, only three families of Negroes had departed, and under Trav and Mr. Fiddler the others were glad to resume their daily tasks. When Lucy now had gone, the overseer followed Trav into the office, and Trav asked: "All ready?"

"Yes. I'm having a table and some chairs set up outside." Fiddler pointed to a list of names on Trav's desk. "We've thirty-nine hands to sign; twenty-three men, including the boys over seventeen, and sixteen women." And he said: "Then there are three or four other men, Sam—" Sam was the blacksmith. "Sam, and the stocktenders. And what about Peg-leg? We're not running the mill."

"We will be. When we get ready to move the cabins, we'll need some lumber."

"Going to move them this summer?"

"Yes. They haven't been moved for eight years. Gets pretty filthy under the floors, as long as that." Trav fumbled among the papers on his desk. "I had a letter from Brett Dewain. He signed with his people on the sixth, fifty-nine men and seventy women. More women than men. I suppose a lot of his men trailed off after the Yankee soldiers."

"Did they make him sign to pay the old people, or the children?"

"No, just the hands." And Trav reflected: "It averages out, I suppose. The children and the oldsters don't more than earn their keep anyway, the little they do."

"I'm afraid they don't even earn that."

"I know," Trav agreed. "And we've a lot of them here; thirty-six children under ten, and Pete and Vincent, too old to do anything but rake leaves." He said, half embarrassed: "You know how I am about figures. I make our average age sixteen—as near as any one can tell about nigras' ages. And we've eight-nine people on the place—"

"Ninety," Fiddler told him with a chuckle. "Viney had another baby this morning."

"She's a fast producer. Who's the father this time?"

"Oh, she don't ever even claim to know."

Trav said, amused at himself: "Don't know why I say 'good' over Viney's baby. Old habit, I suppose. Her baby doesn't belong to me, not now."

"You'll have to feed it, though. I sent her a blanket and six yards of flannel."

"Yes. Yes, we'll always treat the people as if they still belonged to us."

They talked of the work on the place, interrupted by this great day, and of the excitement among the people, and time spilled away till at last they heard the bell ring.

"That's the Bureau man, must be," Trav said. Isaiah went through the hall above them to admit the agent, and Trav rose, shaken by faint misgivings. He knew enough of the follies committed by Yankees in dealing with the Negroes to be prepared now for ignorance, stupidity, arrogance or insult. But when at Isaiah's summons he went up into the hall, he was reassured. This fair-haired young man, in spite of the uniform he wore, was the sort you liked at sight.

"I'm Lieutenant Page, Mr. Currain," the officer explained, and Trav extended his hand. The Lieutenant seemed faintly surprised, but he took it. "We can go ahead at once," he said, and Trav realized in a faint amusement that the young man was embarrassed. Probably he had received, in the course of his duty, some rude receptions.

He nodded, turning to lead the way down to his office. "Well, we're ready," he said. "But I might explain to you, first, how we're operating. We've made an arrangement that seems to satisfy our people." In the office, they sat down, and he asked: "May I offer you some refreshment?"

"Oh no," the Lieutenant hastily assured him. "I don't want to trespass on your time. The contract is already printed. Sergeant Foster—I left my men at the hitch rail—acts as my clerk. There are just the blanks to fill in, and the signatures." He mopped his brow. "May I send for him, sir, and we'll be out of your way in no time."

Trav bit his lip to hide a smile. He spoke to the overseer. "Will you bring the Sergeant, Mr. Fiddler?" Then, since the Lieutenant sat silent, he said quietly: "We have our people on wages, pay them in cash, once a month. We pay them half their wages, and we've promised to pay the rest next December, after the crops are made." The Lieutenant seemed surprised, and Trav waited till he saw the other would not speak, then went on. "We've been paying the men at the rate of eight or ten dollars, paying them four or five dollars a month. The women are on a five- or six-dollar basis."

Lieutenant Page seemed to feel himself on the defensive. "You're required to furnish them food," he said uncertainly. "And a house, too! And medicine!" He added the last word in hasty afterthought.

"Oh, we're doing that, of course. We always have."

"But do you pay them money? Don't they go off to town as soon as they get it?"

"No. No, most of them ask me to keep their money for them." Trav pointed to a ledger on top of the desk. "Every hand on the place has an account there." He smiled faintly. "They've no real use for money. We give them everything they need—as we always did; cabin, food, blankets, cloth, medicine. We charge them only when we give them money."

Fiddler returned with the Sergeant, and the Lieutenant, after a moment's hesitation, said: "One of the contracts, please, Sergeant?" And when he had it, he studied it as though he had never seen it before. "Well," he said uncertainly: "This is what you're supposed to sign." He handed it to Trav. "Read it, will you please?"

Trav nodded, and his eyes ran along the lines, and now and then he read a word or two aloud. " 'Witnesseth.' " He looked at the Lieutenant, smiling. "They'll like that word. One of our women had a baby this morning. I expect she'll name it 'Witnesseth.' " The Lieutenant looked embarrassed, and Trav read on, half to himself. " '. . . said undersigned laborers . . .' Do they all sign this?"

"They're supposed to." Lieutenant Page did not seem sure.

Trav unfolded the long sheet. "Well, I see there's room enough. This runs till January, eh?"

"Yes. You're supposed to make a contract every year."

Trav read, mumbling the words, with many pauses: " '. . . shall not be absent from the plantation without permission . . . good behavior . . . punishment . . .' Who does the punishing?" he asked.

"We act, on your complaint." The Lieutenant added apologetically: "At least, that's the way it's supposed to work."

Trav's eyes twinkled, but he did not smile; his eyes returned to the paper in his hands. " '. . . supply lodging . . .' Well, I'm doing that. '. . . subsistence as usual.' Yes. '. . . medicine and medical attendants . . .' Well, our cook is our midwife, too, but if a doctor's needed we fetch Doctor Towle from Martinston. Preaching? We have a minister here every two weeks, and a church building down in the quarter." He looked up. "By the way, Lieutenant, while you're here, you'd better inspect things down there. We may not be doing what you want."

The Lieutenant wiped his beaded brow. "Mr. Currain, I'm sort of surprised," he admitted. "The other planters haven't seemed so—ready to co-operate."

"Well, you know," Trav reminded him, "it's not easy to take a licking, nor to be told what we're to do with our nigras by men who aren't familiar with the problem. So some of us take it hard. If you tell us in general terms what you want us to do, we'll try to do it; but when you start telling the nigras what you're going to make us do, that just makes trouble for everybody." The other did not speak, and Trav glanced through the remainder of the contract. "This specifies paying them their share of the crop in December. That would suit me better, of course, but I think our people would rather have some of their money, if they want it, right along."

Lieutenant Page drew a deep breath. "I'll write in a new paragraph covering that," he decided. "May I use your desk?" Trav made way for him, and Page seated himself, and then looked up with a sudden smile: "A few more gentlemen like you, Mr. Currain, can make me like this job." Trav decided his first impression of this young man had been right; it would be easy to like him.

When Lucy left her father in his office, she went to the pantry to portion out to old Maria, who presided in the kitchen, the supplies that would be needed for the day. Since their return to Chimneys, Lucy's mother, sulking at the prospect of living out her life in this remote solitude, had flatly refused to direct the business of the household, and Lucy had assumed that duty. Maria, at first laughing at the notion that Little Miss could keep the keys and plan each day's tasks, quickly became Lucy's slave, and since the old woman had over the Negroes on the place a mysterious domination, into the source of which the white folks were too wise to inquire, Lucy's path was made smooth for her.

Her business with Maria done, she turned back into the big house. Her mother often slept till noon. Peter had breakfasted with them; but when she and her father went to their horses, he disappeared. When he and Lucy were children here, before the War, a Negro boy named Bob had been their guardian and servant, and Bob's sister Quinny, a year or so younger than Peter, usually tagged along. Peter and Bob were still partners in every enterprise, and Lucy guessed now that Peter was off with Bob.

In her room she found April sitting at the window. The fat old woman heaved herself out of the big chair and greeted Lucy in an affectionately scolding tone. "High time yuh come in out o' de sun, Missy. Jes' look at yuh; red as some white-trash woman bin hoeing in de cawn fiel'. De sun, and de heat f'om dem hawses, you might full as well stan' oveh de stove all day. Heah, lemme git yuh out o' dem close!"

Lucy submitted to her ministrations, stepping out of underskirts and underbody and chemise, splashing in the tub, tucking up her hair while April briskly wielded the harsh towel. Afterward the old woman would have brushed her hair for hours, but Lucy insisted on getting dressed.

"And do hurry, April. I want to watch. Haven't I anything better than this ragged old blue muslin? Every flounce is torn."

"I'se mended 'em twell dey lak lace, Missy. Hol' still."

"And my hoops, April! I want to look my best."

"You ain' gwine let no Yankee man lay eyes on yuh, is yuh?" April stepped back, hands on hips. "Ef yuh is, you fix y'own se'f!"

"Why, April, of course not! But don't be so scornful! This Yankee's making Papa sign a contract promising to take care of you."

"Huh! I tuk keer o' Mars' Trav 'foah he et out of a spoon, and I'se gwine keep on doin' it. He don' tek keer o' me. I tek keer o' him."

"Well, the Yankees say you have to have a contract, so Papa won't cheat you."

"He ain' cheat me yit! Lemme ketch him at it!" April stood back to admire her handiwork. "Now you look moah lak a young lady b'longs tuh look!" Lucy turned toward the door, and April challenged. "Whah you gwine?"

"To wake Mama, so she can watch. Where's Peter?"

"Him! Dat limb o' Lucifer, he be'n up an' gone sence sunup."

"Gone where?"

"Ast me no questions, I'll tell you no lies. Gone whah he no business, da's sho!" She sniffed eloquently, and Lucy laughed.

"Oh, you don't know any more about it than I do!" She went along the hall to the big front room and opened the door. Her mother was curled small under the sheet, her hair loose across the pillow and touched by the sun. Enid seemed asleep, but Lucy went in, closing the door behind her, humming under her breath, crossing to the windows, to the table, to the chair where her mother's discarded garments lay. Her low hum became a half-whispered song. " '. . . maid with golden hair.' '. . . swallows in the air.' "

Enid stirred. "Oh, all right, I'm awake! What is it?"

"I knew you'd want to see the Freedmen's Bureau man."

"For heaven's sake, why?"

"We can watch from your window here. But he hasn't come yet."

"I should think not! The crack of dawn! Go away! I want to sleep!"

But even while Enid protested, she sat up, swinging her feet over the side of the high bed, yawning and stretching. She could still, when her hair was ordered and laughter in her eyes, be beautiful; but now she was frowsy and disheveled, her eyes dull, her hair lifeless, her cheeks sagging. Lucy looked at her in a strong distaste. "Mama, why don't you ever get up for breakfast? Or at least be up and dressed when Papa and I come back from our rides?"

Enid looked at her in a cruel anger. "Why, Lucy, when I'm with you and your father, I feel such an outsider!" She had always resented Lucy's fondness for her father, and Trav's for Lucy.

The girl ignored the jibe. "You're so pretty and sweet when you want to be. You'd be lots happier if you kept busy, running the house and everything."

"Why should I?"

"Well, you're supposed to, for one reason. You're Papa's wife. You're the lady of the house."

Enid shook her head. "Not his wife, child. I'm just a conquered province." But before Lucy could speak she cried, looking out of the window: "Oh, here they are, Lucy! They're coming up the drive." She rose to draw the curtains across the window by her bed, and Lucy crossed to her side. Themselves invisible, they watched the approaching riders, four men in blue uniforms.

"Why, they're soldiers," Lucy exclaimed. "And with guns! See!"

"Guns? Of course! They're still afraid of us!"

The soldiers, riding two and two and still some distance off, passed briefly out of sight where the drive curved around a clump of trees. They reappeared, coming directly toward the house, and before the overhang of veranda hid them, Lucy whispered: "Mama, that one in front would be real handsome, if he weren't a Yankee!"

"Hush! Listen! They're coming up the steps! Coming to the front door! The impudence!"

The bell sounded, and Lucy darted to the bedroom door and opened it a crack, and heard Isaiah come through from the kitchen. As he opened the front door, she stood on tiptoe, trying to look down into the lower hall, but she could only see the top of a man's head, fair hair with a damp wave at the temple where a hat brim had rested, a glimpse of brow and cheek and ear. His voice when he spoke to Isaiah had a friendly sound, but her heart pounded so hard she could not hear the words. Isaiah went to summon her father, and Lucy wished she might step out where she could really see this visitor, but dared not. Trav came up from his office, and she heard the young man introduce himself. Softly, she closed the door.

"They've gone downstairs, Mama," she reported. "His name's Lieutenant Page." She crossed to the window that overlooked the yard, and Enid put on a cap, stuffing her tangled hair into it any old way, and drew a wrapper over her nightgown and came beside her. A table and chairs had been set against the side of the house, directly beneath their window and two stories down, and around it the waiting Negroes were gathered. Lucy brought two occasional chairs, and she and Enid— secure against being seen, since no one looked up—settled to silent watching.

But for long minutes nothing happened. The Negroes stood in nervous groups, their eyes fixed on the door and the windows that led into Trav's office. Enid, in a sudden impatience at the delay, went to lie down again, but Lucy did not relax her attention.

When at last Mr. Fiddler and a soldier came out of the door below where she sat, and the soldier seated himself at the table and the

Negroes pressed nearer, Lucy signaled her mother, and Enid joined her. The Negroes stared, and nervous waves of giggling ran around the circle, and Mr. Fiddler and the soldier talked in low tones. At a word of direction from inside Trav's office, spoken through the window, the soldier went to the corner of the veranda and summoned his companions. They took post, one at either end of the table. Then Trav and the officer came out of the house, and Lucy trembled so violently that she was afraid her teeth would chatter.

"They're going to begin!" she whispered, her hand tight on her mother's arm. Enid brushed her off.

"High time they did," she muttered.

Trav, the Lieutenant standing beside him, spoke to the waiting Negroes. "I expect you people know what this is all about."

Someone shouted, in a huge relief from the long strain: "Yas suh, Mars' Trav! Day o' Jubilee!" Grins and chuckles and a warning "Hush, man!" answered him, and Trav went on: "You know the way things are now, here on the place. Well, we're going on in the same way, but we're going to put it all in writing, here, now, today. Lieutenant Page has come to tell you all about it, and to see that everything's in order, and then we'll all sign the paper."

"Yas suh, yas suh!" There was chuckling agreement, and one of the young hands shouted: "Fawty acres an' a mule. Da's foah us!"

Lieutenant Page held up his hand, and he spoke for the first time. Lucy, directly above him, could see nothing of him except his hat with its cord, his shoulder bars, the blue of his uniform. "No one's going to give you forty acres of land; no, nor a mule either," he warned them, his voice firm. "Whoever told you that was trying to fool you, trying to get your hopes up. No one's going to give you anything. If you want land, the Bureau will arrange for you to lease forty acres of abandoned or confiscated land somewhere, but there's none around this neighborhood. You'll be better off staying right here, working for Mr. Currain, living on in your old homes."

Trav said something to him in an undertone. Lucy could not hear what they said, but now Trav spoke. "If any man wants some land of his own," he promised, "I'll give him as much as he can work and still do his work for me." And he added: "You all know I keep my promises."

"Da's so! Yas suh, da's sholy so!"

Trav stepped aside, and Lieutenant Page unfolded the paper in his hand. "I'll not read this contract to you," he told the attentive listeners. "It's full of long words you might not understand." Laughter answered him. "But this is what it says. It says that you promise Mr. Currain that you'll go on working for him, doing what you're told to do by him or by Mr. Fiddler—" He looked aside toward the door, and Lucy guessed that the overseer stood in the hallway there. "Till January first.

Besides that, you promise you won't leave the place without permission. Understand?"

"Yas suh!" "Yas suh!" The assents came from all sides, but someone challenged: "Whut he promise us?"

"Mr. Currain promises that you can live on in your cabins as you've been doing, and he'll provide you with food and medicine and he'll pay for funerals, and get you a preacher twice a month, and he'll try to get a school started somewhere near, for your children." He looked at Trav, then went on: "And he'll go on paying you wages, half at the end of every month, and the other half in December."

He studied the papers in his hand. "I think that's all. Now remember, you don't have to sign this contract, but if you do, you have to live up to it, or you'll be in trouble with me!" There was a good-humored chuckle in his tones. "If you don't, as we say down in Maine, I'll bring you up with your toes a-digging."

They laughed in delighted agreement, and Lucy whispered to her mother: "I wish he'd take his hat off. I wish I could see what he looks like!"

"Don't laugh too hard," the Lieutenant warned them, his voice stern again. "If Mr. Currain has any trouble with you, he'll send for me, and I'll tend to you." A doubtful chuckle answered him, and he said: "Now you step up here and make your marks."

He moved back and the Negroes pressed toward the table, at first lagging a little, and then with sudden laughter and shouts, some giggling like children, some solemn as owls. Mr. Fiddler and the Sergeant came to the table and Trav and the Lieutenant moved out of Lucy's sight into the lower hall.

"Now we're ready to begin!" Mr. Fiddler told them. "The ones that are going to sign, get up front here; the rest of you keep back and give them room." He looked at the list in his hand. "When you hear your name, step up to the table." The Sergeant had taken his seat there, the long contract spread before him, an inkstand near, a pen in his hand, and Mr. Fiddler, standing at his shoulder called a name. "Jim."

A quick stir ran through the crowd, and a wiry little man stepped forward and took off his cap. His black scalp shone through his scanty hair. The Sergeant pointed the pen at him accusingly.

"Jim who?"

Jim giggled in embarrassment. "Jes' Jim, suh!"

Mirth ran through the crowd behind him, shrill shrieks of laughter from the women, chuckles from the men. The Sergeant looked doubtfully at Mr. Fiddler, but the overseer said: "Most of them just have one name."

The Sergeant looked at Jim. "Can you write your name?"

"Naw suh, not me," said Jim.

So the Sergeant wrote, then extended the pen. "All right, put a cross right here." He pointed with his finger.

Painfully Jim made his mark; the Sergeant took the pen; Mr. Fiddler called another name, and the proceedings fell into a pattern. The Sergeant challenged each in turn. "Name?" Usually it was only a given name: Jim, Henry, Dicey, Eve, Dennis, Patty, L. Sam,—that was Little Sam; B. Sam was Big Sam, the smith—Zebah, December, Melia, Scipio. But once or twice there was a variation. Lucy heard Peg-leg answer: "Joseph Albion, suh!" She thought he must have named himself after Enid's mother, Mrs. Albion, who had visited them here before they moved to Great Oak. Bill, the driver, called himself Billy Driver, but for the most part the names were simply Titus, Nanny, Tyra, Reveal, Polly, Bib.

The Negroes were slow and awkward and desperately serious about this business of making their mark. They bit their extended tongues, they gripped the pen so tightly that the muscles in their forearms knotted with the strain. One man and then another pressed so hard that the nib required to be repaired or replaced, one man dropped the pen in the dust, to the hooting derision of the watchers. The signers were at once tensely serious and grinning too, embarrassed targets for half-fearful jeers from their watching fellows.

Once the routine was interrupted. A hand named Bib, about to scratch his mark on the contract, hesitated, stood up and looked toward the doorway where Trav and the Lieutenant stood watching. Silence fell all around, and Bib visibly sought words. Trav after a moment prompted him.

"What is it, Bib?"

Bib's brow wrinkled. "Mars' Trav, s'pos'n Ah don' want t'do dis heah?"

"Then you don't have to."

"Ah mean t'say, s'pos'n Ah don' want tuh wo'k foh y'all no moah?" Bib scratched his head, frowning at his own dilemma, and he added hurriedly: "Ah does want to, Mars' Trav; but jes' s'posin' Ah don't? Whut Ah do?"

A howl of laughter burst from his listening friends, but Trav said gently: "If any of you don't want to work for me, don't want to stay here, no one will make you do so. If you do want to stay, you put your mark on the contract there, and live in your cabin and work—the way you always have." He added, sudden amusement in his tone, "But don't make any mistake about it; if you don't want to work, pick up your feet and go!"

Bib said contentedly: "Yas suh, da's whut I want to know." He leaned down to make his mark, and the work went on.

Lucy had till then been amused by the scene below, but now it took on a profound solemnity. She thought it was like a marriage, or a baptism. These ignorant people, till today only a little higher than the animals, now scratched a cross upon a sheet of paper and by the act became men; this, their first wholly voluntary decision as to what their lives should be, lifted them out of one estate into another. In the past they had been bound by law, and without their own consent; this new bondage they accepted of their own free choice. They could reject it if they chose. The act of making their mark was their first step into the world of free men. Henceforward they could stand erect, masters of themselves and of their lives.

Bib made his mark, and others followed him, and Lucy's thoughts took their own course. The signing went on, and she watched heedlessly, till a half-grown Negro boy, more brown than black, came running up the hill from the quarter. Lucy recognized Bob. When a few weeks ago they all came back to Chimneys, Peter, now a tall youngster almost fourteen, had at once attempted to reassert his youthful dominion over the other boy. Bob sought to rebel, and but for Trav's stern intervention Peter would have enforced his orders with a whip. "Bob can be with you as much as he wants to," Trav warned his son. "But not unless he wants to. You're not his master any more."

When Bob now came racing past the corner of the smokehouse, Lucy expected to see Peter on his heels, but her brother did not appear. Bob's first rush broke through the contracting circle of Negroes, and the Sergeant at the table looked up with a warning.

"Hold on there! What's the hurry?"

"I wants tuh sign. I ain' gwine be nobody's slave!"

"Of course not, but wait your turn. We'll come to you!"

"Yas suh. But Quinny—" Bob looked uncertainly around, then saw Trav in the doorway. "Mars' Trav, Mars' Peter kep' us down't the mill, me and Quinny. He tie me up. He say he ain' gwine let me sign. He say he gwine keep us his slaves! I wiggled loose de rope, but he still got Quinny!"

Lucy heard her father's voice. "I'll send for her, Bob. And you can sign, but you understand that means you work in the fields, instead of playing with Peter."

"Yas suh! I'se grown up, Mars' Trav. I'se too old tuh play wid boys."

Trav gave Mr. Fiddler a nod of consent, and the overseer added Bob's name to the list in his hand and gave the list to the Sergeant. Then he departed toward the sawmill, and Lucy whispered to her mother: "I declare, Peter ought to be whipped! Making trouble for Papa, today of all days."

"Peter's growing up, child," her mother said casually. "Quinny's a pretty little packet, and boys and men are all the same." Lucy stared at her, astonished, and Enid rose. "I'm going back to bed. Go into your own room, will you, so I can sleep? After that nonsense is over down there, tell April I'm ready to get dressed."

So Lucy was watching from her own window, April beside her, when Mr. Fiddler presently returned. Quinny, a neat and cheerful brown girl of twelve or thirteen, who except when she slipped away to be with Bob and Peter helped old Maria in the kitchen, walked demurely beside him, but Peter did not appear. Quinny joined some of the older wenches in the circle around the table, and they whispered and giggled together.

Lucy resented something impudent and provoking in the girl's bearing, and she realized with a sudden clarity that she did not like Peter; no, not even though he was her own brother! She remembered how while they were in Richmond during the War he was forever slipping away to watch the shooting of deserters, or the hanging of spies, coming home to detail these spectacles to her, and delighting in her shuddering repugnance. She shook her head now to banish that memory. Lieutenant Page came out of the house and spoke to the Negroes, and Trav told them the signing was over, and they drifted away toward the quarter. Page and her father strolled toward the front of the house. Lucy had not yet seen the Lieutenant's face, so she darted swiftly down the stairs to one of the tall front windows, drawing the curtain a little in order to watch them when they came to the hitch rail, and herself remain unseen.

The front veranda was high above the ground, so when her father and the Lieutenant did come into view, they were below her, and the Lieutenant's hat still provokingly hid his brow and almost completely hid his eyes. But she saw that he had a nice straight nose—for a Yankee—and a crisp small mustache, and a smooth chin. Then when he shook hands with her father he bared his head as politely as anyone. So, Yankee or not, he knew his manners. She thought his brow fine and his hair beautiful, and wished she were near enough to see his eyes.

He swung into the saddle, his men mounted, and at a walk they moved away. Trav stood watching them depart, then came slowly up the steps, and Lucy met him on the veranda, linking her arm in his.

"There, Papa, was it awful?"

"Eh? Why, no! No, that young fellow's all right. I rather liked him. Lieutenant Page. Donald Page." He looked at his watch. "Hullo! I didn't know it was so late. I should have kept him for dinner."

"Papa! Don't say such things! Expect me to sit down at table with a Yankee?" But there was laughter in her tone. "Unless, of course, he's young, and handsome, and gallant."

He slipped his arm around her, laughing with her, and they turned indoors. "Next time I'll make him stay," he said.

2

Summer and Fall, 1865

THROUGH THAT SUMMER after Appomattox, all across the South, Negroes singly and by families and in bands roamed aimlessly, savoring their freedom. Sometimes their former owners had abandoned any hope of keeping up the big plantations and left the Negroes who had been their slaves footloose and hungry; but even when men like Trav sought to bring the land back to cultivation, it was hard to keep the Negroes at home. From Chimneys they might drift off to Martinston, or to the Shandon plantation, or the Pettigrew place, for a visit with the Negroes there. Not only did the Chimneys people wander about the countryside, but they had many visitors. There was a steady trickle of travelers along the highway, travelers bound nowhere in particular. "Jes' up de road a piece," was the usual answer, when Trav, finding one or a dozen of them gossiping with his people down in the quarter, asked where they were going. All over the county—and all over the state and all over the South—the Negroes were on the move, wandering cheerfully, drawing rations from the army or the Freedmen's Bureau, sleeping where they could.

Inevitably every planter or farmer or householder lost an occasional chicken or turkey or goose, or even a suckling pig. The *Raleigh Standard* reported the frequent retaliations. A white woman named Temperance Mealy, down near Salisbury, shot and killed a Negro who forced his way into her home, and a Mrs. Ball was tried in Raleigh on a charge of murdering a freedman who stole her chickens. Whenever Trav rode into town, stopping to exchange the news of the day with his friends among the small farmers along the way, he heard report of local depredations, and felt in these men an increasing readiness for violence.

One morning in August, Tom Shadd, whose house was next beyond Ed Blandy's on the road to Martinston, riding his big mule that could trot faster than most horses could canter, came to ask Trav's advice. "I'm in a little trouble," he explained. "I'd like to find out what you think I'd better do."

"Come inside," Trav invited, and led the way into the office. He whittled a nubbin of tobacco, and passed the twist to Tom. Shadd was a lank, lean man with a conspicuous Adam's apple. When now he spoke, his words came in a steady flow that testified to his anxiety.

"It's Ma, mainly," he said. "Our well's gone dry, and I was down t' the spring by the branch, getting some water." Tom and Mrs. Shadd had raised a daughter and two sons—four other babies had died in infancy—but their children were married now and gone. "These four nigras come by, two men and a woman and a half-grown boy. Ma see 'em coming along the road, so she put my old musket handy, right inside the door. They 'lowed they was hungry. Mostly she'd have give 'em a plate of something, but they didn't look hungry, kind of watching her, and grinning, so she told 'em to go on about their business. One of 'em made as if he was going to come in the house. She grabbed the gun and backed off, but he kep' coming, and the others kind of egged him on—so when he come inside the door, she shot him."

"Killed him?"

"Dead as a rat! Yup!" Tom grinned at a sudden memory. "I heard the shot and come a-runnin', and when I see what had happened, I thought she'd be upset, so I set out to pet her and tell her not to worry and all that, and she says: 'Worry?' she says. 'I ain't a-worrying! Good riddance to bad rubbish! Now drag him out of here so I can scrub up my floor!'" Trav chuckled with him, and Tom said: "So I did. I laid him out under the apple tree and put a sack over him agin' the flies, and then come to see what you think I'd best do. Bury him somewhere?"

Trav shook his head. "No, I'm afraid not. The others ran away?"

"Judge so. They was gone, time I got to the house."

"Well, they'll go to the Bureau and tell their story, so you'd better get ahead of them and tell your story first."

"Do they have to know it was Ma? I could say it was me."

"Best tell the truth," Trav advised. "Freedmen's Bureau doesn't have an agent nearer than Salisbury, but you and me, we'll ride to town and tell Judge Lowman about it. After we talk to him, likely you can bury the man, and the Judge will write a report to the Bureau. Or I will."

"What'll they do?" Tom grinned. "They try to take Ma to court, they'll git an earful."

"Lieutenant Page struck me as a reasonable young man," Trav assured him. "I think it will straighten out all right."

They set out at once for Martinston. Chelmsford Lowman, for many years postmaster, had succeeded Judge Meynell as justice of the peace, and he was a person of authority, since the justices not only presided in the lower courts, but had full charge of roads and of schools. Judge Lowman, having been Postmaster under the Confederacy, was not included in the general amnesty; but when he repaid out of his own pocket post-office funds which at the beginning of the War had been confiscated by the Confederacy, his pardon was prompt.

When they consulted him, he agreed that to report to the Bureau was the proper thing to do; in the meantime the dead Negro could be buried. Trav offered to let him be interred in the Negro burying ground at Chimneys, and undertook to find a preacher. The Judge agreed, and he suggested that Trav write the report to the Bureau. Trav did so, and they both signed it.

When this business was done, the Judge asked: "Seen the Gov'nor's proclamation, Major Currain?" Trav shook his head, and the Judge explained. "Well, it's for delegates to a Convention to meet the second of October, to do whatever we have to do to get back into the Union." He leaned aside to spit an eloquent brown stream into the cuspidor by his chair. "I thought some of sending you." To designate candidates for the Assembly was a function of his office. "If I put you up, no one'll run against you."

"Wouldn't do," Trav assured him. "I haven't been pardoned." While he and Enid were in Richmond in May, he had presented his application for pardon to Governor Pierpont, who, having set up under Union protection a provisional government at Alexandria early in the War, had after the surrender moved his capital to Richmond. The Governor promised to give the matter early consideration, but Trav had heard nothing from him till a fortnight since; then Governor Pierpont returned the application, saying that since Trav's home was not now in Virginia but in North Carolina, it should be endorsed by Governor Holden.

Trav disliked asking any consideration from Holden, whose editorials in the *Standard* during the War had seemed to him to be an incitement to desertion; but he forwarded his papers to Raleigh with a brief covering letter. He had had an acknowledgment from the Governor's office, but nothing more, and he explained this now to Judge Lowman. "So I'm not qualified."

"Your pardon will be here before October."

"I won't count on it." Trav smiled. "If you sent my name in for a delegate, the Governor would think I was taking a lot for granted. No, I'm afraid not."

Their business done, they rode homeward. Trav stopped for a word with Mrs. Shadd—who assured him she never worried about killing a nigger now and then—and Tom shook his hand with an eloquent vigor. At home, Lucy asked where he had been, and, when she had heard his errand: "Do you think they'll arrest her?"

"I sh'd doubt it." Trav added, a twinkle in his eye: "But I expect Lieutenant Page'll come up to look into it. If he comes, we'll keep him to dinner! You and Mama'll have to be nice to him."

"I can just see myself being nice to a Yankee!"

"Wouldn't do it myself, only to help out Mrs. Shadd."

"Well, maybe, for that," she agreed, and she asked: "Do you really think he'll come?"

"I think he will," Trav decided. "Yes, he surely will."

Lucy, though she did not admit this even to herself, looked forward to seeing Lieutenant Page again. When he came, with six Negro soldiers at his back, it was on a morning steaming hot after a night of rain that had lasted till the sun was high. As the clouds burned away, stifling heat drove Trav to the west veranda, and Lucy joined him there.

"Keeping cool?" she asked.

He grunted resentfully. "This is one day, I'll be glad when it's over." He waved a huge palm leaf fan. "You look cool enough!" Her straight dress of white cambric was dotted with small yellow flowers. "Makes a man feel better, just to look at you."

She smiled and took the fan from his hand. "Here, let me."

He relaxed in his chair, his eye following a buzzard soaring above the trees that cloaked the river beyond the bottom land. It scaled ever lower, and three more joined it. "Something dead down there," he said, with a nod in that direction.

"I see," she agreed, the fan moving gently. Two more buzzards came without haste to join the others. The first settled clumsily down below the treetops, and another followed, and she looked around the half circle of horizon, searching the skies for more.

"Cow lost her calf," he guessed drowsily. "Or a pig died."

"Here comes someone," she said. He looked toward the road and saw a little group of riders approaching along the drive.

"That's that Yankee Lieutenant," he grumbled. "Why did he have to pick a day like this? You go tell Maria I'm keeping him for dinner. And tell Mama."

She moved to obey. "Papa—may I stay in my room?"

"Now, now, Honey, you'll have to get used to Yankees; you'll see a lot of them, all the rest of your life. I want to make this Lieutenant feel he's welcome here."

She slipped away, and Trav moved to the head of the steps, and as the horsemen approached, he lifted his hand in a gesture at once of greeting and of welcome. The Lieutenant swung from his horse and climbed the steps, his hat in his hand. Halfway up the steps, as though to approach without speaking made him uncomfortable, he said: "A hot day, Mr. Currain."

Trav extended his hand. "Why, it is, for a fact," he agreed. Clearly this young man was as ill at ease as on his former visit. "It is for us, at least." To talk about the weather for a while might reassure the Lieutenant. "Even the hot ones, we usually get a breeze, 'specially out here on the veranda." He looked thoughtfully at the sky. "I don't know but we'd be cooler downstairs, the sun as high as it is. Let's go down." He remembered the men at the hitching rail. "Let them get themselves and their horses into the shade somewhere."

The Lieutenant spoke to his men, and he and Trav stepped indoors. Trav pulled the bell, and when Isaiah appeared bade him bring juleps. "It's been a while since we've seen you, Lieutenant," he remarked. The young man admitted that this was true, and seemed to have no more to say, so after a moment Trav suggested: "I suppose you've come about the Shadd business."

"Yes," the other agreed. "Partly at least." He hesitated, seemed visibly to take the bit in his teeth. "But I was coming anyway, at the request of Governor Holden."

"Ah!" Trav waited, and when the Lieutenant did not speak, he said: "I hear he's called a Convention, ordered the election of delegates."

"Will you be a delegate?"

"No. It was suggested, but I haven't my pardon."

Page seized on the word. "Yes, your pardon. Governor Holden is considering your application, and he asked the Bureau for a report on your relations with the freedmen."

His tone was an apology, and Trav understood the Lieutenant's embarrassment and liked him for it. "I see. Have our people made any complaints?"

"No, no, none at all. No, of course not!"

"Well, suppose you ride around the place," Trav suggested. "Talk to the hands in the fields; to the women, too. Go down in the quarter, see what they have to say. You'd better go alone, so they can talk freely."

The Lieutenant loosened his collar with his finger. "No need of that," he blurted. "I've already written my report. Would you like to see it?" He reached toward his pocket.

Trav felt a slow pleasure. He shook his head. "We're doing as well as we can," he said.

"I understand your problems a little better now than I did when I was here before." Page was suddenly more vocal. "I've learned a lot." He added in a humorous tone: "I've had to."

"Some of our nigras are dissatisfied," Trav confessed. "We've lost a family or two." Isaiah brought the juleps, and they lifted the beautifully frosted silver goblets, their eyes meeting. "Your health, Lieutenant."

"Yours, sir." And after the first draft of the fragrant, icy drink, the young man said: "If they signed the contract, I could have brought them back for you. But of course, they wouldn't stay."

"No," Trav agreed. He smiled faintly. "They've all got itchy feet, want to keep moving, see the country. That's their idea of freedom, to be able to go places."

"Have you had much sickness here?"

"No more than usual. We're moving all the cabins this summer. They should be moved every five years or so, to let the sun in on the ground under them. There's usually some dysentery while we're moving the cabins, but it's been no worse than usual."

"Lots of disease in Salisbury," the Lieutenant told him. "And in all the towns and cities. Some smallpox, and more all the time. Of course, the Negroes are piling into the towns, huddling together fifteen or twenty in a room. You can't make them move—and you can't make them wash! Or keep their premises clean. They seem perfectly willing to sit there till they starve."

"You feed them, don't you?"

"Yes. If they stay on the plantations, we require their master to feed them if he can, but often he can't. We issue thousands of rations to hungry white people, as well as to the Negroes. Last month, for the whole state, we issued over two hundred thousand rations, nearly fifty thousand dollars' worth. It isn't quite as bad now, but down in Salisbury they crowd in on us like a—" He hesitated, suddenly conscious of his own loquacity. "But I don't need to tell you about Negroes." He looked at his watch and rose. "I hadn't realized it was so late!"

"No, no, sit down!" Trav insisted. "Never hurry a julep; let it ripen! Besides, you must dine with us." This naturally friendly young man was like a dog whose advances have been so often rebuffed that he distrusts any apparent kindliness. He pointed to the commode with its basin and pitcher. "You can get the dust off, there. I'll have something sent out to your men."

He had moved toward the window as he spoke. The Lieutenant said the men could take care of themselves. "They've rations in their saddle bags," he explained, "And I'm afraid I—"

"I see they've already made friends in the kitchen," said Trav, from the window, and the Lieutenant crossed to look. "Good campaigners!" Trav approved. The men were sprawled along the shady gallery outside the kitchen door. Old Maria kept a hospitable watch upon their tin plates heaped with grits and fat-back and corn bread swimming in molasses, and Quinny served them, snatching up empty plates, returning with full ones. When she passed among the men, one or another was apt to reach out to spank her, or to pinch her, laughing when she squealed and dodged away. On the ground, in a wide circle, watching silently, a score or so of the plantation Negroes had gathered; one or two old men of the trash gang, a few women old and young, half a dozen giggling girls. "You'll have some of those wenches following you back to Salisbury," Trav remarked.

The Lieutenant smiled and turned back to wash his hands. There was time for Isaiah to freshen the juleps before the bell ding-donged, and Trav rose.

"There we are," he said hospitably. "Come."

Lucy and Enid, consulting, had decided to wear hoops, in order to impress this young man with their stately charm, but Lucy when she heard the dinner bell wished she had not agreed to do so. Without her hoops the Lieutenant might have thought her a little girl and ignored her; as it was, he would probably pay her all sorts of silly compliments.

When Enid passed her door, going toward the stairs, Lucy followed her down to the landing. There Enid waited till Lucy stood beside her; then they descended the last few steps of the wide stair together, and Trav said formally: "Mrs. Currain, I present Lieutenant Page."

Enid offered the Lieutenant her hand, smiling up at him. She had made herself beautiful, and her eyes were warm and melting. "Welcome, Lieutenant," she said softly.

Lucy wished her mother were not always so obvious with young men. Trav said: "And our daughter, Lieutenant. Lucy, this is Lieutenant Page."

The Lieutenant bowed. "Miss Currain! Your servant, ma'am." Lucy lowered her eyes, glad when Peter, with a clatter of feet, came galloping up the stairs from the office level, his hair still wet from hurried ablutions there. Trav said:

"And my son, Peter, Lieutenant Page."

Peter grinned insolently. "Hello, Yank."

Lucy was furious, but Lieutenant Page smiled. "Hi, Sonny!" he said, and patted Peter's head, and Lucy wanted to shout with delight.

Peter in a rage slapped at the other's arm. "Keep your hands off me, God damn you!"

There was an instant's dreadful silence. Then Trav said sternly: "Peter, go to your room." No one spoke till Peter, his eyes on the young officer, turned slowly toward the stairs.

In the dining room, when they were seated, while Isaiah passed the platter of fried chicken, Quinny the paper-thin-sliced ham, Isaiah the sugared sweet potatoes, Quinny the rice, Isaiah the gravy, Quinny the hot biscuits no bigger than the end of a man's thumb, Isaiah the watermelon-rind pickle, and Quinny the wild strawberry jam, embarrassed silence held them all. Lucy, without seeming to look in his direction, saw that the Lieutenant was fiddling with his fork, and she wanted to reassure him, to tell him how wonderfully he had handled Peter. Why didn't someone say something?

At last her father remarked: "Enid, the Lieutenant says he's seldom sampled Southern hospitality." And to their guest. "I suppose, Mr.

Page, you meet a good deal of discourtesy, from grownups as well as from children."

The young man's tone was mild. "Well, we've no right to expect a welcome, but we're here under orders." He smiled. "It's as hard a pew as I ever was in."

"Eh?" Trav was puzzled, and for a moment so was Lieutenant Page. Then he understood Trav's question, and explained:

"Oh, that's a saying we have, down in Maine. A hard pew is—well, it's like hoeing a hard row; any difficult, unpleasant job."

Enid asked, wanting his attention: "Why do you say 'down in Maine'? Isn't Maine up, from here?"

"I think it's probably because before the railroads were built, we always went to Boston by boat. In fact, lots of people still do. Our fair-weather winds come out of the south and the west, so with sail it's up-wind from Maine to Boston, and down-wind from Boston to Maine."

"I declare, that's real curious," said Enid. "Likely I'd find as many strange things in Maine as you find around here."

"Things here don't seem as strange as they did at first," the Lieutenant assured her, and Trav remarked:

"Everybody's suspicious of strange ways. That's been our trouble; we didn't know you folks up North, and you didn't know us." The other did not speak, and Trav said in a good-humored tone: "We've both a lot to learn. You think we've abused the nigras, but actually they were better off as our slaves than as savages in Africa."

Page said, almost apologetically: "There are many things the Bureau hopes to do for the Negroes which in the past you haven't done. To educate them, for one thing."

"We didn't educate our white people, as far as that goes," Trav reminded him. "We Southerners have always felt that public schools, even for white children, were a waste of money." He said thoughtfully: "I certainly wish the Bureau every success. I'd like to live to see the day when I can hire a hand without having to build him a house, feed him and his family, keep him from getting sick, board him when he's too old to work—" He laughed, lifting his hands. "But it will take generations to do that. Most of them will remain very much as they are, long after you and I are gone. You begin to see their limitations. There's some talk that they ought to be allowed to vote. What do you think of that?"

"I've yet to meet one whom I thought qualified to vote," Page admitted. "But then I think few white men are really qualified."

"There's a lot of truth in that. How do you find that we receive your plans for schools for nigras?"

"Most planters say they're agreeable to the idea, but they don't think teachers can be found."

Enid exclaimed: "I can't imagine a white woman willing to teach a nigger school. Much less a man."

"I'm not so sure about that." Page colored in faint embarrassment. "In fact, I've sometimes thought I'd like to try it myself. I was a school-teacher before I joined the army."

She asked teasingly: "Was that 'down in Maine'?"

"Yes ma'am. My father's a farmer, in Montville. I'd go to college one term and then teach school to earn enough money to go again."

"Is your father a planter?"

"Well, not the way you mean. We had a hundred-acre farm at the foot of Frye Mountain, the best land in the town." As his glance turned from her father to her mother, his eyes for the first time met Lucy's, and checked, and held. It was as though he had not seen her till now, and her eyes fell and she heard him, after the faint pause, go on. "He and my brothers and I did all the work, sharing work with neighbors. I could drive the hay rake before I was seven years old, milked cows before that. I started to school when I was six, walked three miles each way. The ABC's, and the three R's . . ."

Enid asked: "What are they?"

"Reading, and writing and 'rithmetic," he explained, and Lucy was for a moment lost in her own thoughts. Her father had taught her to read and to write, and had tried to interest her in arithmetic—Peter was always her superior in that—and little Madame Carlson, the dress-maker from Martinston, gave her a beginning of French. The modest library at Chimneys was devoted principally to agricultural matters, but at Great Oak there were loaded shelves, and there she read like a glutton. But that was all her education, and probably he would think she was stupid. He was saying: "The Bureau schools—around New Bern—are teaching arithmetic, geography, grammar, just like our schools in New England. We have almost three hundred freedmen, men and women, boys and girls, in school in Goldsborough, with three white teachers and several Negro assistants, and there's a night school for grown people that's always crowded. The Negroes—not all of them, of course—are pathetically eager to learn."

Trav said tolerantly: "They're eager to try anything new."

Lucy saw the young man's color rise like a boy's when his enthusiasms are laughed at by an elder, and she spoke for the first time. "But Papa, just because we've never asked them doesn't prove they don't want to learn!"

Trav looked at her in surprise, and Enid supported Lucy. "Remember Sapphira, Trav! After you sold her, she educated herself; at least so they say. She must have wanted to."

Trav laughed, spoke in apology. "I'm sorry, Lieutenant. With both my ladies against me, I must be wrong."

Enid asked: "Do you really think of leaving the army to teach school, Mr. Page?"

"No ma'am; not till things settle down some, anyway. My time's out in January, but I'll probably re-enlist."

"Aren't thing already settled?"

The Lieutenant looked at Trav as though for help, and Trav explained: "Mrs. Shadd had to kill a nigra the other day. That's why the Lieutenant's here, to find out how it happened, decide what to do about it."

"Why should anything be done?" Enid protested. "He needed killing and she killed him; that's all there is to that!" She smiled at the Lieutenant. "There, I've saved you all the trouble of deciding."

The Lieutenant seemed troubled. "It isn't always that simple." Enid rose and they moved into the hall, and he said apologetically: "Will you forgive me, Mrs. Currain, if I go about that business? Mr. Currain, will you ride with me to see Mr. Shadd?"

Isaiah was in the dining room, clearing the table, and Trav called to him: "Isaiah, have someone bring up Nig."

"May he tell the Sergeant I'm ready?" the Lieutenant suggested, and Trav directed Isaiah to do so. The Lieutenant turned to Enid. "Thank you, ma'am, for your gracious hospitality."

She offered her hand, smiling. "I declare it's been a pleasure, Lieutenant. We so seldom have any guests here. Pray, do come again."

"I hope I may." He turned to Lucy. "Your servant, Miss Currain."

Lucy bowed. He had left his hat in the office, so he and Trav turned to the stairs. Lucy and Enid went out on the veranda together, waiting to see them ride away. There was some delay; the Sergeant had disappeared, and three of his men were also missing, the other two asleep against the shady side of the house. The Lieutenant, red with embarrassment and anger, sent these two to summon their fellows. The soldiers had probably gone down to the quarter to gossip with the people there, but Lucy could understand the Lieutenant's feelings. He knew that she and her mother were here watching, and he must be miserable. She heard her father say: "I expect you have some difficulty, keeping your nigra soldiers in order."

"The colored troops do get into trouble," Page admitted. They had paused just below where Lucy and Enid stood, at the end of the veranda. "They delight in arresting some poor darky at the point of a bayonet, pricking him to make him squeal. And of course they like to make the white folks step around, too. It's particularly bad around Beaufort and New Bern. Not so bad here."

"Just the sight of nigra soldiers exasperates white people," Trav suggested.

"Yes." The Lieutenant smiled at a memory. "We stopped at a house day before yesterday, and while I was talking with the householder, one of my men went over to the well where a bucket of water was already drawn and took the gourd and dipped himself a drink of water. A woman came running out of the house, fairly screaming at me that she had never drunk after a nigger and never would, and what did I mean by allowing such a thing! I was glad she didn't have a broom-stick!" He added, remembering his errand here today: "The women are more violent than the men. Like Mrs. Shadd."

Enid touched Lucy's arm and nodded toward the house. Lucy wished to stay, but if Lieutenant Page looked up and saw her, he would think she was interested in him! So she followed her mother indoors and went up to her room, and April helped her out of her dress and her hoops and loosed her hair. The still afternoon was baking hot, and the old woman cooled Lucy's temples with cologne, and brought the couch woven of split cane under the windows and made her lie there, and fanned her till she slept.

When she woke, the sun was low, and the westward-facing veranda was in full glare; but behind the house, between the house and the orchard, and except in early morning well shaded, an arbor supported some muscadines. Three or four comfortable chairs made the spot in summer an agreeable retreat and Lucy found Trav there, a julep on the table by his side. She joined him, feeling that sense of warmth and reassurance which to be with her father always gave her; his smile of greeting testified his pleasure. There were times when neither of them felt the need of speech, but now Lucy wanted to know what had happened about Mrs. Shadd, and most of all she wanted her father to talk about Lieutenant Page.

As though he read her wish, he said at once: "I like that young man." Lucy, as happy as though he had complimented her, laughed at nothing, and he looked to see why she laughed. "Even if he is a Yankee," he added. "Don't you?"

"He's rather nice-looking, but I don't like the color of the clothes he wears."

Trav said gravely: "Blue looks well on a man with blue eyes. To me, anyway."

"But those awful brass buttons!"

He smiled with her. "I like him," he repeated. "I don't like his job, but I can't complain about him."

"What did he do about Mrs. Shadd?"

"He talked to her, and to Tom, and decided there was no sense in arresting her, taking her into court, making a lot of trouble. So that's all straightened out."

"Did he find his men, finally?"

"Yes. Oh yes." Lucy looked at him, a question in her eyes, and he said in an awkward tone: "They were down in the quarter, joking with the womenfolks. Bob got into a fight with one of them. Fellow was teasing Quinny. You know how Bob is about his sister."

Lucy smiled. "That would tickle Quinny. Was Peter there?"

"Haven't seen him," Trav said, but as he spoke, Peter, flushed and panting, came stamping out to join them. He dropped into a chair, stared at Trav's julep.

"Golly, I wish I could have one of those."

Trav asked mildly: "Where've you been, son?"

"Bob and I went rabbit-hunting. We got five." He was suddenly excited and happy, looking from Lucy to his father, his eyes shining. "You ought to see Bob knock them over with his throw stick, and he saw two in their forms and walked up slow and quiet and jumped on them and caught them! The way he kills them, he takes their head in his hand and sort of snaps them, like snapping a whip, and they're dead! I thought it broke their necks, but he says it snaps their hearts. They bleed out of their mouths. He let me try—"

Lucy cried protestingly: "Oh Peter!" And Trav said:

"Peter, I sent you to your room."

"Well, gollies, not for all day," Peter protested.

Trav did not push the matter. "You'd better be washing up. It's almost suppertime." Peter grunted and departed, and after a moment Trav said, half to himself: "Yes, I like young Page."

So did she, but it would not do to say so. "I suppose he's all right—for a Yankee."

His eyes twinkled. "You were—polite to him."

Her cheeks flamed, and she cried: "Don't be absurd, Papa. You asked me to be, so I was. But don't expect me to do it again. If we ever see him again."

Trav nodded. "I don't suppose we ever will."

The weeks glided by. In mid-September a letter from Brett Dewain reported that Treasury agents were scouring the country, seizing whatever they dared in the name of the United States. "And the sand-hill tackeys have turned to thieving now," he wrote. "If you catch one he says: 'I thought it was Confederate prop'ty, thought I might full as well have it as them Yankee robbers.'"

He said it was cotton the agents chiefly sought, but Chimneys had grown no cotton since the War, so the Martinston neighborhood escaped these visitations. Summer passed and the grapes came to harvest. The peaches were fine, and an enterprising Northerner, traversing the countryside with a caravan of wagons and a troop of pickers and packers, bought them on the trees.

"Some I'll ship to New York," he told Trav. "But I'm building a preserving plant at Statesville. I saw this country while I was in the army, and decided this was the place for me. I'm from New York State."

Trav repeated this at dinner, and Lucy cried: "They'll never be satisfied till they've beggared us!"

Trav smiled. "This one didn't beggar me. He paid my price for everything he bought."

"Just trying to get on your good side! I wish they'd all stay home! Not come near us!"

"I don't," he admitted, his tone thoughtful. "We need Northern capital; not only money, but—ideas, initiative."

One morning when they set out for their ride the ground was white with frost, and the forest trees had begun to adorn themselves with red and brown and gold, and as the sun rose higher the day was finely beautiful; so when at a spot where their trail crossed the highway they came face to face with Lieutenant Page, Lucy almost forgot that he was a Yankee and that she hated all Yankees. To avoid letting him see this, she put herself on guard. He sat his horse, hat in hand, explaining his presence here. Four young men had beaten a Negro to death over near New Castle; then they rode into the town, shot and wounded a white man, fired at another Negro, and for a while terrorized the place. They were known, and the Lieutenant and his men were riding to arrest them.

"But I couldn't come so near and not pass the time of day," he concluded, smiling, meeting Trav's smile of welcome. Lucy watched him, though avoiding his eyes. His hair now was cut short, and she resented this. Southern men liked to wear long hair; for him to have had his cut was vaguely a criticism of them.

"Come up to the house, Lieutenant," Trav suggested. "Let us offer you some refreshment."

"I'm sorry, but I must meet my men at the crossroads east of here; Zion, I think they call it. I just rode by to—pay my respects." Lucy knew he must have come some miles out of his way, and wondered whether he had come hoping to see her. If he had, she would show him he had wasted his time! "Is there a short way to the crossroads, or had I best go back through Martinston?"

"There's a short cut, yes," Trav agreed. "We'll put you on the right track."

Lucy was half-a-mind to bid them leave her at the house; it was like a Yankee to spoil her ride with her father. But Trav seemed to take her assent for granted, so she went with them. They followed for a while a sandy byway and could go abreast, cantering easily; but when the way narrowed, Lucy dropped behind and watched the young man with a critical eye. Probably Lieutenant Page had never ridden a horse till he became a soldier, but now he was well up with his horse, and he kept his mount up to the bit, and his seat was easy. He rode, she admitted to herself, in a fretful resentment, surprisingly well—for a Yankee.

He and her father as they rode talked about the business which took him now to New Castle. "The trouble is," the Lieutenant commented, "that the local police won't interfere with these men—and with others like them."

"Our local police were organized because you ordered us to do so," Trav reminded him. "But you can't expect them to arrest their neighbors."

"Well, whatever we expect—they won't," Page admitted. "I'll find in New Castle that no one knows where these—" He checked the angry word. "Where these gentlemen have gone. And if by any miracle we do arrest them and lock them up, they'll be helped to escape. You know, Mr. Currain, you'll never have a settled state of affairs here till you settle things yourselves."

"Well, we haven't been encouraged to settle things ourselves," Trav reminded him, and he said in a tone that was steady without being combative: "Part of the trouble is that you're dealing with men who till now have never taken orders from anyone. No white man in the South—till now—has ever had a master, and he was proud of that fact. It distinguished him from the slave. When you Northerners come and give him orders, you can't very well expect meek obedience."

"But you've surrendered, Mr. Currain," Page urged. "You tried to settle things your way by going to war, and you failed. If you weren't going to let war settle things, it was folly to fight!" He added gravely: "Of course, war is folly anyway."

Lucy, riding between them, bit her lip in rage at this impudent Yankee who dared thus taunt her father, but Trav said reasonably: "Well, we're all given to folly, Mr. Page. But don't keep reminding us!" And he added: "We turn off here."

They rode now in single file, Trav leading and picking his way steeply uphill through underbrush where no trail ran. They crossed a low ridge and came down into an open valley beside a meandering stream, and there Trav checked and pointed. "Follow this branch up to the bridge, then turn right, and it's only a mile or so to Zion. You can't miss it from here on." He extended his hand. "And come and see us whenever you're up this way."

"Thank you, sir." Page turned to Lucy, lifting his hat. "Good afternoon, Miss Lucy."

She nodded curtly, and he hesitated, but then he turned and cantered away. Trav commented: "Good seat, for a Yankee."

"I don't see how you can hear him talk so and not get mad!"

"Why, Honey, he's a pretty reasonable young man."

"I hate calm people! And I hate men so sure of themselves! And what right did he have to call me 'Miss Lucy'?"

Trav looked at her and she felt his eyes and held her head high, but when he spoke she understood that he was being careful not to sound amused. "I suppose he's a pretty exasperating young man, one way and another. But anyway, one comfort, now he's gone!"

Enid, though she was slender and small, had a lively appetite, and when that evening the supper bell rang and Trav did not at once come up from his office, she said irritably: "Come, Lucy, we'll begin. I'm tired of waiting." But when Trav presently joined them and she saw that he was troubled, she asked: "Whatever's the matter, Trav? You look as though you'd lost your last friend."

"Nothing; nothing, Enid." He noticed the empty chair. "Where's Peter?"

"Nothing, my foot! Peter? Oh, he and Bob went to set a trotline or something. What's wrong?"

"Oh, it's just that we had some visitors in the quarter, seven men and boys, and five of them had guns and two were wearing pistols."

"Well, what of it?"

"The roads are full of homeless nigras, begging and stealing wherever they go. When they start carrying guns, it's dangerous!"

Enid said resignedly: "Well, I fully expect we'll all be killed in our beds if we stay here long enough, with no one but niggers and poor whites for miles. But you're bound to have it so."

"Oh, Mama," Lucy protested. "No one's tried to kill any of us yet." And she asked in good-humored teasing: "If you're so afraid of being killed in your bed, why do you stay in it so much? Half the time, you sleep till noon."

"I might as well be killed as be bored to death."

"We've been lucky up till now, far as stealing is concerned," Trav remarked. "But Mr. Fiddler found a dead cow over by the river today, or what was left of it, hoofs and hide." And he said in a sudden interest: "A curious thing, too; they didn't just shoot it; they put a rope around its neck and dragged it up to a tree—you could see the tracks—and pole-axed it, and then hauled it up to a branch and butchered it properly. Must have been half a dozen of them. They didn't waste any of it, either." And he added: "That's the first time we've lost anything bigger than a hog."

"Can't you keep everything penned up?" Lucy asked.

"Not very well. If this cow had been shot, I wouldn't be so puzzled. A nigra with a gun would as soon shoot a cow as a rabbit. Sooner, probably. Powder and shot cost more than a rabbit's worth, but there's lots of meat on a cow."

Isaiah came in with mail, the *Standard*, an official-looking packet, and a letter. "Peg-leg fotch it f'om town, Mars' Trav," he explained. "When he went to haul de flour. De stage come today."

Trav took up the packet, studying the big official seal, guessing the truth. Lucy asked a question, and he said: "It's my pardon, I think." He broke the seal and unfolded an impressive document, and she came to his side, leaning on his shoulder. "Yes," he said. "Yes, that's what it is!"

Lucy took it from his hands. "Let me!" She began to read the pardon aloud. " 'Andrew Johnson, President . . .'!" Enid tried to protest, but Lucy hushed her. "Sh-h-h! Listen!" And she read, in sonorous tones: " 'Andrew Johnson, President of the United States of America, to all to whom these presents shall come, greeting:

" 'Whereas, Travis Currain, of Martinston, North Carolina, by taking part in the late rebellion against the Government of the United States, has made himself liable to heavy pains and penalties . . .' "

Enid groaned. "Oh Lucy, for Heaven's sake!" But with a frown for silence, Lucy read on.

" 'And whereas the circumstances of his case render him a proper object of Executive clemency,' " Lucy, as though breathless, made a sweeping gesture, filled her lungs.

" 'Now, therefore, be it known that I, Andrew Johnson, President of the United States of America, in consideration of the premises, divers other good and sufficient reasons me thereunto moving . . .' Mercy, what elegant language! 'Me thereunto moving, do hereby grant to the said Travis Currain a full pardon and amnesty for all offenses by him committed, arising from participation, direct or implied, in the said rebellion, conditioned as follows, viz:' "

She shivered with distaste. "Br-r-r, what an ugly word! Viz, indeed!" Her eye ran down the lines, and she explained: "It says you have to take some kind of an oath, Papa, and you mustn't ever buy any more slaves, or have slaves working for you, and you have to pay all costs of something or other, and you must notify the Secretary of State that you've received and accepted the pardon. It says viz all those things, and then it says: 'In testimony whereof, I have hereunto signed my name and caused the seal of the United States to be affixed.' Then there's this enormous big seal, see!" She went to show it to her mother, but Enid turned her head away. Lucy laughed at her. "And look! It's signed by the President, and by the Secretary of State!" She saw Trav smiling at her, and laughed and kissed him, crying: "I never realized what an important old traitor you were, Papa! I'm so proud of you, being pardoned by the President, and everything!"

He took the pardon from her, chuckling at her foolery. "Look out there! Don't get that all mussed up!"

Enid said scornfully: "I declare, Trav, you act as pleased as a small boy who's been let off a whipping! If it had been me, I'd never have begged for any old pardon. I'd have died first! Specially from Governor Holden!"

"Oh yes, you would," Trav assured her. Lucy saw that he was too pleased to be disturbed by anything her mother might say. "You see, this makes me a whole man again. Yesterday I couldn't buy or sell, I owned nothing that wasn't subject to confiscation, I couldn't preach a sermon—not that I wanted to—or get married—even if you'd permit it, my dear—or vote, or go as delegate to this Convention they're having." And he said, thoughtfully: "Reminds me, now we can sell the Clay Street house." Mr. Pierce, father-in-law of Trav's nephew, Burr Dewain, had lived there since June, waiting to purchase as soon as Trav could sell.

"I suppose you're bound to sell it, just because I liked living there."

He nodded absently. There had been a letter in the mail, as well as the pardon, and Trav opened it. "Yes, of course," he said, and then as he scanned the first lines: "Enid, this is from the General." For Trav, "The General" would always be General Longstreet, on whose staff he had served through the War. "He's been in New Orleans . . ." His voice trailed away, and Lucy cried:

"Oh Papa, read it aloud."

He frowned over the pages. "Doesn't look like his handwriting. Sort of back-handed, hard to read. I guess he still isn't over that wound he got at the Wilderness. He's been in New Orleans, and he's decided to settle there, but right now—when he wrote this—he was starting for Lynchburg, planning to stay there several weeks." And he read a line or two. " 'I left my family there, you remember, when I started for Texas with Goree. Business will take me to Washington for a few days, but we'll be in Lynchburg, I should think, till the first of the year. Garland's in VMI . . .' " Again his voice fell, he stared at Enid with blank eyes, and he murmured: "I'd surely like to see him." And then, in sudden pleased inspiration. "Enid, how'd you like a few days in Lynchburg? We'll all go! I'll see the General, and leave you there while I go to Richmond to deal with Mr. Pierce."

Enid was transfigured; she rushed to kiss him, to hug him hard. "Oh Trav, Trav, you darling! How wonderful! How wonderful to get away from here, even for a few days!"

Trav chuckled. "How about you, Lucy? You'll see Tom Buford again."

"I'll love it, Papa." Even as she spoke, Lucy realized with surprise that she had not thought of Tom Buford for a long time; she could not remember when.

3

AFTER HIS PARDON came, Trav wrote to Tony in New Orleans, asking for a deed to Chimneys. He found it hard to draft his request, and he had for the first time some misgivings about Tony's answer. These awakened doubts led him to search out the letter his brother had written him last December, and to study it with care.

Dear Trav:

This is just a note to say goodby, a fond—as the saying goes—farewell. I know you disapprove of me, so I'm going far, far away, so that you need never again be embarrassed by my presence. Though to be sure, I have other reasons. There are so many deserters around here that they rule the countryside, and since Sapphira has become my hostess I am unpopular with them—as I am with you. By yielding to their demands I've so far avoided any trouble; but to do so has reduced our supplies till now we can't feed the people on the place through the winter. I don't intend to starve myself to fill the mouths of a lot of lazy niggers, so I'm leaving. I'm going to New Orleans. Chimneys will probably be looted by the local desperadoes, unless you can resume possession. A few of the people have run away, but you're welcome to take title to those still here; and you may consider this letter a deed of gift to you of the niggers and the place, with my blessing! Don't feel any obligation to repay me. I've dabbled in blockading, and in the cotton trade, and I shall be able to live quite comfortably on my credits in New Orleans.

Be so kind as to convey my farewells to Cinda and Tilda, unless, of course, you feel it would embarrass them.

All brotherly greetings,

TONY

Well, that was sufficiently explicit, though Trav doubted its validity in a court of law. At Appomattox he had heard from Brett, who had it fr⟩m "Buck" Owen of the Washington Artillery, that in New Orleans Tony was backing a Republican newspaper read largely by Negroes; that he had turned against the South, becoming the Southern equivalent of a Copperhead, the serpent which gives no warning before it strikes. The thought was troubling, yet surely Tony would not refuse to confirm his December letter with a deed in due form. Trav had the deed drawn, and he mailed it, with a covering letter, to Tony in New Orleans.

As soon as the tobacco was harvested, they would go to Lynchburg, but wet weather delayed them, and Enid fretted at the waiting. Life at Chimneys was for her desperately lonely. Before the War, though neighbors were few, there was always Emmy Shandon, or Clarice Pettigrew, or—though she did not particularly like her—Marie Lenoir; but Captain Pettigrew had been killed at First Manassas, so Clarice now lived in Raleigh, and the Shandons were traveling in Europe. As for the Lenoirs, Mr. Lenoir was an offensive little man who for some reason liked to boast that he was not even remotely kin to the General William Lenoir, hero of the older wars, for whom the town some thirty miles southwest of Chimneys had been named. A Northern sympathizer, when in 1862 New Orleans fell, he betook himself with his family to Union territory there.

So Enid, who had always refused to share Trav's friendly pleasure in the company of the small farmers of the region, and who was equally scornful of their wives, found her days at Chimneys completely dreary, and looked forward to the trip to Lynchburg. She was disgusted with Peter because he chose not to go with them. "I like it here," he insisted, and when she pressed him for reasons: "Well, you might not get back for the hog-killing. I want to be here for that."

"I'm sure I can't imagine why! A lot of half-naked niggers covered with blood, and hogs squealing, and the smell of steam and pork fat. If you'd any sense at all, you'd come with us. I shall tell your father to make you!"

Lucy added: "And Peter, if that's the only reason you're staying, you might as well come along, because I'll have to be back before then, to see to it that they take care of all the meat." She was proud of her role of housekeeper. "There's so much to do, making sausage, and head cheese, and salting down the fat-back and the sow-belly, and smoking the hams. If I'm not here they'll waste half of it."

But Peter would not yield, and Trav, pleased that the boy wished to stay at Chimneys, let him have his way.

The Convention called by Governor Holden met on the second of October, and they followed the subsequent proceedings in the *Tri-*

Weekly Standard. "But they won't decide anything," Trav predicted, on one of his morning rides with Lucy. "Except to obey their orders."

Lucy protested in surprise: "Orders? From whom?"

"From President Johnson. Before being taken back into the Union, we must repeal the ordinance of secession, free the slaves, and repudiate debts incurred in fighting the War. That's the Convention's job; to do those things."

"I don't see why we want to get back into the Union! We fought a war to get out. Why not stay out?"

He shook his head. "Until we're restored to statehood, we'll have no voice and no vote in Washington." Trav half smiled. "No one likes taxation without representation."

"You mean to say we have to pay taxes to the Yankees?"

"Of course."

"To pay them for whipping us?"

"We have to help pay off the money the Union borrowed to defend the Union. Yes. So they're taxing cotton, and of course the tariff is a tax on the South. And there'll be direct taxes too."

He spoke mildly, and she cried: "You make me so mad, being so patient about things! I want to kick and scream! If it was me, I wouldn't do anything they told me."

"Yes you would, Lucy. We want to return to the Union. Secession was a failure. The sooner we forget it, the better."

"You mean you think it was wrong?"

"Wrong!" In a sudden heat he cried: "Great God Almighty, no!" And after a moment, his wrath rising: "No! We had a right to secede! It's true they wouldn't let us go! But don't ever let anyone tell you we were wrong!"

She laughed and moved her mare to his side, catching his arm and squeezing it. "That's better! That's the way I like to see you. Mad! You ought to get mad more than you do, Papa. It would clear your blood! Like sulphur in spring! Everybody ought to get mad about things."

He chuckled and shook his head. "Not me. It upsets my digestion." His eye swept the horizon. The sun that morning had risen clear, but now clouds began to form. They checked their horses on the ridge above High Fields, a fine sandy slope with a southerly cant where under Mr. Fiddler's eye the hands were harvesting the tobacco, and after a survey of the ominous sky, Trav summoned the overseer with a halloo and a wave of his hat.

When the other reached them, Trav nodded toward those clouds. "We'll have rain today, Mr. Fiddler," he predicted. "Better go hurry the wagons on here. I'll stay, see the hands don't cut more than we can handle before it rains." And to Lucy: "You'd better go along with Mr. Fiddler, Honey. I may be here till dinnertime—or later."

"Yes, I'd better," she agreed. "Maria's making apple butter today, and I'll have to give her the sugar, and the spices." She and the overseer turned down through the field. Before they reached the highway, Lucy's mare picked up a splinter of stone. Mr. Fiddler removed it, but the mare limped slightly, so when they came to the road Lucy bade the overseer go ahead. "I know you're in a hurry. I'll let Nellie take her time."

"If I meet any strange nigras on the way, I'll come back and squire you," he promised.

"I'll be all right," she assured him, laughing at his precaution, and he lifted his horse to trot and canter, and disappeared around the first bend.

Lucy at first felt no uneasiness. The road here followed a little stream, meandering through woodland, with underbrush and scattered trees on either hand, and since before the coming rain no air stirred, the morning was hushed and still and listening. The hoofbeats of Mr. Fiddler's horse died in the distance, and when a covey of quail flushed from the ditch beside the road, the mare sheered away, and danced limpingly, and Lucy's heart pounded hard. She felt or heard the beat of it, and it seemed to grow louder till she realized that what she heard was a horse coming at an easy jog, but still far behind her. She instinctively lifted the reins and leaned Nellie into a trot, but the mare limped so outrageously that Lucy checked her. Horses made a lot of fuss over a slight hurt, but you never could be sure the hurt was slight.

Yet the overtaking horseman was nearer all the time, the hoofbeats steadily louder, till as his horse rounded the last bend they sounded almost on her heels. Lucy wished to turn and look back, yet dared not do so; but then the trot changed to a walk, and a man spoke, close behind her.

"Good morning, Miss Lucy."

She turned to face him, and it was Lieutenant Page, and her relief was so great that she forgot he was a Yankee. "Oh, good morning, Lieutenant! I'm glad it's you." She rubbed her hot cheeks with her palms. "For a moment I was frightened, hearing someone coming, not knowing who it was."

He drew up beside her. "I don't suppose you often ride without an escort?"

"No, Papa'd rather I wouldn't!" She had never before been alone with the Lieutenant. Why were her cheeks burning? Why did it seem so necessary to explain? "Mr. Fiddler was with me—Papa's back there watching the hands at harvest—and Nellie hurt her foot, and

Mr. Fiddler was in a hurry, so . . ." Then, remembering that she hated him, furious at herself: "You can easily go back and find Papa! Don't feel you must stay with me."

"Oh, I'm in no hurry," he said, but that was all he said; and she was angrier than before. Had this young man no manners? Any gentleman would have answered her with charming gallantries, would have vowed that to ride with her had always been his dream of Heaven; Lieutenant Page only assured her he was in no hurry!

"Papa's right over the other side of that ridge back there," she urged, checking, and turning to point with her crop. "You'll see our tracks where Mr. Fiddler and I came down into the road. Just follow them till you get out of the trees at the top of the ridge and you'll see him!" Now surely he must go—or if he didn't, he must say he preferred to ride with her.

But he only said: "Oh, I'll see him on my way back. I want to see your mother, too. They've been mighty kind to a—rather lonely young man."

"Why, I shouldn't think you'd ever be lonely." She was so angry that she wished to anger him. "With your nigra soldiers for company!"

He looked at her in belated understanding. "Have I—offended you, in some way?"

"Offended me? Well, hardly! After all!" She hoped he understood her tone; it assured him that no Yankee was sufficiently important to be able to offend her.

"I'd have been sorry to," he said, and said no more, and they went on at a footpace, neither speaking. She and her father were often thus silent as they rode, but surely Lieutenant Page ought to remember that he was with a lady, to whom he owed the courtesy of a little conversation. Still resentful, she broke the silence.

"You really might as well go find Papa. Mama won't be downstairs for hours and hours."

He pulled up his horse, half frowning. "Then perhaps I'd better not bother her." She realized that he was actually about to accept dismissal. "Will you give her my compliments, and—"

The idiot! "Oh, of course she may happen to be down this morning," she said hurriedly, feeling her cheeks burn. "You might as well come on and see." And she added: "I suppose Mama will want to see you. She loves visitors, loves to hear what's going on in the world, all the news."

So they rode on toward Chimneys. "But I'm afraid I don't know any news," he said. "Or haven't you heard that the Convention finally repudiated all the state's war debts. They didn't want to, but President Johnson telegraphed that they must. And they yielded."

"I suppose he thinks he's ever so brave, giving orders from way off in Washington! I'd like to see him come down here and try to boss us around, where we could get at him!"

He did not argue the point, but after a few paces he remarked that the weather lately had been pretty dull and rainy. She was quick to defend the weather against his slurs. "The sun rose fine today!"

" 'Red sky in the morning, sailors take warning.' "

"What's that got to do with it?"

"It's what we say down in Maine. 'Red sky at night, sailor's delight; red sky in the morning—' " He added: "October's our finest month of the year."

He was so persistently good-natured that it was hard to stay mad. "Why don't you ever forget and talk natural? You always say 'down' as if it had two syllables. Sort of 'day-own'!"

He chuckled. "But you do the same thing with 'him.' You say 'hi-um', and you say 'ha-uv' for 'have'."

"Do I really?"

"Just listen to yourself sometime, when you're talking to yourself!"

This, for some reason seemed to them both a hilarious suggestion. She smiled and so did he, and their eyes met and their young laughter rang. "But why is your October so grand, day-own in Maine?" she demanded. "It's just as beautiful here!"

"I expect it might be," he admitted in a quizzical tone, "if the weather were better." She could not defend the rainy weather of the past fortnight. "But on dull days here there's not much color; just reds and browns. You don't have our maples, yellow as gold, and sometimes red as gold. I expect spring is your finest season, but with us it's the fall."

Where the drive turned up toward the house, they met Mr. Fiddler with the wagons, and Lucy spoke to him. "Mr. Fiddler, please tell Papa that Lieutenant Page is here." The overseer lifted his hat in assent, and the Lieutenant added a word.

"I'm not on business, Mr. Fiddler. And in no hurry."

The overseer nodded, and they watched the wagons pass, and Lucy asked: "Why are you so anxious to thank Papa and Mama, all of a sudden?"

"I had business in Martinston. That brought me up this way, and I may not be here again. You see, I've been transferred."

"Transferred?" She was suddenly empty as a broken cup, breathless, feeling she must hurry, driven by an urgent need for haste.

"Yes'm, to New Orleans," he said, and she must say something!

"My Uncle Tony lives there."

"Perhaps I'll meet him. Is he a planter? I'll be working with the Bureau."

"I don't know." Her eyes were on her mare's nodding ears, and she felt herself tremble, felt in her nostrils the sting of unshed tears; it was as though she were frightened, were afraid of something hardly comprehended, yet dark and dreadful. "When will you go?"

"I report there the first of February, but I'm going home first, a month's leave."

" 'Day-own in Maine'?" she asked, managing a smile as she parroted his phrase, and he met her glance and as though unconsciously he checked his horse. Her mare stopped too, and for a moment Lucy and the young man looked at each other, their eyes steady. Then she saw him about to speak; his lips parted, and her breath checked in her throat with fear and longing. But his lips closed again; the horses moved, the moment ended.

"Yes, down in Maine," he said. She frowned a little, as though this were something she must be careful to remember.

When they reached the house, he secured their horses, and she went to tell her mother he was here. Enid was asleep, but she roused at once and was instantly wide awake, bidding Lucy send in April, whose services they shared, to help her dress. Lucy found April in the big chair by the window, asleep, her head back, her jaw hanging. She was slumped sidewise, and her whole body appeared to be collapsed like a half-empty bag, as though there were no bones to give it form, so that Lucy thought for an instant that April was dead. The old woman's mouth hung open, revealing the gaps between snuff-stained teeth, with a hint of rotting and decay that turned Lucy cold with repugnance and with fear; but then April awoke and came laboriously to her feet, and was at once her grumbling, tender, half-angry yet devoted self again.

Yet that first impression persisted. April was so very old, and Lieutenant Page was going away. There was so much sadness in the world! She must keep him company till her mother was dressed, so Lucy tossed aside her wrap-around and ordered her hair, and April helped her change. When she descended and Lieutenant Page rose to meet her she said ruefully: "Oh, isn't Mama down? I'd have hurried if I'd known." She had forgotten to send April to her mother.

"It's all right, Miss Lucy," he assured her. "I didn't mind at all." She tried to imagine even Tommy Buford missing such an opportunity to pay a compliment, and the thought made her laugh aloud, but of course she could not tell the Lieutenant why.

They traveled by stage to Statesville to board the Danville train. This was made up of five flatcars, a boxcar with board seats in which rode the Negro passengers, a car for baggage, the ladies' car, and a passenger coach. The engine, even at a standstill, leaked steam from so many cracks and crevices that Trav doubted its ability to move the train at all, yet when the time came it developed a creditable speed of ten or twelve miles an hour.

Among their fellow passengers Trav recognized Mr. Memminger, who had been Secretary of the Treasury in the Confederate cabinet till June a year ago. Mr. Memminger had a summer residence in Flat Rock, and Trav guessed he must now be on his way from there to Richmond, or even to Washington. When Enid and Lucy were settled in the ladies' car, he went to pay his respects, introducing himself.

"I'm Travis Currain, Mr. Memminger. I was on General Longstreet's staff."

"I remember you, Major," Mr. Memminger assured him. And when they were seated: "I believe we share an affection for North Carolina. Have you not a plantation hereabouts?"

"Yes sir. I'm just from there."

"Then you have found hands to work your place? I hear from many old friends that the nigras don't do as much as they used to."

"Well, they've slowed down," Trav admitted. "I don't work as much land as I did, have had to let some fields go. But I hope another year will see the people settle down."

"I'm afraid it's the planters who must settle down, who must face new conditions," Mr. Memminger suggested. "Slave labor you could afford to waste; you usually had a surplus anyway. But now that labor is scarce, you'll have to learn to make full use of it."

"We have a lot to learn," Trav agreed. "Most of us in the past never tried to learn to farm, not even after Edmund Ruffin showed us how. We ravished the land instead of wooing it, and when it was worked out, we bought new land that was still virgin. Now there's an end to cheap labor, and the end of virgin land is in sight, so we're going to have to learn in order to survive."

Mr. Memminger smiled. "You've something of the poet in you, Major."

"Well, I think there's poetry in land. I'm like old Mr. Ruffin."

"His death became him."

"Is he dead? I hadn't heard."

Mr. Memminger nodded. "Yes, he killed himself, last June. The first time he tried it, the cap snapped, but he put on a new cap and tried again. The last thing he wrote was a damnation of the Yankees."

"He had the courage of his beliefs." Trav spoke thoughtfully. "I think he did as much as anyone to bring about secession. He and Pryor and Yancey and—" He checked himself, remembering the bitter emnity between Mr. Memminger and Robert Barnwell Rhett.

"And Rhett." Mr. Memminger finished for him. "Yes, between

them they fathered secession—and much good we had of it. Ruffin was the only honest man among them; he meant what he said, and when secession failed, he chose to die."

Trav came back to farming. "Did you make a crop this summer?"

"No, I'm not a planter. I vegetated at Rock Hill—my place in Flat Rock. In fact, we stayed there last winter. I thought it imprudent to move the family home to Charleston."

"I should think so, with Sherman headed that way."

The other nodded. "But it appears I made a mistake. The agent of the Freedmen's Bureau seized our house there, asserting that it was 'abandoned,' although my representatives were living in it at the time. The Bureau has converted it into a home for orphaned nigra children." His tone was calm enough, but his lips were white. "There might have been some justice in confiscating the property because of my former service to the Confederacy, but there was none in asserting that our house was 'abandoned.'"

Trav nodded, deeply angry; yet for such a wrong it was inadequate to offer sympathy. "The pretext of scoundrels," he commented.

"There will be many southern lands abandoned in fact, before we're done," the other predicted. "The power to tax is the power to destroy."

"Taxes may destroy ownership, and owners, but they can't destroy land. The land will still be there. They can't take it north."

"They'll sell it to the nigras."

"Any nigra who buys land a Southerner has been forced to sell will soon regret it." Trav spoke in a hard anger.

Mr. Memminger shook his head gently. "We've found force a fraud, Major; threats will serve us no better."

When Trav rejoined Enid and Lucy, he told them Mr. Memminger's experience. "But I expect he's better off at Flat Rock than in Charleston. Probably every city is full now of hungry nigras."

Lucy said: "Well, no wonder they're hungry! They spend their time watching the trains go by. There've been crowds and crowds of them at every station, today, and at every crossroad, men and women and children. Sometimes you could see them way up the road, running to get to the crossing before we passed. I'm glad Chimneys isn't on the railroad. The people would be so busy looking at the trains you'd never get them to do any work!"

She was laughing, and Trav enjoyed her gaiety. Nowadays, when he laughed, it was from the lips out, but when Lucy laughed, the sun shone brighter. Perhaps that was because she was young. It was only to youth that the future was always fair. If a man could learn to keep youth in his heart, to look forward with youth's fine confidence, how much he might achieve.

"I enjoyed talking with him," he said, and caught Enid's eye. "You know, Enid, I think I miss seeing outsiders as much as you do. I'm looking forward to hearing all the news."

"So am I," she agreed, smiling happily. "It's almost worth living in the country, you have such a good time when you come to town."

Enid and Lucy had spent several weeks in Lynchburg between the day they escaped from Richmond just before the city was surrendered and the day Trav took them to Chimneys. Trav, too, was well acquainted in the city. When Longstreet was wounded in the Wilderness, Trav and Captain Goree brought him there. Mrs. Longstreet was a Garland, and half a dozen houses on Garland Hill were the homes of her kin. They made Longstreet welcome, and Mrs. Longstreet came from Augusta to join the General, and Trav stayed in Lynchburg till it was decided to move Longstreet to Augusta, where he would be safe from the casual raids of Hunter's cavalry.

Upon their arrival now, their first call was on the General and Mrs. Longstreet. Lucy thought her as pretty as ever, and proud of her new baby. Enid asked: "How old is he?" And Mrs. Longstreet told them gaily: "No one really knows. The General thinks he was born June first, but no one thought to look at the clock right away, and I shall always say it was the thirty-first of May!" She made a grimace at the General. "Just to irritate my big husband!"

"Exasperating woman!" the General commented, and Lucy saw the happiness that bound them.

When Mrs. Longstreet took the baby upstairs, Enid went with her, but Lucy stayed with her father and the General, listening to their talk together. After Appomattox, Longstreet had stayed in Lynchburg till late June. "Then we headed for Texas, Goree and Garland and I," he explained. "We had an ambulance, and two good mules, and a boy named Jim to drive them. Goree and Garland rode the two horses I had here. Maurice had taken the others ahead to my brother's, in Georgia." Maurice had been the General's servant from the time of his wound to the War's end. "We were more than two weeks getting to his place."

They had passed through Statesville on the way, and Trav and Lucy reproached him because he had not stopped at Chimneys. "You must have had some exciting times," she conjectured, but the General shook his head.

"None," he said. Then, remembering: "Or perhaps one. Down near White Plains, in Alabama, a drunken man wanted me to share his liquor, and when I declined, he wanted to trade me out of one of the mules, and when I said 'No' to that, he drew a pistol. I had to take it away from him."

Lucy cried: "But how frightful! How could you?"

"Oh, I just knocked it out of his hand. He was very drunk, and he'd forgotten to cock it."

"Weren't you terrified?"

"Absolutely, ma'am!" He spoke gravely, but she saw mirth in his eyes.

"There, you're making fun of me!"

His head back, he laughed aloud. "No, it's true. I don't like flying bullets. Major, remember the night we left Knoxville, in the rain and the mud?" Trav nodded, and Longstreet turned again to Lucy. "We saw a light in a house—it turned out to be the home of Mr. Watkins, who was in Bragg's army; he'd been in Congress before the War—so we knocked, and your father here asked Mrs. Watkins to give us some refreshments. She produced a cold sweet potato pie, and brewed us some sassafras tea, and nothing ever tasted better. Then she made me stretch out for a rest on the couch, in the room with her little girl. Drusilla was the child's name, ten or eleven years old, and she had the chicken pox. She and I both went to sleep, and when I woke up, bullets were flying every which way, and your father here was shouting under our window, abusing some of our cavalry something scandalous!"

He and Trav chuckled together at the memory, but Lucy protested: "What happened? Don't just sit there and laugh!"

"Why, General Gillem, a dangerous man— it was he and his men who killed General Morgan in Greeneville the following September, remember?"

"I remember General Morgan, yes."

"Well, General Gillem had been in the neighborhood a week or so before. Some of Vaughan's cavalry heard that he was hiding in the Watkins house, so they came to catch him. I judge they'd had a drop too many, because without asking any questions, they shot out both windows in the room where I was asleep, and peppered walls and ceiling with bullets till the plaster looked like a bad case of measles. Or as if it had caught Drusilla's chicken pox!"

Lucy laughed with them, and Trav asked: "That pistol you took away from your drunken friend, General; did you give it back to him?"

"I would have, but he galloped away in too much of a hurry, so I kept it. It's one of the pistols Mr. Colt made in London, the Navy. The rammer latch is broken—it hit a rock when it fell—but otherwise it's as good as new." And he concluded his narrative. "We went on to Macon, in Mississippi, where my kinfolks live. My brother had come with us from Georgia, and we had a good visit there, and then Goree and I proceeded to New Orleans. I still—"

"In the ambulance?" Lucy interrupted.

"No, we went horseback to Meridian and then railroad to Mobile and steamboat to New Orleans. We met many old friends in New Orleans. I'm going to settle there." He said in a friendly tone: "Currain, you

and I ought to make some arrangement about the future." And to
Lucy: "Your father's become a habit with me. I can't get along
without him. Tell him he must come along to New Orleans with
me."

"New Orleans?" Lucy remembered with a quickening pulse that
Lieutenant Page was being transferred to New Orleans.

"Yes, I'm going into the cotton business with Mr. Owen and his
brothers." He spoke to Trav. "I'm serious, Currain." Then, as Enid
and Mrs. Longstreet came downstairs, and they rose: "I must go to
Washington tomorrow, but don't leave here till I return. We need to
talk this over."

Trav nodded in good-humored agreement and they said goodbye.
Outside, Lucy asked why the General was going to Washington, and
Trav said: "To ask for amnesty, I suppose. It would be pretty incon-
venient, trying to do business without being able to sign papers."

"He's just the same as he used to be, isn't he? Only jollier."

"Well," Trav reminded her, "I think we're all a little more cheerful
than we were last spring, don't you?"

Trav for a while put off the trip to Richmond; there were here so
many old comrades. Captain Blackford had been of Longstreet's staff,
and during the hard winter in Tennessee, Mrs. Blackford had spent
some weeks at Headquarters; so she and Trav were already friends,
and she came to call on Enid and invited them to dinner.

For Lucy's sake, Mrs. Blackford included Tom Buford. When last
spring Tom returned from a Northern prison, gaunt and half starved,
Lucy had thought him a hero; now she was surprised to see, instead
of the hero she remembered, an awkward boy, still lacking the two
teeth which he had lost to scurvy while he was in prison at Elmira.
In May those gaps had been honorable scars; now they were blemishes.
She was as nice to Tom as she knew how to be, but she found it hard
to look at him, and so her glance strayed up and down the table.
Enid was seated diagonally across from her, and Lucy had never seen
her mother as beautiful as she was tonight, her eyes shining, her cheeks
bright, her laughter gay as a child's. At Enid's left sat a young man
of extraordinary appearance and deportment. Lucy had noticed him
in the drawing room because he was extremely tall, but now that he
was seated, he was no taller than any of the other gentlemen. During
dinner she saw that he talked with a feverish eagerness, his words
tumbling over one another. Enid was seated between him and Captain
Blackford, and when her host spoke to her she listened with parted
lips and wide, enchanted eyes, but when she must listen to this other
gentleman, her obvious boredom so amused Lucy that, watching Enid,
and to Tom's bewilderment, she laughed immoderately at Tom's
every word.

After dinner, when her father and the others came to the drawing room, the long-legged man hovered at Trav's side, and Lucy joined them. "Mr. Cist, you met my daughter?" Trav asked, and Mr. Cist abstractedly assented, but then he looked at Lucy again and corrected himself.

"Oh, no, I didn't."

So Trav made introductions, and Mr. Cist acknowledged them, and watched Lucy in an abstracted way while he continued what he had been saying to Trav. Lucy was sure she had never heard a man talk so fast. He was talking about something that could be done with cottonseed. That seemed to her a dull subject, so when Tommy Buford came to her elbow, she was glad to escape.

But that night she asked her father about Mr. Cist. "You seemed to like listening to him, all those things he was saying about cottonseed?"

"Yes. It sounds potentially important." Trav hesitated, a smile in his tone. "Lucy, did it ever strike you as surprising that—with my interest in anything to do with figures—I've never gone into business?"

She smiled. "You'd be miserable if you weren't planting things. What does business, and cottonseed, have to do with Mr. Cist?"

"Why, he's in the cotton-oil business. At least, he proposes to be, if he can interest a few partners here and there." And he explained: "Here a few years back, some Louisiana gentlemen found how to get the oil out of cottonseed. At first it didn't really pay; the machinery was expensive, and the oil wasn't very good. But now some new machinery has been designed, and the oil is of better quality, and Mr. Cist thinks the business is going to boom."

"What in the world does anyone want with oil made out of cottonseed?"

"Well, to hear Mr. Cist talk, it's what the world has been waiting for these two thousand years. He claims you can't tell it from olive oil, and he says you can use it like lard, or to make soap." He said seriously: "Mr. Cist's building a mill now, across the river from New Orleans." Lucy thought she was hearing a lot about New Orleans lately. "And he's looking for capital. Captain Blackford's putting some money into it."

"Are you going to?"

"Well, I'm going to talk it over with the Captain."

"Mrs. Blackford's beautiful, isn't she? I could see tonight that you and she were old friends."

"She was at Headquarters in Tennessee. Remember I wrote you?"

"I expect you all had some gay times in the army, Papa; so many pretty ladies."

"Wasn't Mama lovely tonight!"

"Oh, Mama thrives on parties, and on new men."

Enid was in fact so happy among the many gaieties which their friends here planned that she declined to go with Trav to Richmond. He would stay with Mr. and Mrs. Pierce in the Clay Street house which he had bought during the War. "I couldn't stand it," she declared. "Mr. and Mrs. Pierce are such bores. And Barbara too." Burr Dewain, son of Trav's sister Cinda, had married Barbara Pierce. "I should think Burr would go crazy."

So Lucy and Trav made that trip together, and Lucy enjoyed the reunion with her Dewain cousins. Julian, who lost a leg at Williamsburg, had subsequently married Anne Tudor, and he was reading law with Anne's father, the Judge, and they lived with the Judge in his Twelfth Street home. Burr and Barbara and their two sons shared with Mr. and Mrs. Pierce the house Trav had come to Richmond to sell. Lucy and Trav lodged with them, and Lucy thought Burr stuffy, and Barbara petulant, and Mrs. Pierce was forever full of doubt and fears. Mr. Pierce had been, till his retirement before the War, a banker. Upon secession, he converted his possessions into gold and hid the gold. Now he labored to conceal the fact that his wealth had survived the War by talking about how poor he was. Lucy and Trav maliciously decided that when the time came to sell him the house, Trav must drive a hard bargain.

The best part of their visit was when Vesta and Rollin came up from Great Oak. Vesta had always been Lucy's favorite cousin. Tommy Cloyd was killed at Williamsburg soon after he and Vesta were married, but toward the War's end she married Rollin Lyle. Now they were living at Great Oak in a cabin which Rollin and Big Mill had built together, and working to clear the fields and bring the plantation once more to production, and Vesta had a thousand fine tales of their adventures, proud of their accomplishments. Lucy saw Trav's happiness in the knowledge that someone now was at Great Oak to call it home.

During their stay, Trav spent much of his time with Judge Tudor. Richmond was thronged with Negroes who would have starved but for the rations issued by the Freedmen's Bureau. They crowded the sidewalks, lounged against the buildings, clustered like sparrows in every sunny corner. Most of them were fat and beaming, and cheerful enough.

"But that's changing," Judge Tudor told Trav, in honest concern. "At first they were delighted to be free, and they were sure that the last one of them was going to be given forty acres and a mule." He smiled grimly. "A nigra making a speech to a crowd down back of the station one night promised them forty acres and a mule and a white man to do the work! They laughed like good ones at that!

"But now they're beginning to realize life isn't going to be as simple as they thought. Some have gone to work, and some have gone to thieving. Every so often you'll see a nigra with a pistol in his pocket."

"I've seen a few," Trav agreed, and he asked: "Do you hear any talk about letting them vote?"

The Judge shook his head. "Oh, maybe some damned fool Yankee schoolteacher, or a Northern Methodist preacher. They're the worst, the Northern Methodists. But even the Yankees, most of them, know better than that!"

"There was a big meeting of colored people in Raleigh last month," Trav remembered. "They demanded the right to testify in court, and to be on juries, and to vote."

"The nigras I've talked with want land, and that's all they want."

Trav smiled. "Well, I don't blame them for wanting land, I like land, myself."

When he and Lucy were on the cars, bound back to Lynchburg, Trav said contentedly: "Well, we had a good time, didn't we? If Mama had been with us, I'd have stayed longer. I'd like to have gone down to Great Oak."

"Vesta's wonderful, isn't she?" Lucy agreed. "And she and Rollin are so happy! Did you make Mr. Pierce pay lots and lots for the house?"

"Lots and lots," Trav assured her.

"I don't like him. But I love Vesta—and Rollin too—and I just love Anne and the way she takes care of Julian."

"Did you like Barbara?"

"Oh, I like her all right." Lucy hesitated. "But I think she's mean to Burr."

"I expect we'll come back often, as things settle down." Trav smiled at his own word. "I keep using that phrase, keep assuming that sooner or later everything will suddenly fall into place again, and life will be just what it was before the War. It won't, of course. 'Settling down' will simply mean that we'll get used to having things the way they are."

In Lynchburg they found that General Longstreet had returned from Washington to report his errand a failure. He had called on General Grant—they had been friends since they were young lieutenants—and had been cordially received, and Grant, in a personal interview with the President. had urged amnesty be granted him.

"He thought the President agreed," Longstreet explained. "And at his advice I went to the Secretary of War, and afterward had two long interviews with the President. He was perfectly pleasant, but he finally admitted that there would never be amnesty for Mr. Davis, or General Lee, or for me. He said we'd given too much trouble."

Trav sought some word of comfort. "He put you in good company!"

"I'd not relish the company of Mr. Davis, not even to receive amnesty." Longstreet added honestly: "All the same, it will be a damned nuisance."

"When do you go to New Orleans?"

"Soon." And Longstreet said in jovial urgency: "Come along with me, Major. We can still do great deeds together!"

"I'm afraid my roots are sunk pretty deep at Chimneys." Trav rose. "We're starting home day after tomorrow." He extended his hand, and the General, his right arm still useless from that Wilderness wound, gripped it with his left. "Goodby, General. We'll meet again."

"Sooner than we think, Major, sooner than we think."

Before leaving Lynchburg, after some talk with Captain Blackford, Trav put four thousand dollars into the cotton-oil enterprise. Enid thought him absurd to do so. "Letting that long-legged I-don't-know-who take your money off to Louisiana! I can't imagine what you're thinking of. He'll go to New Orleans and keep going and you'll never see a dollar of it again."

"I don't believe he's a thief!"

"More fool you!"

Lucy asked quietly: "Do you think Captain Blackford is a fool too, Mama? You seemed to enjoy him, the night we dined there."

"What has that to do with it?"

Lucy looked at her father, and he explained: "We're in it together, Mama; Blackford and I. We're going in together."

"Well, I hope you know what you're doing."

He said amiably: "Thanks, I hope I do."

Trav went to say goodby to Captain Blackford at the other's office. Mr. Cist had left for New Orleans during Trav's absence in Richmond, and Blackford said confidently: "You know, Major, I think we have good prospects there."

"The figures sound good."

"Figures don't lie, not in truthful hands." Blackford hesitated. "My only doubts hang on Mr. Cist himself. He's an enthusiast, maybe too much so. I wish we had someone to stand beside him, hold him down." He smiled. "To make him keep his figures straight. But I've all I can manage here, and so have you, at Chimneys."

"You don't know anyone in New Orleans who could—keep an eye on him?"

"No."

"The General's going there."

Captain Blackford shook his head. "He's had no business experience. No, we must risk it. But I wish we had someone in New Orleans, all the same."

They came home to Chimneys, Enid sulky and silent, Trav and Lucy eager for the first glimpse of the big house; yet Lucy thought it would not be the same here, now that the Lieutenant was gone. She had liked him, Yankee or no Yankee, and she had thought of him many times during their stay in Lynchburg, comparing him with Tom Buford and with the other beaus she met there, and liking him the better for that comparison.

But he was gone, and she was sorry. It would have been fun to see him again, and really get acquainted.

On the stage from Statesville, Judge Lowman was a fellow passenger, and he told them April was dead. "Died in her sleep one evening," he explained. "Sitting in a chair upstairs in the big house." Lucy remembered how often she had found the old woman sleeping there, and her eyes filled with tender grief. To their questions, the Judge said April died ten day ago; she was buried in the Negro burying ground at Chimneys. The funeral had been a big affair, and at the preacher's request, Judge Lowman had himself attended.

Lucy thought April might have preferred to be buried with the family, but then she remembered that that was impossible, because Henrietta, Lucy's baby sister, died and was buried in Richmond, and the rest of them were still alive, were not buried anywhere! It was so ridiculous for her to think of such a thing that she laughed out loud, and saw her father look at her in blank astonishment, and at his expression she went from laughter to tears, and buried her face against his shoulder, weeping helplessly, while he patted her head in awkward comforting.

Enid said sharply: "Oh, Lucy, don't be a little fool!" Lucy smothered her sobs, and Enid reflected: "April was so old and clumsy she was almost a nuisance, anyway. I think I'll have Quinny upstairs from now on. Trav, you can give Maria someone else in the kitchen."

Trav absently agreed; he asked Judge Lowman: "Anything else happen since we left?"

"Well, Mr. Shandon sent an agent to sell off some small farms along his east boundaries to the nigras. They have to pay him instalments and interest—and they have to pay the taxes."

"They'll be debt-bound," Trav predicted. "Worse off than when they were slaves." And he asked: "I suppose the thieving goes on?"

"I think it's on the decline. Some white men caught two nigras, way in back of Ed Blandy's, skinning out a steer they'd shot. They hung one of them and whipped the other, and told him to pass the word to his friends."

Lucy, her tears dry but her head still on Trav's shoulder, felt her father's jaw set hard. "What did the Bureau do about it?"

"A new man—Lieutenant Page is gone—came up with a squad of twenty soldiers and asked a lot of questions."

"Find out anything?"

"I'm afraid not."

When the stage halted in Martinston, Mr. Fiddler met them with the carriage, and on the six- or seven-mile drive to Chimneys he made report to Trav. The people were restless, and the overseer thought that after they received the balance of their pay, many of them would wander off. "They've all got itchy feet, and they're scared, too. We never had a patrol here before the War, but now men ride the roads night and day."

"White men?" Trav's words were more a statement than a question.

"Yes. The same lot that killed Mister Darrell."

Lucy cried: "Darrell? My cousin?"

Mr. Fiddler looked at her and at Enid, and then at Trav. "I'm mighty sorry, sir. S'posed they knew."

Trav said: "I'll tell you about that by and by, Lucy." He met Enid's eyes, wide and frightened, and after a moment the overseer repeated:

"Anyway, the patrollers are out, so the nigras are scared. You heard about the hanging?"

Trav nodded. "Peter all right?"

"Yes, same as always." And as they came up the drive to the big house he added: "I forgot to tell you; Mr. Lenoir was here yesterday. He said it was a business matter, said he'd come again."

"Lenoir? I thought he was in New Orleans."

"No, he's here, lodging in Salisbury. Their house, the roof's gone to pieces. They haven't begun to fix it yet, but he says they're coming back to stay."

He checked the horses at the steps and they alighted. Enid hurried indoors, but Lucy linked her arm in Trav's and came up the steps with him. "Tell me about Darrell, Papa?" she prompted.

Trav hesitated, pausing; she stood one step above him. "Why— Darrell was staying here with Tony," he explained. "He offended a troop of bushwhackers, and they killed him."

"What did he do? I mean, to offend them. How can anyone offend a bushwhacker, anyway?"

Trav took off his hat, mopped his brow, wondered how much to tell her. "Well, someone had been stealing out of the smokehouse and the meal bins, and Darrell fixed a pistol so it would shoot whoever opened the smokehouse door. It turned out to be Mrs. Blandy, Ed's wife. You remember her?"

"Yes, of course. But why was she stealing? Didn't Mr. Blandy—didn't they—"

"The commissary agents had seized all her corn."

"But—why didn't Uncle Tony give her whatever she needed?"

He said helplessly: "There are a lot of questions I can't answer, Honey. I wasn't here. The first I knew about it was a long time after it happened, too late to do anything." He added: "When the bush-whackers caught Darrell, Ed tried to save him, and got a lick on the head that made him wander-witted, the way he is today."

"But why didn't somebody catch them and hang them for murdering Darrell?" Her eyes were hot.

"Everybody was in the army."

"But you know now who they were! Mr. Fiddler said they were the same men that hung that poor nigra, and whipped the other one! You could have them hung now. Couldn't you?"

Trav asked, quizzing her: "What makes you so excited about Darrell? Did you like him?"

"No! I hated him. But people can't kill people that way."

He shook his head. "You know the way it is in the South. Killing a man's nothing to get excited about, 'specially if he needed killing—unless it was a white man who got killed and a nigra who did it." He went on up the steps, Lucy beside him, and he opened the door, but for a moment she stood there, thinking. Suddenly she shivered, and he said: "It's cold, Honey. Come on inside."

She obeyed. "I know what you mean, duels and things," she admitted. "But I didn't know we could just kill people and nothing happen."

Trav faced her thoughtfully. "Lucy, you asked me one day to treat you like a grown person. I will. Darrell was bad. He was bad clear through. There were plenty of other things he'd done. Little Miss Meynell drowned herself because of him, and he killed Judge Meynell. Darrell needed killing. If I'd seen him, about that time, I'd have killed him myself."

She came close to him, wondering, looking up at him, a little pale. "Really?" He nodded, and she shivered, her color gone. "I'm scared, Papa. Don't tell me anything else." She half smiled. "I guess I'd rather you didn't tell me things, rather be treated like a little girl."

He smiled and bent to kiss her and they parted. Going up to her room, Lucy remembered with a shocking hurt that she would not find April waiting for her there.

Trav went down to join Mr. Fiddler in the office on the lower floor, to hear what else the overseer might have to tell. Mr. Fiddler said Bob had had a fight with a soldier, and he told the story. In spite of rust and wind and rain, they had harvested more wheat than would be needed on the place, and Mr. Fiddler took two wagonloads to the mill in Salisbury. Bob drove one of the wagons, Leroy the other. While Mr. Fiddler was negotiating with the miller, he heard a wordy argument in the street outside, and heard Bob's voice, and the sudden tumult of the fight.

"It was the same man Bob fit with here that day," the overseer reported. "He made some brag about Quinny, and Bob went for him." Before he could himself reach the combatants, both the soldier's bayonet and Bob's razor had come into play, and the soldier fell, his cheek laid open and blood flooding from another gash that ran from ear to shoulder.

Then two officers came racing out of the building across the street, and one of them was Lieutenant Page. "That was a bit of luck for Bob," Mr. Fiddler explained. "The Lieutenant had seen the whole thing, heard the soldier name Quinny and make his brags. Then Bob told the soldier he was a so-and-so and a liar to boot, and the soldier jabbed him with his bayonet—it went through his left arm—and Bob fought back."

So Bob was free. Trav asked: "What about the man Bob cut?"

"He'll be all right, the Lieutenant said," and Mr. Fiddler added: "It was a sight to see Bob, Mister Currain. He's a fighting fool. He was all over that soldier—and all the time with a bayonet through his arm. He'll stand up for Quinny, any time."

Trav said: "With April gone, Mrs. Currain thinks of taking Quinny upstairs to do April's work."

The other nodded in an absent way. "Quinny could do it," he said. "Maria says she's the best girl she's had in the kitchen in a coon's age." He hesitated. "Quinny's a pretty little thing—and she'll flirt with anything in britches. Bob's got the boys around the place scared to fool with her, but it might be a good thing to get her into the house, out of the way."

"Bob takes mighty good care of his sister. There are just the two of them, aren't there?"

"Yes, Bella died a week or so after she had Quinny. I guess Quinny takes after her. Bella claimed she never did know who their fathers were." And Mr. Fuller said: "Speaking of babies, we've had two die, down in the quarter, while you were away; Viney's, the one that was born the day we signed the contract, and that tall wench we call Looper. She had a baby while I was off to Salisbury. The babies died the same day, the same way; they got tangled up in the bedclothes and smothered. Or so the women said."

His tone was eloquent and Trav asked: "You think their mothers smothered them?"

"I wouldn't be surprised. Like as not they want to take the road, soon as they get their pay, and they don't want to have to lug a young one along."

Trav passed his hand across his brow. "That's a hard thing to think of. Let's hope it isn't so."

"Might as well, might as well. Nothing we can do."

Trav remembered, after he was abed that night, Mr. Lenoir's call. and wondered mildly why the man had come, and hoped Mr. Lenoir would forget his promise—or was it a threat—to come again. But he forgot any uneasiness he might have felt in the pleasure of being at home again, and next morning he rose early, wondering whether Lucy would join him, and found her ready in the hall. When they came home from that fine ride together, Mr. Lenoir was waiting for him in the office, Mr. Fiddler with him there.

Trav greeted him politely: "Glad to see you, sir." He drew chairs to the fire, produced brandy and small glasses. "A day like this, the chill goes deep. Your health, sir."

Mr. Lenoir—Mr. Fiddler had withdrawn when Trav arrived—lifted his glass, hesitated, then set it down again. "I find myself somewhat embarrassed, Mr. Currain."

Trav looked at him in surprise, at once on guard. "Indeed," he said, and he too set aside his untouched glass and waited silently. After a moment Mr. Lenoir drew from his pocket a letter.

"This will explain the situation."

Trav took the letter, recognizing Tony's hand. He cracked the seal and with a quiet deliberation picked off the fragments of wax and unfolded the letter. It was dated in New Orleans three weeks before.

Dear Trav—

This will be presented to you by my friend Mr. Lenoir—whom you may remember—to whom I have sold Chimneys.

Trav read this far, and he read the lines over again while he absorbed the shock. He looked heavily at the other man. Mr. Lenoir was absorbed in an examination of his own right hand, inspecting it front and back, examining the fingernails, clenching his fist and opening it again. Trav's eyes returned to the letter.

to whom I have sold Chimneys. As you know, his land runs with mine for some distance, so that the two places may be readily combined. Mr. Lenoir, in the few years since he came to New Orleans, has greatly enlarged his fortune. I, on the other hand, have been more interested in politics than in business, so that my capital has shrunk a little. Hence, his offer for Chimneys was attractive; too attractive to resist.

I was surprised to understand, from your letter and enclosure, that you took seriously my remark in my letter of last December. You were always a literal fellow, Trav. What will you do, I wonder? Great Oak is a ruin. Perhaps Brett and Cinda will share the Plains with you. Or, my dear brother, why not come to New Orleans? Sapphira and I have many friends here, who will be yours.

In any case, accept my most elaborate respects,

Your servant,

TONY

Trav read slowly, thinking as he read. After the first moment of shock, the words he read lost all reality. This could not be happening; yet since it seemed to be happening, he must play a part. He read to the end, and refolded Tony's letter, and found Mr. Lenoir now smilingly ready to meet his eyes.

"Ah, yes," said Trav. "You have the deed?"

"Recorded, yes sir."

"Then I expect you would like early possession."

"At your convenience, Major."

Trav rose. "Will this day week be agreeable to you?"

Mr. Lenoir puffed his lips. "I had thought—" he began, and Trav took one step toward him, then checked himself and spoke in even tones.

"This day week will be perfectly agreeable to you, Mr. Lenoir," he said. "Now sir, here is the door."

PART TWO

The Thug

★

I

December, 1865

TIME WAS SHORT, and Trav made haste to get away; let the cut be clean, the wound would the more quickly heal. His rendezvous with Mr. Lenoir would be bitter as death, yet he raced to meet it. Out of his office came books and ledgers and letter files enough to keep a huge bonfire going all of one day and one night, with Peter, intoxicated with destruction, in delighted attendance. The attic, and the storerooms on the ground floor, provided fresh fuel for the fire. Trav would have packed and taken with them his desk, the bed he had bought when he and Enid were married, their armoire, the cradle in which Lucy and then Peter and then Hetty had slept, other things around which memories clung; but Enid shared Peter's zeal for destruction.

"Burn them," she insisted. "Let's make a clean sweep, Trav; leave everything behind. I don't want to think of this place again as long as I live."

He assented readily enough. Since they must leave the land itself, the rest did not matter. So his departure was made easy. The tobacco in the sheds was so recently harvested that it was not ready for the market, but Judge Lowman found a buyer, Colonel Allison, who lived toward Happy Valley and whose crop had failed. With this attended to, Trav had only to pay off the hands and take his leave. He wrote to the Freedmen's Bureau, asking that someone be sent to go over his figures and approve the settlement.

While the surface of his mind was concerned with this business of pulling up his roots, his thoughts had sometimes turned to the future. What were they to do? When they left here, where were they to go? Great Oak? Vesta and Rollin had made their own new world, into which he would not intrude. Belle Vue? Ghosts dwelt there; let them be undisturbed. The Plains? Brett and Cinda would make them welcome, but there he and his would always be visitors.

The answer to his problem, when he found it, was obvious. He had a score to settle with Tony, and Tony was in New Orleans. He had pledged a part of his scant capital to a venture in cotton oil, and that, too, centered in New Orleans. His closest friend was General Longstreet, and the General was in New Orleans. Thus his decision was ready-made; he had only to accept it.

The officer who watched his final dealings with his people—Mr. Lenoir came with him, an army ambulance their conveyance—was as unlike Lieutenant Page as it was possible to be, short and fat and wearing an offensive smugness. Trav took the opportunity to hand Mr. Lenoir an inventory listing the contents of the smokehouse, the corn bins and meal chests, the wagon sheds and the carriages house; he presented a tally of the cattle and mules, the hogs and sheep, the chickens and turkeys and geese and ducks and guinea fowl.

He suggested an inspection, to be sure his listings were correct, but Mr. Lenoir said politely: "I know they are, sir; I know they are."

"We will have left here before nine tomorrow morning."

Mr. Lenoir bowed, and he and the Bureau agent climbed into the ambulance and drove away. When they were gone, Trav and Mr. Fiddler went into the office on the ground floor. Trav sat down, and he stared for a moment at the bare wood of the desk top, then turned to look at Mr. Fiddler. It occurred to him that he had not asked the overseer's plans for the future, and he was suddenly embarrassed.

"I've assumed you'd go with me," he said.

"Yes sir," Fiddler assented. "The place here is nothing without you."

Trav nodded. He had been sure of the other's loyalty. "I've half decided to settle in New Orleans," he explained. "But we'll go first to Mr. Dewain's plantation, just across the river from Camden. I wish you'd take the wagons—" There were two, loaded with trunks and boxes. "And the horses—Nig, and Nellie, and that mare of Peter's, and your Buck, and Pardner and Beauty for the carriage—and go to Camden, meet us at Mr. Dewain's. You'll be a week or so on the way. When we go on from there to New Orleans, you can start from the Plains at about the same time." He added: "Peter wants to travel with you, if you don't mind."

"Glad to have him. I'll look out for him."

"Mrs. Currain's taking Quinny, so you'd better take Bob. I don't want to separate those two."

The overseer nodded. "We'll need two drivers," he reflected. "And with six horses, there ought to be at least three riders; say Bob and Peter and me to ride. For drivers, old Pike hasn't any family since Susie died." Pike was the coachman, a spry little man despite the fact that he was clubfooted. "And he can drive a team as well as he can a carriage. And how about Isaiah? He's a steady man?"

"He's taken up with Daisy, hasn't he?"

Mr. Fiddler smiled. "Yes sir. Fact is, they want to get married. I told him he was getting mighty fussy; he never got married before! But he said long as he was a slave he couldn't marry, but now he's a free man!" The overseer added: "Daisy could ride in the wagon with him, and she's a good washwoman. You could use her, when you get settled. And you're going to miss old Maria in your kitchen."

"Reckon she'd go? The people aren't slaves now. They'll have to decide."

"She'd go, and Isaiah'd go. They're mighty devoted to you, Major. And Daisy's old enough not to be flighty, and Pike will make you a good stableman."

Trav suddenly was tired. "You talk to them. I'll leave all that to you." That night he wrote Captain Blackford his plans, and wrote briefly to General Longstreet in New Orleans, and next day they went by stage to Salisbury to take a southbound train.

There had been time, since Appomattox, to begin to bring the rail-roads back to usefulness. Many of the bridges destroyed during the War had been rebuilt, but the track was still an uncertain quantity, and fifteen miles an hour a dangerously high speed. Any long journey was a wearying experience, and when they were in the cars and settled, Enid took opium and drowsed away, while Quinny, much too excited to sleep, twisted and squirmed by a window.

Trav and Lucy sat together, and he thought she, too, might be sleepy. "You've worked harder than I, these last days," he suggested.

"Oh, I'm too excited. So much happening, and so much that's going to happen. We'll be in time for all the Christmas parties, at the Plains."

"Thought you'd got your fill of parties in Lynchburg."

"Oh, I love parties; so many pretty girls, and handsome beaus!"

Trav chuckled. "Tom Buford handsome? He looks like the side of a barn with the doors open!"

"So would you if you'd been starved till your teeth dropped out! Papa, what makes Yankees do things like that?"

"Well, a lot of Yankees starved to death in our prisons."

"You're always standing up for them!" Then, with a quick, apologetic smile. "Oh, I guess you're just trying to be fair!" Her eyes flashed with laughter. "But I think it's lots more exciting to take sides. Hating Yankees is fun!"

"That why you enjoyed being with Lieutenant Page?"

"Oh, he's not a Yankee!" She spoke, suddenly, in an accent so like the Lieutenant's that Trav laughed. "He's a state-o'-Maine man." She laughed with him, and after a moment, thoughtfully: "Tom's going to the University in January. He wants to learn about engines, and machinery." Trav observed that in her thoughts Tom and the Lieutenant were coupled. "General Lee's President of the University now, and he wants them to teach chemistry, physics, mathematics, engineering, mechanics, practical things like that. And Tommy thinks the South is going to need practical men, men who know how to do things."

"He seems to have some good ideas."

"Oh, he does. But of course he's just a boy." Trav smiled, wondering what Tommy would think, dismissed so casually.

They had days and nights of wearying travel, and even Quinny, after her first excitement faded, roused only when the train stopped at stations. Then she pressed close to the window, and sometimes carried on, in an eloquent and laughing dumb show, elaborate flirtations with the handsome young bucks who caught her eye. There were throngs of Negroes at every station, and sometimes they wore the blue uniform of the Union Army, swaggering among the wenches in the throng.

Toward Greensboro Lucy first saw traces of the destruction left by Sherman's army, dead trees around each of which was wound a steel rail. To her question Trav explained: "The Yankees used to heat the rails red-hot, then bend them around the trees." He added: "Or heat them in bonfires and tie them in knots."

At Greensboro they were required to change into another train. "The bridge over the Catawba hasn't been rebuilt since Stoneman burned it," the Captain explained. "Most of our rolling stock was caught south of the river, so we just run a shuttle from here. You'll get good cars again beyond the river." The shuttle train consisted of a freight car for the Negro passengers, a second-class passenger car with a plain wood bench running the length of each side for the white people. When the train was still half a mile from the river, canvas-covered wagons met them and transported them across an uneasy pontoon bridge. The train waiting on the other side was made up of a first-class passenger car, a Negro car, a baggage car and two freight cars. In this they completed the five- or six-hour journey to Winnsboro. Sherman had left no railroad in operation anywhere within thirty miles of Columbia, and the track had not yet been rebuilt. A stage line carried passengers from here to Columbia; but at Winnsboro they were as near the Plains as they would be in Columbia, so Trav sought someone who would transport them direct to the plantation.

The stage driver suggested Major Taliaferro. "He's sitting in by the stove right now, or was a while ago." The Major, when Trav found him, had his heels propped on the fender. At Trav's inquiry he kicked open the door of the stove, spat into it with casual accuracy, kicked the door shut again, and announced that he was at their service. Did he know the way to the Plains, Mr. Dewain's plantation? The Plains, he intimated, was his second home; Mr. Dewain his closest friend. His voice was a rasping whisper, as a result, he told Trav, of a bullet received in his first duel.

"We fiuhed—" the word as he spoke it had two syllables. "We fiuhed togetheh. His bullet caught me heah!" He pointed to his Adam's apple. "Mine piuhced his haht!" The vehicle which he presently produced was an old market wagon with a canvas cover, drawn by three horses hitched tandem and apparently too fatigued to undertake a journey. They were, he assured Trav, a hot-blooded lot, speedsters every one. "You will find you'self deposited at youah destination quick's a cat can twitch his whiskehs."

Straw in the wagon bed, and warm blankets, made Enid and Lucy and Quinny comfortable. Trav sat with the driver. The Major was full of speech. His home, he said, was in the Low Country; he was in Winnsboro only temporarily. There had been some trouble with the nigger soldiers, and he was glad to be of help. "Needs a man who is accustomed to the feel of a pistol and knows what it's faw."

Trav maintained an absolute gravity. "Do you often find it necessary to—kill them?"

"Not often; just once, suh!" The chuckle was like rubbing bricks together. "Just once to each niggeh!" And the Major explained: "The otheh day, the Sheriff came, nigh weepin', to find me. 'Cunnel,' he said. He always promotes me, suh! 'Cunnel, ridin' in heah jus' now, Ah see seven dead blue-bellies, right outside the gate. Please suh, how come?' I said: 'Why, She'ff, they attacked me!' I declah, suh, he like to cried." The Major added, his whisper not so loud: " 'Cose, on that occasion I was not alone. I had stopped to visit a friend, and he and anotheh gentleman and I wuh discussing a toddy by the fiuh when his lady called to us f'om the gahden. The niggehs—they wuh foot soldyuhs—wuh weaving drunk and wanting lickeh, and one of 'em had touched his lady! We toted 'em out to the highway and laid 'em theah right peaceful, muskets and all."

"I expect you heard from the Freedmen's Bureau about that."

"Why the niggehs wuh daid, and no one in the neighbo'hood seemed to know a thing about it." He said seriously: " 'Cose, I don't shoot tuh kill, only if a niggeh's moah awnery than most. I don't need to." He chuckled again, like brick on brick. "I've got 'em so, they see me comin' and they lay right down with theah face in the mud while I ride by."

Trav asked: "Have you had respectable officers in command of the nigra troops around here?"

"Why, no doubt, no doubt, but I haven't seen one. I have defective vision, suh! When we meet on the highway, I find it impossible to see a man in a blue unifo'm. They seem to fade and disappeah!"

Trav thought a Northern radical would find the Major a treasure beyond price. Certainly the truth was not in him; probably not even his name was his own, and that hoarse rasping voice could be much more credibly attributed to too much rum or whiskey than to a pistol ball. The Major talked on and on, and when he paused, Trav uttered an automatic reply. "You don't say!" "Well I declare!" "You're right, I quite agree!" The miles slid sluggishly behind them; night fell, but there was moon enough to see the road; the horses went their way.

The Major might not be strictly accurate in other things, but when he said he knew how to find the Plains he had told the truth. The road, when it left the sandhills behind, gave firmer footing; they swung to a more southerly course, and the Major explained: "We'll go down this side the riveh." They dipped and climbed, and they crossed eroded gulleys and splashed through little streams and threaded their way through fine pines, turning at last off this meandering byway through an avenue of live oaks. At its end, the big house came into view, pale in the moonlight, wide-winged, with broad verandas reached by twin stairs at either end of the east front.

Trav, thinking it later than it was, had expected to find the house in darkness; but there were many lighted windows, and dogs at the overseer's house a little to one side of the drive announced their coming. Lucy woke, and Enid stirred, and Trav said: "We're here, ladies."

Then yonder at the house the front door opened. "There's Uncle Brett," said Lucy happily. "Wondering who we are! Won't he be surprised!"

Trav waved his hat. "Ho, Brett!" he called. "It's Trav!" Lucy cried out a greeting too, and Brett shouted some word over his shoulder into the hall behind him, and then came quickly down the steps to meet them.

So that was a fine welcome, from Brett before the others appeared; and then Cinda came running to sweep Trav in her arms, and Jenny was close behind her. Jenny had been widowed when Clayton Dewain fell at Manassas; now she and her Kyle and little Janet and baby Clayton lived here with Brett and Cinda. Kyle came beside his mother, a grave youngster not yet ten years old; the other babies, Jenny said smilingly, had been asleep for hours.

They came into the house, while under Banquo's dignified supervision the Negroes brought their luggage. Then Trav's sister Tilda, her hair tucked under a cap, and wearing a wrapper, came down the great stairs. Trav had forgotten she was here, and was the happier to see her now. He went out again to make his duties to Major Taliaferro, and he could not resist suggesting that the other stop to exchange a word with his old friend Mr. Dewain; but the Major excused himself and spoke to his horses and drove away into the night.

So Trav went indoors and the hospitable house received him.

2

L UCY HAD always liked Jenny and Aunt Cinda, but she had thought
Aunt Tilda dull and tiresome, eaten up with stupid envy. At
the Plains she quickly realized that this was no longer true.
Tilda had somewhere acquired a self-respecting dignity, a quiet reserve,
a steady strength. Brett had established on the plantation a school for
the Negroes, and Tilda was the teacher. Lucy, when she discovered this,
asked curiously: "But, Aunt Tilda, can you really teach them anything?"

"Of course," Tilda assured her. "But many people think it's wrong to
do so. Four schoolhouses have been burned right in this county."

"Who did it?"

"Oh, just plain worthless white men. They scared away one teacher,
a Massachusetts man; threatened him with a whipping and he disappeared." Tilda laughed in light scorn. "Probably he went back to
Massachusetts to tell terrible stories about how awful we are. They've
threatened to burn our school here, but I'm sure they never will."

"Does Uncle Brett make the children come to school?"

"Why bless you, Honey, they want to come! Not just the children,
either; the grownups, women and men. They try real hard, and stick
to it, and they learn, too. If the sand-hill tackeys around here were as
willing to be taught, it would be wonderful; but you know the way
they are. Even if he lives in a mud-floored hut, and his wife and children do all the work, every wretched one of them still thinks he's
as good as anybody—and he's ready to kill someone to prove it!"

Lucy laughed at Tilda's sudden anger. "You act as mad as if they'd
done something to you!"

"Well, I am mad!" Tilda admitted. "I hate bad men! Redford
Streean was one! I was lucky he left me!" Tilda's husband, having
made a fortune by speculation during the War, had before the surrender fled the country with his loot. "The worst thing about a bad

man is that he can always find some woman like me to father his worthless children. I'm ashamed every time I think of them!"

Darrell was one of those children, and certainly Darrell had been a scoundrel, but Lucy had always thought Dolly wonderful. "Will you let me go to school with you, sometime, listen to you teaching them?"

"Why, of course."

"There was a Yankee officer in the Freedmen's Bureau at Salisbury, and he told me about the nigra schools. He's been transferred to New Orleans."

Something in Lucy's tone made Tilda look at her with an attentive eye, but she asked no questions. "Come tomorrow," she suggested. "Or any time."

Lucy went more than once. Brett had built for Tilda's use, down beyond the cotton press and near the creek, a neat small structure. The boards and timbers were sawed on the place; the roof was of cedar shakes, rived by a blind old man who sat every fine day in a wind-sheltered, well-sunned corner, his frow and maul steady at their tasks. On Lucy's first visit to the school, Tilda stopped to speak to him, and she said: "Samuel, this is my niece, Miss Lucy. Lucy, Samuel made the shakes to roof our school."

The old man touched a finger to his brow. He was bareheaded, with white hair and a thin white beard, and Lucy saw his sightless eyes. "How do you make them, Samuel?" she asked.

"Jes' lak' dis, Missy." He adjusted the block of cedar between his knees and set the frow and with shrewd strokes drove it home, while the cedar cracked and then split clean.

"You do that so easily!"

The old man nodded proudly. "Yes ma'am. Yes'm, I drove many a peg and many a nail, in de days o' mah youth, building cabins 'n de like, heah on de place." He chuckled. "Couldn't hit a nail wid mah old eyes de way dey is now. It takes a maul, and I hits by de feel. But I uz a good ca'penteh, dem days."

"Have you always lived here?"

"Yas'm. Bawn yondeh in de quawteh. Now I'se spendin' de evenin' o' life wheah I spent de mawnin'!"

Lucy felt her throat sting. "Are you glad to be free?"

The old man smiled. "Why, I'se been free all mah life, Missy. Mars' Brett, an' den Mars' Clayton, dey give me mah wuk to do an' I did it, da's all. Dey done all my fussin' an' frettin' foh me. Bein' free ain' sky-hootin' all oveh nowheah, kicking up yuh heels lak a spring lamb. Dese heah niggehs allus braggin' dey free, dey mighty soon find it out. Only de bound is free."

They left him to his task, and Tilda said: "They're so wise about some things, aren't they?"

"Maybe they're wise as children are wise." Lucy added, only half joking: "Maybe they'd be happier if you didn't teach them anything!"

Tilda looked at her with doubtful eyes. "I know. Sometimes I worry about that, too."

The school was only one of Lucy's many interests here. She liked to ride with Trav and Brett upon Brett's morning rounds. Brett when they reached the Plains was in triumphant humor. During the last year of the War, Jenny had made some cotton, and baled it, and hid it in the woods. "And when we came back in June," Brett told Trav, on their first ride together, "I shipped it downriver on a flatboat as far as the Santee bridge, and then on the cars to Charleston, and off to New York. The first lot was pretty dirty, but it fetched forty-five cents, and some of the second lot went at fifty-three cents and the rest at fifty. There's ten thousand in gold and twenty thousand in greenbacks waiting for me in the Ravenel office in Charleston, and the rest in gold in New York!" He said frankly: "I never expected to have that much in hand again. Jenny deserves all the credit."

When there was room, they rode four abreast, Kyle close by his grandfather's side, Lucy flanking Trav, and always three or four bird dogs coursed around them. Brett carried a double-barreled shotgun, its butt resting on his thigh, its muzzle skyward. When the dogs pointed and the covey rose under his horse's nose he might knock down a bird or two. A Negro boy on a shambling mule always rode with them, to mark down the squandering covey and to pick up the birds Brett killed; but this casual hunting was only incidental to Brett's daily scrutiny of the work in progress everywhere. The year's crop of cotton had been picked and ginned and baled in the old screw press which Jenny and Mr. Peters had put back into service when Yankee soldiers burned the presses in Camden, and now in fine weather the hands were put to knocking down the old cotton stalks, or pulling them up and piling them to be burned.

"And we've a constant fight against erosion," Brett explained to Trav. "Clayton started that, and Kyle here—" He and the boy exchanged grins. "He keeps me at it." So everywhere, small washes were being filled, and the larger gullies were choked with pine boughs and cones and with sod, to start small dams and settling basins.

Their talk on these rides took many turns. Brett applauded Trav's decision to settle in New Orleans. "I'm tempted to go with you," he declared. "They'll be building railroads all over that part of the South, these next twenty or thirty or forty years, and railroad securities have always been my favorite investment." He laughed. "Now that I'm a capitalist again, I can talk big. Another thing, New Orleans is the biggest cotton market in the world, Trav. She'll ship close to half a million bales this fall, and four times that in a couple of years. You ought to get into that business." His thoughts were racing. "And insurance! We need some Southern insurance companies, to keep our money at home. We're paying Northern companies five or six million a year. New Orleans is the commercial and financial capital of the South. The bonds of common interest will tie the South and the West together—and New Orleans is the lock on those bonds." He laughed suddenly. "I'd like to be a young man in New Orleans today, with a lifetime ahead of me!"

Trav nodded. "I'm not as young as I was," he admitted. "I've a lifetime behind me. But I'm looking forward, not back." He reflected: "I suppose New Orleans nigras are used to freedom by this time. They've had four years of it."

"The nigras are a nuisance here," Brett commented. "They've crowded into Camden, expecting to live high on the rations issued by the soldiers, but now they're half starved, a lot of them sick, some dying."

Trav had seen the same conditions in Lynchburg. "They were packed in shanties down along Blackwater creek," he said. "Each shanty bulging with men and women and children, and fringed with cur dogs. Ever notice how curs and poverty go together?"

Brett nodded, and he spoke of the uprising in Jamaica, where the former slaves were spreading death and ruin. He feared something like that might happen in the South, said: "Certainly nigras hereabouts are grumbling more and more."

Trav did not share his fears, and they fell into a discussion of the problems of the planter, now that his hands were no longer slaves. Each had found it necessary to reduce the daily tasks assigned. "A hand used to hoe and haul a quarter-acre in a day," Brett explained. "But this year, mighty few of them did that much in two days, and not a man on the place picked a hundred pounds in any day this year."

"I don't make any cotton," said Trav. "But other work slowed down thirty or forty per cent." He smiled. "I didn't much blame them, seeing this was their first year of freedom."

"I know," Brett agreed. "We got them into the fields early, but they'd dawdle over their breakfast, and take two or three hours at dinner-time just being sociable, singing or talking and laughing."

"I like to hear them laugh; it shows they're contented. Did you have to increase their rations?"

"No. Four pounds of fat side meat, a peck of meal, a pint of molasses and plenty of salt."

"I had to give them half as much again," Trav said. "They had so much company! The roads were full of loose nigras, just wandering around." He smiled. "We've a lot to learn. It's no longer just a matter of riding a fine horse and watching the hands sweat in the fields."

"That's all over," Brett agreed. "We've got to work. We're a bankrupt people. Including our state debts, the South owes more than her entire assessed value. And before we can start paying our own debts, we've got to help the North pay off the debt with which they saddled the nation in licking us. Hullo; that black and tan setter has a point."

He cantered away, and Lucy reined her horse beside her father's. She delighted in these early rides; they were so often the best part of the day. She loved to watch the sun's first rays draw mist up from the river and the bottoms, loved those colder mornings when hoarfrost lay like snow across the land and the frost-crisped grass and weeds crackled under the hooves of their horses, and she loved, too, the occasional warm, steaming dawns that made her want to yawn and stretch and go back to sleep again.

The covey yonder rose, and Brett dropped a bird, and watched another fly toward the distant swamp, its legs dangling, obviously hit. He and Kyle cantered after it, and Trav said: "We'll wait here. They'll come back this way."

Lucy nodded. She had been thinking about Tilda, and now she said: "Papa, Aunt Tilda said something sort of pitiful the other day; she said that every time she thought of her children she was ashamed. I knew Darrell was bad, but I always thought Dolly was lovely, and wonderful. Why is Aunt Tilda ashamed of her? I know she married a man named Bruce Kenyon, and that he died, but—what happened?"

He hesitated, spoke reluctantly. "She—betrayed her husband, and he sought death and found it. And she went away with the other man."

"Who was he?" Lucy asked, after a silent time. "The other man?"

"Remember Captain Pew?"

"The blockade runner?"

"Yes. A partner of Redford Streean. And a scoundrel."

Lucy asked no more questions, but presently she said: "I like Aunt Tilda. I think she's wonderful!"

"She is," Trav agreed. "I'm proud of her."

"And I like Aunt Cinda too," Lucy reflected. "She's nicer than ever, nicer than she used to be. She used to say so many sarcastic things, always hurting someone's feelings."

"She's changed, yes," he assented. "She's even nice to Tilda. Ever since they were girls, Cinda's been ready to jump down Tilda's throat at the drop of a hat every time she opened her mouth."

Lucy protested, laughing: "Wait a minute! I'm all mixed up. Whose hat did who drop down whose throat, and who did the jumping? But I know what you mean." And she said: "Mama's changed too, Papa.

Have you noticed? Since we got here? All the good times, and seeing lots of people. She loves it!" Brett's gun roared, yonder in the swamp, and he and Kyle rode toward them. "She's having such a good time, she looks like a girl again."

Trav made no comment, and the others joined them and they turned homeward, riding all together, till Lucy lifted her horse into a run and she and Kyle raced ahead, Brett and Trav following at an easy canter back to the house again.

From the day of their arrival at the Plains, their waking hours were full, with calls and callers and many gaieties, and Jenny and Cinda had planned for Christmas night a fine dancing party. "By that time," Cinda explained, "Everybody'll be so tired of parties that they'll all go home at sensible hours and we old folks can catch up on our sleep."

Brett laughed at her and declared that she was always the last one to want to see a party end, and in fact when the night came, Cinda had her share of dances, and Tilda too. Once Ronny Hamilton danced with Cinda—Lucy's partner was Boykin de Saussure, and Trav was dancing with Jenny—and when the music paused the three couples drew together. Cinda, flushed and panting, said laughingly: "It's not like Richmond, Trav, where the day she marries, a girl puts on a cap and settles down in a corner. I declare I prefer our South Carolina ways."

The music gave them no long pause, and Ronny Hamilton swept Jenny away. Lucy watched them go, and Trav caught Lucy's eye and came to claim her, and Boy de Saussure made his bow and turned to Cinda. But Lucy said suddenly: "No, Papa, forgive me. You too, Boy. I'm going to have this dance with Aunt Cinda. We've something to settle, she and I. Papa, you go dance with Mama."

She linked her arm in Cinda's, and Trav and Boy turned away, and Cinda whispered: "Please, Honey, let's sit down! My feet are killing me."

"Of course! But I want to ask you something." Pev Boykin besought her, but Lucy bade him wait a while, and she and Cinda found chairs. "Aunt Cinda, am I just imagining things about Jenny and Ronny Hamilton?"

Cinda's eyes twinkled happily. "What things, Lucy?"

"Oh, that Jenny's never so lovely and charming as when she knows he's coming, or when he's here."

Cinda nodded in happy assent. "But don't even whisper it, Honey. Jenny hasn't realized it herself, yet." And she said: "You see, Ronny and Clayton were best friends, and he was married at almost the same time as Jenny and Clayton. But Ronny and his wife had no children for a while, and then just after Manassas, just after Clayton was killed, Ronny's little wife and their baby died together. So of course Ronny and Jenny have always been close. One of these days something will happen!"

"I'm so glad! But why are they so slow about it? They're wasting so much time!"

"I know," Cinda agreed. "I feel like giving them a shove, or a pinch, or something, myself."

Then Pev Boykin returned to claim Lucy. Dancing with Pev— he was a nice boy, though so much taller than she that he seemed to dangle her at arm's length—Lucy looked for Ronny. He and her mother were dancing together, Enid vividly lovely, laughing up at him; but Jenny was now with Brett. Yet her eyes forever turned toward Enid and Ronny, and Lucy felt a faint discomfort. Since they came to the Plains, Enid had seemed to grow younger, sleek and beautiful, her eyes limpid with unspoken promises to which men instinctively were drawn, so that on such occasions as this, she might be surrounded by half a dozen gentlemen, each sure that she would have preferred to be with him alone. Certainly she was flirting now with Ronny Hamilton, and probably he was as flattered as any man would be.

But it was too bad of Enid! Jenny was so wonderful, so gentle and so kind; when she and Ronny were together, she seemed to shine with happiness. It was a shame for anyone to mar that happiness.

Trav had decided to go to New Orleans at first alone, to find a house for them and to survey the situation there. On one of their morning rides, Lucy heard him and Brett discuss how the journey might most conveniently be made.

"I hadn't realized it was such a problem," Trav confessed, "Till last night Judge Chesnut suggested that a good way would be by the cars to Charleston, and then by steamer to New York, and then by steamer from New York to New Orleans. That seems pretty roundabout. I'd as soon take Nig here and ride all the way." Mr. Fiddler with the wagons and the led horses had arrived a few days before Christmas, Peter full of tales of their adventures on the journey, and Trav rode Nig this morning. He stroked the big horse's neck, only half joking. "It wouldn't take much—or any—longer."

Brett's interest in railroads had led him to follow in some detail the progress of rebuilding lines destroyed during the war. "You could get from Atlanta to the Gulf Coast," he said. "To Pensacola; maybe to Mobile. At least I know the cars are running from Atlanta to Pensacola, through Montgomery."

"There's a steamer from Mobile to New Orleans," Trav remembered. "General Longstreet went that way. Isn't there a railroad from Charleston to Atlanta?"

"Yes, but from Charleston to Augusta it's practically destroyed, many gaps, long stage rides in between. But the cars are running from Augusta to Atlanta."

"How far is Augusta from here?"

"Around a hundred and fifty miles."

"I could ride over," Trav reflected. "I want to leave the family here till I can come for them, but Mr. Fiddler and I could ride to Augusta and he could stay there with our horses till I come back."

Lucy said hopefully: "You ought to take Mama with you, Papa. She'd love the excitement, and you'd have such fun together, like a second honeymoon." If he did, that would put an end to Enid's mischief-making here.

He laughed. "Can you imagine Mama riding from here to Augusta? It's years since she's ridden at all."

"You could take it slowly."

He looked at her in surprise at this urging. "What's on your mind, Honey?"

"Why, nothing!" she protested. "I just thought what a good time you could have. Mama'd love it; yes, and so would you, having her with you."

He shook his head, dismissing her suggestion, and turned back to Brett: "I think that's what I'll have to do. Mr. Fiddler and I."

Lucy dared say no more, but when in due course her father and Mr. Fiddler rode away, she felt herself left to face a problem beyond her powers. A day or two after Trav's departure, Cinda and Enid and Lucy were together in the front room, and Enid strolled toward a window, then suddenly turned and went away upstairs. Lucy heard the hoofbeats of a horse on the shell drive, and crossed to look out. Ronny Hamilton was just dismounting at the foot of the steps, and Lucy thought her mother had seen him coming, had gone to primp. Ronny started up the steps and then paused as a Negro boy led Jenny's mare to the hitch rail. Jenny, dressed for riding, came running down the stairs, and with a word to Cinda and to Lucy, she met Ronny at the door.

Lucy watched them ride away, and she wanted to sing. Then Enid appeared in the doorway. Thus quickly she had changed her dress; her hair was freshly brushed, her cheeks bright. When she saw them there alone, she exclaimed in surprise. "I thought I heard Ronny Hamilton."

"You did," Cinda assented. "He and Jenny went for a ride."

"A ride?"

"Oh yes, they often ride together." Cinda cocked an eyebrow. "Isn't that all right?" Her tone was dry.

Enid sat down, her face blank with disappointment, and Lucy, suddenly anxious to protect her mother from Cinda's sharp tongue, began to talk of anything at all, and thus banished silence, till Cinda, and Enid too, were roused to lively conversation.

As was so often true in this hospitable home, other callers presently appeared—Boy de Saussure and Pev Boykin came arm in arm—so there would be guests for supper, and Enid was happy again, glowing and vivacious. But when at dusk Ronny and Jenny returned, Enid went to once to Ronny's side, and Lucy heard a few words. ". . . haven't ridden since before the War, but I'd like to start again! Do you think I . . ." Jenny turned toward the stairs and disappeared, but Enid clung fast to his arm, laughing up at him.

Lucy was at once furious and miserable. At supper, watching Enid, she wished her father were here. But since he was not, perhaps she might do something, find some wise word to say. When the evening was over and the guests all were gone, she and Jenny sat a while together by the dying fire. The big house was hushed and still before, arm in arm, they turned toward the stairs.

In the upper hall, a thick candle burned all night, to give light if light were needed. They parted there, and Lucy went on to her room, Jenny turning the other way. But alone in her room, she stood for a while, her back against the door, her hands pressing the panels, staring at the single candle, trying to think what she could do. Surely Cinda must see as clearly as she did how Enid was behaving, and Cinda was never slow to speak her mind. How terrible for all of of them, for Jenny in particular, if Cinda blurted out some damning word. Perhaps just to tell her mother that Jenny and Ronny were in love with each other would be enough; if Enid knew, she certainly would not risk making them unhappy.

Lucy opened her door and looked out. The hall was empty and she glided toward her mother's room, knocked and at Enid's word went in.

Quinny was gathering up Enid's discarded garments and putting them neatly away, while Enid in her chemise posed before the tall mirror, revolving slowly, surveying herself from every angle. "That you, Lucy?" she asked, lifting her breasts with her hands, her eyes still on the mirror. "You'd never think I'd had three babies—and almost had who knows how many others—would you?"

Lucy bit her tongue. She could not say what she had come to say while Quinny was here. "I'd not think anything about it."

Enid laughed at her tone. "Mercy, child! Did I shock you? Where's my nightgown, Quinny?" She dropped the garment over her head, wriggled out of her chemise, slipped her arms into the sleeves of the nightgown. Quinny brought a woolen wrapper, and Enid said teasingly: "Now Honey, if you don't think me too immodest, come sit by the fire with me while Quinny does my hair."

Lucy obeyed, ill at ease, grateful for Enid's steady monologue. "Wasn't it a pleasant little impromptu party? You and your beaus were having such a jolly time!" Then, sighing: "Oh, it's wonderful to be young, Lucy. You'll never realize it till you too are old and out of everything. Though of course I don't feel out of everything, here! After all, Cinda and Tilda are old enough to be my mother." She laughed. "But they couldn't both be, could they? Either one, then. And Jenny's almost as old as I am, I'm sure."

Lucy realized with surprise that this was not far from being true. Jenny must be twenty-seven or eight, though she was so quiet that she seemed older, while Enid was only thirty-three. Quinny's brush strokes slackened, and Enid said sharply: "Don't stop! Keep on till I'm sleepy. Quinny!" In sharp command. "Don't stop!"

"I'se sleepy now, Miz' Enid."

"Well, don't be! Get your sleep when I don't need you!"

"Yas'm."

The brushing went on, and Enid's voice went on, and Lucy, too, felt sleep enfolding her. And after all, what could she say? She had thought of angry words. "You ought to be ashamed! Do you want Aunt Cinda to order you out of the house?" It had been easy enough to say these things in her thoughts; but you could not say angry things to your mother, whom your father loved. She had decided she need only tell Enid that Ronny and Jenny were in love; but now, while Enid talked on and on, her thoughts blurred and thinned and faded and lost all conviction.

She rose at last, surrendering her purpose. "Good night, Mama!" Enid lifted her cheek, and Lucy hesitated, then leaned obediently down to touch it with her lips. But then in a sudden passion of lone-liness and longing, she hugged her mother close, kissed her strongly, whispered: "Oh, Mama! Mama!"

Enid laughingly pushed her away. "For Heaven's sake, child! What's got into you?"

Lucy whirled to the door; she looked back, smiling, eyes full of tears, and blew Enid a kiss. Then she was gone.

Her own room was at the end of the house which overlooked the gardens. When she went in, the night light burned in pale welcome, but beyond it the window was bright with a frightening radiance. She went quickly to look out. Something, down over the brow of the hill, was afire; a billowing smoke cloud glared redly in the light of lancing flames.

Lucy ran to tell Jenny, and Jenny in turned raced swiftly downstairs to ring the alarm on the big plantation bell. Lucy followed her, and behind them, after the brief interval of waking and of catching up necessary garments, everyone came trooping down. Brett and Kyle went racing toward the flames, but already the fire's glare was fading, and Brett returned to tell them what had happened.

"There were six men, mounted," he said in stern, sad tones. "I knew there'd been a lot of feeling against the school, among the families up in the sand hills. Poor-white people don't want nigras taught anything. But I didn't look for this to happen. These men came up along the creek, through the woods below the hill, and no one heard them except old Samuel. I suppose the crackle of the fire woke him. Apparently he ran out, ran toward them, toward the fire. He didn't know they were there, of course, and of course they wouldn't have known he was blind. They clubbed him down." He looked at Tilda. "We'll build you another schoolhouse, Tilda, but old Samuel is dead." He added, like a requiem: "Old Samuel's dead and gone."

3

IT WAS EARLY JANUARY when Trav and Mr. Fiddler left the Plains; dusk had darkened into night on a blustering and raw and rainy February day when they returned. At the steps Trav swung off his horse, and Lucy heard them there and came running out of the house to throw herself into his arms. Trav bade her go in out of the rain, and she tugged at him, crying: "Come in yourself. You're soaked! You must be frozen!"

Mr. Fiddler took Trav's horse away, and indoors Enid and Cinda and the others gave Trav welcome home. When he would have kissed Enid, she protested that he was wet, but he laughed and swept her into his arms and ignored her resentful outcries, hugging and tousling her, seeking her lips till suddenly her lips seized on his with an awakened eagerness. On the hearth a great fire burned, and Trav laid aside his greatcoat and stood steaming while he drank the toddy Banquo brought without instruction, and answered their rapid-fire of questions, till Lucy cried: "Oh Papa, just start at the beginning and tell everything!"

He laughed. "Give me time, give me time! I'm soaked through." He took his toddy at a gulp, spoke to Brett. "Can Banquo bring me up another while I change?"

"Hurry," Cinda bade him. "Supper'll be ready, time you're dressed."

"Enid, coming up with me?" he asked.

She half rose, but Cinda said sharply: "No, she's not, or you'd never come down! Go along, Trav; do! And hurry! We're all starved!"

At supper and afterward they listened to his Odyssey. He had been an even two weeks on the way to New Orleans. "Going, I took the steamboat down the Alabama River. The railroad to Mobile still had some breaks in it."

Brett said: "I heard, after you'd left, that the cars only ran to Pensacola."

"No. That used to be so, but in 'sixty-two they built a branch line that runs from Tensas station across to the main line of the Alabama and Florida at Pollard. I came home that way, saved some traveling time, but I stayed over in Mobile to look at a cotton-oil mill they're building there, so I didn't really gain much."

"I want to hear more about that whole proposition, before you leave," Brett remarked, but Enid exclaimed: "Well not now, please! For goodness sake, Trav, don't talk about cotton oil—or Mr. Cist—for that matter. I had enough of him that night at the Blackfords'."

Trav grinned. "You'll see a lot of him after we're settled in New Orleans. See him and hear him. He and I spent three days together in Mobile."

Enid and Cinda both spoke at once, and stopped, and looked at each other, and Cinda said: "Go on, Enid."

"No, you! I was just going to ask . . ."

Lucy said laughingly: "Hush, both of you! Let Papa tell it his own way."

Trav looked around. "Well, where was I?"

"You were on the steamboat going down the river."

"We'll go that way when we go," he promised. "It was real pretty." And he said: "And from Mobile I took another boat to New Orleans, and put up at the St. Charles, and . . ."

"What's New Orleans like?" Lucy asked, and Cinda protested in amusement: "There! Who's asking questions now?"

"I expect you and Brett have been there, Cinda," Trav suggested.

"Two or three times," she agreed. "And Jenny and Clayton went there on their honeymoon." Her eyes met Jenny's for an instant, then turned to Lucy. "And Lucy, you're all going there pretty soon, so wait and see for yourself! Besides, no one can describe New Orleans! Go on, Trav, but spare us the descriptions!"

Trav took up his story. "Well, almost the first person I saw—except the bus driver, and the clerk at the hotel, and the boy who showed me my room—"

"I remember the St. Charles," Cinda reflected. "Huge, and that deep, stone-paved gallery across the front, and the white pillars. And that tremendous rotunda. It must be a hundred feet across . . ."

"Seventy-five," Trav told her. "I paced it."

"Oh, you and your figures! It looks a hundred, anyway. And it's full, all day and all night, of men with toddies in their hands; planters, drummers, steamboat men, actors, gamblers, bunco steerers. Rich man, poor man, beggar man, thief; you'll find them all there. It's a sight to behold!"

Jenny asked mildly, "Who's describing now?" and Cinda joined the laugh at her expense.

"Go on, Trav. I won't open my mouth again."

"I was about to say," Trav remembered, "that the first man I saw when I went in for breakfast was General Longstreet." Cinda started to speak, then clapped both hands over her mouth, and they all laughed, and Trav said: "So we had breakfast together. They're all fine, Cinda. Mrs. Longstreet and the children—Robert Lee and Jimmie; Garland's in the college at Lexington—are there with him. They're boarding at the hotel."

Enid exclaimed. "The hotel? Trav, you needn't expect me . . ."

"Oh, I found a house for us," he assured her, and he went on: "He's in the cotton business, Brett; Longstreet, Owen and Co., 37 Union Street, on the second floor." Mirth touched his tone. "And not only cotton. They're agents for 'Pike's Celebrated Magnolia Whiskey'! I expect the whiskey pays the rent when the cotton business is dull."

"Things still pretty quiet, are they?"

"Well, a good deal of cotton came downriver from September on, but of course nothing like the years before the War. And New Orleans is full of cotton factors, so there's a lot of competition. Longstreet's to be president of some insurance company, too." He added honestly: "I don't think he knows anything about business, but they want his name. Though of course New Orleans is full of Generals."

"I hear Beauregard's there," Brett remembered. "They say he bought a cart, after the surrender, and loaded it with smallwares, and peddled his way from Virginia to New Orleans."

Trav nodded. "Yes, he's there, and General Buckner's a cotton factor, and General Hood's just opening an office at One Hundred Common Street."

Brett said thoughtfully: "Remember all the talk we used to hear about going to Mexico. I expect a lot of the men who said they were going to Mexico will end up in New Orleans. How's Longstreet's arm?"

"He's learning to write with his left hand, at least enough to sign his name. Every time I went to his office, he scribbled away all the time we were talking. He wanted to know why I wasn't at Chimneys and I told him. Turns out he knew Mr. Lenoir's reputation. Apparently Mr. Lenoir and Redford Streean did some business in cotton during the War. And the General had met Mr. Cist." Trav laughed. "Lucy, remember what long legs Mr. Cist had, and what a short body? The General says he looks as if he'd been ridden on too sharp a rail! I never did see a man split up so far, but he's got a good head, and people like him."

Enid yawned behind her hand and rose. "Well, if you're going to talk about Mr. Cist again, I'm going to bed. Now don't you and Brett sit up till all hours, Trav."

Cinda too rose, and the others, and Cinda bade Brett remember that Trav, after his weary journey, must be tired. Brett nodded. "But I want to hear more about Mr. Cist and the new venture," he admitted.

So when the others trooped off upstairs, he and Trav stayed where they were. Trav cut a nubbin of tobacco and put it in his cheek, moving his chair nearer the wide hearth, but as he did so Banquo appeared in the doorway with a bottle of Madeira and two glasses on his silver tray, and Trav flicked away the tobacco and bade the old Negro bring a pitcher of water and another glass. Brett laughed. "You remind me of Breckenridge and Sherman."

"How's that?"

"Haven't you heard? Here last spring, Breckenridge went with General Johnston to meet Sherman and discuss surrender terms. The first few minutes were pretty stiff, and he decided there were to be none of the usual amenities, so he filled his cheek. Then just about the time he got his quid into working order, Sherman offered them whiskey, and Breckenridge had to prepare himself to enjoy it." As he spoke, Banquo brought the pitcher, and Trav, chuckling at Brett's story, filled the glass and stepped out on the veranda. When he returned, Brett added: "And that wasn't all. Half an hour later, after Breckenridge had decided he was going to have to fly on one wing, and took another chew, Sherman again produced the whiskey, and he had to throw away that one, too." He lifted the Madeira, filled their glasses, and set the bottle on a small table between them. "Now what about this oil mill?"

"Well, I gave you the general idea. Every time you bale four hundred pounds of cotton, you throw away about fourteen hundred pounds of seed. That's our raw material, We can buy it for around five dollars a ton. The hulls are our fuel; the ashes we can use in refining oil; the meal makes fine cattle food. The oil's worth sixty to seventy-five cents a gallon—or was before the War—and you get about thirty gallons to the ton of seed, and the meal brings upwards of forty dollars a ton in England for cattle feed. It works out that from every ton of seed, we can reasonably expect to gross close to forty dollars." Trav added: "And Mr. Cist thinks that later, when we get the knowledge, we'll have a bonanza."

"Any figures on your costs?"

"Not many. No one already in the business will give you any figures. Five years ago there were seven mills in the United States, three of them in New Orleans. They earned about forty per cent on capital invested."

Brett refilled their glasses. "Of course, competition will reduce that. What are the hazards, the problems?"

"Well, the machines need improving, and there aren't any good mechanics in the South to make them work." Trav hesitated. "I'm speaking mostly out of the mouth of Mr. Cist, though I tried to see every man in New Orleans who's had any experience in the business. Mr. Aldigé, Jules Aldigé, has been at it as long as anyone; Paul Aldigé, too. Mr. Frederick Good and Mr. Wilber tried it, made some improvements in the machinery, but they eventually went out of business. Mr. Good showed me a little bottle of oil which he said cost him twelve thousand!" Brett smiled. "Then there's a Mr. Maginnis. He makes linseed oil. He tried his machines and his processes on cottonseed, and got a dollar a gallon for his product, back before the War."

Brett said decisively: "You'd better save room for me."

"Don't take my say-so. Come to New Orleans and see for yourself."

"Perhaps I will, but save a place for me, anyway. I'm not making any new commitments in South Carolina; not till we see what's going to happen to us. But the Yankees moved into New Orleans three or four years ago. Maybe what's happened there will tell us what to expect elsewhere in the South."

"I had the same thought," Trav agreed. "Looked the thing up. Under military occupation, back in eighteen sixty-three, the state was allowed to elect two Congressmen, a man named Flanders, and Michael Hahn, who was later elected Governor, but Congress adjourned about the time they took their seats, so they never really served. Then in the spring of eighteen sixty-four—still under the Army—they elected Congressman Hahn to be Governor, and then he was elected United States Senator, so he resigned as Governor, and Madison Wells, his Lieutenant Governor, is Governor now."

Brett nodded, and Trav went on: "That same year, eighteen sixty-four, they had a Constitutional Convention. There was quite a scandal over that. They spent nine thousand dollars for liquor and cigars, wasted money right and left."

"Were the delegates Southerners?"

"Some were Southern Unionists, but most of them were Northern born—or so the Southerners say. Anyway, the document they drew up is the State Constitution now. Governor Wells is Louisiana born, a well-to-do-planter, and almost all his appointments have been former Confederate soldiers." Trav hesitated, said soberly: "It wouldn't be stretching it very far to say that Confederates were running the state today."

"I'd heard some talk to that effect," Brett agreed. "It's been accomplished peaceably, too." Trav did not speak, and Brett looked at him with a curious eye. "You don't think it will last?"

"There are a few office-hungry radical Republicans down there who hope it won't. It won't last if they can end it." Trav emptied his glass and rose. "Time I was abed."

Upstairs, Enid was still awake, her fair hair loose among the pillows, smiling a welcome. "You were a long time," she said drowsily.

"Brett wanted to know all about the oil business." Taking off his coat, Trav asked: "What happened to Peter, tonight? He disappeared pretty early."

"Oh, he was up here, waiting to say good night to me. He and Quinny. She devils the life out of him. Did you miss me, darling? I missed you." He went to kiss her, drawing her up into his arms, and when he released her and began to remove his boots she asked: "Did you find a house for us?"

"Yes. I took it on a year's rent, with an option to buy."

She yawned, stretching her arms wide. "Hurry! I'm awful sleepy. Did you see Tony?"

"I met him one night in the rotunda of the St. Charles."

"How is he?"

"Just the same; still dyes his hair, still wears a beard, still shaves his upper lip. Remember, I told you once, he looks vaguely like a sickly Lincoln. I think he tries to."

Enid said cheerfully: "Well I know one thing! I'll be eternally grateful to him for rescuing me from Chimneys. Did you say anything to him about that?"

"No. He brought up the subject. I didn't reply, and that seemed to make him uncomfortable."

"You're a long time getting undressed," she protested. "I never knew you to take so long."

"There was a man with him," Trav remembered, his thoughts in New Orleans. "A Mr. Parker. He'd moved down there from Massachusetts, and he expects a hundred thousand Yankees to move to Louisiana in the next ten years. He impressed me as an able man."

"Am I supposed to be interested in Mr. Parker?" She leaned over to blow out the candle on the table. "There, slowpoke, you can come to bed in the dark."

He laughed, groping toward her. "Sorry. I forgot. I was telling you about Tony."

"Tell me about Tony some other time."

When they were ready to begin their journey to New Orleans, Brett decided to see them as far as Augusta. Enid rode in the carriage which Brett loaned them for the journey, and Lucy or Trav or Brett kept her company. Behind the carriage came the wagons loaded with their belongings, so they made a considerable caravan. This had been a wet spring, and though the weather was briefly fine, the roads were sometimes hub-deep in mud, and even the small trickling streams which they must ford were often treacherous; but there were horses enough, and mules enough, to drag the carriage or the wagons through the deepest mud, and they were never long delayed.

They passed through Columbia, where at Sherman's orders more than two-thirds of that city of thirty-five or forty thousand people had been burned. Whole squares once covered by buildings were now weed-cloaked wastes, pocked with cellar holes, littered with charred timbers, and studded with soot-stained chimneys. The heart of the city was a wilderness of ruins, a mass of blackened, crumbling walls. The residential section was left relatively unharmed, but for almost a mile along the twelve streets that had been the business section, not a building had survived.

Beyond the ravaged city they passed out of Sherman's track, but after another day and another they came into it again, riding once more through waste and desolation. So to reach Augusta was relief after a weary journey. Mr. Fiddler and the wagons took the road to Milledge-ville, as the shortest route to his eventual destination. Peter had elected this time to travel with his father and mother and Lucy. They said goodby to Brett, and boarded the cars.

But the cars were old and shabby, and the road bed in poor repair, and many delays kept them the rest of that day, and the night, and much of the next day on the road to Atlanta. Trav was interested in the rolling upland country and the neglected farmlands through which they passed, but the others sat in an apathetic exhaustion. They reached Atlanta in a downpour, trundling through ramshackle suburbs to the accompaniment of the engine's tolling bell, coming to a stop in what seemed little better than a swamp alive with shouting and beseeching Negroes and surrounded by throbbing steam engines and dingy cars. Bells were ringing constantly, the engines emitted at intervals screams as though of pain. Bales and boxes were piled helter-skelter everywhere, and upon this pandemonium the steady pelt of rain descended, without violence yet without mercy. Two Negro hackmen combined to transport them to a lodging so wretched that when next morning the rain still continued, and Trav said they might as well go on, even Enid was eager to do so.

On the journey to Montgomery, their laboring engine twice broke down, and they sat helplessly waiting while repairs were made. Once a snakehead—the loose end of a rail which had pulled its spikes and was sprung upward by the weight on its further end—came lancing up through the floor of the car, bringing the train to a staggering halt. By the time they reached Montgomery, they were all weary of trains, and glad to agree to Trav's plan to take the stage to Selma, sixty or seventy miles west of the city, and proceed by steamboat to Mobile.

The stage was a bus of the sort hotels sent to meet incoming trains. Their luggage piled up front, just behind the driver, the passengers sat on the benches that ran lengthwise of the vehicle. Thus they faced each other, so that knees touched other knees, and easy conversation became general. A throng of Negroes gathered to watch the stage begin its two-day journey, and as they got underway, the gentleman opposite Lucy, obviously a clergyman, and English, asked at large: "Why were the Negroes watching so intently?"

No one at first elected to answer, but then the comfortable fat man on his left explained: "Looking for somep'n t' steal. They'll steal anything they kin carry away."

"Not really?"

"Positively! Why, my neighbor a mile along the pike from my house, here one night a while back they carried off the windlass out o' his well, draggin' the bucket along with it."

The clergyman's eyes were full of wonder. "I've heard so many strange things—" he said doubtfully, but a thin little man two seats away interrupted him.

"Why, Heck and Prisciller! A windlass ain't nothing! I knowed a man, the niggers stole his front gate and the fence around his front yard, and filled up the post holes after."

"It's shore a fact!" the fat man agreed. "What they'll steal'd surprise you. Paul Albee, down past my place a few miles, six niggers went out back of his house one night and—" He stopped abruptly, meeting Lucy's eye, and gulped, and strangled, and coughed, and exclaimed in red embarrassment: "Well anyway, Paul was in it, and when he yelled at 'em, they dropped the whole shebang flat on its face and put out in all directions. He had to—well, he had a time getting out, I'll tell you."

No one appeared to doubt this, and the thin man said with doleful wagging head: "There ain't a thing they won't tackle, if they git the notion. I sowed a patch of wheat here last fall, and I be dinted if they didn't pick up every seed, like they'd been so many crows."

While the clergyman listened, looking from this man to that, they discussed the shortcomings of Negroes in general. A surly man at the end of the bench said sullenly: "Worst of it is, killing 'em's no good. You kill one, and two come back at you, like flies to a dead dog. It'll come to an outright race war, sooner or later."

The clergyman tried to speak. "You actually mean—" But the thin man broke in.

"Yes, and I'd say it'd be sooner, not later! I'll tell you, inside of two years, either there won't be a nigger left alive in Alabama, or else there won't be a white man. So far, it's just skirmishin', a white man shot from ambush here, three-four-five niggers killed over there; but any day now it'll come to battles." He added unctuously: "Well, me, I'm ready for it."

On the word he lifted from his coat pocket a Navy revolver—Trav judged by the brass frame that it was one of those made in Georgia during the War, when brass was easier to come by than iron—and fondled it affectionately. Three of the others, following his example, produced weapons. "Here's one I made in my own machine shop," a man explained, and passed the revolver from hand to hand. The piece looked at first glance like a Colt, the Army model, except that the rammer lever had an unusual latch, and was not pivoted to the barrel. Yet it seemed to work, for Trav tried it, releasing the latch, levering the rammer home against a seated bullet.

"That's mighty ingenious," he said, handing it back. "But I should think the lever might jar loose, drop out."

"Ain't yit," said the owner. "I rid three years with Forrest and she went with me all the way. She hits like a mule kicks, the powder charge I put in her. Don't have to shoot 'em twice with that. I shot a Yankee in the elbow, oncet, and broke his neck." He added, in the tone of one trying to be fair: " 'Course, he fell off his horse, too, at 'bout the same time. Jim Furber and Wiley May was with me, and they thought that might have had something to do with it."

The fat man sucked at his teeth. "Well now, it might and it mightn't. Necks is funny. I see a man sneeze, once, and break his." He added in a judicial tone: "Long run, though, I sh'd think you'd average better shootin' them in the neck than the elbow."

"Are you gentlemen all armed?" the clergyman asked, in an amazed tone.

Trav smiled. His small revolver was in a flat leather holster pocket inside his coat, its shape well concealed. "Why, I expect you're about the only unarmed white man you'll meet in a week's journey through the South, Reverend," he said, and the others nodded agreement. "We get so in the habit, we can't sleep unless we can feel a lump under our pillow."

The Englishman shook his head in astonishment; he drew a deep breath. "Will wonders never cease!"

They enjoyed the boat trip down the river. The stream's course was tortuous and winding, sometimes returning on itself so closely that in a dozen miles of travel they moved southward hardly at all. They stopped often to pick up cotton at the landings, or to take on wood for fuel. The wood had usually to be carried aboard by hand, but at one landing, it had been piled on top of a low bluff and was slid down to the water's edge along a wooden trough built for the purpose. Trav saw the boat's captain watching this operation, and paused beside him, and the Captain after a moment said reflectively: "If they'd carry that trough far enough out over the water so I could nose up under it, they could let the wood drop right on deck. Save a lot of time; save the mate a lot of swearing!"

"Wouldn't it break your deck?"

"I can lay boards to protect the deck."

"Would it be worth the trouble?"

"It wouldn't use to, but it would now't we have to hire niggers to load it. And anyway, I hate to hire a nigger. All my life, if I wanted somep'n done, I just yelled at the nearest nigger to do it. Every time I hire a nigger now, I Goddamn every Yankee a foot high!"

"I expect we'll have to figure a lot of ways to save labor," Trav agreed. The last wood came aboard, and the lines were cast off, and Trav climbed to the upper deck where presently Lucy joined him. The boat rounded a bend and they saw three deer dipping their muzzles in the water. The deer became conscious of the steamer's approach and lifted their heads to study it and then bounded up the bank and away.

During this indolent passage down the river, he and Lucy were much on deck. The weather was warm, and the river, itself alive, was also a way of life for the flowers beginning to appear along its bank, the deer that came to drink, the ducks forever trading up and down the stream, the occasional fish that jumped beside the boat, the alligators slumbering on every bar, the turtles on many a snag and stump sliding into the water as they approached. Trav reminded Lucy of a day six or seven years past, when they traveled from Richmond down to Williamsburg by the river while he pointed out to Enid the great houses along the banks and told her their stories.

That was before the War, a lifetime ago, but Lucy remembered. "Only I didn't hear the stories about the old houses. You and Mama were by yourselves. Vigil kept us children in the cabin. There must be stories about these lovely places we see every little while along here."

"Not so many," he told her. "Some of those houses on the James River were built over two hundred years ago, but I don't suppose there was any cleared land here till say fifty years back." And he said thoughtfully: "That other trip, we were moving from Chimneys to Great Oak. Now we're moving again, to a new place, a new way of life, a new work."

His voice caught and she laughed at him in quick affection. "Why, Papa—homesick?"

He chuckled. "Guess so. I hated leaving Chimneys. I haven't been so homesick since I was a child!"

They left behind the pleasant bluffs and the wide plantations and came into forests, every tree except the oaks bare of leaf, yet tufted with mistletoe and hung with graceful swaying scarves of gray moss which after last night's shower was now briefly tinged with the green of new grass. Toward dusk the river forked, and they tied up to wait for dawn, and next day they wound a tortuous way through canebrakes and cypress swamps, scattered gum trees and water oaks. They emerged into grassy flats where great rafts of ducks rose before them, flying a mile or two, then settling on the water presently to rise again.

They reached Mobile in time for dinner, and that evening they took the boat for New Orleans. Below Mobile, a channel had been cleared through the barrier of piles built during the War to keep the Yankee fleet at a distance. In the bay beyond, a score or more of ships lay at anchor, waiting for cargoes of cotton. Trav and Lucy were standing at the rail together—Enid, as soon as they came aboard, went to her cabin and to bed, and Peter liked to prowl—when someone spoke beside them, and they turned to face Lieutenant Page!

So there were exclamations of surprise and pleasure, and Lucy wished her heart would not pound, nor her cheeks burn so hotly, and she wondered whether he were as excited as she. His work brought him often to Mobile, he told Trav, and he explained: "I re-enlisted, the first of February, and I'm still assigned to the Bureau, to the General Superintendent's office."

Lucy asked: "Did you go home, the way you planned?"

"Yes, for almost a month! My Uncle Don was there. He lives in California, but he had come home for Christmas, and when he heard I was coming, he stayed on to see me." He chuckled, colored faintly. "I'm named for him, so he calls me his favorite."

"Like it here as well as North Carolina?" Trav inquired.

"In a way. I have to do a lot of traveling. The schools are my special job." Don smiled faintly: "I've just now been in Washington, on school business. You see, sir, the schools for freedmen were supported by the income from seized property, and that's what took me to Washington, to see Mr. Conway. He used to be General Superintendent, till he was discharged, last October. He had charge of over a hundred million dollars' worth of this seized property. He was in Washington to testify before the Joint Committee on Reconstruction, and I went to ask if he could help us locate some of that income that we can't account for."

Hastily, so that the Lieutenant would turn again to her, Lucy asked: "Could he?"

"No. No, he couldn't." Page hesitated. "Or he said he couldn't!"

She saw his frown. "You look mad at him?"

"He's either a liar or a fool." Yet his tone was mild. "He's a liar, anyway! He'd been down here long enough to know better, and yet he told the Committee that two-thirds of the Negroes in Louisiana can read!"

"Can't they?" she prompted. When he was indignant about something his eyes seemed to turn black; black or a very dark blue, she was not sure.

"Two-thirds!" he fairly snorted. "No! Not one per cent of them!" Then in sudden embarrassed apology: "But I don't know why I'm shouting at you, Miss Lucy." She smiled, and their eyes held, and he turned to Trav. "I heard about your selling Chimneys, Major, but how does it happen you're way down here?"

Before Trav could speak, Lucy answered. "We're going to live here! How did you hear about Chimneys?"

"I wrote you a letter and sent it through the Bureau—"

"To me?" Lucy tried not to sound as pleased as she was.

He colored. "Well, really to all of you. I hated the idea of not seeing you—any of you—again. You were mighty kind to me." He turned to Trav. "Will you let me call, Mr. Currain, when you're settled here?"

"Happy, Lieutenant, of course."

"I don't want to embarrass you. Many good Southerners refuse to receive—" He smiled. "A so-and-so blue-bellied Yankee."

"I was here on business a few weeks ago," Trav remarked. "It seemed to me there was more real anger against the nigras than against Yankees."

Page did not comment. The steamer began to swing into her westward course, rounding Cedar Point to enter Grant's Pass. Over the Gulf, the horizon was dimmed by a faint haze, but the islands which walled the Sound on that side were bright and beautiful in the afternoon sun. Page showed Lucy the Dauphins, and Petit Bois ahead, but when he turned to speak to Trav, he saw the other strolling away along the deck, and Lucy quickly asked whether he liked living in New Orleans. He hesitated before he replied.

"I'm not sure," he said then. "I'm sure I would if I were welcome there." He smiled. "Of course, everyone tells you about the way things used to be, duels and gambling and voodoo and—well, things I was brought up to consider abominations. But I'm sure I'd like the place, if it liked me." He added soberly: "But there's anger in the air. You see, the men I know are mostly our officers, and a few civilians with Union sympathies. They all resent the way things are now."

"How are things now?" she asked softly, watching him as he talked, thinking that this was only the second time they had been alone together. The sun was behind her, fair upon his face; his eyes were narrowed against the brightness on the water.

"Why, Confederate soldiers are being appointed to all the offices. Union men in New Orleans say the Confederates who fought against the Union are now receiving all the honors and offices in sight." He added: "I spoke of Mr. Conway. There are a lot of men like him. He was a minister, and you know how bitter ministers can be. He wanted to keep all that seized property, resented the pardoning of Confederates, hated the owners who after they were pardoned compelled him to return their plantations and their homes. The Government in Washington had to remove him. He, men like him, they want to disfranchise every man who fought for the Confederacy, and to give the vote to the Negroes."

"But they can't, can they?"

"I hope not. But it's because of that talk that you hear of Negroes being beaten, or killed."

"No real Southerners would do that; just miserable no-accounts."

"I've never seen it," he admitted. "I don't surely know."

She remembered the school at the Plains, and told him about its destruction. "Mr. Dewain said that was burned by what they call the sand-hill tackeys, the poor whites."

"Well, there are a lot of poor whites in the South," he reminded her. "If they all start burning and killing . . ."

Then Enid, fresh and smiling and looking her best, came tripping along the deck to join them. "I'm just so glad to see you, Lieutenant," she exclaimed. "I had a little nap after we came aboard, but then Mr. Currain told me you were here." The flattering inference was plain, and Lucy felt a wry amusement. "Isn't it the most gorgeous evening?"

"Looks like rain, I'm afraid."

"Oh surely not, for our first impression of New Orleans."

"Well, they have lots of rain there, this time of year." He told them to expect next morning an early rising, an arrival before full day. They stayed on deck till behind gathering clouds the sun disappeared, till first dusk softly fell.

Lucy woke to the steady hiss of rain on the deck over her head, and then someone knocked on the door and her father—he and Peter were in one cabin, Lucy and Enid in another—told them it was time to rise. The steamer from Mobile came from the Gulf into Lake Pontchartrain and across to where a long pier ran far out through the shallow water. Before Enid and Lucy reached the deck—it was gray dark, the rain still falling—the vessel was already tied up at the dock where a train of cars was waiting. The Lieutenant guided them aboard and sat across the aisle. When the train began to move, it was darker because the rain still fell, and Enid resented this.

"I like to see," she protested.

"Not much to see out here but swamp," the Lieutenant assured her. "It's five miles, almost, to the station."

During the half-hour run, light began to come, and through the windows they saw the dark shapes of buildings, increasingly numerous. The train stopped, and at the car steps a bus driver monotonously chanted: "S'Cha's Hotel, S'Cha's Hotel." When they were aboard the bus and their bags bestowed, Lieutenant Page said goodby, and Lucy smilingly reminded him that he was to come and see them.

"We'll be at the hotel at first," Trav explained.

"I will," the Lieutenant promised, and he lifted his hat and turned away.

"But Trav," Enid protested. "Why are we going to a hotel? You said you had a house for us."

"I have, but there's no furniture in it, and Mr. Fiddler won't be here for a week or so, with our people. Meanwhile you and Lucy can start buying what you'll need to furnish the house. We'll board at the hotel till it's ready." The bus trundled through narrow streets, and Trav explained: "This is the old part of town, the French part. We're turning into Royal Street."

"Does the sun ever come out?" Enid asked wearily.

Trav laughed. "You'll see." And after a little: "This is Canal Street we're crossing, and the car line. Royal Street changes its name to St. Charles Street after it crosses Canal. There's the hotel, ahead." When the bus stopped, he rose, relief in his tones. "Well, we're here. We're home!"

Lucy never forgot her first impression of the mass of the big hotel, seen through the drenching rain; of the tall white pillars and the broad wet slabs of stone that floored the veranda. When they came into the octagonal rotunda, she for a moment stood stock still. Peter brushed past her, protesting at her pause, and Trav asked: "All right, Honey?"

"Yes. But this is the biggest room I ever saw."

"It is, isn't it. Come along. We'll get settled and then have some breakfast."

Enid elected to go to bed and rest, but Trav and Lucy and Peter soon descended. Before they finished breakfast, the rain had stopped, and the sun was breaking through. Trav suggested that they see something of the city. "And I think we'll see more if we walk, take our time."

Lucy agreed, so they ignored the solicitous drivers of the hackney carriages waiting outside the hotel. Peter wanted to go directly toward the river—they could hear occasional whistles from the steamboats there, sounding near or far as the wind freshened or died away—but Trav wished to show them the house he had rented, and Lucy agreed to this, so Peter was outvoted. The sun had set the city steaming after rain, and it was warm, warm enough for May at Chimneys, though this was only March. They walked down Gravier Street to Baronne, and Trav paused to point off to their right. "Canal Street's two blocks down," he said. "That's the widest street in New Orleans. It's so wide that when any other street crosses it, it forgets what it's name was and takes a new one."

Lucy felt his high spirits and took his arm, squeezing it affectionately, but Peter asked in a scornful tone: "How can a street forget?"

"Well, they all change their names; I'm sure of that! This is Baronne

Street we're on, but down on the other side of Canal it's Dauphine Street."

Lucy asked: "Why do you say 'down'?"

"Because it's downriver. Downriver's downtown; upriver's uptown. Away from the river is down and toward the river is up."

Peter protested. "How can you go 'up' to a river?"

"You can to this one," Trav assured him. "The levee's like a wall between us and the river. Look at the water in this gutter here; it's running away from the river, down past us. Wait and you'll see."

They left the business houses behind, walking up Baronne Street, and Trav showed them pleasant residences set in gardens where early flowers were already in fine bloom. The crossings were muddy and the gutters deep; the sidewalks, he told them, were called "banquettes," of wood, built up like footbridges above the mud.

Once Peter pointed to what looked like a huge barrel, a dozen feet through and half again as high, set on top of a scaffolding by the corner of a house. "What's that, Papa? I've seen a lot of them."

"They're cisterns," Trav explained. "Everyone catches rain water off the roofs. It rains a lot here, and even when it doesn't rain, it's so damp that you get mildew and blue mold in the houses. I've had fires going in our house all the time I was away, to dry it out and keep it dry."

Lucy asked: "Are we coming to it pretty soon?"

Trav smiled. "Pretty soon. See if you can guess when we do. But I want to show you some of the houses I didn't take, so you can decide whether I made a good choice."

He showed them a house at the corner of Melpomene and Baronne Streets, and Peter said it looked like their house in Richmond. Trav nodded. "But I didn't like the canal over there in Melpomene Street, right beside it," he said, and when Lucy looked into the canal, an open sewer in which floated miscellaneous garbage and a dead cat inflated by decay, she agreed.

He showed them another house where Felicity Road crossed Baronne Street, and by way of Felicity and Prytania they came to Euterpe Street and turned up toward Coliseum Square. In the street and on the banquette near the end of the block, where Euterpe entered the Square, a considerable number of Negroes were gathered, and among them some disturbance had arisen. Peter cried: "Look!" They all halted, but then Peter hurried on. Beyond the disturbed groups of Negroes, a man in the long blue coat of a policeman came lurching toward them, brandishing his club. Trav saw him shoulder a Negro woman aside, so that she fell into the gutter, and a Negro man spoke to the officer in apparent protest. The policeman swung his club and the Negro backed clear, holding his head in pain.

They were not half a block away, and Lucy could hear the drunken, mumbling voice of the policeman; yet at the same time she had a sense of silence, as though the Negroes, weaving and dodging to evade the unsteady rushes of the officer, played a sort of dumb show. She saw Peter, half hidden behind a tree, watching at close range, and then a group of white men came around the corner from the Square and paused to shout approval and encouragement. The policeman, pleased with this audience, began to run clumsily to and fro among the Negroes scattered in the street, striking at them with his club while they dodged aside. Other white men joined the spectators, and Lucy, holding fast to Trav's arm, asked: "What's he doing, Papa?"

"Abusing the nigras. He's drunk!"

"He ought to be ashamed. See Peter watching!"

Trav called Peter's name, but the boy did not hear, and a tall young man in a Yankee uniform came out of the house in front of which the Negroes had been standing, and went toward the drunken policeman. The officer clubbed to his knees an elderly Negro who walked with a cane, and who now with the cane tried to fend off new blows. When the approaching soldier seemed about to interfere, some of the watching white men moved threateningly nearer, and one of them shouted: "Let him alone, Yank!"

The soldier caught the policeman's arm and swung him around, and Lucy cried in sudden recognition: "Papa, that's Lieutenant Page." She and Trav moved quickly forward. The house out of which the Lieutenant had come was a handsome residence, tall columns supporting a balcony at the second floor level. Beyond the veranda, a walk seemed to lead to the back yard, and along this walk a squad of Negro soldiers with fixed bayonets now trotted into the street and at once marched the intoxicated policeman away, a bayonet against his spine. Peter followed them and Lieutenant Page called:

"Peter, is that you? Come back here."

"I want to see what they're going to do to him."

"Johnson!"

At the Lieutenant's word, one of the Negro soldiers turned and without any order caught Peter's arm. Peter screamed: "Let go of me, you God-damned nigger!" Half a dozen of the white spectators moved angrily nearer, but the squad of soldiers swung with bayonets ready.

Then Trav called to Peter, a stern command, and Peter returned toward them and the danger passed. They came where the Lieutenant stood, and Page took off his hat and smiled and wiped his brow.

"Well, Miss Lucy, you put them to flight!"

Trav said: "I'm sorry Peter made it harder for you."

Page dropped his arm across the boy's shoulder. "Oh, he just wanted to see the excitement!" Peter indignantly jerked the arm away, but Page seemed not to notice, continuing: "The policeman was a little over-stimulated. There's always a crowd of Negroes in front of our Head-quarters here. Miss Lucy, I'm sorry you had to see that. It was too bad, but there's a good deal of feeling against the Negroes." He added: "I must ask you to excuse me, now. I've a gentleman waiting on me inside."

"Of course, of course," Trav told him, and the Lieutenant turned away. The Negro men and women who had scattered and fled were now returning to solace those who had felt the policeman's blows, and already, here and there among them, easy laughter began to rise. Trav and Lucy and Peter strolled past them and turned down toward Camp Street at the foot of the Square, and Lucy said wretchedly: "Papa, I never saw anyone abuse nigras before."

"That sort of white man has always done it," Trav admitted, his eye on Peter, who was looking back at the hurt Negroes. He said, in a different tone: "Come along, Peter. We've still a lot to see."

The house Trav had rented to be their home was at the corner of Prytania and Hestia Streets, two stories and a half, with a high-walled garden and a ten-foot iron gate to guard it. The door of the house opened directly on the banquette. Heavy pillars supported the first floor gallery, others not so heavy rising to the roof, and dormer windows lighted the small rooms on the third floor. Three royal palms towered to the level of the rooftree, just clear of the gallery, which faced south-west. The garden was massed with fragrant shrubs, jasmine, sweet olive, crape myrtle and oleander, and with a profusion of flowers, each in its season.

Trav had been pleased with the house from his first sight of it, and as they approached it now, he was as excited as a boy who has pre-pared a surprise for his mother and at the last moment is divided between hopes and fears. He had decided to wait till they were abreast of the house and then pause, then when they looked at him inquiringly, he would say, as casually as possible: "Well, there it is, that's the house, over there."

But before they were abreast, at the corner diagonally opposite, Lucy spoke in pleased tones. "That's a lovely-looking house. I'll bet it would be fun to live there!"

Trav masked his proud delight. "Well, you're going to! That's ours!" Then, in sudden affectionate suspicion, he asked: "Lucy, how'd you guess?"

She stood on tiptoe to kiss him. "Oh, you were getting so excited you were ready to burst, watching it and watching us! But it really is a lovely house. Can we go inside?"

He chuckled and led them to the iron gate in the wall, through which they could see an old Negro, puttering in the garden. Trav called:

"Abram! Abram!" The man came to let them in, and Trav said: "Abram, these are our children; Miss Lucy and Master Peter."

Abram took off his ragged hat, bowing. Lucy saw that he was extravagantly bald, with wisps of white hair behind each ear. "Yas ma'am, yas suh," he said, and Trav told them:

"Abram stays on the place, kept the fires burning while I was away." Finding the house neglected and in some disrepair, he had arranged that during his absence broken windows should be replaced, plaster patched, walls repainted, floors and woodwork renovated, and fires kept up to dry out the damp plaster and banish the smell of mold. "You've got the garden looking fine, Abram."

"Thank'e, suh." The old Negro led them to the covered gallery that connected house and kitchen, and unlocked the door into the back pantry. Before leading the way into the house, Trav pointed to the separate kitchen, and Lucy recognized the likeness to Chimneys.

"So no heat gets into the house," she said approvingly.

Trav nodded. "And the stables and carriage house are there beyond the kitchen, and rooms for the people over the carriage house and in the cabins along the drive. Now we'll go in."

"I want to look at the stables," Peter announced, and Abram said they were unlocked, and Peter turned that way. Lucy and Trav and the old Negro went indoors, from the back pantry through a narrow passage into the L-shaped hall, the perpendicular of which led to the front door, the base to the garden at one side. The parlor and dining room faced the garden, but on the other side of the hall there was a big sitting room and a smaller room at one end of it.

"My study," Trav announced. "And library too."

Galleries at the ground level and on the second floor fronted the garden. When they went upstairs, of the two bedrooms that opened on the gallery Lucy chose the smaller, in the rear. "And you and Mama can have the front ones," she suggested.

"Mama thinks we'll sleep together, here," Trav said. At Chimneys, they had had separate rooms. "I think the big front room will be ours. Peter across the hall."

There was nowhere a stick of furniture, nothing but blank plaster walls and polished floors, but Lucy, seeing how it pleased Trav for her to do so, inspected each room, and planned all the things she and Enid would select.

Peter returned, and they said goodbye to Abram and resumed their way, and Trav asked: "Well, like it?"

Peter said vaguely: "I guess it's all right."

But Lucy cried: "It's wonderful! Mama'll love it!"

"Don't praise it too highly," Trav suggested. "If you do, she'll expect too much, be disappointed." Laughing, she promised to take care.

When at last they approached the river, it was along Common Street, and they saw ahead the twin stacks of a steamboat pouring out clouds of black smoke. Peter cried: "Look, there's a steamer way up in the air!" He raced ahead, eager to see this wonder, and Trav and Lucy followed more slowly.

At the crest of the levee both children were for a moment silent, and Trav smiled. "I expected it to be bigger, too," he said, answering their unspoken thought. "It's not very wide, but it's two hundred feet deep!"

"It's higher than the city," Lucy murmured. "Higher than anything around."

Trav chuckled. "Yes, it runs uphill all the way from its source," he assured them, and when Peter looked at him in quick suspicion, he said: "I'm not joking, really. You see, the earth's thicker through in the middle than it is up nearer the poles, so any river that flows south flows a little uphill. Then too, the earth's spinning around all the time, and it spins faster at the equator than further north, and faster here, and that makes a sort of everlasting high tide here. If the earth stopped revolving, I suppose the river would flow the other way."

"And drain the ocean into the Great Lakes?" Lucy laughed. "What fun! And maybe flood Ohio and Indiana and Illinois and drown all the Yankees!"

They stayed a long time, absorbing every detail of the scene. In each direction for as far as they could see, steamboats and flatboats and other craft of every description were moored. They saw bales of cotton piled everywhere, and Lucy said: "They must raise a lot of cotton around here."

"None right here," Trav told her. "You have to go upriver seventy-five or a hundred miles to see real cotton country. When we get the mill working, we'll have to bring all our cottonseed down river."

Peter asked in wonder: "Who built the levee?"

"I think the first dirt wall along the shore right here was thrown up about a hundred and fifty years ago, and they've been building it longer and higher ever since; first the city, and then the State helped, and for years before the War, the United States Government helped, too."

"I should think people would be scared," said Lucy. "Having the river hanging up over them like this all the time." The yellow flood went swiftly past, not many feet below where they stood. "Suppose it came over the top, wouldn't the whole city just drown?"

"The river's mightier than a million men," Trav said. "But all the same, men have put it in bonds. I've always thought the most eloquent line in the Bible is where someone describes Jehovah's great works, and says He 'set the sand for the bound of the sea.' How many beaches are just built of little grains of sand?" He pointed out across the water. "See how it seems to be rounded in the middle, as though it were higher there than on shore. That shows its still rising." And he said: "The river's like a gigantic snake. Hear the slither as he slides by, sliding along in his ditch between the levees."

"How long is the levee?" Peter asked.

"I heard someone say there are over two thousand miles of it, if you count 'way upriver."

"Gosh, it's big!"

"Yes, its big," Trav agreed. "But it has to be mended all the time, or the little crawfish and the little muskrats would tear the big levee down!" They laughed, but he explained: "It's true. Even a crawfish hole can turn into a big leak, start little and grow big, and all that water out there, running through a big enough leak, would soon wash the whole levee away."

They walked along the waterfront as far as Jackson Square, and came down through St. Peter Street to Royal, and Lucy said so many of the people on the streets looked like foreigners. "And lots of them are talking French," she added.

"They're Creoles," Trav explained. "The Creoles are the real aristocrats of New Orleans."

"Aren't they part nigger?" Peter asked. "Brights, like Quinny?"

Trav chuckled. "Hardly! No, Peter, a Creole is any person of French —or Spanish— descent, who was born here in the colonies."

"This isn't a colony!"

"It was once. Three times, in fact. First it was a colony of France, then of Spain, then of France again."

They came up Royal Street to Canal, and Lucy exclaimed at its width, and Trav said, with the precision that always amused her: "It's a hundred and seventy-one feet wide." So when they crossed toward the statue of Henry Clay, set in the neutral ground in the middle of the street, she said affectionately:

"I expect you know just how high that is."

"The statue's about fifteen feet high," Trav guessed, "and the pedestal's as much more, and the steps and the foundation are at least ten feet. It must be about forty feet to the top of Mr. Clay's head."

"About?" she exclaimed, in pretended surprise. "You mean you don't know exactly!"

He laughed. "No, never measured it." And he said: "Notice the galleries along the front of the buildings that face the street. They're pleasant places to sit, in the cool of the day, now that spring's come." He looked at his watch. "Well, let's get back to the hotel. Mama must be starved."

4

W HEN TONY LEFT Chimneys, he took Sapphira—and 'Phemy,
Sapphira's mother—to New Orleans. There he bought a
house on Felicity Road, near the corner of Constance Street.
The house was built flush with the banquette, with a set-back gallery at
the first floor level and a wide, gently sloping, gabled roof. Toward
the levee and the river, the neighborhood was degenerating. A few once-
gracious residences, now abandoned to disuse and decay, bordered
a jumble of narrow streets lined with saloons which catered largely
to sailors, boarding houses with a heavy patronage of masculine callers,
an occasional cotton press or storage yard, a few malodorous coffee
houses, and a scattering of missions fighting a hopeless fight against
the stubbornly determined degradation all around.

Except Mr. Lenoir, Tony knew at first no one in New Orleans, but
Mr. Lenoir, having been a Union sympathizer, had a wide acquaintance
among Radical politicians. He brought them to meet Tony, and presented them to Sapphira, whose beauty and intelligence were soon
widely advertised. White men who, like Tony, maintained quadroon
mistresses—though Sapphira was actually a quintroon—were no novelty
in New Orleans; the quadroon balls and the "little house along the
ramparts" were still remembered. So they had many callers, but the
gentlemen who called did not bring their wives.

Among the men whom Mr. Lenoir brought to Tony's home was
Doctor Roudanez, a refugee from San Domingo and one of three
brothers who together published the *Tribune,* devoted to the cause of
the Negro. Doctor Roudanez aspired to convert Louisiana into a Negro
state, governed by Negroes, owned by Negroes, and inhabited by
Negroes, and he refused to be discouraged by the fact that no newsboy
would sell the *Tribune,* and that it could be bought from only one
newsdealer in all New Orleans. "My paper is for my subscribers,"
he told Tony. "Not for everyone. Furthermore, I lift up mine eyes to

Washington, whence cometh my strength." And he explained: "I send a copy of each edition to every Congressman. The facts we publish furnish ammunition for our friends there."

Tony was impressed by the man's earnestness, and when the Doctor admitted that the *Tribune* was run at a loss, he began to make up a part of the regular deficits. As one result, Doctor Roudanez came almost daily to consult him, and he brought others, some white men, some Negroes.

One of these was a young mulatto named Pinchback, Pinckney Benton Stewart Pinchback. Before bringing him to the house, Doctor Roudanez told them something of his history. "His mother was a slave, or at least she had been. His white father sent him to Cincinnati to go to school. In eighteen sixty-three, he returned to New Orleans and enlisted in a Union regiment, and since his discharge he has worked as a boatman and then as a house painter. I believe he has a future in politics. He makes friends and keeps them, and when we win the right to vote, his Negro blood will be an asset. My friend Doctor Dostie— I want him to meet you and Miss Sapphira, one of these days—has a high opinion of Pinchback. They were both speakers at an equal-rights meeting back in eighteen sixty-three, and they've been friends ever since. May I bring him to meet you?"

When he did so, both Tony and Sapphira liked the young man— he was not yet thirty years old—feeling in him intelligence and courage and at the same time a deep humility. He meant to devote himself to helping his race. "I want to do many things for them," he told Sapphira, Tony listening. "But before I can help them, I must make myself as good a man as I can—and as powerful as I can. And I must know how to deserve that power."

Tony, watching him as he spoke, observed the hint of seated sorrow in his eyes, and understood the source of that wistful sadness. Such men as Pinchback—and such women as Sapphira—knew the tragedy of complete frustration. For white men and women of their ability, anything was possible, but not for them. Tony in the past had not thought of the Negro as a problem, but now his curiosity was aroused. What had men thought upon this problem of the races in the past? What were they thinking now?

As a result of one of his questions, young Pinchback brought him a book containing selected essays from *De Bow's Review,* many of which dealt with some aspect of slavery. For the most part they were repetitions of dogmas long familiar, which Tony had till now accepted without thought; but now they struck at Sapphira, so that he wished to throw the book angrily aside. Yet he returned to it day after day.

The ground floor of the house on Felicity Road was largely given up to service rooms, but on one side of the hall that led through from the street to the garden behind the house there was at the front a reception room, and then another room which Tony called his office. At early dusk on a January evening he was there, reading *De Bow,* when he came to a passage dealing with slave laws in force in South Carolina, and as he read he tightened to attention.

> When the mulatto ceases, and a party bearing some slight taint of African blood ranks as white, is a question for the solution of a jury. . . . Where the African blood is reduced to, or below, one-eighth, the Jury ought always to find the party white.

His head lifted at a sudden thought, and he went into the hall and called 'Phemy's name. When she appeared, drying her hands on her apron, Tony said in pretended reproof: " 'Phemy, I've told you before! I don't want you touching kitchen work, you hear?"

'Phemy said calmly: "Dese N'Awl'ns niggehs, all dey knows is gumbo an' shrimp, an' bully base. We'uns is et fish till we swim! I's making me some fat-back and cawn bread! Y'all kin eat whut you please."

Tony chuckled. "All right, but you're the housekeeper, not the cook." And he asked: " 'Phemy, do you remember your mother?"

She looked at him in puzzled surprise. "Sho do!"

"Was she black?"

"Nawsuh! Half an' half. My grammaw was black."

Tony clapped her on the shoulder; he left her and went quickly up the stairs and through the drawing room toward their bedroom. To his knock and call, Sapphira bade him in, and he opened the door. The big room was high-ceiled and cool, with tall windows extending to the floor and opening on a gallery that overlooked the court behind. Sapphira sat at her dressing table, brushing her hair. He closed the door and came beside her, his hand touching the faintly rippling black cascade that flowed down over her shoulders to her waist. "I always forget," he told her.

"Forget?"

"Forget what you look like, between times of seeing you. Your beauty forever surprises me." She smiled, and he drew a chair near and spoke her name. "Sapphira."

"Yes?"

"Sapphira, I've just found out, you're not a nigra." Her eyes turned to meet his, and he explained: "Your grandmother was half white. That makes your mother a quadroon, so you're seven-eighths white! The law says you're white!"

She said gently: "What does it matter, Tony? The law doesn't change what I am! The only laws that amount to anything are the ones that say things people already believe, and people won't ever believe a person is white—not if it matters to them whether she's white or not —if they know she's descended from a slave."

"If you were a nigra, the law wouldn't let me marry you, but since the law says you're not, I can!"

She leaned toward him to touch his cheek caressingly. "Our marrying wouldn't change anything, Tony."

He thought how cool her fingers were, how cool and clear her mind. To their serene content together, what could marriage add? "You always know, don't you." His tone was an admission that she was right.

Without direct reply, she began to braid her hair, and he watched with the pleasure he always found in the play of her deft fingers. She asked idly: "Do you expect any gentlemen tonight?"

"I'm afraid so." He rose to stand behind her, looking in the mirror at her and then at himself. "Doctor Dostie asked if he might bring a Mr. Parker." He said with a chuckle and a smile. "Look at me and look at you." He was almost sixty, a lank, big-jointed, spare man not so tall as at first glance he seemed, his hair and beard arrogantly black. "The scarecrow and the angel! I'm a lucky man."

"You're a good man," she told him, and let her hand touch his. "Good to me."

This would not be their first visit from Doctor Dostie, whom Doctor Roudanez had long since brought to call. Born in upper New York State and by profession a dentist, Dostie came to New Orleans in the early fifties, and during that turbulent decade he was conspicuous in his opposition to secession. When Louisiana seceded, he refused to take the oath of allegiance to the Confederacy, and passed into the Union lines; but after the fall of New Orleans and its occupation by Northern troops he returned, and at once made himself a conspicuous figure among Union sympathizers in the city. Though not a member of the 1864 Constitutional Convention, he attended each session, and in the Free State campaign he became a candidate for Congress, campaigning as "the Robespierre of the Revolution." His defeat was a bitter blow.

Dostie had come with Doctor Roudanez a few nights before, when the talk turned to that 1864 Convention which, under the protection of Federal Troops, eventually drafted a Constitution that freed Louisiana slaves.

"After having been ratified under pressure," Doctor Roudanez then remarked, and at Tony's question—the editor's pockets forever bulged with letters and clippings and pamphlets—he produced a mass of material, and selected a letter—or a copy of a letter—and Tony read:

Executive Mansion
Washington, Aug. 9, 1864

Major General Banks—

I have just seen the new Constitution adopted by the Convention of Louisiana and I am anxious that it shall be ratified by the people. I will thank you to let the civil officers in Louisiana, holding office under me, know that this is my wish, and to let me know at once who of them openly declares for the Constitution, and who of them, if any, declines to so declare.

Yours truly,

A. LINCOLN

Tony read the letter, handed it back. "Anyone lose their jobs for opposing it?" he asked.

"Several," Dostie assured him. "Postmaster Parker, for one. Lincoln removed him just before the assassination. Parker's an able man. You should know him."

It was as a result of that conversation that Dostie brought Mr. Parker to the house tonight. 'Phemy showed them up to the drawing room. Sapphira, seated near the best light, was hemstitching hankerchiefs for Tony. He liked to watch the way she dragged a needle across the linen to loosen the threads, catching one thread and pulling it out, and then another and another, and then beginning the swift, deft stitches.

Doctor Dostie introduced his companion. Mr. Parker, then a Lieutenant in the Union Army, came to New Orleans with the forces of occupation, and was assigned to serve as Postmaster. At the time of his removal, he received from the New Orleans papers high compliments on his administration of the Post Office, and perhaps as a result he decided to make New Orleans his home.

Tonight, after paying his compliments to Sapphira, he said to Tony: "I met an acquaintance of yours this evening, Mr. Currain. General Longstreet. He and Mr. Owen were having a toddy together when I stopped in at the St. Charles."

"I've met him, in the past." Tony assented.

"He's going into business with the Owen brothers here. They're cotton factors. I mentioned that I was about to call on you, and he said your brother served on his staff." Tony did not comment and Parker said: "The General was most cordial."

Doctor Dostie, never long content to be silent, took the word as a cue. "That's more than can be said for most rebels. One of them yesterday took care to let me hear him say there were just two kinds of Yankees, damned sons of bitches and damned blue-bellied sons of bitches, depending upon whether or not they were in uniform." Tony, deeply resentful of such language in Sapphira's presence, started to rise, but Sapphira checked him with a reassuring smile, a negative movement of her head. Dostie, completely heedless, went on: "Yes, and insulting Union ladies, too! Chicago friends of mine are staying at the St. Charles, and the ladies tell me they're continually affronted by remarks meant for their ears." He came to his feet, striding to and fro as though the room were a platform. "The damned rebels think they've beaten us," he cried. "With Governor Wells appointing them to every office he controls, the whole state government will soon be in their hands. Yes, and they'll hold on to it, peaceably if they can; if not, by threats or by force. They think the bowie knife and the pistol are proper political instruments."

"Wells is trying to carry water on both shoulders," Parker agreed. "But the rebels themselves are fighting on our side. These new vagrancy laws are just a return to slavery. Congress will resent that."

Tony watched him with a thoughtful eye. Mr. Parker was a man of about forty, who because of thinning hair and a high forehead looked older; his eyes were stern and there was anger in the shape of his mouth, the slight scornful lift of the corner of his left upper lip. His chin was heavy, his neck deeply lined. As though warmed by his own words, he too rose to his feet. "And look at the Opelousas ordinances!" He threw up his hands. "Why the rebels couldn't do better for us if they tried! They'll have every honest man in the North shouting for their blood! And every time they abuse a Negro they throw votes to us." He drew from his pocket a bundle of letters and clippings and selected a letter. "Listen, I received this today from a Chicago clergyman, a Mr. Roy, whom I met here in New Orleans last November. He collected these cases on a three months trip through the South." He came near the light from the wall bracket and read: " 'Doctor Hall of Mobile beat Delia, his housemaid, with a whip. James O'Neil at Stark's landing tried to cut off the ear of a nigger named Joe with an axe. James Sweeney of Mobile took a knife to John Hazel, cut his forehead, stabbed him in the eye. A man named McDonald shot Henry Bowlings because the nigger talked back. George Davis of Mobile beat a boy named Starr senseless with a brick. A man named Sibley in Mobile County killed one Negro and wounded another. A man named Bill Odam cut the throats of a woman and two of her children, threw them into the river and threw her baby, still alive, after them.' " He offered the letter to Tony. "Print that list in your *Tribune,* so Congress will see it!"

"Congress?" Doctor Dostie packed the word with scorn. "What good is Congress? Congress is on the rebel side! It sets up this Freedmen's Bureau, and the Bureau sets up work contracts. What's such a contract but disguised slavery?"

Tony said drily: "And what's a contract to a nigger?"

They had all forgotten Sapphira. "That's one of the things he needs to learn, Mr. Currain," she suggested. "Is it not?" Tony rose contritely, regretting his thoughtless word; he crossed and stood beside her, and Doctor Dostie said:

"It isn't so much a question of the Negro, ma'am. It's a question of politics! The Republican party needs the South, so we need the Negro vote!" His voice rose. "Yes, and we'll have it too; even if we have to disfranchise every white man in the South, and enfranchise every Negro!"

This endless talk of politics sometimes bored Tony. It flattered him to think of himself as in the inner circles of the Radical party, knowing all their plans, yet sometimes his attention wandered. But now when at last the callers rose to go, a word from Mr. Parker startled him to attention.

"You'll be glad to have your brother here, Mr. Currain." Tony stared in surprise, and he glanced toward Sapphira. She had advised against selling Chimneys, sure of Trav's anger, and remembering this, Tony's spine prickled with faint apprehension. Mr. Parker saw his surprise and added: "Or perhaps you hadn't yet heard? General Longstreet had had a letter to say he was coming, said he might settle here, might stay."

"Ah! Well, that will be pleasant." Tony was proud of his casual tone.

When they were gone, Sapphira said with a smile in her voice: "Their friendship won't endure." She came near Tony, holding the lapels of his coat in her hands. "Those two; each wants to hold the floor." Her eyes searched his face.

"I was tempted to show Dostie the door. His obscenities!"

She shook her head. "Never mind him; he won't live long! Men show the mark." And she smiled suddenly and rose on tiptoe to kiss him. "Marste' Trav won't do you harm," she said.

"Eh?" He was surprised. "Oh, Trav? Old Trav?" He chuckled at the absurdity of her suggestion. "Why, God bless my soul!"

Tony's hatred of Trav had long roots. Born a year after his father and mother were married, he was for a while an only child, and the fact that a second son lived only a week and that a daughter was stillborn made Tony all the more precious to his parents. They spoiled him, and so did the house servants and his nurse. By the time he was seven years old he was an arrogant young tyrant, ruling his world.

Trav's birth changed this. "Baby brother" usurped Tony's place in the affections of those to whom till then he had been the all-in-one, and thereafter, his emnity toward Trav was never far beneath the surface. The fact that he did his brother many injuries only sharpened this hatred. When Trav and Enid were married, it amused him to make the bride's mother his mistress, as though in some indirect fashion he thus cuckolded his brother. Thus, to sell Trav's beloved Chimneys gave him a peculiar joy.

Yet when a few days after Mr. Parker's call he encountered Trav in the rotunda of the St. Charles, fright for a moment left him paralyzed. He and Mr. Parker, meeting by chance outside the hotel, had stepped in for a toddy. They approached the bar together, and as they did so, someone jostled Tony so that he jarred the elbow of a gentleman beside him, causing him to drop his glass.

Tony began his apology. "A thousand . . ." But then the other turned, and the gentleman was Trav. Tony for an instant seemed to choke, his Adam's apple pumping. Around them there was suddenly a little space as men backed away. This spilling of the liquor might he seized upon as an affront. But then Tony saw Trav's extended hand, heard his brother say:

"Well, Tony!"

Tony in a vast relief seized Trav's hand and pumped it; he spoke to Mr. Parker, introducing him to Trav. "Now Trav, you'll drink with us," said Tony, and when they were served and had moved back to give room to others, he explained: "Mr. Parker's one of our conquerors. He came to New Orleans as an officer under Butler, but he's decided to make New Orleans his home."

"Ah!" Trav spoke politely to Mr. Parker. "Do you find many of your comrades thus take up their residence in the South?"

"Many, yes," Mr. Parker agreed, and he would have said more—he was a man full of words—but Tony asked: "What brings you here, Trav?"

"Business."

"Can I be of assistance?"

"I doubt it." Trav had decided upon his course with Tony; his tone was perfectly courteous, without heat, yet definite.

Mr. Parker said approvingly! "Business? Ah, yes, the opportunities are everywhere. As soon as conditions are more settled, it won't take long to bring a hundred thousand Northerners into Louisiana."

Tony argued the point. "Doctor Roudanez wants to bring in three million niggers, make Louisiana a nigger state."

Parker smiled. "Governor Wells says that within ten years the Negroes will be driven away or starved out or killed off; says they'll all be gone." He finished his toddy. "There, I must leave you, gentlemen. Major Currain, your servant. Mr. Currain!"

He bowed and turned away. Tony waited in an uncertain silence, and Trav said nothing. A serving man passed with toddies on a waiter and they exchanged empty glasses for full ones, and Trav dropped a coin on the tray, still without speaking. At length Tony said desperately: "Damn it, Trav, the place was mine, if I chose to sell it. Why don't you say something?"

Trav, without answering, drained his glass; he looked for a place to set it down, moved toward the bar, said over his shoulder: "Good night, Tony." He moved away.

Tony hurried home to seek Sapphira's sympathy, blurting out the story, and Sapphira felt him tremble, and shook his arm in a reassuring tenderness.

"Come, Tony, come! It's all right."

"Why, God damn his stinking soul to Hell, what right has he to treat me like a—like a—" Then, in quick contrition: "Oh, I'm sorry! I am sorry." And he cried: "All the same, I'll call Trav out, some day. I'll kill that man."

But he knew this was an empty threat, and so did she.

Sapphira was not only beautiful; she made Tony's drawing room a place which men felt it a privilege to enter. Having come here once, they looked forward to the next occasion. She never presumed, yet to talk with her was to feel the impact of her sound sense and lucid intelligence. Add to this the fact that Tony's wines were well chosen, and it is not surprising that he had many visitors.

That among them were the leading Radicals resulted from the fact that Tony made possible the continued publication of the *Tribune*. The value of the paper, from their point of view, was that it went regularly to every member of Congress, where its news and its editorials could be quoted as effectively as those of the *Bee*, the *Picayune*, or the War-born *Times*, which had leaped to a position of first importance in the city when in the months after Appomattox publication of the *Picayune* was for a while suspended by the military authorities.

To discuss the *Tribune's* contents, Doctor Roudanez came to Tony's almost every day, but there were other visitors. Doctor Dostie, who as a widower led a solitary life, found here an audience, and so did Mr. Parker. Michael Hahn, former Congressman, former Governor, now a Senator without a seat; King Cutler, whose mind was at once the coolest and the boldest among the Radicals; Judge Durell, who had presided over the Convention of 1864; these and a dozen more besides.

One evening in mid-March Doctor Dostie called, in a rare rage at New Orleans voters for re-electing John T. Monroe as Mayor. Monroe came to New Orleans as a boy, worked as a stevedore, and put together among white laborers a political organization the members of which called themselves Thugs. The name was apt, for their favored political weapons were brass knuckles, clubs, Bowie knives, and occasionally pistols. In 1860 their support helped elect Monroe. When General Butler's army occupied New Orleans, the Mayor's refusal to lower the Confederate flag resulted in his arrest and imprisonment, and the empty gesture made him a hero in the city and throughout the South. On his release in 1863, he went to Richmond, and was cordially received by Jefferson Davis, and after the War he came back to New Orleans. Despite his re-election, General Canby had refused to allow him to assume his duties as Mayor, on the ground that he had not yet been pardoned.

While Doctor Dostie was expressing his opinion of Monroe, Mr. Parker was announced, and on his heels Doctor Roudanez and Pinchback. Yet Dostie scarce paused. "The damned rebels, they want too much, too soon! In Georgia, they elected Alexander Stephens to the United States Senate four months after he was let out of jail! And he'd been Vice President of the Confederacy! That was a slap in the face of every man who fought for the Union! And now Monroe! The rebels couldn't be any more completely in control of Louisiana if they had won the War!"

Doctor Roudanez cried: "Congress will use any pretext to throw these scamps out of office."

Parker said drily: "Congress has had enough pretexts, enough Negroes killed, if that were all they wanted."

"Those killings were private acts," Doctor Dostie reminded him. "What we need is something that can be laid right at the door of these rebel officeholders. An execution, something of the sort." He chuckled. "Who'll volunteer to be the martyr?"

Sapphira lifted her head to look at him; she drew over her shoulders a lacy scarf, snugging it about her throat, and Tony saw the movement and came to her side.

"Cold?"

"I felt a little chill."

"Time will work it out," Parker suggested. "But it may be a long wait."

Pinchback commented: "A long wait? Why, Mr. Parker, you white men don't know what waiting is."

"Your waiting is nearly done," Dostie assured him. "It will end sooner than you think, my friend. Equal civil rights, social equality, the vote! They're not far away."

Pinchback shook his head. "They're far, far away." Tony thought he had never heard such sadness in anyone's voice. Pinchback was a handsome man, with dark hair and a warm dark beard, something in the shape of his eyes suggesting the Oriental, and there was a faint furrow between his brows like the mark of pain. "Far away," he repeated. "We are not ready for these gifts. If you gave them to us now, they would spill like sand through our fingers. They must wait on time."

Tony watched him, struck as before by the sadness in this man, but that night when he and Sapphira were at last alone, he asked: "Do you ever think that Pinchback's too humble? Of course there's no such thing as equality, social equality, or any other kind. No man is equal to any other man, except in superficial ways. But the color of his cheek doesn't prove that inequality."

She smiled in one of her rare moments of coquetry. "What is wrong with the color of my cheek, Mr. Currain, if you please?" But as they moved toward the other room she said sadly: "We are humble, yes, Mr. Pinchback and I. It's a lesson we've learned." She looked up at him with grave eyes. "Have you noticed that you never call him 'Mister Pinchback,' as you do Mister Parker and the others. Yes, we've learned to be humble, learned it from our friends who insist that we are better than we are. Such insistence is in itself a little humbling. They protest too much." And as he closed the door behind them: "I think we always suffer less from our enemies than from our friends." He came to help her with hooks and eyes, and she thanked him; then, slipping into her dressing sack, she seated herself at the mirror and began to loose her hair. "'Phemy says Maria is here," she said.

Tony, fitting his boot to the jack, looked at her in sudden attention. Maria had been the cook at Chimneys. "Here in the house?" he asked, puzzled.

"Oh no. Mr. Travis brought her from Chimneys. They brought Maria, and Isaiah, and Daisy, and poor old clubfooted Pike to be their stable man, and Bob, and Quinny to serve Mrs. Currain and Miss Lucy."

"Has 'Phemy seen Maria? How does she know these things?"

Sapphira shook her head. "I'm not sure. Perhaps I have too much white blood in my veins to understand."

In April, Congress passed over the President's veto the Civil Rights Bill, which provided that Negroes should stand before the law in every respect like white citizens, and Tony told Sapphira: "It gives them everything except the right to vote."

She shook her head. "It gives us nothing. It's just a law. Let a nigra try to ride on anything but a Star car, or to go to a white school, or to eat dinner at the St. Charles hotel, and you'd soon see how little it amounts to. I know it's meant to help us, but many will die because they believe it."

He found in her more and more positively this sorrowful foreboding. When in mid-May President Johnson gave John Monroe a special pardon and Monroe took office as Mayor, she said sadly: "That is ugly news. He was a poor man, and poor whites hate nigras. He'll hurt us all he can. Fists and clubs and guns, they're the only arguments he knows." And then, in a strange flat monotone: "He will kill many."

"Eh?" Tony was startled. "Kill who?"

She pressed her hands to her eyes as though to clear them, shook her head, said in hurried reassurance. "Not us; not you, not me."

He learned to share her misgivings, for wherever Republicans came together, it was in an equal resentment at the increasing political preferment given men who had fought against the Union. To the office-hungry Radicals, these former rebels were still traitors. Night after night at Tony's, angry voices went over and over the same ground.

"The mistake was made two years ago," Doctor Dostie declared, during one of these discussions. "The Eighteen Sixty-four Convention should have put a clause in the Constitution disfranchising every rebel, and enfranchising the Negroes. Then we'd be all right. The Constitution would have been adopted just the same."

There were half a dozen gentlemen in the company that night, King Cutler among them. After a moment's silence that held them all, he said calmly: "Why not reconvoke the Convention, do it now?"

That drew many objections, but Cutler, pleased with his plan, met them one by one. The Convention is dead? Not at all, he insisted. The Convention itself gave the President, Judge Durell, the authority to call it back into session.

"That was only if the voters failed to adopt the Constitution," Doctor Dostie reminded him.

Cutler smiled. "We can argue the point—and go ahead in the meantime." He began to suggest objections and then to meet them. "You'll say we can't get a quorum. Well, we can try, and Governor Wells will call a special election of additional delegates. I'll undertake to persuade him."

"The rebels would vote down any such amendment," Doctor Dostie argued. "They wouldn't be disfranchised till the amendment was passed. And the Negroes wouldn't be voting."

Cutler's eyes swung around the room. "Suppose we let Congress worry about that," he suggested. "They'll be on our side, see things our way."

They arrived that night at no decision, but the seed was sown. When the others were gone, Sapphira met Tony's eyes.

"Do you know what will come of all this?"

"Talk, and talk, and more talk?"

"More than that. In the end—killing. And when there's killing, it's always nigras who are killed."

"I expect Doctor Dostie'd welcome some killing," he reflected. "At least he'd like to see enough of it to show Congress that Southerners can't be trusted. You remember he said here one evening that a martyr was needed."

She began to fold and put away her needlework. "I heard him, yes," She moved around the room, turning off the gas. "Too many of his words sound to me like blood flowing."

A day or two later, Doctor Roudanez brought news of a riot in Memphis, after a collision between the police and some discharged Negro soldiers. "And now a mob's taken over," he said excitedly. "They're burning every house where a Negro lives, and there are dead Negroes all over town. That ought to give Congress something to think about."

Sapphira said quietly: "You sound happy, Doctor. Are you happy because nigras have been killed?"

"Their deaths serve us all! I salute them!"

"I do not think they will find any solace in your salute."

The other shook his head. "Madam, you're chickenhearted! This is a war, a war for human rights. A few deaths don't matter; not if they win a victory."

Tony one evening came home from the *Tribune* office to find Sapphira sparkling with amusement. On an errand which took her to Canal Street, she had encountered Enid. "And Mrs. Currain spoke to me," she told Tony. "I'm sure she didn't remember me. She took me for a Creole lady, tried to talk to me in French."

"I didn't know she spoke French!"

"I'm afraid she doesn't." Sapphira smiled. "But perhaps she's trying to learn, and wished to practise on me. When I answered her in English, she didn't know whether to be relieved or disappointed."

"It's a wonder she didn't know you. How long since she saw you?"

"I was thirteen. I had begun to grow up, and she thought Mr. Travis had noticed me, so she made him sell me to Mr. Pettigrew. I was—big for my age," she admitted, looking at her image in the mirror, amused at her own remark. "But my hair was in short pigtails, and my clothes were different." Her eyes shadowed, and she laughed in a curious, abrupt way. "I wore, the day I left Chimneys, an old, stained, torn frock that had belonged to my brother Isaac . . ."

"Frock?"

"You know, a coat, a working coat. It came halfway to my knees.

And a skirt 'Phemy had made for me out of sacking, and nothing much under either of them. And no shoes." Her tone was as bitter as that memory.

He asked in sudden curiosity: "Did Trav ever—pay any attention to you?" He chuckled. "I can't imagine it!"

She smiled. "I don't think you're very complimentary!"

"Not old Trav," he insisted, and he asked: "What was your task at Chimneys?"

"Minding Miss Lucy, till Mr. Travis sold me."

"You've never told me anything about yourself. How did you learn to read?"

"Well, when I was in the big house so much, taking care of Miss Lucy, I stole a book for Peg-leg. He told me which one, and showed it to me on the shelf, and he promised if I'd steal it for him he'd teach me to read it. And he did."

Tony watched her in quiet wonder. "Could Peg-leg read?"

"Yes, some. He knew the letters." She added: "And Big Sam could read, and two of Mrs. Pettigrew's people. They never let white folks find it out, but sometimes they'd teach others that wanted to learn, so they could do the way the white folks did. But when Mrs. Pettigrew found out I could read some, she helped me."

He chuckled, shook his head. "Surprising. But I expect a lot of things went on in the quarter that the big house never knew."

Sapphira laughed aloud in a way Tony had never heard. "They did so!" she cried, hugging herself, her body swaying as though in a remembered ecstasy. "Some things white folks never could know."

"Why not?"

She hesitated, sobering in thought. "I don't know why not. Maybe because a white woman can't ever forget she's white." And after a moment, half to herself: "Maybe I couldn't have the fun I used to have, not now. Maybe you have to live like an animal, to be able to act like one."

A curious embarrassment made him change the subject. "So Enid spoke to you?"

"Yes. Yes, she asked the way to Camp Street, and she said she was Mrs. Currain. She was full of talk."

"Why didn't you introduce yourself?"

"I didn't want to embarrass her."

"Damn it, Sapphira, you're as good as she! Or better!" Tony rose in anger, stalked across the room and back. "Her mother was my mistress for ten years; mine for money, never for love. And I'm dead sure that Enid herself betrayed Trav with Darrell. Darrell all but told me. So don't be so humble! You're as good as she is!"

"Shall I invite her here?" There was teasing challenge in her tone. "Well—" He cleared his throat, embarrassed. "Well, I suppose that's not practical." He sat down again. "But Sapphira," he insisted, "There's a change coming. When the nigras vote, a lot of barriers are coming down."

She smiled. "Men's barriers, perhaps, but not women's. Wait and see."

5

THE NEW HOUSE, and the pleasant excitement of furnishing it and moving in, made the spring months a happy time for Enid. There was so much to do, and it was such fun to do it. She was even for a while sufficiently interested so that she took over the housekeeping, serving out for each meal the necessary provisions, loving the jangle of the keys at her belt. With old Pike driving the carriage and Daisy to carry her purchases, she liked to go before sunrise Sunday morning to the French market. This was an adventure almost frightening, but she came to take pleasure in the clamor of Negro voices, as fat cooks chatted with the fish dealer, or the fruit merchants, or the potato vendors. There was the blended fragrance of oranges and lemons and bananas and pineapples all overlaid with other smells from chicken crates or fish tables. The faces were as fascinating as the wares displayed; white ladies with Negro servants moved among savage countenances of mixed Negro and French and Spanish blood, and one might see a plaintive Sicilian girl and her mustachioed husband, with oranges for sale, or Indian women offering small bags of filé for your gumbo. There might be old men selling shoestrings and cravats, or a land shark waiting to trap a sailor ashore, or a young Creole with haggard cheeks and inflamed eyes sipping hot coffee to forget the night just past. The place was a babel of tongues, French, English, Spanish, a patois blend of Cajan and every other language, with rarely the gutturals of German and occasionally a hint of Gullah.

And each stall had its wares for sale. In one, flowers according to their season; in the next, mutton and beef and pork; in the next, oysters, shrimp, flounder, lobsters, red snapper, pompano, whatever the Gulf or the Lake afforded; in the next, quail, ducks, doves, rabbits, venison, perhaps a bear steak; then onions, lettuce, cabbages, cauliflower, carrots, tomatoes. The variety was dizzying, and at first Enid bought so much that even the servants' appetites were unequal to the task of consuming it all.

The only blemish on her happiness was the weather. When a succession of dull and rainy days deposited upon stair rails and table tops and every exposed wooden surface a slimy moisture like greasy dew, Enid was ready to abandon New Orleans forever. Too often, such days were so humid that to have a fire in the room was unthinkable, and she was likely in such weather to stay abed, with opium to shut away the intolerable world. At such times the house seemed to her a moldy old ark fit only for toads to live in, and New Orleans became a sink of sin from which they would never escape untainted.

But when the sun shone, the world was beautiful. She never tired of strolling along Canal Street, with Lucy or Peter to keep her company, scanning the forever changing faces. The banquettes presented an extraordinary human panorama: ladies and their escorts; Negro bootblacks soliciting business; bouquet sellers, usually Negroes but sometimes white women, offering bust knots of violets or rosebuds; newsboys vending their wares; roustabouts down from the levee, their trade indicated by the shining cotton hooks dangling in their hands; men whom Trav described as ropers for gambling houses, standing idly at corners here and there; well-dressed freedmen, as often as not talking in French; throngs of ragged Negroes who a few years ago were slaves now sitting in the sun or dawdling along the banquettes or waiting pointlessly in favored spots; soldiers in Union blue, and men in gray coats which though innocent of buttons were obviously treasured uniforms; Yankee newcomers staring at everything and speaking in strange nasal voices.

The best time was from noon till two o'clock. Then there were many ladies bent on shopping, tiny parasols tilted against the sun, and the confectioners' shops were crowded, and every belle had her beau, and you could study the newest fashions. Enid and Lucy observed that hoop skirts were no longer so wide that a doorway was a problem, and Enid put herself into the hands of a dressmaker. To meet the current style, she acquired corsets needing for the lacing more strength than Quinny could muster, so Daisy might be called to help. She made Quinny learn to dress her hair high on her head, and with a justified pride in her small feet she allowed the dressmaker to shorten her skirts and petticoats in the new way.

Oh, life was a delight—when the sun shone. To drive out the Shell Road to the lake was delicious, with charming small restaurants hidden in bowers along the way, and Negro boys fishing in the canal beside the road, and boats passing, and the dark green foliage reflected in the water. If Trav were with her, or even Peter, she might sip a glass of soda water in the beautiful summerhouse where the Spanish Fort used to be, and where the dismounted cannon fascinated Peter.

She relished all she saw; Canal Street, the market, the levee, the establishments along Royal Street where fortunes were said to change hands on a roll of the dice or the turn of a card; the fine mansions along Basin Street. "Such beautiful houses," she told Trav at supper one night. "I'm sure they must be the wealthiest people in New Orleans. Yet it was curious; there were no children in the yards."

Peter snickered, and then felt his father's eye and smothered his mirth, and Trav waited till he and Enid were alone before he explained. She had a thousand questions—which he could not answer. "I only know the common talk," he assured her, and because she saw he was embarrassed and uncomfortable, and to torment him, she declared that he probably knew every hostess from one end of Basin Street to the other.

Every aspect of New Orleans life delighted her—on fine days. When the sun shone, she could never drink her fill of this new world; the dark days she thought would never end.

Their first friends in New Orleans were the Morgans, friends of Brett and Cinda. Judge Morgan had in the past handled for Brett some legal matters. His young brother Jimmy had married, last October, Helen Trenholm, daughter of the former Secretary of the Confederate Treasury. Mr. Trenholm's residence was in Charleston, but he had a villa, De Graffin, in Columbia, and Brett and Cinda were among the guests at the wedding there.

"And you'll enjoy each other," Brett promised Trav. "So look him up. I'll give you a letter to him."

When Trav called at Judge Morgan's office to present Brett's letter, the Judge remarked that he had last seen Brett at the wedding, and he said that Jimmy and his bride were now in New Orleans. "Theoretically, he's been reading law with me," he explained, with a smile. "But they're young—Jimmy won't be twenty-one till next fall—and he spends more time driving out the Shell Road to dine at Jules Coché's place, or with some of the gay blades at Victor's or Moreau's, than he does on his books." Trav smiled, and Judge Morgan glanced again at Brett's letter. "Mr. Dewain says you have a daughter. My sisters will call upon her." He hesitated. "Perhaps I should warn you, I'm a Union man, so I've been an outcast through these War years; but I lost two brothers in the War, and Jimmy did his share of fighting, and my sisters were ardent secessionists, so New Orleans is beginning to forgive me. The girls are often at the house, and the Pierce girls are their friends, and between them they attract a coterie of beaus." He smiled. "Plenty and to spare."

Trav said Lucy would be happy to know them, and he asked: "Have your Union sentiments led you into politics?"

"No." Judge Morgan smiled. "Except that one of the local Radicals, a Mr. Parker, approached me this winter to suggest that I turn Republican."

"I remember General Longstreet once remarked that it would be a good thing for the South if some of her best men did just that."

"But not for the man who did it," the Judge suggested. "To be a Union Democrat is bad enough. I speak from experience. But a Southern Republican would be just a plain scalawag." He added: "No offense to the General."

Trav rose to say goodby. "Oh, he spoke half in jest, overstating the case to make his point. A habit he has. Good day, sir. We will meet again."

Judge Morgan's sisters, not much older than Lucy, presently came to call, and Mrs. Morgan too. Through the Morgans and through Trav's business contacts, their circle of acquaintances and friends widened rapidly.

In April, Brett came to see what progress had been made on the cotton-oil mill. "I had business in Mobile," he told Trav. "Couldn't go home without seeing you all. Besides, too many of my investment eggs are in the railroad basket. I need another outlet."

Mr. Cist had been called to Cincinnati by the illness of his mother. "But of course I can show you the mill," Trav assured him. "Though he could explain things more clearly than I. We'll go over tomorrow, if that's agreeable."

Lucy had not seen the mill, and she elected to go with them. Peter, too, might have gone, but Trav had entered him a fortnight before in Mr. Soulé's commercial college, which held its classes in a room over Lyons's clothing store, at the corner of St. Charles and Common Streets. There were thirty-five or forty students, from ten years old into their early twenties, and Peter, at first rebellious, had come to relish this new experience. He had Trav's delight in figures, and Mr. Soulé had paid Trav compliments upon his progress.

Lucy and Trav and Brett crossed to Algiers on the ferry from the foot of Canal Street, and Trav pointed out the roof and the upper floors of the mill building, half seen beyond the levee. "The building's well along," he explained. "And we're putting in the machinery. Having some trouble. We haven't found any really good mechanics."

"Mighty few anywhere in the South," Brett agreed. "During the War even our railroads were largely run by engineers and firemen who'd come down from the North."

They landed at Villeré Street and walked to the mill. In the yard, Lucy recognized Bob, with another Negro, carrying half a dozen long planks, and realized she had not seen him around the house for some time past. Then Mr. Fiddler met them. The former overseer was now assistant manager under Mr. Cist, and Trav suggested that Fiddler show them what there was to see. The other smiled and shook his head, saying to Brett: "Mr. Cist is the man to do that, not me; but Mr. Currain knows as much as Mr. Cist. He can tell you."

"Well, we'll look around," Trav agreed. "But Mr. Fiddler, you'd better come along." During the next hour he told Brett every detail of their plans, showing him every building. "This is our storage space. Our seed will come downriver, will be unloaded at our own landing." He took them to the crest of the levee to see where the wharf would be, then turned to look back at the building. "Three stories and a half," he pointed out. "A hundred feet long and fifty feet wide. We'll have a twenty-horsepower engine—the engine room's outside, to avoid the danger of fire—and run two pairs of five-box presses." He led them back toward the mill, continuing: "We're putting in the Sypher hullers. They're the best."

Lucy, amused and happy and proud, thinking that he was talking as fast as Mr. Cist, prompted him with a question. "What are cipher hullers, Papa?"

"Mr. Sypher invented them. They're to take the hulls off the seeds, so we can get at the kernels. There's a barrel-shaped cylinder, with knives set in it, and it's inside another cylinder with more knives, and the inside cylinder revolves—fast and the seeds go through between the two. The knives break up the hulls, and then the whole mess goes into a sieve that lets the kernels drop through. The hulls go on to the engine room. They'll be our fuel."

He went on without pause. They had reached the hullers, now in process of assembly, so he could point out the details, and Lucy thought he sounded ridiculously like Mr. Cist. His words came in a steady flow. "Then from the sieve here, the kernels will go up on elevators to the attic, and come down through the rollers— they're not in yet—and after they're mashed into a sort of meal, that goes into the heater—this is it, over here—and then into bags made out of woolen duck, and into hair books, and then into the press. It takes about seven minutes to press out all the oil, and then the cakes of meal are set out to dry for cattle feed."

"Do you get all the oil out of the seed as quickly as that? Seven minutes?"

"Not all of it, not with the machines we have now," Trav admitted. "You see, there's a lot of lint on the hulls, and that soaks up some of the oil, and the hulls soak up some more, so you can't squeeze the meal absolutely dry. That's one of the things we hope to change."

"Is the oil ready for the market, just as it comes out of the press?"

"No. No, it has to be treated with soda ash, heated a little and then cooled. Twice is usually enough."

"Have you figured taxes into your costs?"

"There've been no taxes collected in Louisiana since eighteen sixty-one."

"None at all? How's the state paying its way?"

"Issuing currency notes!"

"Good God!" Brett swung to Lucy in quick apology. "I'm sorry, Honey, forgive me."

She smiled. "Are notes as bad as all that?"

"Pretty bad," he assured her, and he said to Trav: "There'll be taxes eventually, of course, and this three-cent tax on cotton will put a lot of planters out of business, curtail your supply of seed, raise the price."

"There are a thousand hazards in the way," Trav agreed. "We discover new ones every day. But so far, we've met them."

When they said goodby to Mr. Fiddler and left the mill, they passed through a fringe of idle Negroes, and Trav remarked: "There's no shortage of labor, at least. We could hire every man in sight here, if we wanted to. There aren't any factories in New Orleans to amount to anything, so plantation nigras who flocked into the city can't get jobs. The Yankees tried a scheme of forced labor to keep them at work, but the folks up north called it reviving slavery, so that had to stop. The plantations will absorb the nigras eventually, but so far most of them are idle."

"I expect it takes capital to make a plantation, just as it does to start any other business," Brett reflected, and aboard the ferry he said soberly: "What the South needs most of all is capital. When we lost our slaves, the value of our land vanished with the slaves, so now we must start over, saving, accumulating. Of course, land is capital, and so are factories, and slaves used to be capital. But it's money capital we need now. The first job of every Southerner now is to work, to earn, to save!"

"That's why I rented a house, instead of buying," Trav agreed. "I'll keep my money capital in hand till the mill is in profitable operation."

"How soon do you think that will be?"

"I'm not expecting to take much of anything out for four or five years."

"We'll spend a lot of money there before we see a profit!" Brett assented, and Trav looked at him in quick inquiry, and Brett said: "Yes, I'm coming in with you."

"Good. There's room enough for all."

They landed at the foot of Canal Street and took a hackney, dropping Brett at the St. Charles to make a business call. When she and Trav were alone, Lucy said apologetically: "Papa, Mama and I have spent a lot of your money these last weeks. Oughtn't we to be helping you save?"

He chuckled. "If it comes to that I'll let you know."

"I didn't know Bob was working at the mill."

"Bob was getting too big for his britches," Trav explained. "He'd begun to bully Peter. I caught him at it, one day, in the stable. He was giving Peter a sound spanking!"

"How dared he?" She was quick with anger. "He ought to be whipped!"

"Peter was ready to kill him," Trav agreed. "I told Bob to get off the place, but he wouldn't go without Quinny, and Mama wouldn't let Quinny go, so I sent Bob to work in the mill."

"Was that why you put Peter in school?"

"I suppose I thought he was old enough to start learning something useful."

"I was glad to see Mr. Fiddler," she remarked. "Where does he live now? We never see him here."

"In a boardinghouse beyond Canal Street."

"I expect he's homesick for Chimneys." Trav did not speak, and she added: "I know I am, sometimes."

He cleared his throat in an awkward way. "Mama's having the Morgans to dinner Thursday night, and the Longstreets, for Uncle Brett."

She made a small grimace, hugging his arm. "Just you old people! That won't be much fun for me! But I don't really mind," she assured him, and smiled fondly. "I like old men like you!"

"You'll have to play Aunt Cinda for the occasion," he suggested, and Lucy, with a sudden twinkle in her eyes, promised to try. When the time came, she dressed the part, Enid entering into the jest, furnishing a gown and helping Lucy pad herself to Cinda's matronly proportions. So they were merry at dinner; but afterward, when the ladies for a while withdrew, the talk turned to politics. Longstreet asked for news of South Carolina.

"Well, Charleston's a ruin," Brett admitted. "Grass growing in the streets, the wharves rotting away. A lot of Northerners have gone in and bought property and apparently intend to stay; but aside from the cotton brokers, they're the only business life in the town."

"Southerners don't take kindly to business," Longstreet agreed. "I know from my own attempts."

They smiled with him, and Brett went on: "The phosphate deposits near Charleston promise to amount to something, though it's Northern capital that's doing the developing."

"Are your neighbors accepting the new order of things?"

"Well, every so often someone kills a nigra—if that's what you mean. Two of them were found with their throats cut, down by the ferry landing, a month ago."

Longstreet said reflectively: "I hear hard things from Texas. Goree and I—he was on my staff, Judge—he and I exchange letters. Thirty or forty counties over there still stick to slavery, and enforce it, and the courts back it. A man named Bray, in Lamar County, had one of his women whipped for insolence, and when her husband protested, claiming they were free, Bray took him to court and had him sentenced to seven years in jail."

"It's a wonder they didn't hang him for being so uppity."

"Treasury agents have been out there, seizing cotton," Longstreet went on. "They claim it belongs to the Confederacy, or else they demand a bribe before they'll let it be shipped. Goree says they made a Mrs. Boyce in Red River County sell four hundred bales at seventy-five dollars, bales worth at least two hundred apiece, cotton she'd raised herself."

Brett asked: "General, have you ever thought of going into politics?"

Longstreet cocked an eyebrow. "How can I? I haven't been pardoned. I'm not a citizen. I haven't even the rights Congress grants the nigras. I'm just a prisoner of war, on parole."

"Parole or no parole, you would be listened to."

The General shook his head. "Silence is the proper role of prisoners." He smiled. "No, I'll stick to business—if it'll stick to me. As soon as I've seen Mrs. Longstreet and the babies bestowed in some cooler spot for the summer, I'll set out on a hunt for cotton."

"I suppose New Orleans in summer is pretty uncomfortable," Brett agreed, and then the ladies appeared in the doorway.

"I heard my name, Jeems," Mrs. Longstreet said smilingly, ridiculously small as she came beside her husband. "And I heard something about stowing me away for the summer. But just now it's time you took me home."

The day she met Sapphira on Canal Street, Enid was with Mrs. Morgan, who had stepped into one of the shops, Enid preferring to wait where she could watch the passersby. She saw Sapphira approaching and recognized her instantly—though she dissembled so well that Sapphira was deceived—and on impulse spoke to her. Afterward, in the excitement of the encounter, she wished she might tell someone about it; not Mrs. Morgan, certainly, but some confidant; someone, for instance, like Dolly Streean. Dolly was far away, none knew where, yet Enid must tell someone. When Mrs. Morgan's carriage dropped her at her door and Isaiah let her in, she bade him send Quinny, and she went up to her room and began to fumble with buttons and hooks and eyes, wondering in an irritable fret why Quinny did not come. The day was warm, the windows open, and she heard Daisy calling from the kitchen gallery:

"Quinny! Quinny! Whah you? Come heah tuh me!"

So when Quinny presently reported for duty, Enid said crossly: "For goodness' sake, where were you?"

"Out in de haymow, Missy."

"In the haymow! A hot day like this! What were you up to?"

Quinny giggled. "Long as Daisy an' Maria kin see me, dey thinks up sump'n f'me tuh do, so Ah gits out o' dey sight, most times Ah kin."

Enid said in an amused tone: "Don't try to fool me! You were up in the haymow with some little nigger boy! Now loosen my corsets. I'm going to lie down." And presently: "Now fix the windows."

Quinny went busily about her tasks, humming to herself, her slender body swaying as though she yielded to some inner rhythm. Enid had taken a pill; it made her comfortably drowsy, faintly blurred her senses. "You're too young to remember Sapphira, aren't you?" she murmured.

Quinny echoed in surprise: "Ma'am?"

"Sapphira. You don't remember her."

"Yas'm I does."

"Oh, you couldn't! You weren't more than three or four years old when we sold her to the Pettigrews."

"Yas'm, I wuz a baby when y'all sold her, but I uz mos' as big as I is now when Mars' Tony fotch her back to Chimneys."

"Oh, of course! I forgot!" Enid wanted to talk about Sapphira, but she was too sleepy "Tell Miss Lucy to wake me when she comes home."

"Yas'm."

"And Quinny, you keep out of haymows! And Quinny!" Enid was barely awake. "If I ever catch you in a haymow with Peter, I'll skin you alive."

Quinny giggled ecstatically. "Yas'm, I knows dat! Yas'm, you sholy will! Yas'm, and Bob'll skin him, too!"

But Enid was asleep and did not hear. When she woke it was at Lucy's knock, hours later. She roused, yawning and stretching. "Ho hum! Hello, Honey. Ring for Quinny, will you?" And as Lucy tugged at the bell, she asked: "Oh, Lucy, do you remember Sapphira, used to be your nurse when you were little?"

"Of course. You made Papa sell her to the Pettigrews."

"M-hm! Well, I saw her today, talked to her. You know, Uncle Tony bought her back, and he brought her with him to New Orleans. She's beautiful, Lucy, and well dressed, in good taste, her hair done high. I do think it was amazing that I recognized her. Last time I saw her she was just a yellow wench in someone's old clothes." Then contritely: "But there, Baby, I shouldn't talk about such things to you!"

"I'm seventeen, going on eighteen," Lucy reminded her. "I'm as old as you were when I was born."

"I know, I know, but you're just a child. But—Oh well, these things happen all the time. Actually, I expect she's been good for Tony." She laughed softly. "Lucy, let's go call on Uncle Tony some afternoon, see what happens!"

"Papa wouldn't want us to do that."

"We won't tell him!" And, half to herself, as though thinking aloud: "We'd have to find out where Tony lives. I'm curious to see whether she would show herself."

Lucy made no promises, but that night at supper Enid questioned Trav. "Have you seen Tony? You haven't mentioned doing so."

"I met him on my first trip."

"I know, but since we came?"

"Only casually, on the street."

"Why didn't you tell me?"

"I had no talk with him. There was nothing to tell."

"Was Sapphira with him? I don't suppose I'd know her, after all these years." As she spoke, she caught Lucy's eye with a meaning smile, making her a partner in that lie by indirection.

"He was with a Doctor Dostie," Trav told her. "Dostie's one of the Radical politicians, a fanatic."

"Where does Tony live, do you know? Do he and Sapphira live together? Or does he put her up somewhere?"

"I've never tried to find out." Trav spoke curtly.

"I didn't mean to irritate you, darling."

"I'm not irritated."

"You seem to be!" Lucy thought her mother was deliberately provoking him, goading him to the point of an explosion.

"I'm just not interested, that's all."

"Not interested? In your own brother?" Trav did not reply, and Enid insisted: "And in his affair with this—"

They were still at table, and Trav came to his feet. "Hush, Enid. Before the children."

"Oh, they're not babies!"

"Hush, I say!" He stood over her, and she sighed and sat in obedient silence, and Peter stared fiercely at his father. When Trav turned and left the room, Lucy rose to follow him, and Enid spoke to her.

"Where are you going, Baby?"

"To bed, I guess."

"Oh. Then good night, dear. I was afraid you were taking sides against me. If you ever did, I think it would break my heart." And when the door closed, she smiled at Peter. "You'll always be on my side, won't you, Sonny?"

"Yes, I will."

"Come give me a hug." And when she held him in her arms: "You didn't even know what we were talking about, did you?"

"Sapphira and Uncle Tony? Yes I did."

"You know who she is?"

"Yes. Quinny told me."

"That imp!" But Enid was at once amused. "You and Quinny are pretty good friends, aren't you!"

"Gosh, no, Mama! We just—well—"

She laughed lightly. "Never mind. I see. Of course. I see."

Enid enjoyed New Orleans on fine days, but Lucy was happy there regardless of the weather. She liked waking at first bird song to listen to the silvery chorus which in spring greeted the coming day. She and her father sometimes rose at dawn to ride for an hour or two, exploring the waking city before the day was well begun. These rides together were not now as regular as they had been at Chimneys, since now they kept later hours, and if Trav went late to bed, he slept longer in the morning.

But Lucy, from long habit of waking early for those morning rides, continued to do so, and if the house were still asleep she might rise and dress and beg a cup of coffee from old Maria and then go for a walk through the neighborhood around their home. Huge oaks in many places overhung the street, branches from either side meeting in the middle to produce a shady grotto. The yards were planted with flowering shrubs, each beautiful in its season, and blossoms spread a heavy fragrance on the morning air. Lucy enjoyed the shrubs and the flowers as she did the birds, for their own sake and without knowing their names, but there was one bird which she heard every morning and which sang over and over in the jolliest way: "Bijou! Bijou! Bijou! Bijou!" She never saw it, and even when she sometimes heard it singing in the nearest tree she was careful not to look, fancying that if Mr. Bijou knew she was curious about him he might be embarrassed and fly away. After all, his song was not complicated and artistic like that of the mockingbird, and Mr. Bijou must know this, but he was doing the best he could! Besides, his song was so jolly, fairly bubbling with good humor, while the mockingbird always sounded a little conceited, showing off. He even sang at night, if the moon was bright. Lucy thought the other birds must hate him, for keeping them awake.

Lucy could be happy alone, but from the first she made many friends. Through Judge Morgan's sisters she stepped into a gay youthful circle of pleasant people. She and Sarah Morgan liked each other at once; she and Miriam were almost equally congenial. The two Morgan girls had lived with their mother in Baton Rouge till the Yankees seized the city, and Sarah, with a lively sense of humor, told the story of their adventures so gaily that Lucy laughed as often as she cried. Their house had been looted and left in an obscene disorder, and Lucy thought Sarah must hate all Yankees forever, but when she said so, Sarah shook her head, her curls flying.

"Heavens, no! Some of them are nice. Like Lieutenant Page." The Lieutenant had called upon Trav at the hotel soon after their arrival, to apologize for that incident of the drunken policeman, and during the busy weeks of furnishing the new house and moving in, he was often able to help, was often there. Since the Morgan girls and others of Lucy's new friends dropped in almost daily, to discuss each new acquisition and help decide how it should be placed or hung, the color of the Lieutenant's uniform was soon forgotten, and he naturally and easily found a place in the group of which they were a part.

"Well, you certainly would never marry one of them—would you?" Lucy demanded.

"I certainly would if I loved him. Wouldn't you?"

Lucy did not reply, but she wondered. Even after they were settled in the new house, she saw the Lieutenant surprisingly often. Nig needed more exercise than Trav could give him, so on Lucy's suggestion she and young Page, he on Nig and she on her mare, sometimes rode together in the evening when the heat of the day was past. Sometimes they were alone; more often there were six or eight or a dozen young people in the party.

Lucy liked Don more and more, yet now in a different way. At Chimneys, no other young man ever came to the plantation, and she had dreamed sentimental dreams about the Lieutenant, dutifully hating him because he was a Yankee, yet with a hate that was half jest, half liking. But now she never hated him, and sometimes she wondered why she was not happier. It had been fun to be sometimes angry with him, and even to let him see it, but now all that was gone; they were friends, happy together, and sometimes they laughed at the least provocation, or they smiled for no reason except that their eyes chanced to meet across a crowded room.

She had not noticed that they did this till one night when they played charades at the Morgans' and there was music, and dancing to heat the blood, and twice their eyes thus met, and she smiled without realizing she had done so till she saw that he was smiling. She wondered if he, too, had realized what was happening, but afterward, while he escorted her home, strolling slowly through the warm and fragrant night, he talked with a mysterious earnestness about his work. So many of the Bureau's schools had had to be abandoned for lack of money to support them.

"And of course," he said, "the Legislature will never vote money to educate Negroes, but the South will always have to live with them, and they'd be a lot easier to live with if they were educated."

Lucy nodded a silent assent, thinking that Southern men never talked to her about such things; they just kept telling her how beautiful she was, joking, so that she joked back at them. She decided she liked being serious, sometimes. He was still talking.

"I can see how Southerners would resent some of the teachers we've brought down from the North; the ones who make their classes sing 'Marching Through Georgia,' and 'Hail Columbia' and the 'Star Spangled Banner' and 'Yankee Doodle.' I think they just do it to make Southern people mad."

"Papa thinks the nigras ought to be taught things," she assured him, and then quickly touched his arm. "Sh-h-h! Wait!" He paused, looking down at her, till after a little she sighed. "I guess not. I thought I heard a mockingbird—" She laughed at her own word. "Sort of clearing his throat, getting ready to sing."

Page nodded and they moved on and he said: "If there were more Southerners like your father—" He hesitated. "Well, I wish there were." And he went on talking about schools, and how the Negroes ought to learn self-respect, and Lucy wondered. Didn't young men make love to girls, ever, down in Maine? She smiled at her thoughts, and he saw her smile and said: "Oh I know it sounds funny, but I think it's the thing they need most!"

She wondered what it was he had been saying. "I'm sure it is," she agreed.

"Men like your father are kinder to the Negroes than any Northern men would be," he said. "But some Southerners—well, they're a lot more ready to kill people than we are up north."

She said, to tease him: "Maybe that's why we so often licked you!"

He laughed awkwardly. "I guess I don't know how to say what I mean so that you'll understand. It doesn't matter, anyway; I was just talking."

So he brought her home and said a decorous good night, and she lay awake a long time, wondering why she was not happier after their pleasant evening together, when she liked him so.

6

EARLY IN JUNE, Trav stopped one day at General Longstreet's office and found the General clearing his desk. "Moving?" he inquired.

"Just cleaning up," Longstreet explained. "I'll be away most of the summer, calling on planters up the river, persuading them to let us handle their cotton."

"We'll miss you."

"You're surely not staying in the city!"

"I think so, at least till the heat drives us away! Mrs. Longstreet going with you?"

"I'll take her and the children to Macon, leave her with my kinfolk there. That's well north of here, two hundred miles or so, a lot cooler."

"Be away all summer?"

"Till late fall, yes. October's an unhealthy month here. Of course," the General added, "some years are better than others. There was only one death from yellow fever last year."

"Doctor Mercer tells me consumption kills more people than yellow fever." Trav had met Doctor Mercer through Judge Morgan. Born in Maryland, the Doctor came as a young man to Natchez and won a reputation as a gallant and a wit, a gentleman of matchless gentleness and courage. After the death of his wife, and then of their only daughter, he moved to New Orleans and became one of its leading citizens. Like Judge Morgan, he opposed secession and was an outspoken Unionist, but after secession he put himself and all his resources at the disposal of the Confederacy, and during the occupation of New Orleans he refused to take the oath of allegiance to the Union. He was now in his middle seventies, benign and kindly, universally respected and admired, and Trav valued his friendship.

"Yes, but consumption takes longer," Longstreet suggested. "It isn't so dramatic! When a person takes years to die, you get used to the idea, but yellow fever hits like a bullet." He finished his task, relaxed in his chair. "Of course, it doesn't come every summer, but this summer, even if Bronze John on his Saffron Steed doesn't pay you a visit—"

Trav smiled. "Fancy words!"

"You'll hear yellow fever called worse than that! But this summer, you're likely to have more men killed by bullets than by Yellow Jack." He saw Trav's astonishment, and commented: "You don't follow politics, do you?"

"I never have."

"You'll come to it. You won't be able to help it. There's an explosion overdue."

"I've had an uneasy feeling, now and then; I've heard a lot of angry talk."

Longstreet nodded. "Yes. You see, the Confederates have reconquered Louisiana. Governor Wells has been appointing them to every office in his power, and most of his appointees are a poor lot, cheap politicians. Now Monroe has been pardoned and has taken office as Mayor, and he's throwing out every city employee who wasn't a Confederate soldier, putting Confederates in. He's the man—he and Lucien Adams— who was responsible for organizing the Thugs here, back before the War, during the Know-Nothing campaigns."

"Thugs? A Society?"

"A collection of murdering blackguards, brass-knuckle orators. And Monroe's putting the most notorious of them on the police force. That's the situation. The Radicals want the offices, and the Confederates are getting them. With men like Monroe on one side and Doctor Dostie on the other, you're bound to have trouble."

"I've heard of Dostie, saw him on the street one day with my brother."

"Your brother should be more careful of the company he keeps. Dostie and a man named Henderson are the most rabid of the Radicals. Henderson is half crazy. He's been in an asylum, and they cry out threatenings and slaughter. I heard Dostie make a speech two or three weeks ago—he was talking to the Republican Association, mostly nigras—and he raged against President Johnson for not hanging Jeff Davis and General Lee." He chuckled in his beard. "Probably he would have included me, if he'd known I was listening. He said traitors have been given positions which should have gone to good and patriotic men, that pardoned rebels govern the eleven rebellious states, that leaders of the rebellion today hold the highest offices throughout the South! All that sort of talk!" Longstreet added in somber tones: "Of course, he has some justice on his side. Certainly, when we elect men like Monroe, we give men like Dostie something to shout about!"

"He sounds like a lunatic."

Longstreet snorted. "Anyone who, as things stand today, expects Louisiana voters to elect Republicans to office is a lunatic."

"The best men in the South are all Democrats, of course."

"Exactly! So no one in Washington pays any attention to them. It's high time some of the best men in the South turned Republican; then they'd be listened to."

Trav smiled. "They never will. It's like that couplet—treason never prospers. If they do turn Republican, then obviously they're not our best men."

"How about Judge Morgan?" Longstreet challenged.

"Judge Morgan's a loyal Union man who puts his country above his state, but he's a Democrat, and always will be."

"I know. I know," Longstreet grunted, half in self-scorn. "I believe as he does, but like him I'm a Democrat, and I suppose I always will be." He rose with extended hand. "Well, Major, I must go. Keep your ears open and your mouth shut! I'll see you in the fall."

Trav easily fell into the habit of stopping on his way home from the mill at the St. Charles Hotel; there were usually friends or acquaintances with whom, over a toddy or a julep, he could talk a while. Longstreet's remarks had made him increasingly conscious of the rising tension in the city, but he had heard nothing concrete till Mr. Fiddler one day at the mill told him that New Orleans Radicals were planning to reconvoke the Convention of 1864. "They're planning," Fiddler said, "to amend the Constitution, so as to disfranchise all former Confederate soldiers and give the vote to the nigras."

To Trav this program seemed patently impossible and absurd, and he said lightly: "I doubt if they try that. I can't believe anyone seriously wants to let nigras vote. And of course the other, disfranchising us all by an amendment to the State Constitution, that's out of the question. We wouldn't vote to disfranchise ourselves."

Fiddler hesitated. "You know, living where I do, I hear talk that you'd never hear."

"You don't hear anyone in favor of nigras voting!"

"God almighty, no! No, but everybody says the Radicals will try it, and they say they'll hang whoever starts it, kill the lot of them."

Trav smiled, unconvinced. "No doubt they'd like to," he admitted. "But they won't have to. No one but a scoundrel or a fool would want to give the nigras the vote. It's just talk, I'm sure."

But a day or two later, his confidence was shaken. One of the foremen at the mill resigned to go into the police force, and he told Mr. Cist that Sheriff Hays, who had been a Brigadier General under the Confederacy, was enlisting many of his old command as deputy sheriffs.

"We're going to be ready if we're needed," the foreman explained, but when Mr. Cist asked what need might arise, he said only: "We'll see. We'll see." Then, in mid-June, Congress passed the Fourteenth Amendment to the Constitution, penalizing any state which barred Negroes from the polls and disfranchising former state or national officers who, having thus taken an oath to support and defend the Constitution of the United States, had subsequently violated that oath by fighting for the Confederacy. This so strongly resembled the proposal of the Radicals that Trav began to believe in the reality of their program, but he was reassured when the newspapers reported that Judge Durell, who had been president of the Convention of 1864 and who had been urged to call it again into session, had declined to do so.

On Saturday, the twenty-third of June, Trav met Judge Morgan just outside the St. Charles and they went in together. As they entered the rotunda, he heard an angry voice. "Sir, I look upon the proposal as wholly unauthorized, unjustifiable, and illegal. No more outrageous action was ever contemplated in any civilized government, and any attempt to justify it would be the most profound and contemptible casuistry. And sir, since that is my opinion of the proposal, I need not state my opinion of the proposers!"

A murmur of approval followed his words, and Trav saw the gentleman to whom those words were spoken confront the speaker for a moment, his angry color high, biting his lip. But then, without a word, this man turned and walked out. There was a stir and movement behind him, and some laughter. Trav asked Judge Morgan: "Do you know the gentleman who just spoke?"

"Yes, that's Judge Abell. He was a member of the Eighteen Sixty-four Convention. The other gentleman—the one who walked away—was also a member, Mr. Fish. He's one of the crowd that wants the Convention reconvoked. I'll make you acquainted with Judge Abell."

When they drew together, Trav saw that Judge Abell was still in a heat of anger. After the introductions, the Judge produced a letter and handed it to Judge Morgan. "This prompted the—remarks you heard as you came in," he said. "You may care to read it!"

"So they're going ahead with it!" Judge Morgan commented, as he read, and with a glance that asked permission, he handed the letter to Trav, whose eyes raced along the lines.

New Orleans, June 23

Sir:

Several members of the Convention, as well as the Executive, wish you to attend a meeting of the Constitutional Convention of Louisiana at the Mechanics Institute, Tuesday, June 26th, at 2 P.M.

JOHN E. NEELIS, Sec'y

"That's what this means, yes," Judge Abell agreed. "They'll remove Judge Durell and put in someone else—probably Judge Howell—as president pro tem, and let him issue the call."

"Can they get a quorum?"

"Quorum? No!" Judge Abell spoke in quiet fury. "Seventy-six is a quorum, and I doubt they'll get half that. About sixty delegates live in New Orleans, but not over twenty-five are taking any part in this outrage. It's an outright conspiracy against the Constitution, yes, and against the people of the state, on the part of a dozen or a score of office-hungry politicians. The Convention of Eighteen Sixty-four is legally as dead as last year's catfish! Not even Gabriel and his trumpet could bring it back to life, much less John Neelis!"

Judge Morgan said: "Judge Durell asked my opinion as to his authority to issue the call. I reminded him that I'm no politician."

"He asked mine, too," Abell agreed. "I told him it wasn't a question of authority, and reminded him of that Shakespearean gentleman who boasted that he could call spirits from the vasty deep, and someone asked: 'Yes, but will they come?' I told him no amount of calling would get a quorum, and that even to try to reconvoke the Convention would start a riot, and he agreed. He went to see General Sheridan, to ask about protection, but the only promise he could get was that if there was a riot, the soldiers would break it up. Then he telegraphed to some Congressmen, asking their opinions, and got no reply. So he refused to act. And now, by God, they're going ahead without him!" And after a moment he said with a quiet violence: "That Constitution of Eighteen Sixty-four was conceived in usurpation and brought forth in corruption, but it has some good points, and by the Eternal, Dostie and his pack shan't tamper with it! Not if I can help it, and I think I can." He looked at Judge Morgan. "I'll charge the grand jury to consider the matter. A few indictments will stop all this."

"Under what statute can they indict?"

"I'll find one! Surely there is power in the state to crush the egg which is about to hatch violence. Any assembly that would have a natural tendency to create a breach of the public peace can be stopped!"

"I suppose," Trav suggested, "that the Radicals would like to see a riot, an outbreak, something to provoke Congress into action."

Judge Abell said crisply: "Of course! But if they push this too far, they'll reap the whirlwind. God help us all."

Trav thought that the meeting Tuesday afternoon might end in a tumult, but it was hardly noticed. Among the newspapers, only Doctor Roudanez's *Tribune* reported it at all. About forty men who had been delegates to the Convention of 1864 met and elected Judge R. K. Howell as president pro tem; but Judge Howell made no immediate move to reconvoke the Convention, so Trav dismissed the matter from his mind.

Lucy and Enid were organizing a picnic for the Fourth of July, at Lake Pontchartrain. Judge and Mrs. Morgan would join them, and Sarah and Miriam, and the Pierce girls. Don Page would be there, of course, and half a dozen other young people, and Trav invited Doctor Mercer, and Judge Morgan suggested Doctor and Mrs. Cenas. Their son Edgar had paid Miriam Morgan some attention, and the families were friends. Enid, as she and Lucy made plans together—though she had after the first weeks surrendered to Lucy the management of the household—was gay with happy anticipation. There were days when she seemed to Trav as radiantly youthful as the child he had married. When wet clouds like steaming blankets lay smotheringly across the city, he avoided her wrath, but the fine days were his compensation.

The day of the picnic was perfection. They chose a shady grove, and from across the lake a cool breeze blew, and Enid declared that people were absurd to leave New Orleans in the summer. Trav and Judge Morgan and Doctor Mercer—Doctor Cenas would join them later—sat in casual talk together. They spoke of Austria's invasion of Silesia, as of a petty incident occurring far away. The Mexican revolt, they agreed, would eventually destroy Maximilian. Mexico was a nuisance; she would neither govern herself nor let others govern her.

A group of riders cantered along the bridle path and Doctor Mercer said: "A pretty creature, the horse! In the old days, I never missed the races; the Eclipse course at Carrollton, and the Metairie, where Lexington beat Lecompte, and the Bingaman . . ."

Trav said suggestively: "I've heard of that race, of Lexington, but not the details, Doctor."

"It's a pleasure to recall it, Mr. Currain," the old gentleman assured him. "It wasn't all one race, you know; they raced several times, four-mile heats, two heats a win. At their first meeting, Lexington won the first heat in eight-o-eight, and the second in eight-o-four, with the last mile in one forty-nine—and that on a slow track."

When Doctor Mercer drew on his memories, he never lacked an audience. Sarah Morgan and her beau-for-the-day came to listen, and Miriam and Lucy rescued Lieutenant Page and Edgar Cenas from attendance on Enid and Mrs. Morgan, and the Pierce girls and their young men saw the circle widen and hurried to make a part of it.

"So they were matched again," the good Doctor explained, his gallant eyes welcoming each pretty newcomer in turn. "This time it was for a special purse of two thousand dollars, and this time, Lecompte won; the first heat in seven twenty-six, and the second in seven thirty-eight and a fraction. Then Mr. Ten Broeck—he had bought Lexington after the first race—offered to run him against Lecompte's best time, for ten thousand dollars, with horses to pace him and two weeks to choose his day. And by Heaven, Lexington did the four miles in seven nineteen and a fraction over, and Ten Broeck won the wager!"

He wagged his head with a chuckle of delight. "They raced once more," he concluded. "The following Saturday, April fourteen, eighteen fifty-five. This time Lexington won going away in seven twenty-three and three quarters. That time, gentlemen, won't soon be equaled in a race that is not paced."

He spoke with unction, and there were exclamations of approval. Trav had listened not so much to the story of that famous rivalry as to the old man's gentle voice, and he thought Doctor Mercer was the embodied past, which still lived and—since such men had been a part of it—would not soon be forgotten.

The Doctor said quietly: "That was before the War. Only eleven years ago, but it seems a lifetime, doesn't it?"

So silence held them, but not long. Sarah Morgan was first on her feet, with some laughing challenge to the others; the circle dissolved, and then Doctor Cenas rode toward them from the direction of the Shell Road. He was a distinguished physician, had studied in Paris and was now Professor of Obstetrics at the University of Louisiana. A member of one of the oldest families in New Orleans, he had married —in his early thirties—a descendant of Lord Carmick of Scotland. Their oldest son was killed at the battle of Murfreesboro; Edgar and two married daughters were their surviving children.

Old Pike, sleeping in the shade, scrambled to his feet and limped over to take the Doctor's horse, and Doctor Cenas, stripping off his gloves, came to join the other gentlemen.

"Afraid I'm tardy," he said, in cheerful apology. "But I stopped by the Fair Grounds. Mayor Monroe was just introducing Mr. Marks of the Fireman's Charitable, to read the Declaration, and he took time to argue that Thomas Jefferson hadn't meant 'all men were created equal' as the literal truth!"

There was amusement in his tones. Judge Morgan asked: "A crowd there?"

"Medium, mostly Radicals and Negroes. I saw Doctor Dostie's bristling beard and flowing locks. He likes to shake that mane of his."

Judge Morgan said thoughtfully: "All the same, I'm inclined to give Dostie a measure of credit. You must say one thing for him—something you can't say for most of that crew—he hasn't changed sides. Judge Howell took the Confederate oath of allegiance, and so did Michael Hahn, and King Cutler organized and equipped at his own expense a Confederate company, and Fish voted to hang my friend Flanders for his Union loyalty. Randall Terry carried the black flag in a parade of Confederate soldiers, and Walters raised a Confederate company. Daunoy hired Thugs, and he was a Thug himself. These men, they're just political adventurers, always trying to join the stronger side, with no lasting principles at all. But Dostie seems to live by his lights. He sticks to his guns."

Doctor Mercer nodded. "Yes, certainly, a sincere man. When he says Jefferson Davis and Robert E. Lee should be hung for treason, he means it!" Then he added gently: "If that's a virtue."

They smiled with him, but Judge Morgan urged: "He's a fanatic, certainly, but he's also a determined, resolute, honest, disinterested man."

"Speaking of Dostie," said Doctor Cenas, "Judge Abell yesterday charged the grand jury to indict these fellows. Mayor Monroe's determined to prevent their holding their damned Convention."

In the momentary silence, Trav felt in each a grave concern. Then young Edgar Cenas came with a message, and Trav thought there was an unusually striking likeness between father and son. Probably the son felt as strongly as his father against the Radicals. The young man reported that the picnic dinner was being spread for them under the wide oaks yonder on the rise back of the beach, so they rose to join the others there.

Unless the weather forbade, Trav enjoyed the half-hour's walk to and from the ferry at the head of Canal Street. If the day were too hot, or if it were raining, he used the carriage; otherwise he walked, relishing the exercise, and he was likely to go a block or two out of his way to stop at the St. Charles and hear the news of the day.

On the Monday following the Fourth, as he approached the hotel, he heard from the veranda an angry challenge.

"All right, you've called your damned Convention! What good will that do you?"

Trav did not know the speaker, but in the person addressed he recognized Doctor Dostie. The Doctor's voice as he answered held a triumphant ring. "What good, sir? Why, we will disfranchise every rebel in Louisiana and give every Negro the vote! And that's just the beginning, sir. We mean to—"

Trav passed them, going on into the rotunda, and distance blurred Doctor Dostie's words, but the news that a call for the Convention to meet had actually issued was deeply disturbing. The rotunda was crowded with excited men, all talking at once, and Trav saw a group pressed close around the bulletin board by the manager's desk, reading something posted there. He made his way into this group and when others finished and gave room, he was able to read the call tacked on the board. Men were crowded all around him, and angry voices in his ear, so he found it hard to concentrate on what he read, but he saw that the delegates were summoned to meet in the hall of the House of Representatives, in the Mechanics Institute building, on the fifth Monday in July, at twelve noon. Judge Howell signed as president, John Neelis as secretary.

Someone reading over his shoulder said: "Judge Durell left town Saturday, gone to Washington."

Someone laughed in scorn. "Wise man. Howell won't get out of this alive!"

"Oh, there'll be no trouble! No delegates will show up!"

Many voices joined the discussion. "What if they don't? Less than forty came to the other meeting, but they went ahead just the same. Why, God damn their impudence, there wasn't even half a quorum there!"

"A lot of delegates stayed away from that meeting, and a lot will stay away from the Convention."

"They can't do a thing without a quorum!"

"They can do anything they please, unless we stop 'em!" The speaker added furiously: "And whatever they do, the damned Congress will say it's the law!"

"They'll be stopped." The word was positive. "If the grand jury doesn't stop them, John Monroe will."

It occurred to Trav that Tony, if he still helped finance the *Tribune*, was an ally of these 'Radicals whom men were cursing. If the anger in the voices he heard here around him meant anything, then Tony might well be in danger, and he considered seeking out his brother, to give him a word of friendly warning. About to turn away, he looked around the crowded rotunda for a familiar countenance, and to his complete surprise saw Redford Streean, Tilda's husband, whom he would have supposed to be thousands of miles away. Trav might have avoided the encounter, but Streean had seen him and came toward him with extended hand.

"Thought that was you, Trav," he said. "How are you?" He clasped Trav's hand and shook it with a friendly energy. "You're looking fine."

Trav said uncertainly: "Good evening, Streean." He thought the other had a puffy, pallid appearance, but refrained from saying so. "What's brought you to New Orleans?" He had no slightest interest in Streean's reason for being here; the question was politeness, nothing more.

"Oh, I had some business dealings with a man named Lenoir, here, during the War, and I'm pretty well satisfied he took advantage of me. Came all the way from Paris to find out the truth."

"Ah!" Trav wondered if there was another Lenoir in New Orleans. "See him?"

"No, I hear he's in North Carolina; has a plantation there." If Streean knew how Mr. Lenoir had come by that plantation, he made no sign.

"Are you going to North Carolina to—pursue your investigation?"

"No, I'm returning to Paris. Dolly and I have a house there, rather a handsome place. We occasionally entertain some old friends. A great many Southern gentlemen are traveling in Europe with their families just now. So much distress at home, you know." He added: "We see Captain Pew quite frequently." And as Trav moved to leave him, "Well, glad to have had this chance encounter. Tony told me you were here. Cottonseed, is it?"

Trav did not correct him; he imagined Streean and Tony discussing his business, and felt his cheeks hot and flushed with wrath. "Good day to you," he said, and swung away.

Trav saw Tony a day or two later, but it was from a distance. Through General Longstreet he had met Moses Greenwood, a cotton factor whose home was on Carondelet Street. Longstreet one night took Trav to join in a game of brag at Mr. Greenwood's rooms, and the host invited him to come again.

"Saturday night always finds a few gentlemen here," he explained. "Except in the summer months, when no one stays in town." He chuckled. "Except me." So through this July, Trav, who liked to stroll in the first coolness after dusk, sometimes stopped to sit a while with Mr. Greenwood on his second-floor gallery which caught the faintest breeze.

Together there the following Saturday night, they saw a number of gentlemen, arriving by twos and threes, enter a doorway in Davidson's Row, across the street. Through windows opposite where they sat, they could look into the upstairs room in which these gentlemen were assembling. While they talked casually of many things, they watched those windows, and among the arrivals Trav suddenly recognized Tony. He was standing in profile, with the light full on his face. Mr. Greenwood saw Trav's attention sharpen, and he asked: "See someone you know?"

"Can't be sure," Trav said, but he was sure. They had been speaking of Prussia's victories in Europe, and he continued that discussion. "It doesn't need a West Pointer to see that the Prussian army is a first-rate military instrument. Everything they do is well planned, and carried through with vigor and determination." The room across the street was full of men; they began to seat themselves. "What do you suppose that's all about, over there?"

"I don't know."

"Know who lives there?"

"I'm not sure anyone does. It may be a small hall. Hullo! Looks like we're going to have a speech!" A man had risen to stand facing Tony and the others, and Mr. Greenwood said: "I know that fellow. He's one of those damned Radicals, Rufus Waples."

"Is he a member of the Convention?"

"No, he's just a plain meddling scoundrel, needs to have his neck stretched. Listen; we can hear him."

This was true; the window yonder was open, the night was still, the street not too wide, and the speaker's voice had a carrying quality. Mr. Waples had drawn a bit of paper from his pocket, and he was saying in mock terror: "I may not be long with you, for I received today the following communication." And he read from the paper in his hand: " 'Rufus Waples! Beware! Ten days! Duly Notified! Begone!' " He paused, and turned the paper, examining it back and front. "There's no signature," he said in a doleful tone. "So I can't even beg for mercy!" Laughter applauded him.

"And yet I am reluctant to depart," he confessed. "I was not a member of your Convention, but I believe that it has work to do, and should resume its sessions. I know many of the members, you gentlemen here and others too, and I have talked with them, and with Judge Howell . . ."

Mr. Greenwood stirred in his chair. "He pollutes the evening air," he growled. For a while, politely conversing with his host, Trav could not listen to the speaker yonder; but perhaps because Trav's attention so plainly turned that way, Mr. Greenwood at last fell silent. Mr. Waples was saying:

". . . and the Governor will issue a proclamation—it is already drafted, gentlemen, needing only the signature of the Secretary of State—Governor Wells will issue a proclamation for the election of delegates in the parishes not represented in your Convention of Eighteen Sixty-four.

"But meanwhile there are delegates enough, already elected, to meet and to act. They were elected to that Convention, and that Convention is subject to recall and now has been recalled. You are recalled. Your opponents will tell you the call is illegal, that your very election was illegal; but you must ignore them. You must be present. You must make a quorum there.

"Why? I will tell you why. I give you a guarantee! Congress will legalize and sanction your proceedings and your actions. So come together! Act! It is high time that every man who aided or abetted, yes, or even sympathized with the late treasonable war should cease to enjoy the franchise; it is time that those loyal citizens who have been set apart from the rest of mankind by purse-proud Southern planters because of the color of their skins should be given the right so long denied them; the right to vote!

"So attend the Convention. General Sheridan will protect you, and Congress will confirm and sanctify your deeds. I say to you, gentlemen—"

But Mr. Greenwood, here beside Trav, came to his feet with a wrathful cry, and Trav felt a deep stir of anger within himself. Moses Greenwood said in a choking voice: "By the Almighty, I've a mind—" He strode indoors and drew a match and set the gas alight, and Trav, following, saw him lift a revolver from the drawer of his desk.

But then suddenly Mr. Greenwood laughed, thrust the weapon back into its place. "Don't know why we should let their lunatic notions upset us," he said. "I'll fill our glasses."

"A nightcap," Trav agreed.

Mr. Greenwood closed the windows. "Don't want to hear any more of that!" he grumbled, then chuckled at his own wrath, and stepped to the sideboard where decanter and glasses awaited their pleasure. "Why do we let these rascals excite us with their nonsense? They can't get a quorum, and even if they did, they can't amend the Constitution without letting us vote on it, and we'd damned soon vote it down."

"Unless Congress takes a hand," Trav suggested, and Mr. Greenwood made an angry sound. Their glasses were full; he lifted his.

"Confusion to all Republicans!" he cried.

Trav chuckled. "Down with 'em all! Sir, to you!"

When Trav said good night and emerged into the street, the window through which he had seen Tony was dark, the men who had gathered in that upper room were gone.

During the days that followed, Lucy, always sensitive to her father's mood, felt his concern. On the twentieth he came home and found her in the garden and joined her there. She wore her prettiest dress and was looking her best, and Trav was usually quick to notice such things and to speak of them, so when he did not, she knew he was angry about something, and asked a sympathetic question. "Anything wrong, Papa?"

"You've heard me speak of Judge Abell?" His tone was a challenge, and she answered with exaggerated meekness:

"Yes, Papa!"

"He's a fine man," Trav asserted, like one expecting contradiction. "An able man."

"Able is Abell?" she suggested, smiling.

He nodded in an abstracted fashion and went on. "Yes, able and intelligent and right-thinking. He charged the grand jury that to reconvoke this Convention is dangerous to the peace of the state, and that public officials involved in doing so are liable to criminal prosecution. Now a radical named Daunoy has had him arrested on an affidavit charging him with treason."

Lucy understood only that her father thought this an outrage, but she said sympathetically: "How terrible!"

"Oh, it's absurd, of course. The United States Commissioner wanted to throw it out of court, but Judge Abell insisted the charge be set for trial, insisted on furnishing bail, wouldn't even accept parole."

"They won't do anything to him, will they?"

"No, no, of course not, but the malice behind the charge is what makes everyone so indignant. It's a malicious outrage. I think it was done just to make Southerners mad!"

"Well it worked, then, didn't it?" she asked, teasing him. "You're certainly mad!"

He relaxed, smiling. "Yes. I have a high respect for Judge Abell, so— well, yes, it makes me mad. And everyone feels the same." Then Lieutenant Page came from the house toward them, and Trav said in some surprise: "Why, good evening, Lieutenant." And to Lucy: "Going out, are you?"

She laughed at him. "You surely didn't think I'd made myself so pretty just for you?"

He grinned apologetically. "Matter of fact I hadn't noticed anything special. You always look fine to me!" She kissed him, and he said: "Have a good time. Take care of her, Lieutenant." As they turned to go, he asked: "Is Mama coming down?"

"She's asleep;" Lucy's eyes met his. "Sound asleep." He understood her tone. Sometimes Enid drugged herself to early slumber.

So Trav and Peter had supper together. Trav was always faintly uncomfortable when he was alone with his son, conscious of the gulf between them, blaming himself yet not knowing how matters might be mended. He asked a few questions: What had Peter done today? What did he plan tomorrow? What would he like to do? Peter answered: "Oh, nothing much," or "I don't know," or "Hang around, I guess," till at last they ate in silence.

Afterward, Trav turned again to the garden. He strolled along the shell paths, then sat for a while, half listening to the night sounds: clopping hooves as a carriage passed the house, the horses splashing in the mud left by a late shower; an awakened bird murmuring in sleepy protest in the orange tree above his head, so near that Trav heard the stir of feathers as it rearranged its wings; the chirping of a cricket under the steps yonder by the veranda; the sound of footsteps on the banquette outside the garden wall, approaching, passing, diminishing in distance; the low voices of the passers; the muffled hoot of a steamboat on the river. All over the world, night was a time of hushing, when sounds were blurred and softer, and one's senses were infinitely more alert. How curious that to listen intently one instinctively opened one's mouth. Could one thus hear more clearly? Were there other senses thus brought into play? If we knew they existed, and taught ourselves to use them, would they not serve us well? How reassuring it would be, for instance, to know what was to happen in this Convention business? How extraordinary that with all his searchings after knowledge, man had never learned to look with certainty into the next moment of future time? How absurd to vaunt ourselves upon our powers, when with all the past at our disposal, to be studied as diligently as we chose, we could never surely foresee tomorrow!

He sat a long time, his thoughts drifting. The machinery at the mill was all installed, and by the week's end Mr. Cist thought it would be ready for a trial, but that was only a beginning. Trav was sure that an unnecessarily large amount of oil would be absorbed by the lint still adhering to the seeds, and he had suggested to the mechanics who set up the machines that there must be a way to remove this lint. He had promised a reward of fifty dollars to the man who devised a method which proved workable, but not even a suggestion had been offered. He thought tonight that Southern men lacked almost completely the instinct to do a thing better, more easily, more quickly—and more profitably—than it had ever been done before.

Slavery, he admitted, was probably responsible for this. To do things better than they had ever been done before meant work, but work was for slaves, not for white men. The highest duty of a white man was to be a gallant, brave and courtly gentleman. Beyond that, nothing was demanded; not industry, not achievement, nothing. Trav remembered something Judge Morgan once had said. He had spoken of the death of his brother in a duel. "I think that tragedy first made me realize that the South had faults. I think that was why I remained a Union man throughout the War, because Southern manners, Southern ideals, cost my brother his life."

Trav rose at last, his own thoughts making him restless, and for a while paced up and down, his hands behind his back. When at last he went indoors, he looked in Peter's room and saw the boy asleep and crossed to the bedside, looking down at his son with a deep sadness in his eyes. Somehow he had gone wrong with Peter. There was in the youngster a sadistic streak and a savage cruelty which Trav could not comprehend; its manifestations aroused in him a shuddering revulsion, as though he looked upon a snake. Because he was afraid of this emotion in himself, he had, when Peter erred, held back his chastising hand, fearing he might strike rather out of that secret abhorrence than in simple justice. Now it was too late. Peter, big for his age, as tall as Trav himself, went almost uncontrolled. He and Trav usually walked together as far as Mr. Soulé's school, parting there while Trav went on to the ferry; but they might walk in silence, Trav strangely tongue-tied and unable to find any easy word to say.

He stood by his son's bed a long time, till Peter spoke. "What's the matter, Papa?"

Trav was startled, felt his pulses pound. "Oh, hullo! I thought you were asleep." And he said: "I was just thinking. A man likes to think about his son."

"I thought you were mad about something."

"What about? What would I be mad about?"

"Nothing, I guess. I don't know."

Trav leaned down to touch Peter's shoulder in an awkward caress. "Shall I leave the door open?"

"M-hm. I get more air that way. Good night."

"Good night, Peter."

Trav found Enid asleep, a candle burning on the table by the bed. She sometimes wanted a night light, but he saw now that she would not wake till morning, so he blew out the candle before lying down beside her.

Sunday in New Orleans was more than a day of rest; the city drowsed under a universal hush. Most people walked to church, their voices lowered, even their footfalls softer than on weekdays. After the midday meal, if the day were fine, little groups might gather in gardens here and there; the murmur of soft voices and the ring of occasional laughter moved gently on the flowing airs. Dancing, charades, cards, masques or formal balls marked other nights, but never Sunday. The day was kept for rest and for reflection.

New Orleans was a city of churches. The most numerous—since French and Spanish families had been the earliest settlers—were Catholic; among the Protestant churches, the Episcopalian. Trav and Enid regularly attended Trinity Church, at the corner of Jackson and Coliseum Streets. The Reverend Mr. Beckwith, on the fourth Sunday of this month of July, preached a sermon which seemed to Trav to have the sound of trumpets. The great war was ended; those who had made their surrender were honorable men; terms had been offered and accepted. Woe, then, to any man who sought to provoke a fresh conflict, for war was waste and ruin and madness, and in time of war all men were liars. Not wounds and death were to be feared, but the corruption of the minds of men, leading them to assert the false and to deny the true. War made credulity a virtue and a lie an act of valor and left truth to be despised. Today a band of evil men, covetous and greedy, sought to revive the envy and the hatred and the lies of war: let them beware the vengeance they invited.

After the service they walked homeward at first along Coliseum Street, Enid and Trav together, Lucy and Peter a few paces ahead, and Enid asked what in the world Mr. Beckwith's sermon was all about. Trav, remembering that she never read the newspapers, thought it must be bliss thus to shut away the outer world. "A few Radical politicians are meeting, a week from tomorrow," he explained. "They threaten to give the vote to nigras and take it away from Confederates. The minister told them they'd better not."

"I should say not!" Enid tossed her head. "Perfectly absurd."

"Some people will try to prevent it," he agreed. "And there may be trouble. That will be a good day to keep off the streets."

He had that night and during the succeeding days a sense of waiting. The city was a seething pot; the voices of men in conversation on the street held the strident rasp of rising passion. At the mill Mr. Cist and Mr. Fiddler daily reported hearing threats and counterthreats, and once Peter heard men talking about hanging some people next Monday.

"I heard one man say: 'I've got the rope for Dostie!' " he told Trav that night. "And another man said: 'Yes and by God I'll help you pull it!' "

"I wouldn't use bad language before your mother and sister, Peter," Trav suggested.

"Oh, for Heaven's sake, Trav," Enid protested, "we haven't glass ears, that will break at a word. Go on, Peter. What else did they say?"

"Well, one of them said hanging was too good for them, and the thing to do was shoot them in the belly and let them suffer." Peter spoke with a lively relish.

"Who were these men, Peter?" Lucy asked. "Anyone we know?"

"Gosh, no! They were just standing around in front of Mr. Lyons's store when we came out of school."

She appealed to Trav. "Do you think there really will be trouble, Papa?"

"I can't believe it, no."

"Don doesn't think so, either," she agreed. Trav thought he had never before heard her speak of Lieutenant Page by his first name. "He says the Convention doesn't amount to anything, and no one will come to the meeting, and that's all there'll be to it."

Wednesday evening on his way home from the mill, Trav stopped at the St. Charles. Almost on his heels, Mayor Monroe, with two or three gentlemen, came in. Trav had seen the Mayor once or twice, and had been puzzled by something in the other's countenance; a sort of ferocity, coupled with a troubled frown, as though Monroe were forever torn by inner conflict.

Men now drew toward the Mayor with quick questions. Would the Convention meet? Would he prevent it?

"I've written to General Baird," he said. "To ask what's best to do."

"What about Sheridan?" General Sheridan was in command of the troops in New Orleans.

"He's gone to Texas. Whatever happens, he can say he wasn't here, and take no blame!"

"What'd you say to General Baird?" A score or so of men were gathered now around the Mayor, Trav among them.

"I wrote him that some men whose avowed object is to overturn the State Government are meeting here Monday. I said their meeting was likely to lead to a breach of the peace, and that if these gentlemen met, I intended to arrest them, unless he approved the meeting, in which case would he please let me know!"

"S'pose he does approve it? What then?"

"I'll wait and see." Monroe's tone was dry and threatening. "He's imitating Sheridan. The only thing General Sheridan would say definitely was that if a riot started, he'd stop it. General Baird's one of those men who never listen to you because they're too busy thinking of the clever things they're going to say. That's why I wrote, instead of going to his office. Didn't want to lose my temper." And he repeated: "I'll wait and see."

Two or three men laughed in saturnine amusement. Remembering the Mayor's political habits, Trav thought Monroe would not hesitate to use violence now. He turned away.

Next day at the mill their first lot of cottonseed had been delivered, and they ran five or six hundred pounds through the huller and examined the results. These were last year's seeds, and Trav thought the kernels shriveled and dry. "That may be one of our problems," he told Mr. Cist. "To get a steady supply of fresh seed, before they dry out."

"The oil can't get away," the other assured him. "If the press was ready I'd show you. Plenty of oil in these seeds. The huller does a good job; see!" He picked up a handful of kernels. "The hulls are gone and the kernels hardly scarred. I think the knives are set just right." He added: "Of course, they'll have to be reset almost every day, and reground every week or so; that's one of the things we'll find out as we go along."

"How near ready are the presses?" Trav asked.

"We'll run our first oil Monday—or know the reason why."

Trav saw one of the workmen just beyond Mr. Cist, a Negro, look up as though about to speak; he called: "Boy, you started to say something. What was it?"

The man hesitated. "I ain' gwine be wukkin' Monday," he admitted at last. "I'se gwine be tuh de Convention." And he added: "Heap of us ain' gwine be heah. We got de call."

If the Negroes were being organized to attend the Convention, then trouble was sure. "Well, no work, no pay," Trav said cheerfully. "Suit yourself."

"Yas suh," the man agreed.

Next morning, in the *Times*, Trav found a boxed paragraph.

Friends of Freedom, Rally!

A GREAT MASS MEETING

of all citizens who are in favor of universal suffrage, of the reconstruction policy of Congress, and of amending the Constitution of the United States to give equal rights to all, without distinction of Race or Color, will be held on FRIDAY NIGHT, July 27, 1866, at 8 o'clock, at the Mechanics Institute. Distinguished speakers will address the meeting. Union men, come in all your might and power.

Trav read the paragraph once and then again, and Lucy saw his absorption. "What's so interesting?" she asked, and came to lean over his shoulder, reading where he pointed. "Why, that's tonight!" she exclaimed, and giggled. "Are you a Friend of Freedom, Papa? Are you going to the meeting?"

"I'll probably walk down that way," he admitted.

"Can I come with you?"

"No! No, not by a long shot. In fact, Lucy, till this business is over, I hope you'll stay pretty close indoors."

After a succession of extremely hot days, a gentle but persistent rain had begun at dawn, and Trav sent for Pike and the carriage to take him to the ferry, but before evening the rain ceased, the heat returned. Governor Wells had that day issued a proclamation calling for the election of delegates to the Convention, but the election would not be held till September, so certainly there was no present occasion for the Convention to meet. The whole confused business roused in Trav an irritated resentment. He thought a monk who for penance wore a hair shirt must endure this same persistent nagging, prickling.

After supper, he took a turn in the garden, then joined Enid and Lucy on the upstairs gallery. Finding them alone, he asked: "Where'd Peter go?"

"Oh, out somewhere," Enid told him listlessly. "He's always roaming around. Trav, I can't stand this heat much longer. I'll expire. We'll have to go away."

He nodded absently. "We'll see, we'll see." He heard from a distance a rising murmur of sound. "I think I'll go see what's happening," he decided.

"Want company?" Lucy asked, knowing what his answer would be. He shook his head, and she said: "Well, you can tell us about it when you come home."

Trav considered riding Nig, but a man on horseback would be conspicuous, so he set out afoot. The Mechanics Institute, originally built by the New Orleans Mechanics Society, was a brick and stucco pile three stories high. Destroyed by fire in 1854, it had been promptly rebuilt, and after the Union forces occupied New Orleans and a state government was organized, it became the capitol. The hall of the House of Representatives, on the second floor, was frequently used for large public gatherings.

The Institute fronted on Dryades Street, between Common and Canal. Trav, from as far away as St. Charles Street, heard cheering voices, and as he passed the Medical College buildings he saw in front of the Institute a black mass of people stirring yeastily in the torch-lit darkness where two gas lamps made a feeble half-circle of light.

He crossed the street to the corner diagonally opposite the Institute and looked up at the building huge against the sky. On the second floor in the front, every window was lighted, Negroes standing in silhouette at each one. Here in the street, from a platform rudely constructed of raw lumber, a man was speaking, the light from the gas lamps which flanked the entrance barely lighting his face. Trav came near enough to hear, looking along the banquette for a spot where there would be no one in front of him, and recognized Tony standing with another man a little nearer the corner. There was a space beside him, and Trav took it. Tony recognized him and spoke.

"Evenin', Trav. Big crowd." Trav nodded, and Tony gestured toward the man beside him. "You remember Mr. Parker."

Trav assented. "Good evening, sir."

Tony became suddenly voluble. "A lot of people here. I saw they'd be all full inside, so Mr. Parker and I hailed some of the niggers, borrowed lumber from over behind that hoarding where they're building the Medical College, set the niggers to putting up this platform. Got it done just in time."

"Are you one of the—organizers of this affair?"

"Helping with the arrangements, doing odd jobs."

"I saw the notice in the paper. Who are the—" There was faint irony in Trav's tones. "The 'distinguished speakers'?"

"Inside, there's Judge Hiestand, and King Cutler, and I think Henry Dibble, and Mike Hahn, and Rufus Waples. Judge Hawkins is chairman out here. That's John Henderson on the platform now."

Trav, turning his attention to the speaker, heard Mr. Henderson shout: "Gentlemen and good citizens, I tell you the world is tired of those white men who in the past have driven you to man-killing labor, and grown fat on the sweat of your brow!" Shrill cries applauded him. "Yes, the men who while your children starved, wasted on wine and gambling and in the putrid purlieus of Basin Street the fruits of your toil. They boasted to the world that the civilization of which they were the self-appointed shining lights was the finest ever produced by man!" Hoots of angry scorn. "But no longer, citizens! Now the world sees them as they are, their hands still grasping the whip imbrued with your blood, the strange woman in their arms, the wine cup lifted to their lips, tossing the gold which they have ground out of your bones and blood and sweat to the base and the vile . . ."

His words were drowned in a rising flood of deafening cries, a hysterical uproar of approval from the solid pack of Negroes massed around the platform. Trav said angrily: "The man's a fool!"

Mr. Parker spoke in quiet amusement: "I'm trying to figure out how many hands that fellow had, the fellow he was talking about, with a whip in one hand and a glass of wine in another and a woman in his arms and tossing out gold!" He added more seriously: "Matter of fact, Major Currain, Henderson is a fool, legally so adjudged. He's been in the asylum. But these people love his raving."

The Negroes were calling out for more. "Yas, man!" "Da's de truf!" "Yas suh!"

"I confess to you," cried Mr. Henderson. "I confess to you that once I thought you not yet ready for the suffrage. But now I have studied the votes of those traitors too long unhung, for whose blood the very stones in the street are hungry, and I say to you that I would rather have representing me in Washington a good, loyal black man than a white traitor.

"The only good men in Louisiana today are the Republicans and the Negroes. The Republicans are your friends; the rebels, men, women and children, they are your enemies! Never forget it! Will you let them—"

Roars and screams drowned his words. With upflung hands he seemed to lead that mighty chorus, but then another man appeared beside him and tried to make himself heard. Trav guessed this was Judge Hawkins, introducing the next speaker, and he heard the name Judd. Tony and Mr. Parker moved away, and Mr. Judd proved too moderate to please the audience; but then a new speaker, by his dress and manner a minister, came to face them and quickly roused the Negroes to a high and higher pitch.

Suddenly from a spot in the thickest of the throng, someone cried out, a thin, gargling cry. The crowd seemed to bubble and swell, and the men pressed back from a common center, and a limp figure was lifted out of the mass and up to the platform. Trav, looking across from where he stood on the banquette a little above the street level, saw the man's heels chatter on the boards, and he heard the word "fit" repeated and repeated.

Then the heels ceased to chatter and he knew the man was dead. Ready helpers lifted the body and hustled it away, and as the platform cleared, Trav saw Doctor Dostie standing there with lifted hands, his face upturned to the sky, his big beard jerking with the movement of his jaws as he spoke.

While the tumult persisted, Trav could not hear his words, but as the crowd quieted they became audible. "Yes, friends, our brother is dead! He's not the first martyr in this cause we serve, nor will he be the last. But if we march shoulder to shoulder, our final victory is sure, as sure as that you are free men. We Republicans, with your help, have freed you from your enslavement under these hell-born and hell-bound scoundrels and traitors. Now, with your help, we will do more!"

He raised a clenched fist, pointed a sternly shaking finger at the Institute across the street. "We propose to meet in that hall up there at noon on Monday, and to disfranchise the rebels, and to enfranchise you!" And when he could be heard, he cried: "But we cannot do that unless we have your support." Bold shouts answered him, but he held up his hands. "No, no, no! It isn't fighting we want; it is your steadfast support, proof that you are with us as we are with you.

"Come here Monday; come to that hall up there where the Convention will meet, give us there your aid and countenance. But be peaceful as you are peaceful here tonight.

"Yet my friends, let there be no cowards among you!" His voice rang, and a shout responded, and he repeated: "No cowards! This is not a time for cowards! So come bravely. Yet remember that you are now citizens, and that except for the vote you have just as many rights as the white man. When you were slaves, a white man could strike you as he chose, but if you struck him, you were killed. Now, that is no longer true! Attack no man; but if you are attacked, defend yourselves! I do not bid you come armed, but you have as good a right as any white man to arm yourself. So come peacefully, attack no man; but if you are attacked, then—remember Fort Pillow!"

A cry like a single scream from five hundred throats rasped Trav's ears; Doctor Dostie once more hushed them to silence, and he finished in the gentlest tones. "Go home, now, go quietly, be orderly. But if any man, white or black, disturbs you, defend yourselves!"

He stepped back as a sign that he was done, and every Negro within hearing, roused to a hysterical frenzy, pressed toward him. Trav moved a few steps away, his hand under his coat resting on the revolver in its holster there. His whole body was hot with the rage that filled him. Those madmen, the speakers, had worked the Negroes to a fever pitch. They were more jubilant than angry, shouting, cheering, hoarse and laughing, but any small incident might convert this exultant mass of men and women into an insane and murderous flood liable to turn in any direction, to slay and to burn. For the men who had deliberately excited the Negroes to this pitch, death was too mild a punishment.

Almost on the moment that Dostie finished, the meeting inside the Institute came to an end, and a new crowd poured out into the street. Voices cried: "Parade!" "Parade!" "Parade!" While Trav watched, torches caught and flared, and the mass of Negroes began to form a column, moving away toward Canal Street.

The head of the procession turned up Canal, and Trav tried to guess how many there were in this marching stream. A thousand, two thousand? He did not know. A column of troops marching by fours or by eights you could estimate with some accuracy, but not this liquid, flowing mass like swarming bees.

He walked up Common to Baronne, parallel with the procession, and looking through Baronne he saw the marchers pass along Canal Street, torches tinting with a red glare the smoke that eddied upward. Mouth organs here and there along the files played march-time tunes; bursts of song arose; some watching woman wailed: "Hi—eee! Yeah ob Jubilee!" Someone called for cheers, and cheer on cheer resounded.

Every Negro near had gone to join in the parade, and Trav heard the steady furious cursing of the white men here around him. "Hang Doc Dostie to a sour apple tree, that's what he needs!" "Kill about a dozen of them white bastards!" "Me, I'm going to shoot me enough niggers for a mess!" Trav half nodded, his anger applauding theirs.

The procession yonder had acquired a band to lead it; the distant strains came back to them. Then the marchers seemed to halt somewhere on Canal Street, and the band was hushed, and when he reached St. Charles Street, looking toward Canal, Trav could see the mob massed around the Henry Clay statue. Someone was speaking to them there.

Then the parade once more began to move, and at Camp Street the marchers turned uptown. Trav saw them pass a block away. He went into the hotel and found the rotunda deserted, but he spoke to the desk clerk. "Quiet night in here!"

"So far, yes sir. I haven't heard any shooting yet. But it's due."

Trav nodded, knowing this was true. He went along St. Charles Street, intending to go home, but before he reached the City Hall, the paraders had flowed up through Lafayette Square to start a new meeting there. As Trav came nearer, from the steps of City Hall, Doctor Dostie began to speak. Over the murmurous and excited stirring of the mass of Negroes, Trav caught occasional familiar phrases. "No cowards . . . the right to arm yourself . . . Streets run with blood . . . hell-born and hell-bound."

Then as the crowd quieted to listen, the words came clearly. "We have here in Louisiana three hundred thousand black men with white hearts, and a hundred thousand true white men, Union men who will fight beside the black race against the hell-bound rebels. We can exterminate them! Judge Abell with his Grand Jury may indict us, Sheriff Hays with his brigade may seek to frighten us, the police may swear in a thousand men and seek to interfere! So, cowards, stay away!

"But brave men, come! If we are interfered with, the streets will run with blood."

When the great shout died, he spoke more gently. "Now, go home. Go home peaceably and quietly. Make no noise, disturb no person. I hear tell that there are prowling bands of armed men out to waylay you as you separate. If you are insulted by these men, pay no attention; go right by them, say no word to them."

His voice rose to a furious cry. "But my friends, if they strike you . . ." He paused, waited, till the roaring throng was again silent, finished then with a steady adjuration. "If they strike you, kill them!"

A great shout rose like a roar of hate let loose, and after a little the crowd began to dissolve and to disperse. Trav, walking slowly homeward, was in a fog of wonder. What manner of man was this Dostie? The other Radicals could be explained as adventurers seeking office and a chance for plunder, or—as in the case of Mr. Henderson—as somewhat less than sane; but Dostie's every word carried a note of sincerity. Trav was sure that the man was moved rather by an intense love of the Union than by any hope of personal gain. It was almost possible to feel for him a reluctant admiration.

But remembering the mood of the white men on the streets tonight, he thought Doctor Dostie had not long to live. What would happen Monday? The question filled his thoughts as before the storm breaks a dark and ominous cloud may fill the sky.

7

LUCY, through these weeks, had not shared Trav's anxiety. For one reason, Don had gone to Mississippi on some business for the Bureau, and her thoughts followed him; but also, the outbreak her father feared seemed to her impossible.

Yet though she did not share his concern, she was sorry for his distress, and this Friday night when he went to the called meeting, she waited for his homecoming, met him in the hall, asked in quiet affection: "How was it, Papa?"

"Well, I'll be glad when Monday's over," he admitted, and laid aside his hat and mopped his brow. "I heard a lot of angry talk on the streets tonight. In fact, I was mad myself! I'm worn out, ready for bed."

"We'll go right up!" She took his arm. "I'll help you," she said smilingly, pretending to support him. "I hate it when you're so worried."

"I don't mind the worry, but getting mad always leaves me in a fog. Guess I take things too hard."

"Remember what General Baird said in his letter to Mayor Monroe?"

He looked at her in mild surprise. "Have you been keeping track of this business?"

"The letters were in the paper," she reminded him. This of course was true, the Mayor's and the General's reply. "He said if the Convention is legal, the Mayor shouldn't interfere with it, and if illegal, it can't do any harm, so why take it so seriously? I mean, that's what he said. I thought it was sort of cute."

"This is no time to be cute," Trav commented. "And he's wrong, too. Either way, the Convention can do harm. The men on the streets tonight were making big talk—and they meant it. I hope Baird has soldiers outside the Institute next Monday."

"Please don't worry so, Papa." She kissed him, smiling. "Please! Nothing's going to happen. I promise!" They parted at his door, and he was somehow reassured by her concern.

When he scanned the newspapers, Trav, like most men, read with the keenest interest the account of events of which he had been a witness. Thus on Saturday morning he studied every word he could find about the meeting Friday evening. The *Times* used jeering headlines.

THE RADICAL MOB
It Lowers, Threatens and Thunders

TERRIFIC APPEALS
The "Distinguished Gentlemen" Not There

Mike Hahn, Col. Field, Rufus Waples, Henry C. Dibble, R. King Cutler, John Hawkins, John Henderson, Ezra H. Hiestand, S. P. Judd, A. P. Dostie *et id omne genus* Get up the Thunder of the Occasion.

The account that followed these headlines was facetiously derisive. "Mechanics Institute was astonished . . ." "The Hall of Representatives was disgraced . . ." The speeches were "an embittered elaboration of the radical fulminations," "a tirade of abuse," "verbose," "drivellings."

The *Tribune* had the most complete narrative, quoting the resolutions adopted at the meeting; resolutions favoring Negro suffrage and applauding the new Convention and commending Governor Wells and Judge Howell for "their performance of a solemn act of duty, regardless of private threats of personal violence, and unmoved by the ridicule, censure and attempt at intimidation of the rebel press." There followed a list of "Vice-Presidents," to the total of well over a hundred, and Trav wondered how many of these gentlemen had consented to the use of their names.

The *Crescent* printed a straightforward story, including some of the incendiary phrases Trav remembered hearing. The *Picayune* was more violent, calling the speakers "fanatics, so infuriated and exasperated at not being able to hold power and position as to counsel everything to arouse the baser passions of the race of which they claim to be the special benefactors. The proceedings last night . . . alarmed the whole community."

One paragraph caught his attention.

A Negro man named Jacob Tasspot was so excited by the violent speakers outside the Mechanics Institute he fell dead in a fit, caused either by an overheated case of a disturbed imagination superceded [*sic*] by the eloquent discourse as furnished by Dr. Dostie.

Trav was impressed by this singling-out of Doctor Dostie. Actually, the speaker at the time had been the minister whose name Trav did not know; but the Doctor, more than anyone else, seemed to have attracted to himself the resentment of the newspapers. He would be well advised to leave town, if not permanently, then at least till tempers cooled. Trav wondered whether Tony could persuade Doctor Dostie to depart, and the thought stayed in his mind.

While he was still absorbed in the papers, Peter joined him at the breakfast table, attacking his breakfast with the fine appetite of youth, but after a moment he asked: "Papa, are they really going to kill all the Union men and the niggers?"

"Eh?" Trav looked up over his paper. "What's that?"

"Well, that's what the boys said in school yesterday."

"Said what?" Looking at Peter more attentively than usual, Trav thought this son of his was at that point of change when the boy is just turning into the man. He had in these few months at first put on weight so fast that he required new clothes; but now he was taller, too, and there was a difference in his voice. "Who said who was going to kill anybody?"

"Everybody. Men in the street last night kept saying so, and I heard a woman say it was the last speech Doctor Dostie would ever make."

"A woman?" Peter nodded, and Trav said: "I thought you were at home and in bed."

"No, I went down to Mechanics Institute right after supper. I thought they might start killing people!" Trav reflected with a deep sense of guilt that it was not Peter's fault he was what he was. Through the War years, he had gone uncontrolled, Trav himself much away, Enid indifferent; so the boy had run at loose ends. In the momentary pause, Peter added: "But everybody's making so many brags, I don't know whether they mean it or not!"

Trav felt between them a certain kinship. "Neither do I, son," he said, some suppressed mirth in the grim admission. "So I don't know what will happen." And he asked: "Do you understand what's going on, in this whole business? It's pretty complicated. You see, they held a Convention, in eighteen sixty-four . . ."

"You know what I think?" Peter interrupted. "Those old Radicals are trying to see how mad they can get us. But they're going to wish they hadn't, when the societies start killing them all."

"What societies?"

"Oh, there are lots of 'em. Some of the men in school are members; you know, the ones that were soldiers. All the regiments have societies." Trav had forgotten that in Mr. Soulé's school there were young men who had served during the War. "General Hays, Sheriff Hays, he has all his men in the Hays Brigade Relief Society, and he's going to swear them all in as deputies, and they say any nigger that goes to the meeting Monday won't get out alive. They keep saying it on the street whenever niggers can hear them."

"It's natural for regiments that have fought together to be friends, and have reunions, things like that," Trav suggested, but Peter said eagerly:

"I bet they'll kill a lot of people! If they do, I want to see them."

"You'll not." Trav felt his cheek hot with anger. "You'll be in school and you'll stay there!" And when Peter tried to speak, Trav said sternly: "That's enough! Mind what I say." Yet at once regretting his tone, wishing he and Peter were not so often at odds, he offered an invitation. He had not meant to go to the mill today, but here was a pretext, a way to interest the boy. "Want to go over to the mill? They're going to start the presses this morning."

Peter hesitated. "All right, I guess so," he agreed. "Might as well."

Walking with Peter down through the city to the ferry landing, Trav thought an unusual quiet ruled the streets. There were few people about, though here and there a group of three or four or five were gathered together, but he heard no loud threatening voices, saw no outward marks of smoldering anger anywhere.

When they reached the mill, it was in full operation, Mr. Fiddler keeping a watchful eye on the huller, Mr. Cist trotting anxiously around the presses. Peter was instantly absorbed, and Trav enjoyed the boy's eager interest. Peter presently attached himself to Mr. Fiddler, watching the huller and the bolting reel designed to separate hulls from kernels. In midmorning Mr. Fiddler stopped the huller and attacked the task of setting up the knives to a new clearance, and Trav came to stand by while the two mechanics worked.

"We have to keep the knives less than an eighth of an inch apart," Mr. Fiddler explained, "or some seeds would get through with the hulls unbroken. The knives have to be set up every two or three days. The blades wear, and they get dull, too. Then we take them out and sharpen them. That's the tough job. The cylinder has to be balanced just right, so we have to weigh the knives after they're sharpened, and put weights inside the cylinder to make up for what we've ground off them. It's pretty ticklish business."

Peter began to question the mechanics, and Trav drew Fiddler a little to one side. "Hear any excitement over the meeting last night?"

"Some of the hands were there, and Bob didn't come to work this morning."

"I see him around the house occasionally," Trav reflected. "Sundays, when he comes to see Quinny. But I'm disappointed in Bob. He's getting pretty uppity." He hesitated. "Mr. Fiddler, do you hear anything about societies that have been organized to keep the nigras in order?"

"Yes, of course," the other assured him. "Like the Fire Department. Our company has over four hundred members, and we're all—or we were—soldiers. Everyone knows these nigras may have to be handled some day." He added: "And I've joined the Southern Cross Association, too. That's an organization of Confederate veterans."

Trav asked curiously: "Does your fire company need four hundred men to fight fires?"

"No, twenty or thirty would be enough for that. But some companies have five or six hundred." Fiddler said in a confident tone: "If there's any fighting needs doing, we could get up an army pretty quick."

Trav heard a similar remark when that night after dinner he strolled down to the St. Charles. A Mr. Tilton, who lived at the corner of Dryades and Canal Streets, diagonally across from the Mechanics Institute, told a group of men in the rotunda that he had asked Chief of Police Thomas Adams to give his house protection during the meeting Monday, and that Chief Adams had assured him there would be no trouble. One of his listeners commented:

"If there is, it won't take long to end it. Break into a few of the stores and get some guns and cartridges." There were murmurs of angry approval, and when Trav went home he wore a sober frown.

Sunday morning while Trav and the children were at breakfast, Isaiah asked permission to go that night to a funeral. "My friend Mr. Tasspot," he explained. "He die."

Trav, as he gave the desired permission, wondered why the name seemed vaguely familiar. He opened the Sunday *Times*. The editor had written: "We are certain that the discreet, even among the Radicals, must condemn the inflammatory appeals made by Doctor Dostie . . ." Doctor Dostie again! Certainly the man was marked for death!

Enid slept late, but Trav and the children went to church, and on Coliseum Street they came face to face with Tony and another. To Trav's surprise, Tony paused, and bowed to Lucy, and introduced his companion to them all. "Mr. Cutler, my brother Major Currain, Miss Lucy, Master Peter." And he explained: "Trav, Mr. Cutler and I have just conveyed our sympathy to Judge Hiestand." Judge Hiestand had been one of the Friday night speakers. "Some scoundrels attempted last night to burn the house over his head, set fire to it in three or four places."

"I'm sorry to hear that. Was he at home?"

"No. Several of us were gathered in Mr. Cutler's office, discussing tomorrow's Convention."

Trav asked soberly: "Gentlemen, is there any chance the meeting will be canceled?"

Mr. Cutler answered him: "Canceled, sir? Nonsense! We will not be deterred by the threats of a cowardly mob."

"Not all men who make threats are cowards," Trav suggested. "I think Doctor Dostie is in great danger."

Cutler laughed. "The only attention we shall pay to these threats is to go to the Convention unarmed."

In church Trav's straying thoughts recalled that Tasspot—to whose funeral Isaiah wished to go—was the Negro who had died of a fit at Friday's meeting. He wondered how that man and Isaiah had become friends, guessed they must be fellow church members. Maybe Isaiah had better not go to that funeral.

After church, while they were homeward bound, stray snatches of conversation twice came to their ears. Once when they met two gentlemen, one of them was saying: "The Convention died two years ago; tomorrow it will be buried. And there may be need for other graves."

After they passed, Lucy asked: "Who was that, Papa?"

"I don't know."

She said in surprise: "He wasn't—riffraff. He looked like a gentleman!" From an open window in the house beside them a voice came to their ears, and the fragment of a sentence. ". . . unless he withdraws that order, the bloodiest day New Orleans . . ." Lucy looked toward the window, she surveyed the house itself, then looked up at her father. "Papa, do you really think there'll be trouble?"

Peter said: "I'll bet the streets'll be full of dead niggers!"

Lucy ignored him. "Do you, Papa?"

"There needn't be," Trav said gravely. "General Baird can prevent it. A couple of squads of soldiers, just a show of force, that's all that would be needed."

"But even if he doesn't?"

He shook his head. "Honey, I don't know."

At home, Isaiah, serving dinner, was gray and trembling. Enid asked him what was wrong and he vowed that nothing was the matter, but he protested so violently that after dinner Trav questioned him. Isaiah, passing through a walled alley on his way to church that morning, had heard men talking in the garden beyond the wall.

"I heah dem say dey gwine hang Doctuh Dostie and Miste' Hahn," he told Trav now, his eyes bulging. "An' dey gwine shoot ev'y nigguh in town. Dey say so!"

"They won't," Trav assured him. "The soldiers won't let them."

"One on 'em say dat, an' t'otheh one, he say dey gwine do it so fas' de sojers cain't he'p deyse'ves."

Trav touched the old man's arm in friendly reassurance. "Keep out of white folks's troubles, and you'll be all right," he advised. Then he asked, with complete gravity: "Do you still want to go to your friend's funeral?"

"Friend?" Isaiah made a scornful sound. "Tasspot? Dat nigguh neve' wuz no frien' o' mine!"

8

Downstairs at first light next morning, Trav sent for the *Times*. President Johnson had telegraphed Lieutenant Governor Voorhees that the soldiers would sustain the courts, but since no indictments had been returned against the members of the Convention, this was an empty assurance. Trav read Mayor Monroe's punctilious proclamation calling upon the good people of the city to act with calmness and propriety, and to avoid perpetrating any act of violence which by creating martyrs might aid the Radicals.

He thought the proclamation had a hollow sound, yet it might accomplish something. He meant to spend the day at the mill. Peter would be safe at school, Lucy and Enid safe at home. He had breakfasted earlier than usual, after a troubled night, and no one had as yet appeared to join him. He rose to stroll in the garden, but when in the hall he opened his watch to see the time, the glass fell out and broke, and he felt a superstitious pang. He bent to pick up the tiny fragments, and Lucy came lightly down the stairs and cried out in sympathy: "Oh, too bad! Let me!" She stooped beside him, but at once protested that it was much too hot to be doing this, that Daisy would do it, and bade him come in and keep her company at the breakfast table.

"A hot day, sure enough," he said. "I'll be glad when it's over."

"You mean about the Convention, don't you?"

Trav nodded. "Yes. Honey, I hope you and Mama will stay close home all day."

Before Lucy could speak, Peter joined them, and said his mother was awake, and that Quinny was to take up her breakfast. Trav went to bid Enid good morning. He found her still sodden with sleep, hot and miserable; she was so creased and sweaty, with matted hair, that as he stooped to kiss her he felt a shamed repugnance, felt relief when she pushed him fretfully away.

"For Heaven's sake, no!" she protested. "There's a time and a place for everything! Why does it always seem hotter in the morning?"

Quinny came with her tray, and Enid propped herself up in bed and took it on her crossed legs. Quinny appeared to be wearing only one garment. "She knows how to dress for hot weather," Trav remarked, as the girl left the room.

"Oh, why not? She's only a child! But you always did have an eye for the wenches!"

He understood that she wished to annoy him. "I'm going over to the mill, may not be home till evening. Goodby."

Quinny came with a pot of hot water, and as Trav left the room, Enid was saying: "I declare Quinny, you're getting a real little belly. If I didn't . . ." He closed the door and heard no more.

Trav often went a block or two out of his way in order to keep Peter company as far as Mr. Soulé's school, thinking that for them to have this half-hour together every day might help him come closer to his son. But today, he was absorbed in his own thoughts, and they proceeded down Prytania and on down Camp Street and no word passed between them till they reached Lafayette Square. There two or three hundred policemen were standing or sitting along the banquettes or in the shade. They wore their summer uniforms; blue coats, white pantaloons, straw hats with a black band. Many of them were armed, with revolvers belted outside their coats. Trav could not remember having seen police officers wearing guns, and he thought the Mayor, or Chief Adams, or whoever ordered them today to do this, had taken a wise precaution.

They came down through the Square, Peter big-eyed and trembling with excitement, and went on toward Canal, and Trav saw several men who wore a bit of blue ribbon in their lapels, and he thought this was unusual. In one group of men, he recognized John Henderson, and heard him say in loud, excited tones: "Five minutes after the signal, every judge in town, and the Mayor, and the Sheriff, and the last constable will be dragged out of their seats! Damn 'em, we'll have none but loyal men in office here!"

When they had passed, Peter asked in a whisper, "Who's that, Papa?"

"His name's Henderson. He's half-witted. No one pays any attention to him."

"Are they going to do what he said?"

"Oh, that's all just talk, son." They reached the corner of Common and St. Charles and were about to part—the stairs that led up to Mr. Soulé's schoolrooms opened on Common Street—and he paused a moment. "Peter, promise me something. When school lets out, go straight home."

"But Papa, if anything does happen, couldn't I just—"

Trav shook his head, said in kindly insistence: "No, son! Straight home." He touched Peter's shoulder in a gesture of affection. " 'By."

He watched Peter turn into the hallway at the stair foot, then went on to a jeweler's shop on Canal Street to have a new glass put in his watch. While this was being done, two men paused in the doorway of the shop and stood there, watching the passersby. A Negro walked down Canal Street toward Dryades, and one of the men said, loudly enough to be heard: "There goes another nigger walking to his own funeral!"

The Negro hurried his steps, and Trav spoke to the jeweler. "Expect any trouble today?"

"I'm putting up my shutters, as soon as I've taken care of you."

Trav nodded. "Sensible. I expect to spend the day in Algiers, keep out of the way."

When his watch was ready, Trav hesitated, curiously unwilling to turn his back on the simmering city. Eventually, instead of going on to the ferry, he returned toward City Hall, thinking to call on Mayor Monroe and ask his estimate of the situation. But the Mayor was not in his office, and Mr. Overall, his secretary, could neither say where he was nor when he might return.

"I see the police are ready, over in the Square, if they're needed," Trav remarked.

Overall made a mirthful sound. "They won't be. If the Radicals start any trouble, our Confederate veterans will handle the situation."

Trav had heard this suggestion before. "I suppose they would," he agreed. "But the police—it's their job." Yet when on his way to the ferry he saw a gun store crowded with young men buying revolvers, he nodded approval. Trouble today would quickly be controlled.

Mr. Cist was at the mill, and Mr. Fiddler, and most of the white mechanics and foremen, but only a sprinkling of the Negro hands. "And if they were coming, they'd be here by now," Mr. Cist pointed out, fretting and angry. "We can't run with the men we have, so we lose a day. How the South ever accomplished anything, with these colored people, I really don't know!"

Trav chuckled reassuringly. "I wouldn't worry. What's one day? Besides, it's too hot to work today."

"Yes, but you know what heat does to cottonseed! I'll put what hands we have to turning over our supply, giving it some air. That may keep it cool."

Mr. Fiddler spoke to them both. "If we can't run, I'd like to take the day. Our fire company was supposed to report at the station house at eight, as many as could get there."

"I saw the police waiting opposite City Hall," Trav told him.

Fiddler nodded. "There's a police station at the corner of Elysian Fields and Dauphine Street, and the men were all there when I passed."

"If there's trouble in town, we might all be needed," Trav decided. "I thought I could play ostrich, stay over here all day, but I guess I'll go back to town."

"I'll stay here," Mr. Cist decided. "When Confederates get to fighting each other, it's no place for a Yankee." And as Trav turned to depart: "Oh, Major, stop at the Custom House, will you; see if they've any report on the *Faraway* bark. That set of huller knives we ordered from Birmingham is on her, and she should be about due. I don't want to take time to sharpen the old ones and go to all the trouble of balancing them if we're going to change them again right away."

Trav promised to inquire. On the way from the ferry slip to the Custom House, he saw Folsom's store crowded with men, men going in and others coming out, and each man who came out carried a naked revolver in his hand. He looked at his watch. It was almost eleven.

The Custom House was built of granite and brick and iron, the whole structure resting on a foundation of heavy cypress logs driven like piles deep into the water-soaked ground. It was approximately three hundred and fifty feet on a side, and rose eighty feet in the air. It fronted on Canal Street, but when Trav entered he found himself in a surprisingly shabby hall, with an unfinished look about it. On either side, a flight of steps led upward, and at the second floor level they united to make one wider flight which continued to still loftier heights. Between these two sets of stairs, a hall led toward the rear of the building. There was no one in sight, and Trav paused, uncertain which way to turn. A man in a hurry came in and brushed past him and trotted up the stairs. Trav called after him: "Shipping office?"

Without turning, the man beckoned and pointed and said loudly: "Marble Hall. Up here!"

The Marble Hall, when Trav found it, proved to be an oval, certainly more than a hundred feet long and fully half as wide, its glass-domed roof high above the floor supported by towering marble columns. The majestic beauty of the whole dwarfed the small wickets all around, but at one of them Trav learned that the *Faraway* was reported through the passes and on her way up river.

As he came out into the corridor again, he saw Tony, standing at the stair head, watching Doctor Dostie; who strode up the stairs to join him. Trav stopped to speak to them.

"Ah, Trav." Tony seemed pleased. "You know Doctor Dostie? My brother Travis, Doctor."

Trav offered his hand, but the Doctor asked in curt challenge: "Are your politics those of your brother?"

"I'm afraid not."

"Then—permit me!" Dostie would have brushed by without shaking hands, but Trav spoke to him, half angry.

"Doctor!" The other paused. "I have heard men say they mean to hang you."

Tony laughed. "That's foolish, Trav! The soldiers will soon crush any trouble."

Trav said strongly: "After trouble starts, it will take time to summon the soldiers. I suggest Doctor, that your danger is considerable; that you would be well advised, today, to stay at home."

Doctor Dostie spoke in calm tones. "Major Currain, I am not a member of this Convention, only a spectator; but I have urged that the Convention be called again into session, so I shall attend. Also, I will go unarmed. I left my revolver this morning with the barber who cuts my hair. If they want my life, Major, they can take it. I think this is a good cause in which to die."

He had spoken quietly, and as he finished, he turned and walked leisurely away along the wide corridor. Trav took off his hat and mopped his brow, for the day was hot as death. "Why is he here?" he asked.

"The Conventioners are waiting in the United States Court room, so they can all go up to the Institute in a body."

"Are you going with them?"

Tony moved his head in a negative, and Trav nodded without blame. No sensible man courted danger without reason. "I'm on my way home," he said.

"I'll go part way with you."

So they left the Custom House together, proceeding down Canal Street. Once Tony remarked: "Lots of men on the streets this morning are wearing a blue ribbon. I wonder what for?" Since Trav offered no opinion, Tony added uneasily: "And a lot of them are showing white handkerchiefs." And when they passed a man to whose lapel was pinned a badge marked with crossed cannon, he said: "That's the badge of the Washington artillery."

They saw, a block ahead, a small crowd gathered about the store of A. B. Griswold & Co. Tony would have taken the other side of the street, but Trav, who was thinking that Peter must be still in school, pushed on, and Tony stayed beside him. The men coming out of the store held revolvers in their hands, and many of them paused to load their weapons. The city was arming itself; no doubt of that. Trav looked at his watch again. Half past eleven. He hurried his steps, Tony's long legs easily keeping pace with him, and they crossed Canal Street and came along St. Charles to Lyons's clothing store.

At the corner, Trav said: "I won't be a minute. I'll just get Peter." He turned into Common and climbed the stairs, but except for a sweating Negro woman with wet sawdust in a pail, sprinkling and sweeping the floor, the schoolrooms were empty. Mr. Soulé, she said, had shut up school for the day and sent the pupils home.

So Peter was safe, and at this assurance Trav knew a great relief. "Peter's at home," he told Tony, when he rejoined his brother. "That's where we all belong."

They went on together. The number of policemen waiting in Lafayette Square seemed to Trav to have increased. He wondered if it would not be well to deploy some of them around Mechanics Institute, but there was no one to whom to offer this suggestion. Tony loosened his collar. "Notice how quiet it is, Trav?"

Trav realized that this was true. For one thing, there were few Negroes on the street; for another, there were no carriages moving to and fro; for a third, the men standing in little groups on corners here and there spoke in low tones. He asked: "Tony, what can these Conventioner friends of yours hope to do today?"

"Well, if they get a quorum, they'll draft amendments to the Constitution."

"Will they resist arrest?"

"No. No, they expect to be arrested. But the Grand Jury hasn't acted yet, so they'll probably not be arrested today. But if they get a quorum, they'll get everything done today."

Trav said in a puzzled tone: "It looks like a fool performance. Even if they do vote to amend the Constitution, we'll vote them down."

"It will never come to a popular vote," Tony assured him. "Congress will take a hand. We've that promise. So—"

But then he paused in surprise, looking past Trav, and Trav turned and saw Sapphira, plainly dressed, a shawl over her head, coming quietly toward them. He saw, too, great thankfulness in her eyes, and the redness of stale tears; and she spoke to him soft and humbly.

"Oh, thank you, Marst' Trav. Thank you."

"Morning, Sapphira. Thank me for what?"

"For bringing him home. I begged him not to go out."

Tony hushed her, and as he and Trav walked on, she followed a dozen paces behind them, not conspicuously. Trav was surprised that he did not resent this meeting, and he thought this might be because Sapphira had called him "master," as though she were still his slave. He was amused to find himself touched by this humble flattery. Where Prytania Street forked off from Camp, their ways diverged, and he said: "Better stay home today, Tony."

Tony nodded and Trav went on. When he approached the house, old

Abram was oiling the hinges of the garden gate, so Trav went in that way. Enid and Lucy were together under the shade of an arbor roofed with rose vines, and Lucy came to meet him. Here was peace, here was home. The world was far away, outside these walls. Lucy slipped her hand through his arm, and they went together toward where Enid sat. He leaned down to kiss her cheek, took the chair beside her. Lucy came with a fan to cool his brow, and he thanked her with a smile.

"Where's Peter?" he asked casually. "In the house? I suppose it's cooler there."

"Peter?" Enid echoed. "Why, at school I suppose. He's never home this early."

Trav felt a strangling grip on his throat. "School is closed," he said. "Mr. Soulé sent them all home, long ago." He rose, his feet like lead.

Lucy came beside him, quick to understand, but Enid said lightly: "I shouldn't worry. He's probably off with some of his friends." Trav turned toward the gate, and she called after him: "Where are you going?"

"To find him."

Lucy asked: "Papa, can I—" But as though she knew the answer, she left the question unfinished. He heard Enid say resentfully:

"Well of all the ridiculous—"

Then the gate clanged behind him and cut off the final word. He found himself, absurdly, trying to finish her remark, to supply the word or words he had not heard. "Ridiculous performances?" No, that did not sound like Enid. "Ridiculous things to do?" Possibly. Or perhaps, finding no satisfactory words, she had just left the question dangling.

He had no doubt that Peter was at the Institute. He looked at his watch; a quarter past twelve o'clock. Perhaps he would be wiser to ride, to take Nig; but to go back now and see the big horse brushed and saddled would require long minutes, so he went on, sweating with haste.

He was at the corner of Camp and Julia Streets when, far away, he heard a shot.

Trav heard that shot at some distance, but old Pike heard it at close range. One of the traces on Beauty's harness needed replacement, and Pike's favorite harness shop, chosen not so much for its location as for its sociable atmosphere, was in an alley away down beyond Esplanade Avenue. A man waiting for his work to be finished could always find good company there, and good talk. The shop was cool and shadowed, and out of reach of even the most peremptory summons from white folks. After Mars' Trav went off to Algiers, Miss Lucy said they would not want the carriage this morning, and that he could do his errand; so Pike coiled the worn trace and tied it compactly—it would be needed for a pattern—and took his cane and set out, limping less and less as his deformed feet resigned themselves to their task.

It was hot, and the heat made Pike's old bones feel better all the time. He paused to pass the time of day with a friend working in the garden at the corner of Calliope Street, who asked whether he was going to the excitement at the Institute, but Pike quoted Isaiah's prediction that this would be a dark and bloody day.

"M'ria, she say so too," he said. "I don' mos' gen'ally pay no mind to skeered niggehs, but I ain' gwine nigh de Insatoot. Not t'day. Niggehs neve' git no fat meat out o' white folks's fusses."

The other man explained that there was a special invitation for the colored people to come and stand by their friends, but Pike shook his head; yet when he continued on his way, he edged down to Baronne Street, and then to Dryades, to pass the Institute. There was a crowd in the street in front of the big building, two or three hundred Negroes standing in scattered groups, talking and laughing, with an undertone of excitement in their voices. Pike wondered why so many of them carried sticks. A few had canes like his, but a much larger number had hoe handles, or axe helves, or just staves cut from some tree; in short, clubs.

Pike stopped to watch for a while the stir and movement in this changing throng. Some of the men started away, and an old Negro on the steps of the Institute called them back.

"Come back heah, men! You heah me! Yo' friends ain' fo'got! Dey'll come, crack o' noon, an' den de high times comin'! Hallelujah!"

He went on to make quite a speech. Pike could see that he was mightily excited, and once when he threw his arms high in a strong gesture, something heavy in his coat pocket thumped against his side. Pike saw another man with a bulge on his hip that was certainly a small revolver. When Negroes with revolvers in their pockets started talking big, trouble was due. Pike judged it was getting along toward half past ten, and everyone said nothing was going to happen till noon, so he had time to go on about his business and come back later. Forgetting his good resolutions in a rising excitement, he wanted to see what happened when some white man came along and sent these uppity, gun-toting niggers about their business.

It did not occur to him that to return might involve any danger to himself. White men never bothered a colored person as long as he behaved. So Pike went limping on his way, refreshed and stimulated by what he had seen.

He thought as he crossed Canal Street that there was a feeling of gaiety in the air, like the day of a revival meeting, or a fish fry, or a big picnic, or a barbecue, or a wedding, or maybe a high-class funeral. He felt a stirring in his blood and an itching in his feet and an absurd desire to hop and skip. When he met white folks, he saluted them with cheerful, friendly deference. Some nodded, and some even smiled, but a surprising number of them scowled in frank suspicion. White folks certainly were on edge today. He turned right and left, zigzagging toward his destination, and heard somewhere the tap of drums, and wondered if there would be a parade.

At the harness shop, he found eight or ten men gathered. Some were old acquaintances, some he had not seen before. Samson, the harness maker, took the trace Pike gave him and selected from his stock one already made up, needing only to have the end finished off at the right length. Pike, watching him set to with knife and needle and waxed thread to hand-sew it, listened to the talk among the others here. Most of them intended to go home and stay indoors till the excitement was over. This, they held, was a white man's fight, and they were disposed to let the white men fight it out.

But some believed that they were needed at the Institute. "Tuh show ouah friends we's wid 'em."

This suggestion won both approval and dissent. "I ain' wid dem till dey wid us an' it gits us so'thin'."

"You free, ain't you, man? Dey got you dat!"

"Huh! Free? Da's jes' sojers feed you 'stead o' Marste', an' ain' nobuddy tek keer o' you when you sick, an' if you ain' got a papuh say you wukkin' foh some white man, de jail man gits yuh."

There were approving nods to this, but someone cried: "Dey gwine fix it so's we uns gits de vote!" The discussion took a new turn. Was it desirable to have the vote? What good was it? What did you do with it after you got it? "White man tolt me I c'd sell it foh two bits, any time dey set out to have a 'lection!"

About the time the new trace was ready, three boys came in, and one of them was Bob. "How you, Pike?" he called. "How's ev'ybody?"

"Quinny? Fine, I rack'n! Huccome you askin' me?"

Bob grinned. "Who said de name? You always studying 'bout her, even at you' age. Quinny'll devil you t'death, you give her de chance! Anything in pants, young or old."

"Fine way t' talk about yuh own siste'!" Pike labored to his feet.

Bob grinned. "Way you stick up fo' her, anybody'd think yuh 'uz sweet on her yuh own se'f. Whah yuh gwine?"

"Home. Ah'm gwine past de Insatoot! Sump'n's likely tuh be happenin'."

Bob and some of the others were bent that way, so they set out together, but as they went out into the alley, an old Negro named

Timeus, who sold watermelons at a stall just around the corner, stopped them and advised them to go back. He was shutting up his stall for the day because, when he went to the post office a while ago, a white man pushed him roughly away from his box and told him there was going to be trouble today and that a smart nigger would keep off the streets.

They laughed aside his fears and went on, and with the sound of drums as a guide they came to Dauphine Street, where a hundred or two Negroes were assembled around the drummers. Then from Burgundy Street a block away came the shrilling of fifes, and the drummers swung into a march beat, and with the crowd trooping on their heels they went to join forces with the fifers. On the way, a man with a bass drum fell into line.

Bob and Pike joined the parade, and old Pike forgot his sore feet. It was fine to be a part of this happy excitement; the piercing notes of the fifes made sweet music, the thudding of the drums made you want to prance and dance, the dust scuffed up by marching feet was incense in the nostrils. Someone with a flag came to lead the procession, and at Toulouse Street, a score or so of stevedores, their cotton hooks hanging on their shoulders, joined the marchers. The parade passed a house where carpenters were working, and one, his saw still in his hand, fell in beside Pike, asking where they were going, what they meant to do.

Pike had to hurry to keep up. It was hard to hold the pace, jostled and off balance much of the time. He lost sight of Bob, but in this jolly, friendly crowd he needed no companion. A pulse of joy, mysterious and unexplained, awakened by the drums, quickened by the shrieking fifes, strengthened by the rhythm of this shoulder-to-shoulder marching, filled him as he hobbled on.

The head of the procession reached Canal Street, and something checked them there, and Pike heard shouts of "Fight! Fight!" and angry cries. Then from up there at the corner, startlingly near, came the sharp sudden sound of a pistol shot.

That shot, fired at about half past twelve on a still, hot day, was heard by many ears. Lucy heard it as far away as the garden of their home. She had been there since soon after breakfast. Before Enid joined her, before Trav returned from Algiers, old Maria had come to ask where Pike was gone. Lucy explained that some piece of harness needed mending, that she had given him leave. When she said this, the expression on Maria's wrinkled countenance startled her; the deep wrinkles suddenly were deeper, the bronze-red skin suddenly was gray, and huge tears formed in Maria's eyes.

"Dat pore old man," she whispered. "Dat pore old man!"

Lucy, frightened, and resenting her own alarm, spoke in a quick irritation. "Pike's all right!"

"He all right up to now, Missy. All right up to now. But nex' time yuh see him he ain' gwine t'be."

Lucy tried to laugh. "Oh, you're an old croaker, Maria! Always predicting trouble! Predict some jolly things for a change!"

But Maria threw her apron over her head and moved wretchedly away.

A little after that, while Lucy was in the garden cutting flowers to freshen the bouquets in the house, Lieutenant Page called. It was not yet ten o'clock when he arrived, and Lucy said smilingly that he took a lot for granted, assuming she would receive him at such an hour! "How could you know what state I'd be in?" she protested.

"Well, I was anxious to see you—"

"I sometimes wonder whether you are or not. Weeks at a time and I never lay eyes on you." His duties often sent him away from New Orleans. "I haven't seen you since the picnic, have I?" She enjoyed putting him on the defensive, particularly since he sometimes reacted with a firmness that surprised her. "I'm not sure. Let's see. You haven't called, I know, and Pike said yesterday that if Nig didn't get some exercise pretty soon he'd kick his stall down, so you haven't ridden with me. And you weren't at the Pierces' party." She was snipping blossoms as she talked, dropping them into the basket on her arm. "And you didn't—"

"Hush!" he said. "I must hurry. I came to—"

"Yes, sir, Lieutenant!" she assented, in an ironic tone. "Wait till I put my basket down so I can salute you properly!"

He did not smile at her foolery. "Miss Lucy, I came to urge you and your mother to stay at home today. I'm on duty, so I can't stop and talk, but I hope you'll do it."

"Stay home?"

"Yes ma'am."

She had laid her basket aside, and she watched him, her hands clasped against her chin, the tip of one finger touching her lips, her eyes grave. "You really mean you're afraid that if we went out, we might be—annoyed?"

"I don't know what's going to happen—but I don't want you to see it happen, if it does."

"Pike's gone on an errand," she reflected. "And Maria thinks he's as good as dead!" She smiled. "But I expect you Yankees don't take much stock in the queer ways old nigra women know things."

"You know better than I whether to take her seriously."

Because Maria had sometimes been unpleasantly right, Lucy was for a moment angry with him. "Are you scared too?" she challenged.

"Of course I am," he assured her. "So is your father. So's any man of sense."

"You needn't be. No one will hurt you!"

He colored, hearing the scorn in her tones, but he and she had in the year since they first met, learned to know each other. Thus he knew now that she would come to sweet contrition, so held his temper in check. "I'm thinking of you, all of you," he said. "Of the South. I don't want the South hurt!"

"You're mighty tenderhearted, all of a sudden. You Yankees certainly hurt us every way you could, there for a while!" She was enjoying herself. This was fun, but in a minute now she would make it up to him.

He said, surprising her: "This is a game you play, I know. I think you like to pretend to quarrel. I don't like games of this kind. Let's not play this one any longer."

"I haven't the faintest idea what you're talking about."

He frowned in a troubled way. "Some mighty good friendships have been spoiled by just this foolish, idle bickering. Please don't! This is not a day for games. Miss Lucy, I've come to feel a deep affection for this South of yours. I don't want her hurt. But between the asininity of the Radicals and the folly of your city authorities and the horn-headed stupidity of our army officers—and the malice of Congress—the South can receive a bad wound today; a wound from which she'll take a lifetime to recover."

She hesitated, then came near him, smiling, her hand touching his arm. "I'm sorry, Don. I know you're not scared! I was just teasing. You know, when you said that for some reason you had come to love the South, I thought for a moment you were going to think of a gallant reason, but you never say gallant things, do you?" He colored redly, and she explained: "I mean saying something awfully elaborately, so that we both know you don't really mean it. It's a sort of game; sort of fun, too!" But since he did not smile she said hastily: "Is this really—dangerous today?"

He began to explain. "Why, the Radicals hope to get seventy-six members of the old Convention—that's a quorum—to meet at the Institute, and pass resolutions to change the Constitution and—"

"Oh, I know all that! Edgar Cenas told me all about that! I mean, I don't see why you and Papa and everybody, why you're all so worried about it! People keep telling me all these things, but I just don't believe them. I hear them but I don't believe them!"

He half smiled. "Maybe your refusing to believe what might happen will keep it from happening."

"That's almost a gallantry, Mister Don."

"You're bound to joke me, aren't you. Everything's a joke to you."

"No-o-o," she said, half to herself. "No, I don't think it is. In fact, I'm sure it isn't. But—isn't it all right to laugh even when you're most serious? Don't Yankees ever laugh in battles, for instance? Papa says they did. I know you did, or you couldn't have beaten us!" She tugged at his arm. "Come, please Mister Lieutenant. Can't you laugh a little, please sir?"

He chuckled. "All right, to please you." He laughed aloud, and they laughed together. "But stay home today, please? Now I must go, shouldn't even have stopped by. May I call later, see that you're all right?"

"Of course!" She added, meaning to tease him: "But I won't promise to be here!" But she walked with him to the gate, and when the gate had closed between them she said softly: "Of course, if you'll promise to come, I'll promise to be here."

"I promise," he said. "I'll come."

She stayed to watch him stride away, and wondered if people down in Maine were all like him. Didn't anybody in Maine ever flirt a little, or maybe even ask anyone to marry anybody? Half a dozen beaus had besought her, in these few months since she came to New Orleans. Why didn't Don?

She clipped her basket full of flowers and went in to arrange them, but though this was usually a pleasant task, she was frowning now. Was it possible that Don and her father were right, that this would prove to be a tragic day? When she finished with the flowers, she gave her basket to Daisy, and Enid joined her, and they sought to find a cool spot in the garden. The day was deathly still, with no stir of air, and as the sun rose toward the zenith, the walled garden held the heat like an oven. Enid groaned in misery, and Lucy suggested that it might be cooler indoors, or on the gallery where the jalousies gave pleasant shade, but Enid was too wretched to move.

Then Trav came home, and learned that Peter was not here, and hurried away, and a few minutes later, Lucy heard the shot.

Peter heard that shot at closer range than any other individual, for the muzzle of the pistol was hardly an inch from his ear. School that morning followed the normal routine, except that since his seat was near an open window, he heard occasional snatches of angry conversation from the street below, and he could see along St. Charles Street to Lafayette Square and catch glimpses of the police officers congregated there.

But at eleven o'clock, Mr. Soulé rapped for their attention.

"Young gentlemen," he said. "I'm dismissing school, and I want all of you to go directly home. Probably you all know that there's likely to be a riot in New Orleans today, and I don't want you around the streets getting hurt." Mr. Soulé had served with distinction in the Confederate army, rising to the rank of Lieutenant Colonel, and his voice had the ring of authority. "You understand, you are under orders. Go home. I'm dismissing school so you can go home, and I expect you to do so. Sheriff Hays has sworn in five hundred deputies, and Mayor Monroe has sworn in about seven hundred special police. When that Convention meets, they may have to arrest or kill every member, and all their friends. It will be dangerous to be abroad, so you go home. And hurry. Now, dismissed."

The thirty-five or forty students marched in orderly fashion down the stairs, but on the banquette they paused in brief discussion. Probably a third of the boys were younger than Peter, while a dozen or fifteen were in their late teens or early twenties. The older boys proposed now to escort the youngsters to their homes, assuming responsibility for their safety.

But Peter had no intention of going home. "I've got to meet my father at the Custom House," he told them, and since he was tall for his age and physically competent, no one sought to keep him. He walked up Common Street, but once out of their sight he crossed Canal and turned down Bienville, to come circuitously toward the Institute. Whatever was to happen would center there.

When, having recrossed Canal, he reached Dryades Street, he saw among the Negroes in front of the Institute a blue uniform, and recognized Lieutenant Page. The Lieutenant was moving from group to group, speaking to the Negroes, but Peter suspected that if Page saw him, he would be escorted home. He dodged back around the corner and up toward Baronne Street, and then, somewhere across Canal, he heard the distant sound of drums, and raced that way.

The sound was muffled and distorted by intervening buildings. But when the squeal of fifes was added to the rataplan of the drums Peter, having gone as far as Dauphine Street, came to the fringes of the crowd which in an uneven procession began to move up Burgundy toward Canal.

Peter hurried along the banquette to overtake the musicians. He was careful not to jostle any white people, but when Negroes singly or in groups were in his way, he elbowed them aside. Sullen murmurs rose as he passed, and angry protests followed him.

As the straggling procession approached Canal Street, the banquettes were crowded with white men, including a few policemen. Peter, anxious to get out into Canal Street before the procession, left the banquette for the street, pushing swiftly forward along the flank of the marching men. In doing so, he sought to shove aside a Negro boy who was just ahead of him, and the Negro braced himself against that thrust and Peter's temper flared. He threw all his weight against the other, crying: "Get out of my way, you black son of a bitch!"

The Negro, caught off balance, stumbled and half fell; he scrambled to his feet and whirled, and Peter recognized Bob.

Bob, even before he saw the face of his assailant, had begun to swing an awkward blow, but when he recognized Peter, he caught himself; the swinging blow became a protecting arm across Peter's shoulder. "You come along out o' dis, Mars' Pete," he urged. "You ain' no business in dis! I'se gwine tek you home."

Peter struggled to be free, and in a red rage he hit Bob hard in the face, crying: "Let go of me, you nigger bastard!" He pounded at Bob's face with both fists, and a white man on the banquette shouted encouragement.

"Kill the nigger, young un!"

Peter swung another blow. As he did so, he saw Bob's eyes widen in sharp terror. Then Bob ducked, and a revolver exploded, deafeningly, close by Peter's ear.

Lieutenant Page saw Peter, though at some distance, at the moment the shot was fired. When he left Lucy, he went first toward the City Hall. His commanding officers had given him no specific directions except to look around, to keep an eye on things, to try to keep the freedmen out of trouble. On the way toward City Hall he noticed the considerable number of men who wore a bit of blue ribbon in their lapel, and one of them was an acquaintance. The Lieutenant spoke to him.

"Going in the wrong direction, aren't you, Mr. Dunster?"

"I'm going home, and I'm going to stay there."

The Lieutenant nodded toward the little knot of blue ribbon. "That have anything to do with it?"

Mr. Dunster hesitated. "Well, a gentleman gave it to me last night, said if I didn't want the nigras to have the vote, to be sure to wear it today." He was obviously uncomfortable, lifted his hand in farewell. "Good day, Lieutenant."

Don went on till he saw the throng of policemen assembled in the square across from City Hall. When he approached them, his uniform made him at once conspicuous, but in the glances he encountered there was only a friendly derision. He saw one or two policemen who had reversed the badges on their hats, so that the numbers could not be read, and he saw another adjusting his belt, adorned with two revolvers, outside his coat. To this man, he spoke, his tone casual.

"You look able to do whatever's necessary."

"Aim to be," the policeman assented. "Aim to knock the dog water out of the damned Convention."

"You really expect trouble."

The man looked at him with a calm eye. "Why, no. But if some of your pet niggers get uppity, you might see a real hell of a fuss today."

Page thought there were certainly several hundred police here awaiting orders. Some stood, some sat on the banquettes with their feet hanging over the gutters. Some moved to and fro. The Lieutenant made his way through the crowd, hearing occasional snatches of conversation. ". . . here since midnight last night." ". . . orders to come in at daylight." "Mayor says we're going to attend the Convention." ". . . to hell with your pistols. I'll take my Bowie knife every time." ". . . gave out the pistols soon as we came in." The Lieutenant left them behind and went on as far as Common Street, turning toward the Institute. Everyone on the street seemed to be moving in the same direction. There were a surprising number of boys in the crowd, and groups of young men at every corner; young white men, and white boys.

Dryades Street was well filled with Negroes, swarming in front of the big building. The banquette across the street from the Institute was lined with white men, watching the excited Negroes with expressionless eyes. The crowd of Negroes was made up of many small groups—sometimes a man and a woman and two or three children were clearly a family—and these little clots of people, their eyes shining, laughing and joking, continually merged with others and then drew apart again, so that there was a constant stirring and ferment everywhere.

Page, scanning the crowd, recognized here and there a familiar face; he went among them, speaking to this one and that. "You know me, know the Bureau is on your side, know we're your friends. Now take a friend's advice and go home; go on about your business, go home."

A few of the men to whom he spoke obediently led their families away, but some were stubborn, and a big Negro whom Page knew as Pecko said seriously: "Naw suh, Miste' Lieutenant, we uns is staying heah! Dey done give us dese—" He produced a revolver. "And dey told us to 'fend de Convention, an' we gwine stay!"

"Nobody's going to bother the Convention, Pecko," Don urged. "If they need guards, the Army will guard them. You boys go on home."

But with Pecko he failed, and with others, too. Some Negroes departed, but others were constantly arriving. The crowd grew no larger, but it did not diminish. He thought many came here only to see what was happening, then were either bored or half frightened by what they saw and so went away.

Negroes were going in and out of the front door of the Institute, and others looked down from the windows on the second floor, calling to friends in the street. The scene, as far as they were concerned, was a jolly one; this might have been a holiday. A little before noon, a group of white men, thirty or more, came from Canal Street toward the Hall, walking by twos and threes. Page recognized King Cutler and Doctor Dostie and two or three others, and knew these were delegates. One of them, obviously a minister, paused on the steps of the building to urge the Negroes in the street to go home, and persuaded some of them to do so. When he followed the other white men into the building, Don went with him.

They entered the wide lower hallway of the Institute, now packed with grinning Negroes who parted to let them through. Halfway along the hall, a flight of stairs led upward, Negroes lining it on either side or trooping up behind the delegates as they ascended. When Don reached the second floor, most of the delegates were waiting, while a throng of Negroes who had taken possession of the hall of the House of Representatives were herded out into the corridor. The way clear, the delegates—and Don went with them—passed through a lobby and through double doors into the House chamber. This was a handsome apartment, tall windows reaching from just above the floor almost to the timbered and beautifully paneled ceiling. The speaker's platform was at the Dryades Street end of the chamber, with lofty windows behind it, and desks below it on either side.

The party of Conventioners, Don following them, came from the lobby into a wide enclosure, separated from the body of the hall by a strong railing. Two men at the doors admitted them, but barred the Negroes in the lobby. The Conventioners and their friends—Don guessed their number at fifty—seated themselves in front of the speaker's platform. Don took a chair at one side, and after a brief interval, and some stir and whispering, a gentleman whom Don guessed must be Judge Howell called the meeting to order and called upon the Reverend Mr. Horton to open the proceedings with prayer. Don was not surprised to find that the Reverend Mr. Horton was the gentleman whom he had followed up the stairs.

After the opening prayer, the Secretary called the roll, an interminable list of names. To most of them there was no answer, but at intervals someone answered: "Here!" Don counted these responses. There were twenty-five in all. Twenty-five was far from the seventy-six necessary for a quorum, yet the Lieutenant as he listened gave a silent salute to each man. Whatever their faults or their virtues, they were brave to the point of being foolhardy. Certainly every man here had been threatened, both directly and indirectly; certainly there were in New Orleans twice or three times that number of delegates who now were kept away from this meeting by the threats which the group of valiants here had dared ignore.

The roll call ended, and King Cutler rose to move that the Sergeant-at-Arms be sent out to arrest and bring in all absent members. Since this would obviously be a considerable task, the motion was amended to allow the Sergeant-at-Arms to name assistants. When they departed on their quest, the members here present were forbidden to leave the hall, but almost at once, the meeting voted to recess till one o'clock. The crowd of Negroes who had till now been excluded from the hall were allowed to come in and take seats in the railed enclosure.

As the recess and the waiting began, the Lieutenant crossed to stand by one of the windows. He was surprised to see how few people clustered in the street below. After the weeks of angry discussion, he had somehow expected that half the Negroes in New Orleans would be here, and thousands of white people, yet there were no more than two-score white men over on the banquette opposite, and certainly not a hundred Negroes in the street.

Perhaps some had been drawn away by the distant sound of fifes and drums off across Canal Street somewhere. Looking that way, Don saw at a little distance a flash of color; a flag, heading a parade. Out on the neutral ground in the middle of Canal Street, a half circle of men and boys were drawn up to watch the parade emerge from Burgundy, and the banquettes in Burgundy were crowded. Some white boys ran to keep abreast of the leaders of the advancing parade, and one of those boys somehow involved himself in a fight with a Negro, and the parade straggled to a halt. Even at this distance, the Lieutenant suddenly recognized the white boy. Peter!

Then Peter disappeared, a puff of smoke hiding his face and head from Page's vision, and instantly thereafter Don heard the pistol shot.

9

WHEN OLD PIKE HEARD that shot so short a distance ahead, he was already at a standstill; the disturbance caused by the fight had halted the column, and he stopped with the others. But at the sound of the shot, the tail of the procession, of which he was a part, edged warily backward; then those nearest the shot, in a wild haste to leave the neighborhood, stampeded the rear guard into flight, and Pike was jostled by the racing throng. A Negro boy came dodging through the thinning crowd at a headlong run, with a policeman at his heels, and as the boy scudded past, Pike recogized Bob. Bob whipped into an alley, the policeman close behind, a group of white men and boys joining him in the pursuit. Pike saw among them Peter. Probably Peter and Bob had been up to something, and the policeman was after Bob, and Peter—the old man had no illusions about young Marste'— was trailing them to see the fun.

He tried to follow, calling Peter's name. Behind him, as he entered the alley, sounded the sudden blast of a cornet. Brass had been added to the fifes and drums, and Pike loved a band even more than he loved a parade; but he ought to take Peter home. Little Marste' hadn't ought to be out in all this ruckus. So Pike hurried up the alley in a limping haste. The policeman and the others returned past him, giving up the chase, laughing together, but Peter was not among them, so Pike went on to look further. The back yard of a store that fronted on Canal Street, littered with discarded boxes, some of them big enough to hold a piano, seemed like a place where Bob might have hidden; so Pike went poking among them till a white man yelled from the store window: "Git out o' there, nigger!"

"Yassuh, yassuh!" Pike hurried out into the alley, and as he did so, Peter came into view from Dauphine Street and saw him and ran toward him.

"Pike, you see Bob?"

"Saw him cuttin' de dust, an' de policeman afte' him."

"Well I'm after him too! The bastard hit me!"

"Sho now, he don' oughta do dat! Mm-hmm!" Pike hummed with disapproval. "You boun' tuh tan his hide when you ketch him. Mars' Petuh, you an' me's a long ways fo'm home. You comin' home wid me?"

"Well, not right now."

Old Pike sat down on the banquette, fanning himself. "Sho is a hot day. Bettuh you had, Mars' Pete. Gun-shootin' time, wise folks stays indoors."

"Shooting's all over. The policeman just shot at Bob because Bob was fighting me. I wish he'd killed him!"

"Ain' no place foh white folks, let alone niggehs. Best you come along home." Before Peter could answer, they heard from some distance a sudden tumult, muffled by the sound of intervening buildings; they heard shouts and cries, and then a shot, and then a peppering of shots. "Heah dat!" Pike cried. "Dat ole pappy shot raisin' him a fambly. We gwine git plumb away f'om heah!"

But Peter shook his head. "Come on, Pike, let's see what's happening." He was off at full tilt, racing toward the distant sounds.

Pike, calling: "Hol' on! Hol' on! Wait foh ole Pike!" at first tried to follow, but Peter rounded the corner and disappeared, and after a few more steps, Pike slowed and stopped. With all that shooting going on, off yonder, an old man with any brains in his head would know enough to keep out of the way. Pike turned his back to the sounds of trouble and headed toward the levee. He would go as far toward the river as seemed necessary, take that roundabout route home.

At Chartres Street he decided he was out of the danger zone and turned toward Canal. He saw a man run past the end of Chartres Street with a pistol in his hand, but Pike went cautiously forward, curiosity battling with terror, and peeped around the corner into Canal Street to see what was happening. Down toward Dryades Street, policemen in blue coats and white pants were shooting off their guns, and Pike could see Negroes running every which way, so he judged the police were shooting at Negroes. He backed away. Probably the safest place for him, till the excitement quieted down, was Samson's harness shop, and he headed that way. Sometimes he heard distant shooting; sometimes the tumult seemed to cease. Once or twice he dodged into a courtyard or a garden to let white men pass him unseen. His fears and his haste between them brought him near exhaustion before at last he reached his goal.

Samson was there, alone, his door wide, working at the bench, and he did not turn at Pike's arrival. Pike sank down, panting and dripping, and he mopped his brow. "Got to set a spell," he said hoarsely. "Bad times." Samson did not answer, but he was always of a silent habit, as though he were deaf. It seemed to Pike strange that there were no others here today, and he asked: "Wheah's ev'ybody?"

He had not raised his voice, but Samson said: "Home t' dinnuh."

Pike had not till then realized that he was hungry. "What time's it got tuh be?"

"Going on two o'clock."

"Lawdy me!" Home and dinner was a long walk. Pike set himself to some serious resting, sprawling in the chair, his legs outstretched. Two Negroes came in, a man named Freedley and another whom Pike did not know. Samson took snuff and passed the jar around, and then a white man with a white handkerchief tied around his sleeve stopped in the doorway, peering into the darkness.

"What's going on here?"

"Dis heah's mah home," said Samson. "You knows dat, Mr. Sykes. Dese heah mah friends."

The white man showed a revolver. "Set still!" He blew a whistle, and another man came running, and Sykes said: "Here's four of 'em. Get out here, the lot of you! Fall in!"

Samson protested: "Mr. Sykes, how come you ac' so? You knows I'se a good man."

"Our orders is kill all you niggers, so come along, 'fore I dirty your own floor. Watch 'em, Charlie."

Samson stepped sluggishly out into the alley, and Pike and the others followed him, and Sykes with a gesture of the revolver indicated which way they were to go. "Now, march!"

They crossed Rampart and went on toward Claiborne Street, and half a dozen men and boys trailed along. Samson spoke once. "We ain' done nothing, Mr. Sykes. What you up to?" But Sykes slapped him on the ear with a revolver barrel, and a boy in the group on their heels shouted:

"Cut his heart out, the nigger son of a bitch!"

After a few blocks, as the houses thinned, Sykes stopped abruptly. "Turn around," he commanded, and Samson and Pike and the other Negroes swung to face him. Sykes said: "I'm tired of walking. Let's kill the bastards here."

On the word, he lifted his revolver and at arm's length shot Samson in the breast. Samson fell, and the Negro named Freedley turned to run, but the white man whom Sykes had called Charlie knocked him down with the barrel of his revolver. Samson climbed uncertainly to his hands and knees, and Sykes threw three more bullets into him, like beating a rug. The Negro whom Pike did not know cried out and ran, and Sykes fired two shots at him before the hammer of his revolver fell on an empty chamber. Charlie ran after the fleeing Negro, and the half dozen who had followed them thus far now joined the chase; they turned a corner and were gone.

Samson on the ground rolled on his back, and Sykes kicked him in the side, and cried: "Cripes a'mighty, ain't you dead?" He gripped his revolver by the barrel to use it as a club, but a man came out of the house in front of which they had stopped and said softly:

"That's enough! Pick that man up and bring him into the house."

Sykes cried: "Who the hell you think . . ."

The newcomer took a swift forward stride and his cane became a sword. The point touched Sykes's throat. Sykes checked his word and stood still.

Pike had not waited. He hurried away as fast as his feet would let him, turning up Claiborne Street. Home was far away, but home was where he wished to be. He could no longer hear any shooting, but when he crossed Common Street he had to wait to let a wagon pass. In the wagon lay six or eight bodies of Negroes, heaped any old fashion. A policeman sat on one of them, and as the wagon passed Pike, this policeman hastily stood up and looked at the body on which he had been sitting and said in astonishment: "Hey! You alive? Why didn't you say so?"

The wagon went on toward the hospital, and Pike struggled homeward, wishing Prytania Street was not so far away. When at last he ventured to turn up toward the river, he guessed he must have at least another mile to go. The day seemed, even to the old Negro, mighty hot, but the streets were shady, and though there was the steady sound of trouble off to his left, for a long time no one crossed his path.

At last he saw the front of the house, and though it was still a long two blocks off, and almost completely hidden by the great oaks that overhung the streets, his weariness was forgotten. He came nearer and saw Miss Lucy on the second-floor gallery, watching him approach. A white man with a hatchet in his hand appeared around the corner just ahead, and came toward him, but old Pike hardly noticed. He had never seen the man before, and there was nothing unusual about him except the hatchet he carried. Only at the last moment had Pike an insant of fear, when the man suddenly leaped toward him, the hatchet swinging high.

When Lieutenant Page, from the window of the Hall of Representatives, caught that distant glimpse of Peter, there was only an instant of recognition before the puff of powder smoke hid the boy, and the crack of the pistol shot reached the Lieutenant's ear. He raced toward the stairs, thrusting through the crowd, speaking words of apology, and reached the street. Everyone was looking along Dryades and across Canal toward the spot where the shot had been fired, and Don ran in hard haste to come where Peter, if he were wounded or dead, might lie.

As he crossed Canal Street, the Negroes who had scattered at the shot were already returning. The fifers and drummers had held their ground, and a man with a cornet joined them, and they grouped around the Negro who carried the flag. Don came there and saw that Peter was gone and said to a white man, standing by:

"What happened, sir? That shot? Did you see?"

The man nodded. "Yeah. One of the niggers got into a fight with a white boy. Tony Elmore took a shot at the nigger, but he ducked and ran."

"Was the white boy hurt?"

"Huh-uh! No, he put after the nigger, mad as a hen."

Don went on a little way along Burgundy Street, looking for Peter. The boy ought to be at home, out of the tumult here where at any moment death might be let loose; if he could be found, Page meant to see him safe. A policeman with a troop of men and boys on his heels emerged from a cross street, and Page spoke to the officer.

"Find him?"

"No!" The man spat disgustedly. "Son of a bitch got away. I had my gun right in his face, but he dodged!"

"What happened to the white boy he was fighting?"

"Here, ain't he?" The policeman looked around at his following. "One of you, was it?" But no one claimed the distinction, and the drums once more began their familiar Thrrripp! Thrrripp! Thrip-thrip-thrip! Everyone moved toward the sound, and the Lieutenant followed them.

Dryades Street was blocked completely, and he heard a shot or two, and saw missiles—they were as big as brickbats, probably *were* brickbats—flying out of Dryades Street into the crowd. Shots came in a sudden flurry, and on their heels the sounds of bells rang a clamorous alarm. The Lieutenant remembered that the Institute had a rear entrance off Baronne Street and he went that way. As he reached the alley that led to this back door, policemen were running up Baronne in what was obviously panic flight. He turned down the alley and saw five Negroes, two with revolvers in their hands, huddled against the door of the Institute. One was wounded in the leg, and a small puddle of blood had formed beside his shoe. Don recognized Pecko.

"You, Pecko? I told you an hour ago you'd better go home."

"Yas suh, you sholy did. I wisht I had went!"

"What are you doing with that revolver?" Don turned to the other man who held a weapon. "You too."

"Dey give us dese and tol' us to gyahd de Convention." The man's eyes wavered; he extended the gun. "You tek it an' git me out o' heah. Pecko, gi' him your'n, too."

Pecko obeyed, and Don tossed the gun over a board wall that divided the alley from the buildings of the Medical College under construction along Common Street. The steps where he stood were high enough so that he could look across Common Street. He saw that the policemen who had run away were now returning, and he pushed the Negroes here beside him back into the hall, out of harm's way, and closed the door upon them. He stayed outside, watching. The policemen were moving slowly, reloading their revolvers, and a troop of young men and boys flanked them and followed on their heels. They would be ready now for killing, to forget their fears and the shame of their headlong flight, so he watched till they had passed before he opened the door and spoke to the trembling Negroes.

"Now come on," he called. "Watch your chance and go along home! And stay there. Keep out of trouble! Come!"

They hesitated till he reiterated the command, then came timidly after him. He led them down the alley, and they huddled behind him while he made sure Baronne Street was for the moment and in both directions clear. "All right," he said then. "Now scoot!" They raced away.

Don moved down Common toward the front of the Institute, but as he reached the corner Trav hailed him from across the street. "Page! Lieutenant!" Trav threaded his way toward Don and they met and Trav asked quickly: "Seen Peter, Lieutenant?"

"A while ago." Page hesitated. "Half an hour ago. He . . ."

"Where?"

"I was up there." Don pointed to the windows above them. "He was away across Canal Street, in a fight with some Negro. By the time I got there he was gone. I've been hunting him till just now." He saw Trav's desperate anxiety. "He went up Bienville Street, I'm pretty sure, but I couldn't find him."

There was for a moment quiet all around them. Dryades Street, from where they stood to Canal Street, was almost a hundred feet wide. Now, except that at either end white men and police formed a solid blockade, it was deserted. Here at Common Street, the newly arrived police were ranked in a double line; at Canal Street, the same thing was true. Don thought most of the Negroes were inside the Institute. "I guess the trouble's over," he suggested. "With the police here to keep them quiet."

"Where are you going now?"

"I suppose they'll go ahead with their Convention. I'll go up and watch proceedings."

"If you see Peter, keep him with you—if you can."

"I'm sure he's all right."

"I'll go over to Bienville Street, look around there where you think he went."

Page hesitated, thinking to accompany Trav and help that search; but it was almost hopeless. If Peter were found, it would be by chance. When Trav was out of sight, Don went into the Institute. The corridor and stairs were jammed, but he worked his way upstairs to the Hall of Representatives. There were certainly a hundred Negroes, and forty or fifty white men in the Hall. King Cutler and Doctor Dostie consulted on the platform, and a moment after Don entered, Mr. Cutler spoke to the Negroes.

"Don't move around, boys. Sit down, on benches, chairs, on the floor, anywhere."

Don saw that several windows had been broken, saw a few bricks on the floor. He went to look out of one of the front windows. A small company of Negroes, a score or so, now were loosely gathered in the street and on the steps. At either end of Dryades Street, police and citizens still blocked the way. In the gutter opposite, a Negro sprawled, and Don saw the red pool below the body. Two other Negroes, certainly dead, lay a little beyond, toward Canal Street. In a vacant lot on that side of the Institute, a dozen others, obviously wounded, sat leaning against brick piles, or lay passive in the shade, their eyes closed.

While he was studying these men, someone came to the window beside him, and Don recognized John Henderson, and saw by the man's white face and gleaming eyes Henderson's tremendous excitement. "What happened here?" he asked, and Henderson said, all in a rush:

"Some boys started throwing bricks through our windows! Our protectors in the street below drove them away, and a policeman fired on our friends, and the colored citizens, empty-handed, exposing their bare breasts to the rebel's leaden missiles, drove the police headlong down Common Street!" He laughed in a shrill way. "Made them run!"

Don had seen that flight, but he felt madness in the man beside him. He spoke in a mild tone. "When I left here, your sergeant-at-arms had gone to try to round up a quorum."

"He hasn't come back, but he will!" Henderson threw up his arm, he shouted. "He will! We will prevail!"

A bullet cracked against the window frame beside him, and King Cutler called: "Away from those windows, gentlemen; get down."

Henderson obeyed, Page finding shelter against the wall. The windows extended almost to the floor, so there was little protection against bullets. In the street arose a sudden commotion, and from the direction of Canal Street came a burst of firing, and scattering shots from men and boys in Common. The street was for a moment a confusion of running figures, Negroes dodging away through the yards and alleys on either side and pressing into the Institute. The hallways below and on this floor and on the floor above were for an interval shaken by the drumbeat of many running feet.

The scattered firing ceased, and the street was empty of Negroes, but policemen in uniform, and men and boys in a shouting mass, flowed in and filled this momentary vacuum. In the vacant lot beside the building, those of the wounded who could move were crawling this way and that, seeking some safer hiding place. They crept into corners, hid themselves in the weeds, lay as still as Don had seen grouse chicks lie while the mother struggles away with dragging wing to divert attention from her babies. Down by the front entrance men and boys in the street raced toward the steps there. Someone sent a Negro spinning out into the street to meet them, and he fell down the steps, and two men shot him, their revolvers speaking as one. Then one of them leaned down to put the muzzle of his revolver against the Negro's head and fired again. A policeman and a white man dragged another Negro between them out of the Hall, and the policeman shot him twice in the stomach, and the Negro stumbled away and then crawled away, one hand supporting his spilling bowels.

Here in the Hall, Doctor Dostie called reassuringly: "Don't be alarmed, my friends! Every Negro in New Orleans is organized and ready to protect you."

Don thought grimly that the Convention would certainly never gather a quorum here today. He heard shots in the lobby below, and in the corridors on the lower floor, and he crossed to King Cutler and asked a question.

"What do you hope for? Why don't you surrender, end all this?"

"Did you see the dead Negro in the gutter across the street?" Don nodded, and Cutler said proudly: "That dead man ends the power of these damned rebels, once and for all."

The double doors into the Hall were flung open, and two Negroes carried in a wounded man, helpless with a bullet through his leg. Half a dozen other wounded followed, and a Negro kneeling among the shattered chairs began to pray aloud. Don went to the wounded men to help where he could. All but one were Negroes, and one of them died as Don reached him. The next was bleeding badly from a bullet wound in his leg, and Don used the man's suspenders to make a tourniquet. Behind him, a brick smashed through one of the windows and fell harmless, and another struck from someone a cry of pain, and from a second floor gallery across the street a random bullet came through one of the windows and split a panel. John Henderson strode to the platform and threw up his hands for silence, and he shouted in a great voice:

"Friends! Friends! Shall we die here like penned sheep? No! Let us rush out together, overpower the rebels, turn their own weapons . . ."

King Cutler caught his arm. "John, don't be a damned fool! Shut those doors, somebody; pile chairs against them."

Cutler seemed to have assumed command, and Don wondered where Judge Howell was gone. Surely, as the man who had called the Convention together, he should be here. Only a dozen white men still remained in the Chamber, but the Negroes huddled around the platform seemed as many as ever. At Cutler's command, some of them began to try to block the doors. The doors opened outward and had on the inside neither locks nor bars, so they could not be secured; but chairs were piled against them with an eager zeal. Don thought the activity was a respite and a relief; to be doing something, even something that was obviously useless, was better than to be doing nothing at all.

Someone shouted: "Here they come!" A Negro laid hold of the handles of the double doors and braced himself, and a white man came close to him, saying quietly:

"Here, you can't hold that alone. I'll help you."

But their position was hopeless. To grip the handles, they had to reach across the benches and chairs which blocked the doorway, and when someone tugged at the doors from the outside, these obstacles threw them off balance. Their hands slipped and the doors swung wide.

As those near the doors recoiled, Don saw in the opening three policemen in uniform, and a dozen men in ordinary clothes. Each policeman had a revolver, and on the instant, each of them, and several of the civilians fired. Don dropped and rolled to one side, and in the moment's lull before the smoke of that first volley cleared, the minister, Mr. Horton, called:

"Stop firing! We surrender! We surrender!" He was holding up both hands, crying out over and over, "We surrender!" And: "Gentlemen, I beseech you!" Don, watching him, saw something twitch at his right hand, and a trickle of red ran quickly down his upraised arm. Another volley spattered through the smoke and the minister cried out in helpless pain: "We didn't come to fight! We surrender!" His right arm bent strangely between shoulder and elbow, and he nursed it with his other arm, and then winced and twisted as though something had hurt his side and went down on his knees. Don crawled toward him, and someone shouted from the doorway: "Kill that God-damned Yank!"

At the first fire, the Negroes had pressed back from the door toward the platform and the windows, and Don saw two of them firing revolvers toward the door, firing without aim. Now a giant Negro lifted a chair and charged at the doorway still lined with armed men. A volley stopped him, but in the smoke other Negroes broke up chairs and used the legs as clubs. The mass of them drove at the door and by sheer weight of flesh, against revolvers that now were empty, they cleared the door and poured out into the lobby and then into the hallway, driving the attackers down the stairs.

Don helped Mr. Horton to his feet. A bullet through his palm had inflicted excruciating pain, his arm was broken, and he had a minor shot wound in the side. Most of the unwounded Negroes had plunged out through the lobby, and King Cutler and Governor Hahn had followed them. The minister took a small flag on its staff from the clerk's desk on the platform, and tied his handerchief to it, and with Don steadying him he leaned out of a window, calling: "We surrender! We surrender!" Doctor Dostie came to join him, waving a white handkerchief; but after an instant he whirled back from the window, bending double, crying:

"I'm shot!" Then, erect again: "But it's nothing! Everybody get away from the windows."

Don, in a cold sweat of rage at this pitiless massacre, turned again to tend the wounded. Except to improvise tourniquets, and to explain to each man that these must be loosed at intervals, there was little to do, but he did this little. Afterward, trying to remember, he thought there must have been here at least a dozen dead or badly wounded, and he wondered why there were so few. With a hundred and fifty men in the room, most of them huddled together, every bullet should have found some mark.

Don went from man to man among the wounded, and many of the Negroes who had driven off that first attack came back into the chamber. Some of the white men did not return. Judge Howell had been invisible from the first, and now King Cutler and Governor Hahn had disappeared, but the minister was still here, and Doctor Dostie, and John Henderson. The brief lull ended with the sound of shots in the corridor, and a few Negroes poured in through the lobby and tried to block the doors, but the doors were again wrenched open and the fusillade renewed.

At the first shot, Don crouched behind a desk at one end of the platform, but then he saw a man leading Mr. Horton toward the doorway, crying: "Get this man out of here! He's hurt!"

Don went to help. One of the men in the doorway shouted: "No sir! Not alive!" He lifted a rude club made out of a piece of board, that had been whittled to a handle, and swung it lustily at the minister's head; but he missed. Then a surge of Negroes once more swept the attackers back into the hallway carrying Don and Mr. Horton with them.

Behind him Don heard Doctor Dostie cry: "Shut the doors! We've got to hold them till the soldiers come!"

In the darkness of the corridor shots flashed, and men locked in a blind grapple, striking and grunting and straining. Abruptly, the crowd which was thus pressed together at the top of the stairs overbalanced the mass on the treads below, and an avalanche of men, friends and foes together, flowed down the stairs into the lobby, falling and tumbling.

Don was caught in that cascade, but he kept his feet, and at the stair foot he twisted away to one side out of the press. A shot came from the corridor behind him, and he whirled that way and saw a man running headlong. Not caring whether he was pursuer or pursued, heedless with rage, his blood pounding, Don ran after him. The fugitive —a white man—flung out into the alley, and so to Baronne Street. He turned toward Common, Don on his heels.

But then Don halted, staring at a wagon that came up Common from Dryades. The wagon was loaded with motionless bodies. A policeman rode with the driver, and someone hailed him.

"Hey, Paul, you've got enough for a mess! Where'd you get 'em all?"

The policeman jumped down, waved the wagon on. "They was all jumping out the windows, give me some good wing shooting."

Don stepped toward the wagon, and the driver looked at him with a quizzical eye. "Where you been, Yank? Got yourself all bloody."

"Trying to save a few lives. Where are you taking these men?"

"To City Hall, to the doctors. That's the orders." The man clucked to his horse, and Don watched the wagon move away. The half-dozen Negroes in it were not dead; certainly not all of them, for while he spoke to the driver, two of them had watched him dumbly. A thought struck him like an inspiration. The Freedmen's Bureau operated the Marine Hospital, out Common Street beyond Claiborne. He hurried after the wagon.

"See here," he called to the driver. "Why not take these Negroes to the Marine Hospital, where the Freedmen's Bureau can take care of them? After all, that's what the Bureau's for."

But the wagon did not even pause. A fresh burst of firing from the Institute a block away made Don look back. He saw a man climb out of a second-story window and hang, ready to drop, and then a shot sounded from the gallery of a house across the street, and the man fell.

Then a handful of police came toward Don from the Institute, marching a prisoner in their midst, and followed by a train of white men and boys, clamorous and shouting. As they passed, Don recognized the prisoner as former Governor Hahn. Since blood had spattered his countenance, Don knew him at first only by his limp. A man following his captors shouted:

"Give him to us!" There was a general cry. "Hang him!" "Kill him!" A man waving a gun tried to come near Mr. Hahn, shouting: "I'll do it. Make room! Make room!" A policeman caught his arm and took the revolver away from him and threw it over a wall beside the banquette and pushed the man backward so hard that he tripped on his own heels and fell, to the laughter of the crowd.

Behind this group came another, with another captive. This was a white man Don did not know, surrounded by clamoring men and boys. He followed them. At the corner of St. Charles Street, the crowd was so dense that the policemen with their prisoner could not push a way through. They commandeered a carriage, protecting the man with their bodies, screening him from any shots from the crowd till he was in the carriage and away.

Don judged that the police were under orders to protect white men, at least after they were arrested; but there was no protection for Negroes. He made his way through the crowd to City Hall and saw Governor Hahn and the other prisoner led into the Central Police Station. When he followed, no one halted him. Here were a dozen wounded men under treatment. Doctor Berthelot, whom Don knew and who seemed to be in charge, was tending a bullet wound in a policeman's leg, and Don spoke to him.

"Doctor, you can't handle all the wounded here; not all the Negroes certainly."

The Doctor shook his head. "No, not if they keep coming." With a sidelong glance he saw the blue leg of Don's uniform trousers and looked up at him and asked: "Lieutenant Page, aren't you? The Freedmen's Bureau?"

"Yes, Doctor. May I suggest that we can take a lot of wounded, whites or Negroes, at the Marine Hospital?"

"Go ahead; you have my blessing. Shameful business! Here, we've no place to put them except on the floor in the recorder's court, and it's overflowing already. I'll pass the word that the Hospital will receive them." He added grimly: "Everyone here is theoretically under arrest, but you take 'em to the Hospital. I don't think they'll run away."

When Don reached the street, a crowd of boys and young men was jeering the arrival of another prisoner. Don scanned the crowd, hoping to see Peter among them; but if the boy was there, he was not visible.

Page worked his way toward Common Street. At the corner he watched two policemen drag up Gravier Street a Negro, bloody and beaten, marching him between a double line of men and boys with knives and clubs who sought to dodge around the policemen and strike at the prisoner. Once a bowie knife slit the man's shirt across the shoulder, and he cried out, and one of the policemen turned with revolver drawn to drive back the crowd. Here, at least, the police were protecting a Negro.

The Hospital was on Common Street beyond Claiborne; but Common was crowded, so Don went down Gravier, a block further uptown. As he passed Baronne, a Negro ran diagonally across the street a block ahead, and a policeman fired at him. The Negro dropped to his knees, and the policeman tried to shoot again and his revolver misfired. He put a fresh cap on the chamber which had missed fire and stepped close to the Negro and shot him in the face.

Don had started toward them at a run, but when he saw the Negro was dead, the policeman walking away, he stopped. He was shaking with anger, blind to any sense of danger to himself; but what use? What use? The best service he could render would be to help the wounded. As he crossed Dryades Street, he heard heavy firing toward the Institute and found that he could see through the windows of the Hall of Representatives, see the flash of guns in the smoke cloud there. So that slaughter was not yet ended! He heard a shot from Rampart Street, a block ahead of where he stood, and another somewhere behind him, but the heaviest firing was in the Institute itself.

Watching, he thought bitterly that even one squad of soldiers could have prevented all this, could have saved all these lives. General Sheridan was away in Texas, but General Baird had been given specific warning that some such outbreak as this was inevitable. Don had not believed any such bloody butchery as this to be possible in a city that even pretended to be civilized, yet he was sure that if he had been in command, there would have been troops here this morning. Everyone who could read the papers had known that the Convention was to meet at noon. Don's teeth set with rage at General Baird, at Governor Wells, at General Sheridan, at any man who might have prevented this butchery and had not done so.

Still standing on Dryades Street at Gravier he saw a sudden burst of men run out from the Institute, some in the blue coat and white pantaloons of the police, some civilians. Two Negroes fled before them, fled toward him, but at Common Street a shot dropped one of them and he rolled like a rabbit and lay still. The other dove under the banquette and tried to hide there, and three of the men dragged him out and beat his head with their clubs, till in a sudden silence that swept the scene as a cloud shadow sweeps a field, Don a block away heard the soggy, crackling sound of their blows.

And in that sudden silence, Don heard another sound; a distant trumpet call! So at last the soldiers were here, the tragedy was done.

He waited till by the cries and the scurrying he was sure of this, then went on to the Hospital. There, drays and wagons full of dead or wounded Negroes wheeled up to the door to be emptied of their loads. Don helped with this work, lending a hand on a stretcher when a hand was needed. The wounded, even those able to walk, were sometimes as lifeless as the dead, moving like drugged men, their faces bruised and battered, blood caked upon them and upon their garments, stupefied and senseless. Many of them had, except for their hideous swollen contusions, no visible wounds, though here and there Don saw a knife slash. Those with bullet wounds were usually helpless, in collapse. There were a surprising number of broken arms and legs. He thought the arms might have been broken in warding off savage bludgeon blows; the broken legs had presumably resulted from jumping out of the windows of the hall. A few white men were among the number, and about four o'clock Don helped carry in the minister, Mr. Horton. He was unconscious. When Don last saw him, his wounds had been relatively slight, but since then his skull had been beaten in.

Don stayed at the Hospital till the sun was low. When he started for his lodging, he was too weary to think of stopping on the way; that he went past Lucy's home was more instinct than design.

Trav, hurrying toward the Institute to try and find Peter, soon after that first shot heard the far squeal of fifes, and the thud of distant drums, and Negroes and some white men and boys raced past him toward the sounds. The drums grew louder, and then hushed, and two men with drawn revolvers overtook him and hurried on, and one called back to him: "Hurry, or you'll miss the fun!" The other shouted something that ended: ". . . to their long homes."

A block short of the Institute, Trav heard a shot ahead, and suddenly the street was all one tumult of shots and of shouting and of men dodging and running. A policeman with a Negro prisoner came toward Trav, the prisoner at revolver point, his hands in the air. The Negro was making a hoarse, crowing sound, and the policeman kicked him. "Go on! You didn't crow like that yesterday!" The Negro stumbled on, and Trav watched them go, thinking it was as though the policeman were insane. He was not surprised when, a block away, the officer put his revolver against the back of the Negro's neck and pulled the trigger, then stepped around the body and walked on.

Trav started after him, then checked himself. Peter was his concern, and Peter would be where the crowd was thickest; so Trav turned again toward the Institute. Three Negroes ran up the middle of the street toward him and bullets pelted after them, and one of the Negroes jerked up an enormous horse pistol and shot at Trav. Trav whipped out his own revolver, but then he thrust it away again and let the man go. Between him and Common Street, two Negroes sprawled in the dust, one of them crawling toward the gutter, and some boys came running to beat at him with clubs, and a woman screamed and Trav looked up and saw her on the second floor gallery.

"For God's sake," she wailed. "Don't do such brutal things before my very door."

The boys scattered, the Negro crawled away. Trav came to the corner of Common Street, where police and citizens stood like a wall, but the throng of Negroes churning in front of the Institute suddenly raced toward them, and the police here at the corner broke and ran, racing away up Common Street. There was always something vaguely ludicrous about such a spectacle, and Trav found himself grinning in an absurd amusement.

The firing had for the moment stopped; he worked his way to and fro through the crowd, looking for Peter. Eventually he met Lieutenant Page, and heard what the Lieutenant could tell him, and set out to cross Canal to search the streets beyond, but on the banquette across the street from the Institute he met a man he knew, a Mr. Brooks, who as correspondent for the *New York Times* had once come to see the mill and send a dispatch quoting some of Mr. Cist's high predictions. Brooks caught his arm. "What's happened, Major Currain?"

"Hell to pay."

"I know! I know! I was here when they met, and when they adjourned—"

"Adjourned?"

"Yes, they sent the sergeant-at-arms to try to drum up a quorum, and they were going to meet again at half past one. I went to the telegraph office to send a dispatch to my paper, and when I came back there was a regular battle going on here in the street. I hid in the alley back there." He pointed. "And when the police cleared the street, I ran down to the telegraph office again. Looks like they're going to attack the building."

"You're sending off dispatches right along?" Brooks nodded, and Trav said ruefully: "The South isn't making a very good showing for herself today."

Brooks said in a sympathetic tone: "Thad Stevens is licking his chops, by this time, Mr. Currain."

"Think the news is in Washington already?"

"Oh yes."

"Why didn't General Baird have a few soldiers here?"

"Probably he had his orders. Every Radical, north and south, has been praying for something like this. There they go!" The reporter moved a step nearer the Institute, to see more certainly.

Trav said: "The police seem to have things under control."

"Not for long! This mob will take over!"

They stood diagonally across the street from the Institute. At their backs a fence surrounded a well-tended garden, and Trav saw a gentleman on the second-floor gallery watching the crowd. Then Brooks said in a hushed voice: "Look!"

Trav turned. As though on a common impulse every man and boy in sight—there were no Negroes visible—was moving toward the four pillars that marked the entrance of the Institute. There was something frightening in that movement, and a moment later Brooks cried again: "Look! Watch! They're starting!"

The crowd had pressed around the steps of the building, and a few men had gone inside. Now Trav saw a Negro dragged out through the door and flung staggering down the steps, and he heard a quick flurry of shots.

Brooks exclaimed: "There comes another!" He left the banquette, edging his way through the crowd to cross the street. Trav, in a sick repugnance, turned away. He must find Peter. If the boy were here, he would have seen him, so he went on across Canal and along Burgundy. The shutters were up, the curtains drawn, few pedestrians in sight. Trav went up Bienville Street as far as Dauphin, and so back to Canal. The streets, till he returned to Canal, were almost deserted, but in Canal there were many white men and boys. From the direction of the Institute came the sound of shots, sometimes muffled, sometimes startlingly loud, but Trav scarce listened. His eyes forever promised him that the boy yonder was Peter, and again and again he hurried to overtake some youngster whose back was turned, and found disappointment at the end of each pursuit.

Some instinct led him back to the spot outside Mr. Lyons's store where he had last seen Peter when he left him at school this morning, and a big Negro in a checked suit raced in panic up Gravier Street and toward him, three policemen and a dozen men in close pursuit. The policemen flung shots at the Negro, heedless of the crowd in the street, and a lane opened before the fugitive. He dodged into the doorway where Trav had taken shelter, and fell on his knees, and the policemen pressed in on him, and Trav cried: "Don't shoot that man! Arrest him!"

For only answer, the leading policeman thrust his revolver against the Negro's head, and before Trav could interfere, he fired. Too late,

Trav gripped the barrel of the gun, and the policeman jerked it free and backed clear and leveled his weapon at Trav's stomach and said like a madman: "Yes, and you, too! You nigger-loving son of a bitch!"

Trav took a hot step toward him, but one of the other policemen caught aside the ready pistol. "He's blood-drunk, mister," he said to Trav. "Don't pay any attention to him! Come on, Tom." He led the man away, but Trav, caught by that curdling, choking, blinding rage which in the hour of battle once or twice had swept him, pushed after them, drawing his own revolver. The policeman who had killed the Negro, as though that blood-letting had dazed him, stood passive, but the other man urged: "Let him go, mister, please sir. What's your name? He'll come and apologize to you tomorrow."

Trav bit his lip, trembling with passion. "If I ever see him again," he said stiffly, "or you either, I'll blow your brains out! Get out of my sight!"

"All right, all right, sir. I don't want any trouble with you." The policeman, a firm grasp on his comrade's arm, moved off toward City Hall.

Slowly, Trav's senses cleared. A wagon passed, piled with bodies of men who seemed to be dead, and he turned his eyes away from the hideous sight. A knot of shouting, angry men brushed him aside, calling threats at a white man who marched as a prisoner between four policemen. The crowd sought to reach him with clubs or knives, and a man ran ahead and threw a rope over the cross-arm of a lamppost, and as the prisoner passed, he tried to drop a noose over the prisoner's neck, but the police brushed it aside with their drawn guns.

Trav looked for Peter in the crowd, but the boy was not here. Peter was surely somewhere near the Institute, so Trav went that way. He passed a ladder wagon of the Fire Department, and the fireman standing by the horses asked cheerfully: "Need any ca'tridges, friend? Don't run short. Plenty here." Trav shook his head and went on. At the sound of sudden shots, he looked and saw a Negro at a window of the Institute and Trav thought his lips moved as though he moaned a prayer. Shots spattered around him, and he jerked back and someone shouted:

"Give him time! Wait till he gets his legs out and hangs ready to drop!"

Then a Negro—the same man or another—came at a running jump through the window, clearing the fence behind the Medical College; but as he struck the ground his leg snapped under him, and a dozen boys with clubs ran to cluster around him, pounding lustily, while the bystanders here on the banquette cheered.

Trav shook his head as though to shake the sight away. He found

Dryades Street in front of the Institute now jammed with spectators. A woman on a second floor gallery called in a shrill excitement: "There's a pack of niggers in behind the shed in my back yard!" A score or more of men, police in uniform, firemen with white handkerchiefs around their necks, men in ordinary clothes, ran that way, and Trav heard shots and cries, and saw the woman watching and shouting gleefully.

A mass of men which spilled out of the entrance to the Institute, swirled halfway across the street, engulfing him, and Trav recognized Edgar Cenas. He made his way to the young man's side, asking in desperate hope: "Have you seen Peter?"

The other looked at him through glazed eyes. "Peter? Oh, you're Major Currain? No sir."

Trav said urgently: "I'm looking for Peter."

"Maybe he's upstairs." His tone was flat, and Trav saw that he was gripped by the half-stupor, like madness, which held all men today.

Someone called from the steps of the Institute: "Come on, everybody!"

Cenas moved that way, and Trav went beside him. "I think I saw him upstairs," said Cenas. They entered the lobby side by side. "Come on, and I'll . . ."

Trav lost the other's words in the sudden rush of many men that carried them all up the stairs. As they neared the top, a shot flashed in their faces, and by the flash Trav saw a mulatto in the hall above them, aiming a revolver. Edgar Cenas fell back into Trav's arms, and Trav caught him, and carried him up the stairs and laid him on the floor at one side. Double doors across the hall swung wide, and in that sudden light Trav knelt over the young man. A bullet had struck just above the corner of his mouth, and Trav slipped his hand under the other's neck and felt the exit wound. The bullet had smashed down through a vertebra.

Trav lifted the limp body, and when the way cleared, he carried young Cenas through the lobby into the Hall of Representatives. He halted in the doorway, shocked and unbelieving. Blood had splashed the walls, and blood was slippery on the floor; every chair and desk and bench seemed to have been shattered; dead men and wounded lay all about, and many Negroes and a dozen white men, huddling in corners, stared at him in dazed terror. He stepped over a litter of broken chairs and bore young Cenas into the terrible room and laid him down by the wall, ordering his limbs, covering his face with a handkerchief.

Some of the Negroes struggled to shut the doors into the lobby, and Trav surveyed the company here. He had no longer any hope of finding Peter, but he looked from man to man. Most of them were Negroes, but he recognized the minister whom he had heard speak on the platform just across the street, the night Isaiah's friend Tasspot died of a fit. Mr. Horton sat on the floor, nursing a broken arm, and he was very pale. Then Trav heard a wail from a Negro peering out of the window.

"Dey got Doctuh Dostie!" the Negro cried.

Trav went to look out. The Doctor, apparently dead, lay on his back on the banquette almost directly below. Two boys tugged at his feet, trying to drag him toward Canal Street, but as Trav watched, someone shouted: "Hold on there!" The boys stopped, and the man who had spoken said: "I want to make sure of that bastard!" He lifted a sword cane, the blade flashed, and the man drove it home in the Doctor's stomach. "There, by God!"

The crowd cheered, and the boys who held the Doctor's legs lugged him toward the corner, others helping them or racing behind or beside the limp body, kicking at it or striking it with clubs. Trav saw them halt and hail a two-wheeled cart that chanced to pass, and they threw Doctor Dostie's body into the cart and it moved away.

Trav stayed at the window till a shot struck the ceiling of the Hall almost above his head and he realized it had been fired at him. Then there was a rush of feet in the lobby, and the double doors were jerked apart, and a dozen police officers and civilians ranged across the doorway and their guns began to speak. Trav, with no thought of his own danger, watched in a dull amazement. When the doors were thrown open, the few men still in the Chamber had seemed stupid and spiritless, the Negroes peering out of the windows, or weeping, or praying helplessly; but as the first shots sounded, they surged headlong toward the doorway, clubs flying. The armed men emptied their revolvers into this mass, then recoiled down the stairs to seek time to reload.

Out of this brief murderous confusion, Trav all his life remembered words and phrases, just as his eyes photographed single incidents. Thus he remembered a Negro down on hands and knees, shaking his head, his blood flying as though it spouted from his eyes and ears. He remembered shouts: "Another black devil gone to Hell!" "Kill 'em!" "Kill 'em!" "Kill 'em all!" "Shoot the niggers!" "Count off another!" "Wipe 'em out!" The air was full of shouts, of oaths, of cries of fear or pain. He remembered a man waving a white handkerchief from one of the windows, and a bullet snatching it from his hand. He remembered the repeated cry: "No quarter! No quarter!" And the ruthless, savage shout: "Not alive! You can't surrender, long as you're alive!" He remembered clubs flying as the Negroes swept back those whose guns were empty, and the spatter of blood as revolver barrels or butts smashed down on broken scalps, and he remembered a giant Negro, blood-spattered but apparently unhurt, coming back into the Hall, staggering as though drunk, falling on his knees to pray. He remembered a jovial cry: "Sure, I'll protect you. With this!" A double explosion punctuated the reply. He remembered a white man on his stomach trying to crawl out into the Hall through the many legs that blocked the doorway.

There was brief surcease when the doors were closed, but almost at once they were once more wrenched wide, and the shots and the cries began again. "We surrender!" "We surrender!" "No prisoners!" "We want no prisoners!" Trav's eyes photographed a man scrambling backward over the sill, dropping from a window. He saw another backing out of a window, and then suddenly twisting in a contorted agony and bowing forward into the room, his open mouth emitting a heavy gush of blood as he slumped forward and hung across the window sill, feet out, head in. He remembered seeing a one-armed white man in the doorway taking careful aim, firing six slow shots before a Negro's club struck him down.

Time was eternity, but when Trav looked at his watch it was not quite two o'clock. Only a few white men were still in the room, and perhaps a dozen Negroes. They made a rush, all together, into the hall, and Trav followed them. The lobby and the stairs were filled with grappling men, but Trav forced a way down the wide stairs and burst into the street. A pistol exploded in his face, the burnt powder stinging his cheek, and someone shouted: "No, no, he's all right!" He felt a small stab of pain in his leg, and knew he was hit, and crossed the street to the banquette. When he turned, John Henderson had just come out of the door of the Institute. Clubs in the hands of half a dozen men clattered around Henderson's head, against his ineffectually shielding arms, and when he fell, a man with a bowie knife jerked his head up and back and dragged the blade hard across his throat. Then Mr. Adams, the Chief of Police, clubbed one of his own uniformed men aside and came to Henderson's defense and carried him away. Another white man came out of the Institute, dragged by many hands, and while he was beaten to his knees Trav heard approving shouts here beside him, and saw three familiar faces, members of the City Council, applauding the clubbing.

The doorway across the street appeared to be the exit from a sort of gantlet; an eager pack with knives and clubs and guns waited there, and at intervals a victim, usually a Negro but sometimes a white man, was flung out to them. Trav saw a Negro dragged out in the grip of a policeman. Three policemen in uniform gathered around him. One hit him in the face with the revolver barrel and the man fell, and the policeman who had clubbed him down thrust the others aside and fired at the unconscious man's head.

Trav felt a thin twinge where that bullet a while ago had stung his leg, yet his trouser leg was not wet, nor was there blood on his sock or shoe, so he judged it was no more than a scratch. But as he leaned down to make sure of this, a bullet from somewhere struck him in the side. He knew at once that this was more serious, and he walked out to Canal Street and up toward the levee, watching for a doctor's sign, and found Doctor Anfoux at home. The bullet in his leg had passed through the fleshy part, cutting no large vessel; the one in his side had been almost spent, had lodged barely under the skin. While the doctor removed it, they heard a trumpet, and then a drumbeat, and the knowledge that the soldiers had come was like a powerful sedative. Trav's senses blurred, and Doctor Anfoux gave him brandy and made him lie down, and he slept, drugged as much with emotion as with loss of blood.

Mr. Fiddler went from the mill directly to the fire station to join his company. The men were all armed, and a wagon unloaded four wooden boxes filled with packets of revolver ammunition. Someone advised Fiddler to tie a white handerchief around his arm. "If shooting starts, you don't want any of us shooting at you." One of his friends, a policeman, Joe Dorset—he and Fiddler lodged under the same roof— came in to talk a while. He asked curiously: "You boys all got guns?"

"I mostly carry mine," Mr. Fiddler admitted. " 'Specially if I'm going to Algiers. And there's plenty of ca'tridges, if you're short."

Dorset shook his head. "Don't reck'n I'll use what I've got. I'm too old to go shooting niggers for fun."

The waiting dragged, and it was a relief when at last the alarm bell loosed them. They leaped into action, tailing onto the traces for their headlong run toward the Institute, and a train of excited boys and men ran after them. They put the ladder wagon on Common Street, opposite the Medical College, and their captain repeated his orders.

"Take clubs, and if you see a nigger starting trouble, stop him. If the police or Sheriff Hay's deputies need help, help 'em. Anyone that's out of ca'tridges, tell 'em there's plenty here in the wagon, and clubs too. Now scatter 'round."

Fiddler joined the crowd of civilians and police at the end of Dryades Street. From the crowd many voices rose and blended in the toneless roar, like the moan of an insane man, which is the voice of the mob. Fiddler began to tremble with an infection almost irresistible. Men near him were shouting. "Kill the lot!" "Come on, come on!" "Burn it down!" "Hang 'em!" Their cries rose close around him, their voices at once hoarse and shrill. He saw that their eyes were glazed and with the whites showing, as though they had been suddenly startled by a flash of blinding light. They stared up at the second floor windows of the Institute, their mouths open, and each mouth emitted a low, moaning sound.

The mob churned and threatened. Three policemen ran toward the doorway of the Institute and seized a white man there and hustled him toward the corner, leading him through the crowd. Men pressed about them, striking at the prisoner, shouting profane abuse and deadly threats, and Fiddler made his way to their side and went with them, helping them fight off the mob. When one man aimed a revolver, Fiddler's club cracked his wrist and the weapon fell. The man, cursing furiously, stooped to pick it up, but the moving throng hustled him along.

Fiddler stayed with the police. They brought their captive to St. Charles Street and turned toward City Hall. At the corner, one of the policemen, harried and breathless from their long struggle, bumped into someone, and turned with a cry of exasperation. The man with whom he had collided was an old Negro with a palsy that made his head shake monotonously from side to side; the collision knocked his hat off, and he clutched it and said meekly: "Whut I done, Massa?" The policeman shot him in the face, and the top of his head seemed to explode.

Fiddler cried out: "For God's sake!" No one paid any attention to him. The police with their captive sidled around the dead Negro and went on. Fiddler backed clear and let them go, stricken not so much with anger or with horror as with shame. They went on to the City Hall and across to the police station, but he stopped at Union Street. A shot somewhere near—it seemed to come from the corner of Gravier Street—made him look that way. At first he saw nothing except the swirling crowd, but presently from the direction of the shot, two policemen came toward him, one gripping the other's arm. They were arguing, and the man under restraint protested:

"I'll kill any God-damned check-suited nigger I see. Anything I hate, it's a stuck-up nigger!"

"All right, all right, but don't go killing—"

Then the speaker's voice was drowned by a sudden shout, as policemen appeared with another prisoner, a threatening crowd harrying the officers.

Fiddler turned down Union Street and made his way back toward the Institute. The ladder wagon was where he had left it, a dozen firemen, two or three policemen and a score or so of men and boys clustered around it. Between the Medical College and the Institute ran a high board fence, and Fiddler saw men, a dozen or so, standing along the fence, waiting. From inside the Institute came occasional spatters of shots, and clamorous cries, and shouts like screams. He stopped on the banquette so that he could see over the heads of men in the street. For a minute or two there was nothing to see, but then a pair of black hands suddenly appeared, clutching the top of the fence. The waiting men moved quietly that way, and when the Negro on the other side of the fence pulled himself up till he could see over it, he looked into the muzzles of half a dozen revolvers. A policeman called a sharp order: "Come on, boy. Climb over!" The Negro, gibbering with terror, scrambled up to perch on top of the fence, and a revolver cracked. He hurled himself off the fence toward them, and two men fired at him in the air. He struck the ground and tried to stand up, and Fiddler saw the rise and fall of clubs.

When another Negro came over the fence and died in the air, Fiddler had ceased to feel anything except a gasping emptiness; there was no emotion in him at all. A wagon came up Common Street, and a fireman shouted to the driver: "Hold on a minute and we'll have a load for you!" He found recruits, and they dragged limp bodies out into the street and threw them into the wagon. Not all the Negroes were dead; they submitted passively, yet stirred and groaned. Half a dozen of the hurt men were loaded into the wagon, and the driver cried: "I can take one more!"

"Wait a minute," someone shouted. "There he comes!" A Negro was hanging by his hands from a window of the Institute, ready to drop; bullets flicked dust from his clothes, and he fell, to an exultant shout from his slayers. A moment later, his blood pouring out in many small streams, he had been loaded into the wagon.

The driver cracked his whip and turned into Baronne Street and Mr. Fiddler followed, stumbling like a blind man. The wagon had stopped on Baronne, just around the corner, the driver abandoning it to seek refreshment. Drops of blood spattered in the dust under it. Fiddler found the Negro from whom most of the blood came; it poured from a hole in his leg, near the crotch, but as Fiddler located the source of the hemorrhage it dwindled and ceased. He helped the living men to more comfortable positions, and he gave them some reassurance. "Driver'll be right back," he promised. "Get you to the doctor." When the driver did return, Fiddler asked: "Where do you take them?"

"Marine Hospital. That's the order now." The man looked at his human freight with a sympathetic eye. "I see you've tried to help 'em some. Don't it beat hell, the way a crowd will act when it gets started!" He climbed to his seat and drove away.

Fiddler stood to watch the wagon depart, and a man spoke at his side. "Out of ca'tridges, mister?" Fiddler stared at him. "Got no gun? I can get you one!" The man had half a dozen packets of cartridges in his hand, and his eyes were blurred and his lips wet and glistening.

Fiddler shook his head and went through Baronne Street to Canal. He reached the corner in time to see a policeman in uniform empty his revolver into a passing horsecar, a Star car full of Negroes.

Then Joe Dorset came up beside Fiddler, a revolver in his hand. "I'm about ready to start killing me a few policemen," he said in a voice thick with sick anger. "I've stood about my limit!"

Fiddler said: "I don't know but what I've seen more men killed today than I did in the whole War."

"You don't notice it, in a war," Dorset suggested. "They ain't men, so much."

Fiddler pounded his fist into his palm. "Where in God's name are the soldiers?"

"Coming, they say. I hear General Baird claims he thought the meeting was at six o'clock, instead of noon. The lying son-of-a-bitch! It's been printed in every paper in town, forty times. Every white man and nigger in town except Baird knew it was at noon."

Fiddler nodded. "Yes, and Sheridan, little Gor-a-mighty himself, he went off to Texas so he wouldn't get mixed up in it!"

"No one can find Governor Wells! His son's in the Convention, too."

Fiddler said gloomily: "I don't know. I don't blame any man for hiding, running away." He repeated: "We can't just stand here." They moved into Baronne Street. The firing had stopped, and Fiddler said in grim tones: "Sounds as if they'd killed 'em all."

A cry called their attention to a man crouching on the roof of the Institute, silhouetted against the sky. Shots began to peck at him, and Fiddler saw men taking careful aim, and a fireman rested his revolver on the fence and shot slowly and deliberately. Fiddler shouted: "Get back! Get out of sight!" He groaned. "The damned fool!"

The Negro on the roof ran to and fro, witless with terror, and some-one called: "One of you squirrel hunters! Bark the bastard!" The Negro knelt to peer over the edge of the roof, and Fiddler heard his thin wailing cries and thought of a cat in a tree, afraid to come down. A man on the roof of the Medical College fired at the Negro at short range, and he slumped on hands and knees, head hanging over the edge. Then somehow he stood erect upon the roof, and staggered, and with a sudden movement like a bound, he fell, turning over in the air, arms outstretched above his head, legs straight. He fell as a board falls, turning slowly end over end; he fell face upward across the brick fence beside the Institute, and he broke as a log breaks, his legs on one side of the wall, his head on the other, his stomach toward the sky.

Fiddler's teeth set hard. He wrenched his eyes away. Dorset was bent over, gagging, and Fiddler put an arm across his shoulders, helped him stand erect. Dorset, as he moved, stepped in a thread of dust-darkened blood and slipped a little and Fiddler steadied him. Blood was everywhere; it lay in a thick red film across the banquette; it had dripped through the planks, and in one place in the gutter it had formed an inch-deep pool.

After the man was shot off the roof, a long silence fell, and from the rear entrance of the Institute a police lieutenant came toward them. "You men, all of you, every one in and bring out the bodies," he directed. "Dead or alive."

The order was for the police, but Fiddler wished to help. He and Dorset went through the alley and in by the rear door, then through the corridor toward the front of the building, and directly upstairs. The stairs were slippery with blood which as it trickled down the steps had coagulated, thickening like melted candle wax when it cools. Under the passage of many feet this blood had become a grisly pudding, an inch and sometimes two inches deep. The Hall of the House of Representatives was a chamber of horrors; shattered chairs and desks and benches, bullet-scarred walls, blood in wide dulled pools turning brown on the floor. Some wounded Negroes sat braced against the walls; some lay helpless on the floor. They were at first glance indistinguishable from the bodies of the dead, but Fiddler counted nine surely dead.

One of the policemen, seeing him thus engaged, said: "There was one dead white man here. They say he was Doctor Cenas's son. They already took him."

Fiddler nodded absently, moving without purpose across the room, and someone called: "Let's have a look upstairs. Some of the bastards that started this are still hiding around here somewhere."

Fiddler went with that group, half a dozen of the uniformed police and three other civilians. In the attic, they found four white men and several Negroes. One of the Negroes had climbed upon the cross timbers in the rear end of the garret, high above the floor, crouching in the darkness there. He might have gone undiscovered, but when the other Negroes were marched toward the stairs, one of them looked that way, so a policeman went to scan those upper timbers.

"Well, hello, up there," he called cheerfully. "Join us, won't you? Come on down!" Revolver in hand, he waited, but the Negro did not move. "Oh, come along," the policeman urged. "You can't stay there forever!" Mr. Fiddler peered up into the darkness, thinking there was something familiar about the shape of the man perched on the heavy timbers. Then the policeman fired, and one of the man's legs dropped into view; the policeman fired again, and the man fell, hitting hard, seeming almost to bounce when he struck the floor. He lay on his side, and light struck his face. Mr. Fiddler recognized Bob.

The policeman who had shot him caught Bob by one foot to drag him toward the stairs, but then he stopped, his attention caught by a challenge from one of the other policemen to a white prisoner. "Say, you're King Cutler!"

"Of course!" the prisoner replied.

"How long you been hiding up here?"

"Two hours or so."

Fiddler, for the moment forgetting Bob, watched this man, hating him, yet giving him an unwilling respect; Cutler faced these his enemies in a fashion completely composed; they pressed around him, death in their hearts.

"Two hours? What for?"

"To avoid being killed by you and your fellow murderers."

The policeman hesitantly raised a revolver, but the others checked him. "No, no, not now! Take him down to the station."

Fiddler thought the man would be lucky to reach a cell alive, but Cutler started down the stairs as calmly as though he had nothing at all to fear. Fiddler knelt by Bob, and the policeman who had shot the boy asked curiously: "Know him, do you?"

"He used to be one of our people, up in North Carolina."

"Well now, that's too bad. Why didn't he come down?"

"Scared, I suppose." Fiddler turned Bob gently, opened his shirt. "Right under the heart," he said sadly. "And there's blood in his mouth."

"I tried to just scorch his backside."

Fiddler looked up at the policeman without comment, then at Bob again. Blood had streamed over the boy's face from a scalp wound above the ear. "And a bullet in his head," he said. "And he fell all of thirty feet." He stood up. "But I think he's still alive. Mind if I take care of him?"

"Go ahead. Need any help?"

"I can handle him." Fiddler lifted Bob in his arms and crossed to the stairs. The others were already gone.

"I'll take a look out that skylight," the policeman decided. "There may be some of them on the roof."

So Mr. Fiddler went alone down to the second floor. There he had to pause, to rest, and he laid Bob down. The Hall of Representatives was full of people; the doors were open, and in the crowd Mr. Fiddler saw Peter, and called his name. The boy came out and peered at Bob's body on the floor and cried: "Who's that?" Then as he leaned nearer: "It's Bob!"

"Yes, it's Bob. Peter, you ought to be home."

"Is he dead?"

"I don't think so. I'm sending him to the hospital. Your folks are bound to be worried about you."

"Gosh, it's been exciting, hasn't it! Bob acts dead."

"He'll probably die. Bullet through his body, and one in his head."

Peter leaned down and thrust an exploratory finger into the gash in Bob's scalp. "The bullet didn't go into his head," he said, in a curious tone. Fiddler wondered at the boy's extraordinary calm; he could not have brought himself to probe that bloody laceration.

"I'll take care of him. Promise to go home, will you?"

Peter withdrew a cautious three or four paces. "I will pretty soon."

Fiddler hesitated. He was bound to see Peter safely home, even if he had to lead the boy by the ear; but Peter would surely stay here till he had his fill of horrors, so there was time enough to carry Bob down to one of the wagons, send him off to the hospital. "They'll be glad to see you when you do," he said casually, to make Peter feel secure, and picked Bob up in his arms and bore him down the stairs. A policeman stood in the front door, and Fiddler called: "Any wagons out there?"

"Not right now. Might be one out back."

Fiddler, his burden heavier with every step he took, went out through the back door and the alley to Baronne Street. A wagon, already well filled with dead and wounded Negroes, stood just across Common Street, but the driver was not in sight, so probably he too had gone for a drink, like that other driver an hour ago. Fiddler eased his burden gently into the wagon beside a Negro whose face was a battered mask, and whose ears had been sliced away. One of the Negro's eyes opened— the other was a bloody pulp—and Fiddler said in a friendly tone: "Look out for this fellow. He's hurt bad."

The man's blank eyes closed again. Fiddler hesitated, tempted to hunt the driver of the wagon and hurry it to the hospital; but his first duty was to take care of Peter, so he returned to the Institute. The boy was not in the Hall of Representatives, but he might have gone up to the attic, and Fiddler went to see. He even climbed the ladder to look out of the skylight, but Peter was not there.

With his head out of the skylight, Fiddler heard the blast of a bugle on Canal Street, so he knew the soldiers had come. He descended, and from the corner of Dryades and Canal he saw the artillery unlimber at the Clay statue, up where St. Charles Street met Canal. Then the infantry extended its ranks across the wide street and with fixed bayonets began to move toward him; the only sounds were the stir of shuffling feet, and an occasional resonant command.

With sentries posted, there would be peace here, so Peter was no longer in any danger. Mr. Fiddler decided to seek the hospital and see what the doctors thought of Bob's chances. He turned away, glad to leave this dreadful scene behind.

For the hours since the policeman fired at Bob over his shoulder, Peter had been in the grip of an increasing intoxication. The shot so close to his ear not only deafened him; it hurt and surprised and frightened him, and when Bob ran and everyone bolted, Peter ran with them. He hoped they would catch Bob and shoot him, but somehow Bob escaped, and when they all turned back toward Burgundy Street, Peter caught a glimpse of Lieutenant Page and judged it best to keep out of sight.

So he chose circuitous ways. Beside the Institute, between the building and Canal Street, an alley ran, and the stores that fronted on Canal Street had storage yards opening on this alley. Peter found a fine vantage on the second-floor gallery behind one of these stores. From there he saw the first stages of the riot, till the police cleared the street and three dead Negroes lying in the gutter were the only ones left. After an interval, a new tumult arose, and he saw two Negroes dragged out of the Institute and shot. Across from where he hid, in the hall of the House of Representatives, there came a volley of pistol shots, and smoke drifted lazily out of the windows. Down on Dryades Street, a white man came out of the Institute and turned toward Common Street, and a man ran after him and plunged a bowie knife into his back. Someone shouted a question and the slayer yelled an answer. "That damned Loup son of a bitch!"

A Negro came out of the Institute in the grasp of many men, and the man with the bowie knife swung it hard into his side. The Negro slumped to the ground but the knife stuck and its owner braced his foot against the dead man's chest and with both hands wrenched his knife free. A bloodstream ran with surprising rapidity from the body toward the edge of the banquette, and Peter watched, panting and trembling, his mouth open.

There was more shooting in the Institute, and a Negro jumped from one of the windows opposite where Peter crouched. He began to crawl through the weeds toward Baronne Street, and a group of boys no older than Peter himself poured into the vacant lot to club the Negro senseless. Peter licked his lips, watching, hearing their excited cries. Here was a sport in which he might take a hand. Fear for a while held him where he was, but when the boys were gone he swung down into the alley and climbed the fence into the vacant lot. He crept into the weeds and crawled past a dead Negro without seeing him till he came to the man's feet; he passed another whom he thought was dead till he saw that the Negro, though half his face was a spongy, bloody, swollen mass, was watching him with rolling eyes.

Peter, with a muffled cry, sprang up and ran and came into the passage that led from Baronne Street to the back door of the Institute. A man dodged out of the building, and a policeman caught his arm. The man said: "I'm your prisoner, officer!" For only answer, the policeman lifted his revolver and knocked the man down.

A woman with a knife in her hand came running, a troop of laughing men and boys behind her. "Let me put my mark on him!" she cried, and caught the man's hair and pulled his face toward her and cut gashes at either corner of his mouth.

The policeman guffawed. "Where'll you have him delivered?"

"Nell's the name, and everybody on Gallatin Street knows me."

She flounced away, and laughter followed her, and the policeman dragged the half-conscious victim to his feet and led him toward the street. One of the men who had come with the woman saw Peter watching them, and clapped him on the shoulder. "Son, you killed any niggers yet today?" Peter, his throat suddenly too dry to speak, shook his head, and the man said: "Well here, you take this, and kill yourself a mess. Time you learned how. Anyway, I've got all I need. It's loaded, but here's some more loads if you run out."

He pressed into Peter's hand a revolver which the boy thought was the most beautiful thing he had ever seen, slender and graceful, with a curve where the barrel melted into the frame, and sweetly rounded grooves in the cylinder. Peter clutched it greedily, and as the man departed, Peter sat down to admire his treasure. He heard, beyond the fence, the sound of running feet, and a shot. "Missed him, by the Almighty," said a voice, and another answered: "No fun if we killed them all."

A third voice said: "All right, fun's over. Time to clean up inside. Go carry out the bodies. I'll send some men to help you."

Peter paid no attention. He heard other men pass on the other side of the fence and go into the building. He aimed his revolver at a chimney of the Medical College and pulled the trigger, but he had forgotten to cock the weapon. He drew back the hammer and again pulled the trigger, and the sharp jolt against his hand gave him a delicious pleasure. He fired again, and a policeman's head came over the fence behind him.

"What you shooting at, Sonny?"

"The chimney up there."

"That's wasting good bullets. Guess the fun's over, anyway. They're carrying out the dead ones."

The policeman's head disappeared, and Peter decided he wanted to see the bodies. He thrust the revolver inside his pants and buttoned his coat, pressing his hand against the pleasant weight of the weapon. He entered the Institute through the rear door and followed the long corridor toward the stairs. At the top of the stairs he turned into the Hall of Representatives, and just within the door he stopped, staring at the shambles there; dead men and wounded men and shattered furniture and bullet-pocked walls and bloodstains everywhere.

Then he heard his name, and saw Mr. Fiddler in the hallway outside. He went uncertainly toward the overseer, and recognized Bob on the floor at Mr. Fiddler's feet. Mr. Fiddler said Peter must go home, but Peter asked whether Bob was alive. Mr. Fiddler said he would probably die, with a bullet in his head and another near his heart. Peter stuck a finger into that head wound, but the bullet had not pierced the skull, and he frowned in resentful disappointment. Surely one more nigger could as well as not have died today. Why not Bob? Bob had bullied him enough; he had even tried to boss him around today! Peter wished Bob were dead.

Mr. Fiddler again urged him to go home, and Peter answered sullenly. Fiddler picked Bob up and went across to the stairs and down, and Peter watched him from the head of the stairs. When Mr. Fiddler turned toward the rear of the building, Peter slipped down the stairs and followed along the corridor and out to Baronne Street. He saw Mr. Fiddler lift Bob into a wagon already well filled with dead and wounded, and he dodged across into the waiting room of the street railroad, and from that hiding place watched Mr. Fiddler return and go in through the rear door of the Institute.

When Mr. Fiddler was surely gone, Peter stepped out into the street, his hand gripping that beautiful revolver tucked inside his trousers. He cocked it, moving cautiously toward the wagon yonder. At any moment, the driver might return; but he did not. The other Negroes in the wagon either were dead or they played 'possum, for when Peter approached and paused beside them, not an eye opened. Bob lay on the side nearest the banquette, within arm's reach; Peter thrust the revolver against his ear.

Back toward the Institute, a Negro raced out of the alley, bullets spurring him on, and for a moment the air was full of the sound of shots. That Negro fell, drawing every eye, and Peter tucked his revolver back into his belt and waved his hand to fan the smoke away.

Then, somewhere, a bugle sounded. A bugle meant soldiers! Peter instinctively began to run, but at once he slowed to a walk again, pretending he was not afraid. He was suddenly in a hurry to come home.

Home was a long way, and he was tired. He approached the house through the drive and the stable, finding the stable deserted. He wrapped his revolver and the packet of cartridges in one of Pike's wiping rags, and stuck it deep down under the oats in the corner of the bin. Later, he would buy a box of caps, and take the revolver to the house and up to his room, and reload it and hide it there.

He was curiously reluctant to see anyone, so he climbed into the haymow and lay down and drowned in bottomless sleep.

To Lucy's ears, the shot which the policeman fired at Bob was a small sound far away. She asked: "Mama, did you hear anything?"

"Hear anything? Hear what? No, of course not!"

"It sounded like a shot. And I've been hearing a band, too. Or at least it sounds like a band, except that I can only hear the drums. You know the way you feel drums before you really hear them, when you're waiting for a parade or something, and the band's a long way off."

"For goodness sake, child, it's too hot to talk folderol!"

Isaiah said dinner was ready, and they went indoors, but it was almost too hot to eat. Afterward Enid went upstairs. "I'm going to take my clothes off, try to get cool." But Lucy went into the garden. Almost at once she heard another shot, and then many more.

She walked toward the gate, thinking she might hear more clearly there, and two men, half running, passed. She called to them. "Please, gentlemen." And, when they paused: "What's happening, please?"

They lifted their hats in polite salute. "They're smashing those Conventioners, ma'am." Then hurried on. The fire bell began to ring, but instead of the usual few strokes it rang on and on; a clamorous, frightening alarm.

Then it was true! That incredible horror which her father and Don had feared was come upon them? Yet surely not in the dread proportions they foresaw; surely this was no more than a petty altercation, a few shots fired harmless in the air. The wall around the garden, shutting out the world, made Lucy feel smothered and cut off. She went indoors and up to the second floor. From the gallery she could overlook the wall, could look for several blocks along Prytania Street. She stayed there, and the hot afternoon was timeless. At intervals she could hear the steady crackle of distant shots, but then either because the shots ceased or because of some change in the slow drift of the light airs she heard nothing at all. There were no more passersby; the street was a frightening solitude.

She was conscious after a while of some presence near her, and discovered Quinny in a heap on the floor just inside the door, dissolved there in silent tears. Lucy's own anxiety put a sharp impatience in her tone. "Quinny! What's the matter with you?" Quinny burst into wailing sobs, through which Lucy was finally able to get an answer. Old Maria had said Bob would not live out the day.

"Oh, Maria and her foolishness!" Lucy was furious. "She doesn't know any more about it than you do, Quinny. Stop your crying! Bob's all right!"

"No'm, he daid! Ef'n he ain't, he gwine tuh be." She bowed her head in her hands, sobbing. "Mah poah baby!"

"Fiddlesticks! You haven't got a baby!"

"Ah'm gwine have one, ma'am. Poah baby, wid his Uncle Bob, he a'ready daid!"

Lucy stared at her, at once startled by this information and amused by the absurdity of Quinny's weeping because the baby would have no uncle. She said crisply: "All right, that's enough crying! Go wash your face and behave." And when Quinny wailed again, Lucy stamped her foot. "Quinny, you hear me?" Quinny hushed her sobs, and started along the hall, and Lucy said, relenting: "After you've washed your face, you can use some of my cologne, and smell real good."

Quinny squealed with delight. "Oh, Missy, thank'e! Thank'e, ma'am!" She skipped away.

Lucy resumed her steady watching. It was terribly hot. Another year, they must surely seek some cooler spot. She stood peering through the jalousies, looking off along Prytania. The shooting had dwindled to almost nothing. It must be past two o'clock.

Two or three blocks away, a man appeared, coming this way. At first she could only see his feet, under the overhanging branches, but he walked with a cane, and he limped in such a way that she knew this was Pike, returning from his errand. In her anxiety for her father and for Peter, she had forgotten all about the old Negro; it was reassuring to see him coming, safe and sound. If he was all right, so, surely, were they.

Pike, in spite of his limp, came swiftly nearer, and through a rift in the branches Lucy had a clearer view. He had somehow lost his hat, for he was bareheaded, a fringe of white hair circling his dark poll. He was on the other side of the street, hardly a block away. A man came up Hestia Street from the direction of the river and turned down Prytania, so that he would meet old Pike about halfway of the block. Lucy was watching Pike so happily that she did not notice this man till he was near Pike. He carried a hatchet in his hand, as though he were a workman; yet his clothes were not those of a man on his way to work. She wondered idly why a white man would carry a hatchet through the streets, but she paid him little attention, watching Pike, gladness in her eyes.

But as the white man met Pike, without a word or a sign, he took a quick step forward and struck the hatchet into Pike's skull.

The blow was sudden, yet for Lucy, time through an instant stopped. Then Pike began to fall, in a slow, deliberate fashion, as slowly as objects fall in dreams. She saw that the hatchet was stuck in his skull, saw the white man wrench at it, striving to twist it free. Pike for an instant dangled, suspended and jerked to and fro by that blade stuck into his skull as the man wrestled to break it loose. Then the hatchet came away, and Pike fell heavily, and the man struck the hatchet into the ground two or three times as though to clean it, then walked on; but after a few steps, as though on an afterthought, he turned and drew his gun and fired twice at Pike where he lay.

Lucy roused from her stupor of amazement and horror and rage and ran into the house, calling Quinny, racing downstairs and through the kitchen, crying out: "Isaiah! Maria, Daisy! Come on!" But she did not wait to make sure they followed her. She ran through the stable and down the drive, but the tall iron gate was locked. She wrestled with it, calling Abram, calling for someone to bring the keys, reaching through the gate to tug at the bell. As though yielding to her passionate haste, the gate suddenly opened and Lucy ran across the street at a long diagonal to where old Pike lay, and dropped on her knees beside him. The wound in his scalp was bleeding badly, and there was blood on his shoulder and along the side of his leg. Instinctively, she tried to lift him, and could not, and looked helplessly back toward the house, and saw Abram coming, and Maria. Isaiah and Daisy were hesitating in the driveway. She called to them:

"Bring bandages, Isaiah! And we'll have to carry him!"

Abram and Maria reached her, and Maria at once took charge. "Lemme at him, Missy. Don' git you'self in dis mess."

"Oh, Maria, he's bleeding so!"

"Hush, Honey! I be'n tendin' men's cuts an' gashes 'fo you was bawn." She pushed Lucy gently aside and went down on her knees, a wire-thin little old woman. She unbuttoned Pike's shirt and eyed a shoulder wound. "Nothin' but a fleabite!" She pulled up his trousers and moved his leg and looked at the blood which had flowed there and said in a calm appraisal. "He kin git along widout dat little bit of blood. Now le's see dis heah!" She unwound her bandanna and began to clean the cut in his scalp, leaning close, peering, moving his head so that the sun shone into the wound.

Lucy whispered: "Is he alive?"

"He ain' daid," Maria assured her. "I wouldn't go tuh say he uz rightly alive, but I will say dis much; he ain' daid. We git him tuh baid an' tek good keer o' him, an' he'll git well or he won't. Da's all." She sat back on her heels. "Hyah dey come."

Isaiah had brought a blanket. They lifted Pike upon it, and with Isaiah and Abram on either side, Daisy and Maria at the feet and Lucy at the head, they carried him home. Quinny trailed them, weeping aloud, and when at last old Pike was in his own bed in his neat room in the carriage house, Maria without a word turned to Quinny and vehemently boxed her ears. Quinny fled with screams, and Maria said contentedly:

"Dat done me a heap o' good! Any one thing I hates moah'n de nex', hit's a squallin' young un." She swung toward the others, storming at them in sudden rage. "You Isaiah, Abram, git out o' heah! Daisy, fetch me plenty hot water, and some clean beddin'. Time we git him clean an' stop dat bleedin'—" No one had moved to obey her commands and she leaped at them. "Go on, you heah me!"

They scattered and Lucy said: "I don't blame Quinny for crying." There was a sob in her throat. "I feel like it myself." She touched Pike's shoulder in a helpless grief.

"Weep ef it eases you, Missy." Maria's tone was infinitely tender. "Weep and pray."

There was finality in her words, and Lucy looked at her in half-panic. "I'll get a doctor." She turned toward the door, but Maria shook her head.

"Ain' de time yit, Missy. I'se gwine bathe him an' git him clean, and git his bed clean, an' ef he daid befo' I get th'ough, I'll lay him out. Ef he ain't, we'll wait till mawnin', see how he does. Mos' he needs now is a heap o' lettin' alone."

"I'll help," Lucy urged, her heart full of tender pity.

"Go on, git out o' heah 'fo' I lose my patience wid yuh. Go on! Git!" Maria flapped her apron as a woman shoos chickens, and Lucy retreated. Probably Maria was as good as many doctors; yes and better than most. The old woman came through the carriage house after her, grumbling because Daisy was so slow, and she called a final word. "Go on and change, Missy. Yuh all bloodied up. Don' let yuh pa see yuh so!"

Lucy looked down and saw that her gown was stained along the hem and at the knees. She found Quinny, still hiccoughing with sobs, already in her room, and was glad to have her help. Quinny, subdued by Maria's sudden violence, offered no word, and Lucy did not invite conversation. She fell to thinking of that man who, without provocation and for no reason she could guess, had struck Pike down. It was as though he were a wild animal. She tried to guess what had been in his mind. Pike had done nothing to provoke the attack; if he had, she would have seen. Was there some deadly madness in the very air today?

And where was her father, and where was Peter; yes, and where was Don? Her anxiety returned, and the minutes were like hours. When she was dressed, she went out on the upper gallery. She wished to do something, to go search for them, to find them, to bring them safe home; but she could only wait.

It was just past four o'clock when a hackney carriage came along Prytania Street. She saw Trav in the carriage, and she raced downstairs to open the door for him, and threw herself into his arms, and felt him wince, and cried out: "Papa? Are you hurt? Are you all right?"

"Yes, Honey; all right, yes. Couple of scratches, nothing." And, his hand heavy on her arm, he asked: "Is Peter home?"

She shook her head, leading him into the parlor, making him sit down. "Who scratched you? What happened?"

He smiled faintly. "Not that kind of scratches, Honey. Bullets. But they weren't meant for me."

"They might have killed you!" She knelt beside him, tears in her eyes. "Oh, Papa!" And she asked: "Did it hurt when I hugged you?"

He laughed. "If I were hurt, a hug from you'd cure me."

She leaned forward, her hands holding his arms, pressing her head against his breast, and she felt his weary sigh and cried: "You're tired! You ought to go to bed."

"I am pretty tired," he admitted. "Or maybe—just sick."

"Sick?" In quick alarm. "Shall I get a doctor?"

He shook his head. "Sick from the things I've seen." And he said in a low, dull fashion, not looking at her. "They killed a lot of nigras. I don't know how many, fifty, a hundred. And some white men, too."

"Who did?"

"The police, and the deputies, and—well, everyone who felt like it. Where's Mama?"

"Asleep, I think. Papa, don't you want a doctor?"

"I went to a doctor's office," he explained. "Had my wounds bandaged. I had a little rest there. By that time the soldiers had come, so I got a cab and drove up to the Institute to have one more look for Peter." His eyes shadowed. "I saw them arrest Judge Howell. He's the man really responsible for all this, but as soon as the shooting started, he hid in the Governor's office and stayed there, safe and sound." She listened with parted lips and angry eyes. "Mr. Fiddler was there. He says Bob is dead."

"Oh, Bob?" she cried, and remembered Quinny. "Papa, Maria told Quinny that Bob would be killed today, and you know . . ."

He went on as though she had not spoken, and she realized he was intent on his own words. ". . . shot by a policeman," he said. "Mr. Fiddler carried him out of the Institute and put him in a wagon with other wounded. He'd been shot through the body and through the head, but Mr. Fiddler thought he might live, but he was dead before he got to the hospital."

"Why did the policeman shoot him?"

"They were killing every nigra they saw. Mr. Fiddler saw Peter at the Institute and told him to come home. You say he hasn't come?"

"No. Poor Bob!" She cried in sudden memory: "Oh, Papa, a white man killed old Pike with a hatchet! I saw him! Right across the street." She added: "Only he's not dead yet. Maria's taking care of him."

"Edgar Cenas was killed," Trav told her, and she saw he was still half stupefied by his experience, his mind not ready to receive new blows.

"Edgar? Who did it?"

"I was right beside him. We were going upstairs to the Hall of Representatives. The hall was full of nigras, and a few white men. The police would jerk the doors open and empty their revolvers into the crowd and then go back out into the street to reload, and then do it again. I went up with young Cenas to see if Peter was there. Someone shot him, shot Cenas, there on the stairs." He added: "He was studying at the Medical College, you know. It's right next door."

"Papa, Maria knew Bob was going to be killed. How do the nigras know?"

He shook his head, muttered, like a prayer: "I wish to God I knew where Peter is. Mr. Fiddler and Lieutenant Page both said he wasn't at the Hospital."

"Oh, did you see Don? Was he all right?"

"Looked all right. Tired, of course."

"Papa, why were they killing nigras? I thought it was the Convention people that every one hated so."

"Oh, they killed some of the Convention men. I saw them kill Doctor Dostie."

"Couldn't you do anything?"

He chuckled grimly. "It's a little vague, Honey, but I seem to remember that I was once about to kill a policeman, because he'd killed a nigra. But someone persuaded me to let him off."

"Were many killed?" she asked, wondering, trying to comprehend.

"A lot of them, scores, maybe fifty."

"I mean policemen. Did any of them get killed?"

He said in weary amusement. "I heard that one died of a sunstroke."

Lucy had never seen her father so tired. "Papa, come upstairs. I'm going to put you to bed."

He submitted, went with her; his leg had stiffened, and he limped a little, and she bit her lip, close to tears that were half tenderness for him, half anger at those others. She expected to find her mother in their room, but Enid was not there. Lucy offered to bring Isaiah to help him out of his clothes, but Trav said he would rest a while on the couch. Lucy left him already half asleep and found Enid in Peter's room, where on hot days there was a better breeze. Enid woke, and Lucy told her what there was to tell, Enid drowsily protesting that such things were terrible, beyond belief. Lucy watched her with resentful eyes, and as an afterthought she said:

"Oh yes, and Quinny says she's going to have a baby."

Enid turned in swift attention. "Really!" She laughed in amused pride. "Why, that precocious little devil! He's only fourteen!"

Lucy stared at her, at first bewildered, and then, in sudden comprehension, angry. Her mother meant Peter! She felt a surge of harsh contempt for this brother of hers; contempt for Enid, too, because she was obviously almost pleased. "Papa's asleep in your room," she said shortly, and left Enid alone and went down into the garden, aimlessly pacing the paths. After some time she heard newsboys crying extras in the street, and guessed that the papers had rushed into print some account of the bloody business of the day. Probably they would boast of brave deeds done, of helpless Negroes slain!

Her thoughts were bitter company, till from the gate yonder Lieutenant Page called her name, and great gladness filled her. "Oh, Don, Don," she cried, running to him. The gate was locked, but she reached through and caught his hands, clinging to them with both hers. "Oh, I'm so glad to see you! Abram's gone somewhere with the key. I'll let you in the door."

"I can't stay. I have to go and report."

"You can stay a minute!" She saw his weariness. "You must stay a minute!" She ran back through the house, and when she opened the street door he was there. She drew him into the hall and released him only to close the door. "Where have you been? I've hoped you'd come. Papa got hit by two bullets, but not bad ones. And Bob—you remember Bob? Quinny's brother? They killed him! And a man just about killed old Pike with a hatchet, and shot him twice besides, right across the street! I saw him! Where were you?"

"Why—in it!" he said. He was hoarse, and he cleared his throat and tried again. "I saw it start. Since it ended, since the soldiers got there, I've been at the hospital, trying to help." He said, staring at the carpet: "They brought over a hundred men there, some dead, some just wounded. Hauled them like logs, in wagons!" He had sunk into a chair, his hands on his knees, his head bent in that posture of fatigue she had learned to recognize.

"I hate it!" she whispered. "I hate it!"

He looked up at her in surprised concern. "Hate what, Lucy?"

"Hate New Orleans! Hate the South!"

He hesitated, but after a moment he shook his head, said gently: "No, Miss Lucy, it's not just the South! There've been some bad riots in the North too. There was one in Philadelphia, and here in New York a while back they killed hundreds of Negroes."

"They killed hundreds here today! I saw them kill old Pike!"

"There won't be any more of it. General Baird's declared martial law." Don added shortly: "If he'd been a little quicker about it, he'd have saved a lot of lives."

"Did they kill white men too? Papa says they killed Edgar Cenas."

"I didn't know that. Yes, ma'am, they killed some of the Conventioners, or hurt 'em so bad they died, or they will die. The minister,

Mr. Horton, he's got a fractured skull; and Mr. Henderson's throat is cut. He's barely alive. And I hear they killed Doctor Dostie, and some others." He asked: "Is Peter home yet?"

She shook her head. "No, but Mr. Fiddler saw him, after the shooting was all over, so he's probably all right."

"I saw him, the first of it, but he was way off from me, and by the time I got to where he'd been, he'd gone." He rose. "Well, ma'am. I'll have to go report."

She rose with him, then suddenly caught his arms, shaking him, crying out in resentful protest: "Oh, stop calling me 'ma'am'! Yes, and stop calling me 'Miss Lucy,' too!"

He was bewildered. "Why, what do you want me to call you?"

"Oh—" She looked up at him, and hesitated, and then she smiled. "Start calling me 'darling'!" she whispered, and pulled his head down and kissed him; then whirled away to the door and opened it wide. "Now I know you really do have to go!"

He strode toward her and put his hand on hers that held the latch, and closed the door, shaking his head. "Miss—darling," he said gently, his weariness forgotten. "Even a State-of-Maine man can only be pushed just about so far!"

But Lucy, now looking past him, pressed him away. "Peter!" she cried, in a great relief, and ran through the hall toward where Peter had appeared. "Papa! Mama! Everybody! Here's Peter, safe and sound!"

PART THREE

The Scalawag

August 1866 — June 1867

★

I

For Lucy, the horror of that day would always be epitomized in the moment when without a word the unknown white man struck Pike down; but also, Bob was dead, poor Bob who with Quinny had been her childhood playmate and protector, and Edgar Cenas was dead, whom she might have counted among her beaus. They were dead, and her father had been wounded, and Don had helped tend the wounded; so her father and her brother and Don whom she loved had all been that day in peril, and it was Southern men who had killed Pike and Bob, and whose bullets had even touched her father.

Trav before he went to bed had decided he would sleep late, and to make sure he slept soundly, Enid gave him one of her pills; so he did not come down to breakfast, nor did Enid. Peter joined Lucy, but her questions brought only grunts and empty words, and when he left her, Lucy turned to the pile of papers which was always laid by her father's place. Prussia's brief war with Austria was over. The Atlantic cable was now complete; eighteen hundred and sixty-four miles of cable spanned the sixteen hundred nautical miles between Newfoundland and Ireland. The events of the day before, said the *Bee*, were of course in many ways "painful and regrettable," but they taught that "those who rise up against the law must expect the officers of the law to do what is requisite to suppress them." The day gave "gratifying evidence of the complete ability of the municipal government to put down political and other riots."

Lucy laid the paper aside, turned to the others. The tone of each was the same; praise for the police, damnation for the Radicals, mock-sympathy for the Negroes. When her mother came downstairs, Lucy was reading the *Times,* and Enid asked: "Anything in the papers?"

"All about yesterday," Lucy told her. "Oh, Mama, how can men do such things?"

"Pooh! What do they expect? We'll never let niggers boss us around!"

"Pike wasn't trying to boss anyone around!"

"He's a nigger, and they're all alike," Enid retorted. "Every so often, they need to be taught a lesson."

Trav when he woke sent for the papers, and Lucy, going later to bid him good morning, found him propped up in bed. He had slept finely, he assured her; said: "I'll get up for dinner."

She sat on the edge of his bed, tumbled the papers about. "Have you read these?"

He nodded. "Yes." He watched her eyes. "They seem to agree that we've taught the Radicals a needed lesson." When she did not speak, he added: "I expect some of those who survived have left town. I would, in their places."

"Papa, I'm ashamed of us!"

"Whoa, Honey; what have I done now?"

"Oh, I don't mean you! But Papa, can't we go live somewhere where people aren't always killing people and being proud of it?"

"Our going away wouldn't improve things here, Honey," he suggested. "Too many Southerners, since the War, have done just that, have gone away. And it's not all Southerners, anyway." He tried to speak lightly. "I know several gentlemen who never killed a nigra in their lives!"

"But why don't the rest of us stop them, put them in jail, make them behave? Instead of saying how brave they were for beating wounded men to death with clubs!"

He nodded in reluctant agreement. "To kill a man, anywhere in the South, isn't very serious; not if you've any excuse at all." He added in an ironic tone: "And of course you don't need an excuse to kill a nigra." He asked: "Have you seen Don today?"

"No." She colored in happy memory. Yesterday evening, when Peter appeared and they all gathered around him, Lieutenant Page had quietly departed. "No, not yet. But I will. He's sure to come."

"You'll find he won't condemn the South," he suggested. "Certainly not as fiercely as you."

She laughed and came to kiss him. "He'd just better not!" she declared.

Lucy was impatient for Don's coming, but he would surely come as quickly as he could. After dinner she went to her room, preparing to endure the smothering heat of the day, and she remembered with a warm happiness his surprise when she kissed him, and her thoughts made her cheeks burn, so that sitting before the mirror she laughed at her image in the glass. What would he do when he came? Would he sweep her into his arms and hold her breathless, his lips on hers? Or would he kiss her politely, on the brow? Or on the cheek? Or perhaps he wouldn't kiss her at all! That, certainly, would be provoking!

Southern men understood these things so much better; they sighed and said sweet things and made up all sorts of pretty speeches.

But then, she reminded herself, they went out and killed some poor old nigra! Her shamed disgust returned. How could she face Don proudly when he came?

She lay down and fell presently asleep and was wakened by her mother's sudden call. "Lucy, Lucy, wake up!" Lucy roused, and Enid cried: "See here!" She thrust into Lucy's hand a letter. "Jenny's getting married to Ronny Hamilton. Remember him? And Cinda wants us all to come on for the wedding. And I was about going crazy with the heat anyway! So we're going! Papa says we can leave Monday!"

Lucy, by this time wide awake, listened to Enid's happy babbling. They must summon the dressmaker, buy this, buy that; this was Tuesday evening, so time was short. Lucy nodded, welcoming the sudden plan. It would release her for a while from New Orleans which now she abhorred, and certainly it would be fine to escape the deadening heat of these last few days!

Yet to leave New Orleans meant leaving Don. How could she leave him now, when their lives had just begun? She had been sure he would call before the supper hour, but he did not. Afterward, when she was in the garden with her father and mother, the bell rang, and she went across the garden toward the gate, thinking this must be Don and that she could admit him there.

But then she decided he should be received with proper formality, so she turned aside toward the rose arbor. Her father and mother were yonder by the fountain, where there was no nearby shrubbery to deflect the occasional light stir of air. Mosquitoes were worse here under the arbor, but she did not notice them, grateful for the concealing shadows. She saw Don come from the house and turn toward where Trav and Enid sat, and she heard him greet them and ask for her, and Trav said: "She was here a moment ago. I heard the bell, thought she'd gone to let you in."

"More likely," Enid suggested, "she's gone to pretty up! It's mighty hard for a girl to keep looking her best, a night as hot as this."

But Lucy, shyly unwilling that she and Don should be at first alone, was already moving forward to join them. Don heard her step and turned and came toward her so purposefully that in half terror she extended her hand, shook hands with him and thus kept him at a distance, then hurriedly seated herself and left him standing. Trav said helpfully: "Take a chair, Lieutenant. Any more disturbances?"

Don sat down, looking toward Lucy. "Nothing new; no, sir. I've been at the hospital, or at the workhouse, or at headquarters—military headquarters—most of the day. Everything's quiet."

"The workhouse?" Trav's tone made the word a question.

"They had twenty-two dead Negroes there, in coffins ready for burial. The deputy coroner went to conduct an inquest and I served on his jury."

Lucy asked in a low tone: "Did the jury vote that the nigras were murdered?"

His eyes swung back to her. "We found they died of pistol or knife wounds received during the riot."

Enid shuddered. "It must have been pretty unpleasant, in this weather, looking at twenty-two niggers who'd been dead since yesterday."

"They had a big fire in the room, to purify the air."

She came to her feet, rubbing her hands together. "Booh! Horrible! Good night, Lieutenant."

Don rose as she moved away, and Lucy hoped Trav too would go, but he did not move. "That experience yesterday left me numb," he remarked. "I suppose such terrible things are their own anodyne; the shock protects you from the full impact."

Don nodded without speaking, and Lucy said: "Don, if I were in your place I'd be proud of having fought the War against such people as we Southerners turn out to be."

He swung toward her in quick surprise. "I know some mighty fine Southerners, ma'am!"

Ma'am? He had called her "ma'am" again. So he did not even remember that moment in the hall yesterday! For an instant she hated him. Trav said: "Lucy feels pretty strongly about it, Lieutenant." She wished her father would go off to bed or somewhere.

"It was an ugly thing," Don agreed. "I expect everybody feels a little ashamed about it today, specially the men who did it." He spoke to Lucy. "Men are mostly ashamed afterward. North or south."

"I think most of the men who called the Convention were born in the North," Trav reflected. "But they'd turned Confederate when that was the popular side of the political fence. Judge Howell held office under the Confederate government, took the Confederate oath of allegiance. So did Michael Hahn, and he made speeches presenting flags to Confederate regiments. King Cutler equipped a company for the Confederate army, and others of the leaders were the same."

"I hadn't known that, sir," the Lieutenant admitted. "I'm not in politics, either way. But Negroes are abused in the North too, Major Currain; not only in the South." Trav was about to speak, but Page went on: "The difference is that in the South a lot of fine people have owned Negroes, and know their good points, and respect and admire them for their virtues. There's no such class in the North, no one up there who cares about them."

Lucy thought: How can he go on talking and talking to Papa?

Doesn't he want to be alone with me as much as I want to be alone with him? She interrupted, her voice indignant. "I don't see how in the world you two can be so calm about it! I saw a white man meet Pike on the street and drive a hatchet into Pike's head! I'm not calm!"

Don asked: "How is Pike?"

"Oh, he's still alive! Maria hasn't given him up!"

"I expect there are a lot of wounded like him, who've been taken in and sheltered by their white folks, or by their Negro friends. We'll probably never know how many were killed."

"One was enough for me!" Lucy retorted. "Enough to make me hate the South for the rest of my life!"

Don said quietly: "Hating anyone, anything; that's a kind of poison. Hate killed those men yesterday. That's the—"

But she cried out in a sharp impatience: "Oh, don't be so—so—so doggoned reasonable! Excuse me, Papa, but he makes me so mad! Don, don't you ever just get furious about things, and want to kick, and scream, and slap people's faces, and—well, carry on regardless?" He chuckled, and she came to her feet, stamped her foot at him. "Stop laughing! I'm not trying to be funny!"

"I'm sorry, Miss Lucy. I just—"

"Oh, you—! 'Miss Lucy'?" She mimicked him scornfully. "Good night!"

She darted toward the house, and the Lieutenant took two steps in pursuit. Then he remembered that Trav was here, and stopped uncertainly, and Trav said: "She'll be over it by morning, Lieutenant." Don hesitated, and Trav said insistently: "Sit down, do. Did Lucy tell you we're leaving Monday, going to South Carolina?" Don, with a last glance toward the house, returned reluctant to his chair.

Lucy, once safely indoors, had waited for him, standing in the hall, her back against the wall, her hands outspread and pressed against the paneling, hot with anger that was half hunger for his coming; but he did not come, and when she knew he would not, she ran up to her room and without turning on the gas looked out from her darkened window. There was still light enough so that she could see him sitting calmly with her father, their voices even and low. Did he never get excited? Her father never seemed excited, and she thought this a mark of strength and wisdom; but Don was too young to be so calm!

Her resentment held, so that when he came next day, she sent word that she was indisposed. The day after, old Pike was dying, and she and Maria and Isaiah were there. When the bell rang, she did not hear it; but Isaiah went to answer, and when he returned, Don came with him. Lucy's eyes were on Pike and she did not look up; but a moment after Don appeared in the doorway, old Maria began to cry, in a high, thin wail that had the penetrating, shivering quality of a slate pencil on a windowpane. At the same time, she pulled the sheet up over Pike's face.

So they knew he was dead, and it was then that Lucy lifted her eyes and saw Don yonder in the doorway. Without a sound she darted around the foot of the bed and into his arms, her arms around his waist, her cheek pressed hard against his chest, his arms enfolding her. He murmured some word of comfort, and she whispered through sobs: "Take me away! Oh, Don, take me away!"

He led her out into the garden. He had brought her a box of confections, from Mr. Lopez's shop on Canal Street near Dryades, and somehow now with his arm around her he let it fall, and stooped to pick it up. The fall had broken the box and Lucy helped him repair the damage, her tears drying, touched by his gift, forgetting all his offenses.

"But I do mean it, Don," she insisted, hiccoughing with swallowed sobs.

"Mean what?"

"I want you to take me away! I can't bear to live here any longer!" She looked up at him in sudden question. "You do love me, don't you?" And when he had answered, she laughed happily. "That's the first time you ever kissed me! The other time, I just kissed you. But I kissed you this time, too, so I'll always be one ahead of you, and you can never catch up!" Don was drunk, speechless with happiness. "But I mean it!" She was almost stern. "Papa and Mama and Peter are going off Monday to the Plains, but you resign from the army and we'll be married Sunday—Mama'll fuss, but no matter—and you can take me home to Maine and we'll stay there forever and ever, Amen!" Still he did not speak, and she kissed his cheek and laughed and said: "There, it's all settled."

"Miss Lucy, you're so mighty sweet!"

"Not 'Miss Lucy'! 'Darling'!" Her fingers pressed his lips.

"I like calling you that." She tugged at his hand, leading him toward the rose arbor. From Pike's cabin came a keener wail. Daisy had joined Maria there, and Isaiah, moving furtively and with averted eyes, slipped across toward the kitchen gallery. They watched him go into the house. "Poor old man," Don murmured.

She stopped her ears. "I wish they wouldn't cry so! They're laying him out! Let's get as far away as we can. Let's go indoors. It's probably no hotter there." She led the way to the sitting room, seated him in Trav's big chair, pulled a stool near and sat at his knees. "Now we can discuss plans. We'll have to hurry."

He shook his head, smiling down at her, leaning to touch her shoulder, but she drew back. "No, let's be serious!"

"Let's be sensible," he amended. "We can't go ahead, the way you say."

"Why can't we, if we just do?"

"Do we have to think of reasons? My grandfather used to say: 'When in doubt, say no!' That's Maine for you."

"Why can't we?" she insisted. "Don't make jokes, please! Why can't we?" There was warning in her tone, and he became grave.

"Well, for one thing—darling—you're upset just now, sad over Pike, shamed and resentful. But ugly things happen everywhere. The South is your home. You'll feel different about it after a while."

She reached out to touch his knee. "When you're a little wiser, Don, you'll learn never to tell a woman she's upset—'specially when she is. I am. I admit it. I've known these things happened, but you never really know a thing till you see it. The bottom's dropped out of my world. I want to find a new world. With you."

"We will," he promised, and with her head on one side she asked: "But not Sunday? Is that it?"

"What happened here the other day can happen anywhere tomorrow."

"Why not Sunday, Don?"

He hesitated. "Maybe I'm just naturally slow, darling. I never want to hurry. In this, I see so many reasons for waiting. Your mother and father won't want you marrying a Yankee. They'll come to it in time; they'll have to, but let's give them time. Then your friends here; of course they've been mighty fine and friendly to me, but if I let on I was going to marry you—" He chuckled. "Well, your beaus would start calling me out, and I'd have to shoot three or four of them."

She leaned back, clasping her knees, her fingers twined, smiling up at him: "I bet you could!"

"Now who's making jokes? There are lots of things to consider. For one thing—"

He hesitated, his eyes fixed in thought, and he was silent so long that she said at last: "Go on, Honey."

He laughed suddenly. "I was just imagining what it would be like, us being married. I've a little money saved, not much. Pa takes care of it for me. With that and my pay we could rent a little house. But this work I'm doing, I'm away a lot of the time, sometimes a few days, sometimes a few weeks. I'll be away more than I'm at home. That wouldn't be much fun for either of us."

"You'd have to resign from the army," she agreed. "We'd go back to Maine."

"Well," Don confessed. "I don't know as I want to go back to Maine and stay there." He hesitated, his tone grave. "If I stay here, maybe I can help the Negroes learn some of the things they need.

And maybe I can help the white people, too. I think I help some, even now, and I'll do better as I go on."

She interrupted. "What else?"

"Isn't all that enough?"

She shook her head. "No, it isn't." And she confessed: "I never hated the South before. I suppose it was seeing Pike killed."

"I've seen men killed, in the War. It never seemed to me to prove much of anything."

"I know. But Don, the only reason for not getting married that would really count would be your not wanting to marry me!"

"I do want that. You know I do. But we have to be reasonable." He slipped to his knees beside her, kissed her; but after a moment she freed herself, her color high.

"You're too reasonable, Don! I'm beginning to change my mind already!"

"I'm trying to think straight for both of us."

"I see! Trying to protect me from myself? Trying to protect the poor little Southern girl who's lost her head over you?"

"Now, Miss Lucy, I didn't say that."

"You needn't be so noble! It's true! I'm mad about you! You're so brave, and so handsome, and so gallant! And so reasonable! How can I—"

"Don't be sarcastic, Miss Lucy. I can stand your being mad at me, but when you're sarcastic it's just like—"

"Oh, you—" She laughed and kissed him. "You big—I wish I could stay mad at you! Don, did you really re-enlist to help the nigras?"

"Well, I liked the South, too."

"Aren't you even going to pretend that liking me had anything to do with it?"

"I never had any idea that—this would happen to me."

"Why, you're just an old nigger-lover, aren't you, darling!"

He chuckled. "Them's fighting words. But—well, the Negroes certainly need help pretty bad." He added, teasingly: "Who was it you were crying about so hard, a while ago?"

"Poor old Pike!" Her throat filled again. "I suppose I loved him, yes. Will you come see us this summer at the Plains? It's near Camden, in South Carolina."

He could not promise; worse still, he must go tomorrow to Baton Rouge, and his business there would keep him till after their departure. That meant it would be weeks, yes, and months, before they met again. It was late before Lucy would let him say good night, would let him go.

The week before their departure for the Plains was for Peter a trying time. In the moment when he pressed the muzzle of his gun against

THE SCALAWAG • 225

Bob's ear and pulled the trigger, he was half drunk with the bloodshed he had witnessed; but to remember, afterward, the buck of the revolver butt against his palm, and the way Bob's head was rolled away by the shock of the bullet, was to bring the moment itself back in overwhelming reality. He felt a furtive pride, and a shrinking horror, and he felt terror too. Suppose someone had seen him? Suppose someone knew?

The day after Pike died, Mr. Fiddler came to bring a Negro named Saul who would hereafter take Pike's place. Saul was younger than Pike. He had been till a year ago coachman in the family of Jeremy Villard, a sugar planter a few miles downriver, whom the War and the loss of his slaves had left penniless. While his son, Elon, was away at the War, a year after the Yankees came to New Orleans, his wife died, and Villard and his daughter, Eleanor, abandoned the plantation, ruined by enforced neglect, and moved into town. Till the War ended, father and daughter lived on the proceeds of the sale of furniture, jewelry, portraits, tapestries, china, glass and even linens from the big house downriver.

Elon Villard had an instinct for machinery. Home from the War, he set up a small shop and engaged two mechanics, working side by side with them, and Mr. Cist had several times called on him to make adjustments or repairs at the mill. When he heard of Pike's death, Elon suggested that Saul might fill his place.

"We don't keep our horses now," he said. "So I'd like to see him have a permanent home."

Trav agreed, and Mr. Fiddler brought Saul to the house. Peter's revolver was still hidden in the feed bin, so when Fiddler took Saul to show him the stables, Peter followed them, watching while Mr. Fiddler pointed out to the new coachman where everything was kept. Mr. Fiddler had a vague feeling that Peter was uneasy about something, and wondered why, and when he was through with Saul and ready to return to the house, he asked casually:

"Peter, where'd you go to, the other day at the Institute? After I'd put Bob in the wagon to send him to the hospital, I went back and you were gone."

"Oh, I came on home."

Fiddler nodded. He might easily have missed Peter in the crowd. From the Institute, he had gone to the hospital, where he learned that Bob was dead. Bob's death was no surprise; his wounds had been severe. But when Mr. Fiddler saw the body, Bob's head was tipped to one side, exposing powder stains and dried blood around his ear. So Bob had been given a *coup de grâce* after he was put in the wagon, and the knowledge stayed disturbingly in Mr. Fiddler's mind.

"Well, you're all off to South Carolina, Monday," he remarked.

"Major Currain wants me to live here in the house while you're away."
He turned toward the stable door. "Coming?"

"Not yet."

So Mr. Fiddler went on alone. Peter stayed behind, watching Saul,
who had turned to the stalls to become acquainted with the horses,
stroking their flanks, talking to them, petting them. Then he began
to move here and there about the stable, handling everything, looking
into everything; he even opened the oat bin and dipped his hands into
the grain.

"Gwine need us some moah oats right soon now," he commented.

Peter gnawed at his knuckle, scarce breathing till Saul closed the
bin again. The revolver had become an accuser, lying in wait to destroy
him; if he left it in the oat bin, Saul would surely find it. Certainly it
must be hidden somewhere else. He would attend to this the first time
his mother used the carriage, so that Saul would not be here.

His opportunity came that night. His mother and father and Lucy
went to a party at Judge Morgan's, and as soon as he heard the carriage drive away, Peter started for the stairs. But Quinny, in his
mother's room, putting Enid's discarded garments away, heard him and
called him with a teasing singsong.

"I knows somep'n' Petie don' know! I knows somep'n' Petie don'
know!"

He stepped into the room, speaking in an angry whisper. "Stop
calling me Petie!"

"Well, I does," she boasted, mocking him. "Somep'n' you don'
know."

"I bet you don't."

"I bet I does."

"Well then what is it!"

"Ain' gwine tell!"

"Aw, you're just lying." He turned away.

"You'll find out diff'n't."

"When will I?" he demanded.

She tipped her head to one side, rolling her eyes toward the ceiling,
counting on her fingers. "An' Novembe' makes nine! Long 'bout de
middle o' Novembe'," she decided, her smile deriding him.

He stared at her, then flushed with incredulous dismay. "You are
not!"

"I is too!"

"Who says so?"

"Maria! Don' you think she knows!"

"You're not old enough."

"I is ef you is!"

Peter, in outright panic, ran back along the hall to his own room and shut and bolted the door behind him. He lighted the gas and stared at himself in the mirror, but after a moment his fright began to yield to pride. He grinned at himself; he set thumbs in arm sockets and strutted a little, wishing there was someone to whom he could announce this amazing and wonderful thing.

Then fright returned. Suppose his father learned the truth? Or his mother? Quinny had said that Maria knew, so probably all the Negroes knew; but if the baby were born before they returned from the Plains, Quinny could smother it, the way Looper and Viney did last year at Chimneys. He would make her promise to do so!

Since now he was a man, his thoughts took ever bolder shapes. To go out to the stables and retrieve his revolver from its hiding place was nothing. In his room, he reloaded each empty chamber, thrusting the small end of the paper cartridge into the cylinder, setting the rammer against the bullet, ramming it home. When they set out for the Plains, the loaded weapon was packed among his belongings. Having left New Orleans behind, he easily put away the thought that he was a murderer, and soon would be a father, and the full days at the Plains wiped his mind clear of all worries till, with summer gone, chance let him overhear a conversation between his mother and Aunt Cinda and Aunt Tilda.

He was in Brett's gunroom, fondling the shotguns and the rifles and the half-dozen revolvers there. The day was balmy as a fine fall day may sometimes be, and a window of the gunroom was open. His mother and the others were sitting on the veranda, unconscious of his presence so near. Peter paid no attention to their talk till he heard his mother say something about their imminent return to New Orleans.

"Trav says we'll simply have to start Monday. I declare I dread it." Then she giggled. "I suppose I ought to be excited about seeing my first grandchild!" Peter heard Cinda's surprised exclamation, and Enid said: "Yes. You remember Quinny, that little maid of mine? Of course, I knew she was full of the old Nick, but I thought Peter was just a baby! Can you imagine? That infant!"

Peter froze with terror! His mother knew! Had she told his father? What would his father do to him? He heard a murmur as either Aunt Cinda or Aunt Tilda said something, in a tone too low for him to distinguish the words. Then his mother spoke again.

"Oh, yes, Quinny told me herself! I suppose it's the climate down there, or something; they grow up so young." She laughed delightedly. "I've a mind to make Trav set them up in a little house on the ramparts, the way they used to after the Quadroon Balls. All the pretty little brights were brought up ever so properly, and once a year they had these big balls, and the young gentlemen took their pick! But of course they were young gentlemen, not little boys. Just think! Peter! Isn't it amazing?"

Peter's first terror at the discovery that his mother knew about Quinny was forgotten in his realization that she was not horrified, or disgusted, or angry, or anything like that. Actually, she seemed proud of him. Neither Aunt Cinda or Aunt Tilda had expressed surprise, or admiration; in fact, they had not expressed anything at all. But certainly his mother was proud. Now, against their silence, as though she read their disapproval, she talked faster and faster. "I suppose he ought to be spanked, really. He's so precocious! I don't know what we're going to do! You could have knocked me over with a feather! Of course the girl's to blame!" She rattled on, but always behind her pretended reprobation he heard the pride in her tones.

At the first pause, Cinda spoke, rising. "I declare, it turns chilly mighty quick when the sun gets low." They moved away toward the door, and Peter stayed unseen, relieved by the knowledge that whatever his father might say, his mother was in this matter on his side.

Don's letters that summer were long, and Lucy read them with delight that was only tempered by the fact that they were completely free from rapturous assurances of his devotion. He began with "Darling," and he closed, "With love," but otherwise she thought his letters were such that anyone might have read them; yet when she tried reading one of them aloud to her father, she found many passages where Don spoke of his thoughts, or of his beliefs, or of his hopes and dreams in a way she knew was meant for her alone.

Lucy was on her part incapable of writing impersonally. There were so many things she wished to tell him, yet she could find no proper words for the telling; against the wall of his steady "Darling" and "With love" she could not fling the ardent declarations which she wished to pour into his ears. He wrote her each detail of his days, but she was sure he would not be interested in what she did, with whom she rode, who went on what picnic where, who came to do charades. If she wrote about Boy de Saussure, or Pev Boykin, or some of the other boys who were nice to her, it would surely make him unhappy, and they meant nothing to her, really.

In late October he wrote that Helen Morgan, Jimmy's wife, was dead. "I called on Miss Sarah and her sister today," he said. "They'd just heard. Jimmie and Helen were at the Trenholm's in Charleston, and their little girl baby was born, and then a few days later Miss Helen died of the fever."

That was sad enough, but it was almost worse to read that Don was being sent to Texas, and would probably be away at least two months. He hoped to be back in New Orleans for Christmas, but could not be sure. Uncertainty made her the more eager to come home.

The journey back to New Orleans was not so tedious as it had been in January, for now the railroads were again in operation; but Enid suffered. Even laudanum would not always put her to sleep when she must sit bolt upright in a bucking, swaying, bouncing train. She hated, too, the wretched business of making a public toilet, of washing her face and hands in the basin on the bench at the end of the car.

"You act as if you were alone in your room," she told Lucy, in a jealous wrath. "I don't see how you do it."

"I'm sure they're not thinking about me," Lucy explained. "So I just don't think about them."

The boat trip from Mobile to New Orleans was this time less pleasant; a cold wind, cold rain, a troubled sea. In New Orleans, Mr. Fiddler and Saul with the carriage were at the station to meet them, Saul grinning and beaming to welcome his new white folks home again. While he handled the luggage, they gathered around Mr. Fiddler to hear the news. Everyone was well, he said; there was no great excitement, except that Quinny had had a baby.

"A baby?" Enid pinched Peter's arm. "Really? Why that little imp! I suppose it's practically white?"

"White?" Fiddler chuckled. "No, ma'am. That young one's black as the Ace of Spades!"

To Enid, that Quinny's baby should be black seemed a deliberate affront. She had been so sure Peter was the father, and now the memory of her boasts to Cinda and Tilda left her crawling with embarrassment and humiliation. Not only had this wretched nigger wench affronted her; Quinny had betrayed Peter! In fact, the miserable little drab was an abomination, her further presence in the house not to be endured! At Mr. Fiddler's word, Enid held silent and fought for self-control, and even on the way home—Trav and Mr. Fiddler had departed together for the mill—Saul on the box might hear any word that was said, so she held her tongue. But when they reached the house and Isaiah admitted them and Daisy and Maria came to make them welcome, Enid nodded pleasantly enough, but she asked at once: "Where's Quinny?"

Maria answered. "I'se kep' her in baid, Missy; she so little, an' dis uz a mighty big boy!"

"Then it's true that she's had a baby?"

"Yas'm!"

Enid nodded. "Then get her out of here," she directed, in a quiet fury. "Get her out of this house; her and her brat! I don't want her under this roof another night!" Lucy touched her mother's arm in silent remonstrance, but Enid pushed the girl's hand away. "You hear me, Maria?"

"Yas'm, I heahs you. She ain' unde' dis roof. She in my cabin."

"Well, go along and get rid of her."

Daisy began to whimper, and Lucy said: "Mama, I'll see Quinny, see how she is."

Old Maria spoke. "She fine, Miss Lucy. But dat bebby, he uz mighty nigh bigger'n she wuz. She ain' fit tuh git out o' baid yit."

"Well, fit or not, up she gets!" Enid insisted. "I won't have a slut like her around me!"

Lucy took her mother's arm. "You go upstairs, Mama. I'll take care of it."

Enid, recognizing the fact that Maria was on the edge of outright defiance, yielded and turned toward the stairs. When she was gone, Lucy went with Maria through the kitchen, and across the yard. Quinny lay on a pallet in Maria's room, the small black bullet of a baby in the proud cradle of her arm. There was a sparkle in her eye, and a laugh in her tones, but Lucy saw that her lips were pale and bloodless, and after they had talked with her for a minute or two, her respiration quickened. Certainly she could not be moved.

Back in the kitchen Lucy told Maria: "I think we can keep her here for the present."

Maria said firmly: "Da's right! She gwine stay right heah, anyways twell yore pa come home. Marste' Trav ain' gwine 'low such goings on! Th'ow dat young un out o' dis house, mah foot! Whah he now?" The old woman spoke in a lively wrath.

"He went to the mill, but he'll be home to supper."

"Huh! He bettuh be!"

At supper, Trav put a quick end to the discussion. "Quinny's not in the house, Enid, so you needn't carry on. When she's well enough to be moved, we'll see." And when Enid protested, he said lightly: "Oh, Enid, hush! Why such a fuss because the girl has a baby? It happens all the time."

She said in mustered rage: "Quinny's brushed my hair, helped me dress, washed my clothes! I feel her filthy hands all over me."

"Fiddlesticks!" Yet he watched her with thoughtful eyes. "What's in the back of your mind?"

She was suddenly frightened. Trav's curiosity, once aroused, might lead him too far, so to protect Peter she evaded the question, spoke in pretended surprise. "Why, Trav, whatever prompts this sudden interest in what I think about anything? In what I feel? In what I want? You're so sweet even to ask. Though of course I know that what I want will make no difference!"

He met her eyes in strong anger. "No, Enid; no, it won't; not if you want to throw that child and her baby into the streets." Enid touched a handkerchief to her eyes, with a sidelong glance at Peter, but Peter was attending strictly to his plate. "When they're both stronger, we'll manage something."

"Must I let her be my maid again?"

"Of course not!" Resenting her effort to put him in the wrong, he said furiously: "Quit twisting things around! As long as she's too weak to get out of bed, we'll keep her, then let her go. Find yourself another maid."

Thus, through Maria and Saul, there came into the household another Villard servant, a tall mulatto named Filly, who had been Mrs. Villard's personal maid for twenty years before she died. Filly was a handsome woman of forty or so, who, except to answer questions, seldom spoke, and Enid liked her from the first. So though for a few days after their homecoming they lived under the shadow of Enid's anger, this passed, till on Sunday, as they rose from the dinner table, she said in a cheerful tone: "You know, you people have been very patient with my bad humor, but I'm all over it now. Lucy, let's go out back and see Quinny and this fine baby of hers."

There fell an empty silence. Lucy looked at her father, and Peter quietly slipped away to escape the coming storm. Trav stood thoughtful. Enid saw them all thus troubled, and she moved toward Trav. "What is it? What's the matter?"

"Well, Enid, they're gone."

"Gone! Oh, Trav, not dead? I'd never forgive myself!"

"No. No." He lifted his shoulders as though under a burden. "No, Maria and 'Phemy talked it over, and Quinny's gone to Tony's. She and the baby." Enid stared at him, and he said: " 'Phemy likes her, and Maria says Sapphira does too. Quinny's a good laundress, specially on the fine work, and quick with her needle, so Sapphira's mighty—"

Enid cried in a harsh voice: "Trav, you fool!"

"Eh? What's the matter?"

"That tongue of hers, rattle, rattle, rattle! Everything we've ever said or thought or done, Sapphira'll hear all about! Everything! You idiot, Trav!"

"Well, I promised you I'd do something about her!"

"Oh, you did! You certainly did!" Enid slumped into a chair, beating her forehead. "What can I do? What can I do? How do men ever live to grow up, when they're so utterly stupid! Lucy, why did you let him?"

Trav spoke quickly. "I did it, Mama. Maria and 'Phemy and I. Lucy and Peter didn't know anything about it till it was done. Lucy said you wouldn't like it, but by that time—"

Enid wailed. "Oh, Trav, Quinny knows things about me I don't want anyone to know—much less Sapphira!"

Lucy tried to reassure her. "Things always seem worst at first, Mama. You liked Sapphira when you saw her, remember?"

"Liked her! What's that got to do with it? She's a nigger, putting on airs, and your father—" She bowed her head in her hands. "Oh, I could scream!"

One evening in mid-December, Trav, stopping at the St. Charles for a toddy before going home to dinner, saw General Longstreet in talk with General Beauregard and two or three other gentlemen. He had never been presented to General Beauregard, and he did not know the others, so he waited at a little distance till the group broke up and Longstreet turned toward the stairs. Then Trav came beside him and spoke, and the General turned. "God bless me, Major," he cried, and their hands met. "You're a treat for sore eyes."

"When did you get back?"

"This morning." Longstreet took Trav's arm. "A toddy with you, Currain. This calls for a celebration. I tried to find you when I was here in October, but the old nigra in your garden said you were in South Carolina."

"Yes." They took their glasses and looked for a place to sit down, turned into one of the reception rooms. "I'd gone to bring the family home," Trav explained. "We went to the Plains early in August, came home last month."

"Louisa and the babies stayed in Macon till just now. There was a little yellow fever here."

"Almost two hundred people died of it," Trav assented. "But small-pox was worse. Over five hundred deaths, the last time I talked with Doctor Mercer."

Longstreet smiled. "You and your figures! I thought the family might as well stay in Macon. Garland was there for a while. I was all over Mississippi, hunting cotton; spent some time with Uncle Gus, in Oxford. You remember him?"

"Judge Longstreet? Yes. How are your Macon kin?"

The General chuckled. "Well, they're in a fuss. Specially Sister Sarah. You know, the Methodist Church is split into Southern and Northern wings, and they're at pitchforks with each other. No quarrel as bitter as a church row! The Northern Methodists say that the only South-erners who haven't surrendered are horse thieves and Southern Method-ists, and the Southern Methodists are just as hot against their Northern brethren. The trouble is, Sister Sarah married a Northerner, Judge Ames. He was born in Ohio, and his brother is a Northern Methodist bishop, and during the War, Secretary Stanton made Bishop Ames custodian of all Southern churches that didn't have Union men as preachers." He shook his head, laughing in his beard. "So the War's not over, not for Sister Sarah! She and Judge Ames live under one roof, but in a sort of armed truce! He don't dare say a good word for his brother the Bishop, because Sister thinks the Bishop is a black radical, and a liar, and slanderer, and blackguard—like all Northern Methodist ministers!"

Trav smiled with him. "Hope you didn't get mixed up in it."

"No, no, no. I was off hunting cotton, all over Mississippi and Alabama. Wherever you see a field of cotton, just wait a while and you'll see me."

"Big crop, this year," Trav commented "At least, everyone says so."

"Big crop, little price," Longstreet reminded him. "With labor costing cash money, and the tax to pay, and the price as low as it is, a lot of planters are ruined—or will be." He raised a finger at a passing waiter, ordered fresh toddies. "By the way, how's your cotton-oil business coming?"

Trav smiled faintly. "We've learned enough now so that we know how little we know." And he said: "Judge Longstreet is along in years, isn't he?"

The General nodded. "Close to eighty, yes." He chuckled. "And he fought the War all the way through—in his head. Remember how he used to write me advice when we were in Tennessee?"

"Sometimes good advice, too."

"Sometimes, yes. He knows Napoleon's campaigns by heart. He took the War hard, and he's taken peace hard too. You know he's an ordained minister, still preaches a sermon now and then, and he goes into a rage every time he's reminded of the Yankee orders that our ministers must pray for President Johnson. And then of course he gets mad every time he goes out of doors, because half the town was burned when 'Lys Grant's army went through there—including the Judge's house, with all his correspondence—and the sight of a chimney rising out of ashes makes him boil."

"Don't blame him," Trav agreed.

"But he's cooling down," said Longstreet. "Enjoys his grandchildren, reads *Mother Goose* to them, plays his flute for them. And he likes to play euchre. And he sees something of the students. The University buildings weren't burned, and they have two or three hundred students. One of them, young fellow named Mayes, does the Judge a lot of good. Mayes thinks the South ought to forget her wrongs and go to work; says freeing the slaves was the best thing that could have happened to us. He and the Judge have some roaring arguments."

Trav said strongly: "Young Mayes has the right idea."

"Exactly!" Longstreet spoke with sudden vehemence. "Our cue is to sing low, work hard, stop holding back in the traces." He asked: "Did you see any of that foul business last July?"

"A lot of it, yes. Too much."

Longstreet looked at him with a sharp eye. "Was it as bad as it sounds? I hear the Congressional Committee is due here to start its investigation?"

"The first hearing's Saturday," Trav assented, and he said: "Yes, it was as bad as possible. I saw men shot, stabbed, beaten to death. I've tried to count them, to remember just how many murders I actually saw but after a while the thing fogs over. I only remember flashes, incidents, the way a man's eyes pop out when his head is pounded with a club."

"Are you going to testify?" Longstreet's voice was like a growl.

"No. No, I haven't talked about it. Not many people know I was there. Anything I could say would hurt the South. It was a damnable piece of business, any way you look at it."

Longstreet watched him with a thoughtful eye. "I read the news-papers," he said. "But I haven't talked with anyone who was actually there. The *Picayune* said the Negroes were all armed."

Trav made an angry sound. "That's not true. Oh, I know the *Picayune* said it, and a hundred years from now some Southerners will still be saying it. It's true that a few nigras had revolvers or horse pistols. I saw one or two myself, and in fact one of them took a shot at me. But not one nigra in ten had a firearm, while every policeman I saw had at least one revolver, and some had two. Besides that, almost every civilian in sight had a revolver. I had one myself. No, few of the nigras were armed. The best proof of that is that forty or fifty nigras were killed, and a hundred more were wounded, but not one policeman. One died of a sunstroke, and seven had slight shot wounds, but if the nigras had been armed, they'd have done more damage than that."

"Doctor Cenas's son was killed."

"Yes. I was right beside him when he was shot. And other white men were killed; Doctor Dostie, and John Henderson, three or four of the Conventioners. I think they were mostly killed by civilians. I saw police trying to protect the white men, but no one was protecting the nigras."

"How many killed altogether, does anyone know?"

"The army surgeon had the names of thirty-four nigras killed or died of wounds, and he reported at least ten others whose names he didn't learn. But you know as well as I do that those who could do so, no matter how badly wounded, would crawl off and hide somewhere. They had a hundred and fifty-one killed and wounded listed by name at the Hospital, all of them nigras except four or five. Most guesses put the total at about three hundred. Killed and wounded."

"That business will elect a lot of Radicals to Congress this fall," Longstreet commented. "Congress has already passed the bill to let nigras vote in the District of Columbia; the next step will be to let them vote everywhere!"

"A lot of Northern states will balk at that."

"Northern states, yes, but Southern states won't be allowed to balk; not as long as the South continues to boast that we're a stiff-necked and rebellious generation."

"President Johnson will veto this District of Columbia suffrage."

"Congress will override the veto," Longstreet predicted. "In fact, I think Congress will impeach Johnson, before they're through. You read his St. Louis speech. He said in so many words that Congress made the riot here."

Trav started to speak, checked himself, said in a controlled voice: "I read it, yes, but I'm tired of hearing who made the riot. Whoever made it—the Radicals if you like—it was General Sheridan and General Baird who might have prevented the killing but didn't. But it wasn't General Baird, or General Sheridan, or the Radicals, or Congress who murdered forty nigras and half a dozen white men. They were murdered by New Orleans policemen and New Orleans deputy sheriffs and firemen, and by New Orleans citizens. Men and boys. We did the killing! If we hadn't, there'd have been no one killed!"

His own words fed his anger, and General Longstreet spoke almost in apology. "I was surprised, when I was here in October, to hear so little talk about the whole affair. Of course there's more now, with this Committee coming."

"The talk died quickly," Trav agreed. "By the time I took Enid and the children away to the Plains, a week after the riot, it was already half forgotten." He added in an ironic tone: "The newspapers had persuaded their readers that the police had valiantly resisted and defeated an organized attack on the state government. There was a lot of talk about the 'scoundrels' who by attempting to hold a meeting 'provoked' the riot. Some of the Conventioners were even arrested, but none of the men who did the killing. I half believed that sort of talk myself. It was easy to shut your eyes—and your mind." Trav's voice hardened as he recalled those shameful days; he said grimly: "Lucy, more than anyone else, made me see the damnable business in its true light. She was so disgusted with the whole thing that she wanted us to move North and forget we were Southerners!"

Longstreet said in affectionate amusement: "She's a mighty sweet young lady, Major." He added in a different tone: "And the North has many traits we might imitate. Northern reluctance to commit murder, or to applaud it, is one of them." Trav did not speak, and Longstreet added: "The sorry part of it all is that before this happened, we Southerners, the Democratic party here, had regained most of what it lost by maneuvering the state into secession. Every major office was held by a Democrat. But this massacre threw away all that had been won. It will be a long time before the Democrats again control the government of Louisiana."

2

IT WAS TWO OR THREE WEEKS after their return to New Orleans
before Don came back from Texas. Lucy had longed to see him,
thinking what rapture it would be to throw herself into his arms,
but when he appeared, an absurd terror overwhelmed her, and she was
grateful because he shook hands with her mother and with Trav before
turning politely to her and then to Peter.

Enid and Peter presently said good night, but Trav stayed, and Lucy
was not sure whether she wished him to go or to stay, and when at last
she and Don were left alone, she began to tremble. Don had risen to
say good night to Trav. He turned back to her, she looked up at him
with wide eyes, and felt her color fade, and he saw this and said softly:

"Lucy, don't be afraid!"

So everything was fine! Before that blissful hour ended, they had
decided that some day soon they would talk to Trav and Enid about
themselves, about the way they felt, about what they should do. "But
not now," Lucy urged. "Not right away. Let's wait a little while, and
not tell anybody. Let's wait till after Christmas, at least."

There was no hurry, Don agreed. "I'm going to be pretty busy for a
while, anyway." And to her questions he explained. The House of
Representatives, as soon as Congress met, had appointed a committee to investigate the riot of last July. Before leaving Washington,
the Committee heard there the testimony of seven New Orleans Radicals; now they would pursue their investigations here, and Don had been
assigned to help them.

"Will you be a witness?" she asked, in a dubious tone.

"I don't know. I hope not."

"Will people be allowed to go and listen?"

"Do you want to?" he was surprised.

"Oh, I don't suppose so; not really. But will they?"

He shook his head. "I doubt it." To her many other questions he
could only confess ignorance, till she said with a smile:

"Well, you don't really know anything, do you?"

"One thing," he said gravely. "I know one thing." So they spoke no more of the Committee at all.

Next morning, Lucy's thoughts returned to that Committee soon to begin its sessions here, and she asked Trav: "Papa, are you going to be a witness at these hearings?"

They were at breakfast, and Enid heard the question. "What hearings?" she demanded, and when Trav had explained: "Oh, why can't they just let the old riot be forgotten? People will tell them all sorts of lies!"

"I don't think I'll be called, no," Trav told Lucy. "Not many people know I was at the Institute that day."

"Don's going to be helping the Committee, but he doesn't want to testify against us."

"Against us!" Enid exclaimed. "You talk as if we had done something to be ashamed of!" And she added: "Oh, of course, I'm sorry for the poor niggers, but as for Doctor Dostie and that crowd—well, it's a pity they weren't all killed, instead of just a few!"

"Oh, Mama, you talk the way the newspapers did," Lucy protested. "Next thing, you'll be bragging about our brave policemen, just because three or four hundred of them killed forty or fifty helpless nigras."

Trav said reasonably: "Keep things straight in your mind, Lucy. A good many other people besides policemen killed nigras that day."

"You didn't! Not even when one of them shot at you!"

"Oh, that poor fellow was too scared to know what he was doing. Besides he missed me!" Trav smiled, then added: "And Lucy, the police saved the lives of some of the white men; don't forget that."

Enid cried: "They ought to be ashamed of themselves for doing it, too!"

Peter said in a surprisingly deep bass voice: "They ought to have killed 'em all!" The sound of his own voice seemed to startle him, and Trav looked at him in surprise, and Enid said with a quick smile:

"Why, Peter! Sweetie, you're growing up!"

"Well, it's so!" Peter repeated, and this time his voice squeaked, and he reddened and was still.

"Shame on you, talking so biggity!" Enid chided.

"I saw boys as young as Peter with clubs," Trav told her. "Some with revolvers too."

"I'm glad Peter wasn't one of them shooting people, anyway!" Lucy said, smiling at her brother. Peter seemed about to make some hot retort, then held his tongue, but Enid said:

"I'd be proud of him if he had!" Trav made a protesting sound, and she retorted: "Oh, I know you were too—too something or other, to do your share!"

Lucy said in a wondering tone: "You know, I wish I could hear all the testimony. I don't know why. I certainly don't want to hear about the horrible things. Maybe I'm sort of hoping that if I could hear all about it, I'd see some excuse for what happened."

Trav nodded soberly. "I'd like to hear that myself," he agreed.

The Committee, arriving on Friday, put up at the St. Louis hotel. Don had engaged their rooms, and he met their train and saw them settled. Lucy had made him promise to come, no matter how late, to tell her all about it. It was an hour or two after supper and only Trav and Lucy were waiting when he reached the house.

"There are only two of them here, so far," he explained. "A Mr. Eliot from Massachusetts and Mr. Shellabarger from Ohio. But another's coming. They had several callers while I was there—General Sheridan, and General Sherman, and a Committee of Aldermen, and the Governor."

They would conduct their investigation in their rooms at the hotel, he said, and without an audience. The first witness tomorrow morning would be a Mr. Fish, Stephen F. Fish. The second would be Henry Clay Warmoth.

"Seems to me I've heard of him," Trav remarked.

"Warmoth's a young politician," Don told them. "He's the man who claimed that Louisiana, after she seceded, was just a territory. He organized a make-believe election, with Negroes voting, and they elected him the territorial delegate." There was mirth in his voice. "I called on him yesterday, to tell him he'd be wanted tomorrow. There's a sort of audacity about him." The Committee would meet at nine o'clock, he explained. "I'm supposed to have Mr. Fish and Mr. Warmoth ready in the lobby."

Lucy had many questions, and while Don answered them, Trav watched the two young people with a quiet attention. Lucy's absorbed interest in the Committee and its activities to some extent infected him, and he asked Don at last:

"Big crowd in the hotel this evening?"

"Not as many as you'd think."

"There won't be many tomorrow morning," Trav reflected, and met Lucy's eye. "Lucy, you and I might drop in, early tomorrow; get a little of the excitement second hand. That is, if you want to."

"Would it be all right?" she appealed to Don.

"I saw a number of ladies there this afternoon," he assured her, and Lucy said in laughing correction:

"Not 'afternoon'. 'Evening'! If I've told you once, I've told you a hundred times! Every time you say 'afternoon', you just give yourself away for a Yankee!"

"Well, after all, I am a Yankee," he reminded her, and he rose, a twinkle in his eye. "I must go call on Judge Howell. They want him tomorrow afternoon."

Lucy cried helplessly: " 'Evening', Yank! 'Evening'! In the South there's no such thing as 'afternoon'!"

"My apologies, ma'am," and he asked with perfect gravity: "Miss Lucy, may I call upon you tomorrow afternoon?"

Trav chuckled, and Lucy stamped her foot, and tried to frown, and laughed instead, and linked her arm in Don's to go with him to the door. Trav watched them with understanding eyes.

Next morning Saul brought the carriage around. Trav and Lucy dropped Peter at Mr. Soulé's Academy, and at the St. Louis hotel Trav told Saul to wait, and with Lucy on his arm they went in. The original hotel had burned twenty-five years before, but it was at once rebuilt and became famous for the subscription balls regularly given there by the great Creole families. The hotel was for a time not only a social but a business center, housing the St. Louis Exchange where from noon till three o'clock each day the auctioneers created a Babel of tongues, but with the beginning of the War, its importance had diminished. Till she went there with her father now, Lucy had never been inside its walls. As she entered, her eye was at once caught by the wide, spiral flying staircase which rose gracefully to the floor above, and for a moment it held all her attention.

Then she felt Trav's arm, on which her hand rested, stiffen slightly, and she followed his eyes and saw Don standing at a little distance, talking with three other gentlemen. Don had not yet seen her, but a moment later he did so, and at once crossed to where she and Trav stood. "You did come, then?"

"Did you deliver your witnesses?" Trav inquired.

"Young Mr. Fish, yes. He's with the Committee now. That's Mr. Warmoth I was talking to, the one with his back toward us." And he asked: "See here, would you like me to present him?" Lucy looked at Trav, and when Trav did not at once reply, Don said: "You'd find him interesting, I'm sure."

So Trav nodded, and a moment later young Warmoth, a surprising physical force in his bearing, tall and strikingly handsome, was bowing over Lucy's hand. She listened with a lively interest as he and her father talked together. "I understand from Lieutenant Page that you're to testify before the Committee," Trav remarked, and at Warmoth's assent: "Were you a member of the Convention?"

"No sir. I attended the noon meeting, but only as an interested outsider. At the recess, I went to the home of a friend on Canal Street—and stayed there."

"Then you won't be able to tell them very much."

"Very little," Warmoth agreed. "I only saw two Negroes killed." His words held a dry humor, and when his eye met hers, Lucy realized resentfully that his ironic tone had almost made her smile.

"You saw them killed?" Trav's tone was a question.

"We were on the gallery of my friend's home. I can't testify as to what provocation the Negroes had given. I saw them come out of Baronne Street at a hard run, followed by numerous citizens and policemen who threw rocks at them till first one and then the other fell. I then saw men in the uniforms of policemen walk up and discharge their pistols into the Negroes as they lay on the ground, and I saw the Negroes quiver and die."

"Quiver and die." That was a phrase Lucy would not forget. To Trav's continuing questions, this young man explained that he saw no more than this; his friends would not allow him to stay on the gallery and watch.

"They feared for my life if I were seen," he explained, and Lucy wondered why anyone should want to kill him. He seemed a thoroughly charming young gentleman, and his tone and his manner of speaking made everything he said sound profoundly true—and sometimes faintly amusing, as when he told her father: "I did not hear that any policemen had been killed. I heard that one or two had been slightly wounded, and I believe one died from the heat."

To one of Trav's questions he said he was a lawyer, "but not now in practice," and Trav asked:

"Have you found any feeling in New Orleans against employing Union men? I mean, as lawyers."

Mr. Warmoth said in an even tone: "The people here very wisely abstain from employing Union attorneys, because before a jury in New Orleans to do so would ruin their case. Certainly I would never engage a Union man to carry my cause to court, not if I hoped for victory."

"Then you'd say the refusal to employ Union lawyers is more common sense than prejudice?"

"Undoubtedly, yet the prejudice is always there."

"Do you encounter a social prejudice, as well?"

The young man's glance touched Lucy; his tone was comically mournful. "The dear ladies are, I fear, the most bitter of all."

This time she did smile. His impudence was charming. When a moment later, in answer to Trav's question, he suggested the wisdom of a temporary military government in Louisiana, she agreed with him; when he said Mayor Monroe headed an organization of men called Thugs, who had elected him to office and who had been rewarded with places on the police force, she believed him; when he said that a former

Confederate soldier who killed a Union man could never be convicted by a New Orleans jury, the very lightness of his tone made her accept the hard truth of his words.

While Trav and Mr. Warmoth talked together, Don stood beside Lucy, his eye upon the stair yonder, and presently he stirred and spoke. "Mr. Warmoth, I see Mr. Fish has finished his testimony. May I escort you upstairs?"

Warmoth said easily: "Don't trouble yourself, Lieutenant. I'm acquainted with the Committee members. You remember, I spent some weeks in the corridors of Congress, awaiting acceptance as Territorial delegate. So, pray, stay with your friends."

He bowed and turned away, and Lucy asked why the rioteers might have wanted to kill him. "I liked him," she declared.

"So do I," Don agreed. "He's not one of the Convention crowd, stands by himself." He spoke to Trav: "You know, Mr. Currain, if the Negroes ever do get the vote, they'll elect him anything he wants to be."

Trav, watching Warmoth go up the stairs, said, half to himself: "I wouldn't be surprised."

Mr. Warmoth had interested Lucy, but now he was gone, and Don had an errand he must do, and Trav wished to go to the mill, so they came out of the hotel and found Saul and the carriage. Trav helped Lucy in, then left them together, and Lucy asked: "Don, can't I carry you to do your errand?"

"It's just down Royal Street. I can walk as well as not."

"Wouldn't you rather ride with me?" And she said teasingly: "Why do I always have to prompt you?" At his rueful expression she laughed. "There, never mind! Where do we go?"

He stepped into the carriage beside her. "Well, much obliged. It's the corner of Royal and Hospital Streets; the Haunted House, they call it. The Bureau's been using it as a school for Negro girls, but we've had to give that up, and put it up for rent. I want to see that it's been cleaned and put in order for the tenants."

Lucy leaned forward. "Saul, you know where the Haunted House is?"

"Yas'm."

"Lieutenant Page has some business there."

Saul made a doubtful sound, but he clucked to the horses. "You, Pa'dner, you, Beauty, don' you put yoah eahs slanchwise at me! Us'ns go wheah little Missy say, so pick up yuh feet."

Lucy asked: "Who haunts the Haunted House, Don?"

"Well, once upon a time—"

"Oh, like a fairy tale?"

"One of the gruesome ones, yes. Once upon a time, the mistress of the house was a woman who liked to abuse her slaves. She'd give big balls, and while the music drowned all other sounds, she'd go up in the attic where the slaves lay in chains and whip them till the blood ran. She was very beautiful and charming, and full of good works; but she was found out, and they say the Devil finally got her. A mob attacked the house, trying to break in, threatening to burn her at the stake or something, but all of a sudden the stable-yard gates swung open, and there was her carriage—some say she was on the box, and some say it was her Negro coachman—and the horses were rearing and plunging. The crowd scattered, and the carriage whirled out into Hospital Street and off toward the Ramparts and disappeared in a cloud of dust—and no one ever saw her again!"

"Oh, lovely," Lucy applauded. "Didn't anyone ever see the carriage or the horses, either?"

"I think they found the carriage, but she was gone!"

"Br-r-r! Makes me shiver! But there isn't a word of truth in it, Don, because ladies don't whip their slaves. I'm sure the abolitionists made her up. Didn't they, honestly?"

He smiled with her. "That's the tale as it was told to me."

"You know," she remarked, "except going to and from the station, I haven't been in this part of town at all. Everything's different, isn't it."

"This is the old town, the original city," he explained.

"The houses all look sort of empty; closed shutters and blank doors. Doesn't anyone live in them?"

"Yes! Yes indeed. The old Creole families, the aristocrats. Since the War, many of them have moved back to France, but not all. The houses look shut up because they're built around courtyards, all planted with flowers and shrubs and even trees, and with iron-railed galleries going up two or three stories. And notice the galleries overlooking the street. At night you'll often see ladies sitting out on them in lacy shawls, the kind my mother would call a throw! And sometimes wearing veils."

"Why are some of the street doors so huge?"

"So carriages can drive right into the courtyard." And he added: "Some of these houses haven't got any inside stairways; just stairs going up from the court, and the galleries serve as halls."

As he spoke, he touched her arm and with a smile and a gesture bade her watch Saul. She had not noticed, till then, that Saul was following an eccentric course. He turned right or left at every corner, approaching their destination on an S-track like a snake's. Lieutenant Page called: "Aren't you going a roundabout way, Saul?"

Saul grunted without reply, and Lucy whispered to herself in pretended despair: "Will I ever be able to teach this man manners? Imagine a gallant gentleman, riding with me and yet in a hurry to reach his destination."

Don chuckled. "I'm sorry, Lucy. But in fact I am in a hurry. Forgive me." And he spoke again to the Negro. "Saul, go on another block and turn left." And when they presently swung down Hospital Street, he pointed. "There's the house, on the corner." She saw a three-storied mansion with a delicate iron railing along the gallery at the second-floor level, and after a moment Don said: "Stop here, Saul." Beside them was a lofty portal wide enough and high enough to let a carriage pass. "The house fronts on Royal Street," Don explained. "Back here is for the servants, and the stables. This is the carriage entrance."

"The one she came out of?"

"The very same one." He pointed upward. "See that big window on the upper floor, looking toward the river. That's a beautiful room. It was hers, they say. All right, Saul."

The carriage turned into Royal Street, and Lucy said: "Look, Don; see the bars in the fanlights over all the ground-floor doors. Or are they windows, with the shutters closed? I'll come in and inspect the house with you. May I?"

Saul pulled up his horses behind another carriage which stood directly opposite the recessed entrance door, and Don said: "I'm afraid the new tenants have arrived, so maybe you'd better not. Thanks for bringing me down. May I call tomorrow?"

"Of course."

He raised his hat. "Goodby." Her eyes said more than that. Then as he turned away, she looked up at the windows along the gallery of the big house and made a small, startled sound. Don turned back. "Did you call? What was it?"

"I thought I saw—" Lucy laughed. "But of course I didn't. That house really is haunted, Don. I thought I saw a lovely, wicked cousin of mine, but I couldn't have. She's thousands of miles away."

He smiled, looking up at the windows. "I haven't yet seen the new tenants. I dealt with their agent. Maybe she's here."

"Oh no, I didn't really see anything. Tomorrow?"

"Tomorrow, yes." He lifted his hat and turned to cross the street, and Saul touched the horses with the whip; he swung the lash on one and then another, and the horses were startled, and the carriage lurched ahead.

"Saul! Slowly!" Lucy protested.

"I ain' gwine stay here twell dem hants malleroo me."

"Malleroo? What's that?"

"Wuss bad luck dey is!" He gentled the horses, speaking to them softly.

"I never heard of it."

"Yas'm you is. It's when somebody gives you de malleroo!" With the big house well behind him, he was now at ease. "It's de way de French say 'hoodoo', da's what!" Lucy was still puzzled, but she asked no more.

The Committee during its stay in New Orleans heard more than a hundred and fifty witnesses, some whites and some Negroes, some Radicals and some Democrats. Forty-seven of these witnesses were called at the request of New Orleans citizens anxious to clear the city's reputation. The newspapers printed an occasional paragraph, but since the hearings were behind closed doors there was little they could say.

Lucy had from Don regular reports on the Committee's work, and he brought her a copy of the testimony of young Mr. Fish, who had been the first witness. "And I can get others if you want them," he said.

She nodded absently, her eyes upon the manuscript, and as she read a phrase here, another there, her pulse began a slow pound, pound. "—The Reverend Mister Horton, who had opened the meeting with prayer and who was afterwards murdered . . ." She looked at another page, and another; then thrust the manuscript back into Don's hand. "I don't want to read it!"

"Reading can be worse than seeing it."

"I can't imagine anything worse than seeing these things with your own eyes."

"I suppose it's like being in battle," Don said thoughtfully. "In battle, you're all fired up and excited, and you don't comprehend what you see, but remembering, afterward, can be terrible. Hearing them tell about what happened that day made me feel even worse than when I saw the things happening."

The last witness, Governor Wells, was heard on the second day of January. As the year ended, the weather had turned bitterly cold. The wind was from the north, and before dark that night—the General and Mrs. Longstreet came to supper—a thin rain began to fall.

Lucy found that the General's feeling about the hearings had been much like hers. He, too, had at first wished to attend. "To judge for myself which men were lying and which were not."

"I don't suppose there was much lying," Trav suggested. "The truth was bad enough."

The General nodded. "They had some testimony Friday that clinched the thing for me. I heard it from General Sheridan. Mr. Herron was on the stand, the attorney general of the state, and he testified that he didn't prosecute anyone for the murders that were committed. He said he couldn't get enough evidence to indict anyone!" There was an angry roar in Longstreet's tone. "When thirty or forty or a hundred men are murdered in broad daylight, before hundreds of witnesses, and not one individual is even arrested for the crime, the city in which such a thing occurs forfeits all claims to be civilized."

Enid cried out in protest. "But General, they were fighting for the South!"

"Nonsense, ma'am! Or if they were, they did the South great harm! No, they did their killing because they enjoyed doing it! But I don't blame the murderers so much as I do those who let them escape!"

Mrs. Longstreet said drily: "You know, I think we've worn out the subject of the riot. If you're not careful about criticizing the South, Jeems, folks will start calling you a scalawag. Enid, don't argue with him; it just makes him worse. When he argues, he keeps saying things that are more and more outrageous till I'm ready to scream!" She laughed at her own words. "Let's talk about the weather, instead. Isn't it unusually cold for the time of year?"

So they spoke of other things, and when they left the table, a mood of high good humor held them all. The wind was howling at the windows, and the roaring fire drew them in a close circle. Trav and the General fell into reminiscence, recalling amusing or tragic or pitiful incidents that had happened during the years of the War, and the others were glad to listen, and time sped so that it was toward midnight before Mrs. Longstreet rose to say good night.

When they opened the front door, a wet snow was falling, and Trav said: "I'd better have Saul carry you home."

Mrs. Longstreet laughed in amused scorn. "Nonsense, it's only a step. If I find the mud too deep, I'll just climb into Jeem's pocket!" She was so small beside him that this seemed not impossible.

After they were gone, Enid and Peter turned at once upstairs, but Trav stayed to bank the fire, and Lucy to watch him and to ask a question. "Papa, what's a scalawag?"

Trav was surprised. "Eh? A scalawag? Well, a scalawag's a friend who turns against you. He's not quite as bad as a copperhead. A copperhead is secret about it, sneaking; he bites without rattling. But a scalawag at least rattles, tells you where he stands."

"What can a Southerner do, without being called a scalawag, if he thinks the South is wrong about things?"

Trav considered. "It's hard to answer, Lucy. I think the South is wrong about lots of things, but most Southerners would say I'm wrong, so maybe I am. I believe in—democracy, in majority rule, whatever you want to call it. But we've never tried it in the South. We've always been afraid of letting people vote; not just nigras, but white men, too. That's one reason we went to War, to try to check the increasing political power of the ordinary man. Lincoln believed in government by the people, but we thought it hateful, so we hated Lincoln." His voice changed, held a hint of mirth. "I'm a little ashamed of believing in majority rule, because Southerners of our class are against it, and it's hard to differ with your own kind. Our class, men like me, feel sure that a small group of men like us could run the state, or the South, or even the United States, better than it's being run. I think that's probably true, but even if it is true, it wouldn't be good for any of us to let them do it. We're running things, and if we run them badly we can always change and do them better. Every man has a right to make a fool of himself. That's the real inalienable right; not just life, liberty and the pursuit of happiness, but the right to make a fool of himself. A real good absolute monarch, a King or an Emperor or something of the sort, he could make a lot better country than we've got. But I'd be glad to die fighting to keep him from doing it." He paused, laughed, said: "Where was I? Oh yes. That question of yours. What can a man do if he thinks his country is wrong. Well, if he believes in democracy—and I do—he'll just have to decide he's wrong in thinking so."

She shook her head. "I'd rather be wrong and think I'm right than be right and think I'm wrong. And you know, Papa, I believe General Longstreet is like me!" She crossed to say good night, smiled. "And thanks for explaining things so clearly. Now I'm more confused than ever."

"I used to know, positively, a lot of things," he remarked. "But the older I grow, the less I'm sure I know. I've had to change my mind so often, these fifty years—"

"Fifty-two! Don't start cheating on your age."

"Oh, I didn't have any real, firm opinions till I was two years old!" They laughed together, moving toward the door to look out at the snow again. In the garden, every branch and twig bore its white burden. "We must get up early," he suggested. "See this before it's all melted and gone."

"It's a long time since we've had a morning ride, Papa."

Her tone was a challenge, and he accepted it. "Excellent! I'll go tell Isaiah, have him tell Saul."

When next morning they set out, the horses danced in a fine excitement, bowing their necks to stare at the white carpet under their hooves. The snow was two or three inches deep, and the wind had plastered it against trees and shrubs and against the sides of houses. In a yard on Eugene Street, even thus early, someone had built a snowman, and children were everywhere, pelting each other with snowballs. There was a lift of laughter in the air, and Lucy felt this. "You know something, Papa?" she asked; and when he looked at her inquiringly: "This is about the nicest time I've had since before the War."

3

AFTER THE RIOT last July, the more conspicuous Radicals had either gone north for greater safety, or if they stayed in New Orleans they avoided being seen in public places and waited on healing time. Even when the November election proved how much Northern indignation provoked by the riot had strengthened the Radicals in Congress, they were slow to return. When the investigating Committee reached the city, only eight of the twenty-five or six Conventioners who had answered the roll call on the thirtieth of July could be found to testify.

But when Congress convened, the picture quickly changed. Using their added strength, and overriding the President's vetoes, the Radicals first conferred the vote on Negroes in the District of Columbia, then passed the Fourteenth Amendment, and finally enfranchised Negroes everywhere.

Tony during the summer had had few callers, but the night after this bill passed, a considerable company gathered at his house in exultant celebration. Doctor Roudanez was there, and Pinchback, and J. M. G. Parker, and former Governor Hahn, and others came and went. Among them was Ezra Hiestand, who after testifying before the Congressional Committee in Washington had now risked returning to New Orleans. Tony, presenting him to Sapphira, said:

"Mr. Hiestand has a distinction; he is almost if not quite the only Radical in New Orleans who has never before been our guest."

She smiled, and Hiestand said soberly: "Mr. Currain, that is not my only distinction. On the night of July twenty-seventh, four of us spoke to the crowd in the street outside the Mechanics Institute. The others were Doctor Dostie, John Henderson, and the Reverend Mr. Horton. I'm the sole survivor of the four."

"So you are," Tony agreed, and Sapphira asked:

"Were you there, in the Convention?"

"Well, no," Mr. Hiestand admitted. "I left my office at about twelve o'clock, intending to go, and I even went half a block toward the Institute; but then for some reason or other—I don't really know why—I turned aside into an alley and—well, I never did get there." He added: "I returned to my office, and a friend came to warn me to stay away, so I went home."

When he and Tony moved on, Mr. Parker came to Sapphira's side. Between them a mutual respect had long ago developed. He asked her tonight: "Did you read General Beauregard's letter in the *Times?*" Beauregard had written advising the South to remain a passive spectator during the struggle for political ascendancy in Congress.

"Passive people accomplish little," she suggested. "Not as long as they stay passive."

He smiled dissent. "A dam is passive," he reminded her. "Nevertheless it holds back the flood." And he urged: "In times like these, a man must make his choice: take that road, take this road, or—just sit still!" She did not speak, and he looked across the room to where Hiestand had joined Michael Hahn. "Governor Hahn and I are going into partnership in a new enterprise, a newspaper," he said. "I've chosen my road. I can't be passive, and I won't turn back. We're going to call the paper the New Orleans *Republican.*"

As was usually the case, she was sewing, her needle busy, and she did not raise her eyes. "I'm afraid your competition may mean the end of the *Tribune.*"

"Not in the near future," he assured her. "We'll have a few years, here, of Negro rule, and Doctor Roudanez will ride that tide. But Negro rule can't endure, and there will always be a place in New Orleans for a *Republican.*"

"Will you be the editor?"

"No; no, Governor Hahn."

She looked along the room to where the other stood. "I don't feel I know him; he has been here so seldom."

"He's a Bavarian, Miss Sapphira. His father and mother came to this country when he was a boy. When Louisiana seceded, he went with his state, but after we occupied New Orleans, he took the oath, and under the Free State Constitution he was elected Governor." He smiled. "I wouldn't call him a scrupulous man," he admitted. "But he has a big following. Of course, he—"

Then he saw she was not listening; she was looking at someone down the room, and he swung to follow her glance. 'Phemy had entered with decanters and glasses, and Quinny, carrying a waiter with nuts and crackers and cuts of cheese, came on her heels. 'Phemy's strong face and strictly dressed hair were accented by the black bombazine with a white collar and white cuffs which she always wore. Quinny, erect and stiff with dignity, was attired exactly like her, and she matched 'Phemy's manner so completely that Mr. Parker smiled.

"There's a mighty pretty young one," he said approvingly. "Isn't she new?"

"New here," Sapphira assented. "But I've known her since she was a baby."

'Phemy came to them, and Sapphira filled her glass, and his, and 'Phemy moved on while Quinny in turn presented her tray. He took a few nuts, making a long business of the selection, watching the girl, and when she turned away, he said: "She acts so like 'Phemy that it's funny."

Sapphira smiled. "She amuses me." 'Phemy and Quinny disappeared, and Sapphira added: "And Mr. Currain; she amuses him, too." Her eyes were again upon her sewing.

"Speaking of General Beauregard," he remarked, "and of politics. I used to be a Democrat, then turned Republican, but I was already a Yankee, and my doing so surprised no one. But if General Beauregard, or someone like him, would turn Republican, it would at least . . ." He smiled. "Well, it would confer on the Republican party at least a suggestion of respectability."

"That's hardly likely," she commented, "I mean, that General Beauregard, or any man of equal station, will turn Republican." And she asked: "What will Congress do next?"

"The Radicals can do whatever they choose," he reminded her. "The riot here last July put Northern sentiment overwhelmingly behind them. Suffrage for the Negroes was the first step, but everyone knows the Negro will never vote in the South unless soldiers guard the polls, so I expect the next thing will be military government, to protect the Negro in his voting."

Sapphira nodded, eyes on her sewing. "I expect so, yes; but soldiers can't protect us after we're dead." She folded the fabric in her hands, jabbed her needle through it. "Everybody does things too fast! White folks and us, leave us to ourselves, give us a little time, we'd get along together; but if the North handcuffs us together, and says we got to get along, we'll hate each other for a hundred years."

He looked at her in quickened attention, and after a moment he asked: "Miss Sapphira, you—think of yourself as a Negro, don't you."

"I am one."

"Were you conscious, a moment ago, of talking more like a Negro than like the—cultivated person you are?"

She considered, frowning with thought. "I wasn't, no. 'White folks and us.' 'We got to get along.' I see what you mean." And she said: "Maybe when I see things most clearly, it's the Negro in me. We're children, and in many ways children are wiser than grownups." She shook her head. "Giving us the vote, Mr. Parker, is as foolish as giving monkeys a fine set of china to play with." Then, in a questioning tone: "Yes, Tony?"

Parker had not heard Tony's approach. " 'Phemy just announced two gentlemen," Tony explained. "My brother-in-law, Redford Streean; you remember him?"

"He was here in May, last year, yes. Young Darrell was his son." There was something somber in her eyes.

Tony nodded. "And Captain Pew's with him, a gallant hellion who enchants the ladies." A stir at the door made him turn, and he went to meet his guests and bring them to Sapphira. Parker had waited. Streean bowed over Sapphira's hand, and Captain Pew greeted her with a grave courtesy. Tony introduced Mr. Parker. "One of our conquerors, gentlemen. Mr. Parker came here as an officer in Butler's army, became postmaster, made us his friends." And he told Parker: "Mr. Streean during the War proved himself one of the best businessmen in the South, while Captain Pew was probably our most successful blockade runner." He turned back to Streean. "Where's Dolly?" He explained to Sapphira. "She's Darrell's sister."

Streean asked her: "Oh, you knew Darrell?"

"I was at Chimneys at the time of his death."

Her tone was serene, but Streean looked at her acutely, and then at Tony. "I never thought of that possibility. Darrell must have—admired you, Miss Sapphira. Did he die at Chimneys?"

Tony said in a heavy tone. "He was in good health when he left Chimneys."

Streean nodded. "Ah yes, I remember. You told me." And, recalling Tony's question: "Dolly? She retired early. We've been doing some remodeling, tearing out walls, laying new floors, making the house more suitable for our purposes, and of course choosing the furniture, the floor coverings, the curtains, the wallpapers, all that has fallen on her." To Mr. Parker he explained: "My daughter is my hostess, sir. We have just taken a lease on a house on Royal Street. Perhaps you know it. At the corner of Hospital Street?" 'Phemy and Quinny came to offer them Madeira and old brandy, nuts and crackers, and as they moved on around the room, Streean, watching them, turned to Sapphira. "Which reminds me, Dolly finds some difficulty in locating satisfactory servants. Can you advise her, Miss Sapphira?"

" 'Phemy can help her, I expect."

"Will you speak to 'Phemy?"

"I think Miss Dolly had better do that, so 'Phemy will know what she wants."

Mr. Parker looked at Sapphira with an amused interest. Here was a subtlety. Sapphira never forgot she was a Negro—but she had resented the reminder from Streean. If Dolly wished help in finding Negro servants, let her consult a Negro servant!

He turned toward Captain Pew. "Captain, may I make you acquainted with the gentlemen yonder?" he suggested, and as the Captain turned with him, he explained: "You've fallen into a boiling pot of politics, Captain. We're all violent Republicans." Then, beginning introductions: "Former Governor Hahn, who escaped being murdered in the slaughter last July; Mr. Hiestand, who was equally fortunate; Doctor Roudanez, the moving spirit back of the *Tribune*, a newspaper devoted to the Negro cause; Mr. Pinchback, a young man with a promising future; Mr. Dalloz, editor of the *Tribune*. Gentlemen, this is Captain Pew, who I am told was a successful blockade runner during the War."

Captain Pew bowed. "Gentlemen."

Governor Hahn asked directly: "What are your politics, Captain?"

Pew smiled. "During the War, profit was my politics. These last two years I've lived abroad, but my politics remain unchanged."

Hahn grunted. "Hunh! Profit is your politics, politics is my business. It comes to the same thing. Hiestand, it's time we took our leave."

Doctor Roudanez and Dalloz departed with them, but Parker and young Pinchback stayed, and the two groups united, drawing chairs near Sapphira's. Captain Pew asked questions. "For I've seen more of foreign lands, of late, than of my native country." Parker recognized the cool audacity in the man which somehow made his questions inoffensive. "For instance, I do not remember that such a group as this—" his glance touched Pinchback and Sapphira—"would have gathered together in the South I knew."

Sapphira said, faintly amused: "I am colored, yes, and of course, so is Mr. Pinchback. So were two of our departed guests. I think that is new. Yet in New Orleans, free people of color have long been respected."

"I believe it's a good beginning," Pew commented. "In the *salons* of Paris, the tint of a man's skin has little importance. The French as a nation are more mature than we."

"It's a beginning, but only a beginning, Captain." It was Pinchback who spoke. "My mother was a mulatto, so there were at least two white men among my immediate forbears, and my father sent me to Ohio for several years of instruction. So I am removed by at least two generations and by at least some education from the Negro who works in the fields. Yet I am not—by intellect, or character, or capacity—the equal of a white man. Congress is trying to make me his equal by laws. The only result will be to persuade me—" His tone changed: "To persuade all us niggers that we's not only as good as white folks; we's better!" Faint smiles responded, and he said more quietly: "It needs time and time and time. We're a race just freed from slavery. To adjust ourselves to that single fact is task enough to occupy us for a generation or two. Those who hurry us too fast, thrust us ahead too fast, are our enemies rather than our friends."

Pew listened with respectful attention, and Parker said thoughtfully: "Men decide nothing. We're just chips on a flowing stream. Soil and climate and man's natural indolence made the South largely agricultural. Other forces made the North industrial. Opposed interests made North and South enemies, so they went to War. The North, as a war measure, to capture the sympathy of the world, freed the slaves. The South was beaten; they surrendered.

"But the Southerner could not accept the end of slavery. That was asking too much of human nature. As Miss Sapphira said, as Pinchback said, a change as great as that needs time. The South tried Black Codes, to retain the fact of slavery, if not the name, and the North, resenting the trick, was all the more bent on having its way. That's human nature too; so now, since you won't let the North free the slaves, they'll give the slaves the vote and let them be the bosses for a while."

He shook his head. "But no one man caused any of these things to happen—neither one man nor many men. It was a thousand forces working together; it's those forces which write history, not men."

For a moment they were all silent and thoughtful; then Pew asked: "You seriously expect that nigras will be allowed to vote in Louisiana?"

"Certainly, and soon."

"I hope you're mistaken. But I fear you're not!" Pew rose, caught Streean's eye. "Miss Sapphira! Mr. Currain! Gentlemen! We will hope soon to return your hospitality."

Parker and Pinchback left with them, and when she and Tony were alone, Sapphira said thoughtfully: "I should not have reminded Mr. Streean of Darrell's death. Now he will wonder. Is Dolly attractive?"

"Pretty as a witch." On a sudden memory Tony chuckled. "Remember some of the dresses I brought you, long ago, from Richmond? I told you the prettiest girl in Richmond tried them on?" She nodded. "Well, that was Dolly!"

She smiled. "I remember you said she couldn't hold a candle to me."

"No more she can. She was the prettiest girl in Richmond, but you weren't there."

"She's Captain Pew's mistress?"

"Oh yes, naturally." He chuckled. "I can't even guess what you're thinking. I ought to be scared of you."

"Do you like Mr. Hahn?"

"No, I suppose not. He's not my style. Gruff fellow."

"Governor Wells came here once," she remembered, and added, without heat: "The chin-whiskered old hypocrite! He was shocked at your establishment, Tony."

"This Convention business was his idea."

"I know. Why do I hate those of your friends who organized the Convention worse than I hate the policemen who killed my people? I suppose it's because this that you're doing to the South, you and your friends, I hate that; and yet I want it, too, want you to win, want you to have your way."

Later, when they were abed, she said lightly. "Governors aren't so much? Governor Hahn! Governor Wells! Tony, how'd you like to be governor?"

"Fine. Why?"

"You might be, some day, you know."

He laughed drowsily. "I'm about as likely to be governor of Louisiana as—as—." He tried to think of someone sufficiently improbable. "Why, as Pinchback is," he said.

Trav and Enid had not heard that Streean and Captain Pew and Dolly were in New Orleans till Dolly came to call. Enid was asleep in her room, and Trav was at the mill, so Lucy received her. Except for that glimpse through the window, she had last seen Dolly three years ago, when the other left Richmond with Jenny to go to the Plains. Dolly was pretty then, but only pretty; now she was as beautiful as a glass of wine, not sparkling, like champagne, but warm-bodied and richly satisfying. Lucy remembered Trav's words, that whatever Dolly's sins, they did not show.

"Mama's napping," Lucy explained, after their first greetings. "I'll go wake her."

"Oh, Enid and I are old friends," Dolly protested. "Let's both go right up to her room."

But Lucy, remembering that Enid, freshly waked from sleep, looked less than her best, would not permit this. The thought that Dolly, herself so exquisite, should see her mother all disheveled was intolerable. "No," she insisted. "I'll tell her you're here."

She ushered Dolly into the drawing room, then darted up the stairs, and returned to say Enid would be down in a minute. Dolly nodded.

"I expect you're wondering wherever I came from," she remarked. "And how long I've been here, and everything. Well, you see, Papa had some investments in New Orleans during the War, and he came back here last June—we were living in Paris; I sort of keep house for him— to see about them, and he saw so many opportunities here—you know he's a wonderful businessman—that he decided to just move back here. So we did. We came six or eight weeks ago and rented a big house . . ."

"I know!" Lucy exclaimed. "At the corner of Royal and Hospital Streets? I saw you at the window, one morning just before Christmas."

Dolly eyed her warily. "You were in the carriage with Lieutenant Page?"

"Yes."

"I thought so, but you've changed!" She smiled flatteringly. "All grown up, and so beautiful! I wasn't sure. Lieutenant Page is real sweet, isn't he? He's been so helpful! I had to refurnish that whole enormous house . . ." Her words came tumbling, but Lucy briefly ceased to listen, wondering why Don had not told her about Dolly? He must have seen her many times, yet never a word. When she began again to pay attention, Dolly was saying: ". . . used to belong to a terrible woman, Madame Lalaurie. She had dozens of slaves and gave perfectly enormous dinners and balls. Her husband was a doctor, but no one paid any attention to him, because she was so beautiful and clever and gay. She was always doing things for poor people, taking them food and things, and she was ever so devout, but after a while people began to hear screams from the house, and noises like whips snapping on flesh, and then one day the house caught fire, and when they broke in to put out the fire, they found niggers in chains, and covered with cuts and running sores, and even flyblown . . ."

Peter appeared in the doorway, gnawing furiously at his nails, his eyes gleaming. He asked: "Was she crazy?"

On the question, his voice broke to a tone so nearly soprano that Dolly thought Lucy had spoken. "Love-crazy, if you ask me! She had a great handsome brute of a mulatto butler, and he was her coachman too, and—"

Then Enid cried from the doorway, brushing past Peter: "Dolly, you devil, you're making that up!" She and Dolly threw themselves into a happy embrace. "Shame on you, scaring my little Peter! Look at him; he's white as a sheet!"

Dolly had not seen Peter till now. She cried delightedly: "For goodness sake, is that Peter? Your little Peter, indeed! Why, he's as big as I am! Aren't you, Peter? Come here, Sugar, till I give you a great big kiss!"

She took a step toward him, but Peter scuttled sidewise and disappeared. They laughed together, and Dolly said: "I was telling Lucy about our haunted house. Madame Lalaurie used to live there, and she tortured her slaves. She chased one little girl with a whip till the child jumped to death off the roof."

"That house has been a school for colored girls," said Lucy.

"Oh, I'd forgotten, you do know Lieutenant Page, don't you? I've grown so fond of him. Yes, but the girls would never stay in the house overnight. I'm having a terrible time getting servants who'll stay." She laughed. "I thought Uncle Tony's Sapphira could help me, but she said for me to see her cook!"

"Did you see Sapphira?"

"No, I sent Papa and Captain Pew."

Enid tipped her head on one side. "Oh, is Captain Pew still dancing attendance?"

Dolly's quick glance touched Lucy. "Not at all, but he and Papa are partners."

"I suppose you've never looked at another man since poor Mr. Kenyon was killed." Enid's tone was one of exaggerated sympathy, and Dolly smiled.

"Well, one can't go around with one's eyes shut," she admitted, and she cried: "There, stop talking about me! Tell me all the news about everyone. Is Aunt Cinda as sharp-tongued as ever? I suppose Mama lives with them, poor woman. Do you ever hear from her?"

"We were there all summer," Enid assured her. "Cinda's just the same. Everybody's fine. Poor Barbara had a little girl baby born dead last August."

"Heavens," Dolly protested. "She already has a litter, hasn't she? Isn't she Burr's wife?"

"Yes, she has three boys," Enid agreed. "But she wants a girl. Oh, and Vesta has a son, named Rollin, for his father. She married Rollin Lyle, you know."

"Poor Rollin! He was heartbroken when I wouldn't have him! Mercy, that seems so long ago."

Lucy rose with a swift motion, wishing to escape, but then at the sound of key in lock, and men's voices, she went quickly into the hall. "It's Papa," she said, over her shoulder. "Oh, and General Longstreet." They heard her say: "Mama and Dolly, Papa. General, did you know my cousin, Dolly Streean?"

Then she reappeared in the doorway, and the General and Trav followed her into the room. "But it's Dolly Kenyon, now, General," Dolly explained to Longstreet. "I was widowed in the fighting below Wilmington."

"But—still Mrs. Kenyon?" he protested in elaborate gallantry. "The fighting ended long enough ago."

She laughed in appreciation of the gallantry. "I've been waiting for the right chance," she assured him, her eyes suggesting that her waiting now was done.

Trav rang and bade Isaiah bring toddies. He turned to Longstreet. "General, I'll find those records you want to see." He went to his office, and Dolly said some laughing word to Longstreet, and Lucy asked him:

"General, I heard you say something to Papa as you came in about General Sheridan being so—stupid. You sounded mad."

The big man nodded grimly. "I was," he admitted. "Good and mad!"

"Why? What about?"

"We're moving General Johnston's body from New Orleans to Austin. I'm one of the honorary pallbearers; Dick Taylor, Beauregard, Hood, Bragg, Buckner, and I. Now Phil Sheridan says there'll be no bells tolled, no band music, no fanfare. As if for us to honor a hero could harm the North! The jackass believes in the iron hand, but without the velvet glove!" Trav came to the door of the office, a sheaf of papers in his hand, and Longstreet took them from him. "Thank you, Currain. I'll return them."

Isaiah came with toddies, and Dolly rose. "General, my carriage is outside. May I drop you at your home?"

He turned with a smile of pleasure. "Thank you, ma'am. I'll be the envy of the town."

Trav said: "Your toddy's here."

There was an instant's silence; then Dolly moved toward Enid with a rustle of petticoats. "It's been so fine to see you again, Aunt Enid!"

Enid laughed. "Stop it! Next time you call me 'Aunt' I'll box your ears. Come and see me tomorrow and we'll talk to Maria about some servants for you."

"I will. Goodby, Lucy. Say goodby to Peter for me. Goodby, Uncle Trav. General, are you coming?"

"Save my toddy till another day, Major," the General decided, and offered her his arm.

Enid went with them to open the door, but Lucy stayed with Trav, drew near him. "She really is beautiful, though, Papa," she said appeasingly.

"I suppose her life has taught her malice; she has been so often wounded, it pleases her to wound."

The door closed behind Dolly and the General, and Enid returned, humming with an exaggerated nonchalance as she came along the hall. "Well!" she exclaimed. "Wasn't that a surprise? I didn't have time to even get started asking her questions. What a lot she'll have to tell. And Trav, how wonderful to have her in New Orleans."

Trav said seriously: "Enid, I don't want you to see her, or Redford Streean, or Captain Pew."

Her brows rose in mock surprise. "Really? Of course, I've no desire to see Mr. Streean, but Captain Pew is charming. As for Dolly, we always were the very best of friends, and—I hope—always will be."

Trav hesitated. "I didn't mean to seem to give orders, Enid. I'm just making a request."

She said lightly: "Your tone was pitched rather on the master-and-servant key, it's true, but I didn't take you seriously."

"Streean is a scoundrel," he reminded her. "And Captain Pew is a rogue."

She laughed in derision. "Perhaps someday you'll tell him so? Streean is whatever you like, but Captain Pew's a gallant gentleman."

He ignored her words. "And Dolly has forfeited the right to be on terms with you and Lucy."

"Oh, fiddle! Dolly's a flirt, of course."

Lucy came near him. "It's all right, Papa!" She smiled up at him. "I don't like Dolly, or admire her, or anything; she's not going to do me any harm."

He met her eyes, looked again at Enid. "I can't be your jailer," he admitted, "and I can't control Dolly. But I can speak to Streean—and to Captain Pew."

Lucy wondered why Don had not told her that it was Dolly—Dolly, who thought he was real sweet—who had rented the Haunted House, but she tried not to let the thoughts disturb her, vowing she would not even ask him any questions. It was a fortnight since she had seen him. When the Congressional hearings ended, he had gone to Alabama and to Mississippi, on Bureau business.

The night he returned, Lucy had not known he was coming. When they finished supper, Peter and Enid had gone upstairs, and Trav to his office, and Lucy was reading in the sitting room when the bell rang. Isaiah came to answer it, and Lucy heard Don's voice and called: "Oh, it's Don, Papa." She went into the hall to meet him, went quickly toward him, and—first making sure Isaiah was gone—came into his arms, kissing him with happy whisperings.

Then Enid, somewhere above them, said in amused surprise: "Well!" Lucy looked up over Don's shoulder and saw her mother at the stair head, for a moment motionless, then descending toward them. Lucy linked her arm in Don's and waited, and Trav came into the hall behind them and spoke.

"Good evening, Lieutenant. Home again, are you?"

Enid laughed. "Very much at home, Travis! You should have seen them a moment ago!" Coming to the lowermost step, she took Page's hands and drew him toward her. "Welcome, Don!" And she leaned down to kiss him on the mouth, catching him with mouth open in astonished embarrassment. "And my little kitten!" She kissed Lucy too. "Aren't they darlings, Trav?"

Lucy wanted to cry, or to slap her, or something. Little kitten! Darlings! As if they were about two years old! Don, beside her, spoke soberly to Trav. "Major Currain, Miss Lucy and I have come to love each other."

Trav laughed, his arm around his daughter. "God bless you, I know it; knew it a long time." He extended his hand. "I'm in love with Lucy myself, Lieutenant; never expected to be so well pleased with the man who took her away from me."

Enid protested: "Oh, but Trav, it hasn't come to that, not yet." She took Don's arm, told him: "You and I are going to have to get acquainted all over again. Knowing you as a nice young man—even though a Yankee—was one thing, but having you as kissing kin is quite another!" She smiled up at him. "But I'm sure I'll like it!"

Lucy was red with anger hardly controlled, and when she spoke, there was ice in her tone. "I'm sorry you saw us, Mama. It was our secret; we wanted to keep it so, for a while."

"But not from us, surely!" Enid held fast Don's arm. "Don't be selfish, Honey! We'll share him, you and I."

Trav spoke hastily. "It's just that Mama needs a little time to get used to it, Lucy. She's surprised; that's all."

"Surprised?" Enid echoed the word. "Why, 'course I am! I never dreamed!"

Trav nodded. "See, Lucy?" He took her arm, feeling her wrath, leading her toward the drawing room. "We don't have to stand here in the hall. We can sit down."

Lucy submitted; he was right of course, but Mama had a way of spoiling things, making them seem—oh, nasty, or something. Kissing poor Don on the mouth that way! Lucy, remembering his astonishment, suddenly wanted to giggle.

In the drawing room Enid made Don sit beside her, held his hand. "I must get used to the idea," she reminded them all. She lifted his hand and shook it, in a tender, scolding fashion. "Why, I don't feel as if I knew you at all!" Her eyes put on that melting look Lucy had long since learned to recognize. "What will we do about these two, Trav? Lucy, you look so glum! You mustn't be mad because I like your beau! After all, you've taken my beau away from me! Trav thinks ever so much more of you than he does of me! But now it's my turn. I'm going to be so nice to Don that you'll be simply furious at me, much of the time."

With her many words she held them all for a while in silent misery, till Trav at last maneuvered her away upstairs. Lucy, when she and Don were at last alone, said wretchedly: "Oh, I didn't want it that way!" The bright delight was gone. "I feel as though we'd lost something we could never have again. Why should having other people know about us make it seem less sacred, or something?"

Don was wise enough to see that protest would only fix this mood beyond shaking. "I don't feel that, so much," he said. "But I did want them to leave us alone a while, so I'd have a chance to talk to you. That's the hardest part of being away from New Orleans; I haven't you to talk to, to talk things over with."

"Why do I hate Mama so, sometimes, do you suppose? I'm ashamed of myself, but I do. Here, sit here." Despite his protests, Lucy made him take the big chair that was her father's favorite.

"I always feel like a trespasser."

"No, I like having you in Papa's chair." She drew a hassock near and sat at his feet, pressing her cheek gratefully against his knee. "You do like to talk to me, don't you?"

"That's what I most look forward to, when I come back from these trips. I can talk to you better than I can to anyone else. I'm—gagged, when I'm away from you."

She sighed, relaxing and content. "I hate it when you're away." She remembered wondering because he had not told her about Dolly. That no longer mattered; yet smilingly she said: "My cousin Dolly thinks you're real sweet!"

"Eh? What?"

"She says she's grown very fond of you."

His hand on her shoulder moved to her chin, tipped her face up toward him. "Who, Lucy?"

"Who? Why, the pretty girl in the Haunted House!" His face was blank with surprise, and she realized he had not known she and Dolly were related, so of course that must be the reason he had not told her. Happiness stirred in her contentingly, and she said, looking up over her own eyebrows to meet his eyes as he bent above her: "She's my cousin, didn't you know? Why didn't you tell me you knew her? Afraid I'd be jealous?" Suddenly she sat upright. "Perhaps I should be!" Her eyes were dancing, but he asked gravely:

"Is she really your cousin?"

"M-hm! Why?"

"Have you been—together much? I mean, do you see lots of each other?"

"Heavens, no!" She laughed. "She called on Mama the other day, and Papa was furious!" She saw relief in his eyes. "Didn't you really know they were our kin? Mr. Streean married my Aunt Tilda." And in amused conjecture: "I know! You thought you shouldn't mention such low characters to me!"

"No, I just didn't know you were cousins. There was no reason she should tell me; she didn't know I knew you."

"Mr. Streean's our family skeleton," she explained. "He made money speculating, during the War. And Captain Pew—"

"Is he kin, too?"

"Oh no. No, she was married to Bruce Kenyon—"

"I know she's Mrs. Kenyon."

"Yes. Mr. Kenyon's dead, but she ran away with Captain Pew. He was a blockade runner. Captain Pew, I mean. What are they doing here?"

"I haven't seen them lately; just helped them get settled, get furniture in. That house is a regular palace, black and white marble floors in the entry, and the walls and ceilings all decorated with plaster figures; huge glass chandeliers, black marble fireplaces, brocaded furniture, fine tapestries. They practically built it over, inside; the second floor. And new furniture. Most of that they bought at auction. Many of the old New Orleans families are selling their possessions now, living on the proceeds."

"I know. We bought lots of things, ourselves, when we first came." And she said, mischief in her eyes: "Don, take me to call there sometime." And seeing his hesitation: "I mean after we're married. Promise?"

"It's no place for you," he said gravely.

"Oh, Honey, you're sweet!" She caught him close. "Protecting me against the wicked world! Don, won't we have fun? Will we live in New Orleans after we're married?"

"I thought you didn't want to live in the South."

"I don't," she admitted. "But perhaps I'll change. When will the Committee make its report?"

"Soon now, probably."

"What will they say?"

"Well, I'm afraid they'll say the riot was a massacre, planned by the police and carried out by the police and citizens. They'll say the Convention was a peaceful, legal gathering of law-abiding men, and that the policemen—and others—set upon them and murdered them."

"Don, that's all true!"

He shook his head. "Nothing's ever all true, Lucy."

"What will Congress do about it?"

He hesitated. "Well, the Radicals in Congress have argued right along that the whole South is conquered territory, that it ought to be under military government. This gives them an excuse to order that." Lucy shivered. "Cold?" he asked. "It's late; time I should go."

"I'm not cold, no. Just—scared, nervous! I don't know what! Don, I wish you could take me away, to Maine or somewhere. It's going to be awful, here!"

"I don't know," he admitted, and he smiled. "Of course, you'll be under military government. I've been in the army a long time now, under military government. It's a relaxed life. You're given orders and you obey them; you never have to decide what you'll do." He laughed. "I don't mean that some general or other will be telling you what to do!"

She laughed with him. "I'd like to see one try it!"

"Of course," he reminded her, in sober tones, "after we're married, you'll be under military government by me!"

She came swiftly to her feet, came to attention, gave him a smart salute. "Yes sir, General! Very well, General! Yes sir!" So they were happy together, till he said good night.

When a few days later the Committee's report was published, she found that his forecast was accurate. One phrase stayed in her mind. Having recommended "a provisional government established and maintained by military power," the majority report added:

> The imperative necessity of such legislation, to the end that Louisiana shall be within the control of loyal men, and not subject to the rule of the same rebel leaders, military and civil, who conducted the war against the government during the rebellion, is fully demonstrated by the facts in proof before the Committee.

She echoed that phrase, "the facts in proof," and nodded, assenting; there was no denying those deadly facts. Her father, her lover, Mr. Fiddler, her brother, each had been a witness to them, to cruel, needless, planned and deliberate murders; to the facts in proof that could not be denied.

One morning in mid-February, arriving at the mill a few minutes earlier than usual, Mr. Fiddler saw among the Negroes squatting in the morning sun while they waited till time to go to work a scarred and battered countenance somehow familiar. He stopped, and the Negro looked up at him and grinned—there was a gap in that white-toothed grin where three teeth were gone—and Fiddler said questioningly: "Mose? You're Mose, aren't you?"

"Yas suh! Mose Mooney."

"You look as if the paterrollers had caught you."

Mose chuckled. "Wuss'n dat! De riot cotched me."

"Way last July?"

"Yas suh."

Mr. Fiddler stared at him, frowning and puzzled. One of the man's eyes was half closed by scar tissue, and the eyebrow seemed to have been spattered by a blow. A thin, crooked scar, a knife cut, ran from cheekbone to chin. Mose's nose had been pushed to one side and had stayed that way, and someone had sliced away each of his ears. Mr. Fiddler, groping for an almost forgotten memory, said: "They hurt you bad, didn't they?"

"Yas suh."

"Didn't you used to work here?"

"Yas suh, Bob and me come to work 'bout de same time."

"Where've you been since the riot?"

"My mammy kep' me home. Ah felt mighty low a long time." The whistle had blown, the other Negroes were gone to their tasks, but Fiddler kept Mose. "Ah had to let de skin ketch, whah Ah uz cut. Heah on mah eye, hit kind o' mawtified for a while. An' mah laig din't knit real good."

"Was it broken?"

"Kind of, yas suh."

"Did you have a doctor?"

"Ah uz in de hawspital fust off, two days. But Ah uz skeered day'd whop me some moah, so soon's Ah c'd crawl, Ah skun along home."

Then Mr. Fiddler remembered what it was he had forgotten. "You were in the wagon where I put Bob!"

"Yas suh."

"Why didn't you speak to me?"

" 'Bout den, Ah uz layin' mighty low."

"Bob was alive when I put him in the wagon."

"Mebbe so." Mose turned to limp away. "Mebbe so," he repeated, his tone blank.

"Hold on!" Mr. Fiddler came beside him. "Bob was alive. He had a scalp wound, and a bullet through the body, but he was alive." Mose edged off. "Wait a minute! You hear what I'm telling you?"

"Yas suh."

"Someone shot him after that, after I left him in the wagon. Stuck the pistol right into his ear."

"Ah dunno."

"Don't get the idea I killed him!"

"Naw suh! Ah knows better."

Mose walked away, and this time Mr. Fiddler let him go; but what did Mose mean by his last word? "Ah knows better." Had he seen the man who killed Bob? Fiddler took one step after Mose, to ask the question; but then he stopped. If the truth were what he feared, he did not wish to know it; he hoped no one would ever know. For if that truth became known, not Peter but Trav would be the heaviest sufferer, and to protect Trav against loss or grief or pain was the high hope of Mr. Fiddler's loyal heart.

Trav spent all that day at the mill. For months now they had been trying to devise a way to clean the lint off the seeds, so that the crushed seeds would not absorb so much oil. Elon Villard, upon whom they called more and more frequently, had built an experimental linter like a refinement of the cotton gin, and he was making final adjustments and readjustments. Trav watched him at work, offering an occasional suggestion, and Mr. Cist spent as much time with them as his other duties permitted.

Once when he returned after an absence, Trav remarked that Captain Blackford would be here for a few days near the end of the month.

"And I hope we'll have this ready to show him," he added. "We will, too, once we get the brushes so they'll keep the teeth of the saws clean of lint. I wonder how much lint we'll get."

Young Villard looked up over his shoulder. "If we can make this really work," he predicted, "we'll get fifty pounds of lint off every ton of seed."

"I'll settle for half that." Trav laughed and he added thoughtfully: "I think we'll have a pretty good mill here, before we're through, but I'd like to live long enough to see the factories they'll build a hundred years from now." His eye met Mr. Cist's, and they smiled together. They had already decided the mill must be enlarged, probably next year. "Well," Trav reflected, "we'll blaze the trail for them, anyway."

Trav and Mr. Cist and Elon were all that day absorbed in the work on the new linter, but Mr. Fiddler had Mose on his mind, and eventually he decided that any certainty would be better than this uncertainty. He bade Mose wait after shutdown, and when Trav and the others were gone, he called the Negro into the office.

"I want to get your name on the books," he explained, leaning over an open ledger, and then in a casual tone: "Did you see who killed Bob?" With the words his eyes swung up and hit Mose like a blow.

The Negro, startled, said: "Yas suh!"

"Know who it was?" A deadly thrust in his tone.

"Yas suh! No suh! Mebbe so, Mistuh Fiddluh, suh." Then, watching Fiddler's countenance, guessing what Mr. Fiddler wanted him to say: "No suh, Ah dunno's I does."

Fiddler nodded, sure now that Peter had killed Bob, and that Mose knew it. "You told anybody but me?"

"Jes' only mah mammy an' mah pappy."

"What did they say?"

Mose grinned with embarrassment. "Dey say I talk too much wif my mouf."

"Not going to tell anyone else, are you?" Mr. Fiddler's tone was treacherously mild.

"Naw suh."

"Nobody's going to bother you till you do." Fiddler closed the ledger. "Go on, get out of here."

He watched Mose hitch hastily away. Probably everything would be all right. Mose was scared enough to mind his tongue. No white man would come asking him questions, anyway, and if he did babble to his friends, there was no harm in that. Nigras did not matter.

That day Trav, on his way home from the mill, stopped to see Streean and Captain Pew. He had hoped to encounter one or both of them at the St. Charles, or at the St. Louis, but since chance refused to bring him an opportunity, he made his own.

When he rang the bell of the Haunted House, Dolly was sitting with Captain Pew and her father in the innermost of the three second-floor drawing rooms. The day was raw and cold, so the carved sliding doors were almost closed, and a huge oak log burned on the hearth. Dolly sat facing the fire across a long marble-topped table with carved walnut legs, and as she sat she rolled across the table top a pair of dice, watching the spots as they fell.

Streean asked resentfully: "Do you have to keep rattling those damned things?"

"Why, Papa, such language! Matter of fact, you'll hear a lot of these damned things from now on. Dice will be our *specialité de la maison!*"

"You'll find gentlemen prefer a gentlemen's game!"

"In New Orleans? Nonsense! Till a dozen years ago, there was a Rue des Craps no more than a mile from here." She laughed lightly. "Old Monsieur de Marigny had a sense of the fitness of things. From Rue des Craps it was only a step to Rue d'Amour, and from the street of love only another step to Rue des Bons Enfants."

"Oh, talk English!" Streean sprawled in his chair, puffing uncomfortably. He had put on weight in the last year, so that he breathed more easily standing up than sitting down. "I get sick of your airs."

She ignored his protests. "And Monsieur loved the little dice. He taught New Orleans the game—to his sorrow. The Frenchman's game, the game of Johnny Crapaud, so what shall it be called but craps?" Streean made a snarling sound, and Captain Pew looked at him with a quiet eye, and Dolly said: "You know, Papa, sometimes I do not like you very much."

He grunted, sat up in his chair. "Well, now, how shall we open for business?" he challenged. "It's time to decide. The rooms are ready, the cellar is stocked, dealers and waiters engaged. I vote for a grand opening ball."

Dolly shook her head, then harked to the sound of the doorbell. "No, Papa, a ball's nonsense! Where would you find ladies?"

Roderick opened the sliding doors. He was an enormous Negro, well over six feet and lean and strong. Captain Pew had found him acting as major-domo in a handsome establishment on Basin Street.

"Major Currain," he announced. "To see Mr. Streean, or Captain Pew, or both."

Dolly cried: "Oh, Uncle Trav! How sweet of him! Roderick, bring him up here."

The butler departed, and Captain Pew said mildly: "He asked for us, Miss Dolly; not for you."

"Nonsense! He meant us all, of course!"

"Dolly, go to your room," said Captain Pew, and when she hesitated: "Quick! To your room." His voice did not rise, but without a word, Dolly obeyed, slipping quietly away.

Roderick reappeared. "Major Currain," he said.

Captain Pew rose, bowed. "Major, your servant."

"Gentlemen!" Trav returned the bow, and Streean, still seated, said casually: "Hullo, Trav!"

"Will you sit down, Major?" Captain Pew suggested. "A little refreshment?"

Trav chose a chair. "Nothing, thank you. I will explain my errand. We are all to be, at least for a while, residents of New Orleans. It seemed to me wise to discuss that fact, and to consider how we might avoid possible mutual embarrassments."

Streean asked in a jeering tone: "What's the matter, Trav? Afraid someone will find out we're . . ."

But under Trav's steady eye, his voice died to a mumble; he grunted something and was still. Trav looked from him to Captain Pew.

"I do not see why there need be any ill feeling in this matter." He spoke almost without expression. "Certainly I mean no reflection on anyone. If either or both of you requested me not to come again to your home, I should not feel you meant it as a reflection on me. We all like to choose our intimates. You and I, gentlemen, live in different worlds. I came to suggest that we—and our households—continue to do so."

There was, when he finished, a litle silence; then Streean stumbled, red-faced and puffing, to his feet: "Why, sir, you—"

Trav's voice cut sharply into his. "Streean, I will hold you responsible for any word you speak."

"You? Hold me? Why, I'll—"

He hesitated, looking at Pew, waiting to be interrupted, and Captain Pew drawled: "Now, now, Redford. Mind that temper of yours. Or in plain words, don't always be an ass." He glanced at Trav. "Major Currain has come here today to face a situation we all recognize. It is a situation which could be gravely embarrassing to any of us not too thick-skinned." He caught Streean's eye, spoke lightly. "You're a scoundrel, Streean, and some fair criticism could be made of me. As for Dolly, though she has my complete devotion, I would not want her

to be on terms of intimacy with my daughter. If I had a daughter."
He turned back to Trav. "I will undertake that none of us intrude
upon you, Mr. Currain."

Streean protested: "Don't speak for me!"

Captain Pew cocked his head on one side. "Why, Redford, I won't
even speak to you—unless you mind your manners."

Trav was already on his feet. "Thank you, Captain! And I will see
to it that none of my household intrudes upon you."

Captain Pew bowed. "Always your servant, Major. Allow me to
escort you to the door." They strolled away, ignoring Streean. Captain
Pew spoke critically of the weather; Trav thought sunny days were
coming. They parted with words of mutual esteem.

Captain and Mrs. Blackford arrived to find spring in full flood. They
stayed only a fortnight—Captain Blackford had business in Texas,
and then in Missouri, before returning to Lynchburg—but their days
were full ones. Trav and Captain Blackford spent most of the daylight
hours at the mill, where the new linter was under daily trial and
adjustment. Its results were as yet disappointingly small—they had not
succeeded in getting as much as twenty pounds of lint off a ton of seed
—but there was always the hope that some new amendment might
suddenly achieve perfection.

Young Villard shared in all their discussions. Captain Blackford liked
him at once. "Good man," he said to Trav, as the ferry one evening bore
them back across the river. "He has a mechanical aptitude that doesn't
come naturally to Southerners. Young Tom Buford—reminds me, he
sent particular messages to Lucy; don't let me forget to tell her—he's
developing the same thing. They speak well of him at the University."

"I think highly of Villard," Trav assented, and he added: "Not only
because he's a good mechanic, but because he came home from the War
—he was in the Washington Artillery—and started right in to earn a
living, to make a business for himself." And he told Captain Blackford
something of Elon's family. "He has a father and a sister. She's said
to be charming, but I haven't the pleasure of knowing her. Mr. Villard—" He smiled. "Well, he's one of those Southerners who decline
to be reconstructed. He had a big sugar plantation down the river, but
he refused to try to contract with his people. Instead, he moved into
their town house, and now he's selling the furniture out of that to
support himself and Miss Eleanor. His plantation has gone back to
wilderness, and he's on the way to being a beggar."

"Rotting in his cups?"

"I'm told he's a sparing drinker. No, I don't believe he has any
vices, except the inertia that became second nature to so many

planters." He chuckled. "Blackford, when the Yankees made these gentlemen go to work, they committed the unpardonable sin."

"There doesn't seem to be any inertia in young Villard."

"I expect what money he earns is all they have."

"How about the daughter? A good many Southern women have looked around for some gainful occupation."

"I know," Trav agreed. "My favorite niece, Vesta, Cinda's daughter, married Rollin Lyle, and she's working with her hands. She and Rollin are salvaging Great Oak, our old place down near Williamsburg. Of course the house is gone, but they're cleaning the fields, putting them under cultivation. Vesta does her share—and boasts of her callouses."

Blackford nodded. "And no one frowns. A woman can run a plantation, or a dairy, or plait straw hats, or keep bees, or raise flowers for sale and she's all right. But hire out, find a job, go to work for some man? Heaven forbid!" Trav smiled, and Captain Blackford said: "Mrs. Blackford keeps all my books for me. If I hired her, she'd be worth a good salary, but if I hired my friend's daughter, who is perhaps quite as competent as Mrs. Blackford, it would make a scandal. The South still thinks work is a disgrace." He grinned. "Particularly for women, and particularly if they get paid for it."

That evening, Captain Blackford remembered to deliver to Lucy his messages from Tom Buford. "He sent you his everlasting love, Lucy, and his eternal devotion."

Lucy laughed with pleasure. "Tom's really a darling boy. Give him my love, too."

"He's turning out a fine man. Some day you'll be proud of him."

"I know I will. I'm real proud of him right now."

While Captain Blackford and Trav spent their days at the mill, Enid and Lucy drove Mrs. Blackford everywhere about the city to admire the gardens just coming into early bloom. They took her to market, and with her they explored the old city, and Lucy pointed out the Haunted House and told its story. Mrs. Blackford was delighted, and Enid explained:

"That's where Mr. Streean lives, and Dolly, and Captain Pew. Streean's my brother-in-law, and Dolly's his daughter, with whom Captain Pew is infatuated; two skeletons in the haughty Currain closet! I'm forbidden even to call on them!" Malicious amusement made her smile. "And another Currain black sheep lives here in New Orleans too; Mr. Currain's brother, Tony. He has a bright mistress!"

Mrs. Blackford nodded politely. "There are no rules in New Orleans —or so I've always heard."

They dined with General and Mrs. Longstreet, and Longstreet told them General Sheridan was back from Washington. "I called on him today. Congress is going to divide the South into districts, abolish or ignore the state governments, put us under military rule."

"The bill hasn't yet been passed, has it?"

"The details aren't settled, but the decision is made. Louisiana and Texas will be the Fifth District, with Sheridan commanding."

Trav said soberly: "I doubt whether General Sheridan is qualified. He hesitates to make decisions, and then speaks or acts too boldly."

"Boldness is a good trait in a leader of cavalry," Blackford suggested.

"Yes, but even in war," Longstreet argued, "no harm was ever done by taking thought. I agree with the Major; Sheridan was an able commander, but sometimes he's a damned fool." He added: "But whatever his qualities, he'll be for a while our high command."

Captain Blackford asked: "Did he have any information about the impeachment proposal?"

"He says Ashley—that Ohio Congressman who introduced the original resolution—isn't taken seriously, not even by Thad Stevens. Those two Missouri Congressmen are a pair of jackasses, worse than Ashley. Ashley's charging Johnson with corruption was ridiculous. The President of the United States may have faults, but thievery isn't one of them."

"But Ashley's resolution passed," Trav reminded them. "A hundred and eight to thirty-nine."

"They'll keep it going all summer," Longstreet predicted. "Keep it hanging over the President's head, if only as a warning." He laughed. "But from all I hear, Andy Johnson is a hard man to scare."

4

THAT NIGHT while she and Trav prepared for bed, Enid said: "That was pleasant, Trav. We must have a party, too. After all, the Blackfords are our guests. Just an intimate group. I know they'd enjoy the Judge Morgans."

Trav agreed, and they began to plan. "Lucy'll want Sarah and Miriam," he reminded her. "And Jimmy's here." After his wife's death last fall, Jimmy Morgan had returned to New Orleans, a long siege of yellow fever delaying him in New York on the way.

"Oh, we can't make it a children's party, Trav! You'll be wanting Peter next, and his friends."

"Hardly Peter," he smiled. "Don, though, if he gets back from Baton Rouge." Bureau business had taken Don upriver.

"But Heavens," Enid protested. "That's seven, and the Blackfords and us is eleven. We'll have a mob!"

"And Mr. Cist," he reminded her. "After all, we met him at the Blackfords'. We can't leave him out."

Enid surrendered. "Oh, we might as well have everyone! What fun! And the Longstreets make fourteen!"

"Young Elon Villard?" Trav suggested. "He and Blackford liked each other, and I like him, too."

"We can't very well ask him and not his sister."

"And his father? The old gentleman might be pleased."

"How many is that?" Enid asked. "I've lost count! Wait till I make a list." She crossed to her desk—Trav was already in bed, lying at ease —and found paper and pen and began to write, talking to herself as she did so, pairing the names. "Judge and Mrs. Morgan; Jimmy and Sarah; Miriam and—oh, Don, of course."

"What about Lucy?"

"Oh, she can't monopolize Don! Besides, she'll have young Villard. What's his name? Leon?"

"Elon."

"Elon and Lucy." She wrote the names. "Captain and Mrs. Black-ford; General and Mrs. Longstreet. That's twelve, and us is fourteen. Who else did we say? Oh, Mr. Villard and Miss Villard. Sixteen. But I counted seventeen. Who have I left out?"

After a moment he remembered. "Mr. Cist."

"Seventeen! But an odd man!"

"Maybe Don won't get back."

"It will be perfect if he doesn't!" She rose and, list in hand, came to sit on the side of the bed, checking off the names, and he watched her in a warm content, thinking how beautiful she was, excited by these happy plans.

The night of the dinner, Jimmy Morgan had to tell them his adventures. The boy's twenty-one years had been crowded: midshipman at fourteen, Annapolis, service on a Confederate cruiser, back to Richmond in time to escort Mrs. Davis on her flight, guarding the last Confederate gold, married and then widowed, stricken with yellow fever in a New York hotel while the *Evening Star* in which he had taken passage for New Orleans sailed without him and was lost with all on board.

"I must have cat blood in me," he said, laughing. "I can count the *Evening Star* and the yellow fever and five others out of my nine lives that I've used up already."

Now he was to join two cousins-by-marriage in raising cotton on the Hope Estate, four miles below Baton Rouge. "I all but grew up there," he remembered. "Colonel Hicky was a grand host, the most hospitable gentleman in the South. I've seen more than thirty people at his dinner table—and we were not just there for dinner; we were there a-visiting! One lady paid the Colonel and Mrs. Hicky a call that lasted fifteen years, and there was an elderly gentleman, a guest in the house when I was a boy, who had begun his visit there while still a young man!"

His tongue ran merrily, and the older people were content to listen, while Jimmy's sisters continually interjected memories of their own, and young Elon Villard and Miss Eleanor entered in. Eleanor had a gay, laughing way that matched Jimmy's. Sometimes these young people all talked at once, sometimes one or two or three. Trav thought with a secret smile that Jimmy talked all the time; and his sister Sarah was almost as vocal as he. Jimmy and Sarah together began to describe the lively jollity of the sugar-making season at Colonel Hicky's plantation, and Elon Villard and Eleanor recalled equally amusing memories of their own place down the river. Listening, Trav could visualize those days scented with the sweet smell of syrup cooking, nights lively with the strains of music and the whisper of dancing feet and of romping games to the tune of happy laughter. He thought the corn-huskings and the hog-killings at Chimneys, though they had been jolly enough, were dull, utilitarian occasions compared to such festivities as these; it was as though the sweetness of the sugar set the key for all.

Looking along the table, he saw Enid listening as eagerly as Lucy, and he thought she seemed tonight as young as Lucy. Lucy, though she laughed as readily as the others, was quiet, for Don had not returned from Baton Rouge. Even while she laughed, her eyes often swung toward the door, as though still hoping he might appear. Trav thought the gaiety of the others had valor in it. Jimmy Morgan's wife had died only a few months ago, and before that, he and his sisters could mourn three brothers, and Elon Villard and Eleanor could if they chose grieve for the fine life which had been theirs and which now was forever gone, their mother dead, their father vanquished and spiritless.

Yet there was now no sadness in their youthful eyes. How quickly, in youth, the deepest scars were healed. Was not this in fact a test, by which a person's age might most accurately be measured; his ability to forget grievous hurts, and to laugh again? By that test, Jimmy and his sisters, and Elon and Eleanor were certainly the youngest here. Enid, and Mrs. Blackford, and little Mrs. Longstreet, Captain Blackford and the General, they were on the surface almost as carefree as children. Mr. Cist wore that hopeful smile which is the last resort of a stranger in a group where the others are old friends, and talk together of things familiar to them alone, yet he seemed to be having a good time.

But Mr. Villard, by that test of one's capacity for laughter, was certainly the oldest man in the room; so after dinner, doing his duty as a host, Trav drew the other into conversation. Thinking of young Morgan's description of the merry life of a sugar planter, he asked: "Is your plantation completely out of production?"

Villard looked at him with a weary scorn. "Sir," he said, "four years of neglect will ruin any sugar plantation."

"I know little or nothing about the culture," Trav said apologetically. "How do you begin?"

"You can make a start in three years," the other told him. "Seed cane, first, and from that you grow your plant cane. That's your first year. Next year, your sprouts are called rattoon; the third year comes your cane. It takes three years to start, and if you neglect it for a year, it begins to go. Neglect it for two years and it's gone."

"I suppose you lost your people?"

"When the Confederacy failed, I lost my slaves, and thus lost everything. Now we devour ourselves, my daughter and my son and I, selling our possessions. But when everything else is sold, I shall still have my revolver."

Trav thought Mr. Villard had a look of softness about him. It was not that he was fat, yet the flesh on his bones seemed to hang there, and his thin cheeks pouched along his jawbone. "I expect you found the life of a planter to your taste," he reflected, then realizing the implication, he added hastily: "It always contented me. Man belongs to the earth, the earth to man. There's nothing else so completely satisfying."

"It's the perfect life for a gentleman. His land, his people, his crops, his home, everything his eye touches belongs to him." Mr. Villard shrugged. "Now, gone!"

"Have you thought of selling your land?"

"It's worthless without slaves, but I would sell, yes, if I met a man fool enough to buy."

Trav tried to keep the conversation alive, but little by little he ran dry. He looked wistfully along the room. Captain Blackford and Mr. Cist and young Villard were together in eager discussion; no doubt they were talking about the mill, and Trav wished he could join them. Judge Morgan and General Longstreet were absorbed in some topic, Jimmy listening with silent attention, and Trav tried to catch the young man's eye, hoping for a rescue. These few minutes with Mr. Villard had left him physically tired as he might have been after hours of toil. The ladies were staying away a mighty long time.

When at last they returned, Lucy moved at once to her father's side, and he said in heavy jest: "Well, well; Mr. Villard and I were discussing sugar and here you are." Lucy dutifully laughed, and Elon Villard came to them, and Trav, smiling to assure Lucy that his word was not meant seriously, asked: "How'd you like me to turn planter again, Honey?"

"You'll never be happy till you do."

"Mr. Villard says his plantation is for sale."

Young Villard said eagerly: "Let me show it to you some day, sir. When labor can be found, it will make a fine property again."

Lucy laughed. "Oh, Papa's just dreaming, Mr. Villard. He's not serious."

Trav saw the abrupt disappointment in the young man's eyes, and to please him, he said: "All the same, I'd like to see the place some day. When the time is right, we'll do it. Fine."

When the last guests were gone, Trav and Captain Blackford settled themselves for a nightcap. Lucy and Mrs. Blackford and Enid went upstairs together, and Mrs. Blackford said good night, but Lucy stayed a while with her mother, relaxed on the long couch, while Enid prepared for bed. "I like Elon Villard," she said. "And his sister's nice. She and Jimmy enjoyed each other, too."

"Mr. Villard did his best to put a damper on things. I never saw such a sour old gloom!"

Lucy nodded. "He's pretty crotchety. But Mister Elon is fun. He told me about the carnival seasons they used to have here before the War." She spoke like one half asleep. "Gay, mad days, people in masks, dancing in the streets. Sort of wicked, but everyone having a good time: parades and costumes and masquerades, and big balls at the St. Louis hotel. They started by imitating the Mobile Cowbellions—"

Enid, brushing her hair, swung quickly around. "The what?"

"Cowbellions!" Lucy giggled. "They sound awful, don't they? They used to have parades in fancy dress; so two or three years before the War some young gentlemen here in New Orleans—Mister Elon was one of them—organized the Mystic Crew of Comus. They had a parade that was supposed to be characters out of *Paradise Lost*, devils, and tormented sinners and things. They had to stop during the War, but last year they had a little parade, just as a beginning, with four cars, all about the history of Comus, and this year it's going to be 'Triumphs of Epicurus'! It's all secret. I suppose it'll be cakes and pies and things. They have the parade, and then tableaux at the ball afterward." She added happily: "And he's invited me. Won't that be fun?"

"Like him, don't you?"

"Yes, he's nice."

Enid, watching Lucy in her mirror, said: "It certainly sounds like fun, but what will your Yankee say, if you take up with a new beau?"

Lucy laughed. "Heavens, Don won't mind! Of course, he may not be back. I'll write and tell him, but you'll see. He won't care a smidge!"

"Not very flattering, is it?"

"Oh, Don never does things just to be gallant."

"Dead sure, are you?" Enid asked, with a sidewise smile. "He's a handsome thing, you know, and I'm afraid he has a wandering eye, away all the time, seeing all the pretty little Yankee school-mistresses . . ."

Lucy laughed at her mother's folly, and to emphasize her unconcern she yawned behind her hand. "Well, it was a lovely party, Mama! Good night!" She kissed Enid on the cheek. "Sweet dreams."

Enid smiled wisely. "Good night, Honey! And don't worry about Don! Of course even a Yankee likes to flirt a little, but I'm sure he'll come back to you."

On the second of March, Congress passed over the President's veto the bill providing that the South should be organized into five military districts. Louisiana and Texas would form the Fifth District, General Sheridan commanding. After delegates had been elected by male citizens voting without distinction of race or color—Negroes would vote, but no white man who had been disfranchised for his part in the Rebellion would be allowed to go to the polls—the delegates in convention assembled would frame a constitution. When this constitution had been accepted by the people of the state, and approved by Congress, and when the State Legislature had adopted the Fourteenth Amendment, and when sufficient states had endorsed that amendment to bring it into effect—then the state would be granted representation in Congress. Until then, each state would remain under military rule.

The passage of the law had been predicted and foreseen, yet like the long-expected death of a loved one, it came as a heavy blow. In the rotunda of the St. Charles, Trav heard men swear that rather than submit they would die with weapons in their hands, that they would leave the country. Mr. Villard was the center of one group, and Trav drew near enough to hear him.

"Better yet, gentlemen," Mr. Villard cried, with an orator's high gesture. "We will ignore them! Let the rebound from their own foul deed cloak them with a mantle of iniquity! They may put sentries on our every street corner, and experiment upon us with every ingenious torture they can devise; their actions will only redound to the shame of those who commit them; they will hereafter wear the self-imposed stamp of eternal infamy upon their brow."

Murmurs of approval answered him, and Trav in secret amusement wondered how many of the listeners knew the difference between "rebound" and "redound." Southerners loved oratory, regardless of its content. Remembering that the dog which barks loudest is the least dangerous, he looked around to discover men who were silent, or who if they spoke at all spoke in whispers. He saw surprisingly few in this category, and before he went home he was satisfied that there would be no open resistance to the law.

At dinner, to Lucy's questions, he expressed this opinion, but Enid disagreed. "There may be no men ready to resist, but the women of the South will never submit! I certainly don't propose to have Northern soldiers in my home!"

Trav asked in a dry tone: "How about Don?"

"Oh, Don's not really a soldier; he's just a sort of guardian for the nigras."

After supper that night Don appeared. Lucy had gone upstairs, but Trav greeted the Lieutenant with a hearty liking. "Well, young fellow, we've missed you." And he called up the stairs: "Lucy! Lucy! Friend of yours down here."

They heard her cry: "Oh, Don! Darling! Down in a minute."

"Guess she didn't expect you," Trav remarked. Then Lucy came running down the stairs and into Don's arms. Trav waited a moment, then he coughed. "Well, you young people have a lot of catching up to do. I'll leave you to it."

They laughed and turned, and Lucy cried: "Now, Papa, sit down! We're all caught up." She colored and looked at Don. "At least, for now! And you know perfectly well you want to ask Don a lot of questions and things."

But Trav shook his head. "No, I don't know as I do." He chuckled. "The St. Charles rotunda was full, this evening when I stopped in, and everybody there knew everything there was to know. To hear them talk, anyway."

"I suppose it was bound to happen," Don admitted. "But it's a pity, all the same. And worse for the North than for the South."

"How's that?"

"When you do a person a wrong, it hurts you more than it does him."

Trav considered this. "Like turning the other cheek," he suggested. "In a backward sort of way."

They talked for a while together, but when Trav presently left them, Lucy sighed. "I love Papa, but he does make me mad, always seeing two sides of everything. Now let's talk about us." She had written Don that Elon would beau her to the Masque of Comus. "Mama thought you wouldn't like my going with him. Do you?" Looking up at him with loyal eyes. "Because I won't if you do. I mean, if you don't."

He laughed. "If I say 'yes,' do I mean 'yes' or do I mean 'no'? Anyway, I hope you have a fine time."

"Want to come? I expect he'd like to have you. He's very nice, really."

The Lieutenant shook his head. "Don't forget I'm a Yankee, Lucy. You're welcome in lots of places where if I appeared it would start another war."

"Don't be silly! Everyone likes you."

"All the same, Yankee soldiers are going to be pretty unpopular around New Orleans for a while."

She caught his ears and tugged his face toward hers, laughing into his eyes, pulling one ear and then the other so that his head turned this way, that way, saying through clenched teeth: "Not with me, my darling! Not with me!"

Don had only a few days in New Orleans before new orders once more took him out of town. He departed on a Monday, and Tuesday was Mardi Gras. Lucy and Eleanor Villard were members of a merry group which watched the parade from a gallery on Canal Street, then proceeded to the theatre for the tableaux and the dancing. The parade was a banquet of many courses, the first floats representing the Heralds of Appetite, absinthe and sherry and bitters; then oysters with Johannis-berger; then the Lords of the Ladle, the Knights of the Shell, the Rulers of the Toast, and float after float identified as Canard Grecque, Pâté des Oiseaux, Snipe au Diable. The Knight and Lady of the Green Crests presented a salad, the Knight and Lady of the White Crests offered coleslaw, artichokes, cauliflower, asparagus. There were floats representing jellies and puddings and desserts, fruits and nuts and con-fections, coffee and cigars and liqueurs. At the theatre afterward, the tableaux presented "Two Courses and a Dessert"; then audience and actors danced the night away. Lucy came home deliciously weary, to sleep the clock around.

In the rollicking gaiety of the carnival, New Orleans for a while forgot the Military Acts, but when the festival was over, every street corner became again a forum for hot debate, and Trav, going to and from the mill, heard fiery denunciations and loud threats and sarcastic taunts. If Louisiana desired to be restored to statehood, a prescribed program must be followed, but when any one proposed to take the first steps in that direction, violent protests silenced him.

The newspapers entered the debate. The *Times* urged prudence and deliberation, and an end to "rash and violent ideas and expressions, and crude and impracticable propositions." "There never was a time," said the editor, "when the passionate, the heedless, the demagogical class had greater need to hold their peace and defer to the wisdom of the calm, the sagacious and the thoughtful." And he invited such citizens—listing a score or so by name—to express through the columns of the *Times* their opinions, and to offer their advice. Among those he named were half a dozen Confederate Generals, Beauregard, Taylor, Hood, Hays, Buckner, and Longstreet.

That invitation appeared in the Sunday *Times*. In the fortnight since the law was passed, Trav's opinions had crystallized, and he laid the paper aside and went to his desk and sought to put his conviction into simple words. "The South cannot resist," he wrote, "and without repre-sentation in Congress, she cannot even effectively protest. But the law prescribes the first steps toward securing that indispensable representa-tion: therefore, those first steps should be taken!" That seemed to him a syllogism so flawless that it needed only to be stated to be accepted, and he wrote no more, sitting in long thought. When Lucy came to say it was time to start for church, he was so absorbed that he went reluctantly.

On the way home—Enid and Peter used the carriage to come and go, but Trav and Lucy, since the day was fine, preferred to walk—his thoughts still kept him silent, till Lucy said lightly: "I declare you're not very gallant, Papa. You're so quiet, I feel as though I were alone."

"I'm sorry, Honey. I've been trying to decide what the South ought to do about these new laws."

"Have you decided?"

He hesitated, then drew from his pocket the sheet of paper on which he had written those few lines. When she had read them, she nodded approval. "Why, of course! That's so simple anyone must see it!"

"I always distrust things that sound too simple!"

"Nonsense! Send it to the *Times!*"

"Saw the paper, did you?" She nodded and he said, mirth in his tones, "I wasn't invited."

"Oh, pooh! What if you weren't? Well then, make the General send it!"

He thought Longstreet would prefer to form his own opinions, but she was so insistent that after dinner they went together to call upon the General. They found him in the garden and alone. "Louisa had to go meet some demand or other from young James," he explained. "She'll be back soon." He held a letter in his hand, and when they were seated, he said: "This is from Uncle Gus. They've been celebrating their golden wedding." He glanced at the letter. "They set out to have old Doctor Pierce—he married them, fifty years ago—come on from Georgia and marry them again, just to be sure it took, but they decided they were all too old for such foolishness." He looked at Lucy with twinkling eyes. "You better hurry, Miss Lucy, or you'll be an old maid. She was only sixteen when she married Uncle Gus."

"Mama was only sixteen when she married Papa," Lucy agreed. "But I guess times have changed. Probably it's the War!" Her eyes were dancing.

"Well, we've blamed everything else on the War; why not older brides?" Longstreet asked Trav: "Seen the paper, Major?"

"I read it before church, yes."

"Regular—" the General began, and at the same time Lucy said: "Papa—" they both stopped, and he said: "Sorry, Miss Lucy," and she said: "No, go on," and he laughed.

"Well, we'll get nowhere this way! I started to say the editor's piece was a regular call to arms." He looked at Lucy with a quizzical eye. "Now it's your turn."

Lucy blushed. "I started to say that Papa wrote a letter to the editor, and he won't send it in, and I thought—" She checked herself. "But I expect you're going to write one your own self."

Longstreet turned to Trav. "May I read it, Currain?"

"It's short." Trav handed him the single sheet, and Longstreet read it once and again, then handed it back.

"It's short, yes," he agreed. "Possibly too short."

Lucy protested. "But it's true!"

The big man nodded. "True, yes; simple, and short, and true. But if a man asked you what to do in our situation today, and you just read your father's letter to him, he'd be disappointed. He'd say: 'Yes, I know, but—' and then he'd ask a lot of fool questions. The average man feels that to accept a simple solution to some problem that has bothered him is a confession of his own stupidity in failing to discover the solution for himself, so he refuses to listen to the simple truth." He hesitated. "Things are at a pretty pass, all over the South," he said in sober tones. "Crops were short last year, specially food crops. In some parts, people aren't merely hungry; they're starving! Not only that, but anywhere outside of the towns—and sometimes in them—bushwhackers are stealing, torturing, burning, killing . . ."

Trav said in surprise: "General, you sound like a Radical!"

Longstreet met his eyes. "It's not hearsay, Major. I'm stating facts. I was over in Alabama a fortnight since, and we have correspondents, planters all over the South."

"Papa, I know food's scarce," Lucy said. "Don told me they're issuing rations in Alabama, and not only to nigras; to white people, too."

"So something must be done." Longstreet spoke strongly. "We must re-establish an orderly system of government. You've stated it, Major."

Trav folded the letter he had written and put it in his pocket. "Have you shaped your views, General?"

"I think so; yes. We must bring an end to our troubles as soon as possible, and if we can only do so by accepting what Congress offers us, I'm for doing that!" He added: "Of course, the law is unconstitutional; but in a revolution, constitutions are forgotten or overthrown. Once we get our representatives into Congress—as you say there—our opinions will carry weight. Today, the state of Louisiana doesn't exist; but by accepting Congressional terms, we can bring it to life again." He rose, looking toward the house, and Lucy saw Mrs. Longstreet coming toward them. "I favor taking the prescribed steps," he concluded. "No matter how bitter the pill, I'll swallow it."

Then Mrs. Longstreet joined them, and asked for Enid, and told Lucy she had a letter from Garland who sent his particular regards, and they sat in casual talk a while. But when they rose to go, Lucy asked: "Will you write a letter to the *Times*, General?"

"Bless you, yes! The editor's invitation was a challenge, not to be refused."

She laughed, raising a small clenched fist, shaking it at him. "Well, make it a dandy, won't you?"

Longstreet's letter was published in Tuesday morning's paper. When Lucy came down to join Trav and Peter at the breakfast table, her father handed her the paper, open to the page. Standing beside him at the table, she read the letter through. After two or three paragraphs explaining why he wrote at all, Longstreet went on to say:

The striking feature, and the one that our people should keep in view, is that we are a conquered people. Recognizing this fact fairly and squarely, there is but one course left for wise men to pursue. Accept the terms that are offered us by the conquerors! . . . Nor is there any occasion for a feeling of humiliation. We have made an honest, and I hope that I may say, a creditable fight, but we have lost. Let us come forward then and accept the ends involved in the struggle.

Our people earnestly desire that the constitutional government shall be reestablished, and the only means to accomplish this is to comply with the requirements of the recent Congressional legislation. It is said by some that Congress will not receive us, even after we have complied with their conditions. But I can find no sufficient reason for entertaining this proposition for a moment. I cannot admit that the representative men of a great nation could make such a pledge in bad faith. Admitting, however, that there is such a mental reservation, can that be any excuse for us in failing to discharge our duty? Let us accept the terms as we are in duty bound to do, and if there is a lack of good faith, let it be upon the others.

I am, very respectfully, your most obedient servant
JAMES LONGSTREET

Lucy read to the end and laid the paper aside. "He just says the same thing you said, only he mixes it all up so no one can understand it. Yours was better. His won't persuade anyone."

"I'm afraid he may antagonize some folks."

"Why?"

"Because he says we're a conquered people."

"But we are!"

"I know. But a lot of these stay-at-home blatherskites who never went any nearer the War than presenting a flag to some militia company will say that by the Eternal, they weren't conquered!"

She looked again at the page in the *Times*. The headline above the letter read: "A Brave Old Soldier Speaks; Gen. James Longstreet on the Situation." Below, there were a few paragraphs of introduction, and some flattering phrases: "pleasure and gratification," "brave and honored," "promptitude and frankness," "prodigies of valor," "example he has set." The General was praised for saying anything, and for saying it promptly and frankly, and his War record was commended, but Lucy thought her father was right. The editor of the *Times* was not ready to join the General in calling the South "a conquered people."

"I see what you mean, Papa," she admitted, and gave him back the paper. "He was all right as long as he just said what you told him to say. But you ought to tell him what not to say, too!"

"It wouldn't do a bit of good," Trav assured her in a smiling tone. "The General is like a cat! The more you pull him one way, the more bent he is on going the other."

"It's ridiculous for a grown man to act that way!"

Trav smiled. "Grown man? Honey, men don't grow up! They stay boys." He chuckled. "When you see a man you're sure is grown up, leave him alone. He's either dead or dying."

When a few days later Lucy read in the *Times* a reference to "the Military Bill and its proposed supplement," she asked Trav what was meant. "Is there going to be a supplement?"

"It's the new bill Congress is passing," Trav explained. "The first law said that before the Southern states could send anyone to Congress—"

"I know; we had to let nigras vote, and hold a Convention, and all that, and instead of doing it, we've been arguing about whether we'd do it or not, when of course we have to! The War settled that!"

Trav, his head on one side, said: "Well, I'm not sure war ever really settles anything, especially where the South's concerned. What's that about a woman convinced against her will? The South's pretty feminine."

"Fiddlesticks! The South's stupid! Women aren't stupid! What is it about a woman convinced against her will?"

"I've forgotten exactly. She still—oh, she 'remains to be convinced still,' or something like that."

"Of course she does, if she's not really convinced in the first place."

"Well, that's what Congress is now trying to do," he told her. "Most of the Southern states have made no move to hold a Convention, so this new law directs the commanding general in each military district to go ahead and register the voters and hold an election and have a Constitutional convention, whether we like it or not." And he added: "They wouldn't trust us to let nigras vote, so they're putting the whole thing in the Army's hands. We're no longer citizens, Lucy; we're just subjects, now."

Saturday, at the calling hour, Enid told Isaiah to have Saul bring the carriage around, but when she directed him to drive her to the Haunted House on Royal Street—she proposed to call on Dolly— Saul first sought to evade the issue with many vain excuses, and at last flatly refused.

"It's Marste' Trav's say-so, ma'am," he told her. "He say Ah cain't do it. He gib me de orduhs a while back."

Lucy, in the garden, heard her mother's voice rise in shrill anger and came running to the garden gate. Enid berated Saul, she even threatened him with her ridiculous small parasol, while he stood patiently waiting out the storm. Lucy heard enough to understand how Saul had offended before Enid, as though she suddenly realized she was conspicuous, turned abruptly away down Prytania Street, her heels clicking angrily.

An hour or so later, she came home in a hired hackney, and cried out her rage to Lucy. "I've never been so insulted! And by niggers! Saul, my own servant, and then that impudent black brute!" And when she became coherent, she explained what had happened. She had taken a streetcar to Canal Street, hired the hackney, driven to the Haunted House and rung the bell.

"A perfectly enormous nigger opened the door," she told Lucy. "I gave my name and asked for Mrs. Kenyon, and he said she was not at home. I asked where she was, and he just repeated that she was not at home, so I knew he was lying! I'd have brushed right past him, but he stopped me, stepped in front of me, and when I tried again, Lucy, he put his hands on me!"

Words would only increase Enid's anger, but if she were given a chance to talk about it, the worst might be over before Trav came home; so Lucy listened, and murmured sympathy, and went with Enid to her room.

"That Saul! He'll never drive me anywhere again!" Enid said venomously. "No, nor stay in this house! I'll see to that when Trav comes home."

When Trav did come home, she met him with cold politeness. He was abstracted, thinking about a problem that had arisen at the mill, so he did not at once notice this; but when she came down to supper, he recognized her mood and asked: "What's wrong, Mama?"

"Nothing," she assured him. "Why should there be?"

"I know you're upset about something."

"Oh, I'm often upset! I try not to show it, of course, try to keep a smiling face; but it's hard to be treated like a prisoner!" And when, suspecting the truth, he looked at her sharply, she added: "And to be handled by niggers!"

"Who handled you?"

"Saul did, and—"

Lucy, joining them, heard this and interrupted: "Mama, that isn't so! Saul didn't touch you! I thought you were going to hit him with your parasol, but he didn't touch you!"

Enid looked at her with swimming eyes, wailing suddenly: "Oh, Lucy, you too . . ." She fled back upstairs. They heard her speak to Peter in the upper hall, and then go on to her room, and Peter came down to join them. Lucy thought he grew taller every day. He stopped on the lowest step to face them there.

"What's the matter with Mama?"

Trav looked at Lucy, and she realized he did not know Enid's grievance, so she told him Saul's refusal to drive Enid to the Haunted House. "And then she took a cab and went anyway, and the butler there wouldn't let her in."

Trav felt a new respect for Captain Pew. "I'll speak to her," he said, and went upstairs. Peter and Lucy looked at each other, each touched with terror as children must be when parents quarrel, and in sudden gladness that Peter was already so much a man, Lucy went to him and put her arm around him, wanting his comforting.

"I hate it when they're mad at each other," she said.

"He'd better leave her alone!" Peter spoke in a tone harsh and truculent, and Lucy drew away. He would always be on their mother's side.

Trav and Enid eventually reappeared, but during supper Enid spoke little or none, and Peter was as silent as she, Trav and Lucy laboring to keep alive a conversation. When they were done, Enid asked meekly: "Now, Trav, may I please go to my room?"

Trav reddened, and Lucy wanted to slap her. "If you want to, of course," said Trav, and without waiting to see what she did, he left the table and went across the hall into the sitting room.

Enid after a moment followed him, leaving Lucy and Peter still seated at the table. From the sitting room came Enid's question. "Trav, would you mind very much if I asked you to sleep in some other room tonight?"

If Trav answered in words, they did not hear him, but the silence had the sound of whispers, and Lucy and Peter stared at each other in a shared wretchedness. Then, abruptly, the doorbell rang, and Isaiah went through the hall, and Lucy heard Don's voice. Hurrying to meet him, she was careful not to look into the sitting room, but she cried out Don's name to make sure her father and mother knew he was here, and at once Enid came into the hall, radiant and smiling.

"Oh, Don. I'm glad you're back," she cried. "This child's been just pining for you." She slipped her arm through his, leading him into the sitting room, and Trav greeted him there. Behind them, Peter passed through the hall and went out, and Trav asked:

"Where's Peter gone, Enid? Do you know?"

"Heavens, Trav, I didn't question him. He's old enough to take care of himself. Don, tell us all about yourself. Where have you been, and what's the news?" Lucy watched her in a puzzled wonder. How could she change thus quickly, put on this easy charm?

Don answered her by speaking to Trav. "We had a dispatch this evening. Congress passed the new military act over the veto."

Trav nodded. "Of course. There'll be worse to come, if the suggestion in the *Times* today leads to anything. Did you see it?"

"I haven't had time to look at a paper."

"The editor proposes a meeting of the prominent men of the ten excluded states, and he says: 'These states have heretofore, in times that threatened their peace and assailed their homes, made common cause'. That sounds enough like fighting talk to make the North see red."

Enid rose, smiling. "Oh, if you're going to talk politics, I'll bid you good night. Coming, Trav?"

She was so completely her usual self that Lucy marveled. Trav said: "Yes, of course," in the tone of one reminded of something forgotten, and she took his arm and they departed amicably together.

Don rose to see them go, returned to Lucy's side, and she whispered: "Would you believe it, when you came they were having a terrible quarrel!"

"Married people's quarrels never go very deep."

"Do your father and mother quarrel? You've hardly told me anything about them, or your home, or anything."

"I could talk a long time and not tell you all of it."

"Tell me some of it."

"Well, where shall I begin? The house? The farm?"

"Oh no, just tell me about the people."

He nodded. "Why, there's just Ma and Pa there now," he said. "My brother Jonathan's married and lives in Fraternity, and my brother Horace clerks in a hotel in Augusta." There was suddenly a chuckle in his tone. "Ma think his wife is kind of wild. And my sister Emma is married to a runner for a store in Portland. They live in Belfast. His name's Pugh."

"What does he run?"

"Eh? Oh, a runner. I mean, he travels around to the country stores, selling them clothes wholesale. Oscar Pugh. They call him Oss for short."

"It's not much shorter," she murmured, snuggling her nose into his shoulder. "Have you lots of uncles and aunts?"

"Uncle Josh and Aunt Maisy live over in Albion, but the rest of them are scattered all over. Uncle Don—I'm named after him—he went to California in the gold rush times. He was home on a visit when I was, a year ago last January." She relaxed against his shoulder and he thought she might be asleep, but she asked:

"Did he dig lots of gold?"

"No, he turned storekeeper. He used to take me fishing when I was a boy, still writes me letters every so often. I was named after him."

"Go on."

"Well, that's about all there is to tell."

"M-hm!" She was still for so long he thought she must have gone to sleep, but at last she asked: "Have you nigra servants?"

He hugged her closer, chuckling. "Wake up, Honey! We're not talking about a plantation down here; we're talking about a little farm down in Maine."

"Well, you have to have servants, wherever you are."

He laughed in amused delight. "Ma's the best cook you ever saw."

Lucy, after a moment, sat up and looked at him. "Why, Don! Does she do the cooking?"

"Cooking, dishwashing, sweeping, everything." He was flushed and uncomfortable. "We don't live the way you do, Honey. Pa does the outside work—except that Ma helps some whenever she's needed—and Ma does the housework." He saw her eyes warm and tender with happiness, and he added, in the same words. "Except that Pa helps some whenever he's needed, inside, too."

"Oh, I'm going to love them," she declared. "And I'll—" But she checked her word. "Don't they get awfully tired?"

"Every day of their lives, 'course they do. Up at the crack of dawn, and asleep at dark." He laughed at her wondering astonishment. "It's good for you. Never was a Page yet that didn't live to be a hundred."

She caught his hands and gripped them hard. "Me, too," she promised. "I'll be a Page too. And we'll live a hundred years together."

"It won't be long enough," he said, and she reached up to draw his lips down to hers.

A letter from Brett announced that he and Cinda would presently arrive for an extended visit. One night a few days before they were expected, General and Mrs. Longstreet came to call. Enid had gone upstairs, and Lucy proposed to Mrs. Longstreet that they go up to her room.

"I think we'd better," Mrs. Longstreet smilingly agreed. "Jeems is in one of his rages, and at such times, his language . . ."

They turned toward the stairs. Trav had heard in the General's tone a timbre he recognized. Longstreet in ordinary conversation spoke quietly, but when his native combativeness was aroused, his voice, without being louder, acquired a resonance, so that like the voice of a great

singer in a small room, it might bruise the ear. This was its pitch now.
"Louisa was in a mind for sociability," he explained, "and I was restless. I saw Beauregard today. He wanted me to read a letter he's
written to the *Times*."

"I see. What's his opinion?"

"Damned if I know. He admits we were beaten, but he goes on to
say that the conditions imposed by our conquerors are harsh and
ungenerous!" Longstreet demanded, in an explosive violence: "Why in
Tophet do we have to start calling names? Why not just say: 'You
licked us! We'll do what we're told!' and go on and do it and hope
for the best?" After a moment he went on: "He says with nigras voting
we'll 'defeat our adversaries with their own weapon,' by teaching the
nigras to vote intelligently. That's more than we've ever taught ourselves to do!" He rumbled in his beard. "Beauregard's like General Lee.
He's for submission. If you arrest a man and he submits, that only
means that he doesn't resist; he goes limp and you have to drag him
to jail, and thus exhaust him and yourself. But damn it, Major, as
long as the South merely submits, it will be a dead weight which the
North must carry—and which must, in time, destroy our common
country! We wanted our way; the North said we couldn't have it, and
they've backed up their brags, trimmed our combs good and proper.
Well, let's try it their way for a while! Who knows, maybe we've been
wrong!"

Trav smiled. "Fighting words, General! Never tell a Southerner he's
been wrong!" The General made a harsh sound, and Trav said mildly:
"If we'd all stop talking and go to work, things would straighten out.
Laws won't hurt us—or help us."

"Laws never settled anything!" Longstreet agreed. "Nor does talk,
but some people never get enough of it! Right now, the New York
Herald's trying to organize a grand debate with Wade Hampton and
Henry Wise and me on one side, Ben Butler and General Schenck and
Senator Wilson of Massachusetts on the other." His voice shook with
sudden mirth. "What a cat fight that would be!"

Their talk ran on, exploring many byways, till they heard Lucy and
Mrs. Longstreet on the stair, and rose, and after a few minutes, the
General and Mrs. Longstreet said good night. "Thanks for listening,"
Longstreet told Trav. "I needed to blow off some steam on this
Beauregard folly."

The *Times* published General Beauregard's letter, but it was forgotten in the outburst of indignation when General Sheridan summarily
removed from office Attorney General Herron, Mayor Monroe, and
Judge Abell. He made no public statement of his reasons for doing so,
but since these men had either sought to suppress the Convention last
July, or had failed to prosecute the murderers, the reason was plain

enough. Brett and Cinda arrived to find popular resentment at a peak, and Brett shared Trav's opinion that, regardless of the guilt or innocence of the men involved, Sheridan had no right of removal. "If he can go that far, this is no longer a republic; it's a military despotism."

"If it is," Lucy urged, "New Orleans people brought it on themselves."

Trav said sternly: "Lucy, there are some oppressions which not even the worst crimes can justify."

Cinda took Lucy's part. "Don't talk nonsense, Trav! I'd put it the other way around. There are some crimes which can never be adequately punished."

When General and Mrs. Longstreet came to welcome Brett and Cinda, Longstreet had talked with Sheridan about his action. "I felt it was ill-considered," he admitted, "but he said he had given it a great deal of thought."

Trav nodded grimly. "Typical. He hesitated—and then acted in haste. He did not know what to do, and to conceal his own doubts, he did the wrong thing. The man's unfit for his post, General."

Longstreet said thoughtfully: "I can't agree, Major. Sheridan says Judge Abell for weeks before the riot encouraged the murderers, and promised them immunity—and subsequently kept the promise. He says Herron, instead of indicting the murderers, indicted the dead and wounded. And of course Sheridan says Monroe encouraged the police in the riot and massacre."

Lucy wished to cry out that these things were all true, but Trav insisted: "All the same, for the Army to remove from office an official elected by the people is plain tyranny."

Cinda drawled: "Oh, Trav, can't we forget the whole thing? I didn't come all the way down here to talk politics."

"You'll hear nothing else in this house," Enid warned her.

Cinda laughed. "Then we must just outtalk them, Enid; you and I. Do you see anything of Tony? I'd like to see him, while we're here."

"We'll go call," Enid suggested, with a sidelong glance at Trav, but Cinda said cheerfully: "Hardly! Under the circumstances! But may he not call here, Travis?" She laughed at his troubled frown. "Or shall I write him a *billet doux*, offer him an assignation elsewhere?"

"You know, Cinda," Brett suggested, "Trav has to live in the same city with this gentleman."

Cinda spoke in quick contrition. "I'm sorry, Trav. Forget I said anything."

"But don't you want to see Dolly, too?" Enid asked, and at Cinda's quick surprise she added: "Yes, and Redford Streean, and Captain Pew? They're all here in New Orleans now."

Cinda turned inquiringly to Trav, and after a moment he explained:

"Mr. Streean and Captain Pew have opened a gambling house on Royal Street, and I believe Dolly sometimes appears as a sort of hostess. They've attracted a considerable clientele, soldiers, politicians, adventurers from the North, even a few young Creole wastrels. It's a handsome establishment."

"You speak as though you'd been there!"

"I have," he said. And Enid's eyes widened in sudden understanding. He must have gone to request them to bar the door against her.

"Poor Dolly," Cinda murmured.

"She called on me," said Enid icily. "She's as lovely as ever, and she seemed sublimely happy. But I am not permitted to return the call."

"I should hope not!" Cinda agreed.

Enid, seeking an ally, spoke to Longstreet. "She took you home in her carriage, General. Didn't you find her charming?"

The General met her eyes. "I found myself remembering what she was like as a little girl."

"Little girl? You never knew her!"

"I met her in Richmond in eighteen sixty-one. She seemed to me then like a little girl. But she's older now."

After a moment, Trav said: "Cinda, I'll let Tony know you're here."

Before Cinda could reply, Brett spoke to Longstreet, turning the conversation. "General, I suppose you saw that General Lee recommends accepting these laws in good faith, going ahead to meet the conditions they impose?"

Cinda spoke in an exasperated tone. "There they go!" She asked Mrs. Longstreet: "Louisa, aren't you sick of politics? Every time I hear the word I want to spit!" And at the other's quick assenting smile, rising: "Come on, Enid, let's escape. Lucy, coming with us?"

So Trav and Brett and the General were left alone. "Yes, the General said, answering Brett's question. "Yes, I saw General Lee's letter. Every sensible man agrees with him." He turned to Trav. "Major, I'm writing another letter to the *Times;* so many people have asked me to expand my views—though why they should expect wisdom from a blunt old soldier is more than I can tell you!"

Trav smiled, understanding the General's pride. "But tempers are hotter than they were before these removals by Sheridan," he suggested. "Speak gently, or you'll give offense."

Longstreet nodded, and Brett said: "General, I saw a reprint of your letter in one of the New York papers. Was it well received here?"

Longstreet looked to Trav to reply, and Trav said: "By most people, yes. No one could disagree with it, though some objected to being called a conquered people."

"I suppose so," Brett agreed, but Longstreet said positively:

"Until the South accepts that fact, there's no hope for her! I'm restating my position in even stronger terms in the letter I'm now preparing."

There was heat in his tones, and Brett caught Trav's warning eye and spoke of other things. Trav rang for Isaiah to bring the decanter and glasses, and the talk ranged safer fields till the evening was done.

Sunday morning, Trav found the General's letter in the *Times*. He was alone at the breakfast table, the others not yet down. After two or three paragraphs, he came to a passage which made him frown. Longstreet had written:

> The political questions of the War should have been buried upon the fields that marked their end. Our most cherished objects on this earth, blood of our blood, life of our life, if not duly deposited as ordained by an All-wise Providence, become offensive. So must it be with this dead matter. If the last funeral rites of the Southern Confederacy have not been performed, let us with due solemnity proceed to the discharge of that painful duty.

Trav shook his head in a strong distaste. Here was "bluntness of a soldier" with a vengeance, this suggestion that the unburied corpse of the Confederacy had begun to offend the nostrils. The General had allowed his pen to run away with him, and Trav felt a profound repulsion and regret.

He read on. The General saw no virtue in mere submission, in "masterly inactivity." He thought the chief hindrance to the work of reconstruction was the conviction of Southern people, not only that they could do no wrong, but that the North could do no right. But it was too late to discuss right and wrong, since what rights the South once possessed were gone. "The only available law is martial law, and the only right, power," the General said, and he concluded:

> Our duty resolves itself into two very simple propositions, viz: to relieve ourselves from our present embarrassments by returning to our allegiance in good faith . . . or to seek protection under some foreign government. Those who determine to remain should speed the work of reconstruction, and put our people in condition to make their own laws and to choose their own officers for their execution.

Trav could discover in the letter nothing that had not been said before, nothing that needed saying. The General had succeeded only in emitting a confusing cloud of words. He had enclosed in his letter to the *Times* another from Judge John A. Campbell, the leader of the

Southern bar since long before the War. Judge Campbell began his letter by saying: "My opinion as to the proper course to be adopted by the citizens of the Southern states coincides with yours." But there was more. Trav fixed upon one sentence which seemed to him to compass the whole.

> My counsel therefore is that the citizens of the state, on whom the burdens and calamities of this time must fall, shall exercise every right, exercise every faculty, and employ every power that these military bills allow of, with undaunted courage, unwearied in duty, and undisturbed tranquillity of soul, to terminate the existing conditions.

Lucy joined Trav, and he gave her the *Times* without comment. While she was still reading the General's letter, Brett appeared, and when she finished, she handed the paper to him. As Trav had made no comment to her, so she made no comment now, and Brett, seeing their grave faces, asked: "Bad, is it?"

"Wait till you've read it," Trav suggested.

They were silent till he had done and laid the paper down. Then he looked inquiringly at Lucy. "Well?" he prompted.

"I don't think people will like that part about the Confederacy having gone too long unburied!" she suggested, and Trav said regretfully: "But I expect he was rather proud of it."

Brett recaptured the paper to scan the letter again, and he snorted with sudden mirth. "Sorry! I hadn't fully appreciated that paragraph till Lucy spoke of it. Cousin Jeems is badly out of his depth."

Trav nodded. "I hope he's had his fill of writing letters," he said, and they agreed.

5

TRAV HAD PROMISED to tell Tony that Cinda was in town, but he dreaded going to his brother's house to do so. Chance favored him. He and Brett, on the way home from the mill, stepped into the rotunda of the St. Charles and came face to face with Tony and Redford Streean, approaching the door and about to depart.

Brett, first to see them, said quietly: "Hullo, see here!" He greeted Tony, and they shook hands, and Brett said, but without offering his hand: "Ah, Streean!" Trav spoke to Tony, but not to Streean, and Tony said:

"Happy to see you, Brett. Cinda with you?"

"Yes, she's here." Brett added, not looking at Streean, who, though he had deserted her, was Tilda's husband: "Tilda stayed at the Plains."

Streean, as though going on guard, stepped warily back a pace or two, but Brett ignored him. Trav was puzzled by the pendulous soft fat which the man wore like a heavy garment. Streean was not merely obese; surely some disease had laid its hold upon him.

"I'd like to call on Cinda," said Tony, and met Trav's eyes. "That is, Trav, if you permit?"

Trav nodded. "Certainly."

"Tony, you're looking well," said Brett.

"We live a retired life," There was a sardonic note in Tony's voice. "Particularly in recent months, though now times are changing."

"Politics?" Brett asked. "Buck Owen told me at Appomattox that you were taking a hand in local politics."

"Yes," Tony assented. "I'm what is called a Radical, or, as some say, a black Republican." His eyes touched Trav with a hint of mockery. "That scandalizes you both, no doubt, but I like to be on the winning side." And he added: "I had the pleasure of consulting this morning with General Sheridan, of urging him to put a nigger on his registration boards. He's directing the boards to exclude from registration any applicants about whose eligibility there is the slightest doubt."

Trav watched him with a thoughtful eye. The registration boards had begun to list all qualified voters, and it was taken for granted that every Negro would be listed, that most white men would be excluded.

"You're one of the backers of the Radical newspaper here, aren't you?" Brett asked, and at Tony's nod, he said gently: "I shall subscribe, learn your views." He stepped aside to clear the way. "I believe you were just leaving."

Tony hesitated, but there was dismissal in Brett's tone, and he swung toward the door. Brett's eyes touched Streean and the fat man moved to follow Tony, but some instinct of shamed defiance made him pause, facing Brett, and speak.

"Give Tilda my love," he said. "I'll drop by, some—"

Brett slapped him, slapped his cheek so hard that Streean staggered sidewise. The rotunda was as usual well filled, and the sound caught every ear, and every eye swung toward them. Streean turned red and white with rage and fear; he hesitated, then scuttled hastily away. Brett brushed his hand against his side as though it were soiled. "I've wanted to do that for a long time," he said, cheerfully content, and Trav nodded.

"I'll drink to your very good health," he said, and caught a waiter's eye.

During this visit, Brett and Trav spent much of their time at the mill. The linter, under Elon's watchful care, was increasingly successful. "I think we've got the kinks out of the whole process now," Trav told Brett. "From now on it's just a question of improving our methods."

"Or of expanding," Brett suggested. "How about doubling your plant?" He smiled. "Or quadrupling it? I can provide—or raise among my friends—as much capital as you require."

Trav considered. "To increase production will increase the market," he reflected. "No doubt of that. But we've a lot of problems that ought first to be solved."

Brett smiled. "You solved this one, this new linter."

"What do you think of our letting the other mills study it? Copy it?"

"That sounds to me more like the idea of a generous gentleman than of a good businessman." Brett chuckled in long affection. "But go ahead. I'm for you."

Brett enjoyed these days at the mill, and the daily crossings on the ferry were a continual delight. "It's the grandest harbor in the world," he commented. "Twenty-five or thirty miles of shoreline, and deep water so that an ocean-going vessel can tie up to the bank anywhere, and a river half a mile wide, wide enough so that all the fleets in the world can pass to and fro, and deep enough for anchorage."

"Not in this current," Trav suggested. The river was in flood, and had been so for weeks, with breaks in the levee here and there, and inundated areas, and people driven from their homes.

Brett ignored him. "Your danger—I mean the danger to the port— is that you'll rely on the river. New Orleans is the nearest shipping point for a full half of the United States, but your river alone won't bring the trade this way." He smiled. "I'm a railroad man, so maybe I'm prejudiced; but you need railroads, pouring freight into New Orleans from all directions." He added: "I had a talk with Casey, the other day; you know, Grant's brother-in-law. He's planning a line through Houston to the Pacific, counts on getting a big grant from the incoming legislature, hopes to use Longstreet's name, and Grant's. Such a line would bring Texas to your door. If it isn't built, Texas will ship through St. Louis to the east coast, or she'll build her own ports. Of course, Casey sees in it only a chance to eat at the public trough, but it's surprising how often a corrupt politician unintentionally does great good."

"You don't like Casey?"

"He ought to raise his sights," said Brett. "His plan has more virtues than he knows."

After that encounter with Tony, Brett read the *Tribune* daily, and once he asked Trav in honest wonder: "How in the world has the editor of this paper stayed alive till now? Who is he?"

"A man named Dalloz," Trav said. "A nigra, of course, but pretty level-headed. He came here from Texas in '64. I think Doctor Roudanez, the chief owner, comes from Haiti. I hear he really believes in his dream of making Louisiana a nigra state, of expelling all the whites."

"And yet they're both still alive!" Brett laughed. "New Orleans doesn't live up to its reputation. According to Congress, your favorite pastime down here is murdering nigras."

"No one has bothered those two," Trav agreed.

The day Brett and Cinda were to begin their homeward journey, Brett, having finished his packing, joined Trav in the garden. He held two copies of the *Tribune* in his hand, and he said at once: "You know, Trav, this fellow Dalloz—or Doctor Roudanez, or whoever writes the editorials—is pretty greedy. Getting the vote for his race doesn't satisfy him; he wants mixed marriages, mixed schools, mixed everything. Listen to this." And he read: " 'We want to ride in any conveyance, to travel on any steamboat, dine at any restaurant, educate our children at any school.' That was two or three days ago. Now this, today. 'We expect to see proud planters, haughty chevaliers, humiliating themselves to the point of flattering their former slaves, and crouching to their very feet.' " He looked at Trav with a quizzical eye. "Been doing much crouching lately?"

"I suppose the fellow's crazy," Trav reflected. "Drunk with triumph.

Saul, out in the stable, and Isaiah, they've both registered to vote. The nigras are riding high." He added: "If Tony's right about General Sheridan's order, I suppose I'll be disfranchised."

"They expect at home that General Sickles will exclude everyone who voluntarily served in the Confederate armies." Brett folded the papers with an angry rustle. "It's hard to decide whether to laugh at this, or go shoot the man."

"Wonder if Tony ever writes any of their pieces." Trav chuckled in sudden amusement. "Or maybe he's the haughty chevalier who's been crouching at their feet. Wouldn't be surprised to see him run for office, one of these days; yes, and get it."

"Cinda thinks Tony's improved," said Brett. Tony had called on his sister and Enid a few days before. "She found a great change in him— a change for the better."

"I expect Sapphira's good for him," Trav assented. "I can see what Cinda means."

Brett glanced at the *Tribune* in his hand. "Have they organized the Loyal League here?" he asked. Trav did not know. His eyes still on the paper, Brett said: "According to this fellow, they're already planning how to run the Convention. Tony told Cinda some of his ideas, and the *Tribune* here says the same thing. They'll put nigras in as chairmen, put them on committees, give them a chance to talk big, flatter and cajole them."

"Maybe this is all just a nightmare," Trav suggested.

"I'm afraid not. Nigra voters will be in a big majority with us in South Carolina, and here in Louisiana too. That's no nightmare; that's a certainty."

Enid and Cinda joined them, and then Lucy, and presently Don called to say goodby. He, too, was leaving on the night boat to Mobile, and Cinda said in quick pleasure. "Oh, then we'll be fellow travelers."

Lucy asked: "Is this about the rationing, Don?"

"Yes." He explained to the others: "The Bureau's feeding over sixty thousand people in Alabama, Negroes and whites. But our stations are mostly in cities and towns, so the poor people, Negroes specially, have come into the towns to be fed, and there's nobody left on the farms to plant food crops. That's my job now, to give them free seeds and to work out some way to distribute rations in the country, so they can stay on the farms and not starve."

Brett nodded agreement. "I noticed as we came down that many farms were deserted."

Lucy said resentfully: "Isn't it shameful, Uncle Brett, that with all the land lying idle in the South we don't even raise enough to feed ourselves, have to depend on the North's charity? I'm just about disgusted with Southerners!"

"Lah, Honey," Cinda protested. "Southerners don't have time to work, we're so busy being charming!"

They laughed with her, but Trav added a sober word. "And most of us older people are pretty tired, Lucy. We took a hard beating for four years. It wears you down."

Don could only stay for a moment, and Lucy went to see him to the door. "I like that boy," Cinda announced. "Has he declared himself?"

Enid laughed. "He's forever kissing her in corners, if that's a declaration." Lucy rejoined them, and Enid exclaimed: "Mercy, what a tousling!"

Lucy's color rose, and her hands flew to her hair, but Cinda said in laughing reassurance: "Don't pay any attention to her, Lucy; you're neat as a pin! I like your young man. Are you and he making any plans?"

Lucy shook her head. "Not immediate plans," she admitted.

"If you do marry a Yankee, you'll break a lot of Southern hearts." Cinda smiled as she spoke. "Reminds me, I haven't conveyed all the messages from Boy de Saussure and the others." She added teasingly: "There were none from Pev Boykin. He's gone to marry a little Miss Somebody in Charleston."

"We had such a good time with you all, last summer."

"Come home with us now! It's going to be fine on the boat tonight, and your young man will be on board."

Lucy's heart leaped with sudden longing, but she shook her head. "We'll come by and by," she promised, her eyes dreaming. It would be wonderful to be on the boat tonight with him; some day he and she would sail away, far away, and leave all this behind.

Among the boys of his own age in school, Peter made few friends. He was larger than they, with an arrogance of speech and manner which made them dislike and fear him. He cared as little for them as they for him, feeling that by killing Bob he had achieved manhood, while they were only children. He wished to recite his deed, in order to impress them, but he had already learned that silence may be more impressive than braggadocio, and he had found by experiment that an icy politeness is more compelling than loud threats. Boys and young men five or six years his senior paid him a cautious respect, and the more reckless youngsters among them were his friends.

Colonel Soulé, himself a fine mathematician, had seen with pleasure Peter's aptitude, and his eager interest in that course of study, but apart from his studies he watched the boy's development with some concern, and once he summoned Peter into his office and in a kindly way suggested that his companions were badly chosen.

"I need name no one," he said. "But you know, as well as I, the

young gentlemen whose company most often leaves a bad taste in your
mouth. I need not recite their offenses against good taste, good manners,
good morals. But you may not realize that to some extent we all
imitate those around us. That's why it's important to choose for our
friends individuals who are admirable, rather than—well, reprehen-
sible."

Peter thanked him politely, hiding his amused scorn. He had no
least intention of following the Colonel's advice. The older boys with
whom he consorted had introduced him into a world completely fascinating. He knew the gaming houses along Royal Street, and had even
ventured, here and there, an occasional wager; he was a familiar visitor
in a few of the mansions along Basin Street, and he and his companions
had once or twice—taking care to go well armed—strolled through
Gallatin Street, lined with its wretched tenements.

When Quinny was banished to Tony's, Peter—under pretense of
calling upon his uncle—followed her there, and Tony found a malicious
enjoyment in this situation. Sapphira and 'Phemy between them made
sure that he never saw Quinny alone, but for Peter it was sufficiently
exciting merely to enter this irregular establishment, and he imagined
he might some day thus set himself up with Quinny; yes, or even
with Sapphira. Uncle Tony was pretty old, and she was beautiful.

Enid knew something of Peter's secret life. He liked to watch her
leisurely preparations for the night, and after she was abed he sometimes lay beside her, answering her questions about this other world
of his, and she affected to chide him even while she wished she could
share these adventures. One night she had an inspiration.

"Sonny, do you know the place they call the Haunted House, down
on Royal Street?"

"It's a gambling house," he said. "Roulette tables, and cards, and
dice. Cousin Dolly lives there. Fellows have told me, but I've never
been inside."

"I'm glad of that! It's no place for you! At least, not yet a while!"

"I've tried," he admitted. "But the butler wouldn't let me in."

She remembered that butler; but though he had halted Peter at the
door, he would at least carry a note to Dolly—and bring an answer. So
she wrote Dolly, proposing a joke at Trav's expense.

He's given Isaiah orders not to let you in if you come here, and
Saul's not allowed to drive me to Royal Street, and your butler
refused to admit me when I took a cab to your door. But I do want
to see you, often, so let's meet at Tony's. We'll just go and call and
ask for Tony. Sapphira won't dare show herself. I can walk from
here, and you can take a Magazine Street car from Canal Street.
I know the house. You get off at Felicity Road—do you suppose
Tony bought the house because he liked the name of the street?—

THE SCALAWAG · 297

and I'll meet you. It's only a block from there. Whenever you say. You set the day. It will be a joke on all our menfolk. I long to see you, darling; so much to tell, and so much I want to hear.

She told Peter: "Tell that big nigger butler it's for Mrs. Kenyon, and that you'll wait for an answer, and then you can bring the answer back to me." She wagged a warning finger. "But this is a secret, mind! Between you and me! Here's your pay!" She kissed him, hugged him hard. "There! And another when you come back!"

"Oh, kiss me the way you kiss Papa. Not just a peck! A long one!" So she laughed and called him a little devil and kissed him again, and had to push him away.

Enid and Dolly first carried out their plan on a day toward the end of April. Enid, strolling along Magazine Street and watching for the car from downtown, timed herself so that they met at the car steps. They embraced, and as the car moved away, Dolly said laughingly: "I feel like a conspirator! Isn't this fun? Darling, you'd be a perfect witch if you ever let yourself go!"

Enid laughed. "Heavens, you don't know Trav! He's so prim and proper he's shocked when I kiss him! Come on! It's the next block down."

"After all," Dolly suggested, "We could just stroll, and talk as we go along. We don't have to go indoors!"

"Oh, calling on Tony's half the fun! It won't bother me even if we do meet her! Will it you?"

Dolly hesitated. "We-ell, I'm not sure what Captain Pew would do to Uncle Tony if he heard I had. Of course, he and Papa have seen her. They come to see Uncle Tony about politics and things." She giggled. "They've both registered to vote. Tony vouched for them. I think it's hilarious, them standing in line with a lot of nigras."

"There's the house, across the street."

"It's real comfortable-looking, isn't it?"

They hesitated, looking at the house and then at each other. "Do we dare?" Enid asked, trembling.

Dolly laughed. "Why not?" Her head high, she led the way, and Enid regained her courage. When 'Phemy opened the door she said easily:

"Good evening, 'Phemy. You remember me?"

"Yes ma'am."

"This is my niece, Mrs. Kenyon. Is Mister Tony at home?"

"Yes ma'am." Under 'Phemy's calm scrutiny, Enid had an uncomfortable feeling that her bonnet was askew, her hair disordered, a ribbon out of place.

"Please tell him we're here."

'Phemy stepped aside, bidding them enter, and with a gesture she showed them the small reception room, then went quietly up the stairs. They heard a distant murmur, 'Phemy's voice and Tony's answer; then 'Phemy returned.

"Y'all come up, please."

When Enid saw Tony, he was standing in the doorway at the other end of the room, as though he had just come through. He closed the door with obvious reluctance, and came to greet them, but he was almost scowling, and Enid's teeth threatened to chatter. Only Dolly quickly found her tongue.

"You must be astonished to see us here, Uncle Tony."

"Say rather, honored, Miss Dolly." His courtliness had in it something overelaborate.

"We didn't really come to see you, though."

"Ah? Then why—"

"It's ridiculous, actually," Dolly explained. "But Aunt Enid and I were always congenial, and now Uncle Trav won't even let us see each other. So we—" She hesitated faintly. "So we want to meet somewhere, every so often, and have good visits together, and we decided to come and see you and ask if we could meet here."

Enid spoke quickly. "Trav would be furious if he knew, so don't ever tell him. But can't we come here sometimes, and even just sit in the reception room downstairs, not bother you at all."

"I've no particular desire to make an enemy of Trav, you know."

"Peter has such fun here, it makes me want to come!"

The door opened, and 'Phemy and then Quinny, with coffee and small sandwiches and cakes, entered. Enid turned at the sound, and cried in pleased surprise: "Why, Quinny, how nice you look!" Surprise had made her gracious, but after all, they had come to ask a favor. She must be polite. "How's the baby?"

"He fine!" Quinny added proudly: "He got de talipes."

"What in the world . . . ?"

Tony said: "She means he has a clubfoot. Two, in fact. Sapphira had the doctor look at them, and he called it talipes—you know how doctors are; how they love to make mysteries—and Quinny's tickled to death."

Enid began to laugh; her laughter was an explosion, for a moment almost uncontrollable. Dolly and Tony were mystified and half alarmed and Enid shook her head, gasping, choking. "Nothing! Nothing!" And when she could speak: "Just a joke on me! I'll tell you sometime."

Quinny had caught the infection and was near hysterics, without knowing why, till 'Phemy laid an eye upon her. Then she and 'Phemy passed the coffee and cakes and left the room. Enid and Dolly sipped, and tried to keep alive a conversation, till Tony looked at the French clock on the mantel and remarked: "Gentlemen often drop in here toward four o'clock, so unless you care to meet them—"

They rose together, and he rang for 'Phemy to show them out, and then Dolly remembered their reason for being here. "You haven't said, Uncle Tony, whether we could come again."

"If you like," he assented. "You'll be undisturbed in my office. It's also on the ground floor. I'll tell 'Phemy . . ."

Then he stopped, staring at the door, and Enid turned to look that way. A mulatto stood there in the doorway, another young man behind him. Tony recovered. "Come in, come in!" he said. Enid thought he was amused. "These ladies were just leaving." He turned to Enid and to Dolly: "Mrs. Currain, Mrs. Kenyon, this is my friend Mr. Pinchback. And Mr. Villard."

Pinchback was obviously a Negro, so Enid ignored him, but Mr. Villard might have been Elon's brother. "How do you do, Mr. Villard," she said, and added inquiringly: "I know Mr. Elon Villard, and his father, Mister Jeremy, used to."

"My mother and I belong to them," said the young man, and Dolly giggled, and Enid caught her breath, and Tony offered her his arm.

"You were leaving," he reminded her, and escorted them down the stairs. 'Phemy waited at the foot to let them pass, and Enid saw a malicious amusement in her eyes. At the door, Tony said in half apology: "I'm sorry for your embarrassment, but Pinchback and I share the same political beliefs. He is often here. I'll tell 'Phemy, next time you come, to show you into my office. You'll be undisturbed there."

"Thank you," said Enid, still breathless and trembling, and Dolly echoed the word. He bowed, and as they turned away he closed the door behind them.

They walked at first in silence, neither daring look at the other as long as they were in sight from the house they had left. Not till they had turned into Magazine Street did their eyes meet. Then they smiled, and then laughed, and Enid cried: "Well, I never!"

"All the same," Dolly declared. "Pinchback is a handsome nigger! That sad, hurt look in his eyes."

"I didn't even notice," Enid admitted. "I was looking at the other one."

"Will we ever dare go there again?"

"I certainly will! Maybe next time we'll meet Sapphira!"

"Captain Pew says she'd captivate any man she chose."

"She's beautiful," Enid agreed, and she protested in sudden realization: "Honey, you haven't told me anything about anything, Captain Pew, or where you've been, or anything! We didn't have any chance to talk at all!"

"I know it. And you haven't told me why you laughed so, at what Quinny said about her baby. There comes the car, and I must take it. Hurry, tell me!"

"Oh, about the clubfoot! We had an old coachman named Pike. He was killed in the riot last July, and he was clubfooted, so her baby is his!"

Enid began to laugh again, and Dolly smiled in sympathy, but she asked in a puzzled tone: "But why's that so funny? Why is it a joke on you?" The car stopped beside them.

"I thought it was Peter's!" Enid whispered. "Goodby! See you next time!"

Dolly's eyes widened and she began to laugh, and—still laughing—she stepped aboard and the car rolled away.

Enid, walking homeward, had an absurd desire to sing. Her blood was racing, and the skies were blue, the day was fine. Wouldn't Trav be furious if he knew? How surprised Tony had been, and how absurd of him to banish Sapphira before receiving them? And just think of old Pike, with his clubfoot, seventy if he was a day! And that Quinny! She was a hussy, certainly! The baby must take after Pike in more ways than one; it was black as the ace of spades, Mr. Fiddler had said, and so was Pike, though Quinny was almost white, as white as that young Mr. Villard.

He had made no bones about telling her he had been a slave. Possibly nigras one of these days would brag about it! How handsome he was, his features so fine, his lips so red, his eyes so deep and warm.

One night toward the middle of May, General and Mrs. Longstreet came to call. Enid had as usual gone to her room, and Lucy took Mrs. Longstreet up to be with her mother, then returned to listen to the talk between her father and the General. They were discussing the recent turbulence in the city. Negroes had in the past been permitted to ride only on cars marked with a star, but in the last few weeks, they had frequently tried to board cars reserved for white people. The street railways had asked General Sheridan to enforce the system of Star cars, but he declined, and among the Negroes a rumor spread that Sheridan had ordered the drivers to allow them to ride on all the cars without distinction. Last Sunday night, squads of them, fifteen or twenty in each group and armed with clubs, lined the tracks on Love Street, boarding the cars and threatening the driver.

Longstreet spoke of this, and Trav nodded. "There's more trouble coming," he predicted. "Mr. Fiddler had to discharge one of our nigras at the mill the other day. Mose Mooney. He was terribly beaten at the riot last July—both his ears were cut off—and it's made a sort of hero out of him. He's getting pretty uppity, and Mr. Fiddler heard him telling a bunch of Negroes they had a perfect right to ride on any car they chose and urging them to go ahead and do it. Mr. Fiddler paid him off." He smiled grimly. "Now they say Mooney will go into politics."

Longstreet chuckled. "Well, not all the news is bad," he remarked, after a moment. "Cotton's up to almost double the December price."

"That's bad news for the planters who sold," Trav commented, and Longstreet nodded.

"But it will help pay the tax," he remarked. "That runs about twelve-fifty a bale, and the whole bale's only worth about sixty-five dollars. But at the December price, the planter was left out of pocket on his crop. After taxes."

"The North intends we shall pay for the War," Trav commented. "Congress levied on us for a direct tax of twenty millions, and the treasury agents, in collecting that, stole at least that much more. And this cotton tax and all the others are extras. Inescapable."

"You can't get away from taxes," Longstreet agreed. Lucy, listening, thought there was a curious, abstracted quality in the General's tone, as though his thoughts were elsewhere. He said thoughtfully: "Some of our factors are buying and holding for the rise; yes, and some are selling cotton they haven't got, expecting the price will go down before they have to deliver. I agree with the older gentlemen in the business that that's straight gambling; yet if a man had known, last December, that the crop was short, he could have made a fortune."

"I suppose so." Trav, like Lucy, felt in Longstreet a divided mind, felt that the General spoke of one thing while his thoughts were elsewhere, so he was not surprised when Longstreet asked:

"Going to the meeting tomorrow night?"

"What meeting?"

"Senator Wilson's to speak." Longstreet fumbled in his pocket. "You know Mr. Parker, the former Postmaster? He and Governor Hahn are running this new paper, the *Republican*."

"I know Governor Hahn by sight, and I've met Mr. Parker, talked with him once or twice."

Longstreet said: "I had this letter from him today."

Trav took the letter, and Lucy asked: "May I read it too?" At Longstreet's assent, she came to lean over Trav's shoulder. After the customary greeting, Mr. Parker had written:

In your admirable letter of the 6th ultimo, you remark that "our efforts at reconstruction will be vain and useless unless we embark in the enterprise with the sincerity of purpose which will command success."

The spirit which inspired the above paragraph, together with the fact that thousands of brave soldiers are still ready to follow their leader whenever he may see fit to call them, has emboldened me to extend to you an invitation to attend a mass meeting in Lafayette Square tomorrow evening, at which the Hon. Henry Wilson, a distinguished leader in the Republican party, will address the citizens of New Orleans.

As soldiers, we were opposed to each other during the late War; but as citizens may we not wisely unite in efforts to restore Louisiana to her former position in the Union through the party now in power, and for many years to come? If you accept, I shall be glad to hear your views on the condition of public affairs.

Trav read this through with a grave attention, and as he finished, he said thoughtfully: "'the party now in power'? Why, General . . ." He laughed, incredulous yet amused. "Why, General, he wants you to turn Republican!"

"He has repeatedly suggested that I do so," Longstreet agreed. "Remember I told you once that it would be a good thing for the South if some of her big men did turn Republican?"

Lucy cried: "I think so too! If I were a man, I wouldn't be a Democrat for anything."

Trav smiled faintly. "You'd be pretty lonesome, anywhere in the South, Honey." His eyes met Longstreet's. "Though I hear Thad Stevens is bragging that he'll make the South Republican for generations."

His tone was so full of scorn that Longstreet colored, but then he laughed. "I suppose he hates us because we burned his iron furnace on the way to Gettysburg." He reached for the letter in Trav's hand. "The President himself has assured me I'll never receive amnesty, so without the vote it doesn't much matter what my politics may be. But I think I'll go to that meeting, Major. Care to keep me company?"

"Happy to. I suppose it's the first gun of the campaign, and as a possible voter, I should listen."

"Suppose you join me in the St. Charles rotunda for a little refreshment beforehand."

Trav agreed, and they turned to casual conversation. The General asked for Don, and Lucy said he was still in Alabama. "They're feeding people, distributing rations, and he has all the schools to visit, besides."

"Miss him?" His tone was teasing.

"Terribly!" She smiled. "I'm so lonesome! I wish you'd come see us oftener!"

"Careful there, Miss Lucy, or you'll have me cutting capers with your other beaus."

While they jested together, Trav sat half smiling as he listened, yet with troubled eyes. When Mrs. Longstreet came downstairs and they took their leave, he and Lucy went with them to the door, and after they were gone, turning back into the hall, Lucy said: "You don't want him to do it, do you, Papa? To turn Republican?"

"No. It would do no good, would only make him hated in the South."

"But, Papa, you can't fight the North; you might as well join them."

He looked down at her with gentle eyes. "Lucy, when your grand-sons are old enough to vote, yes and your great grandsons, the South will still think of the North as its enemy."

"But that's so silly! Hating someone just makes you unhappy, and it doesn't hurt whoever it is you hate. It's like staying home from a party because you hate the hostess; you just miss all the fun. Cutting off your own nose to spite your face."

"I know. But all the same, a hundred years from now, the mammies will be telling their babies: 'Hush now, yuh heah me! Dem old Yankees'll git yuh ef yuh don' watch out!'"

She smiled with him. "And I suppose Yankees and Republicans will always be practically the same thing."

He nodded, chuckling. "Yes. Any time in your life when you see a white man alone on a crowded Southern street, you may count on it; he's either a Yankee or a Republican."

When Trav came home from that Thursday night meeting, Lucy was curled in the big chair in his office. "I wanted to hear all about it," she explained. "So I stayed up. Know what I've been doing?"

He sat down, tired, relaxing. "Afraid not."

"Reading Don's letters," she said. "All the letters I've ever had from him, from the very first up to the one I had today." She touched the writing case on the floor beside her. "I keep them in this. It's getting pretty full."

"I expect they're interesting."

"To me they are. They're mostly about his thoughts. He thinks a lot, Papa."

Trav smiled. "No harm in that."

"They're not the sort of letters a Southern boy would write. I mean they're not all full of fancy compliments." She giggled suddenly. "Do you think I'm neat, Papa?" she demanded.

"Well, I never thought much about it. Guess I'd have noticed if you weren't."

"Well, Don does!" She reached down and picked up the writing case and from the drawer selected a sheet of paper. "He sent this to me.

It's a poem." Her eyes met Trav's. "It's about the nearest he ever came to paying me a compliment, so don't you dare laugh!"

"I won't," Trav promised, and she read:

> I love to see thy gentle hand
> Dispose, with modest grace
> The household things around thy home
> And each thing in its place.
>
> And then thy own trim, modest form
> Is always neatly clad;
> Thou sure wilt make the tidiest wife
> That *ever husband had.*

She looked toward her father, her cheeks bright. "He underscores those words," she said, and repeated, " 'that *ever husband had,*' " and then read on:

> No costly splendors needest thou
> To make thy house look bright
> For neatness, in the humblest spot,
> Can shed a sunny light.

"There, isn't that sweet!" Her eyes shone with happy tears, and Trav smiled.

"So are you, and many of 'em, Lucy," he said in hearty affection. "Yes, and he's a fine fellow. In his way, he's as fine as you."

She folded the poem and replaced it. "He's more serious than I am. Papa, he's almost religious about his work in the schools, about teaching the nigras. When he talks about it, I feel so little and meeching and humble, never thinking of anything but having a good time."

Trav smiled. "New Orleans has the reputation of warming up these New England Puritans, after they've been here a while."

"Oh, he's warm enough!" At Trav's sudden guffaw she blushed redly and cried out at him. "Stop it! You know what I mean! But he does take it seriously. You just notice him, some time, when he's talking about the schools. There!" She spoke in brisk contrition. "I've talked all the time about Don, and what I really sat up for was to hear about the meeting."

"Well, there was a big crowd," Trav said. "It was in Lafayette Square, and I guess there were as many people as could get within hearing. They were mostly nigras, a few white men."

"Did you go with that Mr. Parker?"

"No, just the General and I, although Judge Morgan joined us."

"Did Senator Wilson make a good speech? Don't make me ask so many questions; go on and tell me all about it!"

"Why, I suppose the speech was all right. The Senator started with a history of slavery, and of what led up to the War, and he didn't color it too much his way. Then he talked politics. He said every man ought to vote according to his principles, not just because a candidate was white or black. He said the nigra was as good as the white man, but that the white man was also as good as the nigra."

"I should think someone would have shot him!"

"He was reasonable," Trav repeated. "He's against race dissension, against hate. He said we were all God's children. He urged them to vote only for men who were for national union. He advised them to behave themselves, be kind and tender, never offend, keep away from whiskey, go to work, earn money, learn to see a dollar as far off as a Yankee can."

He seemed to have finished, and Lucy asked: "What did the General think?"

"He approved," Trav admitted. "I didn't blame him. I couldn't quarrel with most of the things Wilson said."

"Is the General going to –do anything?"

Trav rose. "Time we went to bed, Honey. I don't know. I'll persuade him not to, if I can."

"Why, Papa?"

"For his own sake. He can't change the South. No one can. Time will have to do that. But if he turns Republican, he'll be an outcast from now on."

"I don't believe he cares about himself. I believe he thinks he might do some good."

He touched her shoulder in a light caress, then turned off the gas. Darkening the house as they proceeded, they moved to the stairs and up. At the top, he said, agreeing: "If he thought it would do any good, he wouldn't spare himself."

"Isn't it valorous to fight hardest when you know you'll lose?"

He kissed her brow. "Good night, Honey. We'll see. We'll see."

Friday evening, Elon Villard came to the house to ask for Trav. Trav had not yet returned from the mill, so the young man joined Lucy and Enid in the garden. "Mr. Currain spoke once of wanting to see our plantation, down the river," he explained. "We're all going down tomorrow, and I thought possibly Mr. Currain—or perhaps all of you— might like to go."

Enid was delighted. "I certainly would, for one, but I don't know about Trav. Think we can persuade him, Lucy?"

"I think so. He goes to the mill just about every day, but I should think he could do something else for once."

"We'll just make him!" Enid exclaimed. Her color was high, her eyes shining, and she nodded with a pretty emphasis. "Consider it settled, Mister Elon!" They laughed together at her tone and her manner, and Lucy thought—as she had thought so many times before— that even the prospect of a happy experience always made her mother beautiful. "Who all's going?"

"Well, Papa, of course, and Eleanor, and Mr. Cist, if I can persuade him to leave the mill, and the Morgans, though I haven't asked them yet. Miss Lucy, I'm real sorry Lieutenant Page isn't here."

"You must have an enormous boat, to take so many."

"It's our old plantation boat," he explained. "We used to use it to haul freight between New Orleans and our landing, and for picnics and things. After we didn't need it any more, Papa sold it to Cash, and he's been running it on regular trips, freight and passengers."

Enid asked: "Who's Cash?"

"He was one of our nigras. He's Filly's son."

"Filly's? She never told me she had a son!"

"He's a real good boy," Elon assured her. "Well spoken, too." Enid's eyes widened, her thoughts racing. "Mama always liked him, and back before the War she made Papa set him free, and she gave him enough money to go North and go to school. He worked in a boat yard up there, and I guess he knows more about steam engines than the man who invented them! Mama left him a little money when she died. He used most of it to buy the boat." He smiled. "His name's really Casual—you know how nigras like words they don't understand— but we all call him Cash."

"Casual!" Enid protested. "Filly's too sensible to give her baby a silly name like that!"

"She's sensible now, but she was just a field hand when Cash was born, till after Mama brought her into the house." He added, as though this were an explanation: "Mama always wanted more sons. She had three after me, but they all died when they were just a few days old."

"Is Filly's name Villard? I didn't know."

"I think she called herself after Mama's family, Filly Rawle. Mama was a Rawle. But when Cash went North, Mama told him to call himself Villard."

Then Trav appeared, and Elon rose to greet him and to broach his plan, and Enid watched them, her eyes clouded, wondering, wondering. When next morning they boarded the boat, she saw at once her guess was true. The Captain was that Mr. Villard whom she had met at Tony's.

6

JEREMY VILLARD had been an only son, and a profligate, till at nineteen he came into his inheritance, and Cynthia Rawle was sure he had reformed, and engaged herself to marry him. He bought wild land some twenty miles below New Orleans, and cleared it, and planted cane, and built his house and took his bride to live there, and with the arrogant confidence of youth, they called the plantation Paradise; but after the first three or four years, poor Cynthia Rawle Villard would have sooner called it Hell. That her children—as long as they were children—never knew all the tragedy of her life, and never knew their father as he was; these were her monuments. Outwardly she was always gay and laughing and tender, and her every word and action testified to them her proud belief that Jeremy Villard was a noble, gallant gentleman. Thus she was a double liar, and only since she died had Elon and Eleanor come to know her lies, and for them love her the more.

The boat that took them down river was larger than Lucy had expected, a stern-wheeler with a capacious cargo deck two or three feet above the water, a main deck above. The *Paradise*—the boat was named after the plantation—was when they boarded her tied up to the batture, a little above the ferry landing at Louisiana Avenue. A broad gangplank led up easily to the cargo deck where a miscellaneous assortment of freight was already stowed. On the main deck, a pleasant saloon and cabin and four staterooms were provided for passengers. The top deck, exposed to sun and cinders, was seldom used. The pilot-house there shone with white paint and gold leaf.

Elon met them on the levee and took Enid's arm to help her down the batture to the gangplank. The young man whom Enid remembered having met at Tony's stood at the inboard end of the plank, and Elon introduced him. "Cap'n Cash, Mrs. Currain." They ascended to the saloon deck, and Enid said in a whisper:

"He's as white as anyone isn't he?"

Elon nodded, and Eleanor Villard came to greet them, and to show Enid and Lucy the stateroom reserved for their use. "I always take a nap on the trip upriver," she explained, "and probably this evening you'll want to do the same. All day in the open air makes you sleepy."

"Heavens, I'll be having much too good a time to sleep," Enid declared. They turned back into the saloon where Elon and Trav had waited—Peter had disappeared toward the engine room—and Enid asked gaily: "Well, why don't we start?"

"Cap'n Cash carries passengers as well as freight," Elon explained. "He's waiting for the last of them, but we'll cast off—" He glanced at his watch. "In seven minutes."

Elon and Lucy went to the rail to watch late arrivals pick their way down to the gangplank. He and she had been from the first congenial, finding that the same things amused them equally, and as they watched the last passengers arrive, they whispered merry comments. Half a dozen plantation Negroes came aboard, and an old Indian woman, and Elon said: "She knows every sassafras bush in twenty miles, makes a famous filé."

Lucy, knowing by experience how hard it was to find filé in the market, said: "I must remember her. That couple behind her, I'm positive they're Northern Methodists. See how they hang back so as not to came near the nigras. Hypocrites!"

Three young New Orleans dandies came aboard, wearing peg-top trousers and high-heeled boots and carrying canes, and Elon whispered: "Peter'll be imitating them in a year or two." A man greeted Elon with lifted hand, and he explained: "His name's Bandy. He's the overseer at a plantation just above Paradise, on the other side of the river."

Judge Morgan and his sisters were in Baton Rouge, and Mrs. Morgan would not come without them, so the Currains were the only guests. "I decided not to ask anyone else, except of course Mr. Cist," Elon explained. "We'll pick him up at the mill."

Peter joined them in some excitement, insisting that Lucy come to inspect the pilothouse. "Mama's there," he reported, and as they followed the eager youngster, Elon remarked:

"Papa's probably up there, too. He always rode in the pilothouse when she was ours, so he still does." He smiled. "He clings to that particular *droit de seigneur*."

He was right. They found Mr. Villard established on the high seat that ran from side to side against the after wall of the pilothouse, Enid there beside him. Peter pointed out to them the wheel, the signal bells, the whistle; then as Captain Cash stepped in, he cried: "Wait a minute, Cap'n, till I can get down to see the engine start."

He raced away, and Elon's father said in a benevolent tone: "Well, Cash, ready, are we?"

"Yes, sir."

"Then clear out, the rest of you." Mr. Villard made a shoo-ing gesture. "Can't distract the Captain while he's getting under way."

Lucy and Elon rose to obey, but Enid kept her seat. "Mayn't I stay, Captain? If I keep mouse-still?" Lucy saw the Captain's embarrassed hesitancy, Elon's obvious surprise, as they stepped outside.

Captain Villard from the window of the pilothouse directed the taking in of lines, and Elon led Lucy to the rail to watch. "You notice he was tied up with his bow downstream. There's a sort of backwater here, almost an eddy. The strong current's over on the other side, so he's really heading into what current there is."

She saw in him an unaccustomed eagerness and zest, and guessed how happy he must be, returning if only for a day to his childhood home. "You must have loved steering this big boat, when you were a boy."

He grinned. "Certainly did." They angled across the river and headed up into the current again and he said: "He's picking up some cattle over here. See them waiting on the bank." The *Paradise* crabbed in against the batture, and a gangplank, wider than the one the passengers had used, was manhandled into position. The first cow would not move, and a Negro caught her tail and twisted it, another pulling at her neck rope till she bawled and lunged forward. In a surprisingly short time a dozen head had been hauled or driven aboard, making loud outcries at the indignities they received, and Elon laughed and then felt her faint disapproval.

"I know it looks cruel," he confessed. "But a cow's such a fool! As bad as a hen!" They were once more under way; the current caught the bow and they drifted broadside, slowly turning to head downstream. "Back there where we picked up the cattle, there used to be a point," he said. "But it all washed away and built up the shore on the other side, built a batture outside the old levee fully a quarter of a mile." He chuckled. "They had a lot of lawsuits about who owned the new land."

"Just the river did that?"

He said, something like affection in his tones: "It's a great river. Here's water all of half a mile wide and two hundred feet deep and racing along four or five or six or seven miles an hour." He smiled. "When all that water decides to move something, it moves." And he said: "That's why you don't see many piers along the shore wherever the current swings in hard."

"How can people tell where the current will go?"

Elon smiled. "Well, the water sort of bounces from one bank to another. It follows the outside of a curve—like here—but up where we came aboard, the current was all on the other side of the river." He added: "You'll see, at your father's mill there's slack water, and a pier there."

They touched at the Canal Street ferry landing to take aboard four more passengers, then angled across to Algiers, and Eleanor came beside them. Mr. Cist was waiting on the pier head, and as the *Paradise* almost but not quite touched, he stepped aboard and came up the companion stairs to join them, hurrying to point back at the mill buildings which were his pride, describing to Eleanor the function of each one. She made him promise to take her there some day and show her everything, and he and she moved away together, and Lucy watched them go and turned back to Elon, seeing his eyes follow them, wondering whether his thoughts ran with hers. Perhaps they did, for he said readily: "I like Mr. Cist. He's a hard worker, and he's so enthusiastic, it's infectious."

"I didn't like him at first," she admitted. "But I do now." Thinking of her mother, touched by some vague uneasiness, she remarked: "Isn't it wonderful to see how Cap'n Cash steers the boat just exactly where he wants it to go? Does he ever let anyone stay up there and watch him? I mean, except your father?"

"Oh yes, he doesn't mind, after he gets her under way. Like to go up?"

"I would, yes," she assented. "You must be able to see so much better from there." How ridiculous to feel thus uneasy, yet she did. As they entered the pilothouse, the *Paradise* was rounding the point and opening out a long reach of river that stretched for miles. Enid stood by the Captain at the wheel, and Elon helped Lucy up on the bench and sat beside her, and when they had left the fringes of the city behind he pointed out an occasional landmark. He showed her, just visible above the treetops ahead, the shaft of the unfinished monument that marked where, fifty-odd years before, General Jackson and his heterogeneous army turned back the British.

"The river's eaten away part of the battlefield," he said. "The monument was begun before the War, but there's been no work done on it since the War started. Maybe never will be, now."

A little furthur downstream, he pointed out Four Oaks, and the raised-cottage Colomb house. "General Pakenham, the British commander, was wounded in the battle," he explained. "They carried him into the shade and he died under those oak trees."

"The same ones?" she asked, liking his eager interest.

"The same ones," he assured her. "They were big trees, even then." And he added, smiling: "They've made General Pakenham cover a lot of ground along here. A little further ahead is old Versailles plantation and an avenue of trees there is called Pakenham Oaks. And then a mile or so beyond that, his insides are supposed to be buried under a pecan tree."

"Mercy! What happened to his—outsides."

"They were taken home to England in a cask full of rum."

The river, pent between confining levees, lifted them above the surrounding countryside, so that they looked down upon the world. Sugar plantations, all neglect and decay, followed closely one upon the other. Each was like a small village, the owner's home, the rows of whitewashed cabins, the sugar factory. They made numerous landings, zigzagging from bank to bank, and here and there Elon pointed out weak spots in the levee, and Negroes at work upon them. The levee was sometimes at the water's edge, sometimes a hundred yards or a quarter mile inland, and he explained that a levee needs a firm foundation. "Each planter keeps up his own, and most men put their levees close to the water, to save as much land as they can. But when you've had a bad break, it's better to build a new levee well back from the river. I've known high water to undercut a bank for two-three hundred feet, and when the flood passes and the water goes down, all that undercut land just caves right in."

Lucy's attention wandered. She was watching her mother. Enid asked Captain Cash many questions, more intent on him than on the river, and Lucy saw her flattering interest in everything the Captain said. It was a relief when Mr. Villard after a time left his high seat and went to stand by the Captain's elbow, holding him in conversation till Enid sighed and left the pilot house and went below.

Elon and Lucy stayed where they were, and he pointed out plantations along the way, peopling each one with the persons who had lived there. "But gone now," he said again and again. "Their men were killed in the War, or the plantation was abandoned and went back to jungle, likes ours, when their people went away." And when they came to English Turn, where the river swung sharply from a southerly course to run west northwest for three or four miles, he told her how an English expedition, seeking new territory for the Crown, was turned back by the falsehoods of Bienville, the founder of the colony.

And as he finished, he said: "See that big chimney just showing above the trees? Still three miles away, on the left hand point." For the moment she could not make it out, and he said: "No matter. You'll see it soon. That's the sugar factory at Paradise."

"I see something white, on the shore."

"Yes, that's one of our cabins. Our landing's on the other side of the point, the downstream side. It's silting up in the slack water there, makes a wide batture outside the levee. You can't see the house from this side at all. Just a few cabins."

"Is anyone there?" she asked.

"Just Mr. Tremont. He's Papa's overseer. He and his family. He had his right hand shot off in the War, and he's still sensitive about it, so don't offer to shake hands with him." He added in a regretful tone. "You won't like him, not at first, anyway. He acts sort of sullen, but he's really fine, honest and loyal and—well, good."

As the *Paradise* approached the point, Lucy saw the cabins of the quarter, hidden away among the trees. They moved to descend to the saloon deck, and went forward, and presently Elon said:

"There, now you can see the end of the house. It's brick, doesn't show much through the trees."

Lucy was surprised to find many of the passengers still aboard. "I thought everyone must have got off, at all those landings," she said in a low tone.

Elon shook his head. "No. People often come down and back just for the ride. Cash puts a little card in the papers 'Come to Paradise for dinner,' and tells about the steamer, and his good cook, and so on, and he serves a mighty fine dinner right here on board. We'll eat here." He smiled apologetically. "It will be sort of second table, after the others are through. I want to show your father the place, first; want to show you all around."

Mr. Tremont met them at the landing, and horses were ready. Lucy elected to ride with Trav and Elon, and for an hour they explored the plantation roads, traversing runout cane and weed-choked fields, and Elon explained the culture and the care of cane and told what had been done here and what might be done again.

When they returned toward the house, the sugar factory was a little off the path they followed, and Elon asked: "Like to look inside?" So they dismounted and secured their horses. The building seemed deserted, some windows broken or blown out by gusty winds. "We always had parties, in sugar-making time," Elon said, smiling at his thoughts, and Trav, remembering the jolly talk of those high jinks at his own dinner table, recognized the nostalgia in the young man's tone. "My, but we used to have good times." Lucy wished she could find some word to comfort him, but they entered the building and he resumed his role of guide. "The grinding mill is over in the other building. That's where the canes are rolled, crushed flat, all the juice squeezed out of them, nothing left but the bagasse. We burn that for fuel, just as you burn the hulls at the cotton-oil mill. Then the juice comes in here." He explained, step by step the process of converting the juice into sugar. "And that's the story," he at last concluded. "Except details." He looked at his watch. "I expect dinner'll be ready, time we get there."

Back at the house they found the others—Enid and Eleanor, Peter and Mr. Cist and even Mr. Villard—laughing among the great oaks on

the neglected lawn. Enid, panting and hot, came running to throw herself into Trav's arms. "Oh, we've had such fun!" Eleanor followed her,
flushed and laughing, embracing her brother, crying:

"I just had to make them play games, Elon. I'd have bawled if we
didn't."

Elon, his arm around her in firm affection, laughed. "Puss-in-the-
corner?" he asked.

"That and all the others." And she added: "Now Cash is ready for
us. He sent word half an hour ago, but I said we'd wait for you."

Since half a dozen passengers—that couple whom Lucy had been sure
were Northern Methodists, and the three young dandies, and a man
alone—were still aboard the *Paradise,* they put on for dinner a certain
decorum. Afterward, Eleanor took Trav and Lucy to see the house. It
was of brick, two stories high, with a wing extending to the rear. A
brick-paved passage, wide enough for a carriage, ran through from front
to back. On the left of this passage were pantries and store rooms—the
kitchen was detached, reached by a covered gallery—and outside stairs
led up to the second-floor. The living quarters were all on that upper
floor.

"Papa planned it himself," Eleanor explained. "It was mighty incon-
venient to live in, unless you just stayed upstairs all the time. Mama
didn't put her foot to the ground, sometimes, for weeks on end."

Trav marked the difference in her tone when she spoke of her mother.
"She wasn't very well, was she?"

"Not very, the last few years. But oh, she was sweet!" Then the
Paradise whistled to summon them aboard, and she took his arm.
"There, we must go. Elon and I are just shameless, pushing the place at
you, aren't we? But I hate to see it all going to rack and ruin."

"Your father will come home back here to live, some day."

"Oh, Papa!" Her tone was completely empty of emotion, blank in a
fashion deeply eloquent.

When the *Paradise,* got under way, Elon and Trav moved off toward
the stern. Lucy watched them go, and Eleanor watched Lucy, and after
a moment she laughed and threw her arm around Lucy's waist and
squeezed her in amused affection. "If you ever looked at Elon—yes or
at any other man—the way you look at your father, he'd marry you on
the spot." Lucy laughed, and Eleanor asked seriously: "You just love
him, don't you?" Her tone held a wistful envy.

"Yes, of course I do."

They, too, strolled aft. Mr. Villard and Mr. Cist had joined Trav and
Elon there, and Lucy as they approached heard Elon say: "Half the
white men who tried to register have been turned away, but they're
registering every nigra."

Mr. Cist had not seen the two girls approaching. "I had no trouble," he said. "But of course I . . ." Then Eleanor came into his view, and he stopped in mid-sentence. Trav and Mr. Cist and Mr. Fiddler had presented themselves together to the registration board, Trav expecting to be rejected, but they were all accepted without question.

"Well as for me," Mr. Villard announced, "I did not apply. I wouldn't give those scoundrels the satisfaction."

"We can't do anything to better conditions except by voting," Trav suggested. "And we can't vote unless we register. It seems to me we're bound to try."

"Not I," said Mr. Villard firmly. "I'm too old to lick any man's boots."

Eleanor and Lucy moved on, not pausing, and once past, Eleanor asked, in a new tone: "Lucy, do you know Mr. Cist's first name?" Lucy looked at her in surprise, and Eleanor, as though she had not till now been conscious that she spoke aloud, blushed violently. Then they laughed together, laughter so full of amused affection that everyone in sight or hearing looked at them and smiled.

Don, during his many absences, wrote Lucy two or three times a week, but since he was continually on the move from place to place and since the mails were at best irregular, Lucy might go several days without a letter, and then receive three or four at once. On the Monday following this trip down the river, three letters came together, and one of them Lucy gave to Trav to read.

"It's about politics," she explained. "About how the Republicans are teaching the nigras to vote, and the Southerners not doing anything; just sulking, like—" She sought a fit comparison. "Well, like Mr. Villard." Trav had just come home, joining Lucy in the garden. It was the hour of lengthening shadows, the finest of the day. "It's not really interesting till along the middle of this page," she suggested, and pointed to the beginning of a paragraph.

Don's handwriting had a pleasant, flowing quality; it was small, precise, and as legible as type. Trav looked where she pointed and began to read.

Alabama white people don't seem to care [Don had written] how the Negroes vote. But the Republicans—they're mostly people who have come down here from the North—are working hard every day. The Negroes I've talked to around here on other trips didn't care anything about voting. Lots of them didn't even know what voting was. All they wanted was a little piece of land. But now I run into Radical agents everywhere, and some of the Bureau men are helping, getting the Negroes into the Loyal League, with secret meetings, and ceremonies, and the Negroes are tickled pink with all that. The League collects money from them too; five dollars initiation, in some places, and ten cents a month. There are some white people in the League, but the talk is all against whites, so they're getting out.

I've heard some of the Radical speeches. To the Negroes it's: "Be sure and vote, and vote for Republicans. Vote for any man your old master says is a bad man, because your master's lying to you." Or, if it's white men they're talking to, they say: "A poor white man don't belong in the Democratic party. That's the party that kept you poor, poorer than a slave." So far, in the country places, there's been no one telling the Negroes anything else but to vote Republican. I've started trying to explain, whenever I can, what voting means, that it's a new job and they have to learn how to do it. Trouble is, they're so used to taking a white man's word for a thing that it will be a long time before they learn to think for themselves.

And how can they? They can't read, can't write! They'll be just a sore spot till they're taught a little something, how to read, and some true history. I see so many things that need being done, and know so little how to do them. I try to remember that the way to build a house is one brick at a time. If I could think I'd helped just one man to see straight and think straight, I'd feel better. I know so little about myself, and about other men, and how to understand myself and them.

Trav at this point stopped reading and handed the letter back to Lucy. "He's writing this part to you, Honey," he said gently. "He wouldn't want an outsider reading his letter."

"You aren't an outsider! Not really." But she took back the letter.

Trav asked: "Didn't he once tell us he'd taught school?" She nodded, and he said: "I expect he'd be good at it."

"He doesn't think he could do it as well as it ought to be done."

Trav approved. "That's a good sign. Too many teachers think they know all there is to know. It always used to make me mad when I heard about some teacher, maybe fifty or sixty years old and who had never amounted to a hill of beans himself, telling some boy or girl that they had failed! How did he know whether they'd failed or not? They hadn't even begun! No man has ever failed as long as he's still alive! He might do wonders any time, if the chance came his way. General Grant didn't do much at West Point, and neither did Longstreet. They were just about the stupidest students in the class—according to their teachers. Everybody else in their class was supposed to be smarter than they were—anyway, their teachers said so—but no one ever heard of any of the others afterward." He was silent for a moment, then made a mirthful sound. "Besides, Harvey Hill used to say it didn't matter what a man was taught; the important thing was what he learned."

"I remember him. He used to come to Chimneys, when I was little, before the War."

"He and I got along," Trav agreed. "He wrote an arithmetic book once, always claimed arithmetic was about the only thing you could tell a boy was so and be sure you were right."

Lucy said, amused: "You know, Papa, when you're talking about someone you like to talk about, or saying something you enjoy saying, you talk in an entirely different way."

"Different from what?"

"Oh, usually you're sort of pompous, and precise, and—well, dignified. I mean, in the way you talk."

He threw up his hands, and they laughed together. "Stop me, next time, will you?"

"You never called an arithmetic an arithmetic book in your life, unless you were enjoying what you were saying."

"I was, at that," he agreed. "But then, I always do have a good time, talking about things to you." And after a moment, in an abstracted tone: "When's Don coming back?"

She laughed at him. "Now don't start being sorry for yourself, Papa. You'll still have me to talk to for a long, long, time."

When Trav came home from the mill next day, Enid had a message for him from Mrs. Longstreet. "You're to give the General a talking to," she explained. "She says he's going to make a fool of himself. Something about politics."

"He's not with her?"

"No, he's gone to Mississippi, won't be back till the end of the week. She says he's written a letter to the papers, but he's gone to talk it over with Judge Longstreet before he sends it in. They both came to see us Saturday, before we got back from Paradise, but he left that night." She added quickly: "Oh, and here's a piece of news. Redford Streean has moved to the City Hotel! Captain Pew ordered him out of the house, because he let Brett Dewain slap his face and didn't do anything. Isn't that exciting?"

"How did you hear about it?"

"What?" Her cheeks flamed. "Why, it's all over town! Everyone knows about it."

"Who told you?" Lucy saw a twinkle in his eyes.

Enid ignored the question. "Were you with Brett when he did it? I'd have loved to see that. What had Mr. Streean done? I've often wanted to slap his face myself, even when he wasn't doing anything.

He's so hateful-looking. Mrs. Longstreet and I did some shopping, too."

She chattered on, and Trav did not press his interrogation. Lucy saw Peter watching his mother and father, in sly mirth only half concealed. Enid talked almost without a pause, and when she faltered, Lucy spoke of Don's letters, saying that he might be in Alabama for a long time.

"They're still issuing rations," she explained. "And he's working to persuade the nigras to go back to their farms and do their planting."

"I declare, I miss him," Enid commented. "Tell him to write me a letter some day. You never let me read the ones he writes you."

After supper, Trav usually went to his study, Enid to her room; but tonight it was Trav who announced that he was tired, and turned toward the stairs. "Come along, Enid," he invited. "Come show me all the things you bought today."

"Bought?" She had forgotten.

"Yes, shopping with Mrs. Longstreet."

"Oh, I didn't really buy much."

"Come show me what you did buy!"

"Actually, I didn't buy a thing. We were just looking."

He smiled, and offered her his arm. "Come anyway," he insisted. "There are two or three things we must discuss."

She hesitated, then submitted, but from the door she looked back almost entreatingly. When they were gone up the stairs, Peter whispered gleefully: "I bet it was Dolly told her about Mr. Streean."

"Dolly?"

"M-hm. They meet at Uncle Tony's, right along."

Above stairs, while Trav closed the door behind them, Enid started toward the bell pull, but he caught her arm. "Don't call Filly, Enid. I want to talk to you."

"I can't get to bed without Filly to brush my hair!"

He spoke in casual good humor. "Brush your own hair. Don't ring for Filly." He released her, turning away across the room, and without looking at her, he asked: "What else did Dolly have to say?"

She looked toward him with startled eyes, then turned to her dressing table and sat down. Over the shoulder of her own image in the mirror she saw Trav lay aside coat and vest, then sit down and tug at his boots. After a moment's thought, she took out of the dressing table drawer a bottle, poured some capsules into her hand. A pitcher of water and a glass were within reach. She put two capsules into her mouth and sipped water, then asked in a casual tone: "What was that about Dolly?"

"It was she who told you about Streean."

"Yes, of course. Since you won't let me call Filly, you'll have to help me out of this dress. Come, unfasten me." She stood up while he fumbled with many hooks and eyes, then slipped her shoulders free, dropped the garment to the floor and stepped out of it.

"Where did you see her?" he asked, his tone mild.

She drew a dressing sack around her shoulders and began to brush her hair. "Trav, do you really think you can keep me from seeing Dolly when I want to?"

"I think you might have some consideration for my wishes."

"I think you might have some consideration for mine." Since he did not speak, she turned and met his eyes. "I asked you to get a new coachman, remember; asked you to get rid of Saul, after he was so impudent to me."

"He wasn't impudent; he was carrying out my orders."

"You mean I'm a liar?"

"Of course not; but Enid, you must see—"

She dropped her hairbrush, leaned down to pick it up, and toppled quietly off the stool to the floor. Trav, quick at her side, lifted her head and shoulders and cried out in anxious question, but she laughed in drowsy reassurance. "Just—sleepy. I took an extra capsule." Her eyes closed. "You'll have to undress me, darling."

He carried her to the bed, a dead weight in his arms, but as he laid her down, her arms came up around his neck and she tugged at him, making tender sounds. He freed himself and caught her shoulders and shook her. "Enid! Wake up!"

She rolled her head from side to side, smiling in her sleep, and in a red anger he brought the pitcher, as though about to pour water on her face; but she murmured: "You're sweet, Trav." He shook his head, put the pitcher back again, and came to stand looking down at her. At last he tried to remove her dressing sack, rolling her limp body to one side and the other in order to free her arms from the sleeves, but when he pulled the garment out from under her shoulders a seam ripped, and he hesitated, uncertain what to do. He wondered whether Enid had taken a dangerously large dose, but to send for a doctor, if none were necessary, would be ridiculous. Certainly Enid knew how many capsules she could safely take.

Unless she had taken too many with deliberate intent! At that dreadful thought he knelt beside her, caught her in his arms, cried out to her in urgent pleading. She smiled without opening her eyes, and her arms went around his neck and tugged his face down against her shoulder, and she murmured wordlessly; so he was reassured. Still kneeling, he unbuttoned her high shoes. Scrupulous to protect her even from the profanation of his own eyes, he found a nightgown and worked it over her head, manipulated her arms into it, drew it down to her knees.

Then, with much fumbling and straining and groping, he undressed her inside the nightgown, and finally worked back the coverlet and sheet and light blanket, and rolled her off them, and drew them over her.

The question of where and how she had seen Dolly was forgotten in the perplexities of this task. When at last he remembered, it was with amusement at her cleverness in escaping his interrogation. Asleep and warm and helpless, she was so beautiful that it was impossible to keep alive resentment. He accepted defeat, removed his clothes, turned off the gas and got into bed. She murmured something, and he lay a long time awake, holding her close, remembering the years. How strange that one could never continue to be angry when the other party slept warm and trusting in your arms.

On Saturday of that week, Longstreet returned to New Orleans. Mrs. Longstreet had invited them to dinner Tuesday night, but Monday Longstreet called and asked for Trav. Trav was still at the mill, but Lucy came to greet the General. "Mama's out," she explained. "But Papa'll be home soon. Come sit in the garden with me."

He chuckled. "I'm not old enough yet to decline such an invitation!"

Lucy smiled. "Wasn't it lucky I recognized your voice?" They stepped into the garden and she said: "Feel how nice and cool I've made it for us out here. Did you have a good trip?" She remembered Mrs. Longstreet's concern. "Was it all business?"

"No, not all business." He looked at her in thoughtful appraisal. "Seems to me I've heard you make an occasional comment on political affairs," he remarked. She did not speak, and he asked: "Did you ever meet my Uncle Gus?" She shook her head. "I thought you might have. He was sometimes in Richmond during the War. He took me in hand after my father died, brought me up from the time I was twelve years old." He spoke reflectively. "He's a great man, Miss Lucy; an old man, now, but there will always be greatness in him. He was President of Emory College, and of the University of South Carolina, and he was a mighty secessionist before the Lord, until secession was accomplished and he saw the bloody fruit it bore. He's the finest preacher I ever heard." He had been looking at Lucy, but she knew that while he spoke he did not see her; now his expression changed and she saw him realize her presence. "If such a man gave you advice," he asked, "would you take it?"

She considered. "I would if I wanted to," she decided. "Nobody ever takes advice unless they want to, do you think?"

He smiled. "I'll wager the oracles were all females, gifted at evasion. I had hoped you would help me."

"I will if I can. What is it?"

"I've written a letter," he explained, "advising the South to accept the War as settled, and to go to work."

Since if he knew Mrs. Longstreet had forewarned them, he might be offended, she pretended ignorance. "I read it," she assured him. "In the *Times,* wasn't it?" She laughed, to take the sting out of her words. "The one where you said the Confederacy had been dead so long it had begun to smell bad, and ought to be buried."

His color rose. "Not that one, no! I've heard others criticize the figure of speech to which you refer, ignoring the truth it sought to drive home." She felt his anger. "No, this is another. Would you like to read it?"

"I don't think so. Can't you just tell me about it?"

He hesitated. "Probably it's not important to anyone but me. My problem is whether to publish it or to destroy it. I took it to Uncle Gus, and he read it and advised me not to publish. He said to do so would ruin me, said the South wasn't ready to take the advice I give." He added doggedly: "But he had to admit there was a lot of truth in what I said."

"Really agreed with what you said?"

He considered this. "Yes," he decided. "Yes, I think he did. His whole objection to the letter was that it would ruin me."

"I think someone ought to do something to make Southerners act— decently," she admitted.

"You say that as though you meant it."

"I do!" She spoke so quietly that her words acquired an added emphasis. "General, I honestly believe that most people in the South still think they can wiggle it around so the nigras will all be slaves again."

He nodded. "I suppose that's always true. Whenever there has been a great, permanent change in the world, I believe the people who were hurt by it have always tried to assure themselves the change was temporary." He looked at his watch and rose. "I fear the Major is delayed. I'm glad you think I'm right."

She walked with him toward the house. "I know you think you're right," she corrected, emphasizing "you". "But Judge Longstreet may be right, too. If you're both right, then perhaps the letter should be published—even if it does ruin you. It's a hard choice, isn't it?"

"What would you do?" His tone was almost jocular, and she took his cue, and smiled as she spoke.

"Oh, we're too fond of you to want to see you ruined."

He was no longer smiling. "If what I believe is true, then—at whatever cost— it should be said."

"May I say something pretty impudent?"

"Of course, Miss Lucy!"

"Don't do anything just to be stubborn, will you."

He laughed, a great guffaw. "You sound like Louisa! Yes, I'll promise you that! Good evening, and many thanks to you."

Lucy and Peter were included in the invitation to dinner Tuesday night. At table the General spoke of his impending trip to Mexico. He planned to leave in mid-June, to be gone for two months. "So I'm packing Louisa and the babies off to Lynchburg," he told them. "Garland will join them there. I wouldn't want them here in the hot weather anyway." It was business that took him to Mexico. "But I look forward to seeing again some remembered scenes," he admitted, and turned smilingly at Mrs. Longstreet. "And some remembered faces."

"Jeems likes to twit me about his Mexican sweetheart," she explained. "He was wounded there, you know, spent months recuperating in a Mexican home." And she said in the dolorous tone of one who fears the worst: "Jeems, I do hope you don't find her too much changed."

From Mexico the talk turned to politics. Trav had heard from Elon that a new society was formed, to uphold white supremacy. "It's called the Knights of the White Camelia. Elon says the idea started with Judge Alcibiade de Blanc, in Franklin, in St. Mary's Parish. Some of the young blades here in New Orleans got together last Thursday and formed a chapter." And he commented: "Secret societies, oaths, passwords, such things have a strange attraction for the human mind."

Peter said eagerly: "The Hays Brigade and the Thugs killed a lot of niggers in the big riot, and they were both secret societies."

Longstreet looked at the boy and then at Trav. "There's another crowd," he remarked. "The Ku Klux Klan, organized in Tennessee, and now it's working down into Mississippi."

"Preaching the White Camelia doctrine?" Trav asked. "White supremacy!" Longstreet nodded, and Trav said: "Villard thinks the Camelia will do a lot to unify the Democratic party in Louisiana."

Longstreet said strongly: "Major, the Democratic party is as dead as the Confederacy. It will never again accomplish anything—except perhaps to commit a few more murders."

Mrs. Longstreet rapped on the table. "Jeems! Major! Politics at table is bad for the digestion! You can gnaw that bone together after dinner." And she said, smilingly: "Tell us more about that Mexican sweetheart of yours, Jeems."

"Happy to oblige, ma'am, but I could never do justice to Manuelita without a guitar."

"I thought her name was Carmen!"

He shrugged. "Details, always details!" So politics were for the time forgotten, but when he and Trav were alone, Longstreet said at once: "I saw Hood today, Major. Wanted his advice—and yours. You remember Mr. Parker? It was at his suggestion that we went to hear Senator Wilson." Trav nodded. "I've written him a letter." He took from his pocket folded sheets of foolscap. "Here."

"Parker and Governor Hahn edit the *Republican*," Trav remarked. "So you intend this for publication?"

Longstreet nodded, and Trav began to read.

My dear sir—Your esteemed favor of the 15th ult. was duly received. I was much pleased to have the opportunity to hear Senator Wilson, and was agreeably surprised to meet such fairness and frankness in a politician whom I had been taught to believe uncompromisingly opposed to the white people of the South.

I have maturely considered your suggestion to "wisely unite in efforts to restore Louisiana to her former position in the Union, through the party now in power." My letter of the 6th of April, to which you refer, clearly indicates a desire for practical reconstruction and reconciliation. Practical men can surely distinguish between practical reconstruction, and reconstruction as an abstract question. I will endeavor, however, with renewed energy, to meet your wishes in the matter. The serious difficulty that I apprehend is the want of that wisdom which is necessary for the great work. I shall be happy to work in any harness that promises relief to our distressed people and harmony to the nation. It matters not whether I bear the mantle of Mr. Davis or the mantle of Mr. Sumner, so that I may help to bring the glory of "peace and good will toward men."

I shall set out by assuming a proposition, that I hold to be self-evident, viz: The highest of human laws is the law that is established by appeal to arms.

The great principles that divided political parties prior to the War were thoroughly discussed by our wisest statesmen. When argument was exhausted, resort was had to compromise. When compromise was unavailing, discussion was renewed and expedients were sought, but none could be found to suit the emergency. Appeal was finally made to the sword, to determine which of the claims was the true construction of constitutional law. The sword has decided in favor of the North, and what they claimed as principles because they are opposed to law. It is therefore our duty to abandon ideas that are obsolete and conform to the requirements of law.

The military bill and amendments are peace offerings. We should accept them as such, and place ourselves upon them as the starting point from which to meet future political issues as they arise.

Like other Southern men, I naturally sought alliance with the Democratic party, merely because it was opposed to the Republican party. But as far as I can judge, there is nothing tangible about it except the issues that were staked upon the War and there lost. Finding nothing to take hold of except prejudice, which cannot be worked into good for any one, it is proper and right that I should seek some standpoint from which good may be done.

If I appreciate the principles of the Democratic party, its prominent features oppose the enfranchisement of the colored man, and deny the right to legislate upon the subject of suffrage, except by the States, individually. These two features have a tendency to exclude Southern men from that party; for the colored man is already enfranchised here, and we cannot seek alliance with a party that would restrict his rights. The exclusive right of the States to legislate upon suffrage will make the enfranchisement of the blacks, whether for better or for worse, a fixture amongst us. It appears, therefore, that those who cry loudest against this new order of things as a public calamity are those whose principles would fix it upon us without a remedy. Hence it becomes us to insist that suffrage should be extended in all of the States, and fully tested. The people of the North should adopt what they have forced upon us; and if it be proved to be a mistake, they should remove it by the remedy under republican principles of uniform laws upon suffrage.

If every man in the country will meet the crisis with a proper appreciation of our condition, and come fairly up to his responsibilities, tomorrow the sun will smile upon a happy people, our fields will again begin to yield their increase, our railroads and rivers will teem with abundant commerce, our towns and cities will resound with the tumult of trade, and we shall be invigorated by the blessings of Almighty God.

I am, sir, very respectfully, your most obedient servant,

Trav read to the end without a pause, and without lifting his eyes. Then, returning the letter to the other, he said mildly: "So you're turning Republican?"

"Of course, of course." Longstreet spoke in a hot impatience. "That goes without saying! What about the rest of it?"

Trav clasped his hands together, studied them thoughtfully. "Most people won't get any more out of the letter than just that; that you've turned Republican! And they won't forgive you that."

"My politics don't matter," Longstreet protested. "I'm not even a voter. What about the rest of it? Isn't it sound?"

"I don't think so. Certainly, many will refuse to agree with you that the highest law is that established by war. You can't expect the South—whom you called a conquered people—to agree with—"

Longstreet interrupted. "Hold on there, Major. That isn't a question of agreeing or not agreeing. It's a fact."

"Hardly, General." Trav leaned forward, his elbows on his knees, speaking rather in persuasion than in argument. "You make an initial mistake, for you think the War is over. The War isn't over. It began two- or three-score years ago—perhaps longer ago than that—and it will go on for a few more generations. The War isn't over; only the fighting is ended. At least it's ended for the time being—the fighting I mean—but the War won't be over in our lifetimes."

He leaned back in his chair. "And I think you forget that. The War will go on, the Democratic party on one side and the Republican on the other. And when you're fighting a war and one of your men runs away, or goes over to the other side, you call him a traitor, or a deserter. The Democrats and the Republicans will be fighting this War long after you and I are dead, and any time a Democrat turns Republican, other Democrats are going to call him just that. Traitor and deserter."

Longstreet's jaw set. "The man who continues to seek to disrupt the Union is the traitor."

Trav saw the uselessness of argument, yet he persisted. "Of course that's true, but the South will not agree with you. You say the sword has decided in favor of the North. Those who disagree will remind you that the War was not fought over the questions at issue now, here, today. Not at all. Before the War and during the War, no one ever suggested that we were fighting to decide whether or not the nigra should have the vote. The War settled just one question; it decided that unless a state can muster sufficient force to make good its desire, it cannot secede."

Longstreet sat frowning, but at last he said, in grudging admission: "You're not an argumentative cuss, Major, but once started, you put up a pretty good case."

"I've done a lot of thinking, since I read your other letters."

"Yet surely," Longstreet urged, "you'll agree that the stronger party can lay down the law."

"Of course," Trav assented. "But if it's a bad law, it will still collapse of its own weight. In the long run, only those laws endure which are basically right."

"But Major, even a bad law, as long as it does survive, is the law, and must be obeyed."

"A good many men have martyred themselves, during the last two thousands year, because they disagreed with you."

"Yes, but—"

Trav held up his hand. "Wait. I've no wish to thrash out these points with you, General. That can accomplish nothing, except perhaps to get us overheated. Let me just state my opinions, for what they're worth. Here's one other thing. I'm sure the Democratic party has more substance than you think. Even without secession, there are certain rights guaranteed to the States; the Democratic party stands for those rights. It's the opposition party, and as such it has the duty of examining every step taken by the governing party, of seeking to correct every mistake. The South needs good Democrats today more than it needs good Republicans." He smiled disarmingly. "There, sir, I'm through."

Longstreet nodded. "Thank you, Major. I told you I saw Hood today. He says that if I publish this, the South will throw me to the everlasting fires. Uncle Gus said much the same thing. But Currain, you're the first one who has argued that I'm wrong."

Trav did not speak, and Longstreet rose, with extended hand. "Maybe you're right; maybe I am wrong. I'll make you a promise. I'll wait over Sunday, think it over before I decide." They clasped hands. "Now come along, or Louisa'll wonder where we are."

Since that first occasion, Enid and Dolly had several times returned to Tony's, and each time, 'Phemy showed them to the ground-floor room which Tony called his office and left them secluded there. Dolly had several times declared that they were stupid to allow themselves to be thus poked away in a corner. "Captain Pew sometimes comes here," she urged. "Sapphira seems to run a regular *salon*. He says she's perfectly ladylike."

"Of course," Enid agreed. "And she's a tearing beauty."

"Next time, let's ask for her," Dolly proposed. "Besides, we might meet some interesting men." She giggled. "Even if they are niggers. Like that 'Mister Pinchback.' " She elaborated the name with mock respect.

"I've found out all about the other one," Enid told her. "His name's Casual Villard, Cash for short. Filly—she's my maid—Filly's his mother. They call him Cap'n Cash, because he has a fine big steamboat, a stern-wheeler that he bought with some money Mrs. Villard left him when she died. Oh, and she made Mr. Villard send him north to school!"

"Really!" Dolly's eyes were dancing. "Scandals!"

They teased this engrossing topic for a while, exploring all its ramifications. Then Enid asked: "Have you seen your father since Captain Pew put him out?"

"Oh yes, Papa still comes to play poker, or craps. I love to play craps; I nearly always win. I wish we could just refuse to let him in, but of course he still owns a third share, so we can't, really. Enid, shall we make Uncle Tony let us see Sapphira?"

"Oh, Dolly, I forgot to tell you, Trav's found out about our meeting here. When I told him about Captain Pew putting your father out, he guessed you had told me, and he marched me off upstairs, perfectly furious. He's fierce when he's mad, just knocks you clear across the room. Of course, I really love it, but I was scared too."

She began to laugh at her own thoughts, and Dolly laughed by infection, demanding: "What happened?"

"I took some pills and pretended to go to sleep, right in the middle of his scolding. He had to carry me to bed and undress me. He was so clumsy, and it tickled awfully! I almost died trying not to laugh, but I just went all soft and sleepy, and he finally came to bed, and he kept whispering sweet things till I almost had to wake up. But I didn't."

Dolly laughed in an inattentive way, returning to her original proposal. "But about Sapphira," she insisted. "Let's! Once, anyway!" And she promised: "If you want me to, I'll do the talking."

Enid hesitated. "I don't dare think what Trav would do to me if he ever found out."

"Oh, beat you, probably," Dolly laughed. "But you like that!"

So they agreed, and when on their next coming, 'Phemy opened the door, Dolly asked for Miss Sapphira. 'Phemy looked from one to the other with wary eyes; then, without a word, she ushered them into the reception room and herself turned up the stairs.

"You're white as a sheet!" Dolly whispered.

"So are you!"

Sapphira and Tony had elected that day to dine on the gallery which ran outside their windows, overlooking the garden. Afterward, they stayed a while in their room, Tony seated, Sapphira standing, while Quinny, on her knees, with quick stitches corrected an irregularity in the rows of ruffles which covered Sapphira's gown from the hem to the level of her knees.

Tony was in a calmly triumphant mood. The registration of voters had already proceeded far enough so that it seemed likely that Negroes would outnumber whites by almost two to one.

"So the game is in our hands, Sapphira. Unless we throw away the victory by fighting among ourselves. Doctor Roudanez sticks to his extreme position; he wants Louisiana for the niggers. That can't be. I've asked Mr. Warmoth to meet him here—" He looked at his watch. "An hour from now, to help me make Roudanez see reason. If he persists, if he can somehow drum up a following, he can ruin things for us all."

"I like Mr. Warmoth," Sapphira commented. "So many men sound like liars, even when they're telling the truth; but he sounds like a man telling the truth, even when I'm pretty sure he's lying."

Tony nodded assent. "He doesn't take himself too seriously. That's Doctor Roudanez's weakness, but Warmoth will never batter his head against a stone wall!"

Quinny settled back on her heels. "Now go off a little an' turn 'round slow, please ma'am, an' lemme see." Sapphira obeyed, and Quinny frowned with concentration. They were thus silent when 'Phemy tapped on the open door. Her head was high and proud, and that resemblance between Sapphira and her mother which Tony had sometimes remarked was just now plain for all to see.

"Sis," she said, her voice resonant. "You got callers!" Her eyes swung to Tony. "Miss Enid an' Miss Dolly, they asking for Miss Sapphira."

Quinny, intent upon her task, crawled on her knees back to Sapphira's feet and busied herself with one more ruffle. Sapphira looked at 'Phemy and then helplessly at Tony. "They mustn't, Tony! They oughtn't! Mister Travis would just despise it!" Tony rose and came to her, and she insisted: "It isn't a fit thing for them to do!"

"Enid's no paragon, my dear; and Dolly's Captain Pew's—"

She shook her head. "You know what I mean."

'Phemy with a quick movement gripped Sapphira's shoulders. "Sis, you too good f'dem white trash! Dey know it! But don' you look down you' nose at dem. Real ladies is polite to eve'y lady, an' you a real lady!"

Tony said approvingly: "Show them up, 'Phemy. We'll be out in a minute."

'Phemy disappeared; she closed the door behind her. Quinny, still on her knees, backed away to get a better view of her work. "Hit's straight now, ma'am," she reported.

Sapphira asked: "Tony, you want them to see me, don't you?"

"Yes. I'm proud of you. I wish all of them, Trav, Dewain, my sisters; I'd like them all to know you as well as I do." And he urged: "The world's changed, Sapphira. It's not turned upside down, the way some think; it's just been remodeled a little." He chuckled. "We've knocked off the top story, and brought everybody up out of the cellar, that's all. Come."

Sapphira went to her dressing table and sat down. She looked at herself in the glass, then raised her eyes to Tony's at her shoulder. "Am I all right? Shall I change into something? Tell me what to do."

He drew her to her feet, kissed her hand. "Come," he said.

At the door, she would have held back to let him go ahead, but he made her precede him. Enid and Dolly were standing at the window at the other end of the room, and at the sound of the opening door they turned. For a moment no one moved. Then Enid took a step forward, and Tony came by Sapphira's side, and he and she went to meet them. Tony, seeing them all equally at a loss, said in a dry amusement: "Enid, you and Sapphira already know each other. Sapphira, this is my niece, Mrs. Kenyon. You remember her father, Mr. Streean?"

Enid said lightly: "Sapphira, I knew you'd be beautiful. That's why

I made Mr. Currain sell you; it was plain self defense! Men are so easily enchanted."

At the patronage in Enid's tone, Sapphira forgot her reluctance in a faint stir of anger. "You have found that true?" she asked, and Tony wanted to laugh aloud; clearly, Sapphira needed no protector. Enid's color rose, and Dolly said, as though she admired a beautiful garment, or a fine horse:

"You really are quite beautiful."

Sapphira smiled. "Mr. Currain tells me he used to take you to try on the pretty things he bought for me. Now that we've met, I can better appreciate the compliment."

Enid laughed and said: "You know, Sapphira, you remind me of Mrs. Dewain, my husband's sister. Doesn't she, Tony?"

"Actually, that's a high compliment, Sapphira," Tony explained. "Everyone likes Cinda." He drew chairs for them, amused at the cold rage behind Dolly's smile. When they were seated, Sapphira took command of the conversation, and politely kept them all in play, and Tony watched and listened in delighted admiration. Enid seemed completely won; she was friendly and at ease, but Dolly, though she smiled and smiled, struck out again and again and with a lively venom, till at last Sapphira was driven to retaliate.

"Tell me, Mrs. Kenyon," she inquired, "was there a Mr. Kenyon? Or is that just a *nom de guerre?*"

Dolly made a quick movement as though to spring to her feet, but before she could do so, 'Phemy opened the door. One of the newcomers was Governor Hahn; the other, young Warmoth. Tony greeted them warmly. "I'm glad you could come, Judge. Doctor Roudanez should be here in another twenty minutes. Miss Sapphira was speaking highly of you, not half an hour ago."

Warmoth bowed over Sapphira's hand. "Many people speak highly of Miss Sapphira, every-half hour of the day."

Tony touched his arm, turning him toward Enid. "Mrs. Currain, this is Judge Warmoth." He asked Warmoth: "I don't know whether you know my brother Travis?"

"I have that pleasure," Warmoth replied. "Charmed, ma'am."

"And Mrs. Kenyon, Judge Warmoth," said Tony.

"Oh, the Judge and I are old friends," Dolly retorted.

"Mrs. Kenyon has taught me that conversation with a lady can be more interesting than a game of poker," Warmoth assured them, and he asked Dolly: "How is your father? And Captain Pew?"

She avoided a reply. "You were telling me about politics, remember? I only listened."

"There is no higher art!"

Tony interrupted to introduce Governor Hahn, and Enid drew Judge Warmoth's attention. "I wish someone would explain them to me. Or is it 'it'? I mean, is politics 'them' or 'it'?"

"Politics?" Warmoth reflected. "Politics is an 'it.' It's the art of being politic." He added, smiling: "Politics in Louisiana today is the art of being conservative under radical conditions."

Without warning the door swung open and a man came striding in, a man whom Enid did not know. His eyes were shining; he held a letter. "Governor, see here! Read this." He thrust the letter into Governor Hahn's hand, turned then to Tony. "I apologize for my—impetuosity, Mr. Currain. I raced past 'Phemy on the stairs. But I bring great news." He nodded toward the letter the Governor was reading. "General Longstreet has turned Republican!"

Warmoth without a word went to read over Governor Hahn's shoulder, and Tony touched the newcomer's arm. "May I present you, sir?" They turned to Enid and to Dolly, and Tony said: "This is Mr. Parker; Mrs. Currain, Mrs. Kenyon. Mr. Parker edits the *Republican.*"

Dolly asked: "Is this some more politics, Mr. Parker? Is it really so important?"

Judge Warmoth answered her, amused at his own words. "Madame, General Longstreet has made an honest man out of every Republican in Louisiana."

7

WHEN ENID REACHED HOME, Trav had already returned from the mill, and she found him in their room, refreshing himself after the day's stifling heat. He saw an unusual liveliness in her eyes and came toward her. "You're looking mighty pretty this evening, Mrs. Currain!"

She laughed, pushing him away. "Oh, you always think I'm pretty when I'm red as a boiled beet! Hurry, so I can call Filly to help me change."

He turned to wash his face at the commode. "Been doing anything interesting?"

"Don't splutter so!" she protested. "I hate it when you blow your words through soapsuds! Do hurry! Isaiah will be ready for us any time now."

Trav rinsed his face and groped for a towel. He understood that she was unwilling to answer his question, guessed she had something to conceal; but there was never any profit in quarreling with Enid. It was like quarreling with one's child. Defeat was disaster, and victory was a hollow heartache. "I'll be out of the way by the time Filly gets here," he promised. "Go ahead and ring."

She was so full of her news—Mr. Parker and Governor Hahn would publish Longstreet's letter in the *Republican* tomorrow—that it was hard not to tell him; but if she told, he would insist on knowing how she knew. So when Filly came, she bade Trav go. She wanted to tell someone, even Filly; but instead, she spoke to Filly of her son. Since the trip downriver they had more than once discussed him.

"How's Cash getting along?" she asked.

"Jes' fine, Miss Enid."

"He's so good-looking, it's a wonder he's not married."

"He ain' studyin' 'bout dat!" Except when they spoke of Cash, Filly always preserved a certain remote dignity, but any mention of Cash was sure to set her giggling like a schoolgirl. "Dey's enough of 'em afte' him! Be'n two cutting scrapes account o' him, but he don' pay dem black trash no neveh-mind!"

Enid said lightly: "I wish he didn't have that old boat he's so proud of; I'd like him for our coachman. He's so handsome, I'd enjoy looking at him."

"Yes'm, he sho is!"

"But he'd never give up his boat, would he? But maybe it will explode or burn!"

Filly, still giggling, caught the last hook, tied the last ribbon. "No'm. Yes ma'am."

Before going downstairs, Enid went to speak to Peter, who had been two days abed with a severe dysentery. Trav had worried, thinking this might be a precursor of cholera, but Enid laughed at his fears. She found Peter on the mend, and told him the news. "General Longstreet's turned Republican, Petie! It will be in the paper tomorrow."

Peter's eyes widened. "Golly! Does Papa know?"

She shook her head. "I heard about it at Uncle Tony's— so don't tell your father."

The boy grinned. "I guess it will upset him, all right; he thinks Longstreet's so wonderful!"

The supper bell rang. "Don't tell," she repeated, and went down to join Trav and Lucy. Trav said Peter seemed better, and she said he was fine. "So you don't need to look so gloomy! Is anything wrong?"

"No. No, just worrying about Peter, and why the linter doesn't work better, and this wet heat smothers me!" Trav hesitated. "I expect what started it was Sheridan's removing Governor Wells. The longer I think about it, the madder I get." He laughed shortly. "Wells couldn't be trusted, and everybody's glad he's out, but Sheridan had no right to throw him out! That's what makes me mad."

Lucy reached across to touch his arm, smiling, saying: "There, there! Let me tell you some good news for a change."

"Letter from Don?"

"Two! And he's been promoted. He's a Captain."

"Fine! You're too good for any Yankee, but if any of them is good enough for you, I expect it's Don."

Enid next morning came down to breakfast, and this was so unusual that Trav asked: "What got you up so early?"

She smiled and kissed him. "Breakfast with my husband? What's wrong with that?" Yet he was not convinced, watching her with puzzled eyes. She asked lightly: "Anything in the papers?" This was completely out of character, for Enid never looked at a paper.

"Nothing special," he said. "Why?"

"Oh, just making conversation," Enid assured him. "I declare, you make me feel like an intruder at my own table."

Since the *Republican* did not come to the house, Trav presently departed for the mill without having read Longstreet's letter; but at the mill, Elon called it to his attention. Trav read the letter through as attentively as though he had never seen it before. Elon watched him, and as Trav finished, he said: "There's an editorial, too."

Trav found it, and a phrase here and there fixed themselves in his mind. ". . . reconstruction through the party now in power." ". . . Military Acts a peace offering. . . ." "In the Democratic party he sees no living principles."

The concluding paragraphs Trav read a second time.

> In view of the frank and manly stand General Longstreet has deemed it wise to take, it is almost unnecessary to say that he is now where he can be of infinite service to the South in the great work of rebuilding her fallen fortunes, and that a field has opened before him, personally, upon which higher honors are to be won than those which crowned the brow of the soldier, even in his most successful battles and campaigns. We trust not a week will have passed after the opening of Congress without restoring to General Longstreet the full rights of citizenship, and without his being cordially recognized as a valued leader in the Republican party.

Trav folded the paper, and Elon asked: "Well, what do you think of it?"

"This editorial, those final paragraphs, they sound like what the Devil said to Jesus, when he led him up into the mountain and offered him the earth." Elon waited, and Trav spoke half to himself: "If General Longstreet had read this editorial before he wrote the letter, he'd never have written it. I knew about the letter, had read it. I wish I'd had the wit to say to him: 'Fine! You mail the letter and I'll guarantee you'll have a pardon within a month!' He'd have laughed at me and torn up his letter." He said ruefully. "Instead, I told him he'd suffer hideous pains and penalties. I should have known better."

Villard said thoughtfully: "Nobody blamed him—or will blame him now—for advising submission. Even General Lee did that, and Beauregard. All the generals. But this!" He shook his head. "The South will never forgive Longstreet for turning Republican."

"That's what I told him," Trav agreed in grim regret. "It just made him the more determined to bull ahead. I ought to have promised that to publish the letter would elect him Governor, or Senator, or something." He shook his head, returned the paper to the younger man. "Well, he'll never live it down."

He was convinced that this was true, but when at home that night he said the same thing to Lucy, she cried hotly: "So much the worse for the South! She'll never amount to anything till she stops sulking!"

Trav said, some humor in his tones: "You ought not to turn against the South, Lucy. Just because you're going to marry a Yankee!"

"Oh, I don't mean it, really, I suppose."

Enid said: "Well, if I had my way I'd never let General James Longstreet enter my house again!"

"Well, I would!" Lucy insisted. "I know he's stubborn, but all the same, I think it was a brave, wonderful thing for him to do."

"I've always hated him, really," Enid declared. "Everybody talking about what a great general he was! I don't believe he was good at all, if the truth were known!"

Trav said in the flat tone which she knew was final: "He was great, Enid; make no mistake about that. And also, he will always be welcomed in my home; make no mistake about that, either!"

She flushed helplessly. "Oh, you! But of course I didn't mean it! I'm really fond of Louisa. Poor Louisa!"

Lucy cried: "Poor Louisa, indeed! I say, 'lucky Louisa,' to be married to such a man!"

The *Times* next morning, without naming Longstreet, spoke in a grave paragraph of "one of the bravest and stoutest of the late Confederate Generals, who gives in his adhesion to a party whose whole policy seems to be one of vindictive persecution and abuse of his late confederates in arms." Trav read this at the breakfast table, and passed it to Lucy.

"Well, the hunt is up!" he said. "I'll drop in on the General today."

"Can I go with you? Oh, I know I can't, but tell him I think he's wonderful!"

Peter joined them, now fully recovered, and Trav greeted him. "Morning, son. Feeling fine?" Peter nodded, and Trav suggested: "I expect you'll want to do a lot of resting for a day or two."

"Mama said if she woke up we might take the river trip on the *Paradise*, try to cool off."

"It can be as hot on the river as on shore," Trav commented, and rose. "But it's worth trying. Will you go with them, Lucy?"

"No. I don't like the glare off the water."

He hesitated, thinking it would be pleasant to stay comfortably at home, with nothing to do except keep cool and be with Lucy. "You know, you and I haven't had a ride together for a long time," he reminded her.

She smiled. "There's never time! You don't realize how busy you've been. At Chimneys, we always seemed to have plenty of time to do anything we wanted to do—and yet there was always so much to do that we just barely got it all done every day. But here we miss so many things."

"You don't like living in a city, do you?" She shook her head. "Neither do I," he agreed. "At first, when the mill was new and strange, it kept me interested; but now it's just the same thing, day after day." He laughed. "Here I go, grumbling again. I'll see you this evening."

Trav went directly to the offices of Longstreet, Owen and Company, on Union Street, a few doors from St. Charles. It was still early, and as Trav had half expected, Longstreet was not yet there. Except for two clerks, the offices were empty. Trav strolled across to the St. Charles Hotel to sit comfortably on the cool veranda while he waited. Even thus early, men were here in lively discussion, and Trav heard fragments of these conversations. General Sheridan, when he removed Governor Wells, had appointed in his place a Radical politician named Thomas Durant, who promptly declined the office. This morning the rumor ran that Sheridan would appoint in his place Benjamin Flanders, New Hampshire born, who came to New Orleans in 1843 and was driven away in 1861 for his devotion to the Union, barely escaping with his life. He returned in 1862 and since then had served as a federal appointee in the Treasury department. Durant, who before the War had been a slaveowner, since he became a Radical was despised by most Southerners as an apostate and a coward, but Flanders was hated, and Trav heard one man say now:

"I was one of those who made him run for his life six years ago, and if he takes this appointment I'll be one to make him run again."

Trav, idly listening, thought how quick the Southerner was to threaten death. Probably every man of any prominence in the South had received many anonymous letters, and public threats were not infrequent; but in the South, as elsewhere, most threatened men lived long and peaceful lives. This morning, threats against Sheridan, against Flanders, against Congress, against all Yankees, ran gustily up and down the veranda. Well, it was a way to blow off steam. The threats were not meant seriously; they were mere hyperbole, an exaggerated expression of distaste for things as they were.

Several times he heard Longstreet's name. It was significant of the respect in which the General was held that there were no threats against him, and he was defended as stoutly as he was attacked; yet his defenders were more like apologists, while his critics were numerous and bold.

Trav rose at last and returned to Longstreet's office. This time the General was in, seated at his desk, a half-filled sheet of foolscap before him, his pen in his hand. When Trav entered, the other looked up, his eyes somber; he rose, his movement guarded.

"Ah, Major!" he said, in an empty tone, but Trav extended his hand, and the General took it with obvious relief. "Well, Currain, I'm glad to see you!" And he said, almost defiantly: "I suppose you saw that I decided to publish the letter."

"I read it, yes."

"You were right in your prediction," Longstreet confessed. "Three acquaintances have already refused to recognize me on the street, and you're my first caller." He laughed shortly, tapped the paper on his desk. "Even the *Times*, the very editor who first solicited my views, this morning damns me. He deliberately misunderstands." He nodded toward a chair. "Sit down. I'm writing him now, to explain my position."

Trav shook his head. "Don't do it, General!" He smiled. "You know the old rule: never explain; your friends don't need it, and your enemies won't believe it."

The General brushed this aside. "I'm not a man who accepts an insult without retort." And he asked, like a challenge: "Do you still think me wrong?"

"General, as between you and me there's no question of right or wrong. Either way, I'm on your side."

Longstreet's eyes lighted gratefully. "Thank you. There's no one I'd rather have beside me." He smiled. "I remember that when it comes to the heat and mettle of battle, you wield a stout sword! You were a surprise to me, that day—was it Seven Pines?"

Trav said, flushing: "Blame Nig. He ran away with me."

"But it takes a battle to get you started!"

"Well, you were somewhat of a sluggard yourself, General, till the guns began to roar." Trav's voice hushed with memories. "Then you were an army!" And suddenly he laughed. "I'll never forget the retreat after Gettysburg, the night we crossed the river. Fairfax said that when you swore at a mule, the mule galloped all the way to Winchester."

The General chuckled. "It's a pity you can't accomplish as much by cussing a man as you can by cussing a mule." He picked up the sheet of foolscap. "There's not a cuss word in this! Maybe it needs a few. Read it, Major."

Trav obediently began to do so, but almost at once he broke off. "You say here 'the War was made upon Republican issues.' That's not accurate. We made the War on the issue of secession. The abolition of slavery, the enfranchisement of the nigra, the Military Acts, these are all issues raised since the War. If you and I had a fight over a horse, and I won, I couldn't fairly claim that I'd won not only the horse but the carriage and the stable."

Longstreet said irritably: "I know. I know. What else?"

Trav read on. Longstreet had written: "These are unusual times, and call for practical advice," and he proceeded to elaborate at some length his insistence that the verdict of the sword was final. Trav said: "I'd leave out this part, General. In fact, I wouldn't send the letter at all, if I were you. The trouble is, sir, no one cares now whether your advice is good or bad. They only remember that you've turned Republican."

"But that's my whole point!" Longstreet insisted. "That's my 'practical advice.' That's what a lot of Southerners ought to do." And he urged: "Why, see here, Major; suppose you were commanding a division, and every time you gave an order, one regiment said: 'No, we won't!' You'd win damned few battles! As long as the South says 'No' to everything the North wants to do, this Union of ours will make mighty little progress!"

"The South doesn't consider it 'this Union of ours,'" Trav reminded him. "We tried our level best to get out of it."

"But we didn't succeed in doing so! We're still in it! So what's good for the Union is good for us—and what's bad for the Union is bad for us! Suppose we refuse to help; the Republican North will go ahead just the same, develop industries, build railroads, become increasingly prosperous. The North won't suffer, but the South will!" He came strongly to his feet. "And the United States will suffer!" He flung up his hands. "There's nothing left of the Democratic party except States' rights, and if a state can't secede to enforce its rights, then it has no rights worth the name. The party's dead! Whatever's accomplished in the United States in the next twenty years will be accomplished by the Republican party!

"So, yes, I've turned Republican, and I hope to see a lot more do the same."

He stared at Trav for a moment, then sat down. "Guess I got pretty hot!" he muttered. "I feel strongly." Trav laid the unfinished letter on the desk. "I'll look it over," Longstreet promised. "Maybe not send it, or maybe edit it a bit. I want the *Times* to publish the letter I wrote Parker. So few people read the *Republican* that they don't know what this excitement is all about." He said, head on one side: "You're not saying much, Major."

"I didn't want to interrupt!"

Longstreet guffawed. "I don't often get wound up like that."

"You're a public figure, of course," Trav admitted. "And you feel a responsibility to express your opinions, in case they may do some good." Longstreet nodded, and Trav went on: "My opinions are of no importance to anyone—except to me. I've made so many mistakes in handling myself and my own business that I don't feel I can handle other peoples' business for them. I've always felt that if I did the best

I could with myself, I'd have about all I could handle." He added humbly: "I wonder, if a man makes as good a man as he can out of himself, if that isn't about the best way he can be of service to his family, or his friends—or his city, or his state, or his nation." Longstreet did not speak, and after a moment Trav chuckled at his own serious tone. "I don't often get wound up myself. Maybe it's catching."

Longstreet laughed and came to his feet. "Damn it, Currain, I could never be a man like you! You can keep your mouth shut! I have to snort and stamp on the ground, just to prove to myself that I'm somebody! That's why generals have staffs, so somebody will do the work while they do the strutting!" He thrust out his hand. "Proud to know you, Major!" Their hands struck and held.

At supper that night, Enid was enthusiastic about their day on the river. Passengers had been more numerous than on the former excursion. "But Cap'n Cash let me sit in the pilothouse both ways," she reported. "I was glad, too, for there were a lot of mighty ordinary people on board."

"Cool, was it?"

"Oh yes. Here, the trees shut off the breeze. I can't stand it much longer. How soon can we get away?"

Brett and Cinda had urged them to come again to the Plains, and they planned to do so. "Sometime in July," Trav told her. "Mr. Cist is going home to Cincinnati for a visit, and if the heat is bearable, we'll stay till he gets back." He asked Lucy: "Has Don any idea when he'll be here. I'd like to see him before we go." He smiled. "And I expect so would you."

"He doesn't know at all," she admitted. "But, if I can let him know when we'll be going through, he might be able to meet us in Montgomery. His headquarters are there."

Trav promised to tell her as soon as he could set the date. He asked Peter: "Did you ride in the pilothouse, too?"

Enid answered. "No, Peter was mostly down in the engine room with some boys from Mr. Soulé's school who happened to be aboard." She laughed. "You were all so cute, Peter, swaggering around the decks like so many strutting beaus. Trav, I even saw Peter smoking a seegar! He didn't seem to be sick, either."

Peter colored resentfully. "Oh, Mama, you don't get sick after you're used to it!"

"Peter's probably an old hand," Trav agreed, and he smiled. "One thing sure, son; it hasn't stunted your growth. Try one of mine?" He offered Peter a slender black stogie. "It may be stronger than you like," he admitted, but Peter took it.

They moved into the drawing room, and Enid was so amused by

Peter's smoking that she did not go upstairs till Peter finished that
cigar and accepted another. Then he and she went up together, and in
her room he said in tolerant accusation: "You have to tell everything,
don't you?"

"I didn't tell Papa you were gambling."

He chuckled. "No harm in gambling, as long as you win. And I
always do."

Saturday morning, Longstreet's letter was published in the *Times*.
The General had eliminated a few lines to which Trav had objected,
and now concluded: "I ask that you will do me the favor to publish
this, and my letter (to Mr. Parker) as soon as you may find convenient
space for them."

The *Times* accordingly printed both letters. A long editorial comment began with two paragraphs which touched Trav deeply.

> It is with extreme reluctance that we yield to the demands of
> candor and of justice to ourselves in expressing our respectful and
> kindly dissent from the views uttered by General Longstreet in his
> letter published in another part of our paper. There is an obvious
> spirit of sincerity and honesty in this letter which appeals to our
> charity and forbearance, and in connection with the high proofs of
> earnestness and devotion afforded by the acts of the distinguished
> writer in other spheres, requires that we should treat even the grave
> error it contains with tenderness and deference.
>
> General Longstreet, a brave and reliable military chief, is evi-
> dently inexperienced, we may say unsophisticated, in the devious
> ways of politics and politicians. His letter is full proof that the
> manly style of warfare in which he has been trained and skilled, is
> calculated to unfit him for the very different strategy of the new
> arena upon which he has ventured his fame and fortunes. As the
> commander of the famous Corps which he led so heroically and
> skillfully in many a bloody struggle, he challenged the admiration of
> the world and the respect of his foes. As a party chief and leader
> in the petty struggles for political power and patronage, we fear that
> the laurels he has so worthily won and worn are exposed to serious
> peril.

These words seemed to Trav profoundly true. General Longstreet
himself might resent being looked upon as an object of "charity and
forbearance"; but certainly the editorial had been written in a friendly
spirit.

Below, separated from it by a dash, there was another paragraph:

> A portion of the Republican party seem to claim full right and
> title to General Longstreet. Since the publication of his letter to

Mr. Parker, the more enthusiastic have on several occasions spoken of him as a very suitable candidate for the position of United States Senator, and there seems to be little doubt among them that full pardon and amnesty will be granted him by Congress immediately upon convening another session. The wishes of the General do not seem to have been consulted.

Trav thought that final paragraph, with its suggestion that for what he had done, General Longstreet might receive a reward, was deeply disturbing. A familiar couplet ran through his mind; of the exact words he was not sure, but it was something about treason never prospering, because if it did prosper none dared call it treason. The General had committed what many men would call a sort of treason, yet grateful Republicans might thrust upon him prosperity. There was an ugly irony in the fact that if the General did prosper, his prosperity would damn him more completely than before.

He did not see the General again till Tuesday, when after supper Mr. and Mrs. Longstreet called to say goodby. Mrs. Longstreet and the babies, with two nurses, would leave next day, taking the cars to Memphis and thence east through Chattanooga, with many changes of train and many hours of waiting for connections, and Enid and Lucy promised to come to the station, a dozen blocks down Calliope Street, to see them off.

When the ladies went upstairs, Trav and the General turned to Trav's office, and Isaiah brought decanter and glasses. Trav thought Longstreet looked tired and harassed, but that was not surprising. The *Republican* on Sunday had proudly remarked that the General's opinion on the rights of Congress to legislate upon suffrage corresponded with the opinions of Sumner, Wendell Phillips, Chief Justice Chase and Thaddeus Stevens. No four men in the North were better hated in the South than these, and no Southerner could find himself, without embarrassment, placed in such a company. The Sunday *Picayune*, while paying honest tribute to Longstreet's stature as a soldier, had dismissed his reasons for his course as "puerile," characterized his arguments as "historically false, logically unsound, and filled with capacity for all conceivable mischief," and expressed a courteous and obviously honest regret "that a brilliant reputation in war should have been put to such peril by political utterances so feeble." Trav in reading that editorial found nothing in it with which he could disagree; his affection for the big man could not alter his conviction that Longstreet had been wrong.

For a moment after their glasses were filled, neither spoke; then Trav said: "Well, sir!" He lifted his glass and they sipped the brandy. "I haven't seen you for several days, not since Friday."

As though the other's words were a question, Longstreet assented. "Yes, I've been busy. I find myself involved in a wordy sort of brawl." He smiled angrily: "It seems that in politics as in war, it is not enough to occupy a position; one must be prepared to defend it. I'm summoning reinforcements." Trav looked at him, inquiry in his eyes, and Longstreet said: "You and Hood are my friends, yet each of you disagrees with me, and Beauregard doubtless feels as you do, but I've written to some of my old comrades, asking them—if they approve my views—to publish their position."

Trav wondered to whom those letters might have gone, but he did not ask. Longstreet moved uneasily in his chair. "Of course, I've support in the North," he said, and he explained. "The *New York Times* thinks I express the conviction of an influential class, though I'm afraid they draw up that dogma out of a well of ignorance. They agree with me that a party which clings to the idea of slavery can't hope to carry the country." He made a mirthless sound. "I've given up the idea of going to Mexico, partly because of the troubled times there—they'll shoot Maximilian before the month is out, may have already done so—but also, if I went now, there'd be those who would say I was running away from a fight."

"I don't believe you ought to think of the situation as a fight, General," Trav suggested. "Of course there are loose talkers, but the *Times* and the *Picayune*, though they disagree with you, do so in friendly terms. Even this O'Brien, in his letter in the *Times* this morning, speaks of you affectionately, says you were a brave leader, revered as a soldier and a general."

"Who is he, do you know?" Trav shook his head, and Longstreet colored with anger. "He says he was a private, but now declares himself my equal." His tone changed; he laughed without mirth. "Major, you know me well enough to know that I hold every man who disagrees with me an enemy."

Trav laughed with him. "That includes me, remember?"

"No, not you." But Longstreet's tone was dull and spiritless.

Trav asked, after a moment: "Where will you go this summer, if not to Mexico? To Lynchburg with your family?"

"Parker wants me to come to New England. He and Casey." He laughed in dry scorn. "Oh, the Republicans have big plans for me. I'll stay here for the present, till no one can accuse me of flight, but I'm in the humor to say goodby to New Orleans forever. I've no roots here."

"What about your business?"

"If the cotton crop is as poor this year as last, there'll be no business. But in any case, I know the Owen boys find me an embarrassment. They insist that they're with me, but I suspect they'll be relieved if I—well, if I take a long leave of absence." He added: "And as far as business goes, I've seen mighty few customers this last week, either here or at the insurance office. You'd think I had yellow fever, the way they avoid me. Hood says he'll handle the insurance business while I'm away."

"I never saw you discouraged before."

Longstreet for a moment did not speak, turning in his fingers his half-empty glass. His eyes met Trav's. "I did not do this lightly, you know; not without taking thought, not without prayers. I thought some good for the South might come of it. Louisa warned me, and Uncle Gus warned me, and Hood, and you, that I'd be outcast, branded a scalawag. I was ready for that, if only some good did come." He shook his head. "But it appears now that without helping the South, I've ruined myself. Yet I'll never be sorry for my stand."

Through May and into June, there had been some cholera in the city, but it had all disappeared. Now, two Union soldiers died of yellow fever, and Trav decided to hurry his family's departure. He discussed plans with Mr. Cist, then told Lucy that they would spend Sunday, the twenty-third, in Montgomery; this in case Don could meet them there.

Meanwhile, he saw Longstreet when he could. The General was deluged with letters, some few approving; but the great majority were either reasonable protests, or damning and obscene. "What puzzles me," Longstreet confessed, "three months ago, after the Military Acts were passed, many of us—General Lee, General Beauregard, many others besides me—each of us counseled the South to accept the verdict of the sword, and to make a new government on the pattern laid down for us by Congress. At that time, there was no such clamor of disagreement and abuse as is the case now. Now, the vials of general wrath are being poured in a flood over my head. Why's that, do you suppose?"

"Well," Trav suggested, "perhaps the first shock of the Military Acts was so great that we weren't capable of orderly thought. We were frightened, too, frightened at finding ourselves suddenly under army rule, so we walked softly.

"But now we've found out that military government doesn't necessarily mean courts-martial, and firing squads. We've found we can argue with the army without getting shot. In March we were both angry and afraid; now we're just angry!" He hesitated. "So advice that then seemed reasonable is resented now."

Yet his voice did not fall; it was as though he had stopped in mid-sentence, and Longstreet said in dry amusement. "Go on. You were about to add, for a further reason, that this time I turned Republican. True, of course. Here!"

He handed Trav another letter, a long one, written in a small neat hand, two foolscap pages closely lined. It recited the familiar arguments, lucidly and yet at such length and with such a multiplication of words that Trav sensed behind it the legal mind, which is never satisfied with saying a thing once but must repeat it in every conceivable fashion, till the meaning is obscured behind a spray of words as the transparency of a window pane is destroyed by a gust of rain. It was signed simply "B. J. S.," and when Trav saw this—he had paused in his reading to look for the author's name—he tossed it into the wastebasket.

Longstreet, busy with another letter, looked at him in surprised inquiry; but before he could speak, two men stepped in through the open door, and Longstreet rose to greet them. Trav recognized Judge Warmoth, whom he had met at the time of the riot inquiry. His companion was a mulatto. Warmoth, having shaken Longstreet's hand, swung at once toward Trav.

"And Major Currain. Sir, I'm happy to meet you again!"

Trav, even while he smiled at the tact of the politician, was flattered and pleased. He acknowledged the greeting, and Warmoth introduced his companion. "And gentlemen, this is my good friend, Mr. Pinchback."

Longstreet said: "Good morning, young man." Trav bowed, and Pinchback said good morning, and Longstreet bade them take chairs. Trav made a move to depart, but Warmoth said amiably: "Don't let us hurry you away, Mr. Currain. Ours is only a social call."

Longstreet said: "Yes, Major, stay."

Trav was glad to do so. At their first meeting, he had been sufficiently interested to inquire into Warmoth's history. A former Lieutenant Colonel in the Union army, with something vaguely discreditable in his record, Warmoth had come to New Orleans early in 1865 and had, single-handed, organized a political party dedicated to universal suffrage and to the Sumner theory that the Southern states by seceding had reduced themselves to the status of territories. On this theory, he organized a convention which adopted a platform and planned and carried through an election at which Warmoth himself was—not surprisingly—named territorial delegate to Congress. At this election, Negroes voted freely, and Warmoth, claiming a total vote of 19,000, proceeded to Washington, presented a memorial to Congress, and for weeks lounged about the lobbies, making many friends. Though it was obvious that he presented the memorial with his tongue in his cheek, the effrontery of the whole proceeding was so outlandish that the Democrats were more amused than angry.

Listening now, Trav heard in Judge Warmoth's remarks the suggestion that he found himself and the rest of the world an infinite jest. "General, I wanted you and Mr. Pinchback to know each other," he explained, as they sat down, and he added: "Now that you're fellow Republicans." Trav saw Longstreet's faint frown, but Warmoth added easily: "I expect the word surprises you as much as the first time she's called 'Mrs. Jones' surprises a bride!'" So they laughed together, and he explained: "Mr. Pinchback is a moderate Republican. He would give the vote only to those Negroes qualified to use it! I've pointed out to him the absurdity of that distinction. Suppose, for instance, it were applied to white men!"

Longstreet asked Pinchback, in a dry tone: "Do you consider yourself one of the qualified?"

The mulatto said gently: "I have never voted—except for Judge Warmoth, for delegate—but it's possible that voting is like so many other things; one learns by experience. I can only say, General, that I believe I'm qualified to learn."

Trav thought Pinchback spoke like a man of considerable intelligence. Longstreet, beyond a suspicious grunt, did not reply, but Warmoth broke the momentary silence.

"Well, General, you step into Louisiana politics at a time when the situation is rich in opportunities. General Sheridan has ridded us of that whiskered old bumbler—"

"Governor Wells?" Longstreet asked, and Warmoth nodded.

"The same." His eyes twinkled. "All's well that ends Wells! The rest of the chaff will soon be cleared away, and then there'll be work for us to do. Louisiana—and New Orleans—are bankrupt, their obligations selling at twenty-five cents on the dollar. There are only four paved roads in the city, and prolonged bad weather makes our other streets all but impassable. We've the finest harbor in the world and not one good wharf. Open ditches stinking with foul waste are our only drainage. Our streets are lined with gambling dens and the houses of harlotry. Epidemics regularly kill their scores and their hundreds. New Orleans is controlled by a corrupt, ignorant and bloody-minded gang. The public buildings are in disrepair, the levees are crumbling. The police force is recruited from the ranks of thugs and murderers, and if there is an honest public official in the city, I don't know him. We have no clean water to drink; swarms of flies; no screens; filthy slaughterhouses! The city is fouler than a well-kept cesspool."

He had spoken in measured words, but now he rose, moving restlessly to and fro. "All this must be remedied, and to find the remedy is the responsibility which the Republican party must now assume. That, General, is why we need such men as you! New Orleans needs railroads, docks, warehouses, hospitals, sewers, paved streets—but above all, she needs men; men like you, General!" He swung toward Trav. "And you, Major Currain! Men! For there's work to do."

He broke off, strode across the room and back, laughed in an awkward way. "My apologies for the harangue." He dropped into a chair, looked at Trav. "Major, is not Mr. Anthony Currain your brother?" Trav nodded, and Warmoth said quizzically: "I suspect you do not share his political opinions."

"I do not," Trav agreed.

"Yet you and the General?" Warmoth's words were a question, and since Trav hesitated, Longstreet answered.

"The Major and I were comrades in arms," he said. "And we are friends. But in politics we travel different roads."

"The late War shattered many friendships," Warmoth commented.

"A pity that the peace should shatter more." He rose, and Pinchback with him. "I hope, General, we can do some great work together. Now we'll bid you good day."

When he and Pinchback were gone, Longstreet and Trav looked at one another in a thoughtful fashion, and Trav said at last: "It seemed to me that that young man—both of them, in fact—were men of parts."

"I find more substance in Warmoth than in any of his associates," Longstreet agreed. "He has an invincible good nature. There's easy mirth in him, but there's force too. He'll be heard from."

"What did you think of Pinchback?"

"A clever child. He may succeed, but if he does, success will ruin him."

Trav spent Saturday at the mill. A few more cases of yellow fever had appeared among the Northern soldiers in the city, and there were some cases even among the Creoles, who had lived here for generations and were usually immune. The disease was still in a mild form, yet there had been a number of deaths, and Trav was anxious to get away. Mr. Cist, knowing Trav's eagerness to see his family safely to the Plains, had offered to give up his trip to Cincinnati. Trav declined, but today Mr. Cist reopened the question.

"In fact," he urged, "there's no need of either of us being here; not with Fiddler to take care of things. And Elon can help him out, if the machines give trouble."

He looked at Trav in an expectant way, and Trav asked: "Are you thinking we might bring Villard into the Company?"

"As a matter of fact, I am," Cist admitted.

Trav nodded. "I've been thinking the same thing." The mill had grown, and their production had steadily increased, but so had the burden upon each of them. "I didn't realize, when we began, how much I'd have to learn." He smiled. "There's quite a difference between running a plantation with slave labor and running a factory with hired labor. And until the bills began to come in, I'd no suspicion how much

we'd have to spend for repairs, or new machinery, or replacements."
He grinned. "We lost money on the first oil we sold, and I didn't even
know it, didn't know what that oil had cost us: I mean, in interest on
the money that built the mill and bought the machinery, and in the
time and money you and I had put into it, and for seed, and freight,
and handling, and storage, and all the other charges that would come
later on. But now when we make a gallon of oil I can tell you exactly
what we have to charge for it in order to give ourselves a profit."

"I couldn't do that," Mr. Cist confessed. "I sell oil to get money to
build a bigger mill to make more oil so I can sell it to get money to—"

Trav laughed. "Round and round. But, Josh—" He had never
thought Cist's given name amusing till one day Lucy asked him what it
was, and laughed with delight when he told her. "But, Josh, as it is
now, you do the selling, and I do the figuring, and Mr. Fiddler runs the
mill, and when a machine breaks down we send for Villard. So every
time the machine breaks down it costs us money. Besides that, maybe
if we had him here all the time, we wouldn't have so many breakdowns.
Maybe he'd save us his salary."

So they were agreed, and when they presented the matter to Elon,
he grinned with delight. The details were easily settled. Lucy, when
she heard, said warmly: "I'm so glad, Papa. I like Elon, and I'm proud
of Southerners like him, who've gone to work instead of just sitting
back and twiddling their thumbs and talking about what wonderful
people they used to be."

With this matter settled, Trav, his mind at ease, was eager to start
for the Plains. He had invited Longstreet to sup with them the night
before their departure. Longstreet was half an hour late, and Trav
thought him ill at ease, and could not guess the reason till when they
were seated at the table, the General said, heavily jocose: "Well, since
none of you have congratulated me, it must be that you haven't heard
my news." They looked at him, waiting, and he said awkwardly:
"Actually, it's of small consequence, but I had a telegram today from
'Lys Grant. My pardon has been signed!"

In the momentary silence, Trav wondered whether Lucy and Enid
were as shocked as he. This boon came too promptly; the pardon was
too much like payment. He was relieved when Lucy came quickly to
kiss the General's cheek, to hug him in warm affection. "Oh, I'm so
glad!"

"Hah!" He chuckled with pleasure, his arm for a moment around
her. "That young Lieutenant allows this, does he?"

"Oh, he won't mind, since you're no longer a criminal!"

Even Enid, seeing how troubled he was, kissed Longstreet, and they
united to make a jolly hour for him.

After Lucy and Enid had retired, Trav and the General sat late, in quiet talk together. When he rose to say good night, Longstreet said with an uneasy laugh: "I made a ridiculous mistake today. I wrote a letter to my sister Sarah,—that's what made me late—and then mailed her own letter back to her, stuck my answer in my pocket. Didn't discover it till I took it out to look at it, after I'd rung your doorbell." He produced a folded sheet of paper, and to Trav's astonishment the other's voice suddenly was husky. "Here's my answer. Read it. It will give you an idea how her letter cheered me up."

Trav unfolded the letter, written in pencil on the Carondelet Street letterhead, in that awkward backhand which the injury to his right arm had forced upon the General.

New Orleans, La., June 26th., 1867

My Dear Sister:

I have just received and read your sweet letter of the 22nd. It brought tears in abundance to my eyes and made me quite a boy again. It is truly refreshing to find one who can breathe such sentiments of simplicity and Godly love and sympathy. There is more of wisdom in your simple virtuous judgment, than in the minds of thousands of statesmen whose minds are swayed by prejudice and passion. For months, I have prayed to God to guide me and help me to devise honorable means, by which our people might be saved from the extremity of distress. The letters that are published are the result of my meditations, and His divine aid. They were written because I thought it a duty, that I owed to our people and if I had failed to discharge it, I should have been troubled with the neglect of so important a duty, upon my deathbed. If the people accept my counsel, God will bless and prosper them. If they reject it, I tremble at the contemplation of our future. I am relieved in any event, as it can not be charged upon me that I failed to counsel them in their hour of need. The harsh things that you speak of as being said of me, I can endure with the utmost patience, for I know, that those who speak evil of me, do not know what they do. It is not in their hearts to injure me, it is only the result of misguided judgment. I thank you again for your letter for it is not unusual to receive letters (anonymous) threatening me with the assassin's dagger, under the cover of darkness, so you may judge that I am in a most appreciative mood for such words of sweet consolation as your letter bears. The threats of course have but little effect, but I can not say that it is pleasant to receive them. Give my love to Judge Ames.

I remain your most affectionate brother,

JAS. LONGSTREET

Trav read this, guessing that Longstreet had made a pretext to show him the letter, thinking it might serve as an explanation and a defense, and he found this deeply moving. When his throat cleared, he folded the letter and handed it back, saying, not as a question but because he must say something: "Judge Ames is her husband."

"Yes." The General put the letter away. "I'll go past the office, put this in the proper envelope, send it to her." And he said: "Well, Major, you're off tomorrow. I don't know when we'll meet again. Probably next winter."

"We will, be sure of it."

Their hands struck, and thus they parted. There was next day a small flurry of new cases of yellow fever, and Trav was glad to leave New Orleans behind.

PART FOUR

The Carpetbagger

July 1867 — January 1872

I

D ON WAS UNABLE to meet them in Montgomery. In a small town near the Mississippi line, a white woman had been outraged. The culprit had not been identified, and there was danger of haphazard violence against the Negroes; so Don and a squad of soldiers had quartered themselves in the town till the first excitement passed. His letter explaining this reached Lucy a few days after their arrival at the Plains, and he went on:

It's a wretched little place. Before the War, there were two big plantations near, but now they're abandoned and their owners dead or moved away. Not more than two or three of the sixteen male white residents can read or write. They're undernourished physically as well as mentally, half-starved, some of them half-witted, worse off than the most miserable Negroes. I don't suppose very poor people and tremendously rich people ever lived as close together as in the old planters' South. Why didn't the rich people at least see to it that the poor had schools? There's terrible poverty all through this region. I haven't seen an unpatched garment on anyone, child or adult. There's no school, of course. A boy baby born here, and raised here; how can there ever be any hope for him? Take a boy like him and a boy like Elon Villard, for instance, and compare what their lives have been. Elon's a fine man, none finer; but suppose Elon and one of the young men here had been changed in their cradles; would Elon be like one of these?

It isn't only in the South that this is true. I've seen it in Maine, and everywhere I've been, but it still makes me feel guilty, even though I know I can't do anything about it. Giving them money's no good. Maybe giving them friendship, stopping to talk with them, sharing their interests—but I'm not sure they have any. So many people aren't really interested in anything—or at least they don't seem to be. I wish I knew people better, knew how to get acquainted with them, how to help them. But why should I feel competent to help anyone? I've enough on my hands trying to make something out of myself.

She finished, and sat for a while with the letter in her lap, her eyes open but unseeing, her thoughts exploring roads of beauty and of promises to be fulfilled.

Late in August he was recalled to New Orleans. "So I take every opportunity to walk by your home," he wrote. "And if old Abram's in the garden, he lets me come in and sit a while where I have sat with you. Sometimes I go after supper to see Mr. Fiddler." This year as in the past, Mr. Fiddler was living, during their absence, in the house on Prytania Street. "I like to talk with him. He knows so much about the Negroes, understands them; yes, and not only about Negroes. About people."

The yellow fever was by that time raging in New Orleans, and Lucy was worried for him, but he never spoke of it. She had that summer an occasional letter from Elon, filled with news of their friends. He wrote that Jimmy Morgan's venture at raising cotton on the Hope plantation had ended in failure. "As Jimmy tells it," Elon wrote, "the fields were a flower garden one day, the plants all in bloom, and next morning there was not a plant on its feet. The army worm's as bad as Sherman. Jimmy's gone back to Charleston. Eleanor says he's beginning to sit up and take notice, and she thinks he'll marry again."

Elon had a gift for seeing the amusing side of things, so Lucy regularly read his letters aloud. After one of these occasions, Enid remarked: "I declare, if I had a beau who wrote me letters like that, I'd hang on to him."

"Oh Mama," Lucy protested, "Elon's not a beau! We're just good friends. He's writing to us all, really."

Trav, too, had regular letters from Elon, about matters which arose at the mill, and he heard occasionally from Mr. Fiddler. Mr. Cist had decided to prolong his vacation, to stay in Cincinnati till the yellow fever abated. Cases had multiplied and on September fourth, the disease was characterized by the New Orleans Board of Health an epidemic. A few days later, Don wrote that Mr. Fiddler had been stricken.

"I saw him Sunday afternoon," he explained, "and I thought he looked feverish. He said he felt all right, just tired and a little headache, but I went to see him Monday after supper and his face was flushed and his eyes red, and his nostrils and lips, too. I got Doctor Berthelot—the doctors are all pretty busy—and he said it was yellow fever. I'll let you know how he gets along."

Two hours after that letter reached them, Trav started for New Orleans. Lucy at first wished to go with him. "Because now Don may get sick too," she urged. She and Enid were helping Trav pack.

"No, Honey, you stay here," he told her. "I'll be busy enough, without having to worry about you."

Enid said petulantly: "You're a perfect idiot to go at all, Trav."

"Mr. Fiddler and I have been friends a long time."

"There's nothing you can do for him! Before you get there he'll either be over the worst of it or dead."

Lucy spoke in fond reassurance to them both. "Don't pay any attention to her, Papa. She's just worried for you." And to Enid: "And don't you worry about Papa, and I won't worry about Don. God won't let anything happen to people like them."

"What's God got to do with it?"

Lucy smiled. "Well, He knows I trust Him, and He wouldn't want to disappoint me!"

The third day after Trav's departure, a letter from Don reported Mr. Fiddler's death. The letter was addressed to Trav, but Enid opened it and read it aloud to them all. Don gave details.

> His temperature was up to a hundred and six, Tuesday night [he wrote]. And a pounding pulse. Old Maria was taking care of him, and I sent one of my men to help her. Elon went every afternoon —I mean, evening—and I was there every night. We kept sponging him, and we got some ice to cool him off, and we tried Darby's Fluid, and the doctor gave him ergot. His fever was higher Wednesday, but that night he cooled off. But his pulse had just about quit, and his skin was cold and yellow, and he vomited some black liquid, and the doctor said that was a bad sign. His kidneys quit working, and when I came to the house tonight he was dead.

Lucy's flooding memories brought back to her so much of Mr. Fiddler, a familiar figure in her life since she grew old enough to remember anything, and all her memories were kindly ones, but Enid, having finished the letter, said in exasperated tones: "I knew it! So Trav needn't have gone!"

Trav's first letter said he had found many things that needed his attention. He would stay on, perhaps till Mr. Cist's return; he had seen Don, and Don was fine.

The fever epidemic had not yet begun to wane when in late September the election brought the enfranchised Negroes, for the first time, trooping to the polls. Of that occasion Don wrote at length.

> Everyone except the Southerners seemed to think it was a day of jubilee, but it scared me. It seemed to me frightening to see, all of a sudden, these people put in charge of the government of a whole state; these people who had never governed anything but their mules, who didn't even know how to govern themselves.

Not only that, but these eighty thousand men who two or three years ago were slaves are now going to govern their former masters!

Lots of Southerners who registered did not vote at all, and only about four thousand in the whole state voted against having the Convention, while seventy-five thousand—and all of them were either Negroes or Radicals—voted for it. They had it arranged that the delegates to the Convention would be half Negroes, half whites, forty-nine of each, and that's the way it is. There are only two Democrats in the whole ninety-eight delegates. It couldn't come out any other way, and of course it was great fun for the Negroes.

It will take generations to teach these poor people what it means to be free. I remember you told me once what old Samuel said,— that blind Negro whom the school burners killed—that only the bound are free. Every soldier knows what Samuel meant. If you're a soldier, you need only obey orders. You don't have to feed yourself, or clothe yourself, or house yourself—or your families—because you can't. When these Negroes were slaves, all they had to do was work, and not very hard, at that. Now they have to manage their lives, take care of themselves and their families—and govern the state of Louisiana!

How long will it be before they learn what they will have to know? They can be taught, but who will teach them? Why should I feel so responsible, Lucy? There's so little any one man can do—but I'd like to do my little.

Late in October, Trav came back to the Plains. The yellow fever showed no sign of abating. "Four hundred and thirty-one died in the week before I left," he told them. But Mr. Cist had returned. "And Elon is developing fast," Trav reported. "So the mill's in good hands."

They asked him many questions about the plague which still harassed the city. The disease this year had been of the mildest type, but deaths among children were more numerous than among adults. "Doctor Matas claims the fever is caused by germs in the nose and throat," he said. "All sorts of remedies were tried. Boiled verbena leaves were supposed to help, and of course carbolic acid, and sulphur, but when I left, up to seventy-five people were dying every day. About a fourth of the people in New Orleans have had it, usually light attacks, but over three thousand have died. They say the first good frost will put an end to it overnight."

There was a long moment of silence, and then he said in a new tone: "Well, what's been happening here?"

Cinda said: "Well, let's see; Julian and Anne have a new baby, a boy, named Theodore for Anne's father." She added, with an amused sidelong glance at Brett: "Having grandchildren makes Brett and me feel older and older, but they keep coming. There'll be another in January, and another in May."

Lucy added: "Vesta in January, Papa, and Jenny in May."

Trav had another bit of news. "By the way, Lucy, Tommy Buford's coming to New Orleans."

"Really? How nice. To visit?"

"No, to work in the mill. Captain Blackford says he's developed a real talent for mechanics, machines, engines. He and Elon between them will keep us running with mighty few interruptions."

"It will be wonderful seeing him again."

Cinda said laughingly: "Lucy's running out of beaus around here, Trav. The de Saussure boy and young Boykin are both married. So many boys were killed in the War, the ones that weren't are being snapped up pretty fast." And she asked: "Who's this Tommy Buford?"

"An old beau of Lucy's," Enid told her, and to Lucy: "Cheer up, Honey. Maybe having Tommy around will bring your Yankee up to scratch."

Lucy smiled, feeling her father's eye upon her. "Plenty of time," she said. "After all, I won't be twenty for almost a year."

"Twenty? Ha!" Enid laughed. "When I was twenty, you were almost three."

Before they left the Plains, the South Carolina election had been held. Seventy thousand Negroes and a hundred and thirty whites voted for the Convention. "And those hundred and thirty white men will rule the state from now on," Brett predicted. "The delegates to the Convention are almost all nigras. They'll do what they're told." He made an angry sound. "I'm like Ben Perry. I'd rather have a military government than one that rests on nigra votes."

Enid was glad to say goodby to the Plains. "Brett's so low-spirited all the time," she complained. Under the regulations promulgated by General Sickles, Brett had been refused registration; and though Trav assured him this was a compliment. that under the Sickles orders the only white men eligible to vote were conscripts and deserters, Brett felt the stigma.

"And besides," Enid confessed to Trav, once they were away, "I always feel that Cinda's being virtuously patient with me." She added with a laugh: "And Tilda makes me feel like a sinner, she's so eternally good!"

"I've thought we might go to the mountains, next summer," Trav remarked. "Somewhere up near Chimneys."

"I'd rather come back to Camden. Anywhere else, we'd have to start making friends all over again. Couldn't we rent a house here?"

"We might, I suppose."

"I'd like that. I hate being a guest all the time."

They came from Mobile to New Orleans by boat, and Lucy was

sure Don would meet them at the station; but he did better, boarding the steamer as soon as she tied up at the pier. They met in the saloon and he swept Lucy into his arms and she clung to him, happy tears streaming, whispering: "Oh darling, darling, it's been so long, so long!" They forgot the passengers hurrying up the gangplank and smiling as they passed.

On the train for the five-mile run into the city Lucy was content beside him while he gave Trav the news of the day. The Convention was in session, but had made little progress. "The Negro delegates do a lot of listening and not much talking," Don explained. "But one of them has made a good impression, a man named Pinchback. The Pure Radicals, the *Tribune* crowd, wanted to have all the subordinate officers in the Convention divided equally, half black and half white, but Pinchback fought them, arguing that officers should be chosen for ability rather than for their color, and the Convention went his way."

"Good!" said Trav. "That's the most hopeful thing I've heard; not just the fact of Pinchback's opinion, but the fact that he persuaded others to agree with him. I met him one day, in Longstreet's office. There's force in him." And he asked "Have you attended the sessions?"

"Some of them. I'm interested in watching the Negroes."

Trav nodded. "The sooner we realize that our future depends on them, the better we'll get along."

When they alighted at the station, Saul was there with the carriage, and Enid and Lucy and Peter went directly home, but Trav and Don walked as far as the St. Louis hotel, through the dark streets to which day had not yet come, and breakfasted together. Trav was glad to have this hour with Don. He liked the young man, yet if Don loved Lucy, why did he not marry her? Her rapture when she and Don met this morning had been eloquent of her eagerness. Certainly to discuss the matter with the young man would ease his mind.

Till they reached the hotel, they spoke little. There was a bite in the air, and Trav said once: "Frosty morning."

"We've had two good frosts," Don assented. "They say cold weather drives away the yellow fever."

But beyond this, hardly a word was said till they entered the dining room and ordered their breakfast. After a moment then, Don suddenly laughed, and Trav looked inquiry.

"Oh, nothing," Don said, answering the unspoken question. "I just feel like laughing, now Lucy's home again."

Trav said in dry amusement: "I noticed you were glad to see each other."

"I'm sorry. That happened before we knew it, sir. Had you friends, acquaintances who saw us?"

"I met none."

Don hesitated, coloring. "I've never really asked your consent to my—paying my addresses to Lucy."

Trav chuckled. "We're a long way beyond that, Don." Then he said gravely: "But I would like to know your — plans?"

Don said frankly: "Well sir, we haven't any immediate plans. I can support Lucy, though not quite in your way. Not yet. I've always saved money, and I send home as much as I can. My father keeps it at work for me." There was an apology in his tones. "When we're married, I want Lucy to go home with me, to live in Maine. You know the way she talks now, about the South, but when she goes North, she'll feel differently. In Maine, she'll be a farmer's wife. We won't be poor, but—we don't have servants there. She'll be doing the things that the Negroes do for you here."

He waited, but Trav did not speak, and Don said: "I haven't wanted to hurry her into anything like that. I want to make her love me so much she'll want to go with me, wherever I go, and be happy." He hesitated. "But we don't want to be married till I get my discharge, a year from January. I don't know how you'll feel, sir, about letting her go so far away."

"Neither do I," Trav admitted, and he smiled in reassurance. "I think how I'll feel will depend on how Lucy feels, when the time comes."

"I know. Yes sir." And Don said doubtfully: "In the meantime— of course I'm away on duty a lot of the time, anyway, but if you'd rather I didn't come to the house so often . . ."

Trav smiled. "If I tried that, Lucy'd teach me my P's and Q's, and mighty quickly. No, Don. We'll go on as we've been going, see how things look a year from now." Before they parted, they struck hands, and Trav said: "I appreciate your frankness."

"If you ever want me to—"

Trav shook his head. "If anything comes up, we'll discuss it together, you and I."

The second Sunday after their homecoming, General Longstreet called. Trav was napping on the couch in his study, and he did not hear the faraway jangle of the bell till Isaiah came to rouse him. Behind Isaiah, the General was already in the doorway, chuckling at Trav's slow awakening. "How are you, Currain? Lost a little flesh, haven't you?"

Trav grinned and knuckled his eyes. "Some, yes, I'm glad to say. We're just back from South Carolina, and Brett Dewain and I rode almost every day. Here, I seldom find time to do that."

"Make time your servant, man; not your master." Isaiah stood by, nodding and grinning, and Trav bade him fetch toddies. They sat down and Trav asked: "Is Mrs. Longstreet with you?"

"No, no." The General shook his great head. "No, New Orleans made it plain, last June, that they did not count me a useful citizen. No, Louisa and the children are established in Lynchburg. I came back only to clean up the rags and tatters of my affairs here."

Trav said strongly: "I think you make a mistake, General. There's a place for you here, given a little time."

"Maybe so, but I'm not sure that I want it. Currain, have you travelled in the North?"

"Only as far as Gettysburg," Trav reminded him.

"Ah! Yes. You remember those fine, rich, well-tended Pennsylvania farms, so neat, so proudly kept, in such contrast to our sprawling, slovenly fields. I've been in the North this summer. I went through New York and Connecticut and Massachusetts, and found many warm friends there. Mr. Parker of the *Republican,* for one. His home is in Lowell, in Massachusetts. Other friends, some old, some new." His tone was reflective. "I saw white men everywhere working with their hands, working with zest, with a sort of calm ferocity, driving their farm wagons, handling a plow, operating machines in their factories. New England doesn't lend itself easily to agriculture, all hills and mountains, yet there are farms everywhere, scores and hundreds and thousands of them, white-painted, neat, their small fields in order! To be sure, there are few or none of our great houses, but neither are there shabby huts and cabins full of poor whites." He smiled. "I sound like someone making a stump speech, but Major, there is much in the North which we might emulate."

Trav nodded, faintly uneasy at this indirect criticism of the South. "Well, General," he asked. "What are your plans?"

"I've sold my insurance business to Sam Hood, and I'm closing accounts with the Owen boys. We'll live in Lynchburg for the present. Beyond that, I don't know."

They talked of many things, of Mr. Fiddler's death, of the Convention which now had lost itself in wordy debate, of the refusal by Congress to bring impeachment proceedings against President Johnson. Lucy and Don came in, and Lucy gave the General a happy greeting, and went to wake Enid, and the General asked Don questions about the Freedmen's Bureau and its work among the Negroes. "Or do they still require your paternal care?"

"There'll be distress this winter," Don told him. "We'll be feeding hungry people—and not only Negroes. Half the rations we give out now go to white people." His voice was gentle. "Some of them are ladies left without kith or kin, who before the War were mistresses of great houses. Some have discovered ways to earn a little, selling flowers, or vegetables, or sewing, but often it's not enough to feed those they must feed. So they come to us."

Lucy and Enid returned to join them, and they kept the General for supper; yet Lucy thought there was tonight a difference, as though he were a stranger, and she saw that Trav was troubled and sad. When the General said good night, she came to her father's side, touched his arm.

"Cheer up, Papa," she said in smiling reassurance. "You'll see each other again."

His hand rested for a moment on hers. "No, he's gone," he said. "Part of him at least. He's no longer a Southerner."

"Must everyone be either Southerner or Northerner? Can't we just be Americans?"

Trav smiled, and he drew Enid's arm through his own. "Not your mama and I, certainly. We're too old. You, perhaps; you and Don. But the change will take time." He looked toward the door. "When I think back, I can see that the General was always more an American than a Southerner. I suppose no West Pointer could ever fight against the Union with a whole heart."

Enid impatiently freed her arm. "Don't be silly, Trav. Plenty of them did, from General Lee down."

"Many of them fought," he agreed. "But not with a whole heart. You know, even with a broken heart, a man may live for years."

2

TOMMY BUFORD, as soon as he arrived in New Orleans, came to call upon them, and on that first occasion his eyes never turned away from Lucy. Since he last saw her she had changed. Her countenance was no longer that of a lovely child. The bony structure of her face, the delicate yet strong line of her jaw, and the wide clear brow gave an impression almost of solidity, as though her features had been carved of a warm and living marble. Tommy, though he was two or three years older than she, and though his shoulders were broad and his head high, was like a boy beside her.

Trav saw this, but Enid did not. "You know, Trav," she said one night, Trav already in bed: "It wouldn't surprise me at all if being with Tommy opened Lucy's eyes." Trav grunted heedlessly, and she said: "Oh, Don's nice, of course, but he and Lucy aren't really in love with each other, or they'd have been married long ago. Besides, he's a Yankee. He'd never want to settle in the South, and I can't imagine Lucy leaving us. Leaving you, at least. She's always been in love with you!" He did not comment, but she insisted: "Oh yes she is! I've been frightfully jealous, ever since she began to grow up. But now I think she may realize that Tommy's her own kind."

Trav had before this drifted off to sleep, so he was surprised, when he came home from the mill a day or two before Christmas, to find Tommy established as a member of the family. When they were alone, he said: "I wish you'd discussed this with me, Enid. I'd have——"

"But Trav, I did," she assured him. "One night while we were going to bed. You were probably half asleep. I asked you if you didn't think it would be a good idea to ask him to live with us, and you grunted, so what was I to think? Besides, I want Lucy to see a lot of him."

"Enid," he warned her. "Don't make trouble between Don and Lucy."

"Trouble? Of course not! But if they don't love each other, they'd better find it out now than later on. Besides, we must be nice to Tommy, way off down here all alone."

So Tommy, as well as Don, shared their Christmas gaieties. The two young men were drawn together by that mutual respect which those who as soldiers have been antagonists so often feel. But more important to Trav was the fact that Tommy and Peter were congenial, with the result that Tommy served as a sort of bridge between Peter and himself, giving them a common ground. Peter, though Trav had not known this, went regularly to the Sunday cockfights; now he took Tommy, and Tommy one Sunday suggested that Trav join them.

Trav saw Peter's alarmed consternation, and deferred to it. "What do you say, Peter?"

"Golly, Papa, did you ever see a cockfight?"

"A few," Trav admitted, in a tone which made Tommy catch his eye and smile.

So Peter accepted his father's company. At the main, they joined a group of older boys who were obviously Peter's friends. They looked at Trav a little warily, so when, as the fights progressed, wagers were offered and taken, Trav sought to reassure them. One boy offered a bet against a cock which no one seemed ready to back, and Trav accepted it. He felt, at once, Peter's disapproval. The cock he favored basely refused combat, and after that the boys avoided meeting Trav's eye. On the way home, Peter said: "Golly, Papa, that was an awful cold rooster you bet on."

Trav assented. "I notice you picked mostly winners."

"I'll show you some of the things you have to watch for," Peter promised, and Trav felt a glow of pleasure. Peter grinned at him. "I'm supposed to know something about fighting cocks. Can't have my father betting on barnyard birds."

With this beginning, they presently drew closer. When General Longstreet departed for Lynchburg, Trav saw him to the train, and at supper that night he mentioned this. Peter said critically: "Golly, Papa, I shouldn't think you'd have anything to do with that old nigger-lover."

Once, this epithet would have drawn from Trav a stern reproof, but now he only said: "He's my friend."

"Well, what if he is? People like us have got to take a stand!" Trav looked at his son in astonishment. "The Republicans and the freedmen and the niggers have all coalesced against the white race, and he's one of them!"

Enid protested. "For Heaven's sake, Peter, are you going to start talking politics too?"

So Peter was silenced, but next morning as they walked down town together, Trav spoke of this conversation. "Son," he said, "that remark of yours—about coalescing—sounded like a quotation. If people like us ought to—take a stand, I thought you might want to tell me about it."

"Yes sir, it is," Peter said eagerly. "A quotation, I mean." With an eye on the pedestrians they passed he spoke in an undertone. "It's in the preamble of our Constitution. I'm not supposed to tell anyone about it, not even that there is such a thing, but it's the Knights of the White Camelia. I just joined since we came back from the Plains, Tommy and I. Elon Villard's in it, too. You have to take an oath, and you have recognition signals and everything." And he said urgently: "You ought to join, Papa! The Republicans have got the niggers all organized into clubs, and we white men will have to organize clubs too. I wish you would."

Trav had heard some talk about the White Camelia, and he felt an amused wonder at this son of his. But to do what Peter asked might enrich this new comradeship, worth any price. "Think they'd take me?"

Peter was jubilant, and after Trav's initiation, the boy delighted in exchanging with his father the sign of recognition—"by carelessly drawing the index finger of the left hand across the left eye"—and in drilling him in the questions and answers that followed. "Where were you born?" "On Mount Caucasus." "Are you free?" "I am." "Were your ancestors free?" "They were." "Are you attached to any order?" "I am." "To what order?" "To the order of the White Camelia." "Where does it grow?" "On Mount Caucasus."

Once when they were murmuring their way through this abracadabra, Lucy, having come down the stairs unheard, asked curiously: "What in the world are you two talking about?"

"Oh, nothing," Peter assured her. "Nothing at all!"

She looked questioningly at her father and Trav said: "Just finishing a conversation, Lucy." His eyes silenced her, but later he told her the truth. "It's a lot of nonsense, of course," he admitted. "But it tickles Peter, and we're better friends all the time."

She hugged his arm in tender understanding. "I know. I'll never say a word."

When under the Military Acts, the Negroes were enfranchised, Pinchback, at Sapphira's advice, and financed by Tony, organized the Fourth Ward Republican Club, and thus began his political career. He became a member of the Republican State Committee, and was elected a delegate to the Constitutional Convention. The Republicans in Congress wished to have at command for next year's election the Negro vote in the South. For this reason, they must hurry the readmission to the Union of the states at present excluded, so the necessary procedures were foreshortened. In September, the voters were asked to decide not only whether there should be a convention, but also, who should be the delegates. In a similar foreshortening, the Convention now in session would not only draw up a Constitution, but would also nominate candidates for the offices which that document, if accepted by the voters, would create. The voters would then be asked to decide not only whether to accept the Constitution, but also, which candidates they preferred.

It was over these nominations that the split between Pinchback and Doctor Roudanez occurred. The Doctor, with the *Tribune* as his instrument, avowed his purpose eventually to make Louisiana a Negro state. Pinchback was more moderate, and one November day, the issue between them came to a head.

Tony's home, the drawing room over which Sapphira presided, was the battleground. The first callers that day were former Governor Hahn and Thomas J. Durant. Durant, a pioneer in organizing New Orleans Republicans, before the election had enrolled more than fifty thousand Negroes in Loyal Leagues and marching clubs, easily conducted to the polling places. Sapphira had long ago warned Tony to put no faith in him. "He may point out to you the road to victory," she warned Tony. "But he will never lead you there. Not for him the fearful front of battle; his is a limber spine."

Judge Warmoth had begun to organize the Grand Army of the Republic, and Durant today spoke of him with open contempt. "That man would roll a peanut the length of Canal Street with his nose if he thought he could win a few votes by doing so."

Hahn grunted. "Not unless he were sure of the votes," he corrected. "Not just on the chance! But he knows more politics in a minute than most men ever learn. He'll be the first President of that Grand Army he's organizing, and he'll be the next Governor here, and in a year he'll be a millionaire. Wait and see!"

"Yes, and you and Parker and the *Republican* will support him— for the sake of the jackal's share of the loot."

Hahn laughed shortly. "Jealousy is a canker in you, Tom; it'll eat away all your innards if you don't watch out."

Tony said thoughtfully: "Any newspaper that opposes the next Governor will have to live on hog scraps and dishwater. I'm trying to make Roudanez see the light."

"That nigger's getting too big for his britches," Governor Hahn commented. "You saw what he said a day or two ago. 'The colored masses are the masters of the field.' And ten days ago he began arguing that every colored delegate should vote on a straight black-versus-white basis."

He spoke in hard and sullen tones, a lethargic lump of a man, his utterance thickened by his still strong German accent. 'Phemy at the door announced Mr. Pinchback and Judge Warmoth, and as they came in, Hahn and Durant fell into a sullen silence. The newcomers crossed to make their duties to Sapphira, and when Warmoth turned back to greet Tony and the other gentlemen, Pinchback stayed by her side.

Warmoth spoke at once of Doctor Roudanez. "I heard you name him as we came up the stairs. Mr. Pinchback is troubled by the good Doctor's extravagances." He spoke to Tony. "He tells me, Mr. Currain, that you occasionally give the *Tribune* some financial aid, but when I said extravagances, I had in mind the Doctor's political views. If you are his friend, you can perhaps influence the man."

Tony hesitated. "I've become increasingly uneasy about him, this last year or so," he admitted. He looked toward Pinchback, prompting him. "Mr. Pinchback and I."

'Phemy returned with fresh toddies for the gentlemen, and Pinchback waited till she had come and gone. "Yes," he said then. "Doctor Roudanez would put everything on racial grounds, decide every issue for the Negro and against the white. That is surely wrong."

Governor Hahn gulped his toddy and rose to say goodby, and he told Sapphira, as near a chuckle as he ever came: "Doctor Roudanez and I are rival editors, so I prefer not to eavesdrop on this discussion." Yet he asked: "Do you take his side?"

"I think he goes too far," she said. "We should be eager to be led, but we are not yet ready to lead."

"We?" he repeated, considering the word. "You never allow us to forget your Negro blood."

"I never forget it, myself."

Mr. Durant came to make his bow, and he and Governor Hahn departed. Judge Warmoth spoke to Tony. "You expect the Doctor?"

"Yes; yes, at any moment. Perhaps you can help us reason with the man."

Warmoth rose, shrugged. "I'll be glad to try. It's been a long battle, but the victory is won, the Negro enfranchised: now our care must be not to abuse that victory."

As he spoke, he crossed to stand with Pinchback near Sapphira. She watched him approach, a tall young man, broad shouldered and powerful, with a heavy mustache and a smooth chin. When he came nearer, her head tipped back to look up at him, and Tony, who had begun to speak, realized that they were not listening. He saw Sapphira, her head leaning against the antimacassar on the tall chair in which she sat, change in a fashion he had sometimes seen before; her eyes half closed, her color drained away.

After a moment Warmoth fell into easy conversation with Pinchback, and she watched him, still pale, her eyes veiled. She did not speak, nor did he speak to her. He and Tony and Pinchback, standing, talked together, till 'Phemy announced Doctor Roudanez.

Roudanez crossed at once to Sapphira; he nodded to Pinchback, then greeted Warmoth with a stiff politeness which could not be ignored. Warmoth said at once, in a friendly tone: "I fear you dislike me, Doctor."

"Not you, personally," Doctor Roudanez assured him. "But all men like you, who will try to rob us of the fruits of our victory."

"I was under the impression that we, and white men like us, won that victory for you."

"You've opened the doors of our prison, yes; but you did so because you expected to make us your property, to use us as you chose. Instead, sir, you are now our property. There are a hundred of us to every ten of you!"

"None of us own any of us." Warmoth spoke quietly. "There are no more slaves, white or colored. We are partners, to go forward together."

"No sir!" Doctor Roudanez flung up his hands. "No sir! Not partners. Not to advance together. Oh, we've been generous; yes, too generous. Eighty thousand of us elected as many white delegates to this Convention as we did Negroes. It were better if we had done as our brothers did in South Carolina. They elected only fifteen white delegates; next time we here in Louisiana will do the same. We colored people are infinitely the more numerous; we will rule."

"There is no question of white or colored," Warmoth insisted. "From now on, we can all work together for the greatness of Louisiana, for the honorable place she is destined one day to occupy."

"Sir," said Doctor Roudanez, his voice rising, "Louisiana is destined to be the fourth civilized nation governed by men of my race! Not at once, it is true; not at once! But this Convention will make a beginning." He turned sharply, facing Pinchback as though in challenge. "From this time forward, our right to govern must be recognized! The Convention officers will be chosen not for fitness only, but in proportion to—"

Pinchback spoke, accepting the issue. "Doctor, I must disagree. As a delegate, I will vote for fitness; I won't vote by the color of a man's skin."

Roudanez raged at him, with clenched fists. "Traitor!" he cried. "Recreant poltroon! Fool! Who are you to decide what you will do? You're merely a voice, the voice of the colored men who elected you! Your vote will not be decided by what you think, but by what they think!"

"You are mistaken, Doctor."

Roudanez faced him, furious, seeking words, sputtering, and Warmoth looked at his watch, and said hastily: "God bless me, I must be off." He bowed before Sapphira, clasped Tony's hand, said meaningly:

"Useless, my friend. I'm not one to kick against the pricks." To Pinchback: "You and I will travel the same road." So, finally, to Doctor Roudanez: "You feel strongly, Doctor," he said. "Well, I like a man with firm convictions; I know how to talk to him. You and I may disagree, but we will never be enemies."

Doctor Roudanez said hotly: "If you disagree with me, I shall hold you an enemy of my race—and so of me."

Warmoth bowed. "Then sir, I shall respect my enemy."

Their eyes followed him as he crossed toward the door. When he was gone, Pinchback was the first to speak. "Doctor, I shall always owe you a great deal, but I must choose . . ."

Roudanez laughed in open contempt. "Young man, you may do as you like. Choose which you will do, remain a nonentity—or follow me." He threw back his head. "We have come into our kingdom; we who were slaves are now masters. Let that not be forgotten."

Tony, watching Sapphira, said in a tentative tone: "Then if you are masters, Doctor, you will no longer need any friendly assistance from me."

Roudanez flushed. "If you have thought you were buying me, you were self-deceived," he said. He strode across the room and opened the door for a final word, but before he could speak, Sapphira said:

"Wait, Doctor!" He hesitated, and she added softly: "Close the door." Doubtfully he obeyed her, and she explained: "I was afraid Judge Warmoth had not yet left the house. I'm sure you wouldn't want to collide with him, downstairs."

"Madame," he said in a steady wrath: "I avoid no man! Nor do I court any man!" His eyes turned to Tony. "And I can neither be bought nor frightened from my course. I shall go forward, and if I must I will go alone."

Sapphira said: "I'm sure Judge Warmoth is gone now, so you may go." She emphasized the final word.

For a moment he glared at her; then the door closed behind him. Pinchback turned to Sapphira. "Am I wrong, to separate from him? Am I—disloyal?"

"A man's first loyalty is to himself, to the best in himself. Take that rule for your guide."

He stayed a while with them. "He's been kind to me," he remembered. "But Judge Warmoth is so much the abler man. When it's a question between them, I'll always be on the Judge's side."

When he was gone, Tony said: "You know, we've helped that young man. He has real quality."

Sadness touched her tones. "If he had deeper roots, he might grow tall and strong. I think he will lift his head high, but his roots are shallow, and the winds may topple him." And she said: "No one of us can become great in one generation; perhaps not in two, or three, or even in a dozen. But there is plenty of time; there's eternity."

"I saw you studying Warmoth."

She nodded. "Yes. He is greatly gifted. He will win many easy victories, with those gifts of his."

"And keep his winnings?"

Sapphira met his eyes. "That I do not know."

In January, the Convention interrupted its deliberations long enough to nominate candidates for Governor, and for the other state offices created by the Constitution still in process. During the maneuvering which preceded the nominations, Tony's home was the scene of many gatherings, and every evening and often till late at night men—white men and Negroes—crowded Sapphira's drawing room. The debates and discussions on the floor of the Convention were here rehearsed, the arguments shaped and tested, the opposing forces measured.

One evening soon after the turn of the year, Doctor Roudanez brought to Tony's another Negro, Major Francis Dumas, whom he introduced with some ceremony as the first colored Governor of Louisiana. Major Dumas had been, even before emancipation, a freed-man, and wealthy, owning—like most other well-to-do Negroes—large blocks of real estate. Tony, when Doctor Roudanez had made his introductions, said good-humoredly:

"You speak not as a reporter of past events, Doctor, but as a prophet of the future?"

"To do so calls for none of the attributes of the seer, Mr. Currain. Within the fortnight, Major Dumas will have been nominated; after that his election is certain."

Sapphira spoke to Major Dumas. "I had not known you were a candidate."

Dumas smiled. "It is only just decided. We have been in conference with Judge Taliaferro. I may tell you, ma'am, that we proposed to Mr. Pinchback that he accept the nomination, but he declined."

"Why?" Sapphira asked. Doctor Roudanez frowned, glancing at Major Dumas, but Sapphira insisted: "Why did he refuse the honor?"

"He thought it unwise to nominate a colored man for Governor."

Doctor Roudanez cried: "That was pretext, not reason. I warned you that you invited refusal. He's gone over to Judge Warmoth, and now subordinates his own interests—yes, and those of his race—to the white man."

"Yet you and Major Dumas are confident of victory?" Tony's question was faintly derisive.

"Completely!" The Doctor's temper was short. "We've absolute promises from fifty-seven delegates, and qualified assents from eleven more." He shrugged, forced a smile. "Oh, there will be many names suggested, perhaps several ballots; but forty-five votes is enough. We have them, and a dozen to spare."

"Are political promises always to be trusted?"

"I trust the man, not the promise," said Doctor Roudanez, "Some men are liars; so are some politicians." And he said like a challenge: "I suspect your sympathies are with the Warmoth faction."

"Why, I like the Judge, yes; we both like him. By the way, we expect him presently."

The Doctor looked at Major Dumas, and as though Roudanez asked a question the other said: "Let us stay, by all means. I shall be happy to see him. We're old friends."

When Warmoth presently arrived, Tony watched these antagonists with quiet amusement. Pinchback came with Warmoth, and another Negro, Oscar Dunn, whom Warmoth introduced to Sapphira.

"You see in us the three musketeers," he explained. "One for all and all for one." He turned to greet the others with extended hand. "Ah, Major Dumas! Your servant! Doctor!"

Major Dumas was as polite as he, but Doctor Roudanez ignored Warmoth's hand, watching them all, his eyes darting to and fro. Dumas and Judge Warmoth, standing near Sapphira, were each completely at ease, and there was no talk of politics till, scowling at Pinchback, Roudanez said fretfully that it was time for him and Major Dumas to leave. Then Warmoth proposed a toast.

"To ourselves, gentlemen! No matter how sharp our differences, let us stand as one against our enemies!"

Doctor Roudanez responded, his eyes shining. "And to the future of our race!" he cried.

When he and Dumas were gone, Warmoth and the others stayed a while, and Tony asked: "Are you too making prophesies, Judge? The Doctor says Dumas is a certainty."

"Well, I'm still a candidate," Warmoth admitted, smiling.

"Will the Democrats put a ticket in the field?"

"There'll be no Democratic ticket, I'm sure. I expect the race will narrow down to Major Dumas and me. If Mr. Pinchback here—" Warmoth looked toward Pinchback with a smile. "If he were their candidate, I would probably be defeated. With him on my side, I expect to win the nomination." Tony nodded, but Warmoth added: "Yet the nomination is not enough. There'll be no Democratic ticket, it's true; but if I'm nominated, I expect the *Tribune* crowd, Doctor Roudanez and his friends, to put up a ticket of their own."

Tony considered that: "I suppose so," he agreed, and he asked: "If the *Tribune* faction—"

"Pure Radicals, they call themselves," Warmoth reminded him.

"Then the Pure Radicals; if they beat you in the Convention, will you run on your own ticket?"

"Certainly," Warmoth admitted. "I agree with Mr. Pinchback that it is too soon to elect a Negro Governor. Yes, I should oppose Major Dumas with all my might."

Sapphira said: "But you expect to win the nomination."

"I expect to win, yes." And Warmoth said seriously: "Doctor Roudanez depends for victory on his dream, his proposal to convert Louisiana into a Negro nation. Faith is beautiful, but works are better." He spoke to Tony. "I'm organizing a Louisiana branch of the Grand Army of the Republic. We'll hold an encampment January eleventh, and I will be elected Grand Commander. That alone will give me most of the white votes in the Convention, and my friends here—" He turned with a graceful gesture. "Mr. Pinchback and Mr. Dunn will bring over enough of the colored delegates to carry the day."

Sapphira, looking at Pinchback, asked: "Do you feel as confident as Judge Warmoth does?"

"Yes ma'am," he assured her. "Yes ma'am. It will come down to a question of him or Major Dumas, and enough of us feel the way I do, that we ought to elect a white man. Ohio and the other states up North voted against letting colored people vote. Well, we've got to show them we won't do the wrong things. The Convention won't nominate a Negro for Governor." He chuckled. "Not as long as I keep my voice."

Oscar Dunn agreed with him, and Warmoth repeated his confident prediction. When they were gone, Tony asked Sapphira, "Do you still pin your faith on the Judge?"

She smiled. "Yes. He will win." And she said: "I don't suppose it would be right for me to go see the Convention, watch its proceedings?"

Tony, reluctantly, shook his head. "No. No, it will be a man's crowd."

"You must be there," she said. "To report everything to me."

Lucy, too, wished she might watch the nominating Convention in action, but when she proposed this to Don, he demurred, his answer surprisingly like Tony's. "I'll take you if you say so," he said. "And if your father agrees. The proceedings—whenever I've been there—have been dignified and completely orderly. But it's a masculine crowd, Lucy. You'd see no other ladies there, and the hall is dirty, worn old matting on the floor, mud and—well, everyone uses tobacco. You can imagine what it's like."

She yielded, but she required Don's promise to report every detail of the proceedings. The Convention would meet to make nominations Monday night, January thirteenth. Sunday evening, Don called at the house, and since the day was not uncomfortably cold, he and Lucy strolled in the garden.

"After the meeting, you must come past here," she told him. "I won't actually try to keep awake, but if it isn't too late, you may see a light in my window. If you do, don't ring the bell; just knock, and if I'm awake, I'll come down." She laughed at her own words, pressing his arm against her side. "Won't that be fun? So sort of clandestine! A secret rendezvous!" And she added ruefully: "We almost have to now, don't we, with Tommy underfoot all the time."

"I like Buford," he said. "He's a fine young man."

"He is," she agreed. "I like him too." Her eyes met his. "But Don, I love you."

The Convention was called to order Monday night at seven o'clock, in the Senate Chamber on the first floor of the Institute, but after a few minutes of empty formalities—the calling of the roll and the report of the Committee on Credentials—the room became intolerably crowded, and the Convention adjourned to the hall of the House of Representatives, on the second floor. As Don climbed the stairs to that apartment, he remembered another gathering here, eighteen months ago, when these stairs were slippery with blood, when blood spattered the walls of the chamber and spread in viscid puddles across the floor.

As candidates for the gubernatorial nomination, six names were presented to the Convention. Everyone knew that the contest lay between Judge Warmoth and Major Dumas, so that three other nominations— George Wickliffe was the only familiar name—were accepted as mere compliments. But with these five names already before the Convention, a Negro whom Don did not recognize rose to add another. He began with a few flowery phrases, and when he finished with "Pinckney Benton Stewart Pinchback," the name was received with shouts and cheers and handclapping.

Yet these cheers and this applause had about them something perfunctory, and when Pinchback rose and addressed the chair, Don suspected that the incident was a piece of stage management. For Pinchback had risen to decline.

"I appreciate the honor done me," he explained. "But for the good of the party, I must speak. We colored people have suddenly found ourselves promoted to great power. But power is a responsibility. We must make no blunders that we can avoid. No colored man has as yet any real experience of politics, and I am convinced that it would be a blunder to begin our work here by electing a colored man as Governor. I therefore beg leave to withdraw my name from your consideration."

The roar of applause which greeted his withdrawal was tremendous, and it seemed to Don obvious that Pinchback had been named only in order that he might withdraw and state his reasons, thus indirectly opposing Major Dumas. Behind the incident he felt Judge Warmoth's shrewd hand.

The nominations were closed, and tellers began to distribute ballots. Pinchback was one of the tellers, Stephen Packard another. Packard was a State-of-Maine man, chairman of the Republican State Central Committee and thus the titular head of the party in the State, yet Don disliked him, sure that Packard had come to New Orleans with no other purpose in mind than to make a fortune out of politics.

When the ballots were tallied, Major Dumas led with forty-one votes—forty-five were necessary for a choice—while Judge Warmoth had only thirty-seven, the other candidates dividing ten votes between them. Don had expected the vote to be closer, so he was surprised. Without forming any fixed opinion, his respect for Judge Warmoth's capacities had made him expect the Judge's nomination; now Major Dumas seemed the likely choice.

Yet there was something unnatural about the conduct of the delegates which puzzled him. The Warmoth men seemed undisturbed, while the friends of Major Dumas were clamorous. A motion that on the next ballot the three minor candidates be dropped was carried, and as the decisive balloting began, a whispering hush blanketed the hall.

The ballots were collected for the count. During the count of the first ballot, the hall had been in some disorder, no one showing any eagerness to know the result; but now delegates crowded around the table where the tellers were at work, and in the hush Don could hear one of the tellers, as he unfolded the ballots, calling off the names: "Warmoth," "Dumas," "Dumas," "Warmoth." Don tried to keep account, but too often some stir or movement prevented his hearing the call.

Then suddenly someone shouted: "Warmoth!" The crowd about the tellers scattered, the chair pounded for order in the hall, and Packard reported the tally. "For Major Dumas, forty-three votes." There was a feeble cheer. "For Judge Warmoth, forty-five votes."

He shouted that figure, to make himself heard above the shouts of triumph from the Warmoth delegates, and from the spectators who had crowded into the hall.

The chair named a committee of three to notify Judge Warmoth of his nomination, and while they were gone, nominations for Lieutenant Governor were in order. Major Dumas was nominated by a Warmoth man, and Don nodded. Clearly, Judge Warmoth had from the first directed every move. Dumas would be Lieutenant Governor to mend the division in the party's ranks.

The notification committee escorted Judge Warmoth into the hall—

to another storm of cheers—and he stood waiting on the platform till the applause was done. When he could be heard, he spoke briefly. He was grateful for the honor they had done him; he would try to be worthy of their trust. He considered it a high compliment, that they had chosen him over the distinguished and honorable gentleman, his opponent. He hoped they might now all work together for the general good.

As though his words had been their cue, the delegates on the first ballot nominated Major Dumas for Lieutenant Governor, and a committee was sent to give him this news, while the Convention proceeded to nominations for Secretary of State. But Don decided he had seen enough, so he made his way to the door. At the foot of the stairs he saw the notification committee and half a dozen others clustered around Doctor Roudanez, who spoke in low, angry tones.

"Don't go back at all!" the Doctor insisted, addressing the Committee. "Major Dumas will decline the nomination, you may count on that. We will have a ticket of our own!"

Don heard this as he passed, and without pausing. It was later than he had thought, and no doubt Lucy would be asleep, but he decided to make sure. He found, in fact, the whole house lighted, so he rang the bell, but before there had been time for Isaiah to come from the pantry, Lucy herself opened the door.

"Come in, come in," she said happily.

"I thought you'd be asleep."

"No, no. Judge and Mrs. Morgan dropped in, and Elon and Eleanor, and they've just left. Everybody's gone to bed except Papa and me." And as Trav appeared in the doorway, she added with a smile: "And Papa's just going! Aren't you, Papa?"

Trav clasped her arm, shook it gently. "Don't rush me, Honey!" And to Don: "Warmoth get it, did he?"

So while they stood there, Lucy mischievously shouldering Trav toward the foot of the stairs, Don gave them a straightforward account of the proceedings. "But I think Judge Warmoth could have been nominated on the first ballot, if he chose," he concluded. "They nominated Major Dumas for Lieutenant Governor, but I don't think he'll take it. When I came away, the Pure Radicals were talking a bolt. I suppose they'd put him up as their candidate."

"I doubt it," Trav commented. "They might name Judge Taliaferro." The gray-haired Judge, president of the Convention and a leader in the Pure Radical faction, was respected even by his political enemies. "He's a steady Union man, like Judge Morgan, but he's a Southerner and he'd get some Democratic votes."

Lucy said woefully: "I'm awful tired of standing here, Papa." So he laughed and said good night and left them.

3

WINTER DRIFTED BY. When Enid invited Tommy Buford to live with them, Trav guessed her motive, and it amused him to see that if Don came to the house, Enid at once demanded his attention, trying to leave Tommy and Lucy no recourse except to turn to each other. He thought Enid had become a different woman—a much more attractive woman—since coming to New Orleans. The warmer climate agreed with her. She no longer began each day as torpid as a snake in winter; instead, she woke refreshed and relaxed and happy. One reason may have been that at Chimneys, mornings meant for her only the beginning of another empty day; now she had always some plan or other, even though it might be nothing more definite than to spend an hour or two on Canal Street, either in the carriage with one of her friends, or promenading with Lucy, or with Peter as escort.

She saw Dolly almost every week, usually at Tony's, and eventually Dolly proposed that on the next fine day they meet for a stroll on Canal Street together. Enid, in a moment of reckless daring, agreed, and they did this more than once. Physically, they were perfect foils, and Enid's blond beauty somehow accented Dolly's dark loveliness. Dolly had many masculine acquaintances, so there were chance encounters, and pleasant interludes at the confectioner's, at Victor's, or Dumonteil's, or Moreau's. Enid delighted in these brief contacts with strange men whose gallantry was habit and whose eyes were bold.

"I expect Trav would half kill me if he ever found me out, Dolly," she confessed, after one of these occasions. "But I simply love being with you, meeting all these men. Don't they just terrify you?"

Dolly smiled. "No, men don't frighten me—except, sometimes, Captain Pew!" She giggled. "You know, he's forbidden me to see you! I don't know what he'd do if he knew, but he's up all night, half the time, gaming, so I count on his sleeping in the day."

"You don't stay up all night, do you?"

"No, no. Gentlemen who have come to gamble soon tire of feminine company, no matter how charming—and in fact I soon tire of them!" She laughed. "Only sometimes I play the game of craps, for a little while, to amuse them."

"I wish I could be there, just once, hidden away where I wouldn't be seen, but where I could see everything."

"Impossible, my dear," Dolly assured her. "No ladies come there, and besides, Captain Pew forbids you the house—just as Uncle Trav forbids me—"

"Oh, Trav!" Enid laughed. "I can handle Trav. I've begun to call him 'old man,' and he loves to prove he isn't. He's rather nice, sometimes." She asked: "How's your father? Do you ever see him now?"

"Oh yes, he comes frequently to play. He's enormous, Enid; incredible! A monster! Like a bubble, walking! A bubble full of water! He has himself tapped, every little while."

"Tapped? Whatever for?"

"Oh, he has the dropsy. His fat is all water. Don't talk about him. He's hideous!"

"Why do you let him in?"

"To win his money. Of course, he has a third interest, so we have to give a third of it back to him, so it takes time, but we'll get it all, eventually. He's a poor gambler; always wants to double the bets when he's losing, and to halve them when his luck is in."

"Does Tony ever go there?"

"Sometimes, but he never gambles."

"You must have such fun!" In an instinctive desire to hold her own, Enid said: "We have many gay times at our house this winter, too. You know Tommy Buford lives with us now. The Lynchburg family. His mother was a Garland, and you remember the Bufords in Williamsburg. Such a nice boy. He's working in Trav's mill, and doing such fine things. He and Lucy were sweethearts from the time he came home after the War. They're so cute together."

"I thought Captain Page was practically Lucy's shadow."

"Oh, she and Don are friends, of course. So we have nice parties, Lucy and Tommy, and the Morgan girls, and Eleanor Villard, and Elon, and the Pierces, all with their beaus." She laughed in quick recollection. "Do you know Mr. Cist, Trav's partner at the mill? He comes too. Such a funny little man, talks a perfect stream when anyone will listen, but mostly he just sits and stares at Eleanor. I think she'd have him at the slightest hint. They've nothing, you know. Her brother works in the mill, too."

"I know old Mr. Villard," Dolly told her. "He comes to the House sometimes; criticizes our Madeira and our brandy like a connoisseur, and never risks a penny. Captain Pew and I went down river in his boat one day last summer. Remember Cap'n Cash? We met him at Tony's. He had Sapphira's Quinny in the pilothouse. She's a pretty little twist."

Enid was indignant. "That limb of Satan! I had to put her out of the house, having babies all over the place." After she and Dolly parted, she thought again of Quinny, making up to Captain Cash! He was a lot too good for that shameless wench. It was months since she had seen him; strangely, the time seemed long.

In March the price of cotton rose to twenty-five cents. "And I've held on to ours," Brett wrote from the Plains. "So Cinda and I have voted ourselves a vacation. You can expect us almost any day." They arrived in early April, and without further forewarning, a hackney depositing them at the door. Trav and Tommy were at breakfast, the others not yet downstairs. When Isaiah answered their ring, Trav heard their voices, and his shout of welcome brought Peter running, Lucy close behind him, and Enid called over the banister:

"Oh, come in, come in! Cinda, come up while I dress?"

"Can someone bring me up a cup of coffee? I won't be civil till I've had it!"

"Of course! Lucy, tell Isaiah!"

"I'll bring it myself," Lucy promised. "Go on up, Aunt Cinda." She hurried to the kitchen—Isaiah was helping the hack driver with their bags and boxes—and Cinda went up to join Enid. Trav and Peter and Brett turned to the breakfast table, and Tommy rose at their entrance, and Trav introduced him to Brett, explaining: "After Tommy came back from the War, he went to the University and studied mechanics, and Captain Blackford sent him down to help Elon Villard in the mill. He's a good man."

Brett grasped Tommy's hand. "Good! We need all the help we can find." And as he sat down, he said: "Well, we're here! I had some railroad business in Mobile, and I took time to look at the cotton oil mill there, too." Old Maria came beaming with a platter of spiced sausage and a bowl of grits, to greet Marste' Brett and make him welcome, and Trav asked:

"How did you leave the children, and Tilda?"

Brett said they were fine. "And Vesta writes that your namesake is a buster."

"She should have named him after you."

Brett laughed. "She promised me the next one! There's already a Brett Dewain, you know; Julian's boy." He looked at Peter. "Vesta's borne a Travis Lyle, but Peter, you'll have to father a Travis Currain, one of these days." And in sudden realization: "I hadn't thought of it, Trav, but you and Peter are the last of the Currains. Tony'll never marry, and Faunt's dead." Enid and Cinda and Lucy came to join them, and Brett kissed Enid and held her at arm's length and exclaimed: "Why, what have you been doing to yourself? You look ten years younger—and ten times as beautiful!"

"Really? Trav's never mentioned it!"

They laughed together, and Cinda said: "Oh, Trav would never notice! I told her the same thing, Brett." She added laughingly: "Trav, you'd better keep your eyes open! She looks to me like a girl in love!"

"I've sort of thought she was looking unusually well," Trav assented. "But then Enid always looks wonderful to me."

Cinda, with a side glance at Tommy, asked news of Don, and Lucy assured her he was wonderful. "He's away a lot. His work takes him all over Louisiana and Mississippi and Alabama—and Texas too. He's down in St. Bernard parish, right now."

"Still the Freedmen's Bureau?"

"Oh yes."

"Really!" Cinda drawled. "Yet he seemed like a nice young man."

Lucy laughed. "You can't tease me, Aunt Cinda!"

Cinda smiled. "Of course he's wonderful—but isn't he maybe a little, just a very little, slow on the uptake?"

Lucy colored happily. "We've lots of time!" Cinda looked across at Tommy, and Lucy, understanding, cried: "Oh, Aunt Cinda, this is Tommy Buford."

Tommy rose, and Cinda said quickly: "Don't get up, Tommy. I've heard Lucy talk about you for years."

"I was hoping someone would introduce me," he assured her, and spoke to Trav. "Major, I'll see you at the mill?" Trav nodded, and Tommy and Peter departed together.

Brett asked: "How's Tony?"

"As usual, I think," Trav told him. "One of our new political lights, a nigra named Pinchback, is said to be his protégé."

Enid rose in haste: "Cinda, they're going to talk politics!"

Cinda came to her feet. "I'm sick to death of the sound of muffled drums," she agreed. "When our men get on the subject, it's to the tune of the 'Dead March'!"

They departed, Lucy with them. Brett and Trav turned to Trav's study, and Isaiah brought a decanter of brandy. "Case you gemmen gits a dry th'oat, talkin' so!" He chuckled and backed away, and Trav filled the glasses.

"Just an eye-opener! Here's damnation to the Radicals!" Brett smiled and they drank. "Think they'll remove the President?" Trav asked. President Johnson in late February had ordered Secretary of War Stanton to vacate his office, and this direct violation of the Tenure of Office Act was an open challenge to Congress. That same day a resolution to impeach was offered in the House; next day the resolution was passed; the day after, a committee of two, Thaddeus Stevens and John Bingham, appeared at the bar of the Senate and read the articles of impeachment, and President Johnson's trial had begun last Monday.

Brett said thoughtfully: "I don't know. In any case, the verdict will be purely political." He added dryly: "If there is such a thing nowadays as pure politics."

Trav smiled. "We've had a lull here, since our Constitutional Convention finished its work. The voting on the Constitution comes on the sixteenth and seventeenth, but of course there's no doubt about the result." He added: "Tony's friend Pinchback is up for the State Senate, and for delegate to the National Convention."

"We'll swallow our bitter pill about the same time you do," Brett commented. "Our Convention met in mid-January. It was quite a menagerie; three nigras to every two whites, and even so, only twenty-three of the white men were South Carolina residents, and one of these is a jail bird, and another is a pimp for a troop of mulatto—ladies." He spoke in a dry voice that ached with pain. "Probably we might have elected some better men, but Wade Hampton and Governor Perry, all the political wisdom in the state, advised those who opposed the Convention to stay away from the polls. It seems that unless a majority of all those registered actually voted, the election would have been invalid. But votes enough were cast, and the Convention met." He said grimly: "You may have known its leader. Beverly Nash? Remember him?"

"I don't think so."

"He used to be a hotel porter in Columbia," Brett explained. "Fifty-seven of the nigra delegates in the Convention were slaves three years ago. Now, they've drawn up a Constitution, and by midsummer the Army will get out and leave us in their hands."

"Have your state officers been elected?"

"Nominated. It's the same thing. General Scott's to be Governor. He's an Ohio man, an assistant commissioner in the Freedmen's Bureau, a bigoted rascal. The other nominees are all from out of state— a New Yorker, a couple of men from Massachusetts, a nigra or two. The election's just a formality."

"Well, at least we've a contest here," Trav reflected. "But it's between two Radical tickets, one headed by a carpetbagger—though Judge Warmoth is a man of good abilities—and the other by a Louisiana Republican, a fine gentleman, Judge Taliaferro." He added with a smile: "Not that Southerners will have any voice in the decision. Our

Constitution's disfranchising clause is so severe that even Pinchback voted against it."

"Have you seen this fellow?"

"Yes, I was in General Longstreet's office one day when he and Judge Warmoth called. He's young, but he seems to have intelligence, and some sense of responsibility. Oh, I suppose most Southerners would damn his hide, but from what I've heard of him, if there were none worse than he—yes and if all our white politicians were his equals— we'd have little to fear." Trav added gravely: "My real concern arises from the fact that our Constitution gives so much power to the Governor. Whoever he turns out to be, he'll have more absolute authority than was ever held by any ruler of a civilized nation. What he'll do with it—well, Heaven only knows."

"At least, your two candidates have some of the virtues. Our next Governor has none!" Then someone came running down the stairs, and Brett looked around; but the steps turned toward the front door, and they heard the door swung wide, heard Lucy cry:

"Oh, Don!" And after an instant: "I just happened to look out and see you coming. Come in."

"I'm afraid I can't, Lucy. I just got in, stopped on my way to Headquarters."

"But come in for a minute! Uncle Brett and Aunt Cinda are here, came this morning. You want to see them." And she called up the stairs: "Aunt Cinda, Don's here!"

Brett and Trav rose to greet Don, and Cinda came down, and Brett asked a question, and Don said: "Oh, there's been some trouble in St. Bernard parish, and I was sent to look into it."

"Tell us about it," Brett suggested, and Lucy tugged at Don's arm.

"Yes, do," she insisted. "Sit down. You don't have to report yet! It's awfully early." She pushed him into a chair, perched herself on the arm of it. "Now."

Before he could speak, Enid joined them, and Don rose, and she kissed him and told him how glad she was to have him back, till Cinda said: "Oh, for Heaven's sake, Enid, let him tell his story."

"What story?" Enid echoed, turning back to Don.

"I've been down in St. Bernard," he explained. "They had some trouble there, but it didn't amount to much. One Negro got a shot wound and some others were clubbed, but no one was seriously hurt."

"Begin at the beginning," Cinda urged.

"Well, it all started over a barbecue, last Sunday, at the Marrero plantation. As near as I can get the background, there's a Mr. Ong—"

"A Chinaman?" Brett asked.

"I don't know. I didn't see him. But at any rate, after the War, this Mr. Ong rented a plantation down there from a Mr. Proctor, and went into politics. He was a delegate to the Constitutional Convention, and he organized a Radical club in the parish, and they planned to meet last Sunday at the court house, about two miles from the Marrero plantation, and keep the other Negroes from going to the barbecue."

"Were the planters staging this barbecue?"

"Yes sir, the Democrats, the white men. For the Negroes."

"I should think Mr. Ong and his friends were asking for trouble," Brett commented.

"Well, it was a big meeting," Don assured them. "Judge Warmoth was there, and Judge Pardee, and Mr. Sypher—and Mr. Ong. There's only one road, so Negroes on their way to the barbecue had to pass the Court House, and the crowd there tried to stop them. They did make some of them turn back. Then while the speech-making at the barbecue was going on, everybody from the meeting came marching down the road, the white gentlemen in carriages, and the Negroes tramping along behind. The carriages went on to Mr. Ong's house, and I don't think Judge Warmoth knew what was happening till afterward, but the tag end of the Negroes who were following the carriages, when they came opposite the barbecue field, they started to shout and halloo and raise a hubbub, and someone fired a shot!

"Well, that started a big tumult around the gate of the field where the barbecue crowd was gathered. The Radical crowd were trying to catch some Negroes who had turned Democrats. They were looking for a man named Griff Robinson, and another by the name of Taylor." He made a spreading gesture with both hands. "Of course, I'm just telling it as I pieced it together. One Negro was badly beaten, but I saw him and he'll get over it. The white men running the barbecue finally got things quieted down." He added regretfully: "The affair left a lot of hard feeling down there, especially between the Negroes."

Brett met Trav's eye. "Politics was bad enough even in the days when only white taxpayers could vote," he said gloomily. "It will be worse now."

"How do you know, Uncle Brett?" Lucy challenged. "Maybe it will be better."

"I'm afraid not, Lucy. Most nigras are so abjectly ignorant that they'll believe the first loud-talking scoundrel who comes along."

"But if they're so ready to do what they're told," she argued. "Why don't we teach them to vote the right ways? We never have taught them anything! It's always been against the law even to teach them to read and write." She colored, suddenly abashed. "I'm sorry! I didn't mean to get started, but Don and I have talked about this so much."

"It's a job we've refused to do in the past," Brett agreed. "Now we've got to do it."

Trav watched Don, and after a moment Don said: "I find most

Southerners think it won't be necessary to educate the Negroes. They think the whites can scare the Negroes away from the polls, scare them out of even trying to vote."

Brett spoke slowly. "I don't think our nigras at the Plains have ever been scared, but . . ."

Lucy, with a tender cry, came quickly to his side. "Don didn't mean you, Uncle Brett! You know what he means."

"I know," he admitted, smiling. "But I was about to say, *mea culpa*, all the same, Honey. All of us who were the old South, we're all to blame!"

When they heard Brett and Cinda were here, the Villards proposed a picnic at Paradise. Elon spoke to Trav at the mill, Eleanor called at the house to discuss plans with Enid and Lucy, and Brett received a stately communication from Mr. Villard himself, reminding Brett of a former business contact and hoping he might have the honor of entertaining Mr. and Mrs. Dewain at his plantation home down the river.

Before the day arrived, Eleanor confided to Lucy that it had been her idea. "Because the other time we all went down is the only time Mr. Cist has seemed really human! If I could just make him forget his old mill for a minute!"

Lucy laughed and squeezed her arm. "He's speechless when he's with you. You'll have to do the asking!"

"I won't!" Eleanor declared, her color high. "I never will. But I'll get it out of him somehow, even if I have to fall off a horse into his arms, or something!"

"If we were sure he could swim, you might fall overboard so he'd have to save you," Lucy suggested. "Men are awfully slow, the nice ones. Don never could have—till I sort of gave him a push."

"A push! Heavens, I've pushed and pushed, but Joshua just blushes and starts talking very fast about the mill or something."

"Use a hatpin," Lucy advised, and they laughed together, and Eleanor said wistfully:

"But he is so sweet, Lucy, really!"

Mr. Villard's letter puzzled Brett. "He speaks of our contact in the past," he said. "But I don't remember him."

"The poor old soul's probably hoping you'll buy the place," Enid suggested. "Why don't you? It's really lovely. You and Cinda could use it for a winter home!"

Cinda smiled. "Why doesn't Trav buy it?"

"I wish he would," Enid declared, and suddenly remembered that they would go down on the *Paradise*, that she would see Captain Cash again. She felt her cheeks hot, felt herself hot all over, and thought in complete consternation: something's the matter with me; what is it; somehow I've changed.

Brett was still trying to remember that past contact with Mr. Villard, questioning Trav, and Enid rose and strode across the room to look in the mirror above the mantel. Certainly there was a change in her, but it was a change which she found extremely pleasant. She realized that she felt better than she had felt for years, and the mirror assured her that she was prettier than she had ever been; in fact, she decided, she was beautiful! She remembered that it was a long time since she had taken any of her pills, a long time since the apothecary had refilled her bottle of laudanum; she no longer needed it to help her sleep away long dull forenoons. Returning to her chair she was conscious of the movements of her body. Walking, this almost involuntary, unconsidered act, when you noticed it, became pleasure. It was delightful to take one step and then another, to allow your body's weight to rest first upon one foot and then the other, to feel the thigh bone a firm support under the joint in your hip, to feel your spine curve this way and that as your weight was transferred from side to side. It was a delight to feel this wonderful machine which was your body so efficient and graceful and controlled.

She thought: "I know what has happened. I no longer feel like a girl; I feel like a woman! How different it is!" She wished to be alone, to rejoice in this new self-knowledge, and with an abstracted word, she left them, going to her room. That night when Trav lay asleep beside her, she wondered whether he would recognize the change in her. She lay awake a long time, thinking of Trav, and of Lucy and Peter, not in judgment, or in appraisal, but with a new understanding; she thought of Don, of Tommy and Elon and Eleanor and Mr. Cist, of Casual and of Quinny, and it was as though she saw each one clearly for the first time. She went further afield, thinking of Dolly, and of Captain Pew and of Redford Streean, and to think of Streean, to remember Dolly's description, made her shiver as she drifted off to sleep.

Before the day of the picnic, Don was sent off to Baton Rouge. Lucy was disappointed, but if she kept Elon and Tommy occupied, Eleanor could have Mr. Cist to herself; so when the *Paradise* began her run downriver, she led Elon to tell Tommy—as he had once told her—the story of the famous battle, and the histories of the various plantation houses along the way, and why the British turned at English Turn. Elon had all the lore of the river at his tongue's end, and he spoke of Lafitte and his pirates, who were as patriotic as they were piratical, and from Lafitte he wandered through the many tales, half history and half legend, which were told and retold about the city and the stream, and she listened so intently that when Peter took Tommy away to inspect the engine, she scarce knew he was gone. When Elon paused, she asked in wonder:

"How do you know all these stories, Elon? You must have studied and studied."

"No. It's mostly liking old books; yes, and liking old people. Old people like to tell you about their young days, and about all they've seen and done and known, and I've enjoyed listening, to Grandfather Rawle, and to Grandmother Villard, and to the nigras on the place. I've listened by the hour to M'sieu' de Marigny, in rags and patches and poverty and squalor, chuckling over the good times he's had in his ninety years. See! There's Paradise ahead!"

His tone made her look up at him. "You love it, don't you?" Her own words reminded her how often she had asked Trav that same question, while they lived at Chimneys, and she thought Elon and her father were in many ways alike.

He nodded. "Yes, of course. I grew up here." And he said: "I love it best in the spring. You can feel things growing all around you, feel the earth swelling under you. It's usually high water. You know, when the river's rising, it's higher in the middle than it is at the sides, so that you can actually see the bulge of it."

"I know. Papa told me." So like her father.

"Well, it's as though the whole plantation were swelling like that, as it comes toward its time of bearing."

"You talk about land the way Papa does."

His eyes met hers with a curious gravity. "I expect I do," he assented. Then he stirred. "Well, it's time to go watch Cap'n Cash make his landing." The strong flood had borne them swiftly on. She thought he was not only like her father; he was like Don too, in the things he talked about. They strolled forward as the *Paradise* passed the point and moved crabwise into the slack current and so to shore.

That was a fine day for them all—except perhaps for Cinda. On the trip downriver, Mr. Villard, as before, established himself in the pilot-house, and Enid and Cinda joined him there, Enid beside Captain Cash at the wheel, Cinda devoting herself to Mr. Villard.

"I made up my mind I'd get some conversation out of that—that obelisk—if I had to give him laughing gas!" she told Brett that night. "Or do I mean odalisque? I always mix them up! Which is which?"

"It's a question of sex," Brett said gravely, and she protested:

"Stop it! You're laughing at me."

He grinned. "Obelisk is what you mean," he admitted. "Though it's an unusually polite way of expressing the thought!"

"I know that look in your eye!" she warned him. "You're being obscene, and you think it's funny, but I haven't the faintest idea what you're talking about. I never did thaw him out, not really. His world consists of people who have wronged him, and history was arranged a-purpose to ruin him and him alone. I wouldn't buy his old plantation if it could be bought for thirty cents! I'd see him starve, first!"

"Was Enid any help to you?" he asked.

"Oh, she talked to Captain Cash. What an idiot she is, sometimes! But he's a superior nigra, isn't he?"

"I wonder," he remarked, "whether nigras like him, intelligent, well spoken, aren't sometimes pretty unhappy. They're so nearly white."

"Pooh!" said Cinda. "Blow out the candles and let's go to sleep. Many of the whitest people I know—as far as their souls are concerned, at least—are nigras." And a moment later she murmured drowsily: "Enid certainly enjoyed him, today!"

He whispered: "Meow!" She put her arm across his shoulders and they slept.

Across the hall, Enid was brushing her hair, still far from sleep, her every nerve and bone and muscle as intensely conscious of Cash's strong body as though he still stood close beside her. Watching her image in the glass, she said: "Trav! Trav!" And when he stirred. "Trav, let's buy Paradise."

He grunted, half asleep. "Tonight?"

"I'm serious, Trav."

"Well, we can't do it till morning. Good night now!"

She said no more, not then, but she was resolved; someday Paradise would be theirs.

4

BRETT HAD ARRANGED to have the Charleston *Mercury* sent after him, and at the breakfast table, he and Trav were usually busy with their papers, each reading an occasional paragraph to the other. Once Brett read the final paragraph of a heated editorial.

> If it is the purpose of the United States Government to negro-ize the Southern states, they may as well know now that it has to be done with the bayonet. The Southern people do not intend to be mongrelized.

There was angry approval in his tones, but Trav said mildly: "Curious how that fear of miscegenation haunts us, like the fear of a nigra rising. You'd think the whole of Southern manhood was being threatened with shotgun marriages to nigra women."

Brett, after a startled moment, grinned at himself. "You do me good, Trav. I get worked up over things, but Cinda calms me down, and so do you."

The *Mercury*, with its news from South Carolina, regularly disturbed Brett, and when the election resulted in seating over a hundred Negroes in the state legislature, as against about fifty whites, he said wretchedly: "I've half a mind to stay here in New Orleans."

"Wait and see if we do any better," Trav suggested. This was the first day of voting in Louisiana. And he added: "Or if you want our side of the picture, there's a little ceremony going on today that you might care to see. They're destroying the plates on which our city money has been printed, cutting them up with a chisel." And he explained: "Our city debt is around twelve million—and no funds. They've been issuing city money to pay expenses, printing it as fast as it was needed, and any of it that comes back to the city in payment of taxes or bills or the like is burned in the gas works regularly once a week."

"We haven't come to that yet," Brett admitted. "But we will."

"I'm going to vote on my way to the ferry," Trav said. "Better keep me company."

"There'll be a crowd of niggers at the polling place," Peter predicted. "Anyway, they were there last night."

Brett asked: "Why do you bother, Trav?"

"Oh, I will vote. That's the only weapon I'm allowed to use, so I can't afford not to use it." Trav added soberly: "If I don't, I can't complain of what happens."

They found the street near the poll as crowded as Peter had predicted. The morning was overcast and raw and almost cold, and in every corner that was sheltered from the wind, vendors crouched, some with a small charcoal brazier or a stove no bigger than a basket, offering hot coffee, or fried fish, or sowbelly and salt pork. Here and there a swarthy Sicilian woman had oranges to sell.

"It's like a country fair," Brett commented.

"Like the levee," Trav agreed. "These small victualers are everywhere along the levee, every day."

Near the polling place, policemen had funneled those on their way to vote, Negroes and a sprinkling of white men, into a double line. Two by two, the sluggish, slowly moving stream approached the poll. Trav took his place in this line, the others from across the street watching his slow progress. A white man beside him—Trav thought he was a mechanic on his way to his work—continually grumbled and cursed, muttering under his breath, treading on the heels of the Negro in front of him, whirling in threatening rage at any touch from behind. Whenever this happened, the Negroes behind him recoiled in quick humble apology. Trav, scanning these dark faces, saw in each one an emotion that was part fear, part hope, part triumph. If any eye met his, its owner quickly looked away, as though apologizing for his presence here. Trav thought apology, and humility, and gratefulness were dominant among these newly enfranchised people. Sometimes their garments were indescribably worn and shabby, hardly recognizable as garments at all; one could not be sure whether that which covered a broad pair of powerful shoulders had originally been a shirt or a jumper or a jacket. Their hats held a ludicrous variety, lacking brim or lacking crown, often pierced by many holes. Sometimes these holes in the felt were cut in patterns, crescents, or stars. Many of the voters were barefoot; the shoes worn by others had sometimes lost even the look of shoes, and through worn leather or ripped seams, toes protruded.

Here and there among this press of men Trav saw well-dressed Negroes, men who had been for generations free, men of parts and men of means, respectable and respected. How long since they had been like these others here; how long till these others here might—given a chance—come to be like them?

The poll was in one of three identical houses set side by side; the double line filed in through one door and out another. As he stepped through the door, Trav could see challengers checking each man's name against the list of registrations before the voter went on to face the judges. There were delays while men rummaged their tickets out of a torn pocket, or drew them like a treasure from inside their shirts. The old Negro immediately in front of Trav had his ticket wrapped in a voluminous dingy rag, and he was so long unwrapping it that the judge facing him said impatiently: "Come, come, Uncle; get a move on!" But when the ticket was at last unwrapped and proved to be Democratic—the Republican tickets were shorter and much wider than those provided by the Democrats, and so were easily recognized—the Commissioner said cordially:

"Well, Uncle, I see you know your friends." He received the ticket, slid it into the ballot box.

The old Negro touched his hat. "Yas suh. Yas suh!" He moved on, and Trav handed his ticket to the same Commissioner. The official took it and dropped it into the slot, and the mechanic beside Trav also presented one of the longer, narrower tickets. Trav heard the Commissioner say to someone beside him:

"Three in a row. That's more Democratic ballots than we've seen all morning."

Back where the names of the voters were being checked, a disturbance rose, and Trav paused to listen. A Negro's vote had been challenged; he stood, fumbling with a tattered straw hat.

"Your name isn't on the list," the judge told him severely. "You haven't registered."

"Yas suh, Ah is," the man protested. He appealed to the man behind him. "Jeddie heah, him and me done it de same time."

The judge asked this ally: "What's your name?"

"Jeddie Right, Jedge, please suh."

"Your name's not here! Now, you two, I believe you're lying. Go to the registration headquarters. Ask them if your name is on the lists. If it is, they'll give you a certificate, and you can come back here and vote. If it isn't, and I see you around here again, I'll take a cowhide to you."

"Yas suh! Yas suh!" The two men giggled in hasty mirth. "Yas suh, y'all sho will!" They hurried past Trav and away, looking back over their shoulders with anxious eyes.

When Trav rejoined Brett, Peter and Tommy were gone. "Tommy thought he'd be late at the mill," Brett explained, "and Peter went with him." His eye touched Trav. "Those two seem congenial." They went on toward the ferry together.

"Tommy's been good for Peter," Trav said gratefully. "One thing, he's made it a lot easier for me to get acquainted with Peter." He smiled. "You know, they've persuaded me to join the Knights of the White Camelia, complete with recognition signals, challenges, countersigns and I don't know what all."

"I've heard of it," Brett agreed. "Some perfectly respectable people in it, or so I'm told. Dedicated to the cause of white supremacy." Trav nodded, and Brett said: "Speaking of white supremacy, that was a strange thing to watch, back there. Even from outside."

"They seemed pretty humble about it," Trav reflected. "As though they didn't quite believe it, even now."

Brett nodded. "I expected they'd be like nigras at a fair, or a barbecue, laughing and singing and dancing; but they weren't, they were quiet. After they came out, a lot of them waited to watch others. It was as though they expected to see some change in their friends; as though they expected them to be taller, or handsomer, or something."

"Remember the first time you voted?"

Brett nodded. "Yes. Three or four of us went together, and I think we were all impressed. I know I was. But we tried to act completely casual about it. These men today were not pretending to be casual. They were impressed." He hesitated. "I suppose the high jinks will come after the novelty wears off."

The voting continued through that day and the next. Judge Warmoth was elected Governor, defeating Judge Taliaferro by a lop-sided majority, and Oscar Dunn, since Major Dumas had declined the nomination, was chosen to be Lieutenant Governor. About half the members of the Legislature were Negroes.

But the Republican majority was relatively slim, a margin of only four in the Senate, and of only nine in the House, and in this the Democrats found hope for elections still to come.

Tony came one evening to pay his brotherly respects to Cinda. She and Enid had spent two hours among the shops along Canal Street. The spring styles dictated a tight bodice above a full skirt, small straw hats tipped down over the eyes, and Enid declared that all her old clothes would just have to be thrown away. "And Lucy's too! She must look her best, even if that stodgy old Yankee of hers doesn't ever notice!"

She spoke in affectionate jest, but Cinda retorted: "He notices a lot more when he's listening to her than when he's listening to you. If you're trying to give Tommy a chance, you're wasting your time."

Enid tossed her head. "Don and I are better friends than you think," she retorted, pausing at a new window: "Look at these. You know, they say our New Orleans shops are the next best thing to Paris, and I believe it's true."

"New Orleans is a boom town," Cinda suggested. "Now that the carpetbaggers have their feet in the trough, men who never had a nickel are suddenly rich, throwing their stolen money around."

They returned from that expedition pleasantly wearied, and retired to refresh themselves, so when Tony called, Isaiah bade him wait, and it was some time before Cinda came down.

She accepted Tony's brotherly peck, then frankly surveyed him. "I declare, you certainly keep your looks, Tony! Sapphira takes good care of you. You've always been lucky with your women. Even Enid's mother was good for you. You know, after she took up with Faunt, I met her once or twice, and I really respected and admired her." She added: "It's a pity wives don't learn their jobs as well as mistresses."

"That's one reason I've never married."

"Oh, you were wrong! The right wife is better than the most admirable mistress. Ask Brett!"

His eyebrows lifted in sardonic question. "Trusting spouse! Well, I've heard that the betrayed wife is always the last to know!"

She threw back her head in a burst of mirth. "What a vicious beast you are! I expect you love to pull wings off flies. I've a notion to set Brett on you! That reminds me, how's Redford Streean?"

"I don't follow? What reminded you?"

"Oh, because the last time they met, Brett slapped Streean's face!"

He grinned, not amused. "Ah! Streean? Well, he's gone downhill: drink—and gambling. Pew kicked him out, you know. He no longer lives in the Haunted House—though he's still a partner. Gambles away his profits."

"Dolly live with him?"

"No, she's Pew's—hostess. Streean lives in a fourth-rate boarding-house somewhere."

Lucy joined them, and Tony bowed over her hand and said she was more beautiful each time he saw her, and his tone embarrassed her, till Cinda said reassuringly: "Don't mind him, Honey. He thinks that's just gallantry, but it's the honest truth! Is Dolly, Tony? More beautiful than ever, I mean?"

"Why don't you go see for yourself," he suggested, and Enid appeared in the doorway, crying out a question.

"See what for herself? Hello, Tony!" Her greeting was so casual that Lucy looked at her in surprise, and Cinda answered her.

"See Dolly, Enid."

"Go call on her? Trav won't let her come here."

"I may," Cinda said lightly. "Tony, I suppose the carpetbaggers are Captain Pew's best patrons."

A key clicked somewhere, and Trav's voice sounded in the hall. Tony said to Cinda: "Send your name in to Dolly and you'll be welcomed, I'm sure." Then as Trav and Brett entered, and after greetings had been exchanged, he told Brett: "Cinda asked about Dolly, and I suggested she go to call."

"I'd dare go," Cinda declared, "if you'd take me, Brett."

Brett laughed. "I'll have to think that over. Well, Tony, did the election suit you? I suppose you're pleased. You're on the Radical side, are you not?"

"I was much pleased, yes," Tony agreed. "I'm a Warmoth Radical, not one of Doctor Roudanez's faction. By the way, Trav, the Doctor tells me the *Tribune* will have to suspend publication." There was malicious triumph in his tones. He spoke to Brett again. "One of our particular friends, a young mulatto named Pinchback, will be a delegate to the Republican National Convention."

"A nigra, you said, Tony?"

Tony nodded. "A mulatto, yes." His tone became almost dreamy. "It's not impossible that if the fight is close, this mulatto son of a nigra woman and a white father will by his vote name the Republican candidate. Pinchback may choose our next President!" He looked from one to the other. "We live in an age of miracles, gentlemen."

When he was gone, Trav said quietly: "You know, I'd go a long way to help carry Louisiana for the Democrats."

"It might be possible to do that here," Brett admitted. "But in South Carolina I'm afraid we're helpless."

"I'm beginning to think—" Trav's tone was somber. "I'm beginning to think we're all helpless, unless we help ourselves."

Cinda remembered her desire to call on Dolly, and asked Brett's opinion. "I'd rather you didn't," he admitted.

"Then you go, and tell me about it."

He made no promises, but next day when they left the mill earlier than usual, he suggested to Trav that they stop in at Captain Pew's establishment. "There'll be no crowd there so early, and I'd like to see Dolly." He smiled. "Cinda wants a report on her."

Trav hesitated, but agreed, and they took the ferry to Jackson Square and walked the five or six blocks, approaching the Haunted House along Hospital Street. "A handsome edifice," Brett commented. "And what a setting for Dolly!" They turned into Royal Street and reached the heavy iron grill which barred the recessed entrance. The entrance was floored with marble, black and white squares set at a diagonal; the great door was heavily carved and touched with gold leaf. Their ring was answered by a gigantic Negro in severe uniform.

"Mr. Currain, and Mr. Dewain," Brett told him.

The Negro bowed. "Gentlemen." There was a curious precision in his speech. He swung wide the iron grill. "Please to enter."

They stepped into a high-ceiled hall, where a heavy crystal chandelier hung from the decorated plaster and a thick-piled rug silenced their footsteps. The Negro closed the door behind them, and another, a stately, white-haired old man, relieved them of coats and hats.

"Now may I show you to the social rooms," he suggested, and turned toward the wide, curving stairs which through an open well ascended to the second floor and beyond that to the third. They had expected to find, at this hour, no patrons here, but a murmur of voices came down to them, and their eyes met in question.

But they followed their guide. On the second floor he ushered them into the drawing room, which through wide sliding doors extended itself into mirrored distances. In the further room, a group of men clustered around someone invisible, and Trav guessed Dolly was there. At a small table to one side some gentlemen were playing cards, Captain Pew among them. He excused himself from the play and came toward them.

"Mr. Dewain. Major Currain. I am honored." A servant at their elbow offered cool frosted glasses. "Or whatever is your pleasure, gentlemen," said Captain Pew.

They served themselves, and Brett, looking all around, remarked: "Your establishment is famous, Captain. I have heard it said that no one who comes to New Orleans can afford to miss it—and that no one can afford not to!"

Captain Pew smiled. "We try to deserve our reputation—especially that one."

Dolly came toward them, not actually running, yet so swiftly that she seemed to run to welcome them, moving so gracefully that each step had a beauty of its own. She came with outstretched hands, one for each of them.

"Oh, you dear men!" she cried. "Here!" She kissed Brett and then Trav, rising easily on tiptoes. "How sweet of you to come!" And, laughingly, to Captain Pew: "Yes, Captain, I know everyone's goggling, but it's good for business, my dear! Each gentleman here is hoping it will some day happen to him! Excuse us, will you?"

He bowed, and she took their arms, leaving him to return to his game. She led them back through the wide hall to a rear room. "Now!" she cried, when they were seated there. "Are you comfortable? Are the juleps just right?" And when she had their assurances: "Now, Uncle Brett, tell me all about yourself, and about everyone. Is Aunt Cinda with you?"

"Yes," Brett admitted, laughter in his tones. "And she's wishing she were here. She'd like to see you, spoke of coming to call."

Dolly held up both hands in pretty dismay! "Lah, no! Don't let her do that! She'd be horrified at my goings on." She laughed softly. "You see, I play craps a little while, every night. I challenge all comers, and we play with huge dice—oh, this big—" She held her hands a foot apart. "Maybe not quite this big, but enormous, so everyone can read them, and I roll them the length of the drawing rooms, and everyone cheers. It's wonderful!"

Brett chuckled, enjoying her beauty, her bright cheeks, the glow in her eyes. "Do you always win?"

"Heavens, no! I almost always lose, but Captain Pew says it will soon be my turn to be lucky." Her laughter rang: "But imagine if Aunt Cinda knew! No, this is no place for ladies! Besides, I'm much more at ease with gentlemen. Now you two dears . . ."

Brett wagged his head. "Now, now, none of your pretty games with us! We're not as safe as you might suppose." He asked, more seriously: "Are your hours all filled, all so festive?"

She hesitated, thoughtful. "I wish you could all come sometime. We'd come back here and have a little supper, and a nice visit. Wouldn't that be—fun? But it wouldn't do," she decided, shaking her head. "No, it wouldn't do. We sleep till noon or later, and—as you see—guests may appear at any hour. Our time's never our own."

They talked a while together. She and Captain Pew, she told them, would in another fortnight close the Haunted House and sail for Paris, to be gone for months or for years. There was something wistful in her tone, and Brett thought it infinitely touching. When he and Trav were in the hackney coach on their way uptown, he said sympathetically: "I expect she has a lonesome time of it. She looks like a child. How old is she?"

"Twenty-five. She was born in 'forty-three."

Brett smiled. "Never forget a figure, do you? I wish it were possible for Cinda to see her, give her a kind word, if nothing more."

"I don't think of Cinda as one who—radiates kindliness," Trav suggested, in a dry amusement.

"She'd be gentle with Dolly," Brett assured him, and he said with a chuckle: "I'd like to see one of those crap games, even if I didn't lay a wager. Wouldn't you?"

The hack pulled up at Trav's door, and he paid the driver. "I suppose so," he agreed. "But the ladies will keep us otherwise engaged."

"Probably," Brett assented.

Trav fitted his key into the lock. "Enid will want to know all about our call," he said. "Cinda, too, I expect. Ready for the cross-examination?"

"Oh yes," Brett assented, and as they went in he repeated: "All the same, that's something I'd like to see."

So it was like an answer to his wish when in the hall, Enid met them with a laughing announcement. "You gentlemen will have to entertain yourselves tonight," she said. "Mrs. Morgan's having a party for ladies only—Judge Morgan's out of town—so we won't have to listen while you talk politics."

Trav's eyes met Brett's. "Tonight!" he repeated.

"Yes," she said. "Right after supper, so you can just make the best of it."

"Oh, we will," Brett assured her, his tone so grave Trav wished to laugh. "We surely will."

They reached the Haunted House at half past eight, and sent their names to Dolly, and Roderick led them to her pleasant sitting room where after a moment, radiant, she joined them in quick, excited welcome. Brett exclaimed with pleasure. "My but you're a picture, Dolly. A beautiful gown! A new style?"

"Like it?" Dolly dropped them a laughing curtsey. Instead of the elaborate, ribbon-decked dresses which had succeeded the crinolines, their full skirts so stiff with cascading banks of ruffles that they would almost stand alone, her gown of a soft rose color was elaborately simple, high-waisted and falling in graceful folds to within an inch of the floor. "It came this morning, by Captain Pew's steamboat, just in from France." A maidservant brought coffee, and Dolly saw them seated and at ease. "I must go into the social rooms in a moment now." She laughed at her own words. "Nine o'clock is my hour for making an entrance."

"We came to watch that game of craps of which you spoke," Brett told her, and she nodded, a twinkle in her eye, and was about to reply when Captain Pew came to join them. He accepted a cup of coffee, but would not sit down.

"I must return to my guests," he explained. "But Miss Dolly, I thought it necessary to tell you. Mr. Streean is here, and he is in his cups." He turned to Trav and Brett. "I can only offer my apologies. Mr. Streean is a one-third proprietor, so he cannot easily be refused admittance." He spoke to Dolly. "Several of our guests, who find him objectionable, have already left the rooms."

Dolly came swiftly to her feet. "Papa's intolerable," she exclaimed, her tone iced with anger. She bit her lip, frowning with thought, her toe tapping; then suddenly she crossed to the tall cabinet beside the door and took out of it two polished *lignum vitae* cubes a full four inches on a side, marked with white spots. For a moment she turned them in her hands, and Brett asked:

"Are those your dice?"

"Of course." She looked at Captain Pew as though consulting him, then turned to the door, saying over her shoulder: "Come! If you like!"

From her sitting room a narrow passage led to the drawing room. Captain Pew opened the door for her, then stood awaiting their pleasure.

"Will it be agreeable to you?" Brett asked.

"Certainly. And except for Mr. Streean's presence, you will find it amusing."

They stepped into the passage. Dolly had opened the further door and paused there, one of the big dice cupped in each hand. When they came beside her, they saw Streean, a bloated, pear-shaped figure, facing her from a little distance. A servant paused with a tray of full glasses. He took two, emptied one at a gulp and replaced it on the tray, kept the other. As he turned, the clock above the mantel began to strike the hour of nine.

At the stroke, as at a signal, a stir ran through the crowded rooms, and gentlemen still at cards abandoned their play. Dolly went directly past her father, looking through him as though he did not exist, and Captain Pew walked beside her toward where in the further room a heavy table had been placed. There he gave her the stirrup of his hands as she stepped up atop the table and stood facing them all."

When she spoke, it was quietly, in tones completely matter-of-fact. "This is the hour!" she reminded them. "The Haunted House is haunted by the ghosts of those whom these dice have ruined." She held high the *lignum vitae* cubes for all to see. "For those who are newcomers here, I will explain. I keep the dice. You place your wagers here." She stamped her foot, pointed down at the table on which she stood. "You win or you lose, but the dice are always mine." She leaped lightly to the floor, stepped toward the wide doors. "Make room," she called. "Make room for the long roll."

Trav and Brett were standing by the door through which they had entered, so that Dolly was forty or fifty feet from where they stood. She called: "Players here by the table. Roderick will call the throws." Roderick came to stand just in front of Brett and Trav. "If a die touches any man, the cast is foul." From the table behind her she lifted a silver instrument shaped like a scoop, and she laid the dice in this, and cried: "So!" She threw them with a sweeping motion that became a pirouette, her full skirts flying wide, and the dice, rounded at the corners so that they rolled almost as easily as bowls upon the green, came tumbling and thumping from where she stood to Trav's very feet. They stopped, and those nearest burst into excited laughter. Roderick, the giant butler, stepped forward to where they lay.

"Deuce-Ace," he called, and picked them up. A servant at his elbow received them and glided out into the hall passage; another yonder laid fresh dice in Dolly's silver scoop. She shook them so that they rattled with a musical sound, while at the table behind her, prospective players bought counters from Captain Pew.

"White counters are fifty dollars," he announced. "Reds a hundred, blues five, yellows a thousand." And he called in a clear voice: "The house offers a thousand dollars, or any part of it—in fifties. Nothing less goes . . ."

He stacked twenty white counters on the table, and a dozen or fifteen gentlemen, pressing near, drew aside what they chose, matching his counters with theirs. Trav saw Streean move unsteadily toward the table. Pew had said Streean was in his cups, yet Trav thought it was more as though the man staggered under the burden of his own weight. Streean passed Dolly and spoke to Captain Pew, but none heard his words, for as he spoke, Dolly threw the dice again. When they came to rest, Roderick before he touched them called: "Six-Five."

Captain Pew raked in the counters, matched them neatly, and drew ten against the side of the table in front of where he stood. The rest he thrust forward, his deft fingers flying.

"The house offers fifteen hundred dollars," he said.

Reaching hands this time quickly covered every chip, and Dolly, moving like a dancer, the scoop containing the dice held at arm's length, singing softly as though to herself, with a final whirl sent the dice on their way. Trav did not watch the throw, for Streean yonder had caught Captain Pew's attention, and from the drawer of the table at the end of which he stood Pew gave him counters, not white like those already in play, but red and blue and yellow.

Roderick's voice boomed over a general shout of excited laughter. "Six-Six," he announced, and Captain Pew's rake pushed the stacks toward the winners. He spread fresh counters on the table.

"The house offers two thousand dollars," he announced.

Someone laughed and retorted: "I'll wait till next throw." Others nodded agreement, but Streean spilled a handful of counters across the table.

"I'll take it all," he said thickly. "Throw, Doll!"

Trav saw Dolly look at her father in flashing anger, and this time she threw the dice with a spinning violence. The way was clear for them; they passed Trav and Brett and struck the wall and rebounded and were still. Trav saw their faces, and Roderick announced: "Five-Two."

Captain Pew, his face expressionless, raked in the counters; he rearranged the small piles. "The House offers thirty-five hundred dollars," he announced. The gentlemen around the table, since Streean was the loser of the last bet, gave him time to make his wager.

He said loftily: "It's mine!" He laid three yellows and a blue upon the table, and a murmur of surprise and resentment ran through the circle of players. "Roll them, Doll," he called.

Ace-Ace was the throw, and Streean drew the counters toward him with embracing arms. "The house offers a thousand," said Captain Pew, and Streean laughed in scorn.

"Not worth my while," he said. The wagers were laid, the throw was three-two, the point was made.

"The house offers two thousand," said Pew, and Streean shouted: "Mine!"

Murmurs of protest ran around the room, and Captain Pew said quietly: "Gentlemen, I apologize for Mr. Streean's bad manners."

"Don't apologize for me!" Streean said scornfully. "Your money's covered. Roll 'em, Doll!"

The house won and lost and won, and—all save Streean content now to watch—play fell into a pattern. Dolly threw a pair of dice far along the polished floors, and even before they had stopped rolling, a servant dropped into her silver scoop another pair. Brett watched her in a deep sadness, for this had become a duel between Dolly and her father, and an ugly thing to see; but Trav was more interested in the mathematics of the game, and he tallied wins and losses in his mind. He saw at once that Captain Pew's constantly varying wagers were so planned that though losses and wins came with an almost equal frequency, nevertheless Captain Pew was after a dozen throws wagering none of his own money, and only a portion of his winnings. Trav touched Brett to whisper this comment, but Brett shook his head in warning. This was more than a game of dice; to intrude even by a whisper was to start taut nerves jangling.

The dice rolled and stopped and Roderick called "Deuce-Deuce." Dolly's point had been four, and Captain Pew's rake drew the counters toward him. He spoke to Streean.

"Others wish to play, Mr. Streean, and a quarter of the hour is gone. You have lost twenty-one thousand dollars. If you wish revenge, I allow you three more rolls."

"Allow me?" Streean laughed. "You forget, Captain; a third of this establishment is mine."

Captain Pew thrust his accumulated counters out into the table. "Cover what you wish."

Dolly, waiting to cast the dice, bounced them up and down in the silver scoop; she leaned down to them and pointed the scoop toward Streean, and whispered to the dice, her head on one side as though she asked a question, and waited for an answer. She laughed exultantly, the silver scoop in her outstretched hand, singing to the dice a swift, small song in rapid French.

"All of it," said Streean thickly, and covered the pile of counters with his hands.

"Have you the funds?" The Captain challenged, his tone even; but before Streean could reply, he called to Dolly: "The play is made."

The dice came tumbling and bouncing, clattering along the floor, rolling as easily as balls; but this time one of them turned aside and struck someone's foot. The cast was foul; a manservant retrieved the dice, another dropped a fresh pair in Dolly's scoop. She was about to make the cast when Captain Pew held up his hand. She waited, and Pew spoke to Streean in clear tones audible to all.

"Mr. Streean, you make yourself extremely disagreeable. You have a one-third interest in this establishment. The situation is intolerable. Let us end it!" He tallied the counters on the table. "Twenty-two thousand seven hundred. To it I add my one-third interest here, plus as much more as you care to cover. Let one pass decide. If you win, I walk out of the door there, not to return. If I win, you do the same."

Streean mumbled one word. "Done!" He pointed to the pile of counters. "That represents a hundred thousand." Then, drunkenly: "Dolly, cast the dice."

Captain Pew looked around the table. "You gentlemen are witnesses?" Nods answered him.

Dolly whispered to the dice; she lifted one and pressed it to her cheeks; she lifted the other and kissed it like a lover. She nested them together, and patted and caressed them, and then with a smooth sweep of her arm they were away.

When they came to rest, Roderick called: "Six-Four."

The story of what followed would take its place among the epic tales of gambling on the river; Pew's name would rank with those of Hargraves, of Colonel Starr, of Powell, and White. A third-interest in the Haunted House was worth any price you cared to name, so even without the hundred thousand which Streean was pledged to cover, there was a fortune at stake. Dolly threw that Six-Four at nineteen minutes past the hour. Succeeding casts came slow and slower, for after each indecisive throw, she wooed the dice more and more ardently. She fondled them; she cradled them in her arms and whispered sweet seductions; she held them at arm's length in the silver scoop and danced around them, whispering naughty French songs; she abandoned the scoop and held them up before her in her nested palms and danced without moving her feet, her body undulating, her full skirt swinging in graceful lines.

Cast upon cast, and Roderick's steady calls. "Four-Two." "Five-Four." "Three-Two." "Five-Three." "Six-Two." "Six-Three." "Two-Two." The clock above the mantel struck the half hour, and Trav found himself watching the slowly moving hands till he forgot them again in watching Dolly.

Holding one of the dice in each hand as though they were children which she led, she walked slowly to where when she made her casts the dice usually came to rest, and while she walked, she leaned down to speak to each of the dice in turn, explaining to them what they must do for her.

"You're my sweet babies," she assured them. "My twin Fives. You're my little boy Five," speaking to the dice in her right hand; then, to her left hand: "And you're my little girl Five. Now the next time Mama spins you down here, I want you to lie down side by side, like good little children, flat on your backs, with your sweet little Five faces looking up at me. Understand? Promise me?"

She lifted them and held them pressed against her bosom while she retraced her steps, and this time, when she cast the dice, she ran after them, calling them by name. "Pretty Five! Sweet Five! Remember Mama? You promised! Remember?"

Then suddenly she whirled away, her arms outstretched, her skirts flying; and a great shout rose, and Roderick's booming voice roared out the call.

"Five-Five!" Excitement overcame him, elocution all forgotten. "Five an' Five! Da's what dey say!"

Everyone laughed, and Dolly danced and danced, spinning like a mechanical doll, her arms wide, her head tossing till her loosened hair hung all about her shoulders. She danced away from them through the further room and disappeared, and when they looked for Captain Pew, he was gone, and Streean too.

"I think we might as well go," Brett suggested, and Trav nodded, and Roderick came to speak to them.

"Captain Pew begs you will excuse him," he said. "He has some legal business with Mr. Streean. And Mrs. Kenyon sends her apologies and says she is fatigued. I can call you a hackney?" His words were a question. "Or you may amuse yourselves at the tables if you please."

But they said good night. In the hackney, Brett spoke thoughtfully. "That was a terrible thing to see."

"I never expected I'd be sorry for Streean."

Brett nodded. "What will he do, do you suppose? He must be penniless or almost so." But Trav did not know.

At home, they sat with a decanter between them, remembering and discussing every aspect of this evening, till Enid and Cinda and Lucy appeared. Brett, with a glance at Trav as though to ask permission, at once told them the story. There were many interruptions, but when he was done, Cinda said quickly: "We must never tell Tilda. She'd want to take care of him."

"We could invite him to the Plains," Brett suggested.

"For our sins? No, no, I can't do that!"

"I think I'll go see him, before we leave."

"Please don't," she begged. "Let's not ask for trouble. Let's let sleeping dogs lie."

5

WHEN BRETT AND CINDA returned to the Plains, Tommy Buford left New Orleans on the same boat, bound home to Lynchburg. He had told Trav his decision a few days before. "I've decided there's just as much for me to do around home as there is here," he said, explaining his resignation. "And I'm—well, sir, you've all been mighty kind to me, but I'm homesick."

Trav guessed the truth, but he asked no questions. "We'll miss you," he said. " 'Specially Peter. You've done a lot for him, Tommy." And he asked: "Have you told Elon?"

"Not yet, sir; no one but you." Tommy colored wretchedly. "I'd like to tell Lucy myself, sir, if you don't mind."

His opportunity came after supper that same day. Peter was going out, and suggested that Tommy go with him, but Tommy declined, and he and Lucy strolled into the garden to enjoy the long May twilight. She said Elon and Eleanor might come over a little later, and Tommy said: "Elon's a fine man, isn't he?"

She looked up at him, caught by something in his tone. "Yes, of course. I'm ever so fond of him." Then, half understanding: "And of you, too, Tommy."

"But Don's different?"

Her eyes met his, and after a moment she said: "Yes, Don's different."

"I've known that," he admitted. "I mean, I've known that Don was different. But I thought maybe I could stay here and—well, be near you, anyway. But I can't!" He saw tears in her eyes and said hurriedly: "Don't do that! I'm going home and get married."

"Who to?"

"Somebody wonderful."

"You will, too," she promised him. "I know you will, Tommy." Then, in sudden comprehension. "But then you're leaving the mill?"

"Yes. I told Major Currain today."

"Does Mama know?"

"No. Just you and the Major."

Lucy had an absurd impulse to giggle. "Mama'll hate your leaving," she said. "Maybe we'd better go tell her."

They found Enid and Trav with Brett and Cinda in the sitting room, and Enid was full of protests, urging Lucy to persuade Tommy to stay, urging Trav to do something, while Cinda watched her with amusement in her eyes, and Lucy thought her mother's words somehow lacked sincerity. Brett and Cinda were pleased that Tommy would be a fellow traveler as far as Atlanta, and Elon and Eleanor, when they appeared, received Tommy's decision with no apparent surprise.

"It really was sort of sad," Enid admitted to Trav after they were abed that night. "I practically shoved Tommy down Lucy's throat, and I certainly did my best to like him, but I was almost relieved to have him go, and I don't think any of us were really sorry."

"Elon was disappointed with his work," Trav admitted. "And as far as I was concerned, he seemed so young. About Peter's age."

Of them all, Peter was the only one who really regretted Tommy's departure. Tommy told him at breakfast, and Peter's sorrow took the form of anger, which fell on Lucy. "If you weren't so crazy about that nigger-loving Yankee of yours, Tommy wouldn't go," he exploded, and Lucy looked at Tommy, and Tommy reddened, and Peter insisted: "Oh, you didn't fool me, Tommy! I know why you came down here in the first place!"

When the time came, Tommy departed with the others, and Lucy and Enid had prompt letters from him, full of gratitude and friendliness. There were letters from the Plains, too. Cinda wrote that Jenny's baby was a girl, named Lucinda. "My first godchild," she exclaimed, "and I'm as excited as a bride!" Of Streean, she said: "Trav, I do hope you can keep an eye on the wretched man. No matter how much of a scoundrel he is, he's still kin, and sick, and penniless."

Trav had asked Brett to look out for a house for them in Camden, and Brett reported success. "The Legare place on Watch Hill," he explained. "You can have it from mid-June to October. They expect to go to England and the Continent. Of course, it's ridiculous for you to take a place when we've so many empty rooms at the Plains, but Cinda says she can understand Enid's wanting a house of her own."

When Trav read this, Enid commented: "There, you see, she's been resenting having us, all this time!" Happily, she remembered the Legare place, a beautiful mansion set in spacious grounds, and began at once to plan with Lucy which servants they must take with them for their summer there.

Brett spoke, too, of plantation affairs, of the inauguration of General

Scott as Governor, of the impeachment trial now at its climax in Washington. The final vote had been set for May twelfth. "But now it has been postponed till the sixteenth," Brett remarked. "And we hear rumors that the Radicals haven't enough votes to convict; hence the delay." Before the letter reached New Orleans, the telegraph had brought news of President Johnson's acquittal.

Don had been away since before election, but in mid-May he returned and at supper that evening he had to answer a thousand questions. "I've been visiting schools," he explained. "Mostly in northern Louisiana, but this last week I've been in Mississippi." He turned to Trav. "The Democrats there are pretty sure they're going to defeat the new Constitution," he said. "And I believe they are. I've talked mostly with Negroes, of course, but many of them, certainly the most intelligent, are going to vote against it. At least, they're against it now, but of course the election's two months away, and they may change. The Negroes who were slaves, a lot of them are saying their old masters never lied to them, so they're going to believe them now."

"The majority here wasn't as big as I expected," Trav remarked. "We had only four thousand votes against holding the Convention, but almost forty thousand voted against the Constitution. If the Democrats had organized, worked, they might have beaten it."

"They're organized in Mississippi," Don assured him. "They've persuaded a lot of colored people to stay loyal."

Trav looked at him in mild amusement. "You talk more like a Southerner than a Yankee."

Don nodded. "Well, I think in the long run it's the Southerner these Negroes will have to live with. This carpetbagger crowd, most of them will fill their pockets and go home."

They left the table, and in the sitting room, Peter said: "What we ought to have is the Ku Klux! That's the way to make the niggers behave."

"Ku Klux is mostly bogey man, isn't it?" Trav suggested.

"So far, it is," Peter admitted. "But it doesn't have to go on being! They can take a nigger out and whip him, or anything, any time they want to." He said almost devoutly: "Golly, I wish we could start one here."

"I thought you were a Knight of the White Camelia."

"Aw, they're no good. They just talk, is all."

Enid said irritably: "All men are like that, Peter; especially about politics. Talk, talk, talk!" She rose. "I'm going to bed. Good night all! Coming, Peter?"

He nodded, rising, and they went together toward the stairs, but Trav stayed a while, relishing the chance to talk to Don. "In South

Carolina, they let the vote for or against the Convention more or less go by default," he said. "There were some who argued that if a lot of people failed to vote, that would defeat it; but I've thought from the beginning that since votes are our only weapons, we must use them. We must vote ourselves, and persuade others to vote. And persuade them to vote right."

"I suppose every man has to start with himself," Don suggested. "He has to make sure that he votes right; that he doesn't just vote the way his friends do. As far as telling others how to vote, I think giving them all the facts, telling them the truth and letting them decide, is the fair, wise thing to do."

"What is a fact?" Trav wondered, and Don, after a moment's consideration, asked a counter question.

"Did you ever hear of a true departure?" Trav shook his head, and Don explained: "Well, when a vessel starts out on a journey, the captain makes a note of the last bit of land he sees, and from that point he takes his departure. Then he keeps a record of his course, and of his speed, and of what tides and wind do to him. As long as he knows where he started from, and where he's been since then, he always knows where he is. I call a true departure a fact; something absolute and unchanging." He smiled. "I wish there were more of them, don't you? If we always knew where we started, and how we got here, it would be a lot easier to figure out where we are."

Lucy, listening, watched Don with shining eyes, and Trav saw this, and smiled, and rose. "A true departure," he repeated. "I want to remember that. Lucy, this is a wise young man of yours. Glad you're back, Don. Let us see a lot of you."

When they were alone, sitting together on the couch, Don said in amused self-reproach: "When I get wound up, I'd talk the legs off a stove."

"I love it when you do," Lucy assured him. "When you talk about things, I always have a feeling that something in me that was asleep has suddenly waked up." She pressed her forehead against his shoulder. "Probably that's just because I love you."

"A dollar's worth?" he asked.

"Millions of dollars' worth," she assured him, and had his kiss and laughed, repeating her own words. "Millions of dollars! Listen to me talk. I don't know anything about money, Don. You'll have to teach me."

He said comfortably: "Pa will teach you. Whatever's worth knowing about money, he knows. I've always turned my savings over to him."

"What does he do with them?"

"Well, when I was at home two years ago, he said he'd bought me a lot of greenbacks when they weren't worth much. He was always sure the Union would win." There was a fond chuckle in his tones. "That's the way Pa always said it; not that the North would win, but that the Union would win." He added: "He says those greenbacks will be worth a lot more than he paid for them, one of these days."

"Don." Her voice was muffled.

"What, Honey?"

"Will we live with them?"

"It's a big house," he said uncertainly. "At first we will, I expect. But I know a farm I'd like to buy."

"Does it take a lot of money? I mean, to buy a farm."

He laughed, drew her closer. "Don't worry, Lucy. We'll get along."

For a while, neither spoke, their thoughts exploring that unknown future. For her, it held no terrors, since she would be with Don. He had his doubts and fears, yet other men had married and taken good care of their wives and their families. Surely so could he.

Lucy said at last: "We're not going to be here very long."

"Going to the Plains?"

"No, but to Camden. Papa's rented a house for the summer. We'll leave here early in June." And she said: "I hope you don't get sent away again till after we're gone."

She had her wish, and till their departure Don was able to see her almost every day. The night before they were to leave, a dozen of their friends came to supper, with dancing afterward, and the ring of happy laughter. At supper someone spoke of the nomination of General Grant for President, and the proposal, already being discussed, that the Democrats organize to carry the state in the fall election.

"It can be done," Elon declared. "Organize the nigras into clubs, promise them preference in jobs, and protection against Republican reprisals."

But Enid insisted that for this night, at least, no one should talk politics, and Elon apologized.

Later, dancing with her, he saw her eyes follow someone across the room, and she asked: "What do you suppose Eleanor and Mr. Cist are waiting for?"

Elon swung her around so that he could see his sister, obviously happy in Mr. Cist's pedestrian embrace, but he said: "You're imagining things, Mrs. Currain. I like Mr. Cist, but Eleanor will never marry a Yankee."

"Lucy's going to—unless someone does something about it pretty quickly."

He said lightly: "I'll not believe it till she does."

The music stopped. "Well, you may be right, of course," Enid admitted. "But I don't know. I had hopes of Tommy—or of you." As she spoke, Don came toward them from across the room, and she whispered to Elon, "Someone had better hurry!" Then the music began again, and in Don's arms she said fondly: "I'm going to miss you, this summer, Captain Page. You don't know how much your friendship has meant to me."

"I've thought sometimes you weren't really on my side."

"With Lucy, you mean? Oh, Don, how unfair! Nothing has ever pleased me so much as Lucy's finding you." And when presently the music paused again and Lucy came beside them, she said warmly: "Honey, I just love this young man of yours."

"I know, Mama," Lucy agreed. "We all do."

Enid smiled and strolled away, and Lucy led Don into the garden. The night was warm, and a mocking bird sang sleepily in the fig tree. "We mustn't stay out here," she reminded him. "But they'll go home pretty soon." And when the others were gone, they had an hour together. "This summer won't be as long as the others, Don," she promised him. "We've only taken the house till October. I suppose we may go to the Plains for a while then, but we'll surely be back before December." And she asked: "Know something?"

"Do I?" This was a familiar formula between them.

"Eleanor told me tonight she'll marry Mr. Cist as soon as I marry you to give her courage."

He smiled. "Courage? Why?"

"He's a Yankee!"

For a moment he did not speak; said at last, reflectively: "I suppose that feeling will go on for years."

Peter insisted on staying in New Orleans for a while after their departure. "I don't mind hot weather," he said. "And the servants will be here anyway." The Legare servants would staff the house in Camden.

"But suppose you change your mind," Enid protested. "Papa'd have to come all the way back here to fetch you."

"Oh, Mama, I can take a train trip without a nurse!"

Trav sided with Peter. "No reason he shouldn't stay if he wants to," he told Enid. "There's no sign of another epidemic this summer—and if one starts he can come join us. Let him stay." Yet when he and Peter were alone together, he asked his son: "What are you up to, Peter? What's going on?"

"Some of us are organizing a secret club," Peter told him proudly. "A political club."

"What for?"

"To lick Grant!"

Careful not to smile, Trav asked: "How'll you go about it?"

"We'll scare the niggers so bad they won't dare vote!"

"Careful some big buck doesn't scare you!"

"I can take care of myself." Trav's eyebrows lifted, and Peter flushed and cried: "Well, if you don't believe it!" A revolver appeared like magic from a holster under his arm and, seeing his father's surprise, he explained proudly: "I had a holster pocket made in my coat, just like yours!"

Since it was almost two years since there had been any widespread disorder in the city, Trav no longer regularly wore his revolver, yet he nodded understandingly. "I see," he agreed. "May I look at it?" Peter handed him the weapon, a graceful Colt with a rounded barrel and a half-fluted cylinder. "Handsome gun," Trav commented. "How long have you had it?" Peter did not at once answer, and Trav saw his disquiet, so he abandoned the question. "Can you hit anything with it?"

"A playing card, at ten paces, almost every time."

"As long as the playing card doesn't shoot back?" Trav smiled, and returned the revolver to his son. "Don't get yourself hurt, Peter. We'll worry about you, Mama and I."

So when they departed, Peter stayed behind, and Enid grieved; but after they were settled in Camden, she was happy in the big house on the rising ground north of town. Many Camden people went to the mountains to escape summer heat, yet there were gay occasions, and Lucy had beaus enough; but also she and Trav resumed their early morning rides together.

"And I love them, Papa," she declared, when they had been a week or so established there. "It was never the same at the Plains, when we rode with Uncle Brett and Clayton. Oh, that was fun too, but I like it better when it's just you and me."

"Will you make Don ride with you, after you're married?"

"I'll have to do something, to keep from missing you."

He chuckled. "Not for long, you won't. Don will be husband and sweetheart and father to you—yes, and son, too. Be good to him, Honey. It's mighty easy to hurt a man, and make him suffer, if you're the woman he loves."

She looked at him in tender understanding. "Mama's hurt you a lot, hasn't she?"

"The greatest happiness I've ever had, Mama's given me."

"I know," she assented. "But I know the other, too." And she said: "I wish I could always be near, sort of take care of you."

He shook his head. "No. Forget me! Remember what it says in the marriage ceremony. 'Forsaking all others.'"

Tears stung her eyes. "I'll never forsake you."

"Yes, you will. That's what marriage is, Lucy. Until you do forsake all others—I mean, in the deep ways that count—you'll never be really married to Don. As long as you can even imagine yourself bringing your troubles to Mama, or to me, instead of to him, you'll not be really married. You and he—forsaking all others—will make your own world. That's the way it must be." And he said tenderly. "Never admit anyone else into that secret world you and Don will share; not even me."

That summer Trav's already wide circle of acquaintances in Camden extended itself, but he found in these men a sullen acceptance of the Negro domination of the state. There was some muttering talk of violence, and even of assassination, as a weapon against the carpet-baggers, but in general he thought these were beaten men. Peter's letters—the boy proved a surprisingly good correspondent—were by contrast full of great plans, and brimming with confidence. On the twenty-fifth of June, Louisiana was received back into the Union, and the Legislature at once convened. Peter wrote:

> They're about half niggers in it, and they started right in, making trouble. It was something about Democrats having to take an oath, and the nigger Lieutenant Governor and another nigger who is chairman of the House of Representatives both said they'd have to, or they couldn't be members. We had men there watching the sessions, and they sent word around, and we got people started up that way till there was a bigger crowd around the Institute than there was when we had the riot two years ago. Every policeman in town was there, and they'd have helped us, the way they did in the other riot. There were soldiers too, a regiment of artillery, but they said they'd rather shoot at niggers than white folks. A lot of us wanted to take some of the niggers out and hang them, but they finally gave in, but it surely was exciting for a while.

He suspected that the youngster's account of the threatened riot was exaggerated, but Don's report, a fortnight later, agreed with Peter's, and he added:

> Governor Warmoth was well and duly inaugurated here the other day. No particular pomp and circumstance; a joint session of the Legislature, and he made a speech, moderate enough, all for peace and order. The papers think well of it. Chief Justice Wyman swore him in, and that's all there was to it. He made a good impression; no question about that. I wonder what they'll think of him four years from now.
>
> The Legislature elected William P Kellogg and John S Harris to the Senate, and five Representatives to the House. Only one's a Negro. All state and local offices are now held by civilians. Military rule is over.

Lucy, reading this to Trav, turned the page, glancing through the letter to report other bits of news. "And he says some gentlemen have started a factory to make ice. Mister Labarre is the head of it. Did you know Don worked one winter helping them cut ice in a pond back of Rockport, in Maine, to ship south. That was when he was a boy. The ice on the pond was nineteen inches thick."

"I'd like to see them do that," Trav reflected. "It must be interesting."

"You can see it when you come to visit us, after we're married," she promised, but when his eyes shadowed, she laughed and said reassuringly: "There darling, it won't be as bad as you think! Oh, and Don says to tell you—here, I'll read it." And she read: "'I suppose your father saw that Congress has voted amnesty to General Longstreet, removed all his political disabilities. How pleased he must be!'"

Trav had seen this reported in the Charleston papers, and had written the General his congratulations. Brett in July went to New York on business, and while there attended—though only as a spectator—the Democratic National Convention which on the ninth nominated Seymour and Blair. He saw the General, afterward, in Washington, and when he returned to Camden, he reported that Longstreet sent best regards.

"I had a few minutes with him," he told Trav. "He had hoped Salmon P. Chase would be the nominee against Grant, but since the Democrats named Seymour, he'll vote for Grant."

Trav smiled. "Well, from what Peter writes about all the things they plan to do to Republicans in Louisiana, the General had better not come back to New Orleans to vote!"

"Peter's really turned politician, hasn't he? At—what is he, sixteen?"

Trav nodded. "Sixteen, yes." He added gravely: "I'm concerned about Peter. He seems to have fallen in with some violent young gentlemen. He confessed to me that he goes armed, showed me his revolver, claims to be a good shot."

"Ah!" Brett did not comment, said instead: "I hear they propose to set up a state lottery in Louisiana. Longstreet says they want a Confederate general to act as its titular head. I gather that he feels he might have had the place, but for his politics, or perhaps, his scruples."

"Brett, can you see any virtue in his political position?"

"In the long run, maybe, yes," Brett admitted. "But for our lifetimes, no. In our time, for a Southerner to turn Republican, no matter how high his motives, will always be his damnation."

"Yes. Yes, I'm afraid that's so."

Trav's uneasiness over Peter persisted. New Orleans that summer was substantially free from yellow fever, but Peter's letters and Don's gave frequent warnings that there was a dangerous fever in men's blood. Peter was full of secrets and mysteries; he had joined this society and that, and the avowed program of each was to persuade Negroes to vote the Democratic ticket, using whatever means might prove necessary for that persuasion.

"We don't tell anyone how we're going to do it," Peter wrote. "But we will."

Don's was a different point of view. On an August morning, Lucy and her father returned from their ride to find a letter from Don awaiting her, and some mail for Trav. Lucy was reading to her father a passage from Don's letter when Brett rode up the drive and left his horse at the hitch rail and joined them. Trav said at once:

"You'll be interested in this, from Don, Brett," and he told Lucy: "Start over, Honey, will you?"

Lucy nodded, turning to what was obviously the second page of the letter, and Brett asked in mock surprise: "Why not start at the beginning, Lucy?"

She colored and laughed. "Personal reasons," she told him, and she explained: "Don's been saying that a good many people are being killed." She began to read.

> There are sore spots, places scattered all over the state, where murders are pretty frequent, and no one ever is arrested or seriously prosecuted. I went to Tigerville last week. That's on the Opelousas railroad, about sixty miles from Algiers. I went because a barn was burned, owned by a man named John McIntyre, and our man there thought some Negroes might be mobbed for it. Whenever a barn is burned, they always blame the Negroes. There's been a lot of trouble in Tigerville. Last April someone set fire to the railroad agent's house, and a few nights later they tried to burn some other railroad buildings. The agent's name is Moody. They shot his horse, and shot one of the railroad watchmen, and in the middle of May, a white watchman named Thomas Cosey was shot and killed.
>
> Everything seemed quiet when I was there, but since then someone has killed a Negro named Welborn, shot him while he was standing on his own front porch. He had told everyone he was a Democrat and meant to stay a Democrat. The other shootings seemed to be aimed at the railroad, but this was certainly politics, and I hear, every day, bitter angry talk. Between now and election, there may be some serious trouble here. I almost hope you stay in—

She broke off, smiling, reading ahead. "That's all about that," she told them, and turned the sheet. "But then he says . . ." And she read:

> The papers here report such things, and then say no one is ever brought to justice for these crimes because the police and the courts

are all Republican. But the police weren't Republican, nor the courts, two years ago when they murdered so many at the Mechanics Institute. And no one was ever punished for those murders.

Brett asked: "Does he say why the Tigerville people hate the railroad? I'm more interested in railroads than I am in politics."

"No." Lucy rose to leave them, and Brett remarked to Trav:

"That often disturbs me—the fact that railroads are so unpopular. Without them, most of this country would still be wilderness. They do a great service." He smiled. "And their securities are certainly good investments. But no one has a kind word to say for them."

"I suppose most people think of railroads as a necessary evil," Trav suggested, "Like going to a doctor. Certainly there are few experiences more disagreeable than a railroad journey."

"These new Pullman cars are right comfortable," Brett told him. "I traveled in one from New York to Washington. I'm putting some money in the company."

"I suppose Southern roads will have those cars in time," Trav agreed. "But traveling will never be a pleasure for me."

"That reminds me," Brett explained. "I'd almost forgotten why I came. Tilda had a letter from Tony. He says Streean is in the Charity Hospital, and Tilda wants to go down and take care of him." Trav made a protesting sound, and Brett added: "As long as Streean was well to do, she could forget him, but now she says he needs her and she must go."

Trav met his eyes. "Tilda's pretty fine."

Brett nodded. "Cinda suggested bringing Streean to the Plains. We've a dozen empty rooms." He added, half smiling: "I think Cinda is trying to punish herself because she's always hated him. Tilda wants to go at once. You all better come to supper, and we'll talk it over."

The eventual decision was that Trav and Tilda would go to New Orleans and bring Streean to the Plains. Brett offered to go, and Cinda volunteered to keep Tilda company; but Tilda said she could manage alone, and Trav assured them that he would welcome a chance for a few days at the mill. Enid said he must bring Peter back with him to spend September here, and he agreed. Two days later he and Tilda were on their way.

Until he reached New Orleans, Trav had not realized the virulence of the political campaign. He had telegraphed that they were coming, so Saul and Peter met their train, and on the way to Prytania Street, Peter was full of conversation. "We've been—" he hesitated, glanced at Tilda, said gleefully: "Well, Papa, we've been teaching niggers to be good Democrats! We've converted a lot of them, and not just here in New Orleans, either! We've got secret clubs all over in the state!"

Trav saw his son's excitement. "Persuasion?" he asked.

Peter grinned. "Yes sir, if they'll persuade. But Governor Warmoth sent a message to the Legislature three weeks ago, claiming that at least fifty niggers had been killed, just in Franklin Parish."

Tilda exclaimed in protest. "Killed, Peter?"

He nodded proudly. "Yes'm! And he says we've killed at least a hundred and fifty, counting the whole state, since the middle of June!"

Trav thought Warmoth sounded like a man in a panic, and Tilda echoed: " 'We?' 'We've killed'?"

"Well, you see, we've got these secret clubs everywhere . . ."

"Like the Knights of the White Camelia?" Trav asked, and made the sign of recognition, but Peter only looked embarrassed.

"Aw, that doesn't amount to anything, any more." His tone was full of scorn.

"Elon still in it?"

"I guess so." Peter hesitated. "I don't see him much."

"What does Don think about all this?"

They had reached the house, and between carriage and door, Peter said: "Oh, whenever they kill someone, Don investigates and then talks about how terrible it was." In the hall, his tongue ran on. "We had a big time here a week ago. A Mississippi nigger named Rollins made some speeches for our side, and the Radical niggers started a riot. The police locked him up for carrying concealed weapons, and then when he was acquitted we had a time getting him from the Court House to the Constitutional Club." And as they went in to breakfast: "A couple of thousand of them around us, yelling that they were going to hang him! If they'd tried anything, we'd have sprinkled Canal Street with dead niggers!"

Tilda shuddered. "Were you there, Peter?"

"You bet! Had my gun, too."

She said to Trav: "I declare, I don't know what you're thinking of, to let that boy—" Certainly, Trav thought, he must try to put some check on Peter, try to keep the youngster out of danger if he could.

After they had breakfasted, he went with Tilda to the hospital. Streean was obviously in a desperate condition. Since that night at the Haunted House he had lost a great deal of weight, and loose skin hung in folds on jaw and chin. His color was a lead-gray, the whites of his half-closed eyes touched with a greenish tinge: yet his mind seemed clear, and he spoke to Tilda in a tone Trav remembered.

"Well, well, here's my loving wife! Come to weep over my corpse, my dear?"

"Tony wrote me you were ill. I came to help you if I could."

"Blessed are the merciful!" His drawl was like a lash across her cheek. "And so are the meek, if I remember my Scripture. So you're doubly blessed, my dear."

She drew a chair beside his bed, ignoring the eyes of other patients staring at her from their beds along the crowded, malodorous room. "Why do you pretend, Redford?" she protested. "You're sick, and miserable, and want kindness. I offer kindness. Why not take it? Brett and Cinda ·want me to bring you home to the Plains."

His mouth opened in the pattern of a laugh. "Fools!" he said. "I'm not likely to leave this pauper's bed again; not more than once, certainly. But even if I do, it will not be to accept their patronizing hospitality."

Trav said: "Tilda, I'll talk to the doctors, decide what's to be done." He met Streean's eye, left Tilda with her husband. When after some time he returned, Streean seemed asleep, Tilda sitting beside him with his hand held in both hers. Trav hesitated, stopping at the foot of the bed, and Streean opened his eyes, and seeing Trav's expression, he grinned in malicious triumph.

"So!" he exclaimed. "They told you! Well, so did I. Now, be off! Both of you! I'm content as I am."

Tilda said quietly: "Hush, Redford!" Her eyes threw Trav a question.

"We'll take him to Prytania Street," he said. "A fortnight there should see him fit to travel. They'll send a nurse."

Streean's lips curled in a snarl. "Ghouls! Why can't you let me rot in peace?"

Tilda rose, ignoring him. "No, Trav; no nurse. I'm as good a nurse as any man." And when Streean tried to speak, she said crisply: "Hush, Redford." She looked down at him, her eyes thoughtful. "I suppose you're ashamed because we're trying to help you, but don't be. I'm your wife. It's happiness for me to care for you."

He grinned. " 'Till death us do part'? " he asked in dry mockery, and closed his eyes. "Well, it won't be long."

Streean, helpless to resist, was established in a third floor room high enough to catch what breeze there might be, and Tilda—her cot bed made near his—left him only when she must. Maria and Daisy helped her, and if the strength of men were needed, she could always summon Isaiah, or send for Saul from the stables. Trav, each morning and evening, went as far as the door of Streean's room, till Tilda suggested that he no longer do so.

"It rouses him, leaves him restless," she explained. "I think it's better to let him sleep when he can."

"Is he suffering?"

"Not in his body, no. In his mind, perhaps. He must be. Yet he doesn't change."

Even if he had wished to do so, Trav thought he could not return to Camden and leave her here, but he was glad to have a reason for staying, glad to spend hours at the mill, glad to be here to keep an eye on Peter. Tilda came down to meals, but she was so silent they might have been alone, and Trav found that Peter put no bridle on his tongue. Don was not in New Orleans when they arrived, but ten days later he returned and came for Sunday dinner. After dinner, Judge Morgan called, and Trav asked Don to repeat the report of his latest trip. Don had been in Shreveport, and he said the whole northwestern corner of the state was like tinder waiting for the spark.

"The white people are afraid of a Negro uprising," he explained. "Or at least they pretend to be, and I think they really are. A month or so ago, a couple of hundred Negroes gathered at Bossier Point, and the story is that they had shotguns and muskets. The white people—some of them—sent to Shreveport for troops, but before the troops got there, two or three white men met a crowd of sixty or seventy armed Negroes—so they say—and ordered them to lay down their arms, and arrested them."

Judge Morgan commented: "Odds of thirty to one? Those nigras weren't very warlike."

"As far as I can find out, they seldom are," Don agreed. "That's why it's hard to understand the fears of the white people. These Negroes were tried and sentenced to the penitentiary on charges of preparing to start a riot. The Democrats claim the Bureau had advised the Negroes to arm and organize. Some individual agents may have done that, and of course the Radicals, as well as the Democrats, have tried to form political clubs. And of course most of the Negroes have guns, as do most white men, so, naturally, killings are pretty much the usual thing. A man named Heath thought some Negroes had stolen one of his hogs, and accused them of it, and they beat him pretty badly, and a general fight started. Some other white men joined in, and one Negro was killed and another wounded. The sheriff arrested fifteen or twenty white men, and some of them were bound over for trial."

"That killing wasn't politics," Trav commented.

"No, just a Negro against white, but it's always the Negroes who get killed—or at least, more Negroes than whites." Judge Morgan nodded, and Don went on: "There was another killing up there at about the same time. Some Republican Negroes, pretending they were Ku Kluxes, went to Charles Barker's house and stood outside and shouted threats. He's a Negro, but whether he's a Democrat or not I couldn't find out. When they started away, they fired a couple of shots, and

Barker touched off his double-barreled shotgun. One of the buckshot caught Thornton Spier in the head and killed him." And he said, with an abrupt gesture: "These little affairs are just symptoms, but that whole corner of the state is ready to explode. A man named Dillard publishes a paper in Shreveport, the *Southwestern*. It's the leading Democratic paper in Caddo Parish. You read that, and read the *Banner*, published in Bossier Parish, and you'll get an idea of the feeling there. For months now the *Southwestern* has been urging the Democrats to refuse to employ any Radical Negroes."

Trav saw that Don was more concerned than resentful. "You think that's wrong?" he asked.

"I don't know. I'm sure the editor thinks it's good policy—just as I'm sure he thinks it's good policy to kill a few Negroes now and then, in order to terrify the others. But you can't keep the Negroes terrified; there are too many of them. It would be better to educate them to the point where they can work with you, on a basis of political equality, for the common good."

Judge Morgan asked: "You think it possible to raise their level of intelligence that far?"

There was in his tone a challenge, a readiness for disagreement, and Trav was uneasy till Don replied. "I don't know, sir. I don't know whether or not it can be done, but I know that for the good of the South it ought to be."

Thad Stevens died in August, and at the St. Charles Trav heard men propose to make the day a holiday throughout the South, and there was an attempt to organize a parade. Day by day the tension grew. The political clubrooms, Republican and Democratic, were focal points around which crowds forever clustered. The papers reported many brawls and small affrays, and an occasional spatter of shots stopped all movement on this street or that till the smoke cleared away. From Jackson Parish, late in August, came reports that murders had been committed there, and on the last Sunday in August, Don at Sunday dinner reported another tumult in Bossier Parish.

"It falls into the regular pattern," he said. "The Democrats call it a 'rebellion.' Some Negroes under a Captain Williams gathered at Bossier Point, and the sheriff came along and arrested fifty-seven. He claims they were armed, but as far as we can find out, no shots were fired, no one hurt. There's the usual statement that the Negroes admit they were led by 'infernal scalawags'!"

Trav asked: "You still think these episodes just symptoms, Don?"

Don, about to speak, caught Peter's eyes and hesitated. "I don't know, sir, but I'm sure there'll be real trouble up there, if these small sparks keep on snapping."

Peter drawled: "They'll keep on snapping."

"Does the Legislature take any notice of all this?" Trav asked. "I've been thinking I'd drop in on one of their sessions."

"I believe you'd be surprised at the decorum of their proceedings," Don suggested. "Particularly in the Senate. Lieutenant Governor Dunn is an excellent presiding officer."

Peter thrust back his chair and rose. "Aren't we done, Papa?" he demanded in bored tones. "I need some fresh air."

Trav might have forgotten his wish to see the Senate in action, but Tuesday evening when he landed from the ferry and walked down Canal Street, he heard a flurry of pistol shots. Toward Dryades Street a crowd gathered, and there were angry shouts, but no more shots. He thought of going on to see what had happened, but a mechanical failure had delayed him at the mill and he was late, so he continued toward home.

He was at breakfast Thursday morning when Don appeared. Don asked whether Trav had heard anything about a shooting scrape Tuesday evening on Canal Street, and Trav said: "Yes, I even heard the shots, and saw the crowd."

"Senator Pinchback was one of the principals," Don told him. "No one was hurt, but the *Commercial Bulletin* had an item about the affair yesterday, attacking the Senator, and he's going to reply to it in the Senate today. I thought you might care to hear him."

So when at noon that day the Senate was called to order, Trav and Don were seated in the rear of the Chamber. Through the preliminaries, Trav listened with interest. Certainly the proceedings were dignified—almost excessively so—and except for the occasional misuse or mispronunciation of a word, there was little to differentiate this from any legislative assembly anywhere.

When eventually Senator Pinchback rose to a question of personal privilege, Trav's attention quickened. Pinchback began quietly. Some of the Democratic newspapers, he said, had conducted against him a campaign of personal abuse so malignant that he must attempt to set himself right before his family and his friends. Then, as though speaking to strangers, he introduced himself.

"I was born in Georgia. My mother was on her way from Virginia to Mississippi, and she merely stopped long enough in Georgia to give birth to me and repair her health. My father was a Mississippi planter. He moved to Louisiana, and I was sent to Cincinnati, in company with my brother. I was educated in the Gilmore High School in Cincinnati. My mother had been a slave, but was not a slave when I was born. My father was her former master."

He spoke of his return to Louisiana, his enlistment in the Union army, his entrance into politics. "In politics," he said, "I have felt that the safety of the colored man depended exclusively upon the friendship of the whites. I have sought to allay prejudices and to create a feeling of good will as between the white and the colored elements of the state.

"And, sir, no man, black or white, can truthfully say anything against my personal character, unless it is a disparagement to say that God has put African blood in my veins. I have never intruded my presence upon a white man, and I have never attempted or desired to associate with any individual who did not desire to associate with me."

He was for a moment silent, his eyes sweeping the room. Trav glanced along the rows of spectators, and he recognized Tony, and thought he should have expected Tony to be here. He looked for Sapphira, but could not see her. Pinchback continued:

"In the *Commercial Bulletin* of September second, I find an article traducing my character, from which I will read an extract." He lifted the paper and read: " 'A Shooting Scrape. A Senator in the Lockup. A most disgraceful affair occurred on Canal street yesterday evening at about six o'clock. The parties were three negroes; P. B. S. Pinchback, Jerry Hall, and S. C. Morgan. Some six or eight shots were fired at each other by these negroes in the middle of Canal street, and at a time when crowds of people were promenading. It might have resulted in the death of some white person. It is lucky that it did not, for had anyone been injured, Mr. Pinchback would probably never have occupied his seat a second day in the Senate. Senator Pinchback evidently desires to serve another term in the Workhouse or the Penitentiary.' "

The reference was to an affray in 1862. Pinchback and his brother-in-law had a fight, as a result of which his brother-in-law died. Pinchback was convicted of manslaughter, and served several weeks in prison. He broke off now to explain this reference in the *Commercial Bulletin* and then went on:

"Now, sir, I have lived in this state more or less for thirty years of my life, and during that time I have never had a quarrel with a white man, and never intentionally given offense to one. It is true, I had an encounter the other day with a man of my own color. The facts are these: As I was quietly walking down the left side of Canal Street, I heard the click of a pistol directly opposite, on the other side of the street. I looked in the direction and saw a colored man with a revolver in his hand, in the act of preparing to fire at me. I had a weapon and drew it and endeavored to defend myself as well as I could.

"Did I do wrong in this? Where is the Senator with manhood in him, or any man in the State of Louisiana, who would not have done the same? Yet this is seized upon and made the occasion of additional abuse." From the paper still in his hand he read again: " 'This affair might have resulted in the death of some *white* person.' " He emphasized the adjective, read on. " 'It is lucky that it did not, for, had anyone been injured, Mr. Pinchback would probably never have occupied his seat a second day in the Senate.' "

He paraphrased, laying the paper aside: "If any *white* person had been injured, 'Mr. Pinchback would perhaps never have occupied his seat another day in the Senate.' What is meant by this? Sir, what took place in that affair, or immediately after its conclusion, explains it. If it had not been for the fact that the two police officers who took me in charge happened to be men determined to do their duty, Mr. Pinchback would in fact not have occupied his seat again in the Senate. For, sir, I was set upon by an infuriated mob, who cried out: 'Kill him! Kill the damned nigger! Kill him!' And when I assured them that the difficulty I had had was with a man of my own color, they shouted: 'It's Pinchback, damn him; kill the damned black Radical son of a bitch.'

"And, sir, it required the best exertions of those police officers to prevent them from murdering me in open day on a public street in New Orleans."

Pinchback had spoken quietly enough, no tremor in his tone, yet Trav had for a moment the feeling that it was he himself, and not the speaker, whose life that mob demanded. How did it feel to face scores or hundreds of angry men who shouted at you: "Kill him! Kill the son of a bitch!" How did it feel to look into the eyes of men wanting your life?

Pinchback was a brave man; yes, and he was a brave man to speak here as he spoke now. "They say that if any white person had been injured, perhaps I would not have occupied my seat another day in the Senate. In plain English, the meaning of this is that if I had injured any white man, I would have been murdered by a mob. Yes, that is their doctrine, that any white man may insult and vilify and abuse and maltreat, yes and murder a Negro with impunity, and without the slightest provocation; and if the Negro resents, or defends himself, the cry is, 'Kill the damned black son of a bitch!' "

His voice hardened, it rose a little, and a little more. "Such has been the rule and the practice in this city for a long time past; but sir, it will prove a dangerous practice to pursue much further. Suppose the man who made the attack upon my life had been a white man, should I not have defended myself? I would have done it! The color of his skin would have made no difference to me! I court quarrels and affrays with no man, and by long practice I have schooled myself to patiently endure from white men all manner of abuse which pen can write or tongue utter. But when it comes to an attack upon my life with a deadly weapon, endurance ceases to be a virtue, and I will defend myself with all my power, and with the best weapons I have, no matter what the color of my assailant!"

Something like a half-uttered jeer sounded from a Senator on the other side of the room, and Pinchback whirled that way, his eyes challenging man after man, and he cried:

"If there is a Senator upon the floor who doubts this, let him try it on when we leave this room, or wherever and whenever he chooses!"

He waited as though half expecting an answer, and then in a new voice cried: "And I want to tell, and I will tell, the people of this city, who have been in the habit of murdering, and who manifest a growing disposition to murder men for their political opinions and for the color of their skin, I want to tell them, 'Beware!' I want to tell them they have nearly reached the end of their string." His voice was like a bugle call. "The next outrage of the kind which they commit will be the signal for the dawn of retribution, a retribution of which they have not dreamed; a signal that will cause ten thousand torches to be applied to this city! For patience will then have ceased to be a virtue, and this city will be reduced to ashes, and their—"

Someone rose and said sternly: "I call the gentleman to order!" The interruption had a curiously shocking quality, like a dash of cold water in the face, and Trav felt his heart's quick pound. He had been carried along by Pinchback's words, quickening to the quickening anger in the other's tones; under the spell of the speaker, he looked for an instant into the cauldron brimming with longing and sorrow and bitterness and hate which must forever simmer and stew in the hearts of such men as this one. What Pinchback said was bitterly true; it was no crime to kill a Negro. Oh, legally, yes, of course; but what jury had ever convicted a white man of murder for such a killing? What judge had ever sent a white man to the scaffold for the crime?

The presiding officer warned Pinchback to confine himself to a personal explanation, and the Senator continued, at first in calmer tones.

"If I am out of order, I apologize. And probably I am."

Trav, remembering the passionate outburst of a few minutes before, remembering that glimpse into the soul of this man, for a moment did not listen. When his attention returned, Pinchback was saying:

"I do not seek to stir up the passions of any class, or to bring disaster upon this community. But these triflers do not realize that the endurance and forbearance of those they persecute and abuse is limited, and is now nearly exhausted. I speak because I want to avert the dread calamity I see looming up in the distance. I want the people of this city to know that they are standing upon a volcano.

"We loyal people of this city have been long-suffering, and we are still disposed to put up with any and all abuse, but it must not go beyond words spoken and printed. They must not murder another man on account of his political opinions, or the color of his skin. If they do, fire will make this city cease to be a dwelling place. I want to tell the gentleman who called me to order, and I want to tell the Democratic party, that we propose to have peace if we have to conquer a peace! We cannot and we will not any longer allow ourselves to be scourged and murdered with impunity!"

His words were not shouted, yet they had the impact of a shout, and the presiding officer lifted his gavel, but Pinchback's tone changed. He concluded easily:

"Now, sir, I have been actuated to make this statement to vindicate my family from the charge of having a member who has disgraced them, and also to vindicate my friends in my district from the charge of having sent a man of no character, a scalawag and a felon, to represent them in the Senate of Louisiana. Having done what the circumstances seemed to justify, I thank the Senate for their kind attention."

When, after Pinchback was done, Trav and Don came out into Dryades Street together, Trav looked at his watch. "Hardly worth while going to the mill now. Where are you bound?"

"To Headquarters, I suppose."

"Stop at the house. Isaiah makes a cooling julep." Don agreed. "But it's too hot to go afoot," Trav said, and signaled a hackney. When they were seated in the carriage he said: "Senator Pinchback is an able man, deserving respect. I could sympathize with his anger, but his threats antagonized me."

"They were a sort of profanity," Don suggested. "When one angry man says to another: 'God damn you to Hell,' he doesn't mean it literally."

"When one angry man says that to another in the South, he may die for it," Trav reminded him. "Such talk is killing talk." He hesitated. "And yet," he said. "Pinchback's violence made me realize for a moment what must go on in the mind and heart of a nigra; particularly a superior nigra, a man of parts. Like him."

6

STREEAN WAS still alive, though seldom sensible, and Trav and Tilda were still in New Orleans when one day General Longstreet appeared at the mill. "I didn't suppose you'd be in town," he explained, after Trav's hearty welcome. "But someone said you were in the St. Charles a day or two ago, and I made sure I'd find you here." General Grant had sent him, he said. "He wants to know what's going on down here."

Trav insisted that Longstreet must stay with him, so they picked up the General's valise at the St. Charles, Longstreet acknowledging the guarded greetings of gentlemen in the rotunda. The day was muggy and oppressive, with no promise of rain, so they had taken a hackney from the ferry landing, and kept it to carry them to Prytania Street. On the way, Longstreet remarked with a dry chuckle:

"Cool enough in the rotunda back there. No ovation for the wanderer's return."

"I suppose feeling against the Radicals—the Republicans—is more bitter than ever," Trav admitted. "Even Peter's in politics. He's joined I don't know how many marching clubs—New Orleans is full of them—and they keep him busy. The Democrats mean to carry the state for Seymour at any cost; you can tell General Grant that."

Longstreet nodded. "At any cost, if it means murdering every nigra in the state." Trav did not reply, and after a moment Longstreet said: "The Legislature is recessing tomorrow to receive me. I trust you'll come along and keep me in countenance."

"Honored, of course," Trav assured him. At home, Tilda came to greet them, and after she had gone back upstairs, Trav explained her presence here. Isaiah brought juleps, and Peter presently appeared, and Longstreet said with a heavy jocosity:

"Well, Peter, I hear you're planning to be a politician."

"If I do, I won't be a damned old Republican."

Trav bit his lip, but Longstreet asked, in an amused tone: "Who would you Democrats have to lick, if it weren't for us Republicans?"

"Well, we're going to," Peter assured him, openly truculent. "There'll be mighty few Republican votes in New Orleans in December."

Longstreet said no more, but when Peter had left them, the General remarked: "The young cock likes to crow."

"Whatever Peter is, I'm to blame."

The other shook his head. "No, Major; no, not you. The South produces many men who remain all their lives boys like Peter." He made a grim sound. "In fact we're rather proud of them, make pets of them. That's one of the things about the South which the North will never understand."

Next day, before the hour when the Legislature was to receive General Longstreet, they called upon the Governor. Warmoth greeted them cordially, and when Trav would have left him and the General together, Warmoth bade him stay. "We've no secrets and mysteries here, Major," he said, and chuckled, and in an ostentatiously casual way he drew the first finger of his left hand across his left eye. Trav had almost forgotten the Knights of the White Camelia, yet he recognized something familiar about that gesture, even before Warmoth added: "I wasn't born on Mount Caucasus, but I've been there." At Trav's embarrassed flush, he laughed aloud. "No offense. I'm jesting, Major."

Longstreet asked curiously: "What's all that?"

Trav answered him. "The Governor's referring to an organization devoted to maintaining white supremacy."

The Governor added genially: "A doctrine just now more honored in the breach than in the observance!"

A committee came to escort the General to the hall of the House, and the Governor bade them return afterward. "We've many things to discuss," he said.

Longstreet assented. The Legislature gave him a generous reception, and while they walked back toward the Governor's office, he remarked to Trav: "A flattering occasion, Major. If politics were not so full of hypocrisy, I might come to love it. The men who cheered me today would be equally ready, if the wind changed, to jeer me to-morrow."

They had a long half hour with the Governor. He predicted that the Democrats would carry the state in November. "You can tell General Grant it's certain," he insisted, "unless we have troops to protect Republican voters at the polls—and it seems impossible to move President Johnson to take any action in that direction. I've tried. Within a week of my inauguration I sent a message to our Senate, listing many murders and outrages against the lives of loyal men, and the Legislature passed resolutions asking Washington to intervene.

"But Johnson says there'll be no intervention unless there's an insurrection." Warmoth threw up his hands. "So I'm helpless! I can only warn you that without protection, mighty few colored people will vote." He added strongly: "And at the rate the Negroes are being killed off by the Democrats, there won't be many left alive to vote, protection or no protection!"

"Are all these killings of which you speak political?" Longstreet asked. "Weren't there always a good many such murders, a nigra stole a shoat, or some chickens, and a farmer caught him at it?"

"That's true, of course," the Governor agreed. "The poor whites think nothing of killing a few Negroes on any provocation—or on none. Then, too, the South is full of irresponsible gamblers, loafers, drunkards, aristocrats too proud to go to work, young sparks seeking a way to demonstrate their mettle, and any one of them is likely to shoot a Negro now and then just for the fun of it! It's true that many of these murders are of this familiar sort.

"But many of them arise, directly or indirectly, from politics." He laughed grimly. "Why, Negroes are killing Negroes for political reasons!"

When they left the Governor, Longstreet said in grim amusement: "Struck me that young man has a bad case of nerves."

"I think he exaggerates a little," Trav agreed, "But Don Page has a pretty level head, and he looks for trouble." He added, with a certain sympathy. "I expect Governor Warmoth sometimes feels he's pretty much alone."

"I don't like to hear the Governor of a sovereign state yapping to Washington for help!" Longstreet insisted, and Trav said no more.

Their lease in Camden ran till October first, and Trav must go to escort Enid and Lucy home to New Orleans, but he was in no hurry to depart. As long as the General was his guest, he would stay. He and Longstreet went down almost every night to watch the many parades of Republican or Democratic clubs, long lines of marchers in vivid costumes, their lanterns carried high on poles, the glare tinting the swirling smoke of pine torches. When the paraders were Negroes, throngs of colored people, women and children, screaming and hooting with pride and glee, scurried along the banquettes to keep pace with the marchers, thrusting white pedestrians heedlessly aside; when the paraders were Democrats, the Negroes watched in silence, or withdrew into the side streets and disappeared.

It occurred to Trav one night as he watched, seeing a troop of boys in one of these parades, that Peter might be among them, and next morning at breakfast he asked the question, but Peter shook his head. "No, I'm in the Seymour Infantas, and we only parade when the Innocents do." He explained in proud tones. "It's our job to keep any-one from breaking up their march."

"Who are the Innocents?"

"Mr. Labarre's president. They've got about twelve hundred mem-bers, mostly below Canal Street, from Canal to Esplanade. Their club room's on Orleans Street."

"White men?"

"Oh, yes. Some Spaniards and Sicilians and Portuguese and South Americans, but mostly Creoles and Louisianians."

Trav nodded, but after a moment he asked: "Want to go with me to Camden, to bring home Mama and Lucy?"

"No sir. I don't want to miss what's happening here."

"I ought to be back by the middle of October."

Peter shook his head. "I'd rather stay here."

The General had set his departure for Wednesday, the twenty-third of September, and Trav planned to leave that same day. The night before, he and the General dined with Miller Owen, one of Longstreet's former partners and an old comrade-in-arms. The night was sultry, and at about ten o'clock Owen proposed that they walk as far as Canal Street for ice cream at Mr. Dumonteil's confectionery. "I'm sure Mrs. Owen will join us. It's not far, corner of Canal and Carondelet."

The proposal was agreeable and they strolled along Carondelet. As they crossed Common they heard cheering on St. Charles Street, by the hotel, and Owen said: "The Steadman Guards are having a muster there tonight, with a number of speakers."

"I judge there's something of the sort almost every night," Longstreet remarked, and Owen nodded.

"Yes. One parade after another." He chuckled. "The most picturesque gathering tonight will be at Congo Square. The Grand Club and the Constitution Club—both nigra organizations—are having a union meet-ing, and some other clubs will join them and parade afterward. Their costumes will be worth seeing. We'll probably see them when they pass Dumonteil's."

His prediction was fulfilled. They had finished their ice cream when the strains of a band announced the approach of the head of the pro-cession, and the parade began to pass down Canal Street, only the width of the banquette away from the window where they sat. The marchers carried torches—open-flame lamps fixed to the ends of long poles—and they cheered and shouted and sang as they marched, while along the banquette a pushing, hurrying crowd of Negroes kept pace with them. The torches threw a flickering illumination over the scene, and picked out the bright hues of the multi-colored costumes and the shining faces of the marchers.

A group of men paused outside the window near which they sat, and thus partially blocked Mrs. Owen's view. Trav saw that they were young, little more than boys, and he caught a momentary glimpse of Peter here among them, but this did not surprise him. No doubt Peter's evenings were often spent in just such ways. The end of the procession was in sight, the band now far away, and the tumult in the street slackened. In this sudden half-quiet, Trav heard someone—he was sure it was Peter—shout in shrill challenge:

"Hurrah for Seymour and Blair!"

The response was swift. With angry cries, the marchers came in a swarming rush across the banquette toward the confectionery. Peter and the other youngsters vanished, and swinging blows from the lighted torches smashed the windows. Owen and Trav and the General surrounded. Mrs. Owen and drew her back to safety in a corner under the balcony. The attackers on the banquette made no attempt to force their way into the shop, satisfied to break the windows, and to shout furious oaths and dark obscenities. Outside, Trav heard policemen spring their rattles. In the shattered windows, faces were a black wall broken by flashing teeth and rolling eyes.

Then from the balcony above where Trav and the others sheltered Mrs. Owen, someone fired a shot, and with a shout of mockery and mirth the Negroes along the windows gave way and scattered. A white man appeared among them, and Trav saw a Negro swing his lamp pole like a club. The white man caught the pole and wrestled it out of the Negro's hand, and smashed the lamp down on the other's bare head. The lamp burst, drenching the Negro's hair with oil and setting it ablaze; he ran headlong down Canal, flames streaming out behind him, slapping at his sizzling scalp, and a roar of mirth from Negroes and whites alike went after him.

The whole incident had lasted hardly a minute and a half; the marchers were scattered and gone, but Trav and the others stepped out on the banquette into a shadowed gloom. At the first alarm, every lighted window and store front up and down Canal Street had been shuttered, and only the lamps still burning in the confectionery, and half a dozen torches disappearing in the distance broke the darkness. They walked back to Mr. Owen's house, all a little excited by the adventure, so that their voices were unnaturally high, and Owen commented:

"Senator Pinchback threatened a while back to burn New Orleans over our heads. I thought for a minute they were going to do it." He said in good-natured raillery, "There are your Republican nigras for you, General."

Longstreet did not smile. "I wonder if anyone was hurt."

"I heard a few shots," Owen answered, and added mirthfully: "But in these street pistolades, it takes ten pounds of lead to kill a man."

At the Owens' door they parted, and Longstreet and Trav walked homeward through quiet streets, but next morning's papers reported that the affair at Dumonteil's had been only a beginning. Revolver shots had followed the retreating Negroes as far as Congo Square, and the *Picayune* said several had been killed and wounded, and added:

> The shameless and unprovoked riot is said to have been instigated by unprincipled whites. The white man who cheered for Seymour and Blair may have had the right to do so, but few, even those who are of his opinion in politics, concur in his taste.

Peter had not come down to breakfast, and when Isaiah appeared with fresh coffee, Trav asked: "Mr. Peter home last night, Isaiah?"

"Yas suh, he come in right soon afte' y'all."

Trav met Longstreet's eye. "I suppose I do a lot of needless worrying about Peter," he remarked, but the General did not reply.

Longstreet took the train north. Trav had planned to leave for the Plains on that night's boat, but a little before noon Streean had an ill turn, and early next morning he died. Tilda made no pretense of grief. "He did at least this one considerate thing in his life," she remarked. "He died at a convenient time. Now I can go home to the Plains with you."

In summer's heat, funerals were never long delayed. Streean died at dawn; he was entombed a little after noon, and that evening, Trav and Tilda took the boat to Mobile.

The Sunday after their departure, Don received orders that sent him to Opelousas, and he wrote Lucy:

> It's a prosperous town in St. Landry parish, in good farming country. I think it was the state capital for a while during the War. The chairman of the Democratic committee for St. Landry parish is afraid they're going to have a Negro rising there. He says the Negro clubs have been meeting every Sunday, parading around town and up to Washington—that's about six miles away—and threatening to burn every town in the parish. Such panics among the whites have been the death of a lot of Negroes, but did you ever hear of a real Negro rising, anywhere in the South, in the last fifty years? Back in 1795 a slave insurrection was supposed to be about to break out in Pointe Coupée parish, right next to St. Landry on the east, but the only thing that happened was that twenty-three Negroes were hanged. I'll try to keep them from hanging any of them this time.

He reached Opelousas Tuesday morning, and even at the station there were signs of a high excitement in the town. His uniform drew scowling glances from the little knots of white men huddled everywhere. Mr. Violett, the Bureau agent, was not in his office, but his clerk said hastily: "He's gone to Mr. Hill's house; the justice of the peace."

"What's happened? Something new?"

"The Democrats killed Mr. Bentley, and the freedmen are coming to get the men who did it."

"Who's Mr. Bentley?"

"The schoolteacher. He's editor of the Republican paper here." The other looked uneasily out of the window. "I'm going to shut up the office and go home. You can find Mr. Hill's place all right. I'll show you." He locked the door behind them. "Down that way, just out of town, kind of set back from the road."

Don found a group of freedmen clustered at Mr. Hill's gate, and he questioned them. "Mr. Violett here?"

"Yas suh. Mr. Bentley, too."

"I thought he was killed."

"Naw suh, he jes' beat bad."

Don went on to the house and Mr. Hill admitted him. Mr. Violett and Mr. Bentley were in the kitchen, surrounded by half a dozen Negroes. Mr. Bentley was stripped to the waist, while two of the colored men gently rubbed salve on his welts and weals. The man was trembling, but Don thought this was as much from anger and shock as from fear or pain. He asked Mr. Violett: "What was responsible for this?"

"They resented something Mr. Bentley published in his paper."

"Did he recognize them? Know who they were?"

Bentley himself answered, stammering through chattering teeth. "Y-yes, a m-man named Williams, and M-Mayo, the c-constable, and Judge Dickson. I've s-sworn out w-w-warrants for them. That's w-why I came to Justice Hill." And he said, as though this were the bitter wrong: "They came into the schoolhouse, f-frightened m-my children, sent them s-s-screaming! Little boys and girls."

Violett explained: "They beat him with canes."

"Were you armed?" Don asked the teacher.

"Yes," Bentley told him. "B-but so were they, and their guns were in their hands. I had to s-sign a paper, saying that what I had p-published was untrue, but the story was true in every word!" His voice grew stronger as he spoke. A dark bruise lay across his cheek, swollen and shining. He said thickly: "These madmen know no argument except to beat and to kill! Well, let them kill me!" He rose and turned to pick up his shirt. "I'll go back to my school!"

Violett hastily protested. "You'd better not! Let these boys—" He indicated the Negroes. "Let them take care of you. They'll hide you, get you away."

Mr. Bentley, as though he had not heard, continued to fumble with his shirt, his hands shaking with a frightening violence. One of the Negroes picked up the teacher's undershirt. "Lemme he'p you," he suggested. "Git de sleeves o' dis on, an' I'll ease it ove' yuh haid." Bentley obeyed, and Mr. Violett spoke to Don. "The children thought Mr. Bentley was dead," he explained. "They came running into town, saying he was killed, and Francis Davy,—he's on the Republican parish committee—he sent word all over the parish for the colored people to hurry to town."

Don said at once: "We'll have to stop that!"

"I've already sent men out every road, told them to disperse any armed niggers they see."

Don nodded. "Good. Mr. Bentley—"

But before he could finish, a bell began to ring, and Mr. Hill said: "That's the Court House bell! That's the signal to the white people to get ready for trouble."

Don spoke quickly. "Mr. Bentley, I wish we could show the Negroes you're alive, but there isn't time, and someone might try a shot at you. Judge Hill, can he stay hidden here till night? Good." Then, to the Negroes watching and listening: "Go spread the word Mr. Bentley's alive. Tell everyone you see; every colored person, specially. Go, now, quickly."

He himself was the first to step out of the door, and as he did so he saw a Negro on a mule, riding toward town at a gallop. He hurried to the roadside to hail the man, shouted a question, and the Negro, without checking his mule, shouted:

"Dey fightin' out tuh Ed Paillet's!"

Don turned to Violett. "We'll have to get out there. Do you know where it is? Can we get horses?"

"South of town, about a mile or a mile and a quarter. Yes, we can rent horses at the livery."

Judge Hill had joined them at the gate. "My horse is in his stall, Captain. Glad to have you use him."

"Fine!" They hurried toward the stable. "You can get a mount and follow me," Don told Violett, as he saddled up. With a word of direction from Judge Hill he set out, pushing his horse to a canter, but at a turn in the road he saw approaching two white men. One of them was swaying in the saddle, obviously hurt, and Don slowed to a walk and they pulled up and Don stopped beside them.

"Captain Page," he said, introducing himself. "Inspector for the

Freedmen's Bureau. I see you are hurt, sir. Can I be of any help?"

"Control your damned niggers before they murder us all!" said the wounded man. Then, in a more reasonable tone: "I'm better off than I look. Thought at first the ball had touched my lung, but I haven't coughed blood, so I'm all right." And he added: "I'm Captain May. Captain Lewis and I, with about twenty men, were trying to stop this trouble before it started. Heard there were some armed niggers out at Paillet's, found them, asked them to lay down their arms. They started shooting." He hesitated. "Or at least, someone did. Someone fired a shot, and then we were all firing, shotguns and revolvers. My horse was wounded, and so was I. When the firing stopped and the niggers scattered, I borrowed a horse and here I am."

His voice had weakened, but now it rose defiantly: "And now, sir, you'd better make your niggers lay down their arms, or there'll be hell to pay around here before morning!"

Don said quietly: "We'll do our best, Captain."

He turned and rode on toward Paillet's, and presently he met half a dozen horsemen, one of them a Negro. Two of the men had bandaged wounds in arm or leg. When Don halted, they all pulled up, and again Don introduced himself. "I talked with Captain May," he explained. "If you were of his party."

One of them acted as spokesman. "Yes, we were. I'm Captain Lewis. We're disarming niggers before trouble starts. This one here, I'm taking him in where he'll be safe. Unless you want him."

The Negro spoke quickly: "Nawsuh, I'se gwine stay wid yuh, Cap'n Lewis, please suh."

Don asked: "Is there anything I can do out where the fight occurred?"

"There's a dead nigger, and four or five others were hurt pretty bad, but they're being taken care of."

Don ignored this. "May I ride with you? I might help persuade other armed parties to disarm."

Captain Lewis hesitated, glancing at his companions. "I don't know why not."

Don did in fact continue with them till, toward sunset, they rode back into town. They had seen at a distance three groups of Negroes, some of them armed, but in each case the Negroes scattered at their approach. When this had happened for the third time, Don asked Captain Lewis: "Are you people really afraid of a Negro rising? Those we've seen certainly didn't act warlike—yet there are only a few of us, and that last group must have tallied fifty or sixty men."

Captain Lewis looked at him with unsmiling eyes. "The nigger has been taught to respect a white man," he said. "We take care he don't forget that lesson."

Back in Opelousas, Don found Mr. Violett at the Bureau office. "Anything happen here?" he asked.

The other shook his head. "Town was quiet. They brought in some niggers and locked them up in the jail. I missed you. It took me a while to find a horse. Where did you go?"

"I rode around with Captain Lewis and some of the men who were in the fight at Paillet's."

"I rode out there, but there was nobody around; nobody except four dead niggers."

"Four? Captain Lewis said there was only one dead, and some wounded. He said someone was taking care of them."

Violett said in a dry tone: "Someone took care of them, all right. They were dead."

Don looked at him with puzzled eyes. "They must have been hurt worse than Captain Lewis thought."

The other cut off a morsel of tobacco and put it in his mouth. "Any time a nigger gets hurt in a row with white men, he don't usually get over it," he said. "You ready for some supper?"

While they were at table, two or three shots sounded at some distance, the sound clear in the quiet airs of dusk. Every man in the dining room looked up, but no one rose. When Don and Mr. Violett finished and came out on the gallery, two men rode up and dismounted, and Don recognized Judge Hill, whose horse he had returned with thanks an hour ago.

"Evening, Judge," he said.

The other nodded a greeting. "They got Mr. Durant, Captain. Out by my house. Just now."

"Durant?"

"He was the French editor of the *Progress*, Bentley's paper."

"Killed him?"

"Yes."

"Who did it?"

"I don't know. There was a crowd in the road. I heard the shooting and came out. Durant had come in to ask me where Bentley was, and when he left the house, he must have met them in the road. I suppose they were looking for Bentley, and decided Durant would do."

A man spoke from the shadows of the veranda. "The way I heard it, Judge, it was a private quarrel."

There was something compelling in the voice, and Judge Hill said mildly: "No doubt! No doubt! The crowd was gone when I came out. I didn't even know anyone had been hurt till I started to town. Someone had found him. They were loading him into a cart."

He went into the hotel, and Don and Mr. Violett stood for a moment on the steps, looking across toward the Court House. The Square was crowded, groups of men standing in talk here and there, riders passing to and fro. Mr. Violett said uneasily: "Unless there's something else, I'll say good night."

Don went to his room and made a beginning on his report, a straightforward narrative of what he had seen and heard and done. Twice while he wrote he heard the splatter of a distant volley and paused to listen, and before he went to bed, he walked through the Square and around the Court House. Armed white men stood in the shadows here and there, and sometimes Don was challenged as he passed, and often his uniform provoked derisive murmurs.

At the hotel next morning, Mr. Violett reported that a white man named Dearborn had been killed by three Negroes in a hamlet twelve miles west of town, and Don hired a horse and rode out to investigate. He found Mr. Dearborn alive and well, a lank and wiry individual sprawled at ease on a bench outside his dirt-floor cabin. Don asked whether this was the Dearborn home; it was. He asked for Mr. Dearborn, and the lank man tapped his bony chest.

"Present and accounted faw," he said lazily.

"I'd heard a rumor that you were killed by three Negroes," Don explained. "Obviously, it was another Dearborn."

The lean man shook his head. "They ain't another Dearborn in the parish, not as I know on." He added: "Course, here yestiddy evenin' there was three niggers got tied together and th'owed in the river and drowned. I heard tell so, anyways. Maybe that's how the talk started." He cackled with mirth. "But fur's I know, they hain't killed me—and if they had, three niggers couldn't a done it all by theyselves!"

"You don't worry about a Negro rising?"

Mr. Dearborn spat accurately at a black beetle rolling a ball of manure through the dust. "Not to mention. Rising? Well, whateveh rises up is bound t'come down!"

"Who drowned these three?" Don asked, and Mr. Dearborn made an astonished sound.

"Why, mister!" he protested, in a reproachful tone, and Don smiled.

"Sorry, Mr. Dearborn."

"I was just getting to like you."

Don chuckled. "Mind if I sit down?" He found the other ready enough to discuss the racial mores of this small hamlet. Mr. Dearborn liked niggers, he said; he got along with them first rate. It was only necessary to understand them, and the minute one of them got uppity, take him down a peg; if that did not prove an adequate correction, something else would.

Back in town, Don learned that a group of men had wrecked the office of Mr. Bentley's paper, had smashed the press and pied the type, but Bentley himself had disappeared. All that day, groups of armed white men rode in and out of town, each group with a report of cabins searched and weapons seized. Again and again Don asked members of these groups whether they had had any trouble, had encountered resistance anywhere. The answers were all of a pattern. "No sir." "Not a bit." "No, they were meek as lambs."

Yet the answers were given so gravely that when he was alone with Mr. Violett, Don said doubtfully: "They're too calm about it. I expect a lot of Negroes have been killed today."

"You're calling a lot of men liars," Violett protested, in an almost personal resentment. "Better not do so where one of them can hear it."

"You're right, of course," Don agreed, and he smiled. "Though I'm sure no good Southerner would think it was lying to deceive a Yankee."

After he was abed, remembering Mr. Violett's tone, he thought the agent of the Bureau was surprisingly untroubled by the fact that some of his charges had been killed, and next morning he studied the other with a thoughtful eye. Some Negroes arrested the day before had been lodged in jail, and he spoke of this.

"I suppose they'll be brought into court today," he remarked.

"I don't think so," Violett hazarded. "Probably by this time they've turned them loose. Just locked them up to keep them out of trouble."

"Think so? Well, let's walk down and see."

At the jail, they found Deputy Sheriff Perrodine in charge, a plump man yet with no hint of softness about him. He nodded a greeting, his eye resting a moment on Don's uniform, and Mr. Violett said cheerfully: "Well, you don't look very busy, Sheriff. Jail empty?"

The Deputy said calmly: " 'Twas, last time I looked."

"Turn 'em loose? Or did they escape?"

"Well, I wouldn't put it either way." His eye rested on Don. "There was a crowd come and took them out," he said, completely composed.

Don asked sharply: "White men, or Negroes?"

"Can't say as to that, mister."

"Were they disguised?"

"Well, in a way they were, and in a way they weren't. It was in the night time. They had hats on, and in the dark I couldn't see their faces."

Don thought the day was sickeningly hot. He sat down, and the Deputy watched him with quiet eyes. Don asked: "Where were they taken?"

"I don't know."

"Did you hear any shooting, after they were gone?"

"I didn't listen."

"You didn't go with them, didn't try to protect them?"

"Now, Captain," the other urged, in a persuasive tone. "Some citizens came and asked for these men. They took my keys and opened the door. The jailer was here, and we're both deputies, but what could we do against a hundred men. Maybe two hundred."

"Your duty," Don suggested.

"Will you teach me my duty, Captain?"

Perrodine was still polite, but Mr. Violett said quickly: "Captain Page means no offense, Mr. Perrodine. Of that I'm sure."

Don looked at the agent. "I'll speak for myself, Mr. Violett," he said, and to the Deputy: "Do you think these Negroes were killed?"

"Well, I heard some talk along that line this morning." Mr. Perrodine whittled a sliver into a usable toothpick. "You see, Captain, we're not under martial law here; we're under civil law, and the way we look at it, whatever the majority of white people want, that's the law."

"Did you try to find out whether they were killed?"

"No, Captain. My pappy told me, when I was a boy, not to ask too many questions, and I learnt that lesson good. That's why I'm still healthy."

Don rose. "Who was in command here in town yesterday?"

The Deputy did not answer. With obvious reluctance, Mr. Violett said: "I guess Doctor Thompson—Colonel Thompson—was handling things, sending out patrols, telling them where to go."

Don faced Mr. Perrodine again. "What time of night did these men come to the jail?"

"After dark, but not late. Before midnight."

"Did they have lights?"

"No, no lights."

"Did you know any of the Negro prisoners?"

"I know Joe Gradney and his brother. I took them to their aunt's house, here in town, and told them nobody would hurt them, and to go on home this morning, right along the big road, not trying to hide."

"Where does this aunt live?"

Mr. Violett said: "I know the house."

Don said: "One other question, Mr. Perrodine. Were the men who assaulted Mr. Bentley arrested? Locked up?"

"Seems like they was, for a while," Mr. Perrodine assented. "But in the excitement they might have got away."

When they left the jail, Don was half blind with anger under hard control. Mr. Violett led the way to a three-room shanty on the edge of town. The doors and windows were tightly closed, but smoke, even on this hot day, drifted upward from the chimney. Mr. Violett knocked, and when there was no answer he knocked again.

"Freedmen's Bureau," he called. "We're your friends. Is Joseph Gradney here?"

After an interval, the door opened. Inside, the only light came from the hearth, where an old woman fed a flickering fire with bits of kindling just enough to keep it alive. Three men and two women huddled in the steaming heat, and a stir of movement in the shadows testified that children watched and listened.

These people knew Mr. Violett, but they were slow to answer his questions, till Don took a hand and won their trust. Then Joseph Gradney began to find his tongue. His home was in Washington, he said, but when they heard there was fighting in Opelousas, he and his brother and some others came to see what was happening. He had a gun, the others were unarmed. They were stopped on the road, arrested and locked up in the jail. Between ten and eleven o'clock last night, he said, Solomon Loeb, who was captain of the Seymour Knights in Opelousas, came to the upper room in the jail where they were; he called the names of Joseph and his brother, and of others, and marched them downstairs.

The Negro went on, in a shuddering voice: "In de room downstairs dey was thutty, mebby fawty white men wid guns. Looked tuh me mah time uz come, but den Mr. Perrodine took me and my brotheh out back o' de jail. I ast him would he fotch Tom Cleland an' Risky Jim, dat dey cotched wid us; but den some guns went off some'r's, an' he say: 'Dah dey go! Da's dem! Dem yuthehs, still in de jail, dey gwine go de same way.'"

Don looked at Mr. Violett. "The deputy could have told us more than he did."

"You notice this man didn't see anyone killed."

"I heah de guns go off again, a whiles afteh," the Negro said.

Don asked: "Did you see the place where they were shot—if they were shot? Did you see any dead Negroes?"

"Naw suh! I ain' put my nose outside dis heah house, nor I ain' gwine tuh."

Half suffocated by the stifling heat, Don was glad to escape. Outside, he said: "We'll call on this Captain Loeb, Violett, and on Colonel Thompson. Let's take the Colonel first."

Colonel—or Doctor—Thompson, when they reached his office, proved to be an older man than Don had expected, and there was sadness in his eyes. Don asked at once:

"Colonel, is it possible to make any estimate, for my report, of how many men have been killed in the Opelousas neighborhood since yesterday morning?" The Colonel's eyes fell, and Don added reasonably: "I don't mean exactly, sir, of course. Five? Ten? Twenty-five?" He paused. "Or fifty? Or a hundred? Counting the prisoners in the jail?"

The other met his eyes. "I want to assure you, Captain Page; the killing of the prisoners in the jail was a pure misunderstanding!" And he said in shaken tones: "I told the men not to take any prisoners, and I meant just that and no more than that. I meant them to disarm the nigras and let them go."

"How many were killed at the jail?"

"Eighteen."

"Where were they killed?"

"Down in the woods, half a mile or so." Colonel Thompson mopped his brow. "I wouldn't have had this happen for a good deal, gentlemen."

"Colonel, how many Negroes do you suppose have been killed within, say, twenty miles of town?"

The old man shook his head. "No one knows. Four or five were killed at Paillet's, and a freedman named Victor Dauphin—his body's lying beside the road, just across the river—and a boy named Flander, from Doc Taylor's plantation. I can count eight or ten of my own knowledge, besides the men at the jail. Captain Loeb—he's head of the Seymour Knights—he thinks the total will run close to a hundred."

Don's jaw set hard. Yet certainly there had been some provocation for these killings. Negroes had been summoned to take up arms, and some of them had done so, and had used their weapons. He and Violett left the Colonel, and in the street the Bureau agent said persuasively:

"You know, the niggers really started this."

"I know. Who were the men I saw patrolling the streets last night?"

"The Seymour Knights."

"Do you suppose Captain Loeb is in town?"

"I suppose he is."

"Where can we find him?"

It developed that they had no need to search, since as they reached the hotel, four horsemen cantered down the street and alighted at the hitch rail there, and Violett said:

"That's him; the white hat."

Don waited till the other had dismounted, then spoke. "Captain Loeb?"

Loeb turned, and saw Don's uniform. "Your servant, Captain." His derisive tone held a question, and Don said at once:

"Page. Captain Page. I'm on inspector's duty for the Freedmen's Bureau. I wonder if you can make any estimate of the number of freedmen who've been killed since the trouble started yesterday."

Captain Loeb's glance touched his companions, who stood now at either side of Don and Mr. Violett, and behind them. "Why, I doubtless can," he assented. "I personally know of close to a hundred, and Mr. Bickford here knows of about sixty, and Mr. Prague yonder knows of seventy-five—or was it seventy-six, Mr. Prague?"

"Seventy-six," said Mr. Prague in a sober tone.

"Three hundred might cover it," Captain Loeb suggested. "Why, who wants to know?"

"There'd be some duplication?" Don inquired.

"Might be. It's hard to tell one nigger from another. 'Bout as hard as it is to tell a nigger from a nigger-lover."

"Do you include the wounded in your figures?"

"Well, now I'll tell you," Captain Loeb explained. "The way it is, when we set out to kill a nigger, he either gets away, or he don't. If we just wound him, we don't count it he's dead, so we go ahead and kill him all over again."

"I see. Thank you."

"That all you want to know?"

"It's enough," Don assured him.

"Well now let me ask you one question." Captain Loeb proposed. "Don't you think you'd be real smart if you was to go right on back to N'Orleans?"

"I don't plan to leave till tomorrow or the next day."

"I'd advise you to change your plans. Or you might not have a chance to decide how you'd travel, when you do go. Or where to."

Don smiled. "Now, now, Captain," he said easily: "Don't you know we don't allow civilians to run the army? I'll bid you good day." He turned to walk away. Mr. Prague was in his path, and Don said politely: "Excuse me, sir." Mr. Prague moved grudgingly aside. Don walked slowly, wondering whether they would shoot him in the back, half hoping they would. The murder of a Union soldier on a public street would bring a regiment to Opelousas in short order.

But there was no shot. He heard steps behind him, and someone spoke his name, but Don did not turn till Violett came by his side. Rage still blinded him; he wetted his lips and waited till his voice was under sure control. When he spoke, it was to ask:

"Is there a Democratic paper here?"

"Yes, the *Courier*."

"I'll speak to the editor," he decided, and when they came to the *Courier* office and Violett introduced Mr. Sandoz, the editor, Don said: "Mr. Sandoz, I'm preparing a report on this affair for the Freedmen's Bureau. It seems clear that after the caning of Mr. Bentley, the Negroes—or some of them—armed themselves and threatened the town, and the white people rallied in self-defense, and were successful in preventing the threatened rising. Do you agree?"

"Exactly."

"Have you any figures on the number of killed and wounded? White and colored?"

"One killed and several wounded at Paillet's," Mr. Sandoz began, but Don corrected him.

"Excuse me, but it now appears that there were four killed there."

"Ah! Some of the wounded probably died," Sandoz assented. "Then I've reports of at least four whites killed at Mallet Prairie. That's a settlement of freed niggers. And there've been several casualties around the village. Mr. Durant, for instance. Regrettable! Of course, the number of deaths in these disturbances is always greatly exaggerated, Captain. I can only guess, but I would guess that half a dozen white men have been killed, and possibly a dozen niggers." He made a deprecating gesture. "But now the town is safe and everything quiet."

Don rose. "Thank you, sir. I bid you a very good day."

Back at the Bureau office, Don stood at the window, watching the number of white men, either mounted or afoot, who passed to and fro outside. Violett said at last:

"Captain, you ought to understand that Captain Loeb meant what he said."

Don turned to study the other, and after a moment he asked curiously: "Where do your sympathies lie, in this affair?"

"I suppose I can see both sides," Violett admitted. "The caning of Bentley was a part of the code of these people. And certainly their fear of the niggers had some basis."

"Had it?" Don, without waiting for a reply, capped that question with another, and another, as though Violett were on trial. "It's twenty-four hours since the trouble started. Before killing twenty-five Negroes —or fifty, or a hundred, or three hundred—why didn't they wait till the Negroes had done something? Oh, I know they'd taken up arms, but how many houses did they burn? How many men did they kill? It wasn't Negroes who killed Mr. Durant last night; it was white men who didn't like his politics. It isn't rumor that Negroes were taken from the jail last night and murdered." He spoke quietly, in a monotone, his thoughts putting on words. "Who killed the wounded Negroes out at Paillet's?"

"You have to expect excesses, Captain, when men's passions are roused."

"That massacre at the jail was cold-blooded murder!"

"Not cold-blooded, Captain. They blamed those niggers for firing on Captain May's party, wounding him. He was at first thought to be fatally wounded."

"Not when we saw him!" Don retorted. "But even if he were dead, they had already killed four or five Negroes. Even if Captain May were dead, hadn't he been avenged?"

"They might not think that killing four or five niggers was enough to avenge Captain May."

"Then how many must be killed?"

"Ask his family," Violett retorted.

Don said in a reflective tone: "You don't see both sides, Mr. Violett; you see only one!"

Violett rose in anger. "I'll have satisfaction for that statement, Captain."

Page shook his head. "Don't be theatrical! You've lived too long among these Southerners, with their loud talk of their honor; their honor which seems to require that three men club one, because he has attainted that honor of theirs. They have dishonored themselves! I am allowing for the fear which actuated these men yesterday. I accept it as a fact. But it was not fear which prompted those murders at the jail. The danger was past, their honor was safe; yet they murdered eighteen men." He said calmly: "Don't talk about satisfaction. Next thing I know you'll be saying your honor has been stained."

Violett, after a moment's hesitation, sat down. "I've come to respect these people, Captain," he admitted. "And however false their code, they live by it."

"If their so-called code leads them to whip and to murder defenseless men, then I wouldn't give a damn for it," said Don. He rose. "I want to ride over to Washington," he said. "And to ride around the parish. Care to come?"

Violett, after a moment, rose. "I judge you're not going back to New Orleans, as Captain Loeb advised."

"I'll go back tomorrow or the day after," Don told him. "When my business here is done."

Don wrote Lucy, the following Sunday, a long letter, page upon page, describing his experience in Opelousas. And he went on:

> I'm blowing off steam to you. My report was short and to the point, facts, facts, facts; but I can tell you all the things that are so much more important than facts; the things I guessed, and thought, and felt. This Mr. Bentley, talking to him was an experience. The Democrats say he'd been inciting the Negroes to riot, but I saw the bruises on his back, and from my point of view, they damn his accusers forever. I wonder how it feels to submit to a beating like that. Presumably he would have been killed if he hadn't, and one fire-eating Southerner with whom I talked said that in Bentley's place he would have chosen death. But what does an experience like that do to a man's self-respect, his sense of his own decency and dignity. I haven't heard anyone say that Bentley cried out, or begged; but to submit? Probably there must always be something a little contemptible about a man who has been beaten with sticks. He's like a wronged husband. Instead of sympathy, he gets derision.
>
> There was another riot, a day or two later, in Bossier Parish, on

the Red River above Shreveport. The report we get is that an Arkansas man was robbed, and Negroes were blamed, and some white men killed or wounded a Negro or two, and two whites were killed by Negroes, and after that it was the same pattern, Negroes killed in all directions. Some say twenty-five, some say fifty. I'm beginning to think it's settled policy, in some parts, to take any excuse for killing Negroes, in order to scare them away from the polls a month from now. In this last affair, three Negro prisoners were taken out and killed. That seems to be a favorite pastime among some of these brave men, killing prisoners.

New Orleans is full of parades, and there must be scores of marching clubs. The Legislature passed a social-equality bill—public places not permitted to refuse the patronage of Negroes—but Governor Warmoth vetoed it. Friday night we had a high wind and a heavy rain and the Second Street drainage system couldn't carry off the water, so all that section is flooded. At noon yesterday, water was coming in from the Lake and by dark it had reached Gentilly Road. Some houses went adrift, little ones, of course, and some collapsed. Everything along the lake shore is gone, the papers say. The water began to fall last night. Tell your father there's no damage at the house except some broken shrubs.

Peter, by the way, is very much excited about a party Wednesday night. He's a Seymour Infanta, you know, and some of their young lady friends are presenting them with a banner.

You know what I'm thinking as I write: that this is the last letter I shall ever write you. For your father thinks you will be on the road to New Orleans before another letter can reach you, perhaps before this letter reaches you. Then we will be together, forever, and no need for letters at all. . . .

There was more, which he wrote slowly, a phrase or a sentence at a time, with many pauses to read what he had written, and to let his thoughts wander where they chose. He finished that page and another before the letter was done and sealed.

Through that summer and fall, when Republicans in New Orleans saw day by day the signs that their hold upon the city was weakening, Tony had many callers. Sapphira's quiet composure created an atmosphere of ease and of security wherein a troubled man might find, at least for a little while, release from his anxieties. But Tony himself was increasingly uneasy. For a while he had regularly strolled downtown after supper to watch the many parades, coming home to describe them to Sapphira.

"There must be a hundred different clubs," he told her. "The Grant Club, the Constitution Club, the Seymour Tigers, the Innocents, the

Seymour Infants, the Swamp Fox Rangers. I don't know what all. Some nights three or four different clubs will be parading, and sometimes they raid each other's clubrooms, breaking windows, throwing stones, shooting."

The last time he ventured downtown, he saw one of these raids in process. The headquarters of the First Ward Grant and Colfax Club were on Terpsichore Street, between St. Charles and Carondelet. One night on his way home, coming to the corner of St. Charles, he saw a crowd in the street, and paused. A man on the corner spoke to him in quiet tones.

"We're just cleaning out a nest of Radicals, sir; carrying off their flags and lamps and caps and uniforms. There may be a little trouble." Tony saw the drawn revolver in his hand. "So perhaps you'll want to go on." He added, as though to explain his suggestion: "I think I have seen you in company with some Radical gentlemen."

There was no open threat in his words, yet that night Tony proposed to Sapphira that they go north for a month or two. She quieted his fears, but he no longer ventured downtown after supper.

The Governor and Stephen Packard one day called together, and to Tony's question, Warmoth said frankly: "The city is lost, and probably the state." And he said in a reflective tone: "I had a caller a day or two ago from Franklin, an elderly gentleman named Grayson, a lifelong Democrat. He came merely to pay his respects, but we fell into some talk of murder as a political weapon, and he said that in Franklin Parish, murders were seldom political. Most of their murders were committed by a man named John Word." Warmoth laughed in grim amusement. "This Mr. Word seems to be a one-man epidemic; he kills someone, and then he kills all the witnesses. The extraordinary thing, to me, was Grayson's attitude of complete neutrality."

Mr. Packard nodded. "Murders are a commonplace among these people," he remarked. "If you doubt it, read the rural newspapers." He produced a packet of cuttings, selected one. "Here, for instance, is an editorial from the *Planter's Banner,* published in St. Mary's, commenting on the Opelousas massacre." And he read: " 'The people generally are well satisfied with the result of the riot, only they regret that the carpetbaggers escaped. They are satisfied that the white people tried their best to avert the calamity.' The calamity, in his own words, is—" He read again: " 'A hundred dead Negroes and perhaps a hundred more wounded and crippled.' " He folded the clipping, returned it to his pocket. "There's a picture of the Southern mind, when it's confronted by massacre and murder."

Sapphira asked: "Do white people pay any attention to such newspapers? Do the papers have any influence?"

Governor Warmoth said strongly: "Why, Miss Sapphira, nowhere in the whole world will you find people as completely controlled by newspapers as the people of Louisiana."

Tony asked guardedly: "Governor, do you feel any fear for your person?"

Warmoth laughed. "I certainly do! Of course, I make it a point to be seen on the street every day, and to flap my wings and outcrow any cock in town—but yes, I'm scared. I think I may be attacked, and quite possibly killed, and I know that not a white man in New Orleans would try to help me."

Sapphira looked up at him. "You do New Orleans gentlemen injustice, Governor. I'm sure of that."

The Governor bowed. "Maybe they deserve your good opinion, ma'am."

That night Tony and Sapphira dined alone, and he said again that he wished they might leave New Orleans behind till the election was over; but Sapphira thought that they need only avoid offense. "No one's going out of his way to harm us, I'm sure."

'Phemy and Quinny were, as usual, serving them, and 'Phemy, who when they were alone was always privileged, spoke her mind. "Y'all stay heah and let on you ain't t'home. Stop lettin' all dis riffraff come heah eve'y evenin' and drink up you' good wine and spill ashes on you' purty upholsteries. Dem's de ones de paterrollers gwine git, does dey make up dey minds tuh do som gittin'. Y'all chain-lock you' doahs an' don' let 'em in." She added with an ominous head shake: "Ef you don't, folks gwine think dis heah house is one o' dem nigge' clubs!"

Quinny, pouring fresh coffee for Tony, said: "Cap'n Cash say you git on his boat, he tek you upriver, tek you all de way to Cincinnati ef'n you say de word."

"We can't shut our door against our friends, Mama," Sapphira reminded 'Phemy. "But I'm sure we've nothing to fear." She looked at Tony, saw his eyes flickering. "Truly, Tony," she said.

When Pinchback came one evening and found them alone, Tony asked the Senator's opinion. Pinchback answered in all candor. "I'm afraid for my life," he admitted. "If things get any worse, I'm going to take sick and go off somewhere, and nobody'll see me till the excitement's over."

"Where will you go?"

"I've got my sickbed all picked out."

Tony tried to laugh. "Don't go without me," he suggested. "I feel as if I might have a spell of sickness coming on."

Sapphira tried to quiet his alarm, but two nights later, as they were preparing to retire, a fusillade of rock fragments shattered half the drawing-room windows, and from the street outside, young male voices called in angry derision:

"Nigger-lover!" "Nigger-lover!" "Nigger-loving son of a bitch!"

Sapphira, without haste, extinguished the candles, moving calmly around the room, but Tony's eyes fixed on a rock larger than the others, wrapped in a piece of paper. He picked it up, and in the bedroom he unfolded the paper and saw it bore two or three crudely printed lines. He went toward the end of the mantel to read it by the candles there, but before he could do so, Sapphira came beside him and took the paper from his hands. She creased it lengthwise, then touched it to the candle flame, looking up over her shoulder at him, letting it burn till it was only a corner, then dropping that last bit to burn itself out upon the hearth.

"Do what you decide, Tony," she advised him. "But don't let some name-calling street coward tell you what to do."

7

TRAV AND THE OTHERS reached New Orleans on a Sunday in mid-October. A leaking steam valve had delayed the boat, and it was near noon when they alighted from the train. Peter and Saul met them at the station, and Lucy looked all around for Don. She had been so sure he would be here; but Peter saw her disappointment and explained that Don had gone to Franklin, in St. Mary's Parish, to investigate the killing of Judge Chase and Colonel Pope.

"They're going to be buried here today," he added. "And everybody thinks there'll be a riot, so I have to get out at Canal Street. The Infantas are going to be ready, in case anything happens."

To Trav's questions, he rattled off what he knew about these murders. "Chase was the parish judge," he explained. "And Colonel Pope was the sheriff. They were both Radicals. They'd been trying to stir up the niggers to make trouble, so some of the Seymour Knights—"

"Who are they?"

"Oh, it's a club, like the Innocents here. They disguised themselves and went up to where the Judge and Colonel Pope were talking, on the gallery of the hotel—Mrs. Pope was with them—and shot them, and then made sure of them with their knives."

Lucy cried: "With Mrs. Pope right there watching?"

"I guess so. That's what I heard, anyway."

Enid made a scornful sound. "And after all, Lucy, they were Yankees, carpetbaggers."

"Colonel Pope was a schoolteacher from New York," Peter agreed. "But Judge Chase was born right there in Franklin. But he turned Republican." He added with a side glance at Trav: "Like General Longstreet."

"Then no wonder," Enid commented.

Trav asked: "When did this happen, Peter?"

"Friday night, I guess it was." They reached Canal Street, and saw the banquettes crowded, from Dryades Street to the levee. Presumably the bodies were being brought to New Orleans by boat. Peter spoke to Saul. "Stop a minute, Saul." And to Trav: "Want to stay and watch the funeral? There might be some shooting!"

"I guess not. Who were these men who killed them, did you say?"

"They were some of the Seymour Knights. That's all anybody knows." Peter leaped to the ground. "I'll be home for dinner."

Trav said: "Hold on a minute, Saul. I might as well stop by the mill, see Mr. Cist and Elon."

Lucy laughed at him. "Papa, it's Sunday! They won't be there!"

Trav grinned at his own forgetfulness, and settled back in his seat, and Peter said hurriedly: "Oh, I forgot to tell you. Elon's father dropped dead last Thursday, arguing with someone in the St. Charles. I went to his funeral."

Trav exclaimed: "You don't say!"

"Yes I do. See you at dinner."

Peter darted away, and Saul spoke to the horses. Enid said in an amused tone: "I can't imagine Mr. Villard arguing with anybody. When he got started, he'd hold the floor. No one could argue back."

"Maybe someone did, and that's what killed him," Trav suggested.

Lucy smiled with them. "But let's stop and see Elon and Eleanor on the way home, shall we?"

Enid said querulously: "It's hardly on the way, Lucy!" The Villard house was on Camp Street, facing Coliseum Place. "And after all, that old man wasn't much loss! But I suppose we might as well."

They found Elon and Eleanor at home, and Lucy kissed them both with an equal affection. Trav spoke some word of sympathy, and Elon nodded in abstracted fashion.

"I don't think he'd have minded, even if he'd known it was coming," he confessed. "He'd decided he had nothing to live for." He added, changing the subject: "We've already sold this house and rented a little one—" He smiled. "Just about honeymoon size, on Hestia Street, down across Carondelet from you. Moving in next week."

Lucy wished to take them home for dinner, but Eleanor shook her head. "We've too much to do, sorting all this, deciding what to keep and what to throw away. Look at us!" She extended both hands. "The amount of dust that collects on things is just unbelievable. But supper, maybe?"

"Of course, do!" Enid agreed. "We can get caught up on things." On the way home, she said in mild distaste: "Well, they're not exactly stricken, are they? I'd hate to think I'd leave behind me as little grief as that." She shivered. "Br-r-r! The very thought makes me cold! Hurry, Saul!"

Peter came home while they were still at dinner, reporting that the funeral had been a disappointment. "Nothing happened," he said. "No fights at all. If the Radicals had started anything, we were all ready for them, but they didn't dare!" He laughed gleefully. "We've got the niggers so scared they can't call their souls their own. Even the nigger police! Up by the Dryades Market, Friday night, one of them tried to stop some of us and we beat him half to death, took his revolver and his club and rattle. We drew lots for his things, and I won his club. It's up in my room. Want to see it?" He ran to fetch the trophy, and they passed it from hand to hand.

"Was the policeman killed?" Trav asked.

"Oh no, we just cracked his head." And the boy explained: "You see, Papa, we're trying to scare all the niggers off the streets, so they won't dare try to vote when election comes."

Trav held his tone steady. "Think you can do it?"

"You bet!" Peter told him proudly. "You'll see."

"Is there much of that sort of thing going on?"

"You bet," Peter repeated. "We're around the streets every night, and so are the Innocents and all the other clubs. A nigger alone, or just two or three of them, they can get into trouble mighty quick."

"Killings?"

Lucy asked in a low tone: "Do we have to talk about them, Papa. It makes me shiver."

Peter laughed at her. "Golly, Sis, if talk makes you shiver, you ought to see some of the things I've seen."

But Trav hushed him, spoke of Elon. "I didn't ask him anything about the mill," he remembered. "But I can do that when they come to supper."

That evening he saw a tenderness in Lucy which he had not seen before. Without any wordy professions of sympathy, she nevertheless wrapped Elon and Eleanor in warm and understanding affection. They had been weary when they came. "Simply exhausted," Eleanor confessed. "You all can have no idea of the wrench of deciding whether to keep something or throw it away! It just wears you out!"

"I know," Lucy assured her. "Don't forget we had to leave a house full of things at Chimneys. Only, really, it was easier for us, because we had no choice; we had to leave everything! Except, of course, our clothes." She turned to Elon. "I expect it was harder on you than on Eleanor; men save things so!" Watching them, Trav saw the strong bond between these two. After all, Elon was her own kind, with the same background; strange that it had been Don whom she preferred.

Elon said lightly: "Oh, I didn't mind." And he explained: "Maybe because most of my real treasures are still down at Paradise; things I had when I was a boy, back before the War." He smiled at his sister.

"We did find some old theatre programs today, and some dance invitations, things like that. That was a mighty gay winter in New Orleans; the winter before Sumter."

Eleanor laughed with a break in her voice. "We've been crying one minute and laughing the next, all day," she confessed. "Everything reminded us of something. Adelina Patti was here that winter, singing at the French Opera House. I saw her in every role she sang, sometimes twice, kept all the programs."

"And Maggie Mitchell in *Fanchon* at the St. Charles Theatre," Elon supplemented. "And Blind Tom." His eye met Eleanor's. "Remember how Mama enjoyed him? And Papa went to sleep." He told Trav, with a sudden laugh. "Oh, and I found my bell, my campaign bell, and my collars and cuffs. That wasn't much like this campaign."

Trav asked: "When was that?"

"Eighteen sixty. We organized a club, the Young Bell Ringers. We were for Bell and Everett, of course. Red collars and cuffs were our uniform, and we marched for miles, ringing our bells all the time. There was a Young Men's Breckenridge and Lane Club too. We were bitter rivals."

"Are you campaigning this year?"

Elon shook his head. "The White Camelia isn't very active, no. We're a sober crowd." He asked: "Where's Don, Lucy?" So the conversation turned.

Tuesday evening after supper, Don came to the house on Prytania Street, and Lucy ran into his rib-cracking embrace, and gasped, and he stammered an apology.

"Oh, I'm sorry! Did I half kill you?"

"I loved it!" she cried. "Do it again!"

He laughed and caught her up, cradled in his arms, then hurriedly released her as Trav and Enid came into the hall to greet him. Afterward, in the sitting room, with Lucy beside him on the couch, he had to answer Trav's many questions. Of his business in St. Mary's Parish, he said: "I didn't accomplish anything, except to irritate people, but I found that the men were warned. There's a Negro up there, John Moore; he can read and write a little, a pretty good man. He hunted them up sometime Friday, saw them separately, told them they would be killed that night. But Judge Chase said all the talk and threats were just noise, so they stayed."

"How did the nigra know?"

"I didn't ask him. On the killing itself, I couldn't find any actual witnesses. They were lodging at O'Neill's Hotel. A little past eight o'clock, everyone heard a volley of shots from the direction of Colonel Pope's room, but no one seems to have gone to investigate, till Mrs. Pope's continuing screams demanded attention. The Colonel was dead.

Judge Chase ran for some distance after he was shot. His body was found about four o'clock the next morning, near the bayou; several shot wounds, including one through the forehead, and a knife wound in his back."

Trav asked: "Was there any special provocation, any immediate reason for killing them just now?"

"Well, sir, people up there are pretty bitter about their politics— seven days in the week." From his wallet Don selected a clipping. "Here's what the *Planter's Banner* printed Saturday—before they knew Pope had been killed." And he read: " 'The recent disasters of the Radicals in St. Landry have had terrible effect on that little rat, Pope. He looks as though he had been chawed by a terrier. His liver don't act, he has the colic, the toothache, and the yellow jaundice and he don't feel very well himself. If he dies, the shell of an English walnut would make him a good sarcophagus.' "

Lucy shivered. "How horrible!"

"Who's the editor, Don?" Trav inquired.

"Mr. Daniel Dennett. It's a weekly paper. He and some others were in a store at the Odd Fellows Hall when they heard the shots. They walked toward the Hotel and joined a crowd in front of Healy's Coffee House. The shooting was still going on. They waited till it stopped and waited a while longer. Mr. Dennett says the assassins had plenty of time to stroll away, and he's sure that the crime will—as he says— 'defy investigation.' " He laughed mirthlessly. "It certainly defied mine."

"Couldn't do a thing?"

"Just report the facts."

Lucy drew Don's arm across her shoulder. "So you could just as well have been here to meet me, after all."

He grinned assent, pressing her against his side. "Just exactly," he agreed.

Enid rose. "I'm going to say good night, before you two embarrass me," she said, smiling. "Coming, Trav?"

"Eh?" He seemed surprised. "Oh! Oh, yes!" He rose hurriedly. "Yes, I suppose I am!"

On the stairs she tweaked his arm. "Stupid!" And as they reached their door: "Weren't you ever their age? After all, they haven't seen each other for months."

In their room he closed the door behind them, watching her cross to her dressing table and lean down to look at herself in the glass. She came back to him, smiling.

"I haven't begun to look really old yet, have I, darling?"

He chuckled. "Now, now! Don't try to start a flirtation with an old man like me."

"I'm a little embarrassed, alone with a man in my bedroom!" They laughed together, and she kissed him lightly, and returned to her mirror. "Can you get me out of this dress?" she asked. "Or shall I call Filly?"

"You'll have to tell me where to start."

"I got really acquainted with Lucy for the first time, while we were together in Camden and you down here," she said. "I had her bed moved into our big room and sometimes we talked for hours. She's so young, isn't she?"

"I've always thought she was pretty grown up."

"The hook's not down there," she warned him, trying to look over her shoulder. "Up higher, up on my shoulder blade, under that . . . Here, I can reach it." And with a supple contortion she managed to do so. "I thought so too," she admitted. "In fact, I've always been sort of afraid of her. But actually, she's just a little girl. She's awful sweet! There, I can get out of it now." And before they slept she murmured: "Those two nice children downstairs!"

Trav, at once upon his return, had sensed the sharper temper of the city. He had long since come to a certain intimacy with Captain Kouns of the *Louisa*, the ferry on which he normally crossed to the mill, and Monday morning he spent the few minutes of the crossing in the pilot-house.

"Seems like New Orleans is getting itself pretty worked up over this election," he suggested.

The Captain nodded. " 'Tis so," he agreed. "I went in to buy myself a revolver, the other day. I keep a shotgun here in the pilothouse, and my old Colt Dragoon, that I carried through the War. But that's too big to put in my pocket, and times like these, when I do go ashore, I like to be armed. Well sir, I had to find a storekeeper who knew me before I could buy one. He says they won't sell a gun to a Republican, these days; you've got to be a Democrat." He added: "And then you have to pay twice what it's worth, twenty or twenty-five dollars for a little old Colt that never did cost mor'n ten or twelve dollars before." The *Louisa* under his hands began her swing to come up to the Villeré Street landing. "But a man needs something! You hardly ever see a policeman on the streets after dark. They've been driven into their holes."

"The Metropolitan Police amount to anything?" Trav asked. This force, established by the Radical legislature to supersede the old city police, was controlled not by the Mayor but by the Board of Police Commissioners,—three white men and three Negroes—and Lieutenant Governor Dunn was ex-officio chairman.

"Them!" The Captain's tone was explosive with scorn. "They're just a damned Yankee institution! A third of 'em are niggers!" He chuckled. "You don't see much of 'em. The Innocents have kind of cured the Metropolitans of prowling around." He spun the wheel, rang the bell for reverse. "Here we are. See you this evenin'."

At the mill, Mr. Cist gave good reports of the business, but when Trav spoke of politics, he shook his head. "I have enough to do, tending to my own affairs."

Elon laughed and agreed. "You're wise. No Cincinnati man has any business with Louisiana politics these days." He added, turning to Trav: "You know, Major, some of us last night were able to count seventy-eight Democratic clubs in New Orleans and Algiers and Jefferson, with twelve or fifteen thousand members—all of them armed." He nudged Mr. Cist with a friendly elbow, grinning. "Enough so that any Radicals around here don't brag about their politics."

Trav afterward would remember the rest of that week as a lull before the quickened tempo of the last ten days of the campaign. The papers reported the shooting of a Negro named Robert Gray, on Texas Street in Shreveport, and when Don came to supper Friday, Trav spoke of this.

Don's eyes fell to his plate. "I knew him," he said. "He was elected justice of the peace up there last April. That's why he was killed. They've been killing every Negro who lifts himself a little above his fellows. Our agent up there, Mr. Monroe, reports that a group of white men stopped Gray in the street and asked his name, and he said his name was Bob, and one of the men shot him. Then the murderer stepped out in the middle of the street and waved his hat, and six mounted men rode up with a led horse, and he mounted and rode off. Mr. Monroe found a Negro who said he could identify the killer, and took him to a justice of the peace to make an affidavit, but the justice wasn't in his office, and when Monroe went to hunt him up, the Negro disappeared."

"Have there been many such incidents?"

"Yes, a great many. There was a man named Meadows last spring. Then John Kemp; he was shot on his own front porch. James Watson, up at Shreveport. Charlie Folsom—though he was only partially hanged, was allowed to live. I suppose we've records of fifty. I could—"

Enid cried: "Don't, Don. After all! At supper!"

But Lucy protested. "No, no. Go on, Don. Mama, if the nigras can stand having it done to them, we ought to be able to stand hearing about it!"

"Not at supper," Enid insisted. "And besides, I don't really believe half these horrible stories. Or if they did happen, it's just poor white trash doing them."

Peter at that laughed outright. "A lot you know, Mama!"

Trav said quietly: "Whoever does these things is trash, son. White or black."

"And the nigras are just as dead," Lucy added.

"I wish you'd all stop talking about it," Enid insisted, and for a while they obeyed; but afterward, when Enid and Lucy had left the table, Trav said doubtfully:

"That sort of thing—just aimless, stupid killing—is hard to credit, Don."

"I know it," Don agreed. "I can't believe some of the things reported to us, even when I know they're true. Here a while ago, up in Caddo Parish, a group of men in some sort of disguise went into a house and hanged two Negro women. There's a possibility that the man who killed Bob Gray was one of them. That particular group has done some pretty brutal things. They went to a brickyard where a lot of men were working, took four men and a boy." His jaw set. "They stuck their knives through the hands of these men, threaded a rope through the holes in their palms, dragged them off to the riverbank all tied together . . ."

Peter grunted. "Golly, that must have hurt!"

Don glanced at him, continued: ". . . and shot them and heaved them into the river." He added: "Mr. Monroe says the bodies got into a backwater and are still there, caught in the driftwood. There was a lot of killing in Caddo, all that week. At least a dozen, probably at least twenty, were killed."

"We have to!" Peter insisted. "We have to show them we're still their masters!" He looked from Don to his father, and Don said thoughtfully:

"I suppose you can make them fear you, but I wonder if killing them will ever quiet your fears of them."

Peter cried: "You think I'm afraid of any old nigger?"

"I don't know," Don admitted. "I know I am! I'm afraid of what he may do unless I can convince him I'm his friend. You can't gentle a horse by whipping it."

Peter retorted. "They gentled five niggers over in Jefferson today. Killed them. That gentles them." He rose. "I've got to go downtown and do a little gentling. Good night."

Trav watched him go. "Dark days for us all," he said. "The Bureau's helpless, isn't it?"

"Just about," Don agreed. "By the way, a new superintendent takes charge tomorrow; General Hatch. But the Bureau's not long for this world. We'll be closing up our work after the first of the year. We'll clean up the loose ends just about the time my enlistment expires."

Sunday night, Trav and Enid dined with Doctor Mercer at his home on Canal Street. At the door, Trav told Saul: "Come back at half past ten."

"Yas suh," Saul promised. "Ef'n I don' git mah chunk put out."

"What did he mean, Trav?" Enid asked, as they crossed toward the door.

"His chunk put out? Oh, I suppose the saying comes from the way they borrow a chunk of live coals and cover it with ashes and carry it home." He pulled the bell. "But he's in no danger. He was joking. Half joking anyway."

Doctor Mercer was a courtly host, famous for a wit which wore no barbs, and for a pleasant gallantry. The company was small, and except for Judge and Mrs. Morgan, Trav and Enid had known none of them until tonight; but Enid, sure that she was the youngest and the most attractive woman in the room, enjoyed herself completely.

Even at dinner, the talk inevitably turned to politics. Doctor Mercer had been a Union man. "But I find most genuine lovers of the Union are nowadays, like myself, good Democrats," he remarked. He looked through the drawing room toward Canal Street. "I watch the pageant out there, parades, parades, parades, night after night, but I wonder whether parades swing voters to one side or another."

"Of course they do," said Trav. "Didn't you ever join a parade, when you were a boy? Watch the next parade that passes and you'll see some boys keeping step with the marchers, and to march together is to be bound together. The beat of marching feet is a forging agent as potent as the blacksmith's hammer."

Enid was always surprised by Trav's sudden eloquences. So often, when she became conscious of silence all around her, it was to discover that everyone was listening to Trav. While now he and Doctor Mercer discussed the philosophy of rhythm and its importance in the life of man, she felt a warm, contenting pride.

When the evening ended and it was time to say good night, Saul was waiting with their carriage. As Enid took her seat, she saw, coming down Canal Street toward them, scores of moving torches, and heard the sound of a band, and she asked: "What's that, Trav?"

"A parade," he said. "All right, Saul; go along."

But Enid cried: "No, wait! Let's watch them pass, Trav. I never saw a torchlight parade. Aren't those torches they're carrying?"

Saul said in anxious warning: "Us'ns best git along home, Missy. Might be trouble 'round heah."

"Nonsense! Let's wait and see them."

Trav said nothing, sat watching, and she clung to his arm, trembling with excitement, exclaiming at everything; but suddenly another parade emerged from Dauphine Street, crossing in front of the marchers. The danger of a collision was obvious, and Trav said sharply: "Better get us out of this, Saul." Saul was already trying to turn the horses, but other vehicles had stopped to watch the approaching parade and he could not turn. Trav said: "Try to go ahead."

But then a shot sounded, at the corner not a block away, and on its heels another, and then a volley, and shouts and screams. Trav threw Enid down between the seats of the carriage and covered her body with his. The horses were plunging, and Saul jumped out to catch their bits and steady them. Along the banquette within a few feet of Trav's head, Negroes in costume, each wearing a loose white garment, ran past the carriage, and now and then one turned to fire a pistol back in the direction from which they had come. Enid clung to Trav, sobbing and wailing, and the shooting continued, and the shouts.

Trav found himself counting the shots aloud, counting not in sequence but disjointedly. "One-two-three." "One." "One-two." "One." "One." "One-two-three-four-five-six-seven—" Absurd, to try to count the shots in a rattling volley. A white man, running, paused by the carriage to shoot three times, presumably at the fleeing Negroes; then he returned toward the corner again.

The shooting lasted for two or three minutes. When it had surely stopped, Trav helped Enid up into her seat. "I think we're all right now."

"I want to go home," she wailed.

"So do I," Trav admitted in grim amusement. There was light enough at a little distance, where scores of oil torches now clustered together, but here close at hand he could see only shapes and masses in the milling crowd. The horses were still dancing, and he heard Saul's voice steadying them.

"You, Podnuh, so-o-o! So-o-o, Beauty! So-o-o! Easy! So-o-o."

Trav called: "Saul, you all right?"

"Yas suh!" Saul became visible between the heads of the horses. "Ah jes' kind o' layin' low."

Trav jumped out and went to him. "I'll hold them. Get the reins. Let's go along home."

When Saul took his place, Trav returned to Enid's side. The crowd had thinned, and the horses picked their way through a litter of broken lamps, and placards discarded by the Negroes in their flight. Turning the corner, they shied uneasily, and Trav saw on the angle of the banquette a dead Negro in a loose white robe, blood-dappled. Then they were clear of the crowd, and Enid bade Saul hurry, and the horses settled to a swift trot, their hooves beating in time and then out of time and then in time again. Trav, listening absently, thought Beauty's stride was half an inch shorter than Pardner's. It was rare to get two trotters who could really keep step together; Pardner and Beauty were better than most.

At home he told Isaiah to send Filly to help her mistress prepare for bed. Lucy had been asleep, but she waked on their return, and went to her mother, and then came to Trav to hear what had happened.

He told her what he could. "But I'm not sure of much," he admitted, grinning. "Mother and I were crouched down between the seats, hoping no stray bullets would stray our way."

She hugged him hard. "I'm glad they didn't! Mama's worried about Peter, crying for him, afraid he's hurt."

"I'd better go up," Trav decided, and they ascended the stairs together. Filly was with Enid, putting cold compresses on her head and bathing her wrists with toilet water while Enid writhed and moaned in a frightening hysteria. Trav and Lucy stood beside the bed for a moment, and Trav looked across at Filly, his eyes asking a question. She smiled and nodded, and he led Lucy out into the hall.

"She's just putting on," he said reassuringly. "She'll be all right. You go back to bed."

"You sure, Papa?"

He nodded. "She's play-acting, feeling sorry for herself."

"Well, she has a right to!"

"So have I," he reminded her. "Guess I'll go to bed, too, and kick and scream."

She laughed and kissed him and went to her room. Trav dismissed Filly, and when the door had closed behind her, he began to undress. "It's all right, Enid," he said reassuringly. "You can stop carrying on."

"I want Peter," she whimpered.

"He'll be here in the morning," he promised. "Time now to get some sleep."

Peter was there in the morning. To Trav's question Isaiah said: "Yas suh, he come in jes' befo' sun." Trav had left Enid asleep, but he went back upstairs and woke her to hear this reassuring news, and she said in drowsy fondness:

"I knew he'd be all right, Honey, soon as you told me he'd be."

Lucy slept late that morning, so Trav breakfasted alone, and since this was Monday, he had not even a morning paper to keep him company. At the mill, Elon reported that five Negroes had been killed in last night's riot. "Four men and a boy," he said. "And one white man. There was scattered shooting all night, all over town."

"Peter was out till about daylight," Trav commented.

"I know the Infantas had a meeting," Elon agreed. "They're marching down to Terre Boeuf today." The village lay in St. Bernard Parish, a few miles from New Orleans. "Someone's going to present a banner to the Humble Bee Club, and the Infantas plan to break up the gathering."

"Looking for trouble, aren't they?" Trav suggested, glad that Peter, having been up till daylight, would sleep all day today, and so take no part in that adventure.

"There'll be trouble everywhere, from now through election," Elon reminded him. "Won't have to look for it." Trav nodded, turning his attention to the business of the day.

Yet he was uneasy, and a little before his usual time, he started home. He heard on the ferry that there had been some rioting in St. Bernard Parish, so at the landing he took a hackney, eager to make sure that Peter was safe.

But Peter was not at the house, and Enid reported that he had left before she was awake. He might have gone on that march to Terre Boeuf, but Trav did not tell her this. To alarm her would not bring Peter home.

He and Enid and Lucy were alone at supper. Lucy said Don was on duty. After supper she and Enid went upstairs, but Trav was in his study when the doorbell rang. Isaiah went to answer, and Trav, thinking fearfully this might be some word of Peter, stepped into the hall. It was Elon who came in, and Trav was glad to see him.

"Thought you might be Peter," he explained.

"Did he go to Terre Boeuf?"

"I don't know. Probably. He's not at home."

Elon said uncertainly: "I hear that the Innocents are going to seize City Hall tonight. If I see anything of Peter, I'll try to bring him home."

Trav stared at him, astonished. "Seize City Hall? What for? How can they?"

"What's to stop them? The Mets don't show their faces after dark." The Metropolitan police had proved completely ineffective. Elon added scornfully: "One of them fell over a fence and shot himself with his own gun, down in St. Bernard today. Want to come along and see what happens at City Hall?"

Trav hesitated, but Peter might come home, so he declined. He went with Elon to the door. When Elon was gone, Lucy called softly from the upper hall:

"Wasn't that Elon, Papa?"

"Yes, 't was."

"Why didn't you call me? I could have got dressed."

"He just stopped for a minute. Good night, Honey."

"Aren't you coming to bed pretty soon?"

"Pretty soon," he promised.

But there was no sleep in him. He settled down to read for a while, alert to every sound, and time drifted sluggishly away. It may have been two hours, or three, before the bell rang again. This time he hurried to the door.

This, too, was Elon. "Saw your light, Major," he said quickly. "So I just dropped in."

"Glad you did," Trav agreed. "Come in. We'll have a nightcap." And as Elon followed him toward the study he asked: "Well, what happened?"

So Elon made swift report of the night's events. There had been no real attempt to seize City Hall, he said, though a great crowd gathered there, the Innocents in their red shirts and caps, and many other clubs in uniform, and many men besides.

"There were a lot of speeches," he explained. "Mayor Conway, and General Hays, and General Steedman. General Steedman said Governor Warmoth has turned the government over to the army; says he has told the sheriffs and the police to report to General Rousseau. Mayor Conway wanted to turn over the policing of the city to the Democratic clubs, but the clubs wouldn't accept the responsibility."

"Whoa!" Trav suggested, amused at Elon's rush of words, "Slow down! I never heard you talk so fast, Elon. You must be excited."

Elon hesitated as though embarrassed. "Well, sir, I am! With Governor Warmoth giving up, we've practically recaptured Louisiana! The state's in Southern hands again."

Trav nodded, indifferent. "That's good. I suppose you didn't see Peter?"

Elon seemed taken aback. He flushed, and tried to speak, and choked and coughed. "Well, as a matter of fact, he's in the hack, outside," he blurted, at last, and he added hastily: "He's all right, Major Currain; just a bullet through his shoulder. It didn't touch any big artery, nor any bone."

Trav was already hurrying toward the door. Peter had dismissed the carriage, and was sitting on the doorstep. When Trav opened the door he rose, and as he came into the light, Trav saw with relief that the boy was not badly hurt. His color was good, and there was a lofty pride in his bearing.

"He had the wound dressed," Elon explained, and Peter supplemented that.

"At the coffee house, Artista's, and again at headquarters here. It won't bother me. A few days in a sling is all."

"He'll wear that old sling till it rots off," Elon predicted. "He's the proudest young gentleman you ever saw!"

Trav hushed them. "Let's not wake Mama tonight, or she'd rouse the house. Anything you want, son, before we go to bed?"

"No sir. I'm fine!"

"She's been badly worried. It will almost be a satisfaction to her to know you were wounded. Justifies her worrying. I'll get you to bed."

He thanked Elon, and the other said good night, and Trav and Peter went quietly up the stairs.

Trav had not known how tired he was until he was abed, Enid warm in her sleep beside him. She would be happy tomorrow, lavishing on Peter every attention she could devise, and Trav knew a deep thankfulness because this son of his had passed through deadly peril, yet taken no great harm.

He slept at last, but his long habit of early rising woke him early in the morning. The riot in St. Bernard, said the *Picayune*, had originated when a Negro, jeering at the procession, fired a shot which struck one of the paraders in the shoulder. The Negro who fired the shot was killed and the wounded man—his name, said the *Picayune*, was Martinez—was carried away to receive medical attention.

But Negroes bore the body of the dead man to the home of Thomas Ong, and a crowd of Negroes gathered there and eventually marched to the bakery of Pablo Filio and killed him and set his house on fire. The white people of the parish rallied to put down the uprising, sending their families away to safety by any available conveyance. Several Negroes had been killed, and fighting was still going on.

Trav had finished with the paper before Lucy joined him at breakfast. When she heard Peter was hurt, she asked many questions, but Trav did not try to answer her. "Peter'll have to tell us all about it," he said. "He was too tired to talk, last night—and I was so pleased to have him safe that I didn't make him. I'm staying home today so I can hear the whole story."

Peter might have slept the day away, but when Enid woke and heard the news, she went at once to rouse him and assure herself he was not badly hurt. Peter, once awake, insisted on getting dressed. Enid wished to keep him in bed, but Maria, whom she called to advise her, agreed with Peter.

"Tain't nothin' t'mek a fuss oveh," she declared. "I'se seen a cat scratch dat uz wuss'n dat. I'll rub some o' my own salve on a piece o' rag and stick it in de in-hole an' pull it out de out-hole, an' he be fine." While she talked, she acted, and Peter bit his lip till it bled, and when the bandages were replaced, Maria said contentedly: "Now hit'll mek some nice creamy pus foh th'ee-foah days an' dat'll be the end on it."

Peter, when the time for talking came, would have dismissed the incident with a casual word, but they united in insisting that he tell them every detail. "Well, all right," he said yielding. "We were marching along the road, and a crowd of niggers were sitting on the fence, and we gave a cheer for Seymour and Blair. One of the niggers yelled—" He hesitated, looking at his mother and Lucy. "Well, he yelled a dirty word about Seymour and Blair, and I started for him, and he had a gun in his hand behind his back, and he pulled it around and shot me."

Enid cried: "Why didn't you kill him on the spot?"

Peter grinned weakly. "Why, Mama, what a way to talk!" He looked sidelong at Lucy. "What would Don say? Besides, the shot knocked me down. But they caught him." He added in a contented tone: "A lot of the Infantas are Sicilians, or Italians, or Spaniards. They killed him with their knives."

"It served him right!" Enid declared, but Lucy said:

"Maybe if you hadn't run at him, he wouldn't have shot you, and then they wouldn't have killed him, and all the killing down there last night and today wouldn't have happened."

"You sound like that Yankee beau of yours," Peter retorted. "But we don't let anyone insult Seymour and Blair."

"Oh, you don't care a fig for Seymour and Blair! All you want is an excuse to shoot some poor nigra!"

Enid protested: "Lucy! How can you talk so!"

"Well, Sis," Peter drawled. "There may come a day you'll want someone to shoot a 'poor nigra' for you! But don't count on me!"

"Stop it, both of you!" Enid was furious. "Saying such things to each other! Stop it, you hear?"

"I'm sorry, Peter," Lucy told him. "I didn't mean it."

Peter forgave her with a large gesture. "It's all right, Sis. I didn't mean it either."

Trav had listened in silence, but he said now in a puzzled tone: "Peter, the *Picayune* says the man who was shot was named Martinez."

Peter nodded. "José Martinez was the one who bandaged me at Artista's coffee house," he explained. "The papers never do get things straight."

"Think the shooting's over?"

Peter did not know, but that day troops—infantry and cavalry—were sent to St. Bernard, and by Wednesday evening the parish was quiet. Twenty-five or thirty Negroes had been killed, and there was evidence enough that Thomas Ong, the leading Radical in the parish, had incited them to the murder of Pablo Filio. When Don came to the house Wednesday night, Peter—his wound was feverish and his temper short—asked in a challenging tone:

"Well, what do you think of your poor abused niggers now?"

"I talked with Mrs. Filio today," Don told them. His eyes touched Lucy's. "She's an Irish woman, about thirty, rather pretty. She made it extremely vivid." And to Peter: "That was an outrageous thing, certainly. No possible excuse for it."

"Sure!" Peter agreed. "And it was Ong put them up to it. He ought to be hung."

Lucy asked: "What did Mrs. Filio tell you, Don?"

Don chose his words. "Well it happened Monday night, about eleven. They were all awake, because the Negroes had been shouting and making a great noise around Mr. Ong's house. Finally the Negroes came up the road to the Filio house and banged on the door. No one answered, and the Negroes fired a volley of shots into the house from the road, and from one side. Her husband fired back at them— she and her sister were loading his guns for him—and the shooting went on till the Negroes brought some hay and set fire to the house. Then Mr. Filio told her to take the children and escape, so she and her sister got the six children out of bed and slipped out the back way. The Negroes intercepted them, and they huddled down on the ground—it made me think of a covey of quail, as she described it— and the Negroes kept firing guns over their heads. That was to scare them, I suppose. The house was on fire, and Negroes were carrying out everything they could find that they wanted. She never saw her husband again. His body was found in the ashes."

Peter said furiously: "There you are! You and your niggers! I'd like to kill the last one of 'em myself."

"The white people in St. Bernard feel as you do, Peter," Don agreed. "At least, they killed twenty-five or thirty Negroes—possibly not the same ones, but Negroes anyway—yesterday and today."

"I wish they'd killed them all!"

After that day, St. Bernard was quiet, but in Jefferson, and in New Orleans itself, there were many murders. In an attempt to bring the city under control, General Steedman was appointed Superintendent of the Metropolitan Police. He resigned the next day, reconsidered his resignation the day after, then resigned again, insisting that he was not needed, that good order prevailed throughout the city. Trav, struck by this remark, tallied the newspaper reports. A man had been shot on Sunday, three men shot and a ten-year-old boy killed with a club on Monday, three shot on Tuesday, and another on Wednesday. The *Times* Friday morning listed a Negro wounded, a Negro stabbed to death, an unknown Negro found dead on Rampart Street, one killed on Dauphine Street, and another at the corner of Bourbon and St. Ann.

But now, it was true, the streets were empty; the Negroes had disappeared. Trav imagined them, thousands and thousands of them, huddled in closed and shuttered rooms like frightened animals in their dens, whispering their fears in trembling tones.

Saturday morning, he found on his breakfast table a handbill signed "Council of Seven." He read it with a sort of wonder.

A WHITE MAN'S GOVERNMENT, OR NO GOVERNMENT

The hand of the oppressor bears heavily upon us! Let the Caucasian arise in his strength! Too long have we lain supine! Assert at once, and in unmistakeable accents, your supremacy! This is a government of white men, for white men, and by white men. Let white men vote solidly for their rights, and allow nothing to prevent the triumph of their principles! We have the means, and let us use them effectively.

It is full time that our strength was felt! None but the blue-blooded should vote. See to it, you whose very existence is at stake, that none others do. In order to carry out the designs of the party, the council orders that the independent clubs station a company at and about each polling place for the accomplishment of our purpose.

When Peter appeared, Trav asked: "Know anything about this, son?"

Peter nodded. He was completely recovered from his wound. "They were posting them up all over everywhere last night. I thought you'd like to see one."

"I wonder how many Republicans will stay away from the polls because of this."

"They needn't be afraid. We'll furnish escorts, guarantee their safety."

Trav said drily: "Fair enough, I'm sure." He opened the *Picayune*. The circular signed by the "Council of Seven" had provoked the editor to an explosion.

We print below a document that bears forgery on its very face. It is hardly necessary for the democracy of Louisiana to repudiate the thing utterly, for any man not a natural-born fool or a crazed fanatic must know that it is a trick, a very vile and dirty trick, of the enemy. It could emanate only from the radical party—the party which, while professing to work "in the interest of God and humanity," attains and retains power by undisguised fraud, wholesale corruption and vilification, and by repudiation of oaths and solemn compacts. The thing is worthy of such a party, and the scalawag or carpetbagger who concocted it is no doubt an old expert at such electioneering frauds.

There was more, but Trav read no further. Surely, politics was a madness as infectious as war!

For these last two or three days before the election, the campaign, no longer a matter of clubs and guns, entered a documentary phase. Stephen Packard, as head of the Republican State Committee, issued a circular deploring the violence of the last few weeks, and the circular concluded:

> By outrages, assassinations and murders, the Democratic party has inaugurated a reign of terror in nearly every parish of this State. In many parishes, and perhaps in this city, it will be exposure to outrage and slaughter for Republicans to attempt to vote. But it should be remembered that the Republican party can lose many votes and still triumphantly carry the State; therefore this committee calls upon all Republicans to do their duty manfully. It urges them not to be intimidated, and not to yield to threats of violence, but to go peaceably to the polls on election day and vote as their consciences shall dictate.
>
> If violence shall be used to prevent Republicans from voting as they choose, let the facts be immediately and carefully reported to this committee.

The tone of Mr. Packard's circular seemed to Trav eloquent of surrender, and Monday the *Republican* openly advised this.

TO THE COLORED PEOPLE OF NEW ORLEANS:

Tomorrow is the day of election. You have a right to vote. It is for you to determine whether you can safely attempt to exercise that right.

If you do attempt it, let us advise you that only in so attempting should you appear upon the streets. If you conclude not to attempt it, do not leave your homes.

When on the morning of election day Trav walked down to the polling place, he saw no Negroes along the way, but at the polls a white man escorted two and presented them to the judges. To each one the judges gave a slip of paper, and at Trav's question, the judge showed him a pad of printed slips.

"They're protection papers," he explained. "Any nigra who can show one is safe anywhere—and he gets first chance at jobs."

Trav read the topmost slip on the pad.

Protection Paper

November 3, 1868.

STATE OF LOUISIANA; Parish of Orleans:

This is to certify that ——————————, at the presidential election of this date, did vote the democratic ticket.

——————————
Judge.

"How's the vote?" Trav asked.

"Only four Grant tickets, up to now."

Trav had expected that Grant would run well behind his opponent in New Orleans, but he was surprised at this small figure. "How many for Seymour?"

"Something over three hundred."

Trav moved on, sure that there was some mistake. Not till next morning, when the *Picayune* published complete returns from every precinct in the city, did he appreciate the almost ludicrous proportions of the Democratic victory.

His eyes at first ran along the columns without full comprehension.

FIRST WARD

	1st Precinct			2nd Precinct		
	Poll 1	Poll 2	Poll 3	Poll 1	Poll 2	Poll 3
Democrat	407	403	303	308	305	291
Republican	7	8	7	4	2	6

Below were set the totals:

FIRST WARD

Democratic vote,	2017
Republican vote,	34
Democratic Majority	1983

Trav found pencil and paper and began to copy off totals. Lucy, joining him at the breakfast table, asked:

"Whatever are you mumbling about, Papa?"

"Casting up the Republican vote in New Orleans." He went on, studying the returns, adding the columns aloud: "Two-seventeen. Two twenty-six. Only nine votes in the whole ninth ward. Two fifty-six, fifty-nine. Two sixty-nine, two-seventy." He looked across at her, his eyes blank with incredulity. "Why, Lucy, if this is right, there were only two hundred and seventy Republican votes cast in all New Orleans. Last April, twelve or thirteen thousand Republicans voted here." He shook his head. "An awful lot of voters were scared away."

"Was it the killing?"

"The killing, yes. The threats made some difference, but it was the murders that scared them off. Not even the white Republicans dared vote; at least, not many of them."

They were silent a while, Trav busy with breakfast and the paper, Lucy pretending to eat. She said at last: "Don gets his discharge the end of January, Papa. We'd like to be married early in March."

He looked at her in quiet understanding, said regretfully: "I don't think you'll be sorry to go."

Her eyes filled with tears. "I can't help it, Papa. I hate all this so."

8

IN ALL NEW ORLEANS, only two hundred and seventy men had dared to vote for Grant; that fact alone was sufficient testimony to the effectiveness of the campaign of murder, but as election returns came in from the rest of the state, the testimony was confirmed. In the parishes which had been the scene of many killings, there was a tremendous shrinkage in the Republican totals. In Claiborne Parish, only two Republican votes were cast; in Bossier none, one in Caddo, and in De Soto none. St. Landry and St. Bernard were equally conspicuous. In nine parishes of the state, parishes which in the April election reported almost nine thousand Republican votes, only five individuals now in November had dared cast Republican ballots.

When the full returns were in, Trav calculated that for the whole United States, a majority of all white Americans had voted for Seymour, but half a million Negro votes gave Grant the victory; this in spite of the fact that in Louisiana, the bullet, the knife, the club and the cowhide had kept twenty-five or thirty thousand Republicans, white or black, from the polls. But Trav thought there was little in this record of which a Louisiana man could be justly proud.

He went one day to call upon the Governor, to seek his opinions of the election result and of the general situation. Warmoth's manner and his words were sympathetic.

"I know you have the welfare of the South at heart, Major Currain," he said. "So you must regret as sincerely as I do the conduct of Southern Democrats during the campaign. It has cost you many friends in the North, and of course when General Grant becomes President, he is not likely to go out of his way to deal kindly with Louisiana."

"I suppose not," Trav agreed, half resenting the unctuous sympathy in the other's tone.

"So we must expect to face an enemy in the White House," Warmoth continued, and he said dolefully: "I'm sorry for that, because we'll need a friend there. The Legislature here is on the road to many excesses, and I cannot hold back the tide alone. I've tried to enlist the support of such men as yourself; General Taylor, Doctor Mercer, Mr. Kenner, Judge Morgan, Admiral Semmes. For if I am to stand between the people of Louisiana and this Legislature, I shall need all the allies I can find."

He paused, as though for Trav's comment, but since Trav only nodded, he went on. "It's a pity that General Grant will inevitably look upon the Democrats of Louisiana with an unfriendly eye. To make an enemy of him was completely useless, a gratuitous insult. There was never any chance of his defeat in the nation as a whole, so Louisiana has needlessly offended one who might have been a powerful friend. Violence may frighten voters from the polls, Major Currain, but it wins no friends. I had hoped that the best men in the state would reprehend and condemn this campaign of murder; but no. It's true they have expressed sympathy with the murdered Negroes, but always with a qualification. 'We're sorry for them, but they should not have listened to the Radical orators, should not have allowed themselves to be led astray.' " Anger crept into his tones. "No matter how little sympathy the victim commands, Mr. Currain, the murderer wears the mark of Cain upon his brow, and is damned by every honorable man."

This was profoundly true, but Trav was past the age when he could be as sure of anything as the Governor professed to be. Warmoth had the confident certainty of youth, which has not yet discovered the hazards in the way. Yet certainly he was right in saying the South had harmed itself, and when through November and December more murders and floggings were reported, Trav's anger grew. In mid-November, Don spoke of a whipping which had occurred the preceding Saturday night in Claiborne Parish.

"A Dutchman," he said. "His name is August Teutsch."

"Politics?"

"Yes. Yes, his was one of the two Republican votes cast in the parish. He'd been warned, but he voted Republican anyway, and Saturday night, a crowd of men supposed to be from Sparta took him out of his shop and gave him several hundred lashes."

"Several hundred!"

"They used switches, didn't break the skin, just stung and cut him. The Bureau agent there says he's a phlegmatic individual. The floggers told him they'd kill him unless he left the parish, but he says he's going to stay."

Trav, after a moment, asked: "Don, how long do you suppose this will go on?"

"I don't know. I used to get pretty mad over these things." Don's tone was surprisingly gentle. "But I don't, now. It just seems pitiful and sad that grown men should behave as they do." And, after a moment: "Your people down here are so terribly ignorant. They don't even know enough to keep clean, to keep healthy, to live decently! Poor Teutsch, in his stolid way, went through his whipping without taking any real harm—but it harmed the men who did it, debased them, pushed them a little farther down the scale. Where men lead bestial lives, they become beasts." There was profound sadness in his tones. "They think this election was a victory, but it was a battle better lost than won."

Don and Lucy would be married early in March, and before November ended there was a seamstress in the house almost every day, and through December there was a party somewhere almost every night. Once, at the Pierces', dancing with Elon, thinking how much she liked him, Lucy lost herself in her own reflections, till he saw her abstraction and asked a question, and she said:

"Why, I was just thinking, you're sort of different."

He laughed quickly. "Good or bad, Lucy?"

"I mean, you're not always saying pretty things, paying little compliments, the way most men do. Not to me, anyway!" She smiled. "You're getting to be a regular glum old bachelor!"

He threw back his head in hilarious mirth. "I don't feel glum," he assured her.

She frowned at her own thoughts: "You do say pretty things to the others," she decided. "I remember, now. To Sally and Miriam and all of them. It's just that you don't to me." Her eyes met his, and for a long time neither spoke, gravely following the pattern of the dance, their eyes holding.

He smiled at last. "Sorry! I'll try to do better. You're looking charming tonight, Miss Currain." And since she did not smile he added: "There, that was clumsy! I should have said either that you looked beautiful or that you were charming! Shouldn't I? You should have taken me in hand long ago, Lucy. I need training."

Her eyes were steady in his, and she nodded as though assenting to what he had not said. "I know," she agreed. "I know these easy compliments don't mean anything. It's the silences that are eloquent."

He said gently: "Let's be eloquently silent, Lucy. Shall we?"

"I'm truly sorry, Elon," she said. "Yet I'm proud that this is true, between us; yes, and glad, too." And she said: "There's only one man— one young man—who means more to me than you."

"There's no man whom I hold higher in affection and esteem than Don."

Lucy, remembering this conversation next day, trying on her newest gown, revolving before the full length mirror under Enid's approving eye, cried in sudden happiness: "It's beautiful, Mama! Oh, I can hardly believe it's really happening, and to me!"

Enid laughed fondly. "Neither can I, Honey. I thought for a while Tommy might win you over, and I had hopes of Elon, too. But Don's all right, even if he is a Yankee!"

"I think so," Lucy happily agreed. "I think so too."

Trav, when he came home from the mill, sometimes joined them, to share their happiness and to admire each new gown. "But we'll only buy the really necessary things, Papa," Lucy promised him, one day. "I know we have to be careful."

Trav said laughingly: "Don't worry, Honey. If we run short, you can buy a ticket in the lottery." This institution, authorized last summer, would soon begin operations.

Lucy tossed her head. "Why should I? I've everything, already. What is there left for me to win?"

She and Enid were so absorbed that Trav and Don had hours together. The life of the Freedmen's Bureau would end by statute on the first of January, and one night Trav asked: "Don, are you satisfied that the Bureau did good work?" He added: "I know they did some good, but I mean—as a whole?"

Don considered before answering. "I don't know," he admitted. "Yet I'm sorry the Bureau is being allowed to die. The Negroes need to learn so many things, and they can't just pick that knowledge out of the air."

"I'm not sure we white men haven't more to learn than the Negroes."

"Education was the Bureau's big opportunity," Don reflected. "We ought to have helped the North see the virtues of the South, and we ought to have taught the South some of the good things about the North." He hesitated. "Why, Major, the Bureau could have helped us all forget the War, helped us begin to be friends again, taught us to respect and admire and—well, to love each other." Profound sadness colored his tone. "But a lot of our agents hated the South—probably because they were injuring her—and they taught the South to hate us. So the Bureau, in one way at least, did harm instead of good."

Trav nodded. "Yet it may have been too soon to do good."

Lucy had decided to be married at home, and except for kinfolk, the guests would be few. Don's father and mother could not make the long journey from Maine, but Lucy and Enid wrote hopeful invitations to them and to the Plains and Richmond and Great Oak. A fortnight before the wedding, Enid had a letter from Dolly, and in an ecstasy of excitement she met Trav with the news when he came home.

"And what do you think?" she cried. "She and Captain Pew are married! I'll read you what she says." And she began:

> Dearest Enid:
>
> Look, quick, at the signature at the end of this! Yes, it's perfectly true! Mrs. Percival Pew! Percy and I were married yesterday! I never knew his name was Percival till now! I always called him "Captain," or little names I made up, to tease him or to please him. He says he likes being married; at least, so far. Of course, I'm triumphant, because he's always said he never would, even at the first, when I thought he'd have to, and told him so, but he wouldn't, so I had to marry poor Bruce, or at least I thought I did. Poor Bruce! He was sweet, really.
>
> And now we're coming back to New Orleans. After that night when Papa lost every cent he had in the world, I had hysterics or something, and we just packed up and started for Paris, and we've been here ever since; but I'm all rested up now. We're sailing for New York next week, and then Charleston, and the rest of the way on one of Percy's boats. (He says if I ever call him Percy he'll leave me, so don't tell him I told you.) He has three, you know, real beauties, blockade runners that he bought cheap when the War ended. We'll be in New Orleans the end of the month probably.

Enid folded the letter. "The rest is just talk! Oh, she says Captain Pew has stopped dyeing his hair, so now he's gray. I expect he's handsomer than ever! But anyway, Trav, they'll be here for the wedding, and I want to invite them—and so does Lucy! Now that they're properly married, I know you won't mind!"

He smiled. "Not if Lucy wants them. I told her she could have everything she wants."

"And may I ask Tony?"

"Yes, of course." He chuckled. "Why not ask Sapphira, too? She's worth a dozen of him!"

"Well, hardly." Enid was not amused. "But Dolly—and Captain Pew!" She laughed happily. "Won't we have fun!" She came sweeping to kiss him, and she cried: "I love parties, and a wedding's the nicest party there is!"

"Captain Blackford may be here," he said. "He spoke of coming to see all the changes at the mill."

"I'll write Mrs. Blackford to come with him," she agreed, and asked, teasingly: "Any other of your old flames?" She swung her arms in a wide happy gesture. "Oh, I'd like to invite the whole world."

Brett was the first of the prospective guests to arrive, and he came a full week before the wedding. "I had some business here," he explained.

"Cinda and the children will come on together." And he told Lucy: "Tilda and Jenny want to be at the Plains to welcome you and your young man, so they're not coming. You'll probably get there before we do. Cinda says you've promised to visit with us a while."

"As long as you'll keep us," she assured him. "Except Don wants us to be in Maine by the middle of May, or the first of June, anyway."

Vesta and Rollin were coming, he said, and Julian and Ann, and Burr, but not Barbara. "Cinda professes to be glad of that," he added with a smile. "She's never liked Barbara. Burr says Mrs. Pierce isn't well, needs Barbara at home."

Brett was in high spirits, and Trav spoke of this. "So I judge South Carolina's no worse off than it was?"

"Oh, they're stealing us to death," Brett admitted. "But you get hardened to it. When I can't pay the taxes, they can have the Plains and we'll move out."

"Where to?"

Brett said cheerfully: "North, if necessary. How are your taxes here? Oh, that reminds me, General Alexander is preparing to set up a cotton oil mill in Columbia. I advised him to come see you."

"I'd be glad to see him again. Taxes are high here, too. The state tax is point-five-two-five. City and state paper is going for fifty cents on the dollar. Or less."

Brett nodded. "Legislatures are wasting money all over the country," he said. "I doubt whether even a nigra legislature can outspend some of the states up North."

"We're spending money like pouring water in the river," Trav agreed, and he smiled grimly. "Water, yes. Our latest project is to build some canals. The legislators will vote to do it, as soon as they're paid enough."

Brett nodded. "Yet some of our greatest benefits have come out of corruption, just as fine crops come out of guano. The first instinct of the dishonest politician is to spend money so he can steal some of it, but to make the spending plausible he has to invent a worthy project, and when the project is completed, it's a permanent asset—to the city, the state, the nation." He laughed. "Virtue may be admirable, but as often as not it's the unprincipled rascals who get things done."

Trav smiled with him. "I trust you're not as cynical as you sound."

They heard from somewhere upstairs Lucy's peal of laughter, and Brett shook his head. "No," he said. "No one could be cynical when there's laughter like that in the world."

In the rush of preparations, Lucy was busy every day, and Trav, seeing her so little, thought the house would be empty after she was gone. Her wedding and her departure still seemed remote and far away till Cinda and the others arrived to fill the house with voices and with laughter. Captain and Mrs. Blackford had been unable to come, but even without them there was a jolly company. Brett proposed that he and Cinda stay at the hotel, but Enid cried:

"You'll do nothing of the kind! You'll all stay right here, and we'll manage somehow! After all, no one's going to want to sleep for the next few days, or if they do they can take naps or something."

Cinda agreed with her. "Much more fun this way, and anyone's welcome to my bed any time I'm not using it."

Trav had forgotten how much he liked Vesta—she was almost as nice as Lucy—and he enjoyed listening to Brett talk with his fine sons. Julian with his single crutch was so firmly poised on one leg that you forgot the other lost at Williamsburg. Burr and Rollin seemed years older than he, though Rollin had a lively humor, and he and Vesta always appeared to be sharing a happy secret together. Trav thought Burr withdrawn and aloof, like the child in a new neighborhood, eager to join in the general fun but too shy to do so. Probably Barbara had something to do with that; she was so like her father and mother. Trav blamed himself for the thought, since Barbara's mother just now was sick, and Barbara had stayed home to tend her, but Enid told him one night after they were abed that Barbara's mother was not sick at all.

"Barbara's having a baby in July, and making an awful fuss about it," she explained. "Vesta told me. Barbara could have come perfectly well. Vesta's baby is due in August, and Anne's in September."

Trav chuckled. "So we've really quite a houseful!"

"Yes, isn't it sweet! They're the dearest young ones; Anne and Julian specially. Notice the way Anne never takes her eyes off him. I don't blame her. I'm scared to death he'll fall, any minute. She says he even rides!"

"'Course he does." Trav was half asleep.

"Burr's scarred hands give me the shivers!" In the summer of 1864, a single bullet had taken thumb and forefinger off Burr's right hand, three fingers off his left. "I don't much blame Barbara."

"Blame her for what?"

"Oh, don't you know? She makes him wear gloves in the house, when he's at home. I suppose she thinks the sight of his hands might mark the child."

Sunday, after dinner, Trav and Brett went for a stroll, and when they came home, Lucy met them at the door. Her eyes were alight with happy excitement, but she exclaimed in pretty disappointment:

"Oh, botheration! I thought surely you were Don! He's coming to supper!"

Brett drawled: "Seems to me that young fellow hangs around here a lot of the time!"

"Oh hush!" She laid her fingers on his lips. "Mama and Aunt Cinda and Julian and Anne are all resting," she told them. "Oh, and Papa, what do you think?"

"Well, now, let me see, what do I?"

"Oh, you're awful funny, I know! Stop being so funny and listen! Dolly was here this evening. They got in yesterday. And Papa, they came from Charleston in Captain Pew's schooner, the *Dragonfly II*, named after the one he used to run the blockade in, and she sails for Charleston again day after tomorrow afternoon—" They would be married day after tomorrow. "And she says we can have the cabin!" Her words came in a rush. "No one ever uses it except them! It's kept special! But she's sure we can have it, and going through Charleston's certainly the easiest way to get to Camden."

"But hardly the quickest," he suggested.

She laughed, hugging his arm. "Oh, Don and I won't be in any hurry!" Brett had gone upstairs. "Don't you think that would be wonderful? I haven't had a chance to tell Don yet, but I'm just tickled to death."

"I'm not sure I'd want to be under obligation to Captain Pew," he said, in some doubt.

"But you won't be, Papa!" She reminded him. "Don and I will, but we won't mind a bit!"

He dropped an arm around her waist. "Well, I told you you could have anything you—"

But the doorbell rang, and she cried: "There's Don!" She darted away, and as Trav climbed the stairs, his steps beat a rueful rhythm: day after tomorrow afternoon, day after tomorrow afternoon. Strange how much nearer it sounded when you said "Day after tomorrow," instead of "Next Tuesday"! And tomorrow it would be "Tomorrow," and day after tomorrow it would be "Today."

And what about the next "Tomorrow," after that, when what was now "Day after tomorrow" would be "Yesterday"? He whispered the words, to try the sound of them. "Lucy was married yesterday."

But then he heard her voice as she spoke to Don in the hall below; heard her tones like ringing bell notes of happiness, and he thought in a quiet content. "There! That's what I've always wanted for her! Thank God she has it now."

Don went next day to see Captain Pew, and for a double purpose. The Bureau, as long as it existed, had retained title to the Haunted House, and Captain Pew's New Orleans agent had paid the rent without demur. Don spoke of this.

"But the Bureau has closed, now," he explained. "And the records of the original ownership seem to have been lost or destroyed. I'm not sure what you can do—"

Captain Pew spoke with a friendly smile. "Captain," he said, and then: "Or perhaps I should call you Colonel? Any Southerner who has achieved rank above that of a private is automatically a Colonel."

Don smiled. "No sir. My name's Page. Don Page. In a couple of months from now I'll be down in Maine, and the folks will say, 'Well, I see Don's home!'"

"Well, then, Mr. Page," Pew agreed. "May I congratulate you most sincerely, sir, on your approaching marriage. I do not know your bride, though I met her while she was still a child, but your prospective father-in-law is one of the two or three most respectable gentlemen I know. You have sound reason to be happy, Mr. Page, and I'm glad you have the good sense to appreciate that fact." He looked around the small office on the street floor of the Haunted House, where he had received Don. "As for this edifice and its complications, I will handle them as best I can when the time comes."

Don hesitated. "Captain, Miss Lucy tells me that Mrs. Pew very kindly offered us passage to Charleston on your vessel."

"I know, and I am happy to second the invitation."

"Well, I hope you will forgive me, Captain." Don looked at the other in a comical confusion. "You see, sir, I'm a young man to whom money is regrettably important. I suppose the most impoverished young gentlemen are exactly those who most fiercely resent anything in the nature of a—well, let us say, a financial condescension." He colored miserably. "What I am trying to say, Captain, is that I appreciate your invitation, and am most grateful, but I ask permission to accept your kindness on a business basis."

Pew frankly laughed. "If I didn't like you so well, Mr. Page," he said, "I wouldn't say this. But that's the goddamndest piece of polite circumlocution I ever heard in my life! I gather you want to pay your way?"

Don laughed with him. "Yes," he said. "Yes; I want to pay our way."

"Delighted to have you do so," Pew assured him. "Come along, we'll go aboard her, let you have a look at your quarters. They may not be what you want at all, you know."

The *Dragonfly II* was lying to her anchor off the head of Hospital Street, receiving cargo from a barge alongside, and in response to a signal from Captain Pew—white handkerchief and red, one in each hand, in a brief wigwag—a boat put off from her and came toward them. Don was surprised that the signal was so quickly seen, and Captain Pew explained: "Cabin boy's only duty, if I'm not aboard, is to watch for me. If he misses a signal, he regrets it—with good reason."

And as they were rowed off to the ship he watched her with a fond eye. "A pretty thing," he said. Don nodded, and Pew asked: "Know anything about the sea, Mr. Page?"

"Little or nothing at first hand, but most every New Englander has some seafaring blood. My grandfather was master of a Carleton-Norwood ship, out of Rockport, Maine, before he was my age, till his father died and he came home to Montville to run the farm."

"Sail, eh? I suppose he'd scorn steam."

Don said politely: "Any man with an eye for a ship would admire this one."

"She's a pretty lady," Captain Pew agreed. They ran alongside, swung aboard, and the skipper met them at the rail. "Captain Bonaventure, this is Mr. Page," Pew explained. "Mr. and Mrs. Page will occupy the cabin as far as Charleston."

"Welcome aboard, sir," the Captain told Don. "Trust you'll be comfortable."

Their cabin was on the starboard quarter, with a wide bed and a lounge and a desk, and lockfasts and cubbies in every spare foot of space. It was floored with teak and finished in mahogany, with silvered hardware and gay curtains and upholstery. Captain Bonaventure left them there together, and the cabin boy, a wide-awake, grinning mulatto named Ginger, came to offer them refreshment. Something loosened Captain Pew's tongue, and he began to talk of the days of the blockade, of stealthy runs through a favoring fog, of desperate races to escape when everything inflammable went under the boilers, of the thump of shot and shell against the ramparts of cotton bales, of hot sweltering nights along Nassau's Bay Street, of that run from Nassau to Wilmington when half the crew came down with smallpox in a single short day, of another dreadful voyage when four men vanished one by one and were never seen again, of a lovely but foolish young lady.

"You'll understand, I never knew her name," said Captain Pew, a twinkle in his eyes. "But she stowed away on an outward voyage, in boy's clothes, and when I did the natural, she vowed I must marry her. Which I did not, to be sure, so she found another husband.

"Ah, but the glory of those days, Mr. Page, was the profits to be made. Men like Streean—did you know him? Well, no matter, he's dead, let him rest—men like Streean, yes, and many others, including me, always including me, made ourselves rich off the gaudy spendthrift folly of war."

He looked at Don with a quizzical eye. "Why am I talking so to you? Maybe it's because I was once your age, and I meant to do fine great deeds for suffering mankind. But I didn't! I tell you, Mr. Page, I can't remember anything I ever did of which I'm proud today. Man, man, never let yourself get into the fix I'm in. Money? A pretty, loving wife? Health? Anything a man can want, I've got it,—or I can have it as soon as I know I want it. You know what's wrong with me, Mr. Page? The trouble with me is, I never did any single thing as well as I could. When a man gets to be my age, and feels his muscles and his sinews stiffening, and his eyes fading, and his tongue losing it's brisk pleasing way; yes, and his mind going slack and losing its temper, and he thinks what he could have done with these members of his once upon a time and didn't! Well, there's a thought that's poor company; the thought that you never did anything in your life with all the backbreaking effort, all the sharp-witted planning, all the nimble-footed daring, all the thinking and contriving that you had in you; the thought that never once in your life did you do anything as well as you could!"

He fell silent, staring straight ahead, and abruptly he rose. "We'll go ashore," he said, and he did not speak again till they approached the levee, angling into the current to lay alongside. Then, in an easy tone: "Here we are, Mr. Page. It's a little greasy there, so mind your footing." And to Ginger at the rudder: "Watch for my signal, red handkerchief and white, tomorrow any time."

The boat pulled away, and Captain Pew looked out at the slim vessel where she rode, and Don looked sidewise at the erect, graying man beside him. "She'll be ready at your wish, Mr. Page," said Captain Pew. "After the wedding, I'll come along down ahead of you, and we'll wait on your convenience, sir."

Don thrust out his hand. "I'm more indebted to you than I can easily say."

The other returned his handclasp. "I wish I were your age, Mr. Page," he said. "I wish I were your age, and knew what I know today."

After Dolly's Sunday call, Vesta said thoughtfully to Enid: "I found I didn't hate her at all, Aunt Enid. It's awfully hard for me to hate anybody."

"Why should you?" Enid exclaimed. "Of course we all disapprove of some of the things she's done."

"Oh, but I should hate her," Vesta insisted. "It was her flirting with Mr. Eader, that time at the Plains, that got Rollin into the duel when his jaw was smashed so terribly. Rollin thought he was crazy about her, even after that, till she married Bruce Kenyon."

"I'd forgotten!" Enid confessed. "You know, I never think about Rollin's scar; so many men have scars since the War. But I remember now how mean Dolly was to him afterward, pretending she couldn't bear the sight of him."

Vesta giggled, nodding. "You know, she asked him to marry her, before she married Bruce Kenyon, and he wouldn't. I'm just spiteful enough to enjoy remembering that."

"Did she really?"

"M-hm! It was after she'd gone to Nassau with Captain Pew. What a cat I am to tell you! Poor Dolly." And she said; "All that seems like a lifetime ago, doesn't it, yet that time at the Plains was only just before the War."

"Before the War! Heavens, darling, that's ages ago! Vesta, shall I send word to Dolly not to come tonight?" There was to be a wedding supper, with everyone invited.

"Heavens, no! I want to see how she acts with Rollin!"

"So do I," Enid admitted, and she took care to be downstairs before Captain Pew and Dolly came in. She thought Captain Pew was certainly a fine-looking man, slim as a boy, and as graceful, his dark brows made conspicuous by the gray of his hair and mustache and small wisp of beard. He was wholly at ease, but Enid thought Dolly felt herself on the defensive. She was much too gay, greeting each one with effusive joy, kissing everyone alike, chattering happily. "Oh, Enid, Honey, isn't this fun? Uncle Trav, I haven't seen you in a coon's age! Uncle Brett, I just have to kiss you! Mind, Aunt Cinda? Vesta darling! Burr, you grand old thing, you, why didn't you bring Barbara? Rollin, Honey, bless your heart! Julian, hold on to me while I kiss you. Isn't he sweet, Anne! All of you—"

Peter, coming in from the hall, said boldly: "You haven't kissed me, Dolly!"

"Oh, Sugar, I didn't see you! Here's two to make up! M-mm! Isn't it fun being all together? But Enid, where's the lovely bride? And the bridegroom? I guess we are just awfully early! You'll forgive us, won't you. I jus' couldn't wait to see you all again."

The Morgans arrived together, and the Pierce girls with them. Then Lucy appeared, and then Don with two of his friends, still in uniform, who with Elon and Mr. Cist would be his groomsmen tomorrow. Elon and Eleanor came last of all. At supper there were many toasts, and dancing afterward, and since the night was warm, the dancers between numbers strolled the garden paths.

Enid moved among them in a heedless happiness. She was conscious of looking her best, in a graceful dress of pale yellow pongee. Mrs. Morgan and Cinda were elaborately gowned, their shoulders bare, their corsages pointed at the waist in front, their underskirts intricately ornamented; Mrs. Morgan was in lavender, but Cinda wore white, her heavy silk dress festooned with broad descending bands of lace, and with lace flowers across the underskirt. Enid was sure Cinda should never wear white; it made her look enormous! She thought she was herself the most becomingly dressed woman in the room, except of course Lucy, who looked like a child in a simple gown of dotted Swiss, with a black velvet ribbon outlining her square-cut bodice, girdling her slim waist and descending in a ladder of small bows to the wide hem. Once, between dances, sitting with Cinda and Mrs. Morgan, Enid was so absorbed in watching Lucy and in wishing Trav would come dance with her, that when Cinda spoke to her she did not hear. Cinda said quizzically:

"Yes, Lucy certainly is, but as I was saying—"

Enid recovered herself with a start and a quick laugh. "I'm sorry, Aunt Cinda! I wasn't listening!"

" 'Aunt Cinda' indeed! I ought to box your ears, Enid. Even if you don't look a day older than your beautiful daughter, stop calling me 'Aunt'!" And she said: "Mrs. Morgan was just telling me that Jimmy's thinking of going to Egypt, to serve in the army of the Khedive."

"Really?" Enid spoke absently to Mrs. Morgan. "I thought he was raising vegetables, somewhere near Charleston."

"He was." Mrs. Morgan smiled. "But I don't think Jimmy will ever make a farmer. Two years ago the army worms ate up his cotton, and last summer the potatoes he shipped to New York didn't pay the freight. But he's been happy in Charleston. His friend Captain Dawson edits the Charleston *News and Courier*."

"I've heard Mr. Dewain speak well of him," Enid agreed, "or at least, of his paper." She saw Brett and Trav and Judge Morgan come in from the garden and pause in the doorway. "There, I shall go command my husband to dance with me."

She moved across the floor—Rollin was dancing with Dolly, and she wondered what they were saying to each other—and came near Trav and the other gentlemen; but they were talking together and did not observe her approach, and she was suddenly and absurdly shy, reluctant to interrupt them. Then Brett saw her, and spoke to her, and Trav turned, and she felt her cheeks hot, and laughed in amused embarrassment.

"I don't know why I'm blushing," she declared. "I just came to ask my husband to dance!"

Brett and Judge Morgan smiled, and Trav said awkwardly: "Why, all right, Enid, if you can stand it."

In his arms she murmured: "You shouldn't say such things! I always love dancing with you."

"I'm no good at it."

"It doesn't matter, long as it's you." She looked up at him, laughing fondly. "Why am I suddenly so much in love with you, Trav?" Then, her eyes falling: "Never mind! Let's just dance!" Trav stumbled over her feet and apologized, and she reassured him. "I should have taken you in hand long ago, my dear." And when she saw beads form upon his brow, "There, you've done enough!" She dropped him a curtsey. "Thank you kindly, sir. Shall we walk in the cool?" She took his arm and they strolled into the garden. "Everybody's having a good time, I think. Don't you?"

"Seem to be," he assured her.

"Lucy's lovely, isn't she?"

"And she's happy," he said. "That's the thing that pleases me. She's just overflowing with it, brimming, like a full cup."

"For Don to drink," she murmured. "Lucy's going to be so good to him, Trav." Then, ruefully: "I wonder when we'll ever see them again, after tomorrow. Just think, this time tomorrow, they'll be gone."

"Before that," he reminded her. The decision to travel as far as Charleston on the *Dragonfly II* had modified the wedding plans. They must go aboard early enough so that Captain Bonaventure could take his ship far downriver before dark, ready to negotiate the passes on the morning tide; so the hour had been advanced from four o'clock to high noon.

Enid nodded. "You know, Trav, I've stopped thinking of them separately. It's no longer 'When will we see Lucy again?' Or Don. It's 'them.' "

"We may not see them for quite a while. Right now, I think Lucy will be glad to leave the South. But they'll come back, one of these days." He looked toward the house. "Should we go in?"

She drew him to her. "Kiss me first," she said, and afterward. "You're a dear man. You're a darling, Trav."

"You're mighty sweet tonight."

"Am I?" Their eyes held, in the starlight, and she laughed in a husky way and caught his hand. "Come, darling! We must go in!"

Judge and Mrs. Morgan were the first to say good night, and a little later Brett saw Cinda's head droop, and knew she was asleep in her chair; but when he accused her, she denied it.

"You've a right to be," he told her. "It's past two."

"Who cares?"

"I'd like to get out of my shoes," he confessed.

"I've had mine off for hours," she assured him. "That's one advantage of skirts."

"Maybe if I put my feet back under my chair, I can—"

"Oh, don't be so stodgy! Go dance with Dolly! She'll make you feel young again."

He did not move. "She's enjoying herself, isn't she? She's got Peter to the point where he doesn't know his head from his feet. How old is he? He can't be over eighteen."

"I think he's seventeen," she hazarded.

"He looks twenty. Or older. But I guess you're right. He can't be twenty. Lucy won't be twenty-one till September. She told me so today. Do you suppose we seemed that young, when we were that age?"

"There's Peter wanting to dance with Dolly again." She touched his arm. "Captain Pew's had enough of it! Look!" The three, Captain Pew and Peter, with Dolly between them, were together at the other end of the room, Peter flushed and insisting, Captain Pew smiling and shaking his head. A moment later, Dolly now a captive on the Captain's arm, they began to make the rounds, to say good night.

At once the others, too, began to go, till except for Don—he and Lucy had gone into the garden together—only those who were staying in the house remained. Vesta and Rollin were still dancing, and Burr and Anne. Cinda came to her feet.

"Well, a general good night to all," she said. "I've enjoyed every minute of it, Enid, Trav. Coming, Brett?"

"Let's wait and say good night to Don."

"As if he'd know the difference!"

But then Don and Lucy came in from the garden, and Lucy and Vesta and Anne went arm in arm upstairs, Enid and Cinda on their heels. Don would have said good night, but Trav proposed a nightcap, so they drank a final toast, Trav and Don and Brett and Peter. Then Don departed, and Peter went off to bed.

Brett, at the foot of the stairs, asked: "Coming, Trav?"

"I like to take a last look around. You go ahead."

When Brett was gone, Trav went into the sitting room and to his study, moving absently, surveying the general disorder. Isaiah and Daisy and old Maria would be up early in the morning setting things to rights; yes, and preparing for the wedding. Tomorrow? No, today. He looked at his watch; yes, less than nine hours from now. Probably there was much still to be done, but Enid would have planned every detail. She had been beautiful tonight, in that yellow dress. She had worn a yellow dress the day he and she were married. That was twenty-one years ago, and she was sixteen then, so she must be thirty-seven now, but she had looked no older tonight than on their wedding day. She was changed, perhaps; more beautiful, certainly, but certainly no older.

He turned out the gas, and heard Isaiah in the dining room, and went to speak to him. "I thought you'd gone to bed hours ago."

"Naw suh, us'ns set up to give some suppeh to de music." Isaiah laughed his cackling laugh. "Naw suh, wedding times ain't sleeping times. I'll tuhn out all de lights, Marste'. You go on tuh bed."

Trav stepped for a moment into the garden, and saw dawn already touching the eastern sky. It was a pity to disturb Enid. Perhaps if he were quiet, she would not wake. On the stairs he removed his shoes, and at his door he was careful to avoid any click of the latch. The door opened without a sound and he stepped in.

A candle burned on the bedside table, but the bed was empty and for a moment he thought Enid must be with Lucy. Then she came toward him from the window at one side, where she had stood half hidden in the shadows. "You've come," she said gratefully, and kissed him, holding both his arms. "I thought you'd never come!"

"I thought you'd be asleep."

"Asleep?" She laughed in warm murmur. "No."

He lifted her face, his hand under her chin. "Are you crying?"

"I suppose so."

"You're trembling. There's nothing to cry about."

"I know it." Her face pressed against him. "I know it, but my baby's getting married, and I'm so old; so old!"

He laughed, caressing her, whispering tendernesses. "Honey, you're not old. You looked just the same in your little yellow dress tonight."

"Did I? You're sweet, Trav. Come to bed."

"I'm almost too tired to take off my clothes."

She fumbled with a button. "I'll help you."

He laughed, pushing her hands away. "Stop it! You tickle! You must be cold!" She was in her nightgown. "Into bed with you."

Sitting up in bed, watching him, holding the coverlets snug under her chin, her eyes were big in the one candle's light. "What are you thinking?" he asked.

She shook her head, shivered with a long, sighing inhalation, and reached out to pluck at his arm. "Come to bed," she whispered, and more urgently: "Hurry! Hurry! Please!"

The wedding was as weddings are; the bride was beautiful, the groom was handsome, and they wore happiness like a bright robe that embraced them both. Everyone laughed and no one cried, and Cinda whispered to Brett in the confusion afterward: "Look at Enid! She looks like a bride herself!"

Brett chuckled. "There's something about weddings! I feel like a bridegroom!"

She pinched his arm. "Oh, you!"

When it was time for them to go aboard the *Dragonfly II,* carriages were ready, and they drove down to the levee. Captain Pew was there with boats to set them all aboard ship for a parting toast, and for a while the neat little vessel, decked with bunting for the occasion, swarmed with guests. The cabin was banked with flowers, their scent so heavy that Don at Lucy's direction opened the ports to let the air stir, and there was much talk and laughter, till at last Captain Pew said apologetically: "Ladies and gentlemen, I regret it, but Captain Bonaventure says his anchor's aweigh."

Then the kisses and embraces, and the handshaking, and as the boats received them the crew were at the capstan bars. Before they were halfway to shore, the *Dragonfly* was moving. She drifted, angling a little downstream, and in the boats, handkerchiefs were waved and then hastily applied to laughing, streaming eyes.

So the guests came ashore, and paid their thanks to Captain Pew, and Dolly said they must all be neighborly, and the *Dragonfly* was already far around the point and almost gone from sight. On the way back to the house, Brett and Cinda and Trav and Enid shared one carriage; Vesta and Rollin and Elon and Eleanor were in another; Julian and Anne with Burr and Peter in a third. Vesta and Rollin dropped Elon and Eleanor at their home, and when they were alone, Vesta asked:

"Rollin, was this *Dragonfly* much like the other one? The one that brought you all up to Wilmington, that time?"

"Just about," he agreed.

"It was on deck Dolly asked you to marry her, wasn't it?" He nodded, and she looked up at him. "Do you suppose she remembered?" She hugged his arm close against her side. "I bet she's awful sorry you didn't. Oh Rollin, suppose you had!" He leaned down to kiss her, and her lips met his, and then she murmured: "Heavens, look at us! Right on Hestia Street, in the light of day!"

At the big house on Prytania Street they were all reunited; but Brett and Cinda and the others were to take the night boat to Mobile, and in a flurry of packing, the hours sped. So, suddenly, they were gone, and only Peter and Trav and Enid were left in the empty house. They went early to bed, for Enid was desperately tired, and before they slept she wept again.

"Oh, Trav, I wish our little Henriette hadn't died," she confessed. "She'd be old enough now to be company for us." And after an instant: "Just think, Trav; she'd be ten!" And, weeping: "I wish we'd had dozens of babies." He drew her close to comfort her.

9

THE "DRAGONFLY II", on her way to Charleston, touched at Tampa and then at Havana, where Don and Lucy went ashore under Captain Bonaventure's jolly guidance to see the strange city. Proceeding, they called at Brunswick, and so came at last to Charleston, and said goodby to the *Dragonfly* and the good Captain.

At the Plains, Lucy found a letter from Trav, enclosing one from Don's mother. This she read to herself.

> Montville, Me; February 12, 1869
>
> Dear Daughter—
>
> I hope this will reach you on your wedding day but it is so far from here I can't be sure. It is to welcome you into our family. Don has written so much about you that we already love you very much. The winter has been a hard one, snow seven feet deep in the woods, but I don't go there.

Lucy laughed with happy tears in her eyes, and Don, watching her, demanded to know what she was laughing at, and she said: "Oh, never you mind. This is a joke between your mother and me." And she read on:

> But the crows are beginning to caw on a sunny day, and that's a sign spring is coming and even if they didn't it always has, in these parts, anyway. Crows stay with us, some, all winter. More fools they. If I had a good pair of wings I would fly away.
>
> Don says you won't get here till after mud-time. Well, that's good and I'm glad of it. It ain't fit to set your foot out of doors here after the drifts begin to shrink and the snow goes till things dry off some, and a team can drop in hub-deep any time till the honeypots get out of the roads. But after the mud comes the apple blossoms, and the new leaves on the alders and it can be real pretty then.

We'll be right glad to see you. It's a kind of an empty house with just the two of us, so come when you're ready and you'll be welcome.

With best wishes,

SARAH PAGE

Mr. Page says the same. Tell Don his Uncle Donald died.

Lucy folded the letter tenderly, her eyes shining, and Don asked, smiling: "Aren't you going to let me read it?"

"Oh yes, yes." She gave it to him and came to lean on the back of his chair, reading the letter again over his shoulder. Once or twice he chuckled, and she laughed with him, and snuffled and blew her nose to get rid of her tears. When he read the last line, he said in surprise: "Hullo! Uncle Donald!"

Struck by his tone, she looked at the letter again. "He was the one who went to California, wasn't he? The one you liked."

"M-hm!" He sat a moment silent, thinking; then asked cheerfully: "What does your father have to say?" But that first letter from Trav was brief, simply enclosing the letter from Mrs. Page, and reporting them all well and bidding Lucy and Don have a good time.

While they were still at the Plains, the newspapers reported that President Grant—he had been inaugurated on their wedding day—had appointed General Longstreet to be Surveyor of the Port of New Orleans. Lucy cried in quick gladness:

"Oh, then they'll come back to New Orleans to live! Papa'll like that!"

Brett said doubtfully: "If he's confirmed—and accepts—New Orleans Democrats will never forgive him."

Lucy did not agree. "And anyway, if they're his enemies, he ought to be proud of it! The way they treated the nigras before the election." But a letter from Trav a few days later echoed Brett's comment on the appointment.

"Though I'm not sure he'd value the good opinion of Democrats," he wrote. "And I'm not sure he should! After all, it was Democrats who killed over a thousand Republicans during last year's campaign—just because they were Republicans."

Lucy looked at Don with startled eyes, and he said mildly: "I don't think it was that many. Half that, maybe; maybe three quarters."

"Even half's horrible! Oh, Don, I'm glad we've come away from all that. Forever. Aren't you?" He only smiled.

A letter from Enid in the same mail was all superlatives, with every other word underscored, and Lucy and Don laughed over it together. "It just means she's happy," Lucy explained. "She and I got to be really good friends up here last summer. I used to fairly hate her, mostly because she was so mean to Papa, but I really love her, now."

It was mid-April before they said goodby to the Plains. At Salisbury they broke the journey and went by train and stage to Martinston. They lodged two nights there, and spent a long day in the saddle, riding along every road and trail over which they had ridden together in the past. Once she asked:

"Don, do you realize how few times we really saw each other here? Yet I knew even then that there'd never be anyone but you."

"You used to treat me like dirt!"

"I had to do something! I couldn't just throw myself into your arms, not so soon! But of course, in the end, I had to."

When they left Martinston she said: "This is my real goodby to the South, Don. This was my home, more than any other place."

Julian and Anne welcomed them to Richmond, and Burr and Barbara gave a party for them, and after a few days Rollin came up from Williamsburg and carried them away to Great Oak. There, he and Vesta proudly displayed the neat small house which they had built to replace the mansion Lucy remembered.

They stayed there till early May, and Big Mill was with them all day long, watching over Little Missy. "He's always been here on the place," Lucy explained. "Except sometimes with Papa during the War, or with us in Richmond. He was here when we came to live with Grandma, back before the War. We had lived at Chimneys, but the place here was all run down, and Papa's a wonderful farmer, so he came to bring Great Oak back into condition, and he made Big Mill the overseer here. I expect he was the first slave overseer in the whole South, so he adored the ground Papa walked on, and took care of all of us when Papa was away at the War, except sometimes he went with Papa. But after the War he came back here. He said his roots were here."

"I don't suppose he can read, or write."

"I don't suppose so, but he knows all about farming, and he never had any trouble with the hands."

"I'm not sure that reading and writing really matter," Don reflected. "Reading and writing are the easiest things to teach, so the schools all start with them." He added in some uncertainty: "But—then maybe the things that need to be learned can't be taught?"

"What sort of things, Don?"

"Well, like recognizing a responsibility and accepting it—as Big Mill did when your father made him overseer. For instance, if men took the right to vote—I don't mean Negroes; I mean all men—if they recognized it as a responsibility, and tried to vote as wisely as possible, they'd make this a different sort of country in short order."

She linked her arm in his. "But Don, dear, can anyone teach that?"

He hesitated, laughed a little. "Your father did it with one man, with Big Mill. He gave him responsibility, and Big Mill rose to it. Maybe that's the way to teach, give men responsibility and encourage them to accept it!"

She hugged his arm against her side, said fondly: "I never quite understand some of the things you say, Mr. Page, but I think you're an awfully nice man."

She asked one day, when she had been reminiscing about the life here before the War: "Does it bore you, my talking so much about us Currains and what we've been, and done?"

He shook his head. "No, nothing about you bores me." And he added, thinking aloud: "You know, marriage is a sort of revelation, isn't it? We thought we knew each other pretty well. We'd been together a lot, and we'd discussed things, and we loved each other. But we didn't really know each other at all; we just knew what everyone else knew about us! Then, all of a sudden, after you're married, you do know each other. It's like seeing the reflection on a windowpane from the outside, when all you can see is the reflection, and then suddenly you're married and the reflection is gone—the light changes, or you look at the window from a different angle, or something—and you can see everything in the room. That's getting married."

"And you can see everything that's ever going to be in the room!" she added. "I see what you mean! All of a sudden, we not only know what we're like right now; we know what we're going to be like, years and years from now!" She laughed happily. "You're going to be grand, when you're a hundred years old, Don. I'll be so proud of you!"

After their stay at Great Oak, they spent another day or two in Richmond, and before they proceeded northward, May was half gone. They stayed three days in Washington. "Everybody ought to come here once," Don told her. "And we may never have another chance." His words gave her a momentary qualm at the prospect of burying herself down in Maine, where snow lay seven feet deep in the woods; but how could she be unhappy there if she were with Don?

All the way north from Charleston, Lucy had been alert to the changes in the passing scene. They left behind the moss-hung oaks and the palmettos and for a while saw only pines, and after the pines, the scrub-oak barrens of Virginia. Yet as far as Washington it was still the South: cities and villages with wide, muddy streets; wretched little towns where the best houses needed paint and where there were more cabins and shanties than houses; sometimes at a distance a great mansion built on gracious lines.

This was the South, but when they left Washington behind and traversed the well-tilled farm lands of Maryland and Pennsylvania, Lucy was quick to mark the difference. "And it's happened in just a few miles," she said wonderingly. "Everything's so neat, and the houses are all painted, and most of them have nice lawns around them." The train passed a fine big farmhouse of red brick, backed by barns and carriage houses and storage sheds, but she saw nothing like the Negro cabins at Chimneys, and she asked: "Don, where do the hands live?"

"Honey, these farmers don't have hands, not the way you do down South. Of course, they hire some help if they need it; but mostly, a man and his sons do their own plowing and planting and cultivating, and neighbors help each other with the harvesting."

"You mean the men work in the fields themselves? The ones who own these farms?" He nodded, and she said, eyes wide with wonder: "I remember some of our neighbors at Chimneys used to do their own work, even sometimes when they owned a nigra, but Mama called them trash."

She marked their northern progress by the blossoms. As far as Washington, not only dogwood and redbud and catalpa and the early fruits, but also apple trees were in full bloom or past it, but as they went on through Maryland and Pennsylvania and New Jersey they saw an occasional orchard showing little or no bloom. When she spoke of this, Don said: "Yes, we're outrunning spring, leaving it behind. Our apple trees at home won't blossom for another week or two."

They stayed only one night in New York, were glad to leave it behind. In Connecticut there were more hills, and more forests, and the houses on the farms were smaller. "But they're all fresh painted," she marveled. "And they're so neat! Even the back yards! Around Chimneys, and at Great Oak too, there was always a lot of litter. The trash gang—the old people, and the children—they were supposed to keep things clean, but all they did, really, was to rake the driveway every time a carriage drove over it, or a horse left marks."

"Maybe it's the weather," Don suggested. "Down South, you don't usually have any snow, so the trash accumulates gradually and you don't notice it. But up North, when the snow goes off in the spring, all of a sudden people realize the yard's a mess, so it gets a good cleaning."

When they took the train north from Boston and were settled in their seats, Don said: "Well, we're almost home. I wrote Pop to meet us at Benton Station. We'll be there this afternoon." He smiled. "We don't call it 'evening' here."

"Is Benton where you live?"

"No; no our farm's in Montville, on the east side of Frye Mountain, about thirty miles from Benton. We'll stop the night at Albion, stay with my Uncle Josh."

She pressed close beside him. "Will they like me?"

He held her hand. "Don't you worry, Honey. They'll be a lot more scared of you than you are of them."

"Will your father come in a carriage? I wish I hadn't so many trunks and boxes and things."

"In the buckboard, likely," Don replied. "It'll carry quite a load. Maybe Uncle Josh will come over with his wagon too." He looked down at her, smiling in reasurrance. "I told Pa it would be quite a job, getting you and all your gear to the farm, but I said you'd be worth it."

"I'll try to be." And suddenly, laughing, lifting her chin, tossing her head: "Yes, and I will be, too!"

Through that long day, she never wearied of watching the passing panorama of this new land that now would be her home. There was a frightening strangeness in the very look of it. Once Don pointed to a white patch on the shoulder of a distant mountain and told her it was snow. The sun shone brightly, but by and by, whenever they stopped at a station and someone opened the door, a gust of crisp cool air swept through the coach and made her shiver. Also, the train captain, and the passengers whom she occasionally overheard, spoke in nasal accents curiously clipped and slurred. She remembered that at first Don's way of talking had seemed to her remarkable, but now she did not notice it, and probably she would become accustomed to these others.

They had occasional glimpses of a bright and gleaming river, the water dark and clear like the mountain streams around Chimneys, and the river was full of logs on which, balancing themselves with long poles, men leaped and walked and ran. Don told her these men had spent the winter in the woods, felling trees and cutting them into convenient lengths, and hauling them to the frozen river, to be herded downstream like a flock of sheep now when the ice had gone out on the lifting bosom of spring floods. And once he pointed to substantial brick buildings, set among trees between the railroad and the river, and told her it was Colby University. "They called it Waterville College when I went there for a few terms, before the War," he said. "But they changed the name here two years ago."

Then the train crossed the river on an alarming bridge, and a little later, its bell clanging, it trundled to a stop. Lucy heard a great ringing in her ears, and her heart was shaking her, and Don said, rising, his eyes meeting hers, each of them a little frightened:

"Well, Honey, we're here!"

They came out of the coach into air so cold that Lucy was not sure whether her teeth chattered from nervousness or from the chill. A tall man in a great fur-collared coat, and wearing felt boots and buckled rubbers, came gravely toward them, his head a little bowed, looking at her sidewise, extending his hand to Don.

"Well, you're home, son. This Lucy?"

"This is her." Don's tone was proud, and Lucy tried to look nice enough to deserve his pride. Her hand was lost in Pa's, and his was like a Negro's hand, so hard and calloused. But at least his clasp was reassuringly warm, and he looked from her to Don and back again, and said calmly:

"Well, ma'am, I sh'd judge you've got him gentled some." She saw a far twinkle in his eye, and from that moment on she always loved him.

Uncle Josh, as Don had thought he might be, was here with his wagon. Pa—Lucy would never think of Don's father by any other name —Pa turned and called: "Josh!" His brother came shyly toward them, and Pa said: "This is her, Josh. This is Don's Uncle Josh, ma'am."

Josh muttered: "Pleased to meet yuh!" He took her hand so gingerly and dropped it so quickly that Lucy thought it must be hot. Then the men loaded her luggage and Don's into Uncle Josh's wagon, and then, to her dismay, Don said he would ride with Uncle Josh and she could go ahead with Pa in the buckboard. Pa had brought Ma's buffalo coat for Lucy to wear, and in the buckboard there was a box lined with an old buffalo robe and with a stone jug full of hot water to keep it warm. Into this box she put her feet, and Don tucked the robe around her knees.

"There you are!" he said, so cheerfully she wanted to cry. "See you at Uncle Josh's."

Pa clucked his horses into a trot—to her surprise they were a good pair, well-matched, needing no urging—and they left Don behind. She wondered what she could talk about to Pa, but at first she was too cold to talk. The trotters, after a short climb, turned down a gentle grade and struck so swift a gait that the cold wind on her cheek bones made her forehead ache, as though she had been eating an ice too fast, but after a mile or two her blood was running like wine. They clattered across a bridge and she spoke for the first time.

"Is this the same river? It doesn't look as big."

It was as though she had pulled the cork out of a tipped jug. Pa told her this was the Sebasticook stream. " 'T'other was the Kennebec." And he told her both rivers came down out of the Northern forests to meet here and, as one, race on to the sea. "Carry a heavy freight of lumber, every year, the both of them," he said. "As you c'n plainly see." Once loosed, his tongue did not pause. He seemed to know everyone who lived along the road, their names, and who they married, and how many children they had, and whether their farms were well handled, and where they marketed the crops they made. He spoke slowly, and she was fascinated by the tones of his voice, by the structure of his sentences.

Uncle Josh's farm lay half a mile beyond Albion Village, and his hospitable wife and daughters came out to give Lucy welcome. By the time Uncle Josh and Don arrived, Aunt Missy and Ruthie and the older sister, Betty, the homely one, had things ready to put on the table, but Pa went to help Josh with the milking, and supper had to wait till they returned.

This was Saturday, and Don had told Lucy what to expect for supper. Uncle Josh filled her plate half full of baked beans, and added a big spoonful of salt pork cooked to a jelly, and a thick slice of steaming brown bread, and Pa advised her on how to proceed. "You spread the salt pork on your brown bread. Go ahead! Don't wait for the rest of us. Like this." He took her knife to show her, and the pork spread as easily as soft butter. "Now me, I pile the beans on top of the brown bread, and put some sugar and some vinegar on them, and—"

"Well now, she won't," said Aunt Missy firmly. "Or anyway, not till she's tried some of my tomato ketchup. Betty, pass her the mustard pickle, too, and she'll want some wild grape jelly for the hot biscuits. And there's some mince pie coming, made out of venison from one of the deer Josh killed last fall, with hard sauce, if you like it that way. I put a little rum in it, too. They say champagne's better, but that I never tried. There, ain't that a nice flavor?" Lucy had just lifted the first beans, well seasoned with Aunt Missy's ketchup, to her mouth. "My ketchup suits most folks right down to the ground!"

Lucy was hungry and her healthy young appetite delighted them. When she took another serving of beans and brown bread and this time tried sugar and vinegar, Pa watched for her approval, and she declared they were so good that way and also so good with ketchup that she couldn't tell which she liked better.

No one except Pa and Aunt Missy did much talking during that meal. They ate in silence, and Aunt Missy, the last to finish, moving a half slice of brown bread around and around in her plate to absorb the last trace of the famous ketchup, said comfortably: " 'Clean your plate. Wear it out. Make it do! Do without!' That was the way I was brought up, and my father before me. My mother was always kind of picky. If she didn't want it, she wouldn't eat it. Pa always said she was a wasteful woman, but she was so cute and pretty it kind of tickled him. Ruthie takes after her, but she don't leave anything on her plate long as she eats at my table!"

Ruthie giggled and protested: "Oh, Ma!"

"Well it's true," Aunt Missy insisted. She leaned back in her chair and sighed contentedly. "Well there, I guess I'll do. I've talked my share, too. Josh always says, let me get started and no one else can get a word in edgewise." She laughed at a sudden memory. "Our old stove has a wobbly leg, and one night I was frying buckwheat cakes and talking a blue streak and that stove leg come loose and the whole stove dropped down at that corner, and since then Josh is forever telling about the time I talked the legs off the stove!" And, without a pause: "Well, there, now I guess you young ones can fetch the pie. I been on my feet so much today my ears are droopin'."

The mince pie was delicious. Afterward Ruthie and Betty did the dishes, whispering and giggling in the kitchen. Then they all sat in the dining room listening to Aunt Missy till Pa and Uncle Josh began to yawn, and Don remembered that he and Lucy had had a long day, and Aunt Missy lighted the lamp and led them to the guest room, and told them who had made the piecework quilt, and who made the feather bed, and who had died in the big bed and who had been born in it. Lucy did her best to seem interested, and Aunt Missy said good night and left them, and Don with a fine proud grin swept Lucy up in his arms and whirled her around and around and tossed her at last upon the bed and sat down beside her and told her how wonderful she was.

"But why?" she begged. "What did I do, Don? Just sat like a bump on a log—and ate like an alligator!"

"You didn't try to tell them anything!" he explained. "You liked them, and you liked the supper, and they just loved you, and so do I."

"Aunt Missy's wonderful, isn't she? And Ruthie's beautiful! Why isn't she married? How old is she?"

"Well, Ruthie's older than I am, but she's always said she never would marry unless Betty was married first. Betty's the oldest, but nobody has ever asked her."

"She's sort of—forbidding, isn't she. Just sits there with that patient little smile and never says a word. Patient people make me uncomfortable. I always think they're being patient with me!"

When Don woke her in the morning, the sun had not yet risen; but he was fully dressed, and she saw this and sat up in dismay. "Is anything wrong?"

He laughed and kissed her. "No, sleepyhead, but we've all had breakfast, and we'll be starting soon. Pa and I are doing the milking, and Uncle Josh has gone ahead with the wagon."

She sat up, reaching for her stockings. "Oh, Don, you should have waked me! What will they think of me?"

"They think you're wonderful! Come down when you're ready."

It was a little after five o'clock when they took the road. Aunt Missy went with them to ride back with Uncle Josh, and she sat in front with Pa, Don and Lucy, well wrapped in buffalo robes, behind. As the horses went into their reaching trot, Don remarked: "Good going team you've got here, Pa," and Lucy smiled to hear his tongue so quickly fall into old habits of speech.

The road dipped and climbed as they crossed the long ridges running almost due north and south which washboard that part of Maine, and

Lucy filled her eyes with the pale new beauty of spring that played along the hills. Aunt Missy, turning half around to face them, told Don everything that had happened in the three years since his last home coming, and he asked many questions, pausing now and then to explain to Lucy who this one was, and that one, and Lucy smiled and nodded, saying: "Oh yes." "I see." "Oh, I see!" "Yes, I see."

From the crest of each ridge they crossed, Don made her look back to the west and north, where the blue profiles of distant mountains showed themselves above the nearer hills. She thought Freedom a strange name for a town, and Don told her there were others hereabouts with names just as strange.

"Liberty, and Union, and Unity, and Fraternity, and Hope, and Friendship, and Harmony, and probably more, if I could think of them," he said. "The people who came in here to settle liked to feel they had friends around them. That was during the Revolutionary War and afterward, when people began to work up the George's River and branch out on either side. Pa's farm is at the head of one branch of the George's, the Centre Montville stream. It meets the outlet of George's Lake in Fraternity. We'll catch some trout in that brook this summer." He drew a deep breath, holding fast her hand under the robe. "There are a million things I want to show you. 'Montville' means the village of the mountains, but folks around here mostly just call them the Montville hills. Except Frye Mountain. That's the highest one." And as they climbed the steep grade east of Knox and reached the crest: "There, that's Frye Mountain, off to the right, the one with the notch in the trees." And he made her look eastward to the blue gleam that marked the upper reaches of the Bay.

She thought, presently, that they had passed Frye Mountain, and he said: "Yes, we have. We come back to it at an angle." And a little later: "Here's the turn!" And then: "It's about two miles more." And when the road crossed a trickling brook: "Now another mile!"

She squeezed his hand. "You're eager to get there, aren't you?"

He nodded, grinning. "Ma'll have another breakfast ready."

They passed well-tended farms. The fields to the left of the road and on the lower slope of the mountain to the right were plowed and harrowed, ready for seeding. "Why did they build their fences of rocks, instead of stumps, or rails, or poles?" Lucy asked, and he said they had to move the rocks anyway, to clear the land for the plow, so the stone walls were almost an accident.

"And they last forever," he assured her. "Because stones breed, you know. A lot of young ones are born every winter. We find them trying to tunnel into the ground, every spring, when the snow melts away; trying to hide and not able to get deep enough."

She laughed and slipped her hand through his arm. "You can't tease me!" she assured him. "I'm not as innocent as all that. Stones don't breed! I know how—things are born!" He looked down and pressed her hand hard and happily.

"Now it's the next house," he said, and Lucy's pulse began a steady pound, till presently she saw through the young leaves of the maples that lined the road, the white painted end of the house, the windows like eyes watching their approach. A moment later she could see the whole house, two stories high, with a huge four-square chimney in the center; and beyond, rising even higher than the rooftree of the house, the great barn, and apple trees in orderly rows, faintly touched with bloom, extending up the slope behind.

They turned into the farmyard, and Don cried: "There's Ma!" Lucy saw a plump little woman, brown-haired and pink-cheeked, her hands rolled in her apron, coming toward them from the kitchen porch. Before Pa drew the horses to a stop, Don jumped out of the buckboard and ran to meet her. Then Pa helped Lucy down, and she went uncertainly toward them, smiling at their happiness, and Ma looked past Don's shoulder and saw her and came to her and said, as gently as though she guessed how frightened Lucy was:

"Welcome home, dear."

Then they were in each other's arms.

There were letters waiting for them, two from Trav, and one from Enid and one from Eleanor Villard. "If I hadn't been such a coward," said Eleanor, "I'd have married Joshua the same day you married Don, and we could have had a double wedding. Wouldn't that have been fun? Now Joshua thinks we'd better wait till fall. These Yankees of ours are certainly slow, aren't they. But they're worth waiting for, I suppose, and anyway I can't argue with Joshua. I run out of breath. But I'll get him! Wait and see!"

There was more, which Lucy read with smiling eyes. She had read Eleanor's letter first because it was the shortest, and Enid's was not much longer. Papa was fine, Enid said; he was working hard every day at the mill. General Longstreet was back and had come to dinner, but Mrs. Longstreet might not come till next winter. Papa would always think the General could do no wrong; as for her, she was tempted to show him the door! She had no use for Republicans! Papa said the General and Governor Warmoth were good friends. The very idea!

Trav's letters through the months that followed were as often as not preoccupied with things Lucy cared little or nothing about, but she read them greedily. It was as though she heard his voice saying things instead of writing them. They came irregularly, written—as he once explained— just when he felt like talking to her and had the time to do it. "And of course I write to Don as much as to you," he assured them. "That's why I write so much politics, Lucy. Mind?"

Of the two letters which awaited them in the big house under Frye Mountain, one had been written in mid-April. Trav spoke of the confirmation of General Longstreet's appointment.

> The Senate debated it for hours. Senator Kellogg spoke for him, of course. The General will be high up in Republican circles here. Governor Warmoth is collecting a lot of power into his own hands. I suppose he feels better qualified to use it than the Legislature. Certainly I'd rather trust him. I believe he's a well-intentioned man, though probably ready to butter his own bread. The Legislature passed Senator Pinchback's civil rights bill, but I don't think any negroes will try to force themselves in where they're not wanted. They passed a bill to turn over all the slaughtering business to one company. I expect a lot of Assemblymen collected bribe money out of that.

General Longstreet had not then returned to New Orleans, he said, but in his second letter, Trav spoke of the General's presence there.

> And President Grant has made some other appointments here, and will make more. He appointed James Casey, his brother-in-law, to be Collector of Customs. Lieutenant Governor Dunn and Steve Packard tried to prevent Casey's being confirmed, and Longstreet says Governor Warmoth made a lot of enemies among the Republicans by favoring Casey. Warmoth vetoed thirty-nine bills the Legislature had passed. I'm on his side. Mr. Packard's appointed United States Marshall.
>
> There's no family news. Peter's not much at home, and from some of the things he says, he's gambling a good deal. He must be winning, never asks for money. Don't tell Mama I'm critical of Peter. Naturally she thinks he's wonderful.

A letter written May fifteenth, and which reached them a day or two after their arrival, reported that a Congressional Committee was in New Orleans to investigate last fall's election.

> The papers still report trouble now and then. State Senator François—he's a negro—was badly beaten, cowhided and clubbed, the other day because of some testimony he gave in the investigation by our Louisiana committee here. He's not expected to live. He's suing Sheriff Fournet for assault and battery for beating him. The paper from there, the *Courier of the Teche,* writing up the beating, said Senator Francois received "the best administered and

the best deserved thrashing since Brooks thrashed Sumner." A curious comparison, surely. A hickory stick and a cowhide whip were the implements used. The Sheriff and his brother did the work. They say they were not prepared to submit to dishonor. François is a negro, of course.

Not much news here. The streetcars are being driven so fast people are complaining. General Jordan, who was Beauregard's chief of staff for a while, has sailed for Cuba to serve with the insurgents. They've organized a Southern Historical Association here, but General Longstreet wasn't invited to the meeting. Someone wrote a letter to the *Picayune* saying the city ought to stop poisoning dogs. It seems that the policemen, if they see a stray dog, throw it a poisoned sausage, but sometimes the dog doesn't eat it, and humans do, and several people have been killed that way. No sense in writing you about that, but I like writing to you, so I just write about anything at all.

In mid-June he reported that Mrs. Longstreet had borne a son. "I saw the General today," he explained. "Mrs. Longstreet is still in Lynchburg. He thinks they'll name the boy Fitz Randolph." When Lucy read this to Don, he met her eyes.

"Have you told them about us?" he asked.

"Heavens, no! I shan't, either; not for months! Why, I haven't even told Ma!"

Lucy had settled happily into the routine of the long days at the farm. Ma always made a flower garden, using a hoe or a shovel as readily as a man, and Lucy helped. When she proudly showed Don her first blister, he tried to dissuade her, but she laughed aside his protests.

She had watched Maria often enough to know something about cooking, and one Sunday she prepared for dinner three or four pans of light biscuits, each no bigger than the end of a man's thumb. Don applauded, but Pa snorted scornfully.

"Huh! Call them biscuits! They ain't bigger than a grain o' corn. A hen'd eat two at one peck."

Lucy brought a fresh batch and slid them all on his plate. "There, now butter them while they're hot!"

He picked one up and dropped it again. "Hot? They're afire!" He peered at his hand. "Don't see no blister yet, but it's a wonder. Fixing to burn me, young woman, be ye?"

There was a continual jolly warfare between these two. Pa was a blusterer, but it delighted Lucy to see how he depended on Ma. He was forever calling: "Ma, where's my—" this or that, and Ma always knew, and told him, though now and then she might speak tartly.

"If you wasn't blind as a bat, you'd see it! It's always be'n a living wonder to me you don't lose your specs on the end of your nose!"

The fine, sunny days were a long delight. They were often abed before the sun set, always awake before it rose. Lucy found the old house charming, mellowed by the years. The floors had sagged a little. Just as a used bed molds itself to the form of the sleeper, so these floors had yielded to the feet that trod them. Each room was full of small, used things which testified that here someone for a while had lived. The attic under the eaves was stacked with books, newspapers, empty boxes, broken chairs and beds, lamps without shades, stools with a rung gone, bedroom china cracked or broken, a thousand things which had been used and damaged and saved against possible future need. The litter seemed absurd until she realized that half the things in the house had been patched or mended, and not in parsimony but as a matter of fond treasuring care.

The neat small fireplaces, the woodshed piled full, the cellar and the storage bins, everything in the house was meant to be used, and suited for use. Lucy liked most of all the most-used room, the kitchen with its supplementary pantries, the well-blacked stove, the shining pewter, the barrel beside the sink into which a thin stream of water forever flowed. The water came from a spring a hundred yards up the hillside, traveling through a wooden pipe deep underground, but the little stream had dwindled to a trickle, and Don that summer dug up the old pipe and replaced it with a new one, milled to fit and bound with tin at every joint. The water would swell it tight, he told Lucy; it would last out their lifetime here.

She loved the great barn framed with square timbers ten or twelve inches on a side, the exposed faces wearing a sleek patina where cows and horses, sheep and pigs, had rubbed. She delighted in the coopering shop where on a rainy day she might sit with Pa or with Don while they put together lime casks, for which there was a greedy market in Rockland.

"My Pa taught all us boys the coopering trade," Pa explained. " 'There'll always be a market for casks and bar'ls,' he used to say. 'Farming, or keeping store, or anything else, it c'n go bad on ye, but long as you c'n make a good lime cask, there'll always be a job waitin'.' "

"I should think there'd always be farming," Lucy suggested.

"Nope! Not around here, anyways! One thing, it's hard to keep boys on the farms. This stretch along here is as good farming land as you'll find in the town o' Montville, but like as not yore son, or maybe yore grandson, will live to see the day there ain't a farmer anywhere along this road." It frightened her sometimes, this matter of fact assumption that she and Don would live out their lives here in this lonely spot.

There were no idle days, for there was always work to be done, but never too much. Lucy undertook to teach the trotters to carry a saddle, and they readily accepted first the blanket, then an oat bag half full of grain laid across their backs, and then the saddle which Pa traded from Silas Worthen over at Bean's corner. When Don at last mounted one and then the other, they made no protest, and Don bought a side saddle for Lucy, so that he and she could, after the baby came, explore for miles around.

The days grew shorter, and the evenings longer. For Lucy and Ma there was a great deal of hemming and sewing and knitting to be done. Ma knew everything that would be needed, and one day Lucy and Don drove to Belfast to make many purchases, and came home in the hour of lengthening shadows when beauty filled the land. After that day, gathered around the small table where the lamp was set, they spent long evenings, Lucy and Ma sewing while Don and Pa read. Don had warned Lucy that Pa was a life-long states' rights Democrat so though Pa might read aloud something that had displeased him, and fume and fuss and fret, the others just nodded and pretended to agree.

Trav's letters reminded them of the troubled world. The Haitian revolt was in its second year; the Mexican revolution and the Cuban insurrection went on and on. The municipal election in Washington, with Negroes voting, led to a riot and some deaths. General Longstreet as Surveyor of the Port of New Orleans was removing every Democratic office holder. The grand prize in the lottery was thirty thousand dollars. But these things were far away, making no ripple in the peace and contentment at the farm.

Enid spent that summer at the Plains, Peter and Trav staying in New Orleans. Vesta wrote that Barbara's baby was dead when it was born; she had wanted a little girl to play sister to her three sons, and this was a girl, but it was dead. "I'm awfully sorry for her," Vesta confessed. "And I feel a little guilty, because everything's so fine with us. My new son—we've named him Fauntleroy. You remember Uncle Faunt; I always loved him—was born ten days ago, and I'm already out weeding my garden! My babies never give me any trouble. Besides, being down on your hands and knees—really, your elbows and your knees, the way I always weed—is awfully comfortable."

Lucy was half minded to write Vesta her own news. "But I must tell Papa and Mama first, Don. Do you think it's too soon? I guess I'll wait a while. I like keeping it our secret, don't you?"

In mid-September, Don had a letter from the lawyer who had served as executor of Uncle Don's estate, reporting that all bills had been paid, the store sold and all assets converted into cash. Since Don was the sole heir, a draft in full settlement was enclosed. The amount was for a little more than sixty thousand dollars, but they were singularly unexcited, their thoughts otherwise absorbed. A fortnight later, a light frost killed the zinnias in Ma's flower garden, and tinted here and there a maple tree, and within a few days there was color everywhere. Lucy and Don had liked to walk up to the top of the mountain behind the house, and she suggested doing this again.

"I want to look out over all these reds and bronzes and yellows, stretching as far as I can see," she said, but Don laughed away that suggestion, reminding her that the walk would seem longer to her now. Instead, he harnessed the trotters and drove by a circuitous route to the crest directly above the house. She was silent while she filled her eyes with beauty, and at last she said: "Thank you, Don. Now we can go back to the good world. I'll never be able to even think an ugly thought again as long as I live."

In late October, Tilda wrote from Richmond that Julian and Anne had a new Anne in their family. "I came up from the Plains to be of any help I could," she explained, "and Anne says she couldn't get along without me. I wasn't very successful with my own children, but babies seem to like me, so I think I'll make them my career from now on. Who knows, maybe you'll need me some day, but I hope it's not in winter, way up there in Maine. I can't stand cold weather, never could."

A day or two later, a letter from Trav suggested that Lucy and Don might come South for Christmas. "It'll be pretty cold up there," he reminded her. "You'd better give the idea some consideration. I miss you—or maybe it's just that I'm getting lonesome without Mama. She says she'll be home next month. I may have to go up to the Plains and get her."

He said there was no particular news. The mill was increasingly efficient; they were learning all the time. Peter was as usual. "I saw Uncle Tony on the street the other day," he said. "It seems to me he's failing; at least he's losing weight." Lucy, reading, could almost hear his chuckle as he added: "A thin man always looks about half sick, to me."

Obviously, they could not go home this year, and to explain why this was so, Lucy wrote him her happy news. "And Ma says it will be right around Christmas," she explained. "Won't that be fun? A Christmas baby! Ma says it will be a boy, too. What do you think we're planning to name it? Guess?"

She wrote Enid the same day. Trav's reply came quickly, all happiness and pride, but Enid's, somewhat later, seemed to Lucy curiously stilted and restrained. "I'm happy for you, of course, my dear. I suppose I should come and be with you, but after all, you have Don—and Ma, of whom you speak so fondly—and Papa has only me! So I must go home to him."

Lucy wept over that letter. "I didn't even keep it for you to read," she told Don. "I burned it up! But I refuse to let her make me unhappy."

"You're oversensitive, Honey. I know she didn't mean to—upset you."

"Oh I suppose not," she admitted, and suddenly she clung to him. "I will be all right, won't I, Don!"

"You certainly will. You are, and you'll keep on being."

"Sometimes I'm awful scared. That's when I want my mama!"

"Suppose I write her and tell her so! She's still at the Plains, isn't she?" Lucy nodded, and he said: "She can come right along up here and be with you. I'll write her right now."

Enid's answer came in the first week of December. She could not come, she said; it was out of the question. "I don't know how anyone lives up there in the cold anyway! But you've made your bed, Lucy; you'll have to lie in it."

Over that letter, Lucy refused to shed any tears. "It's all right, Don," she said. "I don't mind, really. I'm not afraid. I'll be fine with Ma."

Christmas was a jolly time. The snow that year held off, so that before Christmas only enough had fallen to make good sleighing, and traveling was easy. They went to the party at the church, and Ma and Lucy took the occasion to consult with Granny Marriner, who would help Lucy when her time came. Granny was sure it would not now be long.

They had spent long evenings stringing ripe red cranberries and pop-corn to adorn the tree, Pa handling the popper while Ma and Lucy and Don with needles and thread raced to keep pace with him. After the party at the church, they went home and lighted the candles on the tree, to make sure they were set properly and would not start a fire, then blew them out again, and so to bed.

Next day, Don's brother Jonathan, with his wife and their two babies—the oldest was four, the youngest two—came from Fraternity, and Don's sister Eva and her husband and their three children came from Belfast, and everyone had packages to hang on the tree before sitting down to Ma's heaping dinner. Afterward there were the gifts to open, and everyone was noisy and jolly and merry as can be. When at last it was over and she and Don went up to bed, Lucy leaned on his arm, laughing at her own weariness.

"I declare, I don't know whether I can make it to the top or not," she admitted, but when he offered to carry her, she shook her head. "No, he might not like it! He doesn't know you yet, but he's used to me, so I'll carry him. But let's rest a minute."

"Three steps to go."

"Do you suppose he'll be as noisy as the children were today?"

"Noisier! But don't forget there were five of them, so you'll have to give him time."

"How funny to think he doesn't know you yet! I'll bet he loves you the minute he sees you. Now, let's try again. One step. Two! Three! There!"

A few days later, propped up in bed with a coverlet around her shoulders and a fresh-lit fire dancing on the hearth, Lucy began a letter.

Dear Mama and Papa—

It's twenty minutes to one o'clock in the morning, December 29, 1869, and I'm having my baby. Don's gone to fetch Granny Marriner. I told him not to wake Ma, because there's lots of time, so he lighted a fire in the fireplace and closed the windows tight, and I'm tucked up snug as a bug in a rug. I'll write to you just to keep myself occupied because I'm so impatient to see him I can hardly wait.

She paused, sat for a moment smiling at her thoughts. Trav had rejected her suggestion that the newcomer should be named after him, arguing that "Donald," after his father, was a good enough name for any baby, especially one with as fine a father as this one had. Since then, everyone had been somehow sure that this would be a boy. So Lucy wrote: "I'm so impatient to see him, I can hardly wait." Then she smiled and looked toward the hearth and after a moment she read what she had written and added:

That sounds sort of as if I meant I was impatient to see Don when he comes back, and I am, of course, but I mean little Donald. I—oh, wait a minute, please.
Now what was I saying. Oh yes. Oh, here's Ma.

Ma opened the door as quietly as possible and saw Lucy awake, and said brightly: "I thought I heard something. What a pretty fire! Don gone for Granny?"

Lucy nodded. "I was just writing to Papa and Mama."

"Go right ahead." Ma brought a chair near the bed. "I'll just sit here. Write all you like."

So before Don returned with Granny Marriner, Lucy wrote much more, Ma sitting fondly by, and smiling when Lucy at intervals reached out to hold tight to both her hands.

And a boy of course it was, born at first light of the new day, and since Lucy had already written them quite a long letter, it was only necessary, when she woke a little after noon, to add a careful line, and Don hurried away to get the letter into the mail.

Long before the answer came, there was a letter from Trav. He began:

Home
New Year's Day
January 1, 1870

Dear Lucy and Don:

By this time, I know your baby has come, and how happy you are. I haven't told you before, Lucy—I didn't know it myself till Mama came home from the Plains at the end of November—because I thought maybe it might upset you. But now that it's happened and now that your baby is surely here—

Well, we have a new baby too! Mama had a little girl, about breakfast time this morning, and—

Lucy had been reading the letter to herself, sitting up in the big rocker by the sunny window. Don was in the shed fitting firewood, and Ma was in the kitchen, and Lucy cried out in her excitement.

"Ma! Don! Come here quick!" And when Ma appeared in the doorway: "Mama's had a baby too!"

Ma took a deep breath. "Land o' Goshen, child, you scared me!" And then as she comprehended this news: "Had a baby, has she?" Her eyes clouded with calculation. "My land, how old is she? She must have married pretty young!"

"Oh, she did! Call Don, will you, Ma? He'll be as happy as I am!" And as Ma went to obey: "Don't tell him anything! I'll just read Papa's letter to him! You come listen and hear what he says, when he hears."

IO

ENID WAS SO PROUD of her own achievement that her first letter scarce mentioned little Donald. "We wanted to surprise you," she wrote. "And we did, didn't we! I feel so well that I'm tempted to have another, maybe two more, start a brand-new family. Papa's so pleased you wouldn't know him! He just sits and holds her and beams—until he has to call Filly to mend matters. Filly takes care of little Enid and me too. Oh, and you'd die to see Peter. He's so jealous it's funny, and simply furious at Papa and me! You'd think we'd done something indecent and shameful! And he won't even look at baby!"

Trav, when he heard their news, rejoiced with them; yet he, too, was more interested in his new daughter than in his first grandchild. Having given little Donald his due, he went on:

> As for our baby, she's as sweet as you were, Lucy, at her age, and no one could be any sweeter than that. You still are, far as that goes. If you don't believe me, ask Don!

It was so unusual for him to write thus that Lucy knew how happy he was. "Don't read beyond this star, Lucy," he warned her, and drew a huge star in the margin. "Because the rest won't interest you, but it may interest Don." Nevertheless she continued to read the letter aloud, Don listening.

> The Legislature's back in session, and the Democrats say they ought to charge admission; that if you've a strong stomach it's as good as a circus to watch the negroes try to act like legislators. I stopped in the other day to see the House of Representatives in action. You know they meet in the Hall where the massacre took place, three years ago. The building was crowded, mostly with negroes, and the negro women were selling cakes and pies and oranges and lollipops in the corridors. But in the Hall, the members seemed to be pretty well behaved. They sat at their desks in a semi-

circle around the speaker, and I'd heard so many stories about what fools they made of themselves that I was disappointed. As a matter of fact, only about a third of the representatives are negroes, and Governor Warmoth tells me there's never been a negro majority in either house. From what I saw, we need more negroes and fewer of the type of white men I heard speak. Certainly the negro members were as well behaved—and as grammatical—as the white men. Of course it's amusing—in a backhanded way—to hear money being spent by the millions of dollars by men who ten years ago were themselves property.

Algiers has been annexed and is now a part of New Orleans, so our taxes on the mill property go up again. Did I write you that Governor Warmoth tried to remove Auditor Wickliffe, accused him of extortion and corruption, had him indicted, put him out of his office, put a negro in his place? Wickliffe was acquitted of the charges and resumed office, so now the Governor's having him impeached. A very pretty quarrel between pot and kettle. May the worst man win! The Governor wants everything he sees, and he's a man of broad vision. He's trying to put through four bills—one's a new election law—and if they're passed, he'll have more power than Nero ever had. The Democrats say the election law is political murder, and the Republicans retort that the Democrats started the use of murder as a political weapon, so they shouldn't complain! A plague on both their houses, say I.

The Republicans are down on Grant's brother-law, Mr. Casey, the new Collector of Customs, because he keeps Democrats in their jobs in the Custom House. They told the President that every leading Republican in New Orleans was against Casey—and then the President produced a letter from Warmoth, praising Casey to the skies. Warmoth made some enemies out of the incident. Casey lives not far from us, on Felicity near the corner of Prytania, but I don't think we'll be congenial. There's a lot of groaning about taxes. I hear Illinois has a rate of forty-five mills. We're still way below that, but the Republicans will keep trying!

Speaking of such things, I hear there's a split between Senator Pinchback and the Governor. Pinchback announced in the Senate that he was not a Warmoth worshipper. When thieves fall out, etc., etc. But doubtless they'll be reconciled.

Don interrupted. "I thought he rather admired the Governor—and Pinchback, too."

"Oh, I expect he still does. But he's so happy about my new little sister that he's joking about things." She lifted the letter again and said in quick interest: "But here's some real news." And she read:

I suppose you've heard from Eleanor. She and Mr. Cist will be married the end of this month and then sail for Europe. Mr. Cist is going to try to open up some new markets for our oil over there. There are twenty-six mills in the United States now—or will be before the end of the year. I think the United States will export a hundred thousand dollars worth of oil next year. Maybe more. I wouldn't be surprised to see us ship ten times what we ship now.

Lucy broke off, said impatiently: "Oh, bother! Why doesn't he tell more about Eleanor, instead of his old cotton oil? That's all he says—except sending his love." She folded the letter away.

"You'll probably hear from Eleanor soon."

She nodded, but they did not hear from Eleanor till after her wedding; then the letter, begun before the wedding and finished afterward and mailed from New York just before they sailed, was richly contenting. Lucy read it aloud, and finished and said: "I wish we'd been there!" But when she saw the question in Don's eyes she added quickly: "But just for the wedding, darling! Then we'd have hurried home again."

The house, the shed, the barn; these were their winter world, bounded by frigid walls and shared by the horses and the kine, the sheep, the pigs, the chickens. When Lucy was strong again, she and Don on snowshoes explored the snow-banked fields and the forest all around, and coming back at dusk saw the house half buried in snow, golden lamp light in the windows, and Lucy cried happily: "Oh, how—" she hesitated, seeking a word; she chose to convert one to her need, an adjective from a noun. "How *home* it looks!"

Within, they were snug; with the great fire in the kitchen, airtight stoves or fireplaces in each used room, cellar and barn well stored against every need, they were safe from any harm. On fine days Don could harness the trotters to the sleigh and he and Lucy might drive for miles, or go a-visiting among their friends, or for the mail. Trav's letters were about equally concerned with the new baby and with matters political. Little Enid attended strictly to her own affairs, but Trav found them engrossing, and he reported when her eyes began to focus, and how much she gained, and how she looked when she sneezed, as seriously as he did the less personal news of the day. Of politics he wrote:

> Governor Warmoth has the Legislature eating out of the palm of his hand. The Constitution says the Governor can't be re-elected, but they've passed an amendment striking that out. It will have to be voted on by the people in the fall, but it will pass. Then he told the Legislature to impeach Wickliffe, and it did, and Wickliffe's on trial now. And in spite of everything, a big mass meeting of protest in Lafayette Square, delegations appealing to the House and the Senate, the newspapers, everything, he's pushed through the four big bills that make him an absolute ruler. Under the election bill,

there's a Returning Board which consists of the Governor, the Lieutenant Governor, the Secretary of State, and Senator Lynch and Senator Anderson, and after an election they decide who won—and there's no appeal from their decision. Under the registration bill, the Governor's appointees decide who is allowed to vote, and under the Constabulary bill his appointees are in charge of enforcing the law in every parish, and under the Militia bill he can raise an army and command it, any time he sees fit. That is, the Governor can. I think Warmoth's a fairly sound man; certainly he has won the friendship of some of the best men in New Orleans. But what the next Governor might do with the same powers is frightening to think about.

In March, he wrote that Wickliffe had been convicted and removed from office, and for Don's benefit he outlined the new law dealing with the state's school system. The state was divided into six sections, of which New Orleans was one; each section had a Superintendent appointed by the Governor, and these Superintendents, meeting together, controlled the whole state.

"That will give the Governor some new offices to fill," Don commented. "But it won't build schoolhouses, nor find teachers."

"Nor pupils," she reminded him.

"The right teachers will attract pupils enough. But the right teachers are few and far between. The school system doesn't matter. Systems, and buildings and all that, they're just trimmings. It's the teachers that count."

In April, when the drifts were shrinking fast, Trav wrote sad news. Kyle Dewain, Jenny's oldest son, Brett and Cinda's grandson, had been killed when his horse tripped and fell upon him. Lucy as she tended her baby knew suddenly how dear all babies must always be to all mothers, and she shared Jenny's fierce passionate grief for Kyle. Thinking of Jenny made her realize how her own mother and father must be missing her, and that night before they slept, holding fast to Don's hand, she said:

"Don, know something?" Half asleep, he muttered a negative, and Lucy said: "I wish we could go home next winter. Just for a visit; just for Christmas, maybe." And when he did not at once reply, she added hurriedly: "I mean, go back to New Orleans. This is home, of course."

"I know." He spoke softly in the darkness. "Maybe we can." He drew her head on his shoulder. "I'm sure we can. I'd like to." And presently: "I'd like to see how they're getting on down there."

Spring came like the tide, rising and receding in recurrent waves. There were warm sunny days when the drifts shrank almost visibly, and every runlet became a dancing little stream. On such days the crows, tumbling and wheeling in the gusty winds, shouted from the sunned skies in hoarse exuberant delight. When the sun vanished, the streams that had run so joyously put on a hushing sheath of ice, and the crows scudded silent.

But the days grew longer, and presently, except in the deep woods, no snow remained, and the spring winds dried the ground, and one day Pa and Don began to plow the upper field, and Ma raked the leaves off her flower beds, and Lucy brought Donny's crib out to the sheltered corner between house and shed that trapped the welcome sun.

Before the fields were dry enough to be harrowed for planting, Trav's letters were saying that the heat would soon drive him and Enid and the baby away to the Plains. "We'll go as soon as Mr. Cist gets back, to take charge at the mill." He planned this summer to return to Martinston, to see his old friends there. "Governor Holden will be defeated at the next election," he predicted. "And that will drive the carpetbaggers out of North Carolina." And he added: "Speaking of carpetbaggers, did I tell you that Warmoth has appointed Longstreet to be Adjutant General of militia? That didn't make any friends for Longstreet."

He sent newspaper accounts of the race between the *Robert E. Lee* and the *Natchez*, from New Orleans to St. Louis; of the vast sums of money wagered upon the contest, and the progress upriver with bonfires at night and salutes by day to honor the rival vessels, and of the seventy-five thousand who cheered the *Robert E. Lee* on her victorious arrival at St. Louis, three days and eighteen hours and fourteen minutes—seconds were not tallied—after the start, with the *Natchez* an ignominious seven hours behind.

"I suppose," he wrote, "there hadn't been so much excitement in New Orleans since that horse race Doctor Mercer told us about at the picnic at the lake. Remember? Seems more than three years ago, doesn't it? I had dinner with some gentlemen at his house the other night. The dinner was for Governor Warmoth. General Dick Taylor was there, and General Adams, and Admiral Semmes and Mr. Roselius; twenty-five or thirty others. Judge Morgan, of course. Warmoth has made some mighty respectable friends."

Summer was a blissful time, long days and short sweet nights. They woke early—the baby saw to that—and Don brought him to Lucy, and then dressed and went to help with the morning chores. Downstairs, Pa would have the kettle singing, and when they returned from the barn with the milking done and the cows turned out, breakfast would be ready. There Lucy joined them, and Donny, in the high chair that had served his father and his grandfather before him, sat watching them eat, pounding and shouting and screaming with delight at the wonder of being alive.

Don and Lucy followed for a while the progress of the war, but through July there was only one minor skirmish. "The newspapers print an extravagant rumor one day and deny it the next," Trav wrote. "I've quit reading anything they print. I'll just wait till it's over and see how it came out." He said that Governor Warmoth, ruling for a few months as an absolute monarch, had raised up against himself envious enemies. When the Republican State Convention met in August, four-fifths of the delegates were Negroes. Governor Warmoth and the Negro Lieutenant Governor, Oscar Dunn, were both nominated for president of the Convention, but Dunn was elected, and every officer of the Convention was a Negro.

Lucy was shocked at this, but Don said reasonably: "It may not be as bad as it sounds. Oscar Dunn has been a first-rate presiding officer in the Senate."

She smiled. "You must be awful lonesome sometimes, Don, away up here where you never see a nigra at all. Don't you miss them?"

He chuckled with her. "All the same, Lucy," he urged, "nothing any more dramatic than this sudden elevation of a slave race to power over their masters has ever happened anywhere." And as she was about to speak, he added quietly: "Oh, insurrections, yes, where the slaves rise and kill everyone; but this change from servant to master has been relatively peaceful—at least on the part of the slaves. They've killed a few white men, of course, but there's been no organized massacre, no official slaughter. Not by the Negroes. Yet how terrible their memories must be!"

"They were never abused," she reminded him. "Even when they were slaves!"

"I know. I didn't mean 'terrible memories' in that sense, but they must have hated being slaves."

"I don't think they did, really."

He laughed in sudden realization. "Of course they didn't! As usual, you're right. I keep imagining that they must have felt the way I would have felt in their places. Yet how strange their new life must be!" This was a Sunday afternoon, and they were sitting under the maples beside the house, the baby on a blanket between them, on his stomach, desperately squirming in his effort to touch a clothespin just beyond his reach. Don watched him for a moment, and he laughed. "Like Donny there! That clothespin, he wants it so, and it just escapes him. These Negroes,—I keep imagining that all their lives, things they wanted were in their sight but just out of reach, and now suddenly all those things are dumped into their lap!"

He reached across the blanket to pick up the clothespin and give it to Donny, who sat up to take it and at once stuck the rounded end into his mouth. After a moment, he took the clothespin out of his mouth and stared at it, then tried the taste of the forked end, then shook the clothespin violently up and down; when this had no result, he threw it away, and Don laughed and said:

"See that! After he got it, he didn't know what to do with it. Don't tell me these Negroes don't need advice, guidance, leading."

She looked at him with grave eyes. "I don't believe you'll ever be happy till you go back and try to help them."

But he shook his head. "No, don't ever think that. I'll always be happy just like this, with you and Donny." He moved around the blanket to sprawl beside her, his head in her lap, and he lay looking up at her and past her toward the sky. "That blue up there, those white clouds to look at, and you here beside me; you and Donny; what could a man want besides?"

She stroked his brow, and Donny made an angry sound. "A man might want supper, pretty soon," she said. "If he's anything like your son. He's getting fussy now."

The papers made headlines of the war news, forever asserting and then denying, supplying half a dozen rumors every day and confirming none of them. France called to arms a million soldiers, and an army of three quarters of a million Prussians marched toward Metz, and a great battle was reported to be imminent, and at that Pa exploded.

"Huh! Imminent! Imminent, my foot! If it's so dad-burned imminent why don't they get at it?"

Early in September, a letter from Trav exulted over the Democratic victory in North Carolina. "Governor Holden turned Kirk and his scoundrels loose in the state, arresting people, torturing them, throwing them into jail," he wrote. "And by doing so, he lost what few friends he had left. The new legislature will impeach him, and that's the end of carpetbag rule in North Carolina. Virginia's free, too. Louisiana will break away, give her time; but from all I hear, the Democrats aren't making any serious campaign this year. I'm glad of it. Another murder spree like the one they had two years ago and I'd be tempted to follow General Longstreet and turn Republican."

Lucy was, as usual, reading the letter aloud, and Don said thoughtfully: "Two years ago the twenty-eighth of this month, I was in Opelousas."

"Please don't!" she begged. "Can't we ever forget?"

"Of course." He laughed, asked challengingly: "Young lady, do you realize we'll have been married two years on the fourth of next March?"

"I certainly do! With Donny nine months old next week, I hope everyone does!"

They laughed together, and she read on. General Longstreet had had a sick spell, but was better now. Senator Pinchback and another Negro named Antoine had set up as commission merchants, with an office on Carondelet Street. Judge Morgan had been appointed an assistant United States District Attorney. The railroad from Mobile to New Orleans would be in operation before they came home; they could ride on it if they came that way. He and Mama were looking forward to their visit, making many plans. Why didn't they come right away, stay all winter?

Lucy wrote that they would not leave Maine till the end of November, and she explained:

It's wonderful here in October, so beautiful you can't even imagine it, and I don't want to miss that. Then there are always a lot of things to do to make everything snug for the winter. With you all down South, winter's the same as summer, except it's a little colder. Here, the animals on the farm, cows, sheep, pigs—yes and chickens too, and we have some turkeys this year—they'll be housed in the barn, with hay and oats and wheat and corn we raised here on the place, and beets and turnips and things enough to feed them through the winter. Then the foundations of the house and the barn have to be banked with leaves to keep the cold out. The potatoes and all the roots have to be dug and hauled into the barn or into the cellar, and the apples must be picked, and dry beans and everything from the garden.

And the wood! You can't even imagine how cold it gets here, way down below zero for weeks at a time, so we have to have huge fires to keep us warm. Don and Pa cut the wood last winter and hauled it out on the sledge, in eight-foot logs, and odd times all summer they've been sawing it up, some four-foot logs for the big fireplace in the kitchen where Ma does most of her cooking, but in summer she uses the stove, and there has to be special wood for that, and for the airtights in our bedroom and in Pa-and-Ma's, and in the dining room, but we didn't use the dining room much last winter after it got real cold. Oh, we keep warm! I've been lots colder at home with you than I've ever been here. Even in the barn, when a cow has a calf, or one of the horses foals, or a mother sheep lambs—I always go out with Don and Pa to hold lanterns and run errands and things —it's warm as toast, with all the animals there. Four horses, and two grown oxen, and a young pair in the tie-up, and nine cows and heifers, and I don't know how many sheep and pigs. The barn's big, you know. You could almost put our whole house into it—I mean your house down there—if it weren't for the timbers.

I don't know how I got started on this, except winters are fun. Don wants to leave everything here so Pa won't have too much to do, but we'll be in New Orleans before Christmas, I promise you.

The day she mailed that letter, the newspapers reported a great French victory at Sedan, but next day the capture of the Emperor and

the surrender of a French army of a hundred and twenty thousand men
was confirmed. By the time September was a week old, Lucy had begun
to preface an occasional remark with the qualifying phrase: "When we
go home."

Autumn was a time of beauty blazing bright, yet quick to fade and
vanish in a shower of falling leaves. It was the time to make the house
secure, to fill the shed with wood and the cellar with supplies; salt
pork and bacon put down in crocks of brine, potatoes in their bin,
apples in their barrels, beets and pumpkins and squash for the humans
in the house and the creatures in the barn. With October a third gone,
beauty filled the world; ten days later the trees were bare, stripped for
the winter's battle against cold that burned like fire. November meant
a leisurely attending to tasks till now forgotten, yet it was also a time
of hasting, quickly gone.

On the long journey to New Orleans, they traveled from New York
in the Pullman Palace Cars, changing only at Louisville. "And inside
another year," the train captain promised, "you'll be able to get on a
car in New York and get off it in New Orleans."

"Why can't we do it now?" Don asked.

"Gauge," the other explained. "Some railroads have one gauge, some
another. But the company's building cars that can be lifted from one
set of tracks to another when the gauge changes."

"Mercy!" Lucy protested. "I hope they let the passengers get off
before they do that."

"If you was asleep you'd never know it happened," the captain
assured her. "Now anything you want, or the little fellow wants, just
you let me know."

II

TRAV AND ENID met their train, Saul in the carriage beaming on them all, and Lucy held Donny for them to admire while Don stood proudly by. Then Enid must be permitted to hold the baby, and it was obvious to any observer that about Donny there was something that made him unique among all the babies ever born into the world. Lucy said modestly that probably her new baby sister was just as cute and pretty, and Trav laughed and said:

"You don't believe that for a minute, but just come along home and see."

At home, Maria and Daisy and Filly and even old Isaiah came to admire, and Daisy took Donny in charge. Lucy asked where Peter was, and Trav with a glance at Enid said drily: "He was so successful as a patron of Captain Pew's establishment that the Captain was forced to put him on the pay roll."

"You mean he's—just a gambler?"

Enid said lightly, like an echo: " 'Just a gambler'? Why, Honey, he's famous! We're proud of him!" Yet her voice broke on the words, and after a moment she confessed: "We seldom see him, Lucy. He seldom comes home now, hasn't, not since little Enid was born."

Don and Lucy did not see Peter till the day before Christmas. Then he appeared for breakfast, gave Lucy a dutiful kiss, greeted Don with "Hello, Yank!" and halfheartedly approved the baby. Lucy that night wept with angry hurt.

"I wouldn't mind so much," she told Don, "if it was just Papa and Mama and me, but I hate the sneering way he talks to you."

He tried to reassure her. "I can understand him. He's young in years, and yet precociously mature, so he's always on the defensive. He'll come out all right, once he grows up."

"Well I wish he'd hurry," she declared.

After Christmas, their lives settled into routine. Lucy and Don would stay till March, or even into April; Don assured her there was no hurry. "As long as we're home in time so I can help Pa get his farming done."

Trav was all day at the mill, but Don found many things to do. "I've a lot of old friends to see," he told Lucy, and smiled. "It's true that some of them are Negroes, but I want to see some of the Negroes I used to work with, and to visit the schools."

But after a few days of this, he was both saddened and angry. Too many of the teachers were lazy and illiterate; the schoolrooms were dirty, the pupils disorderly. In the hope that some way might be found to improve things, he called upon the Governor, spoke of his interest in education.

"I know!" the Governor assented. "That was your chief activity under the Bureau." Don looked his surprise, and Warmoth explained: "I have that sort of memory. Someone told me this much about you, and it stayed in my mental files. What were you going to say?"

"I've visited some of the schools here in New Orleans. They seem to have deteriorated in these two years."

"They have, sir," Warmoth agreed. "Mr. Conway is a bigot. His insistence on mixed schools has forced white children to stay away. If the white children were in school, their parents would be alert to the disgraceful conditions you have seen, and would demand improvement."

"I have an impression that Mr. Conway is not a good administrator."

"Find me a better who will accept the appointment!" And the Governor remarked: "My own opinion is that we attack education from the wrong approach. 'A little learning is a dangerous thing,' and merely to teach our Negroes to read and write is a doubtful service to them. I'd like to see them given training in farming, in household tasks, in weaving and mending and cooking, in practical pursuits."

Don hesitated. "I don't think you can be too specific," he suggested. "I suspect that the real function of the teacher, of schools and of colleges, is to give young people such interesting samples of knowledge that they'll develop an appetite for more."

Warmoth said in quick approval: "That's well put! The key word is 'interesting.' If a teacher doesn't interest his pupils—or her pupils— he accomplishes nothing."

"Exactly," Don agreed. "It's not the pupil who fails, it's the teacher. When a teacher says her pupils are stupid, she's to blame." And he said again: "But it isn't enough just to lead children—or grownups—to learn something; they must be so interested in what they learn that they want to learn more." He hesitated. "I don't think there's any such thing as an 'educated' man, because education is never finished. 'To educate' is a verb without a past tense, or it should be. But if there really were such things as educated men, you could know them by their untiring curiosity."

They returned to the problem of New Orleans schools, and found no answer, but when Don presently made a move to depart, the Governor bade him stay. "I expect a caller presently, but for the moment I'm free. Have you watched our legislature in action?"

Don nodded. "Yes, I've attended several sessions, and listened to the talk in the corridors, the discussion of your candidates for United States Senator. I suppose you're for Mr. Casey." The Collector of Customs was the leading candidate, with Senator Pinchback and Lieutenant Governor Dunn also in the field.

Warmoth cocked an eyebrow. "Why?"

"Well, he's the President's brother-in-law."

"Really? My understanding has it that he's Mrs. Grant's brother-in-law, not the President's. And I doubt that that degree of consanguinity is in itself enough to convince the President that Casey would make a good Senator. But if he does think so, wouldn't you think he'd be asking some of us to support Casey?"

Don was secretly amused. "You want the President to ask you to support Casey?"

Warmoth smiled. "Well now, Captain, I'll tell you. If I support Mr. Casey, and some day I want a favor from the White House, and I speak of this support of Casey as a reason why the favor should be granted, the President might say: 'Support Casey, did you? I didn't ask you to do so!' And that would be the truth. I saw Grant a few weeks ago and he didn't mention Casey's name. If the President wants me to support Mr. Casey, he must tell me so. That's the politics of it, Captain."

"Then will you support Senator Pinchback? Or Lieutenant Governor Dunn?"

Warmoth shook his head. "No. No, I'd be sorry to see Louisiana send a Negro to the Senate. If the President asks me, I'll support Casey, but my personal candidate is General West."

"You'll make some enemies, won't you?"

"Well now, Captain," Warmoth drawled. "A man can be judged by the enemies he makes—and I'll accept judgment on that basis." He turned his chair to look out of the window. "Collector Casey has two faults, Captain. One is minor: he's corrupt. But there is corruption everywhere in the United States today, from the White House down, so that is not surprising. But he has another, a major fault. Like his brother-in-law—" He smiled. "Or to be precise, let us say 'like his wife's brother-in-law,' he is clumsy; either clumsy or stupid, and the result is in each case the same. He—through one of his hired men in

the Senate—is sponsoring the Shed Bill, to form a company monopoliz-
ing the levee front and to spend a million and a half of the state's money.
He plans to buy votes in the Senate at a thousand dollars a vote, and
he has already collected the bribe money from the stockholders. That
was clumsy."

"Will he get his bill?"

"No doubt. And they'll pass it over my veto. But to get the money,
they must issue bonds, and I can stop that—and I will." He smiled.
"So you see, Captain, with both the senatorship and his Shed Bill at
stake, Mr. Casey has been doubly clumsy. And that, too, is the politics
of it, Captain Page."

Don smiled, and General Longstreet appeared in the doorway. He
had a hearty greeting for Don. "Major Currain told me you and Miss
Lucy were coming." He looked toward Governor Warmoth. "Have you
been sounding the Captain on Northern opinion of our problems here?"

"Only on his own opinions."

Don said with a chuckle: "You'll get no comfort from me. In my part
of Maine there are more Democrats to the square inch than you gentlemen would care to meet on a dark night."

They laughed with him, but the General said thoughtfully: "The
South needs to realize that. There's a natural alliance between the
Southerner and men like these State-of-Maine Democrats. They'd never
have followed us out of the Union, but they'd welcome us back in. The
sooner we realize that the Northern Democrats, natural friends of the
South, are solidly for the Union and against slavery, the sooner we'll
better our condition. Right now, the South has political inflammation
of the brain. The way to cure it is to forget politics and go to work!"

"That's the only way to re-establish stable government," Warmoth
agreed. "As long as Southerners keep on fighting the War—" He smiled.
"Well, politically speaking, they're lambs to the slaughter."

Longstreet spoke to Don. "My compliments to your charming lady,
Captain. She's an old sweetheart of mine."

Don rose, recognizing in the General's tone a courteous dismissal.
"I'd like to call and pay my respects, sir. Is your office in the Custom
House?"

"I'm leaving today for Washington. Make it upon my return, and at
our home. Fifty-seven Brainard."

Don thanked him, and took his leave. That night he spoke to Trav
of his talk with the Governor, and of meeting the General there.

"General Longstreet's hand-in-glove with the Governor," Trav
agreed. "I'm sorry, too. Warmoth has a lot of political ability, but he's
short on scruples, and the General's stubborn loyalty may someday get
him into a difficult position. Sooner or later, Warmoth will come to

grief; possibly even to impeachment, like Governor Holden."

His tone made Don comment: "You seem to have a personal dislike for this Holden."

"I have," Trav assented. "He was a Union sympathizer during the War, and I suppose he made deserters out of five or six thousand North Carolina men—some of them my friends. He's a traitor, and he should have been hanged then, and I'd be happy to see him hanged now."

Trav was this winter considering the purchase of Paradise plantation. Elon and Eleanor were anxious to sell, and Trav, with his old love of the soil, was increasingly tempted. The mill was on the verge of greatly increased earnings, and Captain Blackford, handling Trav's cash capital in the tobacco market in Lynchburg, had made substantial profits, so Trav had the purchase price in hand.

He spoke of the matter, one Sunday afternoon, to Don. "Elon says the way to buy it is for him to let the taxes lapse, and then I'd bid it in at a tax sale," he explained. "But I don't know. I've never raised sugar. There's about as much cotton raised in Louisiana now as before the War, but not a fifth as much sugar. In 'sixty-one, thirteen hundred sugar planters sold their products for twenty-five million dollars. That spells opportunity, but if I start now it will be three years before I'd get any return on my money. And with taxes high—and unpredictable —I hesitate to tie up any more capital than I must."

"I suppose taxes here are pretty heavy."

"If they were vigorously collected, we couldn't stand them." Trav admitted. "Our mill pays a hundred dollars to the state, and another hundred to the city, just for the privilege of doing business. Then on the house and furniture—I bought this house, two years ago, though that was probably a mistake—the tax is just under four hundred dollars. Money at interest, and securities, are all supposed to pay a tax too, and there's a two and a half per cent federal tax on income. Not to mention stamp taxes on bills and notes and checks and deeds. If all taxes were collected, it would cost me a fifth of my income, leave me bankrupt in a mighty few years." He shook his head. "So I suppose I'm a fool to consider assuming any further liability."

Don saw that Trav was thinking aloud, not seeking any answer, so he kept silence, and after a moment Trav added: "But I'm about decided to do it. It takes three years to make a crop of sugar, and the canes should be planted in February—so if I'm going to do it, this year, I've got to make up my mind." Don nodded, and Trav said, arguing with himself: "I wouldn't have to make any great outlay at once. It will be three years before I'd need the machinery ready. Elon says it's all there, that Mr. Tremont has kept it free from rust, oiled and ready to use. It's a horse mill, with iron rollers, and I may eventually want steam, though even a small steam mill costs upwards of three thousand. But I can start with what's there, and let it grow." He looked at Don. "Sugar-cane figures to yield about a hundred and twenty dollars worth of sugar and twenty dollars worth of molasses to an acre of land, and in these times land can be bought mighty cheap."

Don's eyes were twinkling. "I see you're going to do it?"

Trav chuckled. "Yes. Yes, I suppose I am."

"Have you talked it over with Mrs. Currain?"

"Not yet. Not a word." He looked at Don, his eyes blank with thought. "Suppose I should," he muttered, and after a moment, suddenly at ease. "No time like now, when I've you to keep me in countenance." Lucy and Enid were upstairs, watching the babies being put to bed, and Trav went into the hall and called: "Enid! Enid?" Don heard her answer, and Trav said: "Come down for a while, you and Lucy; something I want to talk over." And when he rejoined Don: "They're coming right down."

Enid would be forty years old in September, yet she thought she had never been so young. As a girl in her later teens, when Lucy and later Peter were born, she had been physically wretched, but the months before little Enid's birth had been a long delight. She suffered little or no discomfort, and she experienced an extraordinary psychological rejuvenation, and was for days on end as blissfully content as a happy bride.

A year ago, she had written Don and Lucy that she might have another baby, and another; that she might start another family. This was not the exuberance of the moment, but when she spoke to Trav of the enchanting prospect, he shook his head.

"I couldn't go through it again, Enid," he said, with an unfamiliar fondness. "These months before baby came were a lot tougher for me than ever before. When we were young, I didn't worry so much. I was too absorbed in farming, in work. It never occurred to me that anything could happen to you. But now—" He caught her hands and held them fast. "Well, if anything happened to you now, I'd be a lonely old man."

She was so happy at this confession that she accepted his decision, and the first few months of her renewed motherhood were so richly contenting that she forgot her half-formed desire. If there was somewhere in the background of her consciousness an unsatisfied yearning, she did not recognize it; if sometimes she was made uneasy by a vague feeling that there was something she must do, she as quickly as possible dismissed it from her mind.

When Lucy came home, and they were much together with their

babies and with each other, they drew increasingly close. Lucy had at once remarked upon how well Enid looked. "Younger and lovelier than ever," she insisted.

"Well, so do you, darling," Enid assured her.

"Oh, I'm supposed to! A bride with her first baby! It's expected of me. But you look so well you ought to be ashamed of yourself!"

Enid laughed with pleasure. "Well actually I feel better than I've ever felt in my life," she admitted. "As though I could do simply anything I set out to do. I'm so full of energy that Papa laughs at me, all the time." She added: "The only trouble is, I constantly have the feeling that there is something I must do right away, as though someone were telling me to hurry, hurry, hurry! As though there was something I'd forgotten to do." She smiled. "I wish I'd remember. You know the feeling, in the back of your mind. Sometimes it just drives me wild!"

To have Lucy here at first eased this restlessness; Lucy was so happy to be at home, happy with them all. Enid asked many questions about the routine of their days in Maine, volubly wondering how Lucy had ever stood it. Lucy laughed and said: "Why, Mama, it was wonderful. There was never a minute when you just sat around, the way we do here, with nothing in the world to do!" And she said teasingly: "Maybe if you had more to do, you wouldn't be so restless all the time."

"Oh, it isn't that," Enid assured her. "It's more a feeling that I must hurry, before it's too late."

"You need something new to interest you," Lucy suggested, and when she and her mother came downstairs and Trav proposed buying Paradise, her first thought was that this might be the distraction Enid needed.

But Enid looked at Trav in blank surprise. They had not spent a day at the plantation since Lucy and Don were married, and the thought of giving up their pleasant home here for a shabby old house twenty miles from nowhere appalled her.

"Buy Paradise?" she echoed. "What's got into you?"

"Why, it just struck me you might like it."

"Like it?" she echoed. "I'd hate it! Why don't we go back to Chimneys and be done with it!"

The anger in her tones made him blink. "Well, all right," he said hurriedly. "We'll say no more about it!"

"I should hope not!"

"I didn't mean we'd live there, of course. I was thinking of it only as an investment, to buy it and plant sugar cane. We'd never go down except for picnics, parties."

Picnics? The *Paradise?* Cap'n Cash! Enid had not thought of him for months, but this sudden prospect of owning Paradise, of going to and fro on Cap'n Cash's boat, of seeing him whenever she chose, somehow quickened her pulse. "Oh, I see," she said, her tone relenting. "I thought you meant we'd live there."

"Oh no. No, I couldn't do that. I have to be at the mill every day. No, we'd just use it for picnics, or go down on hot nights to see if it's cooler there."

"Does Cap'n Cash still run his boat? The trip was always sort of fun."

"Yes, he and Quinny live down there, since they got married." She had not known this, had not even known that they were married. "Down there or on the boat."

"Well, as long as we wouldn't have to live there—" That wretched little wench! Cash was a thousand times too good for her.

"I thought Don and I might go down one day this week, have a look around. You and Lucy care to go?"

Lucy cried: "Oh, fun! And Eleanor and Mr. Cist! And Elon!"

So it was decided; but that night, long after Trav was asleep, Enid lay awake beside him, accusing Quinny of a thousand crimes! That wretched—nigger! Marrying a fine man like Cash! Her fist, softly pounding the bed, beat time to her thoughts, and Trav roused.

"Eh? What's that? What's wrong?"

"Nothing, darling," she whispered. "Not a thing in the world. Let me come into your arms."

Trav engaged Captain Cash and the *Paradise* for the trip downriver, but the night before, Enid complained of a headache.

"Why, that's too bad, Mama," Trav said in a sympathetic tone. "But—"

"Oh, stop calling me Mama! I'm not your mother!" There was a spiteful irritation in her tones.

"Why, I just started to say that Mr. Cist can't go, either. Some gentlemen he met in England are to be here, and he and Eleanor will be entertaining them. So Don and I will just go down with Elon and have a look around."

They carried out this plan, and while Trav and Elon inspected the mill and rode out with Mr. Tremont to see the condition of the fields, Don walked through the quarter, finding the few inhabited cabins there in good repair, small gardens already started, the Negroes friendly and apparently contented.

But most of the cabins were empty, and he saw only a dozen able-bodied men and women. There were children enough, and an old man and two old women had found a sunny spot and sat contented in the sun. He stopped to talk with them. Yes, they agreed, many of the people who used to be here were gone, mostly living down by the river, or in the swamp, fishing and hunting some, and making a little garden. Yes sir, there were a lot of children still here; twelve or fifteen anyway. School? No sir, not what you'd call a regular school. The preacher came every fourth Sunday, and sometimes he kept school after church was out. Yes sir, it was a good place to be. Mr. Tremont talked hard, but he was a mighty nice man to work for. If someone came along and offered to pay wages, a lot of the hands would come a-running to take the jobs.

Don strolled beyond the last cabins to look at the church, a neatly whitewashed building set close beside the road. Weeds and bushes had been cut back so that the ground around it was clear. On the door a lettered sign read: "Be sure latch catches." Don tried the door and it opened at his touch.

Inside, the church was scrupulously swept and dusted, and Don felt a sudden quick respect and liking for the men and women and children who when the preacher passed this way came to worship here. The church could be used, between times, as a school. When the others returned, he asked Mr. Tremont where the nearest school was located, and the overseer said there was none within a dozen miles.

"Many other plantations? Many Negroes around?"

"None being worked—but there are people enough, yes sir."

Trav bought Paradise just before the end of January. At the tax sale he was the only bidder, and he got the place at his own price, but in addition he made a mortgage note payable to Elon and Eleanor at the rate of twenty dollars an acre for all the land suitable for growing cane. Interest would begin after five years, and the only security for the note was the land itself. Elon protested that this was an excess of generosity, that under conditions as they were the land was all but worthless, but Trav insisted, and he had his way.

Under Mr. Tremont's direction, the hands living on the place began at once to clear away accumulated weeds and underbrush and prepare fields to receive the canes. Through the winter months, since the water was almost always colder than the air, the river was usually shrouded in fog, so that the trip to Paradise was not particularly pleasant, and at Trav's advice, Enid did not attempt it. Once when northerly winds promised to scour the fog away, Lucy went down with Don and Trav, and tried to persuade Enid to go along.

"Heavens, no, it's too cold!" Enid retorted. "I'd freeze, and so will you."

"I?" Lucy laughed. "Oh, I'm used to cold weather."

But she had forgotten the damply penetrating cold of the Southland, against which there is no defense, and she was glad to get back to New

Orleans. After that, she waited for spring, but Don went downriver more than once. The memory of that little whitewashed church attracted him, and twice or thrice he asked Mr. Tremont for a horse, and with a Negro boy for guide, explored the region roundabout. He rode up as far as English Turn, following the levee trail, traversing the overgrown fields of adjoining plantations now abandoned, and he rode as far downriver. The useful land lay between river and swamp, a narrow strip never as much as a mile across, and it was often less than half a mile from the levee to the cane brake that bordered the swamp.

Don was surprised to find that as in New Orleans itself, the land sloped away from the river, and the next time he saw Elon, he spoke of this. "I thought at first my eyes were fooling me," he admitted. "But I found several little streams that flow back toward the swamp."

Elon nodded. "That's right. Give it a few thousand years and the river would build its own levee. Any muddy stream that regularly overflows its banks tends to build up a sort of ridge on each side. When the flood stops rising, the slack water drops part of its load of silt." And he added: "All the land around here, from way above New Orleans, maybe a hundred miles and maybe two hundred, and clear down to the Gulf, and off to the east and west, the whole delta has been built up with dirt that washed away from the country upriver and came down here. First time I'm down at the plantation I'll show you. Down below the point there now, in the backwater, the river's building new land all the time. In places, the levee's a full hundred yards in from the water's edge, and of course in summer it's even farther. Some of the people make their gardens outside the levee; make a fine crop, too, most years."

Because of the swamp, the plantation, except for a man afoot or mounted, was accessible only by water, but Mr. Tremont said there was higher ground off to the southeast, beyond the swamp, and a few settlements. Don was curious to see this hidden hinterland, and with one of the boys as guide, he explored the faint trails. On every patch of dry land in the swamp, Negroes had squatted, building huts and cabins out of logs and driftwood, living on the fish they could catch, the animals they could trap. Here and there dwelt a white man and his family; Cajuns, Mr. Tremont called them, contempt in his tones.

"They're bred out, or the next thing to it; marrying—or not bothering—their sisters and cousins and aunts and the like. They're not so bad other places, but they're bad right around here."

Don could see, without asking, the poverty of their lives, and a slow anger began to burn in him, not at any individual but at this way of life which made beasts of men.

By the end of February, spring was on the flood, and Lucy and Enid now and then came downriver. The house was not yet ready for occupancy, so if they stayed overnight, they slept in the cabins on the *Paradise,* where Captain Cash and Quinny took care to make them comfortable. Quinny was soon to have a baby, and Enid one day told her in malicious tones: "At least, this one won't be a clubfoot, with old Pike dead and gone. Weren't you ashamed of yourself?"

"Pore old Pike, he'uz a real kind man!"

"Where is it, anyway; his baby?"

"Hit lives wid Aunt Lukie in de cabin back yondeh. She Cap'n Cash's aunt."

Enid said teasingly: "You might have another clubfoot. You know they say a cross-bred bitch will always drop one bad one in every litter afterward."

"I ain' worryin'!" Quinny tossed her head. "Long as I's sure dis baby ain' got no Currain blood in him, I's satisfied!"

Enid flamed with rage. "Why you—you— Why, ten years ago, I'd have had you whipped to ribbons for that!"

"Ten years ago ain' now! I don' have tuh tek any big talk f'om de likes o' you."

"I'll report you to Cap'n Cash!"

Quinny looked off toward the levee. They were on the upper deck, and she was polishing the brasswork on the pilot house. "Heah he comes now. Go tell him."

"I'll give you one chance to apologize!"

Quinny laughed. "You ain' worryin' me."

Enid did report the incident to Captain Cash, but she chose her own time, a week later, when Quinny was on the boat and she and Trav were together on the gallery at the house while Cash and one of his crew set up a big four-poster bed in the north room. When he finished and was about to follow his helper down the stairs, she spoke to him.

"Cash, I wish you'd teach Quinny to be a little more respectful." From the corner of her eye she saw Trav's disapproving movement, but she went on: "I had a very disagreeable experience with her when we were down here last week."

"I'm sorry, ma'am," Cash told her. "Quinny has a hard temper, and there's time she speaks before she thinks. I'll talk to her, but I don't know as it'll do a bit of good." He shook his head in amused confession. "She can lead me around by the nose."

Enid felt Trav about to speak, and she said hurriedly: "Oh well, never mind; don't say anything to her. Probably she's forgotten it by now, anyway, and I shall do the same."

Cash left them, and Trav asked: "What did Quinny do?"

"Told me to my face—almost in so many words—that Peter had flirted with her. You know, she did have a baby by old Pike, and now she says it might have been Peter's."

Trav said grimly: "I should think as long as that dog sleeps, we'd better let it lie."

March was a pleasant month, and they enjoyed it. Don discovered Dan Hickok's Place, on the car line out in Carrollton, and took them all to dine there, and to admire the gardens and the conservatory. Roses were in full bloom, and the plum trees were in blossom, so that the evening air was fragrant, and the yellow trumpet vine in the conservatory was a mass of gold.

The Legislature adjourned, having appropriated almost a million dollars, ten times as much as the figure that was normal before the War. Governor Warmoth's foot had been gravely injured in an accident, early in March, and blood poisoning set in. Don went to call upon him and to pay his respects the day before he and Lucy left for Maine.

12

IN THE TWO YEARS after the bloody campaign of 1868, Governor
Warmoth had steadily strengthened his position and extended his
powers—and as a natural consequence he had raised up against
himself a host of enemies. Even Senator Pinchback—though against
Sapphira's advice—in January, 1870, in a speech before the Senate, referring to Warmoth, had said: "I have no partiality for that distinguished
gentleman. I am not a lover or worshiper of his." Speaker Carter, United
States Marshal Packard, Postmaster Lowell, and Collector Casey were
all hostile to the Governor, and after Warmoth united the Democrats
and the conservative Republicans to elect General West to be United
States Senator, against Casey's candidacy, they were his virulent
enemies.

One result of that election, however, was to bring Pinchback again to
Warmoth's side. Sapphira was largely responsible. Tony for some months
now had been in ill health. He had begun a year or two before to suffer
occasional attacks of gout, and his sometimes severe colds, always followed by coughs, began to run together so that his cough became chronic.
'Phemy gloomily warned Sapphira that this might be the beginning of
his end.

"Mebbe I's wrong an' I hopes I is," she said dolorously. "But it
looks t'me he's gwine inta a deecline. Like as not hit's gallopin' consumption—or wuss."

Tony consulted physicians, and he allowed 'Phemy to supplement the
medications they prescribed with her own decoctions, brewed from herbs
and simples. "And I expect you've had some voodoo said over them,"
he told 'Phemy, in friendly jest, but she did not smile.

"Drink it up! Drink it while it's hot!"

"It'll scald the rafters out of my mouth!"

"Drink it! It'll scald de mis'ries out o'you."

There were days when his swollen foot would not let Tony stand at all, but his interest in politics had never faltered, nor his support of Pinchback. When the Negro members of the Legislature in caucus voted to support Pinchback rather than Lieutenant Governor Dunn for United States Senator, he was exultant.

So the election of General West was a shattering disappointment. Pinchback had been till then a temperate man, but that night he came to Tony's, maudlin with drink, dissolved in self-pity, sobbing that he had been deserted by his friends. Tony agreed with him, but Sapphira challenged the statement.

"Which friends?" she demanded.

The drunken man made a feeble gesture. "The Governor!"

"You broke with him," she pointed out. "Not him with you." But he was that night too far gone in liquor to reason or to hear reason, and at last she and 'Phemy put the Senator to bed.

But in the morning, when Pinchback's wits were clear, she labored with him. He clung to anger. "Now I know my friends—and my enemies," he said. "I'll nail Warmoth's hide to the barn if it's the last thing I do."

"It will be the most foolish thing you've ever done if you do it," she told him. "Or rather, if you try to do it." And she said shrewdly: "The Governor has many enemies already. If you join them, you'll be just one more in a crowd. They won't welcome you. But Senator, all his enemies are also yours. You're natural allies and friends."

So she persuaded him, and through the rest of that legislative session he and the Governor stood together. By the time of Warmoth's accident, which for a while laid him low, they were firm allies.

After Don and Lucy in May returned to Maine, Trav's letters kept Don informed. The Custom House gang, he reported, were taking the opportunity offered by Warmoth's illness.

"His leg hasn't healed," he explained. "And Lieutenant Governor Dunn is Acting Governor. Packard's planning to seize control of the Republican organization while the Governor's away. General Longstreet stands by Warmoth, and he's trying to persuade the President that Warmoth is his best friend here, but I doubt he'll make much progress."

Warmoth in August had sufficiently regained his health so that when Marshal Packard and his deputies excluded the Governor and his friends from the Republican State Convention, and read them out of the party, he was able to meet the situation. He led his followers to Turner Hall and organized his own Convention, with Pinchback as president, and Pinchback, at Tony's that night, was quietly jubilant.

"We've got them bottled up," he said. "Stopped in their tracks, at least for now."

"Is the Governor sure he can handle them?"

"He's sure that we can," Pinchback amended.

"Does he realize," Sapphira asked, "that the Democrats will work with his enemies to pull him down? If they can·destroy him, they can deal with the little people by and by."

"We're all right till January," Pinchback told them. "But there's talk of impeaching him then, when the new Legislature comes in. Under the Constitution, they don't have to convict him; they don't even have to try him. If they impeach him, he's automatically suspended, and Oscar Dunn would become the acting Governor."

Tony said in surprise: "I didn't know that. You sure?"

Pinchback nodded. "Yes. And they're talking impeachment, now. I've not been approached myself. They know I'm on his side. But I hear it from some of my friends in the lower house."

"Their real quarrel with the Governor," Sapphira suggested, "is that he vetoes all their steals. But if they do impeach him, Mr. Dunn won't help them. Speaker Carter's a different story, but Mr. Dunn's an honest man. As long as he's Lieutenant Governor, impeaching Governor Warmoth will do them no good."

Pinchback nodded agreement. "But even if it would, there's nothing they can do now," he reminded them. "There's nothing they can do till January, till the new Legislature comes in."

For Don and Lucy, summer in Maine was peace and content, sunshine and rain, cool days and hot ones, and all unhurried and serene. Small Donny throve mightily, and Lucy, teaching him his first steps, said: "You must learn to walk, you know, darling, so you'll be able to take care of your little brother. Did you know you were going to have such a fine Christmas gift?"

They had thought that this baby should be born in New Orleans, but Lucy was not sure. "It's such a long trip," she remembered. "And I'd sort of like Donny's little brother to be born here, so they can start off together."

Don did not argue the point. Time enough for that decision two months from now, or three.

Toward the end of August, Trav reported that Peter had "struck Howard," explaining: "That's the way we say someone has made a winning in the lottery. Mr. Howard runs it, you know. Peter seems to be a lucky gambler. Captain Pew, whom I met in the St. Charles the other day, assures me he's an asset to the Haunted House."

Summer sped, and first frosts touched the trees. To Lucy the season of falling leaves had a sadness and yet a beauty all its own, and she liked to walk through the hardwood growth on the knoll below the road upon a still October day, when she could hear the tick-tick-tick of the leaves as they loosed their holds and fluttered down to rest among their sisters on the ground. One afternoon toward the end of the month she had gone there, picking her way to where the trunk of a fallen beech offered a comfortable seat, while her shoulders rested against the standing bulk of another tree. She sat bundled warm against the frost that, when the sun dropped behind Frye Mountain and left the world in shadow, came to hang like crystals in the air. Her arms embraced her unborn baby, and when he stirred she smiled and loved him.

By and by Don came seeking. "There you are," he called.

"Sh-h!" she whispered. "Listen to the leaves falling."

He sat beside her, drew her close, said presently: "I hear them."

"I can hear your heart beat," she murmured. "And sometimes I think I can hear his; it's there so close to mine."

He kissed the top of her head. "It will soon be dark. Can't have you stumbling through the woods."

"Don, know what I've been thinking? Let's not go South this winter."

"Why, Honey, your father and mother are counting on us."

"I don't want to go."

"Why not?"

"I guess I'm just afraid."

"There's nothing to be afraid of."

"We might not come back."

He laughed, shook his head. "Don't worry, Honey. We'll come back. Now it's time to go in."

She drank deep of the beauty of October, relishing every wine-clear day, and she wished to have Don beside her constantly. "The minute you're out of sight, I'm lonesome," she confessed. "Ma's sweet, and Pa's a darling, and you're just a great big old I don't know what. But help me take care of our baby, mister, will you please?" So they strolled together, or took sedate drives together, or simply were together. If he had work to do, he made a place for her to sit near by; if she were helping Ma in the kitchen, putting up jellies and jams and preserves of every kind, he sat with them, and they might let him pick over berries, peel apples or pears, shell beans. Deep peace dwelt in them all.

When it was decided that this baby would be born in New Orleans, Lucy became restless. They had originally planned to go South early in December, but she thought they might be wise to go before that, so they settled on their starting date.

The last afternoon, they had a letter from Trav. After some paragraphs of happy anticipation of their coming, he added:

> Don, you'll see some exciting times in the Legislature this winter. The Packard crowd have gained some seats in the lower house,

enough so they think they can impeach Warmoth. That would put Lieutenant Governor Dunn in as acting Governor, and he has the reputation of being an honest man, so they may not impeach. If he's honest, he could block their steals.

It's all a question of loot. We deal in large figures in Louisiana nowadays. Our Metropolitan Police cost us around eight hundred thousand dollars a year. I calculated the other day that the City Hall pay roll—it's around two hundred and fifty thousand dollars—would pay the combined salaries of the President, the Vice-President, the entire Supreme Court and the Cabinet, and still have enough left over to pay the Louisiana state officers.

So you'd think there'd be enough for everybody, but now the Customs House gang is out to hog it all. I hear that right now the easy way to make a fortune in Louisiana is to get into the Legislature and refuse to stay bought. I'm told that Governor Warmoth admits an income of a hundred thousand dollars for his first year in office. They say it costs more to get his signature on a bill than to get the bill through the Legislature.

To impeach or not to impeach! Well, it all depends on Lieutenant Governor Dunn.

They arrived in New Orleans on the morning of November 22, and Trav told them at the station that during the night, Oscar Dunn had died.

'Phemy had taken home the word, the day before, that Dunn was sick. When she told them, her hard eyes were soft with tears. "Why, Mama," Sapphira said softly. "Are you crying?"

"He 'uz a good man," 'Phemy reminded her. "De people be'n flocking tuh his house, weepin' and prayin'."

"Did you go?" Dunn's home was on Canal Street, at the corner of Derbigny. After his emancipation, earning his living as a plasterer, he had studied music and had begun to teach it, winning respect and friendship which made him in time an important figure in politics.

"No'm, but I talked to some dat did."

Pinchback came after supper to confirm the news. "The doctors don't know what's the matter with him. Some call it pneumonia, and congestion of the brain. He's suffering awfully, and his stomach's upset, and he says he feels as if he was on fire inside."

"Has he been sick long?"

"No, just since yesterday afternoon. I was with him Saturday night, went with him to the Third Ward Republican Club. He'd had a bad cold a week ago, but he took some Cherry Pectoral and that fixed him up. He made a mighty funny speech that night, had everyone laughing! Then yesterday he was with Marshal Packard till about three o'clock, and then about five o'clock yesterday evening he had this terrible pain, and he had to go to bed. Now they don't think he'll live through the night. Governor Warmoth was there when I left."

When he had gone, while Sapphira moved methodically around the room to snuff the candles, Tony asked: "Sapphira—do you think Dunn was poisoned?"

"I suppose some ignorant colored people will think so."

"I know. But—do you?"

She met his eyes, but made no other reply.

Next morning when 'Phemy brought their coffee, she told them the Lieutenant Governor was dead, and that night Pinchback came again. He had been at the Lieutenant Governor's home since before Mr. Dunn died.

"The Governor and Senator Ingraham and I were there," he explained. "Trying to comfort Mrs. Dunn and the children. They're adopted children. Then the coroner came. He'd heard some say that the Lieutenant Governor was poisoned." Sapphira had been sewing, but at this her hands were still, and Tony watched her. "But Mr. Dunn's friends were sure that wasn't so," said Pinchback. "So finally the coroner agreed to accept a death certificate signed by the attending physician." He added, with a gloomy unction: "They'll give him a grand funeral. You know he was Past Master of Richmond Lodge Number One. He'll lie in state tomorrow. The funeral's at two o'clock."

The funeral began with services at the Lieutenant Governor's home, followed by a public service at the Methodist church. The funeral procession included members of the Legislature and of the city government, several hundred members of the Metropolitan Police in uniform, about two hundred carriages, and two bands. In the cortege, Dunn's empty buggy, the vehicle itself covered with a black pall, and the horse draped with crape, was led by a man on foot. Sapphira, inconspicuous in black shawl and heavy veil, had gone with 'Phemy to watch the procession pass, and sight of that empty buggy moved her to tears. Looking at the weeping Negro women and men who stood on the banquettes all around her, she felt her kinship with these others who grieved now for that first man of their race to rise to a place of honor and of eminence, and while she walked home with 'Phemy, she felt herself somehow the better for having done him homage.

Dunn's death, whether or not he had been murdered, made more probable the impeachment of Governor Warmoth, since impeachment would at once lift Speaker Carter into the position of Acting Governor. But until the Legislature met, impeachment proceedings could not be begun, and a few days after Dunn's funeral, Pinchback came one evening to Tony's in a lively excitement.

Governor Warmoth had that day sent for him. "He talked frankly with me," the Senator explained, pride in his tones. "I was decidedly taken aback. He said I was ambitious, too much so, and he reminded me that I had sometimes opposed measures which he favored, and he said that either as a friend or as an enemy I was dangerous! He thinks I control twenty or twenty-five thousand votes." Pinchback laughed in a nervous way. "But he's calling a special session of the Senate to elect a new Lieutenant Governor, and he will urge his friends to vote for me!"

Sapphira asked: "Can he do that? Call just the Senate, not the House?"

"He says so. He's taken the opinions of the highest legal officers in the state, and of men like Mr. Roselius and Admiral Semmes and other leaders of the bar. He's issuing the proclamation today, calling the Senate to meet on December sixth."

"Did he ask any promises from you?"

"None at all. He said he was telling me his opinion of me so that I would know that he was supporting me, not in expectation of favors, but because he thought me the man for the place."

"What did you say?"

Pinchback chuckled. "I said that if I were as ambitious as he thought, he would make a mistake in electing me Lieutenant Governor, since I would certainly favor his impeachment when it would make me Acting Governor."

Sapphira smiled. "And he replied that you would never do that, because you knew he was a better governor than you could be."

Pinchback grinned. "Almost. He said I wouldn't do it because I was an honest man."

"Will you be elected?" Tony asked.

"It will be close, almost an even thing, but I think I'll have eighteen votes out of thirty-four."

"And if Governor Warmoth is impeached, you'll be Governor of Louisiana!" Tony spoke in a high pride.

"Well—Acting Governor!" Pinchback looked at Sapphira. "But even to be Lieutenant Governor is a great honor."

"Are you proud?" she asked.

He hesitated. "I suppose so. But in another way, I'm more scared than proud." He said in quiet self-appraisal: "I'm ambitious, yes, but I'm not sure of my own capacities. Perhaps that's because we have been taught to think ourselves inferior." He looked from one to another. "In public, I pretend a lot of confidence in myself, but inside, I'm pretty humble."

When the Senate met for the election, the first ballot resulted in a tie, seventeen for Pinchback and seventeen for Senator Coupland, the deputy collector of customs, who was the candidate of the Packard-Casey group. The second ballot was deferred till the following day, and Senator Lewis changed his vote. With Senator Pinchback and Senator Coupland each voting for the other, Pinchback received eighteen votes and became President of the Senate, and *ex officio* Lieutenant Governor.

When the first day's vote was taken, Don was among the spectators, and he reported the result at home. Trav commented: "Well, there'll be some lively bidding tonight." Next day, after the election, Trav heard that Senator Lewis had been promised fifteen thousand dollars—payable at the end of the session—for changing his vote. When he told them this, Don asked:

"Who made the promise?"

"Warmoth. Pinchback. One of them; perhaps both." Seeing Don's face, Trav added gently: "They're both completely venal, Don, though Warmoth's price is the higher. Pinchback's vote is usually quoted at two thousand dollars. He made a fortune last summer in a deal involving buying some land for the city park."

In the corruption of Pinchback, Don tasted the bitter flavor of tragedy.

Don's thoughts through these last days of waiting clung to Lucy, but Enid was always with her, and Eleanor, whose second baby would be born at about the same time as Lucy's, often joined them. Once Dolly came to call, and found them all together. "And she's lovelier than ever," Lucy told Don, when he came home. "I'm glad you weren't here. You'd have lost your head completely—with me the way I am."

"It's already lost," he assured her. "To you and to Mama." Enid had never looked so well as she did this winter; her cheeks were round and smooth, her eyes bright, her lips warm. "She looks like a girl in love, just blooming."

"I'll tell her you think so! She'll be mighty pleased. Far as that goes, she is in love, with Papa. I've never seen her as nice to him as she is now. Notice how happy he is?"

"He's happy about the mill," Don agreed. "They've tripled their production this year, and their European market is booming. And things are going well at Paradise, with a hundred and fifty acres in cane, and more land ready to be planted. Mr. Tremont has twenty-four hands at work, and he's adding a few more." He added in a different tone. "Over a hundred people on the place, and lots of children. One of the young Negro women has started a school, in the church. The Major says she can barely read and write herself, but Mrs. Tremont is helping her."

She touched his hand. "And you're wishing you were doing the helping."

He laughed, shook his head. "Not at all. I've children of my own to take care of, right here at home."

"Only one, so far." Then she whispered: "Ouch!" She pressed her hands to her body. "Stop kicking me!" And to Don: "It's practically two! This one does everything but talk back, already."

Their second son—promptly named Travis—was born on the twenty-second of December, three days after Eleanor's daughter. When Donny was introduced to his brother, he made a determined attempt to poke his finger into the baby's eye, and Lucy hugged little Travis defensively close, while Don explained to his older son that gentleness was the rule. Donny obediently patted the baby's cheek with light fingers, making small tender sounds, and Don and Lucy looked at each other in a great content, with shining eyes.

Peter was seldom at home, but one morning just before the turn of the year, he joined Don and Trav at breakfast. "Morning, Papa," he said composedly, as he approached the table. "Isaiah, fruit and coffee for me." And to Don: "Howdy, Yank!"

Don smiled. "Howdy, Reb." And Trav said: "Morning, Peter. It's been quite a while."

"I'm making a change in my domestic arrangements," Peter explained. "So I'll live at home for the present." He was almost twenty, but Don thought he looked older; a handsome young man with a lean jaw and a mocking eye. "When the Legislature convenes, the Innocents may start up again, and I'll be busy with them." He grinned at Don. "Better stay indoors, Yank," he advised. "This will be a dangerous town for bystanders."

"Especially Negroes?" Don suggested. "I remember they were the usual victims, two years ago."

Peter looked at him with level eyes. "Maybe you ought to have stayed in Maine, you and your memories. Niggers and carpetbaggers; yes, we killed enough for a mess."

Trav remarked: "I hear the Warmoth crowd is ready to spend a quarter of a million to elect a new Speaker."

"A good many people would like to get rid of Carter," Peter agreed. "Ever hear of Figures? It's a secret society. All the members have numbers instead of names. They're after Carter, and they're not the only ones. But of course, the Custom House is on his side."

"Are you?" Don inquired, and Peter grinned.

"Ask me no questions and I'll tell you no lies."

After breakfast, Don went with Trav to the mill, and as they walked downtown Don asked: "Where will you stand, sir, in this row between Warmoth and the Casey crowd?"

"Well, the best men in town, the best Southerners, prefer Warmoth to the rest. He's the lion, Packard and the others are jackals." And before Don could speak, Trav said in a shy way: "Don, I hope you don't let

Peter bother you. He's an unpleasant young man, but I'm always—humbly grateful when he pays us one of his rare visits."

Don said a reassuring word. "I understand him, sir. He'll find himself in time." There was another pause before he spoke again. "I have a request, Major, but please don't think it's because of Peter. Lucy and I have talked it over, and I'd like to go down to Paradise for a week or so." He saw the question in Trav's eyes, and said in uncertain explanation: "I'd like to see how your school there is getting along. I guess you've suspected that I'm more interested in schools than in just about anything. I did a little teaching, before the War." He hesitated, smiled. "I like it," he said. "There's nothing much more fun than feeling, now and then, that you've given a boy an idea that will do him some good."

"I know, son," Trav agreed. "I know how you feel. I don't feel that way myself. It always seemed to me that the best way I could help my—well, my neighbors, was by behaving myself, by being as good a man as I know how to be." He looked at Don with a kindly eye. "One thing I've noticed about you, Don; you think less about how what you do is going to affect you than just about anyone I ever knew."

Don was puzzled. "I don't see what you mean?"

"I know you don't," Trav agreed with a chuckle. "I hope you never do. Just go along the way you are. You suit me." And he added: "Go on down to Paradise, stay as long as you want. You may see some changes I ought to make down there."

"Next Monday or Tuesday?" Don suggested.

"Say Tuesday," Trav agreed. "I'll get word to Cap'n Cash. You know he and Quinny live down at Paradise now." Don nodded, and Trav said: "We have a system, he and I. I fly a signal at the mill when I have a message for him."

When the *Paradise* swung in toward the mill wharf Tuesday morning, Don was waiting. He went up to the pilothouse to speak to Cash, and at the Captain's invitation stayed in talk. The Legislature had met the day before, and at once adjourned till today as a gesture of respect to Lieutenant Governor Dunn, who had died six weeks ago. Don spoke of this, thinking Cap'n Cash must have been pleased by the tribute to one of his race.

"It was partly that," Cash agreed. "But the Senate didn't have a quorum, anyway. All the Casey Senators are hiding in the Custom House. Marshal Packard's entertaining them, with plenty of liquor and seegars. The talk is that Collector Casey'll let 'em have the *Wilderness*—that's the revenue cutter—and they'll take a cruise downriver for a few days."

"Why?" Don asked. "What's back of that?"

"They don't want the Senate to sit till they can get rid of Pinchback,"

Cash explained. "They want to organize the House first, and get rid of Pinchback, and then impeach the Governor."

"I see." But Don was not much interested, looking forward to the days ahead. He led Cash to talk about the community at Paradise, thus forgot politics a while.

In New Orleans that was a stormy week. The Senate was for lack of a quorum paralyzed, but the House first gave Speaker Carter a vote of confidence by a vote of forty-nine to forty-five, and the day after, several hundred members of the Metropolitan Police summoned by Governor Warmoth having gathered in and around Mechanics Institute, revoked the vote. Speaker Carter took the floor to speak in his own defense, and the House became a confusion of shouting, scuffling, angry men.

Next morning Trav, on his way to the ferry, saw two companies of infantry at ease outside the Custom House, and he spoke to one of the officers.

"Expecting trouble?"

"General Emory's orders, sir. We're to put ourselves at the disposal of the United States Marshal."

Trav was in no hurry to reach the mill. He decided to wait and see what happened, but then he remembered that General Longstreet's office was in the Custom House, so he went in to pay his respects.

He found the General troubled and angry. Four members of the House had sworn out an affidavit charging Governor Warmoth, Lieutenant Governor Pinchback, four Senators, thirteen Representatives, the Superintendent of Police, and two of his officers with conspiracy, violence, and bribery in an attempt to eject Speaker Carter.

"It's Packard's idea, of course," Longstreet said angrily. "He and Casey and Carter. I wish President Grant could see for himself what's going on here. They got warrants, and now the Deputy Marshals are going to arrest these people."

"What good can that do? They'll never be convicted."

"Of course not! The charge is nonsense! But the Deputies will hold the thirteen members of the House prisoner while Carter convenes the rest. With Warmoth's thirteen men locked up, Carter will have a majority. He'll unseat four or five Warmoth men, and that will give them control. Then they can void Pinchback's election as Lieutenant Governor, and impeach Warmoth, and Carter will step in as Governor."

Trav asked curiously: "Are you in their confidence?"

Longstreet shook his head. "No, no! But Governor Warmoth has spies in their camp and he told me what to expect. He's ready for them. Carter won't be able to get a quorum, because all the Warmoth men will stay in the clubhouse across the street, so any vote Carter puts through will be void. Then this afternoon the Governor will call them into extra session and undo whatever Carter has done."

"How does he know their plans?"

"Oh, it was all worked out in Packard's office yesterday, and some of the Democrats were in on it. One of them doubtless gave him the information. He has many avowed enemies who are secretly his friends. So he knows what they propose to do, but they don't know what he will do."

"You seem to!"

"Yes, because I'm Adjutant General of Militia. He told me when he gave me my orders for tomorrow. I'll have two regiments of militia and a battery of artillery, prepared to support Governor Warmoth as the lawful head of the state, posted around the capitol before daylight."

"You'll make a lot of enemies."

"Such men as Packard and Casey, yes."

"The Governor himself is not a model of virtue," Trav reminded him.

"Perhaps not, but he at least has stature; he has brains, and energy, and resolution. He will outmatch them all."

Longstreet's predictions proved accurate, and when Don came up river to spend Sunday with them, Trav told him what had happened. "If it hadn't been so damnable, it would have been funny," he admitted. "With forty or fifty Warmoth men hidden away right across the street, Carter couldn't get a quorum. He—"

"Had they arrested the Governor and the others?"

"Oh yes, but the Attorney General telegraphed from Washington not to let the United States courts be used for political purposes, so they were released." He chuckled. "The whole thing ran on a pretty close schedule. Warmoth and the others were arrested at eleven forty-five. While they were getting bail, Carter announced a quorum—the only way he could get it—and put through his votes. He finished about one o'clock, and marched his crowd down to the Gem Saloon to celebrate. Drinks for the crowd, and in two weeks he'd be Governor; so he said!"

"Was Warmoth still locked up?"

"No. No, he was already calling his special session. By half past one, he had his House in session, with a real quorum, and they undid all Carter had done. Now Warmoth's in possession of the Institute, guarded by several hundred Metropolitans, and two regiments of militia, and a battery of guns, with Longstreet in command." He shifted in his chair. "That's the situation here! How are things at Paradise?"

"Oh, fine. Mrs. Harper—the little schoolteacher—does mighty well. Actually, she and the children study together. Mrs. Tremont reads a new page to Mrs. Harper every night, and then they all work on it the next day."

"I expect you found some ways to help her."

"I didn't make any suggestions. They've figured out a trick to teach themselves, and it works. I did get her three or four new pupils, older boys."

"Won't they have to start at the beginning?"

"I told them I didn't think they could keep up with the little children, but they seemed to think they could." There was a twinkle in his eye, but then he said, in an enthusiastic tone: "You see, sir, the way they work, they learn words first, and then letters. Sometimes they'll spend an hour or two seeing who can count up the most 'the's' on a page, or the 'and's,' till they know what the word looks like. Or they'll count the 'a's,' or 'b's,' or some other letter. Mrs. Harper started the older boys on that, and after two or three tries they began to catch on." He added, with a quick chuckle: "And she'll have more pupils, pretty soon. You know the Oaks, the plantation up this way from you?" Trav nodded. "Mr. Tremont says they're getting ready to plant cane there again, and on one of the plantations across the river, too."

Trav said: "I'm not surprised. As long ago as eighteen fifty-three, there were already ten thousand acres in sugar in Jefferson Parish, and around thirty thousand in Plaquemines."

"Those new plantings will mean a lot more children needing school," Don suggested, and Trav smiled and said:

"Plain to be seen you're a young man of one idea."

"Yes sir," Don admitted. "There ought to be a school on each plantation, for the little children anyway, and maybe a big school somewhere to teach the older children some of the things they'll need to know when they grow up. I can see a lot of work that could be done down there."

He talked to Lucy even more freely than to Trav, and as she listened she watched his eyes, and the quick movements of his lips, and when as he became more and more interested in what he was telling her, he began to gesture, she smiled, and he saw this and colored diffidently.

"I must bore people," he suggested. "Talking about it all the time. Tell me what you've been doing."

"Just staying in bed and getting well again."

"Eleanor been to see you?"

"Not yet, but we send messages back and forth through Papa and Elon. She's fine. Dolly was here again. Peter was at home that evening, so he got most of her attention. It's almost the first time I've seen him— but of course he hardly looked at me! I felt sometimes as if I weren't there at all, he and Dolly had such a good time together."

"She's not much older than he, is she?"

"Crazy!" Her eyes were bright with indignation. "She's older than I am! Years older. Six years, I think, and I'm three years older than Peter, so she's nine years older than he!"

He smiled. "Well not quite old enough to be his mother! I suppose she's gone to his head. Can you spare me for another week? I'd like a few days more at Paradise."

She laughed to hide her reluctance. "Of course I can! Who am I that you should prefer me to Paradise!" Then, seeing his distress, she said quickly: "There, Honey, I'm only teasing. Go, of course."

Don grinned. "You act to me like a girl who's got something up her sleeve," he decided. "I guess I'd better stay and keep an eye on you."

He stayed, in fact, through the tumultuous fortnight that followed. Monday night he and Trav—and fifteen thousand others—attended the Democratic mass meeting in Lafayette Square and heard Warmoth denounced, and all his works. Trav saw men in the crowd wearing the red shirts and caps which the Innocents had worn in the bloody campaign two years before, and at breakfast Peter said, answering Trav's question: "Yes, we were there for a while, long enough to see there'd be no trouble."

Don asked curiously: "Which side are you on?"

Peter looked at him in angry wonder. "It would take a Yankee to ask that," he commented.

That day the activities of Carter's sergeants-at-arms, seeking to arrest Warmoth assemblymen in order to destroy Warmoth's quorum in the House, led to a shooting affray on Royal Street in which Mr. Wheyland, a Warmoth member of the House, was killed. The Governor next morning sent police to seize the Gem Saloon, which Carter's supporters had been using as their headquarters. The Mayor demanded that martial law be declared, but instead, Carter and three of his men were arrested and charged with Wheyland's death, held till Friday and then released.

Monday, the Senate, despite the truants—three Democrats and eleven Republicans—achieved a quorum. "Trust Warmoth," Trav said admiringly. "They needed only one man, and Warmoth brought Senator Thomas to town under a safe conduct, and Doctor Mercer invited Thomas to dinner, and about thirty of the finest men in New Orleans assured him they were on the Governor's side. So he agreed to resume his seat." He added: "So today they had a quorum, and they repealed the Election Law and the Registration Law and the one setting up a constabulary. Warmoth keeps his hold as Governor, and repealing those laws will quiet the honest opposition. He's secure."

Yet the margin was still a narrow one. In the Senate, on a motion to elect a new presiding officer, Pinchback cast the deciding vote to break a tie.

Carter, a week later, made one more gesture, announcing that on Monday morning he would seize Mechanics Institute and oust the Warmoth forces. Don went downtown to see whether he would carry out his threat. Several hundred armed men were gathered around the Clay statue, and the crowd grew larger, till Don saw a soldier approach Carter and hand him a slip of paper. Carter read it at a glance, stepped up on the base of the statue and lifted his voice.

"Gentlemen," he shouted. "I have here a message received by General Emory from the Adjutant General of the United States. I will read it to you." And he read: " 'The President directs that you hold your troops in readiness to suppress a conflict of armed bodies of men, should such occur, and to guard public property from pillage and destruction!' " He folded the paper, twisting it between his fingers. "So, gentlemen, we must surrender to superior force. I beg you to disperse, and let there be no violence. Thank you for your loyalty to me."

He stepped down, and under Don's eyes the packed crowd began without a word to loosen and to dissolve. Don, watching, felt a sudden deep pride. A moment ago, a thousand armed men had been ready here for violence and death; now at a word from Washington, those men went peacefully to their homes. Certainly, the Union was more than just a word. When after dinner Enid took the carriage and departed to pick up Mrs. Morgan for a shopping expedition, so that he and Lucy were alone, he told her about that moment. "I was so proud I wanted to cry!" he confessed. "That's the sort of sentimental fool I am."

She smiled and kissed him and whispered: "There are a lot of other things I love about you, too."

They were in the sitting room, and thought themselves alone, but someone in the door asked politely: "Am I intruding?"

They turned and saw Peter there, watching them with an amused eye, and Lucy said, laughing in a pretty confusion: "Of course you are! Can't you cough or something?"

"When I saw I should, it was already too late."

"Wherever did you come from? You weren't here for dinner."

"I had some business downtown." He made a casual gesture. "It fatigued me, so I came home to take my ease." He lighted a seegar, settled himself in a comfortable chair. "Well, Yank, are you enjoying your Southern visit?"

"Oh, I don't feel like a visitor," Don said cheerfully. "I feel more at home here than I do in Maine."

"Ah?" Peter studied the ashes on his seegar. "I hope you won't let that feeling grow on you."

Lucy was about to speak, but a bell rang, somewhere in the back of the house. Peter rose, and Lucy said: "That's the front door. Isaiah will get it, Peter."

Isaiah in fact appeared just then in the hall, but Peter said: "Never mind, Isaiah. I'll go."

"Yas suh!" Isaiah turned back, and Peter went along the hall toward the front door. Lucy drew Don's head down to hers, and she whispered:

"Don't let him make you angry, darling."

He nodded, and they heard the front door open, heard Dolly's voice. "Why, Peter!"

"Hello, Dolly! Come in!" said Peter. In the sitting room, Lucy kissed Don, and their lips for an instant clung. Then they both looked toward the door, expecting to see Dolly there; but she was not there, nor was Peter, and there was no sound in the hall, and the silence was eloquent. Lucy looked at Don, and then Dolly in the hall said something in a laughing whisper, and Peter said calmly:

"Oh yes, Lucy and Don are in the sitting room. Come!"

Don rose, and when they appeared in the door, Dolly at once darted toward him, crying: "Oh Don, Honey!" She threw her arms around him. "It's wonderful to see you again!" She turned to Lucy. "And Lucy, sweet!"

She babbled without pause a while, asking questions and herself answering, leaving room for no word from the others. Had they heard about the new plans for Mardi Gras? This year there would be a King of the Carnival, something never known before. "I only found out about it last night!" She laughed delightedly. "It's a great secret, but I won it from a gentleman at the dice!"

Lucy pretended interest. Who would be King? Who had told Dolly the secret? When would everybody know? Dolly answered her questions without pausing to hear them, and Don wondered as always how two women, both talking at once, could each hear what the other was saying. Peter, lounging at ease, watched with amused eyes. Dolly asked for Enid, and regretted having missed her, and eventually, with Peter as her escort she took her leave.

When they were gone, Lucy said quietly: "There couldn't have been any mistake about that moment in the hall, Don. Could there." It was rather a statement than a question.

"It's easy to imagine things," he reminded her. "The—silence wasn't as long as it seemed."

"It was long enough for us to kiss each other, and then to start listening, and wondering." And she said: "Of course, Dolly didn't know we were here, and Peter's just young enough, and just devil enough, to show off his—well, I suppose he thinks she's his conquest. But even so, she ought to be ashamed." Don did not speak, and after a moment she added: "If Captain Pew ever even suspects, he'll kill him."

"Is there anything you'd like to have me do?"

"Oh no, no; there's nothing we can do. But I hope I never lay eyes on her again."

13

ILL NOW, the Carnival on Mardi Gras had never had a King, but through January there were rumors of the intended innovation, and on the last day of the month, the King's first proclamation appeared in the newspapers. Mr. Howard, the head of the lottery, opened the subscription lists with a contribution of one hundred dollars, and every day during the succeeding fortnight of preparations, the newspapers reported the King's edicts. Don asked Lucy, one night as they prepared for bed: "Want to mask for the Carnival?"

"Heavens, no. I'm too old for that nonsense." Then, seeing the mirth in his eyes: "There, you're just teasing. But I know what let's do!" She spoke in sudden inspiration. "If the weather stays nice and warm, let's go down to Paradise. I'd rather do that, anyway, and so would you! We'll go down just before Mardi Gras, stay maybe two weeks down there? What do you think?" She saw approval in his eyes. "You could visit Mrs. Harper's school some more, and I'll rest and enjoy Donny and the baby. Maybe Mama and Papa will come along."

When they proposed this to Trav and Enid, Trav readily agreed. A Congressional Committee was in town to investigate the recent tumults and incipient riots, and he was weary of politics and bored with Carnival preliminaries. "Fine idea," he said at once. "With the Committee here listening to lies and counter lies, and all this Carnival folderol, I'll be glad to get out of town!"

But Enid protested. "Oh, Trav, don't talk like an old man! Carnival's fun!"

Trav grinned. "Why shouldn't I talk like an old man? Three more years and I'll be sixty!"

"Don't say such things!" she cried. "I won't listen. I'm forty already!" Then, surrendering: "Oh, I'll go downriver if you say so, but it makes me mad! Dolly and Captain Pew dress up in beautiful costumes, and dance all night, and have no end of fun, and I don't believe

Captain Pew's any older than you! One year, he was the Devil, in red tights and a red helmet with his tail hanging over his arm, and Dolly says he was wonderful! They didn't go home till dawn!"

"Makes me creak at the joints just to think of it!"

"Well it doesn't me! It makes me feel about sixteen, and I want to run and sing and dance and flirt and—oh, all sorts of things." And she warned him laughingly: "I feel a little giddy anyway, with Lucy married and all. Trav, wouldn't it be fun to have another baby?"

He chuckled. "And have it call you Grandma?"

They went down to Paradise on the Saturday before Mardi Gras. The big house was ready to receive them. "I've had fires going in every room these three days," Mrs. Tremont said reassuringly. "So it's good and dry."

They settled into peaceful ways, and Lucy sometimes went with Don to watch Mrs. Harper and the children at their lessons. "She doesn't look any older than some of her pupils," she commented. "I don't believe she's a day over sixteen. Is she really married?"

"Oh yes." Don smiled. "She and her husband study together at night," he explained. "Mrs. Tremont says he's quicker to learn than she. He's a good hand, too!"

"How strange it must be," Lucy murmured. "To be a slave all your life, and then suddenly to be free. How frightening, as though you were a child, and suddenly your father and mother and all the people who had always taken care of you died, and when you asked who'd take care of you now, everyone said: 'Why, you'll have to take care of yourself!'"

He nodded. "It's sort of pitiful, yes." He hesitated, seeking for words. "If I saw a tree, or a rosebush or something dying for lack of water, I'd want to give it some. These people are so humble, and they need so much. I'd like to help them find it."

She said in a sudden faint alarm: "But Don, there must be plenty of people who—need things, up in—" She checked herself and smiled. "I mean 'down in' Maine."

He laughed, his arm across her shoulders as they strolled toward the house. "Don't worry, Hon. We'll be going home soon."

"I believe you'd really like to stay here."

"No, no." Shaking his head. "Oh, in winter, maybe, but I hope I'll never have to spend another summer down here. Don't you?" She nodded, happy by his side.

Their days in Paradise were fine; the airs were sweet and cool, and the still nights were heavy with the fragrance of many flowers. Trav and Don usually rose early, but Lucy and Enid might sleep a while, till Lucy went to her mother's room, or Enid came to hers, and they rang for morning coffee. Don, unless there was some other plan afoot, went every morning to watch and listen while Mrs. Harper worked with the children, and these mornings at the church extended themselves so that he might not return to the big house till toward noon. When one day Lucy asked for a report of progress, he explained:

"Well, we're trying different things. Some children learn faster than others—"

She smiled. "So do some grownups."

"I know. And of course, in most schools, the poor students get poor marks!" She had touched him on a tender spot, and he went on, forgetting her in the eager race of his thoughts. "I've never believed in marks, anyway. Trouble with teachers, they think books are important, think that the things in books are the only things worth knowing. If a child of ten, or fifteen, or twenty, doesn't happen to do well at his book lessons, they say he's failed!" His own words made him angry. "Why, doggone it, the world has seen a lot of great men do things, great things, too, who couldn't even write their own names!" He chuckled. "Book larnin'! Shucks! That sort of education is just some fancy clothes a man puts on. They don't change the man; they just make him look better—whether he is any better or not."

They were sitting on a smoothed log on the levee above the landing. The normal spring rise of water was well begun and much of the batture was already covered. The great river slid by with small gurgling eddies and hissing swirls and sighs; the opposite shore was far away. Don rose and walked a few steps away and came back to stand in front of her, his legs spread like those of a colossus, and he went on as though there had been no pause.

"I've read books written by men who were so proud of their book learning that they used a lot of big words to show it off, so many big words that ordinary people couldn't understand them. Anything that's worth saying can be said in words that that deckhand up yonder—" He pointed to a Negro scrubbing the decks of the *Paradise,* moored against the batture. "Words so simple that that deckhand can understand. It's just a little harder to do, that's all; but it's worth doing! Lots of fine men out of the past couldn't read and write. I wonder whether Jesus could? Or Homer? Don't they say there was no such thing as writing in Homer's day, so that he used to recite his poems, and people memorized them, and it was maybe hundreds of years before they were ever written down! The world went along pretty well before men could read or write. Maybe it would get along better now if they forgot how. Maybe then the only things that would be remembered would be the things worth remembering. You know how you forget unpleasant things. A horse kicked me, broke my leg, when I was three years old, but I don't remember how much it hurt; I just remember how nice everyone was to me afterward."

He took four steps one way, four another, and sat down beside her, and after a moment he laughed. "Where was I? I get so worked up, I lose my train of thought. What was I talking about, anyway?"

She smiled. "It's usually about how presumptuous teachers are, when they tell a boy he's a failure."

He nodded eagerly. "That's right! Just because the boy didn't learn something out of books. Maybe he was learning something more important than books. That's what we're trying now, Mrs. Harper and I. Every morning she starts with her spelling book—"

"Where did she get that?" Lucy asked.

"Mr. Tremont had Cash bring it down from town. She prints words or letters on the blackboard, and then passes books around—"

"They haven't any schoolbooks, have they?"

"No, just books, some Mrs. Tremont had, and some from the shelves in the house here. That's one of the things we're doing, outside of their lessons. Someone's always appointed to collect the books, and make sure they're not damaged or dirtied—they wash their hands the first thing every day—and mend the books if they're torn. But then after she has her class, they take turns telling the most interesting thing they've seen this week. Or they can just tell anything they want to tell. Big-foot— he's probably the stupidest boy in school—took us three quarters of a mile across the point, day before yesterday, to watch some red ants moving a nest of black ants they'd captured. They were lugging eggs, and dead ants—or maybe just drugged; I don't know enough about ants to know—as much as ten or fifteen rods through the woods. That was Tuesday."

"Mardi Gras," she commented. "The day you were late for dinner."

He nodded. "And sometimes the children are invited to do things to amuse us. You should see them dance. Then Whistler—no one seems to remember what his name is, not even he—Whistler can imitate any bird you hear around here. And one of the boys whittles out little figures, birds, animals, so well that you can recognize most of them, just by their shape. Almost every one of these children can do something better than anyone else, so each one is champion of something. You'd be surprised how proud it makes them. But we keep telling them every day that they're not trying to beat each other, that the thing they must aim for is to do whatever they do as well as they can, that whoever comes nearest that is really the best."

He hesitated, colored in faint embarrassment, stood up and moved away and came back again. "I was lucky the other day. They were having a jumping match. We let them out in the yard for five or ten minutes every hour, so they won't get bored. One of the boys, Limpy—he's Quinny's son, by the way—is clubfooted. He isn't much more than five years old, maybe less—"

"He'll be six next fall, I think."

"Five and a half, then. But he's small for his age, and he limps with both feet, if you can imagine it. So they all jumped, and I was the judge. I'd measure every jump very carefully, and then I'd measure how tall each boy was. And I gave the prize—it was just a piece of molasses candy—to Limpy, because I said he jumped the farthest—for him! I had to explain that, but when they understood it, it tickled them so they rolled on the ground, laughing. Even Limpy!"

She said happily: "You're an awful nice man. Even for you!"

" I think some of them got what I was driving at," he declared. "And if I get an idea into even one boy, I always feel I've had a successful day!" She saw that he was at a pause, and quickly rose, putting her arm through his, turning him toward the house, and he said with an apologetic chuckle: "I guess I got sort of wound up!"

"I love it when you do," she said. "It's as though I were way deep inside you, in your heart, and in your mind; as though you weren't talking aloud at all; as though I were just thinking with you, being you." She looked up at him gravely; then, with laughing eyes. "But I thought I'd bake, sitting all that time in the sun! Do let's get into the shade; then you can go on."

Captain Cash during the warm months ran daily trips in the *Paradise*, leaving New Orleans in the morning, returning to the city in the evening, carrying passengers as well as freight; but in colder weather, unless there was freight to be moved, or passengers desired transportation, the steamer lay at the levee in New Orleans, or at the plantation, according to the convenience of the Captain. During this stay at the plantation, when Cash made a cargo trip Trav sometimes went with him to the city for the day, and on one of these occasions he remarked at supper after his return: "You missed a call from Dolly, Enid."

"Oh, did you see her?"

"No, but I happened to meet Captain Pew in the hotel this noon. He asked for you, and I told him we were spending two or three weeks down here."

She was puzzled. "How did he happen to mention Dolly?"

"Oh, when I said you were down here, he seemed surprised, and he said Dolly had called on you day before yesterday. But then he seemed to realize he must be wrong, and he corrected himself, said she had gone to call on you, and hadn't happened to mention that she didn't find you at home."

Enid looked puzzled. "How absurd! She knew I wouldn't be there. I told her we'd be down here."

Trav lifted his shoulders. "I'm only telling you what he said."

Lucy caught Don's eye, then spoke to her father. "Did you see Peter?" she inquired.

"No, I didn't go out to the house. Probably he'd have been downtown anyway. I didn't see him." He said to Enid: "Cash left Quinny with 'Phemy, at Tony's."

"I'll be glad when she has this baby and gets it over with. She's been getting more impudent every day. I think she just starts these false alarms to worry Cash, anyway."

"Cash didn't seem worried."

"He's such a superior nigger! It's a pity he involved himself with a wretched little wench like Quinny."

"That reminds me," Trav remarked. "I heard you bragging Cash up to himself this morning."

As though his tone put her on the defensive, she said quickly: "I just told him how lucky he was to have such a fine boat, said he kept it so clean and spic and span that he deserved to be lucky."

"Don't go giving him any big ideas," Trav suggested. "Or he'll take the boat and Quinny and go off up north or somewhere. I've seen many a good nigra, yes and good white men, too, spoiled by too much easy praise."

Enid flushed with anger. "Don't talk to me like a schoolteacher, Trav!"

Lucy spoke quickly, to ease the sudden tension. "Hey there! What's the matter with schoolteachers? Don's one, or at least he'd like to be! Schoolteachers are all right."

Enid laughed, yet she said rebelliously: "But Don never lectures me!"

Toward the month's end, Trav and Enid returned to New Orleans, but Don and Lucy and the babies stayed on another week. When they went back up river, the Legislature had adjourned. "And they accomplished little or nothing," Trav told Don. "Except to re-enact the Election Law, and the Registration Law, with a slight reduction of the Governor's powers. The best thing they did was to adjourn. Every day they stayed in session was money out of pocket for every honest man. I prefer Warmoth to the Legislature every time."

They were at breakfast together, glancing through the papers, and Don remarked: "The Governor's the whipping boy, isn't he? He's being blamed for everything that happens."

Trav looked across the table. "Oh, you're reading the *National Republican*. That's the Carter paper. Don't confuse it with the *Republi-*

can. Warmoth owns a fourth of the *Republican,* so it gets the bulk of the public printing, and the *National Republican* claims he's made a profit of six hundred and seventy-five thousand out of that." He added: "I don't think he'll run for re-election. A few of us prefer him to his enemies, but his enemies have the votes."

They read a while in silence, and presently Don said: "Here's an incredibly illiterate letter from the head of the Carroll Parish school board. He spells 'Parish' p-e-i-s-h, and 'Christmas' c-r-i-t-m-a-s, and 'finding' f-i-n-n-e-n. Head of the school board! Abject ignorance seems so pitiful."

"There's a lot of abject ignorance in the South," Trav assented, his eyes on the paper. Don nodded, his thoughts his own.

Early in March, General and Mrs. Longstreet dined one Sunday at Prytania Street, and the General told Trav he intended to resign as Surveyor of the Port. The day was fine and agreeably warm, and after dinner they all went into the garden to admire old Abram's early flowers. The General slowed his pace so that he and Trav fell a little behind the others. "Major," he said, "remember you once suggested that if I became dissatisfied with the company I had to keep in the Custom House, I had better move my office?" Trav looked at him in surprise, and Longstreet explained: "Well, I've decided to do so." And since Trav still seemed puzzled, he added: "To resign."

Trav, after a moment's consideration, asked: "Why, exactly? Why do you resign? You're not involved with the Packard crowd."

"To stand silent while other federal officials, whose offices are under the same roof as mine, seek to overthrow the civil government of the state, is to appear to consent to their activities. At least it seems so to me, and I'm unwilling to let anyone imagine that I approve their purpose, or their methods."

"You're making quite a sacrifice, aren't you?" Trav laughed at his own thoughts. "You'll confuse a lot of people," he commented. "They've damned you for accepting an appointment from President Grant, claimed it was your reward for turning Republican. What will they say now when you give up a salary of a good many thousands a year for a scruple?"

Longstreet grunted. "Probably decide that I've been bought by Warmoth. But Major, I've never been able to share your apprehensions about what people might think, or say."

"Will you still support Grant?"

"Certainly! The President is not tainted by the acts of these men."

"He probably feels he must stand by Casey."

Longstreet smiled. "Yes, probably. For the sake of peace in the family."

When they said good night, the General remarked: "By the way, Major, I hope that pretty niece of yours hasn't deserted New Orleans for good and all."

Trav, for a moment puzzled, said: "Miss Dolly?"

The General nodded. "Hadn't you heard? I dropped in at the Haunted House last night." He chuckled. "I like a game of poker as well as anyone. Broderick informed me that Captain and Mrs. Pew have gone to Paris for the summer."

"I hadn't heard," Trav admitted, and later he told Lucy and Don of this departure. That night when they had gone upstairs, Lucy asked:

"Don, do you think Captain Pew guessed? Or is he just—taking precautions?"

"Probably just that. If he knew—whatever there is to know—I'd expect him to bring Peter to account."

She shivered. "Surely not! Peter's just a boy!"

He said in dry amusement: "I suspect he thinks himself a man."

Through March and April, Don spent three more weeks at Paradise. When he proposed to do so, he explained: "You know more children are coming to school all the time, from other plantations, and from off in the swamp. They have fun, and they spread the word, so their friends come to share the good times. I like to watch them, work with them."

She laughed, touching his hand in quick affection. "There, you go along. I'll stay here and you can spend all the time you want in your little old school."

"I'm going to take down some schoolbooks, and some pads for them to write on and some pencils."

"Papa ought to get Mrs. Harper whatever she wants."

"Wait. Next winter we can tell better what we need." She looked at him, a little startled to realize his plans went so far.

At the end of the week, he came up to spend the day, and he was excited over a new project. "We're going to build a schoolhouse," he told Lucy. "At least, if your father doesn't object. We're outgrowing the church. More of the bigger boys are coming to school now, and they take up more room. The children will build it themselves, this summer. They'll fell the trees, and Mr. Tremont will have the logs sawed up into boards in the mill, so we won't have to buy anything but nails and window glass and so on, and I can pay for them. Mr. Tremont says old Percy is a good carpenter, can help the boys." He added: "I haven't talked to your father yet."

Lucy, happy in his happiness, was sure Trav would agree, and of course he did, and the following week Don reported that the first trees had been felled. "And we may have acquired a new hand," he explained. "A strange boy appeared one day. He came with two of our boys, but he's white."

"Children play together," she assured him. "At least, boys do, white boys and nigras, if they happen to."

"I know," he assented. "The white boys boss the Negroes around."

"Of course. They always have."

Don nodded. "At any rate, this boy—his name's Pink, he says; Pink Chambers—he came and offered to help. Or at least he hinted. He was watching one of the older boys swing an axe." He chuckled. "The boy everyone calls Pestuh. I don't know why."

"They probably mean Pester-r-r," she suggested, rolling the "r" in comical imitation of his way of talking. "Probably once upon a time his mama told him he did nothing but pester-r-r, pester-r-r, pester-r-r, and other boys heard her and the name stuck."

He smiled with her. "Well, Pester seems to be his name. And Pink was watching him, and I remarked that Pester was the best axeman we had, and Pink said: 'I'm better than him.' So I explained that we were all trying to learn how to do things better, and asked him to teach us, and pretty soon he was giving us all lessons in axe work. He was almost as good as he thought he was, too. He's only about fourteen, I should say, but he's a grown man with an axe."

"Did he just come that one day?"

"No; that was Wednesday, and he's been there every day since. Helps us a lot, too. He teaches by example, so every time he takes on a new pupil, he cuts down a tree to show how it's done."

Seeing his happy content, she said fondly: "I expect you're wishing you could stay there all summer, oversee the work."

He laughed. "No. No, it's pretty hot down here for a State-of-Maine man, even now. I'll be glad to get back where it's cool."

"Oh now," she said, teasing him. "I've been as hot in Maine as I've ever been here. But I'll be glad to get back there, all the same."

They planned to start north early in May. After Don's final week at Paradise, she saw that he was vaguely unhappy, and when three or four days passed and he had not shared his concern with her she asked a question. At first he gave her only denials, or smiling reassurances, till she said in mock severity:

"Now see here, Captain Page, do you really believe that after we've been married over three years you can keep any secrets from me?"

So he surrendered. "It's only that Mr. Tremont thinks we may have some trouble," he admitted. "I told you about the white boy, Pink, who came to watch us and stayed to work with us. One day it rained too hard to work in the woods, so we kept school, instead, and he came in, and seemed to be interested. But Mr. Tremont says we'd better not let him come to school with the Negroes. He says the boy's folks won't like it!" When she did not at once speak, he added: "You know, Mr. Tremont's children don't come to our school. Mrs. Tremont teaches them at home."

"Southern people don't like mixed schools," she agreed. "And besides that, we've never allowed anyone to teach nigras anything anyway. But of course now we have to, and we'll get used to it. It takes time, Honey, but even Southerners do change."

Before Don and Lucy returned to Maine, the preliminary moves of the political campaign were already under way. A Democratic State Convention spent its eloquence in denouncing Governor Warmoth; the Reform party convention, at first called for April twenty-third, was postponed till June; Governor Warmoth's Liberal Party was still an infant, its paternity the only certain thing about it; the Colored Men's Convention on April fifteenth endorsed Grant, and Lieutenant Governor Pinchback called a True Republican convention to meet May twenty-eighth. After they reached the farm, Trav's letters kept them informed of the march of events.

"The True Republicans endorsed Warmoth and Pinchback," he reported, "And Pinchback made a speech endorsing himself with real eloquence! He announced that he was not a candidate for Governor, though he said the odds were ten to one that he would win if he ran!"

Two weeks later, he wrote that Warmoth had formally declined the True Republican nomination. "He insists he's anxious to unite his Liberal Republican party with the Reform and the Democratic crowd. General Longstreet has high hopes of this. He's a Liberal, of course; the General, I mean.

"As things stand, there are at least four parties in the field; the last-ditch Democrats, the Reform crowd, the Liberals, and the Custom House gang. I expect the other three will combine against the Custom House. Meanwhile, taxes keep going up. In eighteen sixty, the state tax here was twenty-nine cents on the thousand dollars of value; now it's two dollars and fifteen cents the thousand, and in New Orleans, parish and city taxes add three dollars to that!"

In mid-July he reported that the Democrats and the Reformers had merged, with John McEnery of Ouachita as their candidate for Governor. "I think well of him," Trav remarked. "I've seen him only twice, but I like him. He's full-bearded, with an almost Christ-like face, at once firm and kind. He was born in Virginia, but he grew up here, then went to college in Indiana, and then studied law at the University of New Orleans. He was a Douglas man before the War, rose to be Lieutenant Colonel of the Fourth Louisiana, returned to the practice of law;

a sound, conservative man. I'll probably vote for him. The Custom House crowd have nominated Senator Kellogg. He's one of those men whose eyes come out of the same hole; a carpetbagger, born in Vermont and brought up in Illinois. Lincoln sent him down here as Collector of the Port, so he's a Louisiana man for revenue only."

Don chuckled at that, but Lucy said resentfully: "I wish Papa'd write more about the things we want to hear. As if we cared who they elected Governor! Or as if it made any difference!"

"It makes a lot of difference to them," he reminded her. He had come in hot from haymaking and after his bath in the shed they were in their room and he was dressing while she read Trav's letter aloud. "The rest of the Southern states are getting rid of their carpetbagger governments. Most of them."

"Not South Carolina," she retorted. "I had a letter today from Sarah Morgan. They're visiting Jimmy. He's home from Egypt, trying to bring back the old Hampton plantation. Remember, Uncle Brett and Aunt Cinda took us over there. It's on the Congaree, south of Columbia. Jimmy has been all alone there—but wait a minute. I'll read what she says."

She found the letter and opened it and read.

> . . . all alone there with one servant, an enormous woman! She must weigh two hundred and fifty pounds, and Jimmy vows that in the first month she carried home—besides birds and venison he shot, and fish and chickens and meat he bought—fifty pounds of bacon, three barrels of flour, and eleven hams. He produces the grocer's bill to prove it. Of course, you know Jimmy and the way he exaggerates, but she looks perfectly capable of eating that much.

They laughed together while Lucy's eyes ran down the page. "And then she goes on about what a rascal the Governor is, and how many carpetbaggers and scalawags they have all around, and about the Ku Kluxes. Jimmy was accused of being one. One day he caught a white man making a speech to his people and kicked him off the place, and he was arrested and fined fifty dollars. The judge was a nigra named Sam. Jimmy's been arrested other times, for driving politicians off the place, and Sam always fines him fifty dollars. Sarah writes almost as much politics as Papa does. She and Mrs. Morgan are living with Jimmy now. They discharged his fat cook, and Sarah says: 'And now her grown sons and daughters have come to Jimmy to go to work in the fields. I guess she was feeding them on what she carried home.'"

As they went downstairs together, she added: "Sarah has met Jimmy's friend, Captain Dawson, and is much taken with him. Wouldn't that be exciting?"

They had settled easily into the familiar routine of life at the farm; the early rising, the long unhurried days, the deep sleep through short summer nights. Sometimes in the night Lucy was roused by the squall of a passing fox or by the noises the deer made as they pulled down apples in the orchard, or even by the soft whoo-whoo-wh-who of an owl down in the lowlands, and she liked to lie awake and listen for the smaller sounds, a cricket's chirp, the squeak of mice or their scurry in the walls, the soft footfall of one of the dogs making his watchful round.

Sometimes when she woke, she fell to thinking of New Orleans, of Trav and her mother and Peter, of Isaiah and Daisy and old Maria. Pa and Ma were nice as they could be, and she loved them both, yet there was in each of them something secret and withdrawn. She thought that if they disliked her, they would never let her know it. The thrift imposed upon them by their way of life and by their surroundings, the necessity of meeting their wants by the sweat of their own brows rather than by the toil of Negro slaves, the necessity of using to the utmost every hour of fine weather in order to accumulate the means of surviving four or five or six months of winter, this thrift had become a part of them. They were sparing of caresses, of small tendernesses, of affectionate words. She was sure they liked her—but why did they not tell her so? Why didn't Ma ever say: "My but you're a nice girl! My but you're a good wife to Don!" Why didn't Pa ever call her something besides "Lucy", or "Lu"? Why didn't either of them seem pleased when she kissed them good night! Ma never even put up her cheek, much less kissed Lucy back. As for Pa, if he gave any sign that he had noticed at all, it was usually just to grunt, in a startled, grudging sort of way.

Yet they were so fine, and the days were so peaceful and serene; how could anyone not be happy here? Why should she sometimes be homesick for people who, if they loved you, told you so? Did Ma ever snuggle up to Pa and whisper love to him? Did Pa ever think up new sweet ways to make sure Ma knew he loved her? Of course, when Ma scolded Pa for not wearing his oilskins when it rained, or for going all day with his feet wet, though she sounded angry, she wasn't, really; it was not real scolding. It was a way of making love.

"But I like our way better," she confided to Don one night, drowsy in his arms. "Don't you s'pose sometimes Pa wishes he was you, and had a nice little wife like me?"

Don chuckled: "I guess he's satisfied."

"He'd better be. Ma's sweet. And so is he."

Trav wrote that Mrs. Longstreet was visiting kinfolks in Michigan. "Mama says there's going to be another baby this summer. That will please him." Longstreet was irritated, he said, by a speech which General Early had made in January and which was just now published. "Early criticized the General's work at Gettysburg," he said. "It's the first real criticism I've ever heard of Longstreet's military career. I wish General Lee were alive to answer it, but of course nobody dared criticize Longstreet as long as Lee was alive."

He and Enid and the baby spent almost three months that summer in the mountains near Martinson. His first letter after they returned to New Orleans in September reported that the Longstreets had a new daughter, named Maria Louisa after her mother. "You never saw a man so tickled," Trav wrote. "Mrs. Longstreet's still in Michigan, and I guess if it weren't for politics he'd have started for there before now. Speaking of politics, it looks as though we might elect McEnery. The Republicans are split, and Warmoth's supporting McEnery. Longstreet says he'll stick with the Republicans, but he doesn't swing many votes."

Tony, he said, had had a stroke. "So I went to see him. They think he'll get over it. It's the third stroke that kills them. He can't talk much, and he may be chair-bound. Sapphira talks for him. The Custom House crowd have put Pinchback up for Congressman at Large. He's backing Kellogg."

Two days later another letter told them that the schoolhouse at Paradise, built by the children themselves, had been burned. "Middle of the night," Trav wrote. "Mr. Tremont lighted his lamp to get up, and someone shot it off the table, so he didn't. The people say there were five of them, white men. After all the work the young ones did, it's too bad."

When Lucy finished reading the letter to him, Don said: "We'll go right down. Pa can get along. He has before. We've got to get a new schoolhouse started right away." Under her eyes he became uneasy. "We must, Lucy," he insisted. "We started this; we can't quit."

"You can't fight men who sneak around in the dark."

"Now, darling, men like that are just cowards!"

"Even a coward can shoot straight!"

"Honey, the children loved the school. They built it themselves, worked at it all spring and summer."

She clung to him, white and shaken. "I'm afraid, Don."

"There's nothing to be afraid of. Believe me, dear." So, inevitably, she surrendered, raised her lips to his.

14

WHEN GOVERNOR WARMOTH allied himself with the Democrats to support McEnery for Governor, he hoped to take with him into the enemy camp a major portion of his followers; but in this he was disappointed, many of his former allies joining the Custom House faction and actively campaigning for Kellogg. Among them was Lieutenant Governor Pinchback.

Pinchback did this against the advice of Tony and Sapphira, who urged that he remain loyal to Warmoth. "I must back Kellogg," he insisted. "The new legislature will be Republican; and their first act, when they meet in January, will be to impeach the Governor. I will then become Governor of Louisiana—if I support Kellogg. If I don't, they'll first move me out of the way."

"Is that your own thought?" Sapphira asked.

"Not at all. I, of course, knew it might happen, but it's been made definite. If I support Kellogg, I'll be Governor of Louisiana from the time Warmoth is impeached till Kellogg's inauguration."

"A few weeks," Sapphira reminded him. "An empty title. Yet for it, you risk your whole future."

He smiled. "Not quite, Miss Sapphira! Not quite! There's a further consideration. The next legislature will elect a new Senator to go to Washington. I've been promised that I shall have the place."

When he was gone, Tony struggled to his feet, Sapphira hurrying to offer him her arm. He had sufficiently recovered so that with her support on one side and a cane in his other hand, he could walk from one room to another. He was still unable to speak clearly, but Sapphira and 'Phemy usually understood him. Tonight as they crossed to the bedroom door, he laughed scornfully.

"Governor Pinchback! Senator Pinchback!" He jerked his head toward the door through which Pinchback had gone. "I'm tired of him!" He shook his head. "Up out of nothing! Watch him go back!"

Tony was in these days as comfortable as a half-helpless man can be. At Sapphira's request, Cash and Quinny had moved into one of the cabins behind the house, and either one or both of them were available if they were needed. She never left Tony's side, and if his temper wore thin he could fret and fume at her without provoking protest or reproach. Like most men, when they are ill, he found an irritable satisfaction in being disagreeable to those who loved him. He had no longer so many callers as in the past. Doctor Roudanez had abandoned politics to confine himself to medicine, former Governor Hahn had retired to his plantation and founded Hahnville, Stephen Packard would not come to a house where he might encounter Governor Warmoth, Mr. Parker was nowadays more interested in business than in politics, Oscar Dunn was dead. But a few of his earlier friends were occasional callers, and Governor Warmoth came now and then to pay his respects to Sapphira, and to talk politics with Tony.

He came one night toward the end of October. Tony lay at length upon a *chaise longue,* Sapphira sitting where his eyes could rest upon her. Her hands were as usual busy with needle and bright threads as she worked upon a piece of *gros point.*

"I'm fortunate to find you alone," the Governor said, after first greetings. "I need to rest and refresh myself, and no place in New Orleans equals, for those purposes, this room of yours."

Tony muttered something, and Warmoth asked: "You're tired of resting? Was that what you said?" Tony grinned and made an affirmative sound, and Warmoth said: "Well, I haven't reached that point yet, though I may. When I presently retire to private life, I shall become the proprietor of a sugar plantation down river. I have my eye on the very property. I shall take my ease there, watch the cane grow, watch the great river sliding by."

He rose and began to walk here and there around the room, leaning to look more closely at the titles of books upon the shelves, at a French doll in an elaborate gown standing demurely on the marble top of the long table, at the engravings on the walls; and as he walked he talked, thinking aloud, now and then glancing at Tony, flinging a question. "Are you interested?" Or, to Sapphira: "Is he tiring? Should I go?"

"You entertain him more than anyone."

He spoke of the campaign, of the election now less than a week away. "I have that all here in my hand," he assured them, extending his open hand with the palm up, then closing his fingers in an eloquent gesture. There was a high mirth in his tones. "Tomorrow, next year, I will be a nobody, a wealthy young man who has retired to his plantation to take his ease, but for the moment I am engaged in electing a Democratic Governor in Louisiana!"

Sapphira asked: "Are you so sure?"

"Positive, ma'am. But not in the traditional Democratic way, the way which prevailed before the War, when according to the Democratic Governors of those days each election was accompained by 'scenes of intimidation, violence and bloodshed,' and by 'crimes committed in broad daylight,' and when 'bloodthirsty mobs overawed the voters,' and when 'the approaches to the polls were completely in the hands of organized ruffians,' who committed repeated acts of 'violence against multitudes of citizens.'" He chuckled. "I quote from the inaugural addresses of some of those pre-War Governors. But I shall elect a Democratic Governor next week, not by such methods, but by the use of a few peaceful devices of my own invention. For after all, what is the function of election supervisors if not to supervise elections?"

The question drew from Tony a cackle of mirth, from Sapphira one of her rare smiles.

"So!" said the Governor. "So this will be a peaceful election! True, some good Democrats organized a White League in St. Mary's Parish last July, but I haven't heard that they've killed any Negroes. The country newspapers breathe out threatenings and slaughter to intimidate the colored voters, but no one is slain. One night two months ago at a Democratic rally here in the city a few shots were fired, but no one was hit. No, this election will go down in history as a bloodless victory. Every registering officer had his instruction and obeyed them, every election officer will do the same. The federal supervisors will be allowed to witness the count for electors, but not the count for local officers; the Returning Board will do the rest."

'Phemy came with decanter and glasses and a dish of nuts and another of sugared cakes, and the Governor stopped his leisurely circuit of the room. "Yes," he said, "we'll elect Mr. McEnery Governor of Louisiana by a good ten thousand votes."

Tony made an angry sound, and Warmoth held up his hand. "Mr. Currain, you are right. Absolutely right. I was a Republican and I am a Republican. I have not deserted the party; the party has deserted me. Did you know that—But that reminds me, have you seen Lieutenant Governor Pinchback, since our return from New York?"

Tony muttered something, and Sapphira said: "No, not for several weeks."

Warmoth said in amusement: "I thought he might have told you. I met him in New York and invited him to come that night to my room. He promised to do so, but did not, and I guessed the truth. There were several bills enacted by the last legislature which I had not yet signed, among them one providing for the selection of a new returning board. The Lieutenant Governor had slipped away, hoping to get back to New Orleans before me, and as Acting Governor in my absence, to sign those bills."

He spoke with relish. "Luckily I had friends in positions of authority on the Illinois Central. I telegraphed one of these friends to make sure that Pinchback missed his train, somewhere along the line. At Canton, up in Mississippi, in the middle of the night, they enticed Mr. Pinchback off the train—something about an important telegram for 'Governor Pinchback.' He couldn't resist the sound of that, so he went into the station to get his telegram. They locked the door, and before he could climb out of the window the train went off without him. I had arranged for a special car, so when I came along next morning I was able to give 'The Governor' a ride to New Orleans. He admitted, of course, that he had hoped to get here first, and sign those bills."

Tony was mumbling, and Sapphira listened for a moment, nodded. "Mr. Currain says it will really be 'Governor Pinchback' before long," she explained.

Warmoth smiled, threw up both hands. "*Touché!* Yes indeed," he admitted. "I expect to be impeached within five minutes after the House is organized, and Mr. Pinchback will promptly seat himself in my chair." He rose, bade them farewell. "But meanwhile, I'll elect a Democratic Governor of Louisiana."

"I expect," Sapphira suggested, "that you think of yourself as Samson in the temple?"

He smiled in appreciation. "You've a sharp tongue, Miss Sapphira: but as between me and Samson, there is this difference. I have not been shorn."

Don and Lucy and the babies came back to New Orleans to an eager welcome, and for a while everyone talked at once. But when Don and Trav were at last alone, without waiting for a question, Trav said: "Well, Don, I went down to Paradise as soon as I heard. You remember a boy named Pink, a white boy?"

"Yes. He helped us cut trees for the lumber to build the schoolhouse."

"Well, it was his father—he and some others like him—who burned the schoolhouse. Chambers, his name is; lives over across the swamp. I rode over to see the men there. I said someone had burned the schoolhouse and the church on my plantation, and that whoever did it must have had a grudge against me, and that I'd like to find out why, and straighten things out so that we'd be on good terms." Don listened in silent attention, and Trav went on: "Most of them didn't say anything, just spat tobacco in the dust as near my shoes as they could without hitting them. But this Chambers, he talked up to me. He said he didn't want me teaching niggers to read and write, and giving them a lot of highfalutin' ideas, and he said he particularly didn't want me teaching his boy to associate with niggers."

Trav paused, and Don asked: "What then?"

"Well, I was just a little hot under the collar!" Trav admitted. "I told him that I'd bought Paradise, and that I aimed to run it my way, and if he wanted to keep his children at home, he wouldn't hurt my feelings."

Don nodded, amusement in his eyes. "You're not much of a peacemaker. Have they made any start on rebuilding the schoolhouse?"

"I haven't been down since, but I doubt it. The people were all pretty frightened."

"I'll go down Monday," Don decided. "Maybe we can get Mr. Chambers and his friends interested in helping."

Trav looked at him thoughtfully. "Think you can get anywhere with him?"

"Well, I'll try not to get him mad."

Trav grinned. "I got mad myself. That's where I failed. Maybe you can do better. Wait a week or two and we'll all go down. This is the best time of the year down there."

Don, instead of replying, asked: "How's the mill?"

"Good enough. Our export trade has just about doubled again this year and we're getting fifty-three cents for our oil."

"Is General Longstreet pleased with his new daughter?"

"He hasn't seen her yet." Trav made a sympathetic sound. "The General's all snarled up in politics. He's been like a bull bothered in fly time!" And he explained: "He's always liked Warmoth, and admired him, and he was disgusted with the Custom House crowd. That's why he resigned as Surveyor of Customs, said in his letter of resignation that he couldn't stomach their trying to 'displace by violence the civil authority of the state.' So he went along with Warmoth in organizing the Liberal Republicans—and then they decided to back McEnery, help the Democrats."

"Warmoth, too?"

"Warmoth and all, yes. But much as he admired Warmoth, the General couldn't follow him that far. If he did, it would be like admitting that when he turned Republican five years ago he was wrong." Trav smiled faintly. "That's something I never knew the General to do; admit he'd been wrong. I'm sorry for him, siding with men he despises, but it's just his own stubbornness!"

Don asked for Tony, and Trav said Tony was as well as anyone could expect. "I call on him, now and then. He still keeps track of politics."

"Has there been much violence in this campaign?"

"No," Trav assured him, and he smiled. "No. This year, instead of killing nigras, they're planning to cheat them out of their votes. Some Democratic ballots are being printed with Grant's picture on them, so a nigra who can't read may drop them in the ballot box, thinking he's voting Republican. Then they've printed tissue-paper ballots so thin that you can fold a hundred of them together to look like one when you drop them in the box. I hear they're going to locate the polls out in the country, in new places, hiding them so you can't find them unless you know where they are, putting them so far out of town that a nigra will have to walk forty miles to get to them." He added cheerfully: "But even Peter—he's the bloodthirsty member of the—"

He broke off as someone came down the stairs, and Enid appeared in the doorway to join them. "Lucy's lying down," she explained. "What was that about Peter?"

Don saw Trav hesitate, and he asked: "How is he, by the way?"

Enid shook her head. "Oh, you'll probably not see him at all while you're here. You know, he'll never forgive you for marrying Lucy. He was always crazy about her, tagged around after her when he was hardly old enough to walk." Don smiled, uncomfortable and ill at ease, and Enid added: "He's running the Haunted House now. Captain Pew and Dolly are in France." She turned again to Trav. "You were saying Peter was bloodthirsty."

"Just saying Peter didn't look for much violence, at this election."

"Nothing worse than burning a few schools?" Don asked, not angrily, and he said: "I believe I'd rather not wait till next week, Major, to go to Paradise. I'd better go down ahead of you, talk to Mr. Tremont, see where we stand."

Trav assented. Lucy, when she heard, wished to go with Don, but he dissuaded her. "I'm not going to run into any trouble, Honey," he promised. "I just want to talk things over with Mr. Tremont. You come down with the others. I'll be fine."

On the trip downriver, Don stayed in the pilothouse with Captain Cash. Mr. Tony was getting better, Cash said; he could move around pretty well. Quinny? She and the babies were well. Limpy was still at Paradise, but the others were with Quinny. Cash had been in New Orleans the night the school was burned. "I'm full as well pleased I was," he admitted. "White men on a rampage, I lay low."

Mr. Tremont met Don at the landing, talking of other things; they walked together past the house and the mill, and down beyond the quarter to where the church and the school building had stood. Don was disappointed to see nothing but a charred chimney and blackened ashes, and he said in an inquiring tone:

"They've not begun to rebuild?"

Mr. Tremont shook his head. "No," he said. "No, and you're going to find it hard to get them at it. These boys, and the girls too, some of them, worked good all summer, got it just about finished; but these men came and burned it down, and let the word get around that they'd better not build it up again, and they're scared."

Don said, not watching the other, but alert to his reaction: "I can't help thinking this was just a drunken prank, setting the fire. Surely they won't do it again."

"I wouldn't put it past 'em," Mr. Tremont admitted, and he laughed uneasily. "Fact is, I'm some scared myself. Leastways, I'd be scared if I set out to go against my neighbors."

Don pressed the point. "But Mr. Tremont, we're trying to help them. If we got some schools started around here, one for Negroes and one for white children, everybody would be better off."

Mr. Tremont spat eloquently. "You'd be surprised to find out how many folks around here—and anywhere else, for that matter—don't want to be better off. Folks most generally like things the way they are, or they'd have changed them themselves. It's like a boy, most always he'll brag about the big things he's going to do when he grows up, but when he does grow up, he takes up with a girl, and they have a passel of children, and he's got all he can do and a little more, and first thing he knows, he forgets all about his big ideas. When somebody comes along and reminds him of all the things he used to think he'd do, and didn't, that just makes him mad." He spat again. "Yes sir, it's surprising how few men want anybody to do something for them."

Don recognized the wisdom in the other's words. "I certainly don't mean to patronize anybody. Not even the Negroes." He colored a little at his own thoughts. "I suppose it's really myself I'm trying to please. I'd be a lot happier if I thought I was helping some of these youngsters —but maybe they're happier the way they are. Maybe, if they knew how much they're missing, they'd be unhappy and discontented and mad."

The overseer scratched his head. "Well sir, I have to say they were a lot happier working with you, building the schoolhouse and all. They was almighty pleased with theirselves. These young ones were so doggoned tickled with the job they'd done, thinking how you'd praise 'em when you came back! I mean to tell you, I was real provoked with Chambers and that crowd."

"Yet I can understand your being—uneasy," Don assured him. "Here with your family, and so much of the time alone."

"Uneasy, my foot! I'm scared! It makes me kind of sick of myself, too!"

"I hate to think of these children being scared."

"It's their grownups, more'n it is them," Mr. Tremont reflected. "Children don't scare easy. They don't believe anybody's going to hurt them till they're hurt. But the grownups know what that kind of whites might do."

Don asked: "Do you think if I rode over to see Mr. Chambers and his friends, it would make any trouble for you? Or for the children?"

"It might make some trouble for you."

"I think maybe I ought to try. I got this whole thing started, and then went off to Maine and left you here to take the blame, to be shot at!"

"They didn't what you'd call shoot at me," Mr. Tremont corrected. "Most of them, when they shoot at a squirrel's eye, they hit it. Not just the squirrel; his eye. No, they didn't shoot at me."

"I thought I'd ride over and explain that you weren't to blame, explain what I was trying to do."

Mr. Tremont hesitated. "Well, it ain't far," he decided. "Three-four miles. I can tell you how to go." He snapped his fingers. "No, 'y Godfrey, I'll go with you!"

"Why don't you stay out of it?"

"Oh, I can help, maybe." There was a wry mirth in his tone. "I can sort of explain to 'em that you don't mean any real harm, that you're just a plain dumb fool and don't know any better."

Don laughed. "Fine," he agreed. "We'll have a talk with them, get acquainted, see how we get along."

The ride was longer than Don had expected, not in distance but in the difficulty of the trail. A mile or so from the house—they had ridden at an angle away from the river—they came to soft ground in which the horses floundered laboriously, and then into the recesses of the swamp, following a winding way through massed trees and shrubs and tangled vines. The trail forked so often that Don wondered how Mr. Tremont knew which fork to take, and the overseer promised to have the trees marked before Don came this way again. They rode through forests of water oaks draped with Spanish moss, through cypress swamps where knees thrust up from the water all around them, through tangled and sometimes thorny vines; and for a furlong or more they waded, stirrup-deep, and Don saw an alligator like a drifting log float quietly away. A silver gar leaped in a flash of sun, an eagle screamed from the sky, and once Mr. Tremont shot a water moccasin that hung draped along a log beside the trail. Herons flopped away, a buzzard soared low above the treetops over their heads, and Don was glad at last to come to a mucky savannah, and then to dry land. The dim trail joined two wheel tracks to lead them on toward half a dozen rude houses widely spaced along the sandy road.

As they approached, Don saw here and there in this small settlement a human figure; a woman hanging out clothes, three or four children, an old man leading a cow; but as they advanced, all these individuals, except the old man and the cow, who went on before them, disappeared into the houses. Don and Mr. Tremont rode side by side, and Don said under his breath:

"I suppose everyone knows we're coming, who we are, whether we're armed."

"Wouldn't you if you was them? They heard me shoot."

The first house was set back fifty yards or more from the road. It was built of rough-sawed boards, two rooms with an open passage between, a 'dog-run' house of the sort never seen in Maine but familiar all over the South. Where a path led from the road to the door, Don pulled up his horse, and Mr. Tremont halted beside him. Inside the house —the door was open—a baby lifted a wailing cry and instantly was hushed. A dog asleep under the house—which was set on posts two or three feet above the ground—woke and stood up and stretched and saw them and barked. Inside the house, a stick of firewood banged against the floor, and the dog dropped and lay flat, its head between its paws.

Don began a conversation with Mr. Tremont, and they turned their backs to the house while he spoke of a curiously shaped cloud in the sky, at which he pointed. Then he pointed again, at a duck wheeling to join friends somewhere in the swamp. He discussed the prospects for rain. After minutes of this he heard a shuffling step behind him, and turned his horse to face the man approaching.

The other paused, and Don said a cheerful good morning, and the man nodded. "Looking for someone?" he asked, unsmiling. A shotgun hung in the crook of his arm.

"Why, yes," Don assented. "Or rather, I'm looking for advice. I've a job on my hands and I don't know how to tackle it. Mr. Tremont here thinks Mr. Chambers could help me. Do you know where I can find him?"

The man's eyes held Don's in a long, completely neutral stare. "Fourth house," he said at last.

Don thanked him and kneed his horse. They did not look back, so if the man to whom they had spoken made a signal they did not see it, but when they approached the fourth house, and while they were still a hundred yards away, a man stepped out and came toward the roadside. He seemed at first glance to be a fat man, but as they drew nearer, Don saw that this was not the case. Mr. Chambers was not fat, but he was big, with heavy shoulders, a deep chest, sturdy legs. If he were armed, his weapon was concealed. His countenance was that of an amiable gentleman.

He was the first to speak. As Don pulled up, he said: "Hear you're looking for Mr. Chambers? I'm him."

It occurred to Don that a man on the ground must look up to a man on horseback, and may subconsciously resent this, so he swung off his horse, extended his hand. "My name's Page."

Mr. Chambers's hand in his was heavy and lifeless. "Yes, I know it is. I give my boy Pink a good hidin', account of you."

"I had many a good licking from my father," Don assented. A log beside the road would serve as a seat. "I need your advice. Can you spare me a little time? Can we sit down?"

"Might as well."

Mr. Tremont had already dismounted; he took Don's reins and secured the horses to a scaly-bark beside the road, exchanging with Mr. Chambers a nod of greeting. Don said at once: "I'm afraid I owe you an apology, Mr. Chambers. You see, I was responsible for building the school over at Paradise. I married Mr. Currain's daughter, Miss Lucy, and she and I have spent some time at the plantation."

"Pink told me all about you," Mr. Chambers agreed. "Or all he knowed, anyway. I told him to keep away from you." His tone was completely free from anger; he merely stated a fact.

"I'm sorry. He's a fine boy. I was proud to know him." Mr. Chambers offered no comment, and Don explained: "I'm a fair hand with an axe myself. My father's a farmer. But your son is as good as I ever saw. In fact, that's one of the reasons I came today. You see, our schoolhouse and church burned down, and I want to see them built again. Is there any reason why I shouldn't?"

Mr. Chambers looked at him in a faint confusion. "What's it to me?"

"If you object, I won't do it."

"Why not?"

Don smiled faintly. "Well, for one reason, I think that if you do object, I'd be wasting my time."

"Might be, yes."

Don nodded. "So I'd like to have your consent before we drive a nail."

"If I've got a say, I say 'No.'"

Mr. Chambers was about to rise, but Don said: "Fine! That's fine!" This surprising word stopped the big man, and he relaxed again.

"Eh? What'd you say?"

"Why, I said 'fine,'" Don told him. "Now we know where we stand, and we can talk it over between us, with no hard feelings on either side. I'll try to see if I can show you why we should build a school over there, and you see if you can show me why we shouldn't."

"You said if I said 'No' that would settle it."

"I didn't mean it quite that way. I said I'd have your consent before we'd drive a nail, and that if you objected we wouldn't do it. But now I'll try to persuade you not to object."

"I already said 'No.' What's the sense of talk?"

"Well, talk is one way of getting acquainted. I'm a stranger around here, so I'd like that. And neither of us has anything more important to do. It's a fine day to sit on a log and talk, don't you think?"

Mr. Chambers was puzzled; he frowned with uncertainty, but then he grinned. "You're quite a word slinger. All right, go ahead and sling a few. I ain't too busy."

"I'm not going to try to persuade you to let us build the school," Don assured him.

"Wouldn't do you any good if you did."

"Naturally. But I would like to ask you a few questions."

"Go ahead."

"Well, for one; how does it happen Pink's so good with an axe?"

"Why, I showed him how to do it, and made him do it till he learned."

Don hid his deep content. If Pink's prowess resulted from his father's teaching, then obviously, teaching was a good thing. He need only lead Mr. Chambers to that admission, and the rest would follow as the night the day. He moved cautiously, careful to lead rather than to drive; he asked another question, and another. Wasn't swinging an axe a thing a man learned naturally, if he did it often enough? No, said Mr. Chambers; there was a right way and a wrong way. "Like anything else," he assured Don. "There's a sleight to it. You've got to get onto that." And to Don's questions he was glad to explain. A man drifted over from the nearest house to stand listening, another came from the house beyond. At the end of an hour, six or eight men were grouped around Don and Mr. Chambers, breathlessly silent for long intervals, their heads turning this way, that way, as Don asked and Mr. Chambers answered. Here, clearly, was a Yankee who wasn't so doggoned cocksure about everything. If he wanted to learn, they were ready to teach him. It was not always Mr. Chambers who answered; two of the others sometimes offered a word. Now and then Don or Mr. Chambers said something that started dry grins or shy chuckles, and once Don evoked forthright, knee-slapping laughter.

He said at last, completely casual: "Well, we've talked about a lot of things, but we haven't said much about the school. Do schoolhouses always catch fire, around here? I wouldn't want to waste anyone's time unless I thought a new one would last a while."

The others looked to Mr. Chambers, and after a hesitant moment, he chuckled in an amiable way. "Why, I don't know as they have to burn down. Depends on what goes on inside 'em." His eye touched this man and that, and nods assented. "I don't know but a schoolhouse that was run right might last a while."

So, with many farewells, Don and Mr. Tremont mounted to ride away, and the men watched them go, and when Don looked back and waved his hat, he had from three or four of them an answering sign.

When Trav and Enid and Lucy came down to Paradise, Brett and Cinda were with them. By that time, work had begun on the new schoolhouse; but there had been a delay, for the Negroes still hesitated, so on Tuesday morning Don went again to Mr. Chambers and told him this.

"Perhaps you'll send Pink over to tell them it's all right," he suggested. "In fact, I wish Pink would stay with us and boss the job." Mr. Chambers, pleased as any father, readily agreed.

When the *Paradise* brought the others downriver, Don went with Lucy to their room. There were always, even after the briefest separations, so many questions each must ask—and answer. Brett and Cinda had arrived yesterday, she said.

"But they're only staying a few days. But Don, I'm going to stay down here with you! I've worried about you." She grasped his arms, shaking them with a tender fierceness. "Are you all right? Are you sure?" So Don told her of his talk with Mr. Chambers and the other men, and of his victory, and she hugged him again, crying: "Oh, I'm so proud of you. So proud! And, my but I love you!"

When he left her, he found Brett reciting to Trav conditions in South Carolina. Brett predicted that Frank Moses would be elected Governor by thirty-three thousand votes. "The election commissioners have settled on that figure," he explained in quiet wrath. "It saves them the trouble of counting."

"Like our Returning Board," Trav commented. "That's why our campaign this year has been so quiet. Everyone knows the Board will decide who's to be Governor, regardless of who gets the most votes."

"Which way will they decide?" Brett asked. "How does the Board stand?"

"Well, Governor Warmoth is for McEnery, and Lieutenant Governor Pinchback is for Kellogg," Trav explained. "There are five men on the Board. Herron, the acting Secretary of State, is a Kellogg man, and from all I hear, Lynch will probably go for Kellogg too. I've forgotten the other member's name, but it doesn't matter. With Pinchback and Herron and Lynch on his side, Kellogg will probably be counted in. Certainly my money would be on him, if I were betting."

Brett chuckled. "You remind me of the story they tell on Major Melton," he commented. "He was a candidate for a judgeship, and he made a fine Republican speech to the Legislature. But everyone knew he was an old-line Democrat, so someone shouted: 'Who'd you vote for, last election?' Well, the Major wanted to be a judge, but he wouldn't lie about it. 'Seymour and Blair,' he shouted, and they roared abuse at him, but he held up his hands for a chance to finish, and when they quieted down he shouted: 'But I bet my money on Grant!' He got the judgeship, too."

They laughed together, and Brett said, in another tone: "Moses is bad enough, but he's a noble gentleman compared to the individual South Carolina will send to the Senate. Name of John Patterson, and they call him 'Honest John.' He runs a 'house of entertainment' over a saloon near the State House. He'll be elected, and I suppose the Senate will seat him."

Their talk turned from politics to the plantation here, and Trav spoke of the burning of the schoolhouse, and Brett remarked: "The same thing happened at the Plains, six or seven years ago. Remember?"

Trav nodded. "Did you rebuild?"

"I proposed to, but Tilda thought it might cause more trouble, urged me not to; so I didn't."

"I think we'll rebuild," said Trav, and looked at Don. "Won't we?"

"Yes," Don assented. "I haven't had a chance to tell you, Major, but we started work Wednesday. Mr. Tremont and I went over to see Mr. Chambers and some of his friends, and had a talk, and they agreed we could go ahead."

Trav waited, amusement in the poise of his head, and when Don did not speak, he said: "I expect you did most of the talking."

"Well, we both talked," Don assured him. "I mostly asked questions." He laughed in some embarrassment. "I think they felt sorry for me, I was so ignorant about so many things. They agreed we could rebuild the school, but I had to go over again Tuesday. I couldn't persuade the Negroes to go to work without some direct word from Mr. Chambers, so I asked him to send Pink over to tell them what they wanted to hear. Seemed to tickle him, to think they wouldn't work without his say-so. So he did, and Pink's our boss on the job."

They smiled, but Brett said warningly: "If these people ever think you're trying to make fools of them, look out."

"I'm not, sir," Don assured him. "I'm asking them to help us, and to let us help them, and I hope they will. I believe they will."

Brett looked at him in quiet approval; he spoke to Trav. "You know, I believe so, too.'

When a day or two later the others returned to New Orleans, Lucy stayed here with Don, and as the days passed they found one reason or another to delay her departure. Cash regularly brought them bundles of New Orleans papers, and Don read everything that was printed about the election and about the confusion which followed. Election day had been peaceful everywhere, and Don commented: "Your father has said several times that the Returning Board will decide things. I suppose the voters realize there's no use fighting over it."

"What does the Returning Board do?" Lucy asked. "What is it?"

"It's a board of five men," he explained. "The Governor and the

Lieutenant Governor and the Secretary of State are members *ex officio,* and—"

"What does that mean? *Ex officio?*"

"Because of their office. And besides these three, there are two Senators. Senator Lynch and—well, I don't know the name of the other one."

"But—what do they do?"

"Why, each parish reports how many votes were cast, and who for, and gives the total for each polling place. Then the Board looks at all those figures and decides which ones are right. Suppose a parish voted three thousand for McEnery and two thousand for Kellogg, the Board, if it wanted to, could decide the figures ought to be the other way around, and change them."

"Why that's ridiculous! Can't anyone stop them?"

"No, they have the say."

"It's the silliest thing I ever heard of!"

He chuckled at her heat. "No doubt about that," he agreed.

The vote, according to the papers, was the largest ever polled in the state, more than a hundred and twenty-eight thousand. The election was held on Monday, and the New Orleans ballot boxes were at once delivered to the Mechanics Institute, but the Tuesday papers reported that no votes had as yet been counted. Mr. Blanchard, State Supervisor of Elections, had ordered the counting to begin, but General Longstreet, who was the federal supervisor, refused to allow this.

"But why?" Lucy asked, and Don could not tell her. "Which side is he on?" she persisted.

"He's for Kellogg," Don explained.

"He and Governor Warmoth used to be such good friends."

"I know. But not in politics. Not now."

Longstreet's reason, according to the *Picayune,* was that his subordinates did not have the proper blanks on which to record the tally, but Wednesday the *Picayune* suggested that the General's refusal was designed to prevent the country from finding out that Louisiana had gone Democratic, for fear that fact might affect the national election.

Don read this to Lucy, and she asked: "Do they mean the Democrats did win?"

"They're sure they did, but the votes haven't been counted. And besides, the Returning Board will have to decide."

The counting of ballots, once begun, was incredibly slow, but within three days after the election, the Republican papers were charging fraud and intimidation. Ten days later the Returning Board—consisting of Warmoth, Lieutenant Governor Pinchback, Secretary of State Herron and Senators Anderson and Lynch, Senator Anderson being that day absent—met to canvass the returns.

Don started to read to Lucy the *Picayune's* report of what happened, but she said:

"Oh, they get me all mixed up. You just tell me."

So he explained.

"Senator Anderson—he's the one I couldn't remember—he and Lieutenant Governor Pinchback had both been candidates at this election. Pinchback ran for Congress, and Anderson for Senator. Their being candidates disqualified them, under the Constitution; so that left Governor Warmoth and Secretary of State Herron and Senator Lynch as the only legal members of the Board.

"Herron and Lynch were both Kellogg men. The Governor is for McEnery, but they could have voted him down. But Secretary of State Herron had failed to make good a shortage in his accounts, so Warmoth removed him on the spot. Under the Constitution he could do that, but everyone except him had forgotten it." He smiled. "Whether you're for him or not, you have to admit the Governor is clever. Another thing; he can remove a man, and when the Legislature is not in session, he can appoint someone to fill a vacancy, and the man he appoints serves until the Legislature sits again, doesn't have to be confirmed."

"I still don't understand what it's all about!"

"It will straighten out in a minute," he promised. "The Board was going to decide who won the election, but Pinchback and Anderson couldn't serve. That left the Board two to one against Warmoth, so then he discharged Herron. That left just him and Senator Lynch. Then he appointed Colonel Wharton Secretary of State. That appointment didn't have to be confirmed, and as Secretary of State, Wharton became a member of the Board and he's a McEnery man.

"That gave the Governor a two to one majority on the Board. Then he nominated two new members and he and Colonel Wharton confirmed their nomination with their two votes to Lynch's one. That gave the Governor four votes out of five on the Returning Board, and they canvassed the returns, and reported that McEnery was elected by about ten thousand votes."

Watching him intently, she said: "What?" And to his puzzled stare: "Say it again! I like to watch the way your mouth works, when you're excited about something."

"You—! Are all Southern girls bound to keep on flirting as long as they live?"

"Just for that, I shan't—"

But he laughed, caught her up and kissed her. "Oh, yes you will."

"We—ell," she said judicially, "if you insist, I suppose I will."

On the face of things, McEnery was elected, but the decision of the Returning Board proved to be only a beginning. Senator Lynch organized a new Board, consisting of Governor Warmoth, Mr. Herron, himself, General Longstreet and Judge Hawkins. General Longstreet, representing this Board, went at once to demand that Governor Warmoth surrender the election returns. The Governor refused to receive him; nevertheless, the Lynch Board met that evening to begin its canvass, and in due course announced that the whole Kellogg ticket was elected!

Captain Cash, when he brought the newspapers which reported this development, brought also a letter from Trav. Trav had hoped to come down to Paradise for a day or two, but could not do so. New Orleans had been swept by an epidemic of epizootic, attacking so many horses and mules that the streetcars were no longer running, and Lucy's Nellie and Trav's Nig were both stricken. Saul, Trav assured them, was doing everything necessary. "They cough, and run at the nose," he explained, "and Saul has to sponge out their nostrils every hour with dilute carbolic, and steam them with hot vinegar two or three times a day, and keep them warm and their legs bandaged. I knew you'd want to know."

Lucy said at once, "We'll have to go home, Don. Or at least I will. I can help Saul. Poor Nellie! But why don't you stay?"

Don of course returned with her, and she began the tedious business of keeping the wretched horses as comfortable as possible, while Don heard from Trav a detailed report of the confusion which had followed the election. The Lynch Board, without having seen a single ballot or a single return, counted Kellogg in. "I asked Longstreet how they did it," Trav explained. "He said they had copies of some returns from the United States Supervisors, and that these showed the political complexion of certain parishes. Then he said they had some affidavits, and some newspaper pieces, and when they had no figures at all, they just made an estimate! He said they threw out about six thousand votes, and counted in about ten thousand affidavits from men who swore they weren't allowed to vote at all."

"How did they make their estimates?" Don wondered.

"Well, they assumed that a man who voted for Grant would also vote for Kellogg." Trav's voice thickened, and he cleared his throat. "Sorry, but just thinking about it makes me mad enough to spit."

"You know, I think the North will resent this as much as you do. Longstreet's badly befooled."

"The General's been a thoroughly confused man for some months now." Trav laughed grimly. "So's the whole situation, for the matter of that."

By Warmoth's next move, the confusion was thrice confounded. Last March, the Legislature had passed a new election law, providing that the Returning Board should be chosen by the Senate. The Governor had not yet signed the bill, but under the Constitution he could do so at any time before the next legislature convened. On the twentieth of November, Warmoth signed this bill, and the effect was to legislate out of existence not only the Warmoth Board, which had declared McEnery elected, but also the Lynch Board which had awarded the victory to Kellogg.

Longstreet came that night to see Trav, storming with anger. "And now nobody knows where we stand," he cried, shaking his head in a bull-like rage. "The air's already full of injunctions flying in all directions."

"Warmoth's a slippery customer," Trav commented. "A hard man to down. I see he's called the Legislature to meet December ninth. That will probably start a new bewilderment."

"There's bewilderment enough already," Longstreet retorted. "Why, do you realize, Major, that the electoral ballots must be cast December fourth—and there's no authority now in either Board to decide who carried the election."

Horace Greeley, who had been the candidate against Grant, had died a few days before, and Trav spoke of this. "So even if you let Warmoth's Board cast Louisiana's vote for Greeley, it wouldn't matter."

"It's a matter of principle," Longstreet insisted. "I've advised Senator Kellogg to appeal to Washington. Someone has to end this chaos. Major, this is a systematic attempt to destroy the Republican party in Louisiana. It ought to be stopped, by force if necessary."

Trav half smiled. "Well, General, as usual, we disagree. Force never settles an argument; it merely ends it."

"When the laws are ignored, or repeatedly violated, force may be necessary to defend them!"

"Laws aren't final," Trav reminded him. "They're subject to change —and that's as it should be. There are bad laws. In this situation here today, everyone concerned has been able to sue out injunctions against the other—injunctions forbidding either of you to do anything. But you can't both be right. Just because you have a judge on your side doesn't prove a thing."

"Perhaps not," the General admitted. "But you'll surely agree that, right or wrong, a judge's decision should be respected and enforced."

"Which judge?" Trav challenged. "Which decision?"

There was more to come. The new election law, signed by Warmoth a few days before, provided for a Returning Board to be elected by the Senate. By signing the bill, Warmoth in effect removed both the Boards then in existence; but under the Constitution, he had a right, whenever the Legislature was not in session, to appoint men to fill vacancies. The day before the date set for casting the electoral ballots,

Governor Warmoth accordingly appointed an entirely new Returning Board, and this Board promptly named the Greeley electors as victors at the polls.

Judge and Mrs. Morgan came to supper that night, and Trav asked the Judge's opinion. "Is there any solution to all this, Judge? Any indisputably legal solution?"

Judge Morgan nodded. "Certainly. Governor Warmoth had the legal right and the legal power to sign the new election law, and he had the legal right and the legal power to name a new Returning Board. That's the law. The Constitution is on his side." He added with a smile: "But of course, that may not be enough."

It was not, for on the following night Judge Durell of the United States Circuit Court, in his cups, and in his own home instead of on the bench, and acting entirely without authority, signed an order directing the United States Marshal to seize and hold the Capitol building. Marshal Packard, using United States troops, carried out that order, and at eleven o'clock next day, this time in court, the Judge granted an injunction, the effect of which was to turn over the government of the state to the Kellogg party.

When on December ninth the Legislature met, deputies and United States troops stood guard at every entrance to the Capitol, admitting none but Kellogg partisans. The impeachment of Governor Warmoth was promptly voted, and Pinchback qualified as Acting Governor.

That night Don asked Trav: "Does this mean Governor Warmoth has run his course?"

Trav nodded. "I should think so. He's full of devices, but with the United States army against him, there's nothing he can do. His power is broken. Power is self perpetuating up to certain limits, and in his case the limits were set by Grant's bayonets. A remarkable man, for all that; a great man. Probably it was that, as much as anything else, which made his Republican allies desert him and eventually pull him down. Little men are always envious of the great."

And he added, grim amusement in his tones: "In his place they give us a nigra, this Pinchback, as Acting Governor of Louisiana. I must drop in on Tony. I know he'll be pleased."

PART FIVE

The White League

December 1872—November 1874

I

F OR TONY, even after he was sufficiently improved so that he could walk without a cane and could make himself understood by callers without resorting to pen and paper, the world had grown smaller. His horizons had contracted, and this was true not only of his physical world but of his mental outlook. He no longer followed the fortunes of the Republican party; it was on Pinchback, of whom he and Sapphira were to such a considerable extent the creators, that his sympathies centered. When Judge Durell's injunctions seemed to decide all issues in favor of the Kellogg party, he exulted because Pinchback as a candidate for Congress on the Kellogg ticket had been elected.

"Why, after Congress, anything is possible," he told Sapphira. "The Senate, yes and even, in another twenty years, the White House!"

Sapphira tried to dissuade him from such dreams. "If they ever take the soldiers out of Louisiana, he couldn't even be elected to the Legislature," she insisted. "You know that as well as I." But he made a scornful gesture.

Pinchback had not called upon them for weeks past, but when Tony fretted at this, Sapphira reminded him that these were busy days for any man in politics. Governor Warmoth had summoned the Legislature to meet in extra session December ninth. Pinchback, when he called the Senate to order, told the Senators that Governor Warmoth had offered him fifty thousand dollars if he would allow the Senate to be organized by the old members before the new ones were sworn in. "But I propose to do my duty to my State, my party and my race," he said.

Before that first day's session ended, Governor Warmoth had been impeached, and Pinchback as Acting Governor stepped into his shoes. Tony, intoxicated with triumph, was sure Pinchback would come to them that night. Since he did not, Sapphira next morning sent a note to the Acting Governor, begging him to come when he could.

"No matter how early or how late," she wrote. "We'll always welcome you."

Pinchback wrote across the top of her note: "Tomorrow at 5 P.M." "Tomorrow" was Wednesday, but actually it was late Saturday night before he appeared. A drizzle of rain that day, on top of the long waiting, had left Tony profoundly depressed, and though he usually permitted Sapphira to put him early to bed, that night he refused to go. Thus, when the bell rang at a few minutes past midnight, they were still in the drawing room.

At the sound from below, Sapphira rose, thinking to go down to the door, but she heard 'Phemy stirring, so she waited till her mother came to announce their caller. Pinchback was on 'Phemy's heels. He entered almost at a bound, his eyes shining, a leather portfolio under his arm. Sapphira thought he was drunk not so much with liquor—though the reek of that was heavy on him—as with a high exultation; his brow was wet, and there were heavy pouches under the outer corners of his eyes, accentuating their faint Mongolian slant. As Sapphira placed a chair for him, she caught the odor of crowded rooms, of seegar smoke and used tobacco and unwashed bodies, clinging to his rumpled garments.

"We've missed you," she said.

"Well, I've been busy," he reminded her.

"Of course," she assented, and Tony on the chaise longue grunted, and Sapphira said: "You must be tired."

"Tired? No, I don't think so. But I can't remember going to bed this week at all, just a nap in my chair! The Governor's chair!" He leaned toward Tony, raising his voice as though Tony were deaf. "The Governor's chair, Mr. Currain!"

Tony made a fretful gesture, and Sapphira said: "He hears as well as ever, Governor. Tell him what's been happening; not what was in the papers, the rest of it." Tony spoke half a dozen chuckling words, and she smiled and interpreted: "He says if you refused that fifty thousand dollars from Governor Warmoth, what did the other side give you?"

Pinchback laughed, throwing back his head; then he leaned forward to whisper a word. "The senatorship!" he answered, and he caught up his portfolio. "Here, I'll show you a few telegrams!" He produced a sheaf of them, fingered them through. "This is my first dispatch as Acting Governor to President Grant!" And he read, in a high pride: " 'New Orleans, December ninth. President Grant: Having taken the oath of office and being in possession of the gubernatorial office—' And I was sitting in the Governor's chair when I wrote this. 'It devolves upon me to urge the necessity of a favorable consideration—' And so forth and so forth, about the resolution asking for protection. Then I go on: 'Be pleased to send the necessary orders to General Emory. This seems to me a necessary measure of precaution, although all is quiet here.'" He explained: "But I'd no sooner sent that than I began to fear it might be too peremptory. 'Be pleased to send the necessary orders' sounds too like a command, and I thought Grant might resent it, so Governor Kellogg wired Attorney General Williams. I have a copy here."

And he read: "'If President in some way indicates recognition, Governor Pinchback and Legislature would settle everything.' Then Mr. Casey telegraphed the President the same thing, asking him to recognize us, either by orders to General Emory or in some other way. But we had no reply that day, and next day Casey telegraphed again." He consulted a slip of paper from his portfolio. "He tells Grant the situation, tells him about Ex-Governor Warmoth organizing a pretended legislature, and so on, and then he says: 'If a decided recognition of Governor Pinchback and the legal legislature were made, in my opinion it would settle the whole matter.'"

'Phemy appeared with decanter and glasses, and he tossed off a glass of brandy and filled the glass again before he went on. "I appointed General Longstreet Adjutant General of Militia, and he sought to take possession of the State Armory, and of the arms and ammunition there, but Warmoth wouldn't surrender the position. Then on Thursday I received a dispatch from Attorney General Williams saying that I had been recognized by President Grant as Governor—until Mr. Kellogg takes office, of course—and that I would be supported by the troops. So this morning Warmoth surrendered the Armory to General Emory, who turned it over to General Longstreet. Emory had a telegram this morning, directing him to recognize my authority."

He closed his portfolio with a triumphant slap. "So the fight's over, the issue settled! McEnery arranged to take a hundred men to Washington to make a last appeal to the President, but the Attorney General wired them it was no use, that President Grant's mind was made up." He emptied his glass and refilled it.

"So you're Governor," Sapphira said, in thoughtful tones. "And of course you're a Congressman, too."

He laughed, with a casual gesture. "I'll never take my seat in the lower House. I told you a moment ago, I'm to be the next Senator from Louisiana." He chuckled. "It was so nominated in the bond, when I joined the Kellogg forces."

Tony muttered something, and Sapphira interpreted: "He says they'll back out of their bargain if they can."

"They can't," Pinchback retorted. "Or if they do, I'll take half their legislature away from them and deliver it to McEnery." He drank again, but when he turned back to Tony, Sapphira moved the decanter beyond his easy reach. "I'll tell you about the senatorship," he said. "Kellogg promised it to me, but he had promised it to another man, too; to

Captain Norton, the man who got Judge Durell drunk enough to sign that midnight order." He winked wisely at Tony. "So Captain Norton's going to pay me ten thousand dollars to withdraw, and after I've got the money I'll go ahead and be elected anyway." He laid a finger along his nose, nodding sagely, then drained his glass and looked around for the decanter. Sapphira said gently:

"Governor, I know you'll forgive us, but Mr. Currain is very tired. To talk exhausts him. You were most courteous to come and see us." Tony spoke, and she nodded, and said to Pinchback: "Mr. Currain bids me thank you for coming."

So Pinchback made his farewells, and Sapphira rang for 'Phemy to escort him to the door. In a momentary concern—he was unsteady on his feet—she asked: "Shall I send for a hackney, Governor?"

He made an expansive gesture of negation. "M'carriage's at the door," he said.

When he was gone, she sat down by Tony, touching his hand. "I could cry my eyes out!" she told him in a weary sorrow. "Cry and cry and cry! He's come so far so swiftly. I suppose it's no wonder, really, that he's—as he is." Tony spoke again, and she shook her head. "No; he's weak! I've always feared it. I suppose a quick growth is never strong."

Nevertheless they followed proudly the events of the next month. Pinchback, in his Executive Address as Acting Governor, spoke of the McEnery Legislature, which met regularly in Odd Fellows Hall, as "the pretended General Assembly," and of McEnery as "the pretended Governor" and he warned them that the militia and the Metropolitan Police would be used to break up any attempt at an inauguration ceremony. But Congress had already begun to move toward an investigation of the recent election, and a telegram from Washington directed that there should be no interference with the McEnery proceedings unless he or his adherents resorted to violence.

So each faction, the Kellogg adherents at Mechanics Institute and the McEnery men in Lafayette Square, formally inaugurated their governors. During the ceremonies, United States troops were posted at strategic points, and the Metropolitan Police were in force around the Institute, but though the day heard many angry words, there were neither shots nor blows. Thus peaceably two state governments began their simultaneous lives.

On his way home that evening, stopping at the St. Charles, Trav met General Longstreet and had some talk with him. The General was about to leave for Washington to testify at the Congressional investigation, and Trav said, smiling:

"I expect they'll want you to explain how your Returning Board could canvass the returns without having any returns to canvass."

Longstreet grunted. "I don't think they'll press us too hard. Senator Morton's chairman of the committee. He's the Republican leader, and four of his colleagues are good Republicans—against only two Democrats. Of course we're taking all our records, and the Lynch Board has been summoned and presumably will do the same, but I'm sure the Committee will approve what's been done."

"Warmoth going?" Trav asked.

"No doubt. After all, he was the most conspicuous figure in the whole drama."

"I looked up the figures on his administration, the other day. Total appropriations, over ten million dollars, in five years. Two millions a year."

"I'm surprised it wasn't more."

Trav said in quiet amusement: "Well, under Wells and Hahn it was. Their legislatures spent almost eighteen million in three years; six million a year. The comparison makes Warmoth and his legislators look like honest men."

"He tells me he's going to buy a sugar plantation, downriver somewhere. You'll be neighbors."

"I'd prefer him to a lot of people I know."

"Hah! So would I," the General agreed. "Jube Early, for instance." And he said: "I get many letters from old comrades, urging me to answer him."

"That speech he made a while back?" Early had criticized Longstreet's work at Gettysburg.

Longstreet nodded, laughed briefly. "The poor fellow lost his army, and now seems to think that qualifies him as a military expert. He'll soon be forgotten."

"You'll never need to defend your record as a soldier."

Longstreet's eyes twinkled. "But as a politician?" Trav smiled, said nothing, and Longstreet said thoughtfully: "I dismissed Gettysburg from my mind ten years ago. There was even then a sly undercurrent of misrepresentation of my course there, but I was glad to accept any blame rather than allow it to touch General Lee. But now Lee's gone, and if I ever have leisure, I may expose Early's fallacies—as well as his outright lies."

Trav nodded. "If you ever decide to do so, I'll be proud to testify." And he asked: "Well, how will Louisiana get along, with two state governments?"

The General grunted. "Manifest absurdity! Who'll pay taxes to a McEnery collector, when a Kellogg collector may call next day? Folly!"

He shrugged his heavy shoulders. "If Sam Grant takes my advice he'll end it mighty soon."

Longstreet went off to Washington, and on January 14 the Kellogg Legislature elected to the United States Senate, for the term beginning March fourth, Pinckney Benton Stewart Pinchback, born of a white father and a mother who had been a slave.

Don stayed in New Orleans for Mardi Gras, and he and Lucy watched the parade of the Knights of Momus, based on *The Talisman,* and they danced for hours at the ball in the Opera House, but when Don next day decided to go back to the plantation, she said at once that she would go with him.

"Better wait a while," he suggested. "After the new school building's done, I think I can persuade Mr. Chambers and his friends to let us build one over on their side of the swamp, for their children. If we do that, I'll want to stay down there and help, till it's time for us to start for Maine. If I do stay that long, maybe you'll bring the babies down. So let's wait and see how things work out."

On his promise to come to New Orleans every week, she agreed. After Don was gone, Trav said doubtfully: "Lucy, I'm not sure Don isn't taking on more than he can handle."

"He just wants to help them."

"I know. And of course, I agree with him." Trav laughed. "Guess I got out of the wrong side of the bed this morning; that's what's the matter with me."

Two days after Don departed, Peter came home, bringing an impressive amount of luggage. To Enid's affectionate questions he said casually: "Oh, I just decided I'd live at home a while." They were at supper when he arrived, and his eyes touched Lucy with a sly malice. "As long as Don stays downriver with his niggers. I don't like the smell of a Yankee in the house."

Enid protested: "Peter, you ought to be ashamed!"

"I? Not at all! Lucy's the one to be ashamed!"

Trav spoke. "That's enough, Peter. You're welcome here as long as you behave in a gentlemanly manner, but—"

"Oh, don't talk to me as if I were a child!"

"Young man, modify your tone!"

Peter flushed, seemed about to speak, then shrugged and was silent. Lucy, remembering that he had been managing the Haunted House, said as a question: "I suppose this means Captain Pew and Dolly have come home?"

Peter uttered an angry sound and Enid cried: "Oh, have they, Peter?" He grunted an assent, and she said: "I'm wild to see her. Where have they been?"

"Paris, I guess; maybe Italy. I didn't cross-examine them."

Don came to spend Sunday with them, and Peter absented himself. Don reported that the church and school at Paradise were, except for final details, finished. "Mrs. Harper has started her classes." He looked at Trav. "And Mr. Chambers and his neighbors have agreed to let us build a schoolhouse over near them," he said. "I suggested that some of our boys would go over, and that Pink could boss them, and he liked that idea." He added: "There's a sawpit at the Four Corners, so we can rip-saw boards and timbers. We'll manage."

"I expect you will," Trav agreed, and he said approvingly: "You have a gift that way. By the way, I ran across something the other day that you may not know. Remember once we were discussing whether the Freedmen's Bureau had done any good?"

"I remember, yes."

"Well, there were less than a hundred public schools in Louisiana when the War ended, and a month ago there were eleven hundred. The Bureau should get some credit for that."

"I suppose so," Don agreed. "If it is a credit. Probably it is. Probably a poor school is better than none." He smiled. "At least, I'm working on that theory." He spoke to Lucy. "And Honey, I ought to stay down there, not come upriver so often. I want to get acquainted with as many of the white people around Paradise as I can, and with the people on other plantations. So if you'd like to come down?" His tone was a question.

Lucy laughed affectionately, said to Trav and Enid: "He's a lot more interested in those young ones down at Paradise than he is in his own children." And to Don. "Of course I'll come, darling. I like being with you. That's why I married you. Remember? But we can take the children down too."

"We surely can."

They planned the move for Monday morning, but Sunday afternoon Mr. Cist brought Eleanor to the house in a hackney carriage. Eleanor's third baby would be born within a few days, but a week ago little Joshua had come down with measles. "And now Cynthia has them too," Eleanor confessed, laughing to fight back her tears. "And I've never had them, and Doctor Fexler says I mustn't have them now. So can you please take me in?"

Enid said of course they could, and she and Lucy made Eleanor welcome and assured Mr. Cist that she would be fine here with them. So Lucy stayed here to keep Eleanor company, while Don went down to Paradise alone. Eleanor's new baby, another daughter, was born on Wednesday, but by that time little Cynthia was desperately ill, and Friday night she died.

Don came upriver Saturday, and that night Lucy wept with racking sobs in his arms, till at last she found relief in words. "She was just the age of our Travis," she remembered. "Oh Don, if anything ever happened to our babies, what would we do? I think I'd surely die. But people's babies do die, all the time, like General Longstreet's, three of them in one week! How did they stand it?" He let her talk, not interrupting, and she wept her tears away. "Doctor Fexler told us not to tell Eleanor, but we'll have to, soon. She keeps asking how they are. Mr. Cist didn't even go up to see her, tonight; he said he didn't dare, because she'd know as soon as she saw him. She would have, too; he was so white, his eyes so red. I told her he'd sent word he couldn't leave the mill till too late to see her today. I don't know why she didn't guess, just from seeing me."

She talked herself to sleep, and Don lay still in order not to wake her. His arm ached and he was in torment till without waking, she turned on her other side and set him free.

But there were grievous days to follow. Eleanor guessed the truth almost at once, and sank for a while into a slough of grief, and was slow to recover her strength, and Lucy felt bound to her side.

The Congressional Committee, although most of its members were Republicans, called the decision of the Returning Board of which Longstreet was a member an outright fraud, and recommended that either a new election be held or that Kellogg be removed and McEnery seated as Governor. But the Senate decided to do nothing, and President Grant supported Kellogg. Longstreet, when Trav saw him after his return from Washington, was almost cheerful.

"It's so complete that it has its funny side," he declared. "They decided that our Board did not exist, that if we did exist the courts had forbidden us to act, and that even if we did exist and had authority to canvass the returns, we had no returns to canvass."

Trav said sympathetically: "That was a bitter dose!"

Longstreet shifted his heavy shoulders. "Well, Sam Grant is still supporting Kellogg. As long as Kellogg's de facto Governor, my duty's clear."

When it became obvious that Kellogg would not be removed, McEnery undertook to organize a militia. To answer this move, the Kellogg Legislature incorporated the Metropolitan Police into the state militia, thus putting all the armed forces of the city and state at Governor Kellogg's disposal, with General Longstreet in command. Trav thought ruefully that the General had thus been made the scapegoat, to be blamed for whatever was to come. The Metropolitans, created by Governor Warmoth, included a large proportion of Negroes. Whoever led them into action against white men would be a target for the concentrated hatred of the South.

"And it may happen any day," Trav told Don, when he came up from Paradise. "I tell you, there's so much hate in the air that you can almost taste it. They'll have to fight, if only to blow off steam."

Trav's prediction was even at that moment being fulfilled. The Third Precinct police station was in the Cabildo, an ancient, thick-walled building erected while Louisiana was a Spanish possession. Colonel Eugene Waggaman led a detachment of McEnery militia in an attempt to seize the building. For half an hour, while their numbers steadily increased, they kept up a rapid fire with rifles and shotguns on the doors. Then the Metropolitans came to the relief of the besieged, and at the order of General Smith of the United States Army, the McEnery forces dispersed.

General Longstreet, before going home that night—he had taken a house on Prytania Street, not far from Trav's—stopped to tell Trav and the others what had happened. "It was a small affair, noisy and spectacular, but of no consequence. I believe one bystander, a young man by the name of Hartmann, was killed by our grapeshot, and two or three others wounded, but the surroundings were the chief sufferers, the trees and the walls." His brow clouded with a slow anger, and he said: "We'll put an end to this nonsense, presently, for good and all."

"How?" Trav asked.

Longstreet looked at him with gloomy eyes. "By force, I suppose. How else? The Governor can't let it go on."

Trav and Don went next morning to see what scars the affray had left on the old Cabildo. They saw bullet holes aplenty. The trees in the Square were pierced and barked, raw wood freckling their surfaces where bullets had struck glancing blows. Windows were broken, and walls spattered with lead, and an iron column had been shattered by a rifle ball.

Trav went on to the mill, but Don, strolling homeward, came to Lafayette Square and saw a crowd around Odd Fellows' Hall, the Democratic stronghold, and he stopped to inquire the cause. Under Longstreet's orders, a detachment of a hundred Metropolitans had just now seized the Hall, arresting Speaker Moncure and several members of the McEnery Legislature, and marching them off to jail. Don remembered Longstreet's prediction. Kellogg had acted. But Don heard angry words, saw scowling faces, and three or four times he heard Longstreet's name spoken with hatred and with scorn.

Don had been secretly relieved when because of Eleanor's need, Lucy had stayed in New Orleans. Their third baby would be born in June, and she could be more comfortable there, but also there had occurred at the plantation a few minor incidents which would have worried her. Lucy, for her part, enjoyed with Enid and the babies long, lazy, happy hours.

One day when she was lying on the bed in her mother's room, with little Travis asleep in the curve of her arm, Peter came to speak to his mother about something or other, and when he turned to go, Lucy asked idly:

"Seen Dolly since they came home, Peter?"

"No," he said, and in a droll tone, "I somehow received the impression that Captain Pew did not welcome my presence, and I didn't want to distress the old gentleman, so—"

Enid laughed, her head thrown back. "Old gentleman? I wish Captain Pew could hear you say that! He can't be a day over—" She hesitated. She had been about to say "over forty-five!" but in no time at all, she would herself be forty-five! Why did life spill so swift away? Why had she been such a little fool, twenty-five years ago, as to marry a man seventeen years older than herself? For now Trav was an old man! In another two years he would be sixty! Of course his hair had not yet turned gray, but it was definitely thin on top; but hair or no hair, he was an old man, content to rise early and go off to the mill and come home early and go off to bed!

It was true that in some ways he seemed to grow no older, and at her own thoughts her heart swelled with tenderness for him. But certainly he was old compared to Captain Pew. How clever Dolly must be, to have held Captain Pew so long, to have won him at last to marry her. She must write to Dolly, plan to see her. If Peter's sly tone meant anything, then Dolly now was risking all her gains.

Enid's thoughts had raced thus far in an instant's time; there was no perceptible interval between her last word and her next. "Over fifty!" she said, finishing the sentence, and then in laughing challenge: "Peter Currain, are you tagging after Dolly's apron strings? Why, she's old enough to be your mother!"

He laughed. "Thanks; one mother's enough for me, and I've got you, Mama. But Dolly is charming in another role!" And in mock seriousness: "I sometimes fear the Captain is too old to keep her happy!"

"Peter Currain, you keep away from her! Your own cousin!"

He chuckled. "Kissin' cousin?" he suggested, and she waved her hands at him.

"Go 'way! Go 'way!"

When he was gone, Lucy said chidingly: "Mama, you ought to be ashamed of yourself."

"Oh, I know it," Enid agreed. "But Peter's such a handsome devil! If he weren't my own son, I'd fall in love with him too!"

She had written once to Dolly, and had had no answer, but now she wrote again. If Dolly could not come to the house here—Captain Pew might have issued an interdict—suppose they met at Tony's. "As we used to," she suggested. "Or as if by accident. Any day you say! Wouldn't that be fun?" And because her earlier letter might not have reached Dolly, she consulted Maria, who agreed to find some messenger.

"Cap'n Cash, he'll tek it," Maria subsequently reported. "He and Mr. Broderick, Cap'n Pew's doorman, dey good friends."

"Well, you just tell Cap'n Cash I'll be eternally grateful to him," Enid directed. She had refused to think of Cash since her last trip to Paradise, but for a while her thoughts lingered on him now, till she faced them, thrust them away. Such thoughts were shameless folly; she would banish them for good and all.

Don came up for Sunday and to assure Lucy that at Paradise all went well. "That boy, Pink Chambers, has real quality," he reported. "With him bossing the job, on the schoolhouse over near his father's place, it's done, all but the windows and the chimney, and we've already started classes for the white children over there. I go over every day, and Mrs. Tremont goes twice a week to help me out. She takes her own children over, and she and Simon—you know, her oldest boy—teach the little ones their letters."

"I like Simon," Lucy remarked. "He's so courteous and gentle. And of course, Helen and Tommy are nice too."

"Simon's only eleven, but he's been his father's right arm ever since Mr. Tremont came back from the War without one."

"Do you have schoolbooks?"

"Oh, yes. I didn't dare offer to buy books for them, but a sister of Mrs. Chambers had old First and Second Readers, and an Arithmetic, and she lets us use them. Those books are handled mighty tenderly, I can tell you."

"What do you teach them?"

Don colored in shy embarrassment. "Well, really, not anything yet, except I try to keep them interested." He grinned. "I guess I make them teach me. They show me how to set trotlines, and how to clean crawfish and cook them, and they tell me the names of the wild flowers and shrubs around there, and which ones are good for medicine, and so on. It's surprising how interested a boy or a girl becomes, when he starts to tell you something that he can see interests you. Every day, when we begin, I ask each one to tell the most interesting thing he's seen or heard or learned since the day before. We really have a good time."

Lucy, loving him and his enthusiasm, said fondly that he was probably the best teacher any little old no-account poor-white children ever had, and he laughed with her, and talked on and on.

He did not tell her, as he told Trav, that he had learned to walk warily. "As long as they can do things for you, they're all right," he said. "But the minute you try to do things for them, they resent it." He had made one success by admiring the chimneys in their homes and asking to be shown the method of their construction. "Mr. Chambers says now he'll have Pink build our chimney in the schoolhouse, to show me, and Pink seemed pleased to do it."

"They're pretty high-headed, men like that," Trav agreed. "You can't condescend to them. They don't think they're any better than you are, but they think they're just as good. But don't ever let them think there's any competition between them and your nigra scholars. They know they're head and shoulders better than the best nigger that ever lived! They've known that since before their great-, great-, great-granddaddies were born." Trav chuckled. "I think I'll go down with you Monday morning, see how my cane crop is coming along."

Not till March was nearly gone did Dolly's message come. It was only two lines, a scribbled note, delivered by a small Negro boy:

> Crazy to see you. So much to tell. Friday, and I'll try to be there by three.

Enid was delighted. Some reluctance kept her from confiding in Lucy, but she asked Peter in a casual tone: "Peter, do you still call on Uncle Tony? I remember when he was so sick, you used to."

Without replying directly, he said: "He's still sick. Or rather, he's sick again. He had another shock, you know."

"Oh, poor man. No, I didn't know that. I must call, see if there's anything I can do to make him more comfortable."

"With two beautiful women waiting on him hand and foot, he should be comfortable enough."

"Two? You don't mean 'Phemy."

"Quinny. She's as pretty as ever." And he said: "May I offer my services as escort?"

"Why, how sweet of you! Of course." She thought to tell him he would see Dolly, but decided not to do so. Let that be a surprise for him. It would be fun to see them together.

So that she might pay her respects to Tony before Dolly arrived, she and Peter reached his door half an hour before the time appointed. 'Phemy admitted them, and Peter elected to wait in the small sitting room on the ground floor. Enid followed 'Phemy upstairs, and when 'Phemy opened the door and announced her, she confronted not only Tony and Sapphira but two Negroes. She hesitated, then hurried to bend over Tony and press his hands and tell him how well he looked, and he grinned in a one-sided way and mumbled something. Then Sapphira said, behind her:

"Mrs. Currain, may I present Senator-elect Pinchback?"

Enid said hurriedly: "Oh, Senator!" Then in sudden recollection: "But I met you here before!" That was the day she first saw Cap'n Cash. She and Dolly were here together. Heavens, how long ago? It was before the first time they went down to Paradise, because she didn't know who Cash was till she saw him by the gangplank when they went aboard the boat; but it was after Captain Pew refused to let Streean stay in the Haunted House, after Brett slapped Streean and Streean failed to resent it. Three years? Four? Five? All this Enid remembered in a flashing second. "I've heard so much about you," she told Pinchback. "So you're really our new Senator?"

"Not yet, Mrs. Currain. I have not yet presented my credentials. That must wait till the next session of Congress, in December." And he added, as though it were more amusing than impressive. "And of course, I was also elected Congressman-at-large."

"How nice!" she said, her tone intended to put him in his place, and she turned to the other Negro, but then her hand flew to her mouth in sharp dismay. Though his hair was grown long, and coiled low around his head and plastered there with grease, it was obvious that he had no cars. A knife cut across his cheek had puckered as it healed, his nose was bent to one side, one eyelid drooped, and the eyebrow above it had been battered into a scarred lump. When he moved, he limped as though one leg were shorter than the other.

Sapphira murmured beside her: "Representative Mooney." Enid tried to speak, could only nod. The Negro bowed low.

"Yas'm, Mose Mooney, da's me! I's one o' Mistuh Kellogg's 'Sembly-men."

His was the rude speech of plantation hands, and Enid was uncertain what to reply. Tony had been watching and listening, an amused expression on his one-sided countenance. He spoke now, his words half formed, and Sapphira turned to Pinchback. "He begs you will excuse him, Senator," she explained. "But he has certain matters to discuss with Mrs. Currain."

The two Negroes at once took their departure. When they were gone, Enid asked Sapphira: "Are there many in the Legislature as ignorant as Mr. Mooney?"

"He was hurt in the rioting in eighteen sixty-six, the thirtieth of July," Sapphira explained. "The police and other white men beat him almost to death." There was no resentment in her tone. She added quietly: "He used to work in your husband's mill, but Mr. Fiddler discharged him."

Enid, feeling herself on the defensive, asked: "Why?"

Sapphira said evenly: "I'm sure he had his reason. Representative Mooney was just 'Mose' in those days, but he liked to preach sermons and make speeches, and someone put his name on the Kellogg ballots, and the Lynch Board counted him in."

Tony barked a summons and Enid sat down beside him. He was full of conversation; his words ran together yet she understood him well enough. "Delighted to see you. Glad Dolly's coming. Only woman I ever saw half as pretty as Sapphira. Oh, you're all right, but you're too white!" He grinned, shifted his weight, moving awkwardly. "Can't turn over without Sapphira or Cash to help me. Needs a man like Cash, with a broad pair of shoulders." Enid remembered Cash's square shoulders in his neat blue uniform, and for a while she ceased to listen, thinking she must go more often to Paradise. It was always pleasant to lead Cash into interested talk, and of course when she did so it always made Quinny furious, and that was fun.

When the doorbell sounded, they heard from the lower hall Dolly's light laughing voice. Enid crossed and opened the door to greet her. 'Phemy was halfway up the stairs, and past 'Phemy, at the foot of the stairs, Dolly was fast in Peter's arms, her arms around his neck tugging his head down till she could reach his lips. Enid had that instant picture; then she drew back unseen, and saw Sapphira watching her, and guessed that her sudden withdrawal from the doorway had revealed the truth.

Then Dolly and Peter were here, Dolly kissing Enid and running to kiss Tony and mothering him with little cries, declaring that he certainly didn't hug like a sick man! Tony laughed a one-sided laugh, and Dolly spoke politely to Sapphira and turned back to Enid with a quick cascade of words.

And again the doorbell rang.

Dolly broke off in mid-sentence, and they saw her white panic. She ran to the window to look down into the street, but already 'Phemy had opened the door, and they heard in the hall below a man's voice. Enid recognized the voice of Captain Pew.

Dolly clutched Peter's arm; she appealed to Sapphira. "Hide him! Please! Captain Pew will kill him!"

Peter laughed. "I think not!" With a movement like magic, he produced a revolver, then concealed it again under his coat. Then steps sounded on the stairs, and Dolly sprang away from Peter to sit by Tony's side, stroking his brow, while Enid went to put her arm through the arm of her son.

"Cap'n Pew, to call," said 'Phemy in the door, and stood aside, and Captain Pew came in. Enid thought he was taller than she remembered, and his hair and mustache and beard now were white. His eyes were the blue of ice, and she thought him in this moment the handsomest man she had ever seen.

He bowed to Enid and to Sapphira; he made his compliments to Tony. Peter and Dolly he seemed not to see at all. Enid's pulse beat in her ears. She was desperately frightened. What could a boy like Peter do against a man like that, even though he did have a revolver under his coat. She must get Peter away.

"Come," she whispered, tugging at his arm, and to Sapphira: "We really must go." 'Phemy appeared with a coffee tray, and Quinny followed with a waiter laden with decanter and glasses. "We really can't stop," Enid insisted. "We should have gone hours ago. Goodby, Tony. I'll come again soon. Goodby, Dolly. Goodby, Captain Pew."

The Captain bowed; he spoke to Peter. "We will see each other soon again," he said politely.

Peter inclined his head. "My pleasure, I assure you."

Enid tugged at his arm. "Come! Do come." So she led him safe away, and once they were outside the house, she cried: "Peter, you must take the first train to—somewhere. Go anywhere, only do it quickly."

"Now, now, Mama, don't get excited! And don't hurry so!" She was walking at a pace that was more run than walk. "Why should I go away?"

She looked fearfully over her shoulder. "He'll kill you! He knows! Couldn't you see?"

Peter shrugged. "Yes, I suppose he had his spies following poor little Dolly. But don't worry, Mama! Or if you're going to worry, worry about him. I'll have a talk with the old gentleman, and that's the last we'll hear of it."

She would not be reassured, pleading with him to leave at once. "You still have time," she begged. "Do, please, Peter! If anything happened to you, I don't know what I'd do."

Before they reached the house, he had yielded to her entreaties. "Well, just to please you, just for a week or two," he agreed. "But don't expect me to stay away too long! I like being here with you." She hovered over him while he packed his bags. "Can Saul drive me downtown?" he asked.

"Of course!" She hurried to arrange this, and when she returned, she asked: "Where will you go?"

"I'm not sure. I'll be with friends." He took up his bags and they descended the stairs. The carriage was at the door, and she watched him depart. "Don't worry," he called. "You'll hear from me."

She shut the door, leaning her shoulders against it, thinking gratefully that Lucy, since obviously she had heard nothing, must be asleep. He was gone; therefore he was safe; she could breathe again.

2

ETER'S COMINGS AND GOINGS were always erratic, and he usually
absented himself over the Sundays to avoid seeing Don, so his
departure drew only casual inquiries from Lucy and from Trav.
Trav—and Don too when he appeared the following Saturday—were
more interested in the reports of trouble in Grant Parish. There, Kellogg
appointees had by stealth taken possession of the remodeled stable
which served as Court House, and now held it by force against the
judges and sheriff appointed by Governor Warmoth, whom they had
dispossessed. The new sheriff had summoned several hundred Negroes
to form a posse and defend the building, and this had an ominous sound.
Sunday evening Trav and Don went to call on General Longstreet, to
inquire about the situation.

"We have our eye on what's going on," he assured them. "Do you
know that region?" Trav did not, and the General explained: "It's a new
parish, set up three or four years ago under Warmoth, so he'd have a
dozen or two parish offices to fill. He named the parish after Grant,
named the Court House for Colfax. It's cotton country, big plantations,
three or four times as many nigras as whites. We've had trouble there
before. We shipped some arms up there in charge of a nigra officer named
Ward, and he turned the arms over to a militia company of nigras, and
they went on a rampage, with this Ward as leader. They robbed, and
looted, and arrested men right and left, murdered Recorder White,
burned Judge Phillips's house. I ordered an inquiry, and we arrested
Ward and broke up the company.

"But now Ward represents the parish in the Legislature, so it's a
pretty touchy situation."

"The *Picayune* said something about seven hundred nigras?" Trav's
statement was a question.

"Shaw—the Kellogg sheriff—has sworn in a lot of them," Longstreet
agreed. "The white people are getting away from Colfax, abandoning
the plantations."

"Have you sent any Metropolitans up there?"

The General spoke in resentful amusement. "Not Metropolitans; Longstreet's Pretorians," he said. "Hadn't you heard? They've been re-christened." And he said: "No, I haven't done anything. I'm damned if I do and damned if I don't. Of course, it's for Governor Kellogg to decide."

Trav saw that Longstreet was as disturbed as he. "When white people are frightened, nigras are apt to get killed," he remarked. "We've heard a lot of talk about nigra uprisings, these last few years, but the end is always the same."

"You talk like a Yankee," Longstreet commented. "Though of course, what you say is true." He lifted his hands in a gesture of surrender. "But what are we to do?"

"I suppose Ward and his nigras are scared, too," Trav reflected. "As long as a white man can kill a nigra whenever he chooses, nigras are bound to be scared. I've never known of a case here in Louisiana where a white man was hung for killing a nigra. Have you?"

"I don't recall one," Longstreet admitted. "There must have been some, while the state was part of a military district, but I don't call one to mind."

At the mill that day, Trav, without acknowledging to himself the turn his thoughts had taken, found himself wishing Peter were at home; but after all, Peter was no longer a boy—at his next birthday he would be twenty-one—and he was old enough to take care of himself. Yet it would be reassuring to know where he was, what he was doing. Trav considered stopping at the Haunted House to inquire, but he put the thought aside. Peter would resent any open solicitude.

He read the news from Colfax every day, trying to sift truth from rumor, but he could arrive at no clear and credible picture of the situation. The *Picayune* said white men in Colfax had been driven from their homes; in the *Republican* the Negroes were the sufferers. Sheriff Nash, the Warmoth appointee who had been evicted, had sent riders through the piney woods to summon reinforcements with which to recapture the Court House. A meeting of both sides to seek some adjustment had been refused by the Ward party. Judge Rutland, after being threatened with assassination, had escaped from Colfax; he boarded the steamer *John T. Moore,* and a mounted mob of Negroes pursued the boat, galloping along the shore. After his departure, his house was sacked. Negroes had abandoned the plantations to flock into Colfax, and the resulting damage to the cotton crop would amount to thousands of bales. Senator Calhoun fled to Alexandria and boarded the steamer for New Orleans, but at Pineville, the sheriff and fifty white men took him off the boat. Officers of the steamer *St. Mary,* when she reached New Orleans, reported that there were five hundred armed Negroes on the

Calhoun plantation. Many believed Senator Calhoun had organized the rising. Fifteen armed men approaching Colfax in a peaceable manner were fired on by two hundred Negroes; no one was hurt, but the white men fled.

Thursday evening, Trav on his way home stopped for another word with Longstreet. He found the General fuming with helpless anger, and when Trav asked the latest news, Longstreet lifted his left hand, let it fall again.

"Early yesterday," he said, in a grim tone, "Governor Kellogg brought Judge Rutland here to report to me. The Judge had barely escaped from Colfax with his life. His house was ransacked after he left." The General hesitated. "And here's an extraordinary thing. He says he had the body of his daughter—or his son, I forget which; his child, any-day—in his house, and that the nigras carried the casket away and broke it open. I suppose they thought it held money. But why would a sane man keep a dead child's body in the house?"

"Was he sane?" Trav asked.

"He seemed so. Yes, and his report on conditions there convinced me that men should be sent at once. I offered to take twenty Metropolitans and go myself, and guaranteed to keep the peace, and the Governor agreed. We could have left last night and been there tomorrow, but for some reason, the—" He hesitated, his face black with rage, and Trav knew from long acquaintance that he was swallowing a blast of blistering profanity. The General for a moment did not speak, and then he began afresh. "But for some reason," he repeated, "the Governor changed his mind."

Trav knew how Longstreet must have revolted at this indecision. The big man was caught in a mire from which he could not escape; Kellogg was a Republican, and Governor of the state, and so must be obeyed. Trav asked, his voice gentle: "Why? Why did he change his mind?"

"Someone persuaded him that the nigras are strong enough to protect themselves, and he's sure they will not attack the whites."

"Any news today?"

"Representative Ward is back in town, he and three or four of the other nigra leaders. They left Colfax Tuesday. I think they decided they'd be safer here. The Governor thought of sending a Deputy Marshal up today, and Colonel Wright, but he changed his mind on them, too."

At home Trav forced himself to a cheerfulness he did not feel, unwilling to let Lucy or Enid guess his concern. Lucy was happy because Don would come to be with them over Easter Sunday. He arrived in time for supper Friday night. Saturday, the *Republican*, the Kellogg organ, reported that the Negroes in Colfax were "well armed, well disciplined, and confident of success," and the editor added boastfully: "The Negroes . . . are no longer the weak and simple creatures they were before the War. The time is past, if it ever existed, when a handful of whites could frighten a regiment of colored men."

Trav thought that was a challenge no white man would ignore.

Next day they all went to church together. Afterward they were at dinner when the doorbell rang and Isaiah admitted Dolly. Enid rose to greet her happily, but Trav saw at once that Dolly was under a heavy strain, and he thought Enid's eagerness had in it something unnatural. Dolly declined dessert, but she sat with them, and after the first burst of greetings she became silent, biting her lip. Trav, wondering at her demeanor, remembered hearing someone say at the St. Charles a few days before that Captain Pew was ill, that Miss Dolly was presiding over the gaming at the Haunted House. If Captain Pew were extremely ill, that might explain Dolly's demeanor now.

In a pause presently she asked for Peter. "I thought he was at home." Enid explained that he had gone to visit some friends, and Dolly asked, almost fiercely: "When did he go?"

"I think it was a week ago Friday," Enid told her. "No, two weeks ago."

"Did Captain Pew go with him?"

Trav saw Enid's hand press her throat. "Why—no! No!" And with a sudden unnecessary vehemence she cried: "Of course not! No, no, no!"

Thus far, Trav had been silent, but now at last he spoke. "Dolly, I heard Captain Pew was ill?"

His tone made the words a question, and she nodded absently. "I know. I told people that, when they asked where he was." She began to cry, dabbing at her eyes, but Trav thought she wept more from fright than from grief. She looked at Enid and said helplessly: "I haven't seen him since that day."

Enid's eyes widened, and Lucy caught Don's glance and they rose and went quietly out of the room. Trav thought Lucy wished to leave them free to speak. "Since what day?" he asked.

Dolly glanced appealingly at Enid, then spoke in a sudden reckless haste. "Uncle Trav, Captain Pew was jealous of Peter. He had no reason to be, but he was. That's why we stayed abroad so long, and before we came back he made me promise I wouldn't see Peter again. And then that day, that Friday, I went to see Uncle Tony, and Peter and Aunt Enid were there—and Captain Pew came in and found us."

Trav looked at Enid. "You didn't tell me."

"I didn't want to worry you. I sent Peter away so Captain Pew couldn't—find him."

Trav asked Dolly: "What happened?"

"Why—nothing," she admitted. "That's what frightened me so. Aunt Enid and Peter went home and left us there, and Captain Pew sat and talked to Uncle Tony till I thought I'd scream. He didn't even look at me. He'd come in the carriage, and when we got in it to go home I waited for him to say something, and he didn't; he didn't even speak. I finally said I didn't know Peter was going to be there, and he just said: 'Ah!' We dined together without either of us saying a word. After the crap game, I retired early, as I always do. Broderick says that after the guests were all gone, Captain Pew went out to walk down to the levee—he always does that before he goes to bed—and no one has seen him since." She had dried her tears, but now she whimpered: "And I'm so scared!"

Trav's shoulders had sagged a little, as though a weary weight oppressed him. "Enid," he suggested. "Suppose you send for Saul, and we'll drive Dolly home." And to Dolly: "I'd like to talk to Broderick," he explained.

So at the Haunted House, while Enid went with Dolly to her room and sought to comfort her, Trav questioned Broderick and others of the staff. He had little help from them, but—knowing how frightened they must be—he had expected little. Perhaps Peter, when he came home, would be able to offer some information; perhaps Captain Pew might himself return. It occurred to Trav to ask whether Captain Pew's *Dragonfly* had touched here in the last fortnight, and Broderick said she was lying in the river now, that Captain Bonaventure was waiting to make his report.

Trav next day went to see the captain of the *Dragonfly*, but Captain Bonaventure proved to be as concerned—and as much in the dark—as Trav himself. Captain Pew owned two other steamers, but neither of them ever touched at New Orleans. One went from Charleston to Nassau—"For old times' sake, I always think, sir," said the Captain—and from Nassau to Bermuda and thence to French ports. The other was a coaster, hailing from Marseilles and staying close to European harbors. "He's not gone to sea, sir," the Captain said positively. "Or I'd have been the one to take him."

So Trav learned nothing beyond the fact that Captain Pew had vanished. But when he went home, his anxious thoughts quickly turned from Captain Pew to Peter, and to Colfax, wondering helplessly how soon the explosion there would come.

The slaughter of scores of Negroes at Colfax occurred on Easter Sunday, but between Colfax and New Orleans there was no telegraph, and by steamer they were forty-eight hours apart. So it was Tuesday evening before the report reached New Orleans. When on the way home from the mill, Trav landed from the ferry, a newsboy thrust into his hands a *Picayune* extra. "The whites have recaptured Colfax, and there is not a Negro to be found for miles around," said the jubilant reporter. The steamer *Southwestern,* Captain Jacobs, had brought the news to New Orleans. Captain Jacobs said the fight lasted from noon on Easter Sunday till five in the afternoon.

"When I left there late Sunday night," he declared, "everything was quiet. There were dead niggers lying all around the landing."

The story he told was fragmentary. Sheriff Nash and a hundred and fifty piney-woods men had marched into Colfax and sent the Negroes flying. Two white men carrying a flag of truce had been shot by the Negroes, and after that, no mercy was shown. The Negroes had fortified themselves in the Court House, but when that was set on fire, those who ran out were shot. Some were burned to death in the building. Thirty-five or forty were taken prisoners, but after dark they were all shot. It was estimated that from sixty to seventy-five Negroes had been killed.

Trav walked home slowly, sickened and sad. Lucy and Enid were upstairs, watching while the babies were put to bed, and Trav, though he listened for a moment from the foot of the stairs and smiled at the babel of voices and the happy laughter, did not call to them. He wished Don were here, but Don had as usual returned Monday morning to Paradise. When Isaiah announced that supper was ready, and Lucy and Enid came down and found him waiting, Enid cried:

"Why, Trav, I didn't hear you come home. Why didn't you call me?"

"Well, I was some tired," he admitted, and Lucy, knowing him so well, said quickly: "Something's happened, Papa. What is it?"

He hesitated, and they went into the dining room together. "Nothing," he said evasively, and then in mild bitterness: "At least, nothing unusual. The nigras got pretty obstreperous, up in Grant Parish, so the whites killed sixty or seventy of them."

Lucy stayed a moment beside him, but Enid said cheerfully: "A good thing, too! If there's anything in the world more hateful than an uppity nigger, I don't know what it is!"

Trav sat down, and Lucy kissed him and took her place, and Enid spoke of the babies, reciting Donny's latest exploit, and how delightfully he and little Enid played together. The doorbell rang, and Isaiah went to answer it, and came back with the whites of his eyes shining.

"Hit's Mars' Petuh," he said, and scuttled into the kitchen. They looked toward the door, expecting Peter to appear. When he did not, Enid rose and hurried into the hall, the others following more slowly.

Peter had slumped down on the bench there, and Enid knelt to catch him in a fierce embrace. "Oh, Peter, where have you been? We've worried so!" And when he did not instantly reply, holding him by the shoulders: "Are you all right? Answer me! What's the matter with you?"

He came unsteadily to his feet. "Nothing!" He was haggard, and his eyes were blank, as though he had been dosed with some stupefying drug, as though he were torpid from overindulgence in food, or drink. Trav thought he was like an animal which drags itself away from a gluttonous feast of carrion long enough to vomit and return to fill its stomach again.

"Come eat some supper," Enid urged, but Peter shook his head, moved back to the bench, sat down. "You must," she insisted. "Darling, you look half starved." Then, realizing this for the first time: "And you're dirty, Peter! Why, you're filthy! Spots all over your clothes!" She scratched at one of them. "Grease?" she asked. "Here, take off your coat and I'll give it to Daisy to clean. Whatever is this mess all over you?"

"Blood," he said, mumbling like one asleep. "Nigger blood! They'd hold a nigger up and I'd ram my pistol into his mouth and blow his brains out and blood would spatter us."

Enid backed away from him, her hands pressed to her mouth. She stopped by Trav in the doorway, caught his arm. Lucy withdrew till she could not see her brother. She stood with her eyes closed, her back against the wall.

Trav asked in a low tone: "At Colfax, Peter?"

"Marched 'em off and shot 'em, two by two." Peter's utterance was thick. "Stood 'em belly to back, and sent one bullet through two or three nigger guts at once. Had to shoot some of 'em over and over and over." His eyes were closed; his words were a mumble; his head dropped on his breast, and after a moment he sighed deeply and seemed to sleep.

Trav summoned Saul and Isaiah, and they carried Peter upstairs. Trav undressed him, Isaiah standing by. Peter's revolver was in the holster under his coat, the cylinder empty. Trav, gingerly, so as not to soil his hands, searched every pocket. He laid aside the heavy money belt Peter wore next his skin and bade Isaiah take the stained garments away and burn them.

Peter had sunk into a bottomless pit of sleep, and when Isaiah was gone, Trav stood for a long time, looking at his son. Then Enid came beside him, and knelt by the bed and stroked Peter's brow, murmuring tendernesses. "Poor, dear, darling boy."

Trav left her there.

Through the rest of April and into May—and for months thereafter —there were echoes of the Colfax massacre. It was more massacre than battle, since practically all the Negroes who were killed were shot after they had thrown down their arms. In more than thirty cases, they were murdered after having been held for several hours as prisoners. General Longstreet sent Mr. de Klyne of his staff to investigate, and to arrest and bring back for trial Mr. Nash, the sheriff appointed by Warmoth and superseded by Governor Kellogg's appointee, and any of his men who could be identified.

Trav saw the General the day de Klyne returned. He had made no arrests, but he and his men had buried fifty-nine Negroes, whose bodies, three days after the tragedy, still lay rotting around the Court House.

"And he brought enough evidence so there'll be some arrests," Longstreet told Trav. "But we're wasting our time. To most Southerners, that pack of murderers are heroes. If we do arrest anyone, the lawyers will drag the trial along till the outrage is forgotten." He looked at Trav with challenging eyes. "Or maybe you don't call it an outrage."

Trav said honestly: "Oh yes. A posse called together by Governor Kellogg's legally appointed sheriff was attacked by men outside the law, and many of them were killed. There can't be any justification."

Longstreet grunted. "They claimed the nigras fired on a flag of truce, and certainly two white men were killed, but what right have lawless men to fly such a flag? Also, those two men, one was shot in the back and one in the side, and it's hard to see how they could have been shot by the nigras in the Court House. Mr. de Klyne thinks they were shot by accident, by their own men." And he demanded: "What's the matter with us Southerners, Currain? Why do we do these things? Of course, these cowards were just trash!"

Trav did not argue the point, but neither did he accept this justification. Peter was not trash; at least, not by birth or breeding.

Peter stayed at home only a day or two after his return from Colfax. With Captain Pew gone, he moved his things to the Haunted House. "Dolly can't run the place alone," he told Enid. "She needs a man, and I'm helping her; that's all."

"But suppose Captain Pew comes back," she urged. "Suppose he just walks in some day and finds you there?"

He told her not to worry. "I don't think any of us will ever see him again. I think the old gentleman decided that there's a time to fight and a time to run away. New Orleans will see his face no more."

"You can't be sure," she insisted, and he smiled and said:

"Yes I can, Mama. I am sure." She looked at him, a sudden terror in her eyes, and he nodded. "Perfectly sure," he said.

She refused to believe that which, clearly, he wished her to believe, and Captain Pew was for a while a specter in her dreams; but on the first of May she was given a hideous sort of reassurance. She and Trav and Lucy went downriver on the *Paradise,* at Don's invitation, to be there for the last day of school. "We're going to have a program," he explained. "And give out some prizes, and it would tickle the children if you could come. And of course it would please Mrs. Harper."

Quinny was not aboard, and Enid for the trip downriver stayed in the pilothouse with Captain Cash. She liked to talk with him, to lead him with questions not too pointed, so that without knowing that he did so, he gave her glimpses of his inner life, of the things he remembered with relish or with resentment, of his thoughts. When she stood beside him, watching his brown hands on the wheel or the play of muscles in his bronze cheeks as he spoke to her, she felt in herself a responsive inner turbulence. Emotions which never shaped themselves into thoughts stirred somewhere deep within her. She would have sworn, in all sincerity, that she was interested in him only because his life had been so strangely shaped, his character so strangely formed; yet when, rarely, he looked directly into her eyes, she felt his glance like a blow, felt fright, and longing too.

She knew, and took a secret satisfaction in the knowledge, that when she stood here beside him he was intensely conscious of her physical presence, and he knew she knew this. There were moments when he hated her because she thus roused and tortured him, while thinking herself, because of the gulf between them, safe and secure. Sometimes his hot thoughts ran a headlong, heedless race. Quinny, when he came to her afterward, had long ago guessed this; so these three people were all equally aware of the truth which between Enid and Cash would always remain unspoken. Between Quinny and Cash, Quinny, in furious explosive jealousy, had once brought it into the open, crying out against them both with shrill obscenities, and refusing to be silenced until with a hard buffet of his heavy hand Cash knocked her senseless. She lay unconscious half the night, and next day her cheek was swollen huge, the skin stretched tight and shining. Thereafter, though her thoughts were her own, she guarded her tongue.

Enid knew that when she was near him, Cash's pulse began to pound, and he knew she knew this, and Quinny knew she knew. So Quinny hated Enid enough to kill her, and Cash hated her because she was beyond his reach. Sometimes, wishing to bruise or hurt her, and not daring to use any other means, he imagined himself doing this with words.

It was this torturing rage which moved him today. They had been thus together for an hour or more, close enough so that when he spun the wheel and the boat heeled, her sleeve touched his. She said: "I saw the *Dragonfly* still anchored in the river when we passed. I wonder what ever happened to Captain Pew."

Cash said, without warning: "He was killed!"

She recoiled as though he had struck her. Not knowing she did so, she spoke his name, like a plea for mercy. "No, Cash! Oh no, no!"

His eyes, like heavy hands, held hers. "Killed. Yes."

"How do you know?"

"Saw him." The rumble of his voice shook her so that she trembled.

"Saw him killed?"

"Saw him dead."

"Oh Cash, where?" She was whispering, breathless. When he spoke, his voice seemed to catch, as though his throat was full; he swallowed hard and began again.

"I'd tied up to the batture off the end of Louisa Street. Current sets in there, so I don't, usually, but one of my steam pipes sprung a joint and I tied up to fix it. Worked half the night, and I was up early in the morning. Current had set him in between us and the bank, and there he was." His words were like clubs. "His head was smashed in, his throat cut open. There were blood suckers in the hole." To see her pale and swaying filled him for a moment with a flooding ecstasy. He flung an arm around her, and in the last instant of time remembered. "You all right, ma'am? Thought you was going to fall." There was nothing but deference in his tones.

She recovered herself, and he freed her. "Oh yes," she said. "I'm all right. What did you do?"

"Pushed it out around our bow into the current and it floated away. It was early, no one around to see."

She thought how quickly 'he' had become 'it,' and a living man had become carrion. "Did you tell anyone?"

"No one, up to now. I didn't want to get mixed into it."

"You said it was floating? I thought they sank."

"If they're drowned they sink, but he was killed. It'd float till an alligator, or some eels or something got at it."

She swallowed hard, mustering her strength. "You're trying to make me sick, aren't you? I'm surprised at you, Cap'n." She crossed to the door, forced herself to smile. "I won't tell anyone," she said over her shoulder. "I won't give you away."

He said: "I wouldn't, if I was you."

She descended to the cabin deck, feeling herself bruised and beaten; it was as though Cash had seized her, mastered her. She thought her garments must be in disorder, and went into an unoccupied cabin to hide herself. She threw aside her bonnet and lay down on the lower bunk, lying on her back, her lungs heaving, her hands clasping her breasts, feeling her heart pound under her hand and her lungs labor.

She lay there, eyes wide, unconscious of passing time, till someone knocked. At her call, Lucy came in, and saw her, and laughed and uttered a sort of whistle. "Whew! What a relief!" She called over her shoulder: "Here she is, Papa!" And as Trav appeared in the door behind her, Lucy explained: "We thought you were up in the pilot-house, and when you weren't there we didn't know what to think! Time to wake up. We're coming in to the landing."

Enid yawned elaborately and sat up. "I had a grand nap." Was it possible that this experience had left no trace upon her countenance? They seemed to notice nothing. "My hair must be a mess." She moved toward the mirror. "And no comb! Well, it can wait till we get to the house." She adjusted her bonnet, turning to face Trav and Lucy in the doorway. "There, will I do?" The *Paradise* glided gently to the landing, touched and was still.

Don and Lucy came back to the farm under Frye Mountain on the twenty-second of May. Pa met them at Benton, and Ma had their welcome waiting. Little Donny accepted Ma's embrace and at once turned to watch Pa unhitch the team and strip their harness off and turn them into the pasture. Lucy could hear his clear child's voice asking many questions, hear Pa answering. Ma took little Travis, to carry him into the house, and after a doubtful look at Lucy he submitted without tears.

Next morning, Lucy thought it was as though they had never been away; everything here was familiar and expected. She told Don that night: "It's like coming home from a dance, when you're tired, and your feet hurt, and you can kick off your shoes and get into comfortable old slippers, and loosen your corsets and just relax." And in his arms, half asleep, she whispered in bitter memory: "Is there any place around here where white men kill nigras?"

"Don't blame your Southern people, Enid. They're just so plain, doggoned, completely ignorant! They don't know any better." He added grimly: "But if I can do anything about it, they will."

"I'm always so glad to come home," she murmured, and in a puzzled tone: "But I'm happy at home too." Then laughed at her own words. "Home here, home there." She pressed close to him. "I guess my home is just where you are, Don." And after a little: "Of course, I was pretty quiet this time, with baby coming. No parties, no going anywhere except to Paradise. But Eleanor and I had good times together. I missed seeing Elon."

"I didn't see him as often as I'd have liked. He came down for a day, two or three times, with the Major, to talk about the planting and ditching." Don chuckled. "Came to school once or twice, for an hour or two. Mr. Tremont says the boys that have had some schooling are the best hands he's got."

"That's the only thing I don't like about being married," she confessed, following her own thoughts rather than his words. "You're supposed to sort of wear caps and sit in a corner and knit or something. I mean, down home. It's nicer here. Even after you're married, you can still have fun." And she said, quietly, in the darkness: "I wonder why no one has ever sort of dusted Elon off and married him."

Don, after a moment, said: "He's a fine man. It's too bad there weren't two of you."

She held fast to his hand, glad he knew, and she laughed in happy reassurance. "If there'd been twenty of me, we'd all love you best." And she added thoughtfully: "I wish there were. Twenty of me, I mean. Then maybe between us all we could love you as much as you deserve!"

Trav's letters that summer came with their usual regularity. He guessed they had seen "in the State of Maine papers"—Lucy smiled as she read this aloud—that President Grant had issued a proclamation recognizing Kellogg as Governor, and ordering everybody who thought differently to disperse and go home. "But as far as I know," he added, "no one has done any dispersing yet. The ladies are too busy raising money for the Grant Parish killers, and the men are probably just plain stubborn. Grant and the army may be able to keep Kellogg in as Governor, but nobody else could."

In June he wrote that Governor Kellogg had appointed General Longstreet to be President of the Board of Levee Commissioners. "The Lynch Returning Board deserved well of Kellogg, and he knows it. He's made Hawkins a judge, and Herron's been handed a ten-thousand-dollar job. Lynch got nothing, but his son's inspector of livestock at around twelve thousand a year. And now, Longstreet."

He and Enid, he said, expected to go to Lynchburg and Richmond in July.

We might even come up and see you and Don, and meet his people. How'd you like that? Or would Mama freeze to death? The Longstreets are spending the summer in Lynchburg with Mrs. Longstreet's kin. It's a sad thing, but he has mighty few friends here now; his old friends, that is. The Metropolitan Brigade is the most hated thing about the Kellogg government, and he's the commander of it. I give him credit for sticking to his guns. Certainly he better deserves respect than General Early, and General Beauregard. They're serving as lottery commissioners, and they get paid ten or twelve thousand a year for drawing the numbers, which any child could do. Just for the use of their names to advertise the lottery. General Longstreet was offered the job and declined it, and General Hood, too. I've worked out some figures on the lottery. They must take in close to thirty million dollars a year—I can account for twenty-eight million—and they pay out less than fifteen million for prizes and charity. The rest of it goes into bribes for legislators, bribes and entertainments—and profits for the rascals that run it.

That letter came a few days after Lucy's daughter was born. The baby was promptly named Sally, for Don's mother. Don's vote was for "Lucy," but Lucy said smilingly that she wanted to be the only "Lucy" in his life. When Trav's letter came, she was already sitting up in bed, and she read it aloud to Don.

"I hope they do come up," Don said when she finished. "Do you think there's a chance?"

"There might be, if we keep hoping hard enough."

But Trav and Enid came no nearer than Richmond. They stayed there only a few days, then went down to Great Oak. Vesta's fifth son was born that summer. "They're a fine lot, these boys of hers," Trav wrote. "And we're enjoying our visit here. Rollin and Big Mill and I ride the place together every morning, rain or shine. They've done a lot to bring the land back to what it was."

On their way home, they stopped at the Plains. Jay Cooke and Company, the New York bankers, had closed their doors on the eighteenth of September, and panic was abroad in the land. "So we're going home tomorrow," Trav wrote. "We don't owe enough money at the mill to worry me, but I'd better be there and on hand. Brett says this trouble was overdue, says we spent too much money building railroads from the Mississippi west, before there was business enough to support them."

All the kinfolk were well, he reported, but Brett had a lot on his mind. South Carolina with one governor was worse off than Louisiana with two. "But I guess a man can get used to anything," he concluded. "Love to all, and we'll see you soon."

When in mid-October the day came for their departure—Don was anxious to get back, to begin work in the schools—Ma decided to go with them as far as Benton station. "So's Pa'll have company on the way home," she explained. "We're both lonesome as all get out, for a spell after you go." And when their train began to move, and Pa and Ma, waving from the platform, slid behind them and disappeared, Lucy wiped her eyes.

"I always hate saying goodby to them," she admitted. "If it weren't for Papa and Mama, I'd hate going home."

Don watched through the car windows the land decked in bright fall colors, soon to be stripped away by winter's icy hands, and he thought absently that there was something pathetic in this brave finery, as though a girl-bride about to wed a phlegmatic old man adorned herself in a vain hope of pleasing him. "I'm almost the other way," he admitted. "Up here, things are finished. The farms are cleared and tilled and prospering, so there's no big job waiting to be done. From now on, a lot of Maine boys will leave the farms, just because there's nothing more for them to do." He met her eyes. "There's nothing here for me to do. The farm doesn't need me, and Pa and Ma don't need me. There's nothing here that needs me. But in Louisiana there's more that needs doing than ten thousand men could do."

"I know," she agreed. "I know how you feel. But I like it here. I'm happy here. Down there, half the time, I'm sorry and ashamed."

Yet it was good to be at home again. When Enid and Lucy and the babies and the servants trooped away upstairs, Don heard from Trav all that was new. Trav's affairs went well. The mill this year would earn half as much again as last year; the cane at Paradise showed fine promise for next year's crop. Governor Warmoth and Colonel Lawrence had bought Magnolia plantation, downriver.

Don asked at last: "How's Peter?"

"He and Dolly run the Haunted House. Captain Pew is dead." And to Don's questioning glance, Trav said quietly: "It's a long time, Don, since I have nursed any illusions about my son."

Tony was better, and to everyone except Sapphira he seemed almost himself again, but to her the change in him was frightening. By almost imperceptible degrees, he had lost interest in the world outside his walls. Senator-elect Pinchback was one of the few of his old intimates who still came to call upon him. Pinchback's credentials from Governor Kellogg, as well as those of General McMillan, who had been elected Senator by the McEnery Legislature, had been presented to the Senate in January, now months ago. At that time, the credentials of the contesting candidates were laid upon the table, but when Congress convened in December, they would be again brought up for consideration, and Pinchback planned to go to Washington to be there at that time.

Meanwhile, he had asked the House Committee that consideration of his credentials as Congressman-at-Large be deferred. "I suppose to do so was presumptuous," he admitted, when he called on Tony a few days before his departure. "But if I can go to the Senate, I certainly don't want to be planked down in a seat in the House."

"Don't take too much for granted," Tony warned him. "The chances are neither the Senate nor the House will have you!" His tone was curt to the point of insolence, for he was in these days increasingly short-tempered. "The damned Radicals are the friends of your race down here when they want your votes; yes indeed! But if you knock on their door up there, you'll find you'll be sent around through the alley to get a plateful of scraps from the kitchen."

Pinchback colored with anger, and he looked toward Sapphira, but she laid a warning finger against her lips, so he controlled his words and his tone. "If they refuse to seat me," he declared, "I'll come back here and secure a re-election. Yes, and I'll continue to do so until they are forced to acknowledge my victory."

"You might do well in the House, Senator," Sapphira suggested. "Two years there would be valuable experience, I should think."

He shook his head. "No!" He looked at Tony. "I'll eat in no man's kitchen. I won't compromise. For me, it will be the Senate or nothing."

Tony chuckled, and at Pinchback's questioning glance he explained: "I don't suppose anyone ever before went to Washington with credentials for both the House and the Senate! They'll tell you that no one but a nigger would have the gall to claim both offices."

Pinchback said stubbornly. "Whatever my race, I have the gall to do it, and I will."

"Luck to you," Tony drawled, and settled deeper in his chair. "Sapphira, the decanter is empty."

"I've rung," Sapphira assured him, and she said: "Senator, Representative Mooney has become a frequent visitor to our kitchen."

"Mose?" He laughed. "Yes, he'd feel more at home in the kitchen than here." 'Phemy took the decanter, and Pinchback said: "It's sad to watch him in the House. He doesn't know what's going on, just sits there day after day, mumbling to himself. You know, he's young, not much more than a boy, with no education at all, but what sense he ever had was beaten out of him that day of the riot, and his scars make him seem older than he is."

"We're glad to have him," said Sapphira. 'Phemy returned, and filled Tony's glass and Pinchback's, and left the decanter by Pinchback's elbow. "He and Quinny get along. She teases him outrageously, often leaves him to tend her babies, but I'm sure he likes it."

"I haven't seen him, these last few days." Pinchback turned to Tony. "I see the Democrats elected Coke in Texas." His tone was faintly uneasy. "The Republicans split there—like the Warmoth split here."

"I was sorry you quit Warmoth," Tony commented.

"I was grieved to do so, but the man was drunk with power. He had abandoned every scruple. I determined he must be destroyed, and I only remained at his side long enough to learn his plans, so that I might defeat them."

Sapphira said: "He had many virtues, and many friends. And he elected McEnery. If it weren't for President Grant and his soldiers, Louisiana would be under a Democratic Governor today, like Texas." Her eyes met Pinchback's. "Ten years from now, Senator," she said. "There won't be a nigra office holder anywhere in the Southern states."

He shook his head, cheerfully insisting she was wrong, and presently said good night. They watched the Washington dispatches for the announcement that he had taken his seat, but instead, the *Picayune* reported that the Senate Committee was investigating the manner of his election. Tony and Sapphira agreed that Pinchback could not stand an investigation, but it was not till weeks later that they heard the explanation. Then Governor Warmoth called to pay his respects, and Tony, knowing he had come from Washington, asked whether he knew the facts.

Warmoth nodded, said in an amused tone: "Yes, I know. The Senator is a little vainglorious. He boasted that he had been paid ten thousand dollars on his agreement to withdraw from the senatorial race, had taken the money and then used it to purchase his election. Someone repeated this to Senator Morton, and Morton questioned Pinchback—and he admitted it." Warmoth snapped his fingers. "So! Poof! Gone!"

When Cash and Quinny were married, they at first made the *Paradise* their home; but after their first baby, they moved into one of the cabins at the plantation. When Tony was stricken, Sapphira asked Cash to come into the servants' quarters at the back of the house, and to Quinny's disappointment, Cash agreed.

"Well, can't I always ride up an' down on de boat wid yuh?" she begged.

"No use in it," he insisted. "You've seen all there is to see, upriver and down. No, you stay here, case they need help some time when I'm away."

"How come you don' want me along wid yuh?" she wheedled. "Ain' I youh sweet sugah?"

"I'll be home every night."

"You bettah be, you heah me! Don' you go chasin' some woman. I'se woman enough foh yuh!" And in sudden suspicion: "I know whut's eatin' yuh insides! Miss Enid alluz tellin' you how wonde'ful you is! You keep on an' I'll cut yuh lights out an' fry 'em foh de hawgs!"

She was half jesting, but he seized her arm in a grip so hard she writhed with pain, and with a heavy hand he slapped her this way, that way. "I'll teach you to lay your tongue on white folks." She kicked at his shins, screaming, and tried to bite, and he cuffed her harder, till her senses blurred. Then he thrust her away to fall across the bed, and he came to lean over her, contorted with rage. "You keep that mouth shut," he told her. "Keep your mouth shut or I'll shut it for you, for good and all."

Quinny was shrewd enough to realize that Cash's anger was confession, but after that night, she usually kept her thoughts to herself. Except when she roused him to wrath, Cash was a devoted and attentive husband. He seldom came home without some small present for her, a ribbon, a gay headkerchief, candy. But one day when he brought home a parasol with a carved handle, he caught her in an ill humor. She inspected the gift, opened and shut it, finally laid it aside.

"Mighty purty," she said. "You mus' be feelin' ashamed o' you'se'f 'bout sump'n. Who all come up on de boat today?" And when in his quick rage he seized her arms, she looked at him with mocking eyes. "I'll screech f' Miss Sapphira!" she threatened, and he released her and turned angrily away. She relented and came contritely after him and made her peace and had his love.

Limpy, her eldest child, stayed at Paradise, a diligent and promising student at Mrs. Harper's school, but the babies she had borne to Cash were here with her. 'Phemy did not allow them in the big house, so until Mose began to be much at the cabin, Quinny was their prisoner. But Mose liked children, and they liked him, and he might spend hours with them, submitting happily while the babies climbed and bounced and crawled all over him. So when he was here, Quinny could whenever she chose leave them in his charge and go for a gossip with 'Phemy, or to do a bit of mending for Sapphira, or even on an errand downtown. They were safe and happy in his steady care.

Cash, too, liked Mose, and was glad to have him around. "He don't put on any airs," he remarked one night to Quinny. "But he does try to act the way he thinks an Assemblyman ought to act. That's why he wears that long black coat, the hottest day. He told me so."

"Was a time," she reminded him, mischief in her eyes, "when yuh wa'n't so willin' t' let a man hang around me all de day long an' yuh away!"

Cash grinned. "Pore old Mose. I guess he won't make up any funny business with you."

"He's real sweet tuh me ef'n I let him be."

"Go on and let him be," he agreed, and pulled her down on his lap. "Let him be. Not too much, but some. But don't you ever forget old Mister Cash has got you under lock and key!" He kissed her, and she writhed around him like a vine.

She said to Mose one day: "I bet yuh uz a right nice-looking fellah 'foah you got so massacreed. Huccome dey done it to yuh anyway?"

"It uz in de big killin' up at de Mechanics Insatoot," he told her. "Long time ago."

"I know when't was," she assured him. "My brothe' Bob got kilt de same day."

"Yas'm. I know."

Her tone sharpened in surprise. "Know? Know what? You know Bob?"

"Yas'm, I knowed him." He was suddenly embarrassed. "In a way, I did," he amended.

But Quinny, like a beagle on a hot scent, was after him, yelping many questions. "Huccome you knowed Bob? Whut you talkin' 'bout?"

"In de cotton-oil mill," he explained. "Bofe of us wukked in de cotton-oil mill." He was perspiring. "I ain' s'posed to tell nobuddy."

"Tell 'em whut? Who say you ain' s'posed t'tell?"

"Misteh Fiddle' tell me ef'n I did he'd skin me alive."

"Did he so? Well, he daid, an' looks to me you jes' as good as skinned alive right now, 'cause you tell me, else I's sho gwine git Cash t'take his skinnin' knife tuh you!"

"You cain' do dat," he pleaded.

"I sho kin."

"Ain' a thing t'tell, Miss Quinny; not a livin' thing!" He was shaking with fear.

She looked at him acutely. "Huccome dey don't go on an' kill yuh all de way, when dey massacreed yuh de way dey did."

"I let on I uz daid and dey thought I was."

"Was Bob wid yuh?"

"Not den, he warn't. Dey drug me out f'om undeh de banquette an' kilt me an' let me lay, and de daid wagon come by and some of 'em th'owed me in. I jes' laid dare same as if I uz daid."

"Jes you in de wagon?"

"No'm, dey was five o' six befoah me."

"Bob?" she cried, and saw his eyes widen. "He in de wagon befoah you wuz?"

"No'm, dey put him in afteh. Misteh Fiddle' did." She hurried him on, question upon question; like a man sliding down a slippery roof, he had no time to catch himself.

"Daid?"

"No'm, he warn't daid yit, till de yether—"

"Who kilt him? You see who did it?" His eyes were an admission. "Somebody I knows? Mister Fiddle'? Cap'n Page? Who was it?" And then by instinct, instantly sure: "Young Marste'? Dat limb? Pete?" She caught his shoulders, her fingers like claws sunk in his flesh. "Da's him! Da's de one!"

Mose was shaking and shivering till his teeth rattled. "Yas'm. He shot him in de haid, kilt him daid." He made a woeful sound. "Miss Quinny, please don' you tell nobuddy!"

Her passion had passed, had given way to a frightening quiet. He sat moaning with mysterious fears, till suddenly, laughing, she threw herself upon him, flung him back, crushed her lips on his, bit him till he bled. She released him, her head high. "Now I done sealed you' lips an' mine! Don' you tell, an' I won' tell! Dis here is me an' you!"

That night with Cash asleep beside her she lay awake for hours, seeking out a plan. The thought which at last gave her peace was a sudden memory. In a drawer in Sapphira's dressing table there was a derringer, a compact weapon, small enough to hide in the palm, and with cartridges to fit. Quinny when she first saw it had asked many questions, and Sapphira told her it was a gambler's gun.

"Mean t'say, dis heah shiny little thing big enough to hurt somebody?"

"Big enough to kill a big man," Sapphira assured her. "If he's close enough."

The little gun was kept always in the same place. Remembering, tonight, Quinny knew she could slip into the house and get it when she chose.

3

DON AND LUCY reached New Orleans in late October, and a few days after their arrival, Enid asked a company of friends to supper. Eleanor and Mr. Cist and Elon were of course among them, and others, young and old. Lucy and Eleanor had each a thousand questions to ask the other, and Don and Elon too.

"My, but we're glad to see you back," Elon exclaimed, and he added with a smile: "I can tell you another who'll be almost as pleased as we are. Mrs. Harper." He chuckled. "You've got her into a bale of trouble, Don. Every nigra on the place suddenly wants her to give them lessons."

Don warmed with pleasure. "You've been down?"

"I go down every so often with the Major," Elon assented, and he said: "You know you're likely to make a lot of sugar down there this year, but Mr. Tremont needs someone to make his decisions. Back before the War, I practically ran the place, even when I was only fifteen or sixteen years old. Papa was never very energetic. I'd tell Mr. Tremont what to do, and he'd see to it that it was done. Your father— that is, the Major—"

Lucy and Eleanor came to join them. Supper was over, and the company had broken into groups talking together. Lucy heard Elon's word, heard Don's reply. "He's more like my brother than my father, but I like it either way."

Lucy, beside him asked: "Pa?"

"No, your father. Elon was telling me—"

Elon said: "We were talking about the plantation. The Major realized that Mr. Tremont needs someone to decide things for him, and I used to run the place, so I've been going down with your father now and then, looking around, making suggestions, dropping in at Don's school. You know Mrs. Harper has to give lessons at night now, to some of the hands, men my age and older. I used to play with them when we were all boys down there."

Lucy asked a question. "Elon, whatever happened to the machine shop you used to run?"

"I still run it," he admitted, and grinned. "It was my first enterprise, so I expect I'll always keep it."

"How did you know anything about machinery?"

"I didn't," he assured her. "Oh, I used to try to fix things that went wrong down at the Plantation, and Cash let me watch him work on his engine. I just hired a little building for a shop, and bought some tools, and hired two mechanics—they were white men—and started in." He grinned. "I wasn't their boss, just their helper. But after I knew enough, I began to make suggestions. Then after we began to do some millwork, I hired two nigras to help, but that didn't turn out well. My white mechanics just sat around bossing the nigras." He made a curious gesture. "So now nigras do all the work that I don't do myself. One of our old foremen runs the shop for me, and Christian Browning—you know him, Don; you've seen him with me at the mill—he can do any thing that needs doing over there. He's learned fast. Cash has taught us both a lot." He looked at Don. "If you ever need someone to teach mechanics, he knows all there is to know."

"I'll try him," Don agreed.

The evening was a pleasant one. Lucy thought Elon seemed older. Once he and Don and General Longstreet had a long discussion of politics, Don listening to the others. At next fall's election, a deter-mined effort would be made to defeat Kellogg, and Longstreet expected as many murders as in 1868, but Elon thought persuasion would be the rule. Across the room, Trav and Mrs. Longstreet sat together, watching them, and she asked:

"How do you think Jeems is looking?"

He hesitated, then said frankly: "He doesn't look happy."

"He isn't," she assented, and after a moment she said: "He had a wretched time this summer. Colonel Withers, whom Jeems has always counted his friend, said in a speech at Warrenton that the General was bribed to turn Republican." She made a small resentful gesture. "You know, no details, no specifications; just one of those outrageous slanders you can never pin down!"

"He spoke to me of that," Trav assented. "There's no defense against such things, of course—except to call out the slanderer, or shoot him down in the streets. But dueling has gone out of fashion since the War." He smiled. "And murder wouldn't be in character for the General."

"He considered demanding specifications," she said. "But I per-suaded him not to do that. Colonel Withers would simply have pointed to the political appointments Jeems has received, would have said: 'If those weren't bribes, what were they?' " And she said: "I don't think he minded that as much as he did the talk about Gettysburg, the outright lies."

"He's been much criticized," Trav agreed. "But I'm afraid that was inevitable."

She laughed at herself, yet with sudden tears in her eyes: "You know, my Garland kin all call me 'poor Cousin Louisa.'" And, watching her husband across the room, she said: "Oh, he's bullheaded, and stubborn, and he'll never admit he's wrong about anything, and sometimes I'd like to shake him till his teeth rattled. But I just love that big man!"

Since she was certainly a foot shorter than Longstreet, and hardly half his weight, Trav chuckled at the picture her words evoked: "I'm as bad as you," he agreed. "It's a long time since I've approved anything he's done—but that doesn't change the way I feel about him."

"He's got a wretched cold, right now," she said. "He and Jeff Thompson have been on a trip upriver, inspecting levees, wading around in the swamps. He ought to be in bed. Sometimes I'd like to pick him up in my lap and comfort him!" And she exploded in sudden laughter. "Heavens, wouldn't he rage if he heard me say that."

Peter occasionally came home to Prytania Street. Trav held toward him a remote politeness, and if Lucy were there—she spent many weeks this winter in Paradise with Don—she ignored him altogether, but Enid welcomed him. He had enlisted her help in refurnishing and decorating quarters he had taken for himself in one of the old houses on Royal Street, now converted into lodgings.

"There was plenty of room in the Haunted House, of course," he explained, the first time he took her to inspect the apartment. "And Dolly wanted me to stay there, but I had to consider her reputation." His solemn drawl made Enid bite back sudden mirth. "Besides, I like this better; my own entrance, no one to spy on me, and I can have guests when I choose."

"It's delightful here," Enid agreed. "I shall come often. In fact you must give me a key! There are lots of times when I want to get away by myself, and you won't mind me dropping in."

He shook his head. "No key. Send me word and I'll come and receive you properly, but there's only one key."

"Men are so lucky," she protested. "This is the sort of thing I've always wanted to do." She laughed softly. "You'd be amazed to know how I've envied Sapphira! She's had a regular salon, for years, the most interesting gentlemen in New Orleans."

"She's a charmer. I think she was the first woman I ever loved."

"Really?" she asked, teasing him: "How about Quinny? When you were barely fourteen?"

"Oh, I said a woman. Quinny was just a child!" He added: "Yet she's as attractive as ever. I saw her, the other day, talking to Broderick, the doorman at the Haunted House." He laughed. "She had him bewitched. That big nigger was fairly sweating with desire."

"Whatever was she doing there?"

Peter smiled. "I asked her," he admitted. "She made a big eye at me and said didn't I know she never would forget me? I told her to be off, and she pulled a long face, as though she couldn't bear to leave me. She has a pretty swing in her walk."

"You'd better be careful," Enid warned him with a smile. "Cap'n Cash'll cut you up for fishbait. I expect he's jealous of every man she looks at."

Peter said icily: "No nigger will make fishbait of me, Mama."

"I know, I know, Sonny. I was just teasing you." She added, in a different tone: "Cap'n Cash is so big and sleek. Like a tiger! She'd probably be tickled to death to make a fool of you, just to make him mad."

"She's a pretty piece," he conceded, and he asked: "When would you like to come again? I'll invite Dolly. You two always enjoy each other."

Enid hesitated. She had seen Dolly only once since the day Captain Cash told her Captain Pew was dead. On that occasion, Dolly came to the house on Prytania Street to ask Trav—it was a Sunday evening— whether he thought she would ever hear again from her husband.

"I don't even know whether he's alive or dead," she confessed, "and Captain Bonaventure wants to know what to do about the *Dragonfly*, and I don't know what to tell him. If Captain Pew made a will, I can't find it. Peter and I—we've looked through all his papers and files and everything—"

Enid listened while they discussed the problem, wishing to tell them Captain Pew was dead, yet not daring to do so. Trav eventually promised to enlist Judge Morgan's services, and to do whatever was legally necessary to meet the situation. Since then, Enid had meant to see Dolly again, but one thing and another interfered, and the fact that she knew Captain Pew was dead raised an impalpable barrier between them.

So at Peter's suggestion now she hesitated, but only for an instant. "Oh, lovely," she agreed. "Of course she can always come to the house, but it would be fun to meet here." And she asked, not looking at him: "Has she ever heard anything at all from the Captain?"

"If she has, she didn't tell me."

"Whatever do you suppose happened to him?"

Peter smiled. "If it didn't make me sound a conceited ass, I'd guess that he didn't want to meet me."

"But where did he go? What is he living on?" She asked the questions as eagerly as though she had never heard of a stranded corpse with a hole in its neck, and she wondered at her own tone, at her skilful pretense.

"Oh, he had agents everywhere, Charleston, New York, Nassau, Europe. He could draw on them. When do you want to come, so I can invite Dolly?"

Enid enjoyed meeting Dolly in Peter's apartment, but when she told Trav about it afterward, her tone held a hint of defiance, as though she expected him to protest. "Peter's rooms are so attractive," she declared. Lucy was at Paradise with Don, and they were alone. "I helped him select some things, but he really has an eye, Trav. Exquisite taste! I often think he has something of the artist in him. A charming drawing room, not large, of course, but with a nice intimate feeling, and two bedrooms. I asked him why he wanted two, and he said the house came that way! The scamp!" She found herself talking faster and faster, as though she were afraid to hear what Trav, if she paused, might say. "And downstairs a storeroom and kitchen. He has a picturesque Indian woman named Minnie taking care of him. I was scared to death of her. She mutters to herself all the time, and whenever Peter tells her to do something she spits at him, like an angry cat. Of course, I mean, just the motion, as if she were spitting. I told him he ought to get rid of her, but he says she amuses him. Dolly found her for him. She gave us coffee and gumbo in little cups, delicious. I never tasted better. Peter says she makes the best gumbo in New Orleans, and I can believe it. Coffee, and gumbo, and little dry crackers. I had a wonderful time, though Dolly did irritate me, acting as though she owned the place—and owned Peter too. You know, Trav, I really believe she's begun to dye her hair, but after all, she actually is thirty years old. She'll be thirty-one this year, and so often black hair does turn gray very early. And after the life she's led, besides." As she talked, she realized that she disliked Dolly, resenting her small proprietary gestures, as though Peter were her property. Of course, Peter was young enough to be flattered by it, but Dolly was really an old woman, and he was just a boy. Dolly was even beginning to have lines around her mouth! "I think she's aged, these last few months," she said, with hardly a check in the tumble of her words. "Her complexion has a dull, muddy look. Probably with Captain Pew gone she has to keep longer hours, though of course Peter must shoulder all the responsibility now. I told you it was she who sent Minnie to cook and tend for him, didn't I? Minnie's daughter is Dolly's maid, and Minnie adores Dolly, and of course she's devoted to Peter, too. Naturally."

She paused, so nearly breathless that she had to restrain a desire to pant, and Trav said, reminding her: "You know, Enid, I've washed my hands of Peter."

She cried out in instant, indignant protest, defending Peter not against Trav but against herself. "Don't I know it! You've always practically hated the poor boy. Washed your hands of him, indeed! What did you ever do to him except beat him? He had to go out and make his own way in the world; yes, and he's done it, too! I should think you'd be proud! Wash your hands! It's he who's washed his hands of you!"

"I've made a bad failure with him," Trav said, as though she had not spoken. "It seems as though he and I could have been friends, but I never found the way. I haven't been a good father to Peter. I wish I'd known how to be."

To her astonishment, she felt the sting of tears, and suddenly she was his defender. "Oh, darling, you've been all right! You and he aren't alike, that's all." Wishing to reassure him, fumbling for words. "He knows how you love him, really."

"As a matter of fact, I don't," Trav declared, but he amended that. "Oh, I suppose I do. Fathers are supposed to love their sons, aren't they? But I certainly don't like him." And in a stronger tone: "No, and I don't love him, either! That night he came home from Colfax, blood-spattered, stupefied with slaughter, I hated him." Her hands pressed against her eyes, and he said helplessly: "It was that half-frightened hate you feel while you're beating the life out of a snake! I wanted him dead!" She began to cry, rose and went into the other room, threw herself down on the sofa with her face buried in her arms. Presently Trav came beside her, not touching her. "I'm sorry, Enid. I didn't mean it, of course. You know that."

She turned on her back, clearing her eyes, staring up at him. "I'm sorry for you," she said. "That's really why I'm crying. I know how it must hurt you, to feel the way you do."

He drew a chair near, sat beside her, "What can we do about him, Enid? What are we going to do?"

"Now Honey, Peter's all right!" But her eyes closed to hide from him the thought behind them, for she was suddenly and completely sure that Peter had murdered Captain Pew. Since that day in the pilot-house, she had known—without acknowledging it—Peter's guilt. She thought now that Cash, too, must know, and she sat up hurriedly, drying her tears. "No, he's not, Trav! He's not all right! He's bad! I hate him too." And she said: "Trav, let's go down to Paradise for a few days. Want to? Be with Lucy and Don. Would you like that?"

Under her eager persuasions, Trav agreed, and that night before she slept, lying in that half-waking state when the mind is dispassionate and clear, unclouded by emotions and instinctive defenses, she faced the knowledge not accepted until now. When Captain Pew confronted Peter that day in Tony's drawing room, she knew Peter meant to kill him. When Peter left her, an hour or two later, she knew he had gone to do that murder. When Dolly came to report that Captain Pew had vanished, she knew Peter had killed him, and when Cash told her of finding Captain Pew's body, she guessed the manner of that killing. Peter must have known the Captain's habit of walking down to the levee after the night's play was done; he could have waited in some dark secret corner till the Captain passed, to strike him senseless and then carry or drag him down to the river, there to cut his throat and thrust his body into the stream to float away.

She had known, and now, admitting that knowledge, she grieved for her son who was lost, and wished to hold him close and guard him. Since she could not, in her half-sleep she drew near to Trav, her arms around him, pressing against him as though it were Peter she held thus tenderly.

On the second day following, they boarded the *Paradise* for the trip downriver. Cash was at the gangplank to receive them, but there were other passengers today, and beyond Cash, Enid saw Quinny with two young Negro women, each with a baby in her arms. Quinny had seen her, and as Enid started up the companion ladder, Trav close behind, Quinny came running to speak to her. "Miss Enid, ma'am!" And when Enid paused: "Miss Enid, is Marste' Peter comin' down t' Paradise? Is he with y'all?"

"No, of course not!" Enid told her, in a mysterious alarm. "What do you want with him? Why should he be?"

"I dunno 'm," Quinny said forlornly. "I knowed y'all was comin', an' I des thought he might be, is all."

"Peter never goes down there," Enid said sternly, and Trav followed her to the cabin deck. They found easy chairs on the shady side, and Enid said in a puzzled tone: "What do you suppose she wants with Peter?"

Trav shook his head; he lay back in the chair and closed his eyes.

Lucy and Don spent happy weeks at Paradise this winter. "Like a second honeymoon," she said contentedly, one night when they sat late on the gallery, looking out across the levee to the pale gold of the moonlit river. "I'm so glad I came down. I hate having you away from me, anyway."

"Second honeymoon?" he echoed. "It's nothing of the kind! We're still in our first! That hasn't ended—and never will, for you and me."

She hugged his arm against her side. "You say nice things, mister. I like the things you say. You do nice things, too."

"Your eyes in this light are so deep and dark I can't see into them."

"You know what's there! You don't have to see."

"All the same, I like to see. I know what we had to eat tonight, but I'll be hungry again tomorrow."

She laughed softly, her breath warm against his cheek. "Do you suppose other old married people sit out in the moon and say silly things to each other, the way we do?"

"No," he assured her with complete gravity. "No, I don't suppose they ever do. I expect we're the first who ever did."

"It always seems as though we must be the first, doesn't it. It seems as if, if there'd been anyone like us, before us, people would have known about them." She nuzzled her nose into his neck. "You smell good," she said, and sighed, and suddenly she giggled. "Wouldn't it be awful if we didn't like the smell of each other!"

"Whoa!" He rose, said sternly: "Such language! Comes of sitting up too late. Madame, my arm!"

She tried to rise and cried out and fell back on the bench. "Ooh, I'm afraid I can't walk! My foot's asleep!" It was a game they had played before.

"Ah, well, if I must!" He lifted her into his arms, bore her indoors.

Don in these days was pleased with the world, pleased with the schools and the pupils, and with the beginnings which he saw. "We've got them asking questions," he told Lucy in happy pride. "All sorts of questions. They're looking around and wondering about things and asking us questions, and if we don't know the answers, we try to find out, and they help us hunt out the answers. We're working all the time to keep them interested; they come to school every day, wondering what's going to happen next." And he said, frowning faintly: "Of course, education's free. Anyone can have just as much of it as he wants; as he effectively wants; as much as he wants hard enough to work and get it. But because it's free, people don't value it, unless they find out it's interesting. The only good teacher is the one who makes things interesting, so his pupils will devour it and ask for more."

Lucy was always happy in listening to him, but not always as attentive as she seemed, and occasionally she interrupted him with some irrelevant word. Thus she said now, in a dreamy voice: "You're awfully interesting to me!"

So that interruption was somewhat prolonged.

Don's days were full, and Lucy's too; she with the babies, he with two schools. "I can't really do all I want with either," he admitted. "Mrs. Harper needs more help than I can give her, and Mrs. Tremont can't do much more than teach them to read. I ought to go to Chambersburg every day, but I ought to be helping with the Negro children, too."

"I wish I could help. But our babies keep me busy."

"You do help," he assured her. "You help by listening, when I come home full of talk. You know, talking to someone starts your thoughts circulating. I get lots of ideas, just talking to you. Talking, thinking of things to say and how to say them—that's exercise for the brain, and the brain needs exercise, just as much as any other muscle!" He hesitated, abstractedly repeating his own words. " 'Thinking of things to say, and how to say them.' " He fell silent, considering, and she watched him with a wondering tenderness in her eyes.

Don and Cash had long been friends; they met as equals, each respecting the other, and next day Cash volunteered an approving word. "You're doing a mighty good thing here, Cap'n Page." In the South, titles have a long life. "It's made a big difference to me, all my life, that I went to school some, and it will make a big difference to the children here."

Don, deeply pleased, asked: "Do you still study, Cap'n? Do you keep it up?"

"Some, I do. Yes sir. I've got seventeen books that I bought myself. I read them, and I read aloud some to Quinny, but she won't sit still long enough to listen. I've got a book about steam engines that I study out of."

Don said thoughtfully: "I've learned a lot of things by teaching them to the children. That's one way." And his head lifted, as though someone had touched him, attracting his attention. He came to his feet, his eyes blank. "I expect anybody would," he said, more to himself than to Cap'n Cash.

"I expect so," Cash agreed.

Don turned to him. "How would you go about teaching a boy to understand a steam engine?"

The other hesitated. "I'd have to think about that," he said slowly.

"Think about it," Don said, with a sudden smile. "I may ask you to do that for the boys here, one of these days."

That day at the Chambersburg school he shared his thought with the children there. The school was by this time beginning to be crowded, children coming not only from the little settlement here but from the Four Corners and beyond. They ranged from six- and seven-year-olds up to Pink Chambers—he would be sixteen this year—and others of his age, and occasionally adult men and women came to listen with a close attention to everything that went on.

"I had an idea, this morning," he told them. "Getting an idea is like picking up a pebble, or a piece of rock, or a chip; you keep turning

it over in your hands, trying to think whether you have any use for it."
He said with a chuckle: "I'll bet everyone of us here has some things
in his pocket, or safely put away somewhere, that he thinks he might
have a use for sometime. It's that way with ideas. You think them over,
and sometimes they turn out to be useful. A man one day saw an apple
fall off a tree, and he thought it fell faster and faster till it hit the
ground, and he thought that over, and watched other apples fall, and
figured out how much they speeded up on the way to the ground, and
that made him immortal, and his name will always be remembered."
He hesitated, grinned. "I'd tell you what it was, but I've forgotten it,
right now." A shout of laughter answered him, and he said: "Well,
that's really a part of the idea I had this morning. I'll find out what
that man's name was, and after that I'll remember it. So in trying to
teach you something, I've taught myself something."

He paused and looked along the waiting countenances. Some of the
youngest children were squirming a little, so he spoke faster. "My idea
was that if we took turns being teacher, here in school, we'd each learn.
We'll try it, anyway, take turns. It doesn't much matter what we teach,
as long as it's interesting. Choose your own subject." He hesitated,
looked along the rows, considering. Boys would be reluctant, shy; better
start with a girl.

"So I asked Vern Bouvet to be the first," he told Lucy when he came
home. "And she elected to have a spelling match, with everyone in it.
But she gave the hardest words to the older children, and the easiest
to the little ones. I don't know where she learned some of the big ones,
but she did. When everyone else failed, she spelled the word herself."
He laughed at the memory. "It came down at the end to Pink Chambers
and Fanny Bishop. Fanny's only seven years old, but Vern kept giving
her words like 'the' and 'and' and 'cat,' till finally Pink missed on
'cupboard'—he spelled it the way it sounds—so Fanny was the
champion.

"That seemed to tickle Pink as much as any of them, so I let him
try it, and he gave a lecture on trees, took us out to the edge of the
woods, showed us how each one was different." He said soberly: "I
learned more today than I've learned in years, Honey. And they all
want to try it again tomorrow."

A few days later he spoke again to Cash, suggesting that he teach
some of the older Negro boys the workings of a steam engine. Cash,
with no pretended reluctance, agreed. Don selected four boys as a test
group. If they relished the experience, others would wish to follow them.
Don himself came with them, curious to see how Cash would begin his
teaching. Cash might himself need guidance and advice.

When they approached the *Paradise,* Don was surprised to see that

Cash had steam up. Probably he intended to take them for a short sail, to illustrate his points. As they reached the crest of the levee above where the little sternwheeler lay, the whistle blew a long blast, and Cash leaned out of the window of the pilothouse, a tin cup in his hands. He called to them:

"See that cloud of steam from the whistle? See how big it is?" They watched it fade and disappear, and Cash said: "Well, look here!" He poured the water out of his tin cup. "This much water made all that steam. Now come aboard."

He met them on the cargo deck, and led them aft. "After we go into the engine room," he explained, "you won't be able to hear much. Too noisy. So I'll tell you beforehand what you're going to see."

He had cut a section of an old bamboo fishing pole and cleaned out the pulp and whittled a plug to fit into the tube. Now he set two boys to blowing, one on either end of the tube. "See which one of you can blow the plug into the other's mouth," he directed.

That was a hilarious game, and everyone wanted to try it. Then Cash pointed out that by blowing into one end of the pipe and then into the other, the plug was made to move to and fro. "And if you blow it with steam, it will move a piston to and fro," he explained. "Now let's go see what happens when it does that."

Don that night described to Lucy all that followed. "It was a wonderful thing to watch," he said. "He took them through the whole process, explaining as he went along, and I don't think there was anything they didn't understand."

"Did they like it?"

"They were fairly goggle-eyed. Cash is a natural teacher. Maybe we can use him for teaching other things besides steam engines." His eyes were twinkling. "You know, they say that's the hallmark of a good school, Lucy; it grows. Poor schools die, but good schools have life in them, a life of their own. They grow like a tree, or like a man."

"I'm not so sure," Lucy said. "Perhaps it's the men who grow; the schools grows with them." Her eyes shone. "You've grown; you're growing all the time. So your school will be just simply tremendous, someday. Just you wait and see!"

Trav, when he and Enid came down to join them, brought the news that nine men, arrested for participation in the Colfax murders and indicted under the Ku Klux law, had been put on trial. "And there's a lot of sympathy for the prisoners," he said. "Money is being raised for their defense. As though they were heroes!"

Don made no comment, but next day while they rode across the swamp to the Chambersburg school, he told Trav that during the winter more than one man had come through the neighborhood, stopping wherever he could find a listener, seeking to arouse feeling against the Negroes.

"The latest fellow came from Terre Boeuf," Don explained. "I heard him talk to Mr. Chambers and the neighbors. He got up on the stump of an old tree—we had cut the tree and whipsawed it into boards to build the schoolhouse—and made a real stump speech. He told them that the Negroes were getting ready to take over the state, drive all the white folks out of Louisiana."

Trav rubbed his chin. "Believe him, did they?"

Don hesitated. "I don't think they did, no; but I think Mr. Chambers was worried, half scared."

"That has a familiar sound."

"Yes. Yes, we've heard it before."

They reached the school building, where fifteen or twenty children watched their approach, and Don alighted, but Trav said: "While you're busy here, I'll ride along over to the Four Corners, talk to some of the gentlemen there."

"Wait a minute, will you?" Don requested, and he turned to the watching eyes. "I want the children to know you," he explained, raising his voice. "And I want you to know them." He called: "Pink, would you mind stepping over here? Tom, you too. Collie. Ed. Eliza. Vern. Mary. All of you." And as they drew nearer, a little doubtfully, Don explained to them: "This is Major Currain. You know he bought the Villard place."

Trav said: "Good morning, young ladies. And gentlemen."

A ragged chorus answered him. "Morning."

"Mr. Page says some fine things about you all." Trav looked around the half circle of faces, and one of the larger boys seemed faintly familiar. "Isn't your name Brook?"

"Yes sir."

"I know your father. Doesn't he keep the store at the Four Corners?"

"Yes sir."

Don said: "I expect you know the fathers of most of them, Major. This is Pink Chambers. You know his father."

Trav, remembering that encounter, made an affirmative sound. He had lost his temper, that day, and Chambers had had the better of their meeting. He spoke to Pink, and to the others whom Don presented, and when he rode on, his thoughts stayed with them. That Chambers boy looked like a fine youngster; fifteen or sixteen, with good shoulders and good color in his cheeks and a high head. His eye met yours fairly, too. A man could be proud of a son like that. Pink and the Brook boy made a good pair. Most children, when you came to think of it, were a pretty good lot; it was their parents and their playmates and their communities which taught them ugliness, put the mark of ugliness upon them. Don might accomplish a lot, with these schools of his. Pink Chambers, for instance; Pink would never again be what he had been before Don came along. As long as Pink lived, he would be at least a little bit different, yes, and surely, a little better, because he had known Don. Any boy would be better for having known Don.

At the Four Corners, outside the store, two Negro men stood by the end of the watering trough, while a mangy mule in a rope harness drank and lifted his head and drank again. Trav tied his horse to the hitch rail and went into the store. Mr. Brook, in his shirt sleeves and wearing sleeve garters, stood behind the counter, while three other men lounged against boxes and barrels along the opposite wall.

Trav spoke to the storekeeper. "Morning, Mr. Brook."

"Mornin', Miste' Currain."

"I came off mighty forgetful this morning," Trav explained. "Forgot my tobacco. That's a rich-lookin' twist." He paid for the tobacco and filled his cheek. "Nice day," he remarked.

"So 'tis," Mr. Brook agreed.

Trav strolled toward the front of the store and looked out where his horse stood at ease; he waited thus for a moment or two, his back toward them all. No one spoke, and at last he came back to Mr. Brook. "Didn't I see your boy, back at the new schoolhouse yonder?"

"He goes some," Mr. Brook admitted. "Him and Pink Chambers kind of travel in double harness." He looked across at the listening men. "Mr. Collins, his boy goes too." Trav turned, and the storekeeper explained to them all. "This is Major Currain, bought Paradise plantation."

Trav said: "Good mornin', gentlemen." They acknowledged the greeting. "Your boys like the school?" he asked, his glance including both Mr. Brook and Mr. Collins. Mr. Brook had not named the other men here.

"Guess so," Mr. Collins assented. "Collie goes 'cause he wants to. I don't make him."

Mr. Brook added: "My boy'll go anywhere Pink Chambers goes."

"I'm interested," Trav explained, "because my son-in-law started the school. He seems to be doing a good work there."

There was a considering silence; then Mr. Brook answered in a guarded tone: "Don't know but he is. Hain't heard he ain't. Boys swear by him."

"If he offended anyone, it would be by accident."

One of the men asked in a dry tone: "Grown man, ain't he? Speak for himself, can't he?" Trav turned to look at the speaker, a sallow, thin man with a twisted mouth. Before Trav could speak, Mr. Brook said hurriedly:

"Meet Mr. Howard, Major Currain. Yes, Cap'n Page has done good. We think real well of him."

Trav waited to see if Mr. Howard would argue the point, but the thin man did not speak, stared at the floor. "Glad to hear it," Trav remarked. "So do I." And he asked: "Hear much politics talked down this way?"

The silence lasted for what seemed a long time, and the men exchanged glances, as though choosing a delegate to reply. When a word was spoken, it was by Mr. Howard.

"Why, there's be'n some talk," he said. "If you was asking me."

"What kind of talk?"

"Well, there's some think the niggers are setting up to run things from now on!"

Trav looked at him. "That so," he commented, careful not to make his words a question. "That so. I remember there used to be talk like that, in that *Tribune* paper, but I thought it had all died out."

"Started up again," Mr. Howard insisted. "Ever so often a man comes along giving us the notice."

"I expect it's a worry to a man," said Trav.

Mr. Brook spoke mildly: "I don't know of anyone that's worrying about it around here."

"I sh'd think not," Mr. Collins agreed. "They go to start a hot spell, we'd damned quick cool 'em off!"

Mr. Howard made a grunting sound; he spat upon the floor. "Any nigger gets uppity around me, I'll cool his chunk for him. God-damned quick, too." And he added, his eyes meeting Trav's: "Yes, and whoever puts him up to it!"

"Don't blame you," said Trav. "So would I." He asked Mr. Brook: "Had any trouble with them around here?"

"Nary a trouble," the storekeeper assured him.

"My people seem contented, at Paradise." Trav moved to depart. "Well, gentlemen, if you're over my way, stop by. I'm not there as much as I'd like to be, but I guess you all know Mr. Tremont, and Captain Page is there much of the time. Good day."

When he closed the door behind him, he felt a definite chill and realized that his nerves were tense. Mr. Howard was an enemy, no doubt of that; but Mr. Brook and Mr. Collins could probably be counted as friends, and the storekeeper's position in the community doubled his influence. Probably most people owed him money; a good man to have for a friend.

It was still early, so Trav did not at once turn back toward the school. He talked that morning with perhaps a score of men, sampling their minds. Most of them knew Don, and none acknowledged any resentment of what he was doing, but Trav thought they were rather neutral than on Don's side. Nevertheless, when he and Don rode homeward, his mind was at ease.

"You've made a good start with them," he said reassuringly, and his eyes twinkled. "They seem to agree that so far you've made no serious mistakes."

Don nodded. "I wasn't worried about that. I'm doing as well as I know how, so if I've made mistakes it can't be helped. But I don't like these loose-talking fanatics, going up and down the countryside trying to scare people." He grinned. "I'd like to catch a few of them and—well, put them on a log and shove them off to float down through the passes and out to sea."

"I never thought you were as meek as you sound." Trav approved. "There 're times when a man's due to get mad." He chuckled. "I'm a meek man myself, but get General Longstreet to tell you sometime about me at Seven Pines." And when Don would have spoken: "No, no, make him tell you. Fact is, I don't rightly know, myself, what did go on. I was in a kind of fog there for a while.

"But these men that are going around now, trying to stir up trouble— I feel the same way you do. The worst that can happen to them wouldn't be too bad."

Don asked: "What did you think of the children?"

"That Chambers boy might amount to something, and the Brook young one. I didn't notice the others much."

They came to water, and the splashing silenced them, but when presently they emerged from the swamp and were again on hard ground, Don said, half to himself: "It's like laying up a log house with saddle-and-rider corners. You shape your saddle and notch your top log and try her on, and she fits! That's the way I feel when I know I've got an idea across to these children." He laughed under his breath. "I don't know anything much more exciting than to sit down and talk with Pink Chambers and feel his mind work, matching up with yours."

Trav looked at Don without speaking, and they went on in silence, but once, at his own thoughts, Trav saw Don smile.

Quinny, from the moment she learned that Peter had killed Bob, knew she would kill Peter; but between deciding to do this and doing it a great gulf lay. Her paths and Peter's seldom crossed, so she would have to seek him out; but finding him would not be in itself enough. Quinny knew—the knowledge was in her blood and had been there for generations—what happened to any Negro who killed a white man. So she must kill Peter in such a way, at such a time, and in such a place that she would not be caught. From the first, her thoughts centered on where and how and when the thing should be done.

As for the means, her answer was the derringer in the wide drawer of

Sapphira's dressing-room table. That drawer, from the time she first became a member of this household, had been Quinny's delight. She liked to examine its enchanting contents; a beautiful silk purse, gold and white; a jewel box containing a brooch and a pendant and set with many diamonds; a silver picture frame with a picture of Tony; an ivory box holding five sachets, perfumed lip salve in an ivory bowl; a ridiculously small ivory elephant with a ring set in his back, to which was attached an inch or two of braided silk cord; a box of pale yellow face powder with a delicious scent; dozens of bits of ribbon, some wide and some narrow, some long and some short; many delicate handkerchiefs, embroidered, and trimmed with lace; a piece of chamois sewed into the shape of a pocket; a necklace of four strands of copper-colored beads that might be gold, and another single strand that certainly was gold; loose beads of every description, relics of other necklaces which had been broken and forgotten; four pairs of scissors of different sizes and shapes; two neatly folded and cobweb-thin scarves, one of which was yellow and the other red; a knife not two inches long, with folding blades and a broken pearl handle; scores of buttons of many sizes; half a dozen pieces of casual jewelry, a pin shaped like a scimitar, another like a bronze flower, a pendant made of an ivory ball with other balls inside it; two pairs of tweezers; a blue-backed notebook almost full, written in Sapphira's precise small hand; two or three pairs of stockings.

When as a child, after Limpy was born, Enid banished her from the house on Prytania Street and Sapphira gave her a home, this wonderful treasure trove was Quinny's first discovery. While Sapphira dressed, with 'Phemy's help on hooks and buttons that were set in awkward places, Quinny hovered over the open drawer, holding up one object after another, asking: "Wha's dis?" "Wha's dis heah?" "How you do wid dis?"

She amused Sapphira, who was tirelessly kind to the child, and now and then Sapphira would say: "You may have that if you like it." And at Quinny's eager question: "Yes, for your very own."

When Quinny married Cash, and they moved to Paradise, she was not so often in Sapphira's room; but after Tony's stroke they established themselves in the cabin behind the house, and she at every opportunity resumed old ways. It was on one of these occasions that she first saw the derringer, a box of cartridges open beside it. She recoiled as though from a snake, but when she leaned nearer, touched the little weapon, lifted it. It was so compact, and fitted so snugly into her hand, and the hole in the barrel was so big; she was fascinated.

"Wha's dis heah?" she demanded, and Sapphira, standing before the pier glass while 'Phemy adjusted the waterfall of ruffles on her gown, turned and saw her.

"Put it back, Quinny. It's a derringer. I got it when Marste' Tony was taken sick, in case anyone bothered us here. Of course that won't shoot very far, but if a man came close enough to touch me, I could shoot him."

Quinny put the gun back in its place, but she leaned over it, staring at it. There is a morbid attraction about pistols and revolvers to which few people are immune. Rifles and shotguns do not have this quality; the reason may be that they are normally used to kill birds or beasts, while pistols and revolvers were invented solely to kill men. To see them, or to touch them, awakens in even the gentlest soul either a shivering terror or a desire to point the piece at something; the desire, in truth, to point the piece at a person and pull the trigger. Scores of people are accidentally killed every year because someone yielded to that deep-rooted desire.

So the little derringer caught Quinny's fancy from the first, and whenever she went to Miss Sapphira's room, she liked to pick it up, to hold it between her palms, to feel its solid weight, to press back the latch and twist the barrel to one side and see the shining head of the shell in its place there. When she first tried to do this, she failed, but Sapphira told her the secret.

"You must cock it, full cock or half-cock. A funny thing, when it's on half-cock, you can't pull the trigger. See?"

She let Quinny try the trigger and find that this was true, but one day Quinny by accident put the derringer at full cock, and when she pulled the trigger the gun jumped in her hand and a roaring explosion filled her ears. For that, 'Phemy would have exiled Quinny from the house, but Tony was amused and took her side.

The episode did not weaken Quinny's interest in the derringer, but it did impress her with its powers; so when she knew she would need a weapon, she had thought of it at once, and looked no further.

Yet to kill Peter with that little pistol meant she must somehow come close to him without his knowing she had it. If he knew, he would take the little gun away from her. She must be close enough to press the weapon against his body; for she must not miss, and she must kill him dead, so that he could not name her to anyone before he died.

A major difficulty was to come at him in such a place and at such a time that none would see her come and go. 'Phemy said he spent his time at the Haunted House, and Quinny, whenever Mose was at the house so that she could leave the children in his charge, hastened down to Royal Street to try to make friends with Broderick at the door. He was ready enough to joke with her in the mornings, but when she appeared one day in midafternoon, he warned her away, in pompous phrases.

She laughed at him. "Huccome yuh talk lak dat. Yuh talk niggeh

talk in de mawnin'. How you talk at night, Misteh Broderick? I'd sho'
admiah tuh know."

"Be off with you," he muttered, looking past her at approaching
gentlemen.

"Ain' yuh got no sweet talk f'me at all?"

He hustled her aside, bowing to the gentlemen, and, erect and proud,
he led them through the great carved door.

So, behind the stout walls of the Haunted House, Peter was safe from
her; but she could wait. She meant to kill him, but not in heedless
haste. Meantime, she could relish the anticipation, waiting alertly for
the chance that someday would surely come.

Toward the end of February, the way opened before her. Tony's
gout had laid him low, and Dolly heard, and she and Peter came
to call. Quinny was in the kitchen. 'Phemy, after answering the bell
and escorting them upstairs, returned to say who they were, and
to bring Marm Tessie, Tony's enormously fat cook, a message from
Sapphira.

"She say send up Marste' Tony's gumbo, an' Miss Dolly say she
lak a cup too, t'see ef'n hit's as good as Minnie's. An' dey all want
coffee."

Marm Tessie grunted scornfully. "Minnie who?"

'Phemy shook her head. "Ah dunno. She jes say 'Minnie.' "

Marm Tessie went grumbling to her task, and Quinny said breathlessly: " 'Phemy, gimme time tuh change an' I'll he'p you." She raced
away to don black gown and cap and apron, and was back before Marm
Tessie had finished stirring in the filé, so she was in time to follow
'Phemy upstairs.

In the drawing room, Tony was on the chaise longue, Sapphira
near him, Dolly with her chair drawn close to his side. Peter was by the
mantel, lounging at ease, and Quinny met his eyes, and her eyes were
briefly so eloquent that he stood more erectly, watching her.

Dolly sipped her gumbo critically. "M-m-m! Almost as good as
yours, Peter!" And she explained: "Peter has this wonderful Indian
woman taking care of him. She used to be with me—her daughter's my
maid—but I knew Peter had to have someone, so I gave him Minnie.
Her gumbo's famous! She makes her own filé, in some secret way. I
know you have to collect tender young sassafras leaves and dry them in
a dark place and rub them to dust and then sift the dust through a
hair sieve, but there's something else. She'll never tell anyone the secret.
Hers is really delicious, though. Perhaps she'll give me some to send
to you."

Tony muttered thanks, and Sapphira, wondering what Marm Tessie
would say to the suggestion that she use filé someone else had made,

nevertheless pretended gratefulness. "I can send for it," she said. "Where is she?"

"Minnie? She's at Peter's place, on Royal Street." Dolly gave the number.

Quinny, passing the tray with sugar and milk to Peter, hearing that address, gave Peter her eyes, and at what he saw in them he stared too long, and absently poured hot milk into his cup until he overflowed it. 'Phemy rushed to repair that damage, and as she and Quinny went downstairs, she hissed angry scoldings into the girl's ears.

"What I do?" Quinny protested. "Ef'n he . . ."

"Hush up! You uz makin' love eyes at him, da's what! I's gwine tell Cash on you!"

"I ain' made no love eyes at nobody."

"Don' you lie tuh me! I see him lookin' at you! He lif' his head lak a terr'pin on a log! Go on wid you now; git out o' mah sight. An' stay out, you heah?"

Quinny scuttled away in pretended fright, but she was well content. She knew now where Peter lived; when the time came she could seek him there.

Peter had expected that with Captain Pew gone, he would find the Haunted House much more attractive, but this proved to be a mistake. With the Captain alive, even a casual encounter with Dolly was an adventure; the interchange of glances, the secret shades of meaning in a commonplace phrase, the occasional brief moments alone, these had a lively flavor which he found delightful. But it was one thing to watch his chance for a moment with Dolly; it was another to be always with her! It was not that she was boringly possessive, not that she demanded constant attention, not that she teased or scolded him; the truth was, simply, that to be with her twenty-four hours a day was not as exciting as to steal an occasional hour.

Dolly was slower than he to come to this opinion. Her long relationship with Captain Pew had always been decorous. They had never shared the same room, and his manner toward her was courteously formal, and hers to him. Thus they had each reserves of privacy. In the beginning, lavishly in love with him, she had rebelled at his insistence on this point.

"I want to share everything with you," she urged. "And I want you to share everything with me."

He shook his head, smiling. "I desire to keep some parts of my life a mystery to you," he assured her. "And I hope you will always remain in many ways a mystery to me."

She found decorum dull, and when Captain Pew was gone, she threw herself into an intimacy with Peter in which there were no reticences. They shared the same room and the same bed, but after a time Dolly confessed to herself that she was beginning to regret Captain Pew and his reserve. So when Peter proposed that he have an apartment of his own, she readily agreed, and helped him find a place that would suit him, and she soon discovered that it was more amusing to go to his quarters than to receive him in hers.

Peter was equally pleased with the new arrangement. He enjoyed playing host to Dolly, or to Dolly and his mother, and he liked inviting two or three young gentlemen of his own age for a round of cards, or for play with the dice. Peter had always been a successful gambler. He had inherited some of Trav's love for numbers, and on any hazard he never forgot the odds; but in addition he had discovered for himself that dice with sharp corners are more amenable than those with round corners, and that a casual scratch on the back of a playing card is rarely noticed unless one looks for it. So for Peter, too, the apartment was a success.

The day he saw Quinny talking with Broderick in the recessed entrance of the Haunted House, he was surprised to see how pretty she was. He knew that since she bore that clubfooted baby—which might have been his—she had married and acquired a numerous family; yet she had kept her looks. The encounter amused him, but he did not think of it again till that day in Tony's drawing room, when the message in her eyes was plain.

His reawakened interest in Quinny revived many memories centering around the Prytania Street house, and on impulse he went home for Sunday dinner. Don and Lucy were at Paradise, and when after dinner Trav went to call on General Longstreet, Peter was glad to be with his mother alone. She had many questions, and he answered or evaded them, and eventually he spoke of Tony.

"Dolly and I dropped in on him, the other day. That gout has him pretty miserable."

"I must go see him," she declared.

"Quinny was there, helped 'Phemy serve. She's kept her shape. Pretty as she ever was."

Enid wagged an admonitory finger. "Peter! Peter! What would Dolly say?"

"Dolly? What's she got to do with it?"

"Oh, don't try to tease me!"

"I'm not, but—what's all this about Dolly?"

"Nothing; nothing at all, if you say so."

"I don't say anything about it!" His tone was cold, and Enid said desperately:

"I'm sorry! Neither do I! I didn't mean anything!"

"Good," he assented, and he said: "If Cash is smart, he'll keep an eye on Quinny. She's started looking around for better company."

"Oh, she'd flirt with the bedpost, always would. I remember Bob was always getting into fights, protecting her."

"I'd almost forgotten Bob. Good nigger, till he got too big for his britches." Peter rose. "Well, thanks for a fine dinner." He kissed her. "Does me good to come home once in a while."

"I wish you'd come oftener. Papa—Oh, I wish you and he understood each other. He's so good, Peter. If you only—"

He laughed. "He and I aren't cut off the same piece, Mama. We'll never get along. I know it's my loss."

"You say so many cruel, sneering things. I sometimes think you like to hurt people."

His head on one side in a gesture that reminded her of Trav, he nodded. "You know, I sometimes think I do."

Tony in these days was fretful and demanding, and Sapphira sought to anticipate his wants and thus forestall his feeble rages, fearing each one might snap the thread of his life. Their relationship, begun without any connotation of real attachment on either side, had developed on his part into dependence, on hers into devotion. Now, remembering his uniform kindness and consideration, and his respect for her personal dignity, she repaid him with a tender loyalty.

She strove to foresee not only his needs but his wishes, and usually she succeeded, but one night after she and 'Phemy had put him to bed, 'Phemy brought him a cup of Marm Tessie's gumbo. At first taste, he remembered Dolly's promise to send him some of the Indian woman's filé, and demanded why it had not come.

"I'll send for some," Sapphira promised. "I'll send, first thing, in the morning."

She thought he might forget overnight, but he did not. Tony's risings were protracted. 'Phemy must always help Sapphira prepare him for the day. So when he woke demanding gumbo and the famous filé, since 'Phemy could not go to fetch it, Quinny was sent for.

"I kin go," she agreed, her thoughts racing. Peter might be still asleep. The drawer of Sapphira's dressing table was open, the derringer there in plain sight. Quinny moved casually to stand with her back against the drawer, her hands behind her. "De babies is fed. Ef dey yell, let 'em yell." When she went on toward the open window and out on the gallery and down, the derringer was in her hand, hidden in a fold of her dress.

She took it, but not with any fixed purpose. Before she saw

Peter—if she did see him—she would encounter Minnie, and if she then killed Peter, Minnie would know it. Quinny had no intention of running such a risk; she took the derringer only on the chance that an opportunity to use it might arise.

But she discovered, when she reached the kitchen of the Royal Street apartment, that Minnie hated Peter. When she rang the bell and told her errand, she was met with suspicion and distrust. There was filé, Minnie admitted, but the filé did not belong to her master; it was not his to give away, though to be sure, he was a thus and so of whom anything might be expected, a man with no appreciation, a man of obscene and degraded habits, given to manifold indecencies, the worst of which was that he did not appreciate his good fortune in being beloved by Miss Dolly, and brought sluts off the street to share his bed while Miss Dolly pined for him. Minnie as she talked was fairly slavering with hate, and Quinny became convinced that the Indian woman would feel no grief for Peter dead.

When he woke, and rang his bell, and Minnie went to take him his morning coffee, Quinny waited in the kitchen, not so much excited as in a calm exultation. Minnie reported to Peter that a yellow girl had come asking for filé for Mr. Currain, and saying it was promised. Instantly sure that this must be Quinny, Peter sat up in bed.

"Where is she?" The Indian woman said she was in the kitchen. "Wait ten minutes and send her up," Peter directed, his eyes gleaming. "I'll talk to her."

At the appointed minute, Quinny tapped on the door, and Peter in his dressing gown opened it. "Come in," he said, his voice husky.

She moved past him into the room, and he closed the door and caught her, drawing her back to him, swinging her around to face him, crushing her in his arms. Her eyes met his, and she smiled, and he felt her hand touch his body, and laughed. The shot was like a heavy blow in the stomach, not painful at all, but his legs turned to limp ropes and he fell, dragging her down with him. The bullet, tearing its way through his bladder and his intestines, had embedded itself in his spine.

He fell, clutching at her knees, and she leaned down and spat in his face. "Da's f'Bob," she said harshly. Then Minnie burst into the room and dropped on her knees by Peter's side, and Quinny said: "Ah fix him! Ah shot him th'ough de gut. He gwine tek his time tuh die!"

The Indian woman looked up in raging comprehension. "You kilt him? He Miss Dolly's love!" She sprang to her feet, but stepping on the hem of her dress brought her to her knees again, and Quinny had seen death in her eyes. She ran swiftly down the stairs and through the courtyard and away.

4

FEBRUARY RAINFALL had been no more than normal, with one heavy shower on the first Monday which accounted for almost half the total for the month; but from upriver came reports that the lowlands below Cairo were overflowed, and the river began to rise. The weather was a major element in making a good crop of sugar. March temperatures were important; spring frosts did more harm than frost in the fall. Subnormal rainfall through the summer and into the fall was usually a favorable sign, and low, wet, cold fields were better put to other crops than sugar. The soil should hold water; yet to remove surface water after heavy rains, good drainage was essential. Deep ditches make rich planters.

So when the river began to rise, Trav went down to Paradise to see to it that his ditches were in order. He spent Saturday in the fields, Lucy riding with him. Next day it rained all day, heavily for a while, and a drizzle persisted till nightfall. Monday was worse. A downpour lasted all morning, and Trav, dressed against the weather, rode abroad to watch for clogged ditches and for overflows. The swamp was filling, but since it extended for miles, wide and shallow, the water rose slowly; the cultivated lands, though they drained away from the levee toward the swamp, were high enough to escape any but the most severe floods.

During bad weather, the *Paradise* seldom came downriver; but Tuesday, after an early shower, the skies cleared, and Trav expected the little steamer. When at noon she had not appeared, he felt a vague alarm. Lucy saw this, and spoke to him.

"What's the matter, Papa?"

"I felt sure Cap'n Cash would be here before now."

"Did you tell him to come?"

"No, but he'd know I want to get back to town."

"There's nothing to worry about. The engine broke down or something; that's all."

"I expect so," he agreed. "But—well, Mama's all alone in that big house."

"Isaiah's there, and Saul, and Filly, and Maria, and Daisy!" She laughed at him. "I don't call that being alone."

He smiled. "I know, but she may be wishing I was there."

"Oh, don't flatter yourself! You're not so important as all that. Stop worrying and enjoy being here with us."

He submitted, but when a little after noon he saw a small steam launch round the point and angle toward the landing, his fears became a certainty. As the launch came nearer, he recognized Elon standing by the steersman, and he had no need to see Elon's sorrowful countenance to know that tragedy had struck. He cleared his throat and went to meet whatever was to come.

The river was high, so the launch could come alongside the levee. Trav waited, and when they were within easy speaking distance, Elon said, not raising his voice: "Bad news, Major."

Trav nodded, accepting this. "Mrs. Currain? or Peter?"

"Peter. He's still alive, but he's dying."

The launch touched. "I'll come back with you," said Trav, and was about to step aboard, but then, remembering, he said: "Lucy and Don will want to come." Elon went to summon them, and Trav sat down on the after thwart. He felt neither grief nor pain, but Enid would need him. Lucy ran down the levee and climbed in to sit beside him, saying nothing, holding fast his hand. Elon and Don were a little behind her, and Don said apologetically:

"I'm sorry. I had to speak to Mrs. Harper."

The launch, with a puff of steam, angled out into the current. "We came down in an hour and a half," Elon said. "But it will take us longer going back."

"Is Mrs. Currain all right?"

"She's with him."

"Was it yellow jack? It's early for that."

"No sir," Elon said wretchedly. "He was shot." And without waiting for questions, he told them what there was to tell. "They say Cap'n Cash's wife shot him. Quinny." And he went on: "He was shot in the stomach, and the bullet is in his spine, in the spinal cord. He's had a bad time, but he's unconscious now."

"When was he shot?" Trav's voice was empty of emotion.

"Friday morning."

"Why didn't someone let us know?"

"I didn't know till this morning. He lived in rooms on Royal Street. The Indian woman who takes care of him stayed with him, poulticing the wound, nursing him. When he didn't come to the Haunted House

Saturday night, Miss Dolly was a little provoked, and next day—that was Sunday—she sent her maid with a note for him. The maid's Minnie's daughter. She came back and told Dolly. Dolly had Peter moved to her place, and she had about every doctor in New Orleans to look at him. She was so distracted that she didn't think to send word to you and Mrs. Currain till yesterday morning, after the doctors told her he couldn't get better. Mrs. Currain's been with him ever since, but no one let us know till this morning." He added: "I didn't know what had happened, so I tried to get Cash to bring me down, but he had to stay with Quinny, so I hired this launch. Mr. Cist and Eleanor are with Mrs. Currain now."

"At the—" Trav hesitated. "At Dolly's?"

"Yes." Elon added: "Minnie—Peter's housekeeper—she told Dolly enough so Dolly knew it must have been Quinny, so she told the police. Mr. Cist—I saw him before I started—said the police had gone to get her."

"I wonder why she did it!"

Elon shook his head. "I don't know."

"It's hard on Cash," Trav reflected. "He's a good man. I'm sorry for him." He was conscious of a certain incongruity in the fact that he was sympathizing with another, rather than with himself.

Lucy began asking questions, and Elon patiently repeated the little he knew. Trav ceased to listen, thinking of Enid, remembering her anger when their baby died, back during the War. She had blamed him; something about a snuff stick little Henrietta's nurse used to use, which somehow injured the baby's eye, and the hurt never healed, and Henrietta died, and Enid in her grief raged at him. Perhaps she would blame him now. Certainly he had always blamed himself for failing to win Peter's trust and love.

Thinking of Peter reminded him of Colfax. Three weeks ago, the trial of the men arrested for that slaughter had begun. Peter might justly have been placed in the dock with them. If he had been arrested and put on trial, he would not be dying now. Trav wondered whether Peter had followed the testimony in the trial with interest, or with concern.

When at last they saw ahead of them the river craft moored along the levee, and the towers of the city beyond, he dreaded facing his son this one more time, but Mr. Cist met them at the landing and told them Peter was dead. Trav was half thankful. A greater thankfulness filled him when they reached the Haunted House, and Enid, with love and pity in her eyes, came into his arms.

At home, afterward, Lucy and Enid went upstairs together, and

Lucy helped her mother prepare for bed. When she came down, she said Enid was already asleep. "She's been with him since yesterday morning, Papa, and I don't suppose she's shut her eyes."

Trav nodded, surprised to find himself already drowsy, as though this stupefying anguish were a drug. Yet he dreaded sleep: in sleep, the bars were down; you were the helpless prey of dreams. He turned, instead, to the pile of dailies which had accumulated during his absence. The case against the men indicted for the Colfax massacre had gone to the jury the day after he went downriver to Paradise. He read the Judge's charge, glancing hastily through a column or so of legalisms until he came to a sentence:

> In the case on trial, there are many facts not in controversy. I proceed to state some of them in the presence and hearing of both sides, and if I state as a conceded fact any matter that is disputed, they can correct me.

Proceeding, the Judge recited—without interruption—the events that led up to the massacre; the approach to Colfax of a small body of armed white men, repulsed without harm on either side by a body of Negroes; the flight of Negroes into Colfax, of white men away from the hamlet. He continued:

> On Saturday, April 5, a band of armed white men, either fifteen in number as claimed by the prosecution, or three in number as indicated . . . by the defense, approached the house of one Jesse McKinney, a colored man, three miles from Colfax, and . . . one of the white men fired upon him, shot him through the head and killed him.

Trav wondered absently whether Peter fired that shot; it was the sort of thing he might have done. He read on, as if he were reading an account of Peter's last hours. More Negroes came to Colfax, said Judge Woods; more white people went away. The Negroes holding the Court House threw up an earthwork near the building.

On Sunday an armed body of white men "variously estimated as from one hundred and fifty to seven hundred," approached the town, and the Judge reported their demand that the Negroes surrender, and the eventual attack. When the Negro line broke, said Judge Woods:

> A portion of them, leaving their arms, fled . . . and were followed by mounted and armed whites, by whom many were overtaken and shot to death. The others . . . took refuge in the Court House.

The Court House was set on fire and some of the Negroes inside wished to surrender. The Judge continued:

One held out the leaf of a book, and the other took off his shirt sleeve and hung it upon a stick as a sign of capitulation. They were ordered to drop their arms. At this point there is dispute between the prosecution and defense. James P. Hadnot and one Harris, whites, approached the Court House, and as claimed by the defense, they had a white flag upon a pole. As they came near the door, they fell, both mortally wounded. The defense insists that while bearing the white flag, they were shot from the Court House. The prosecution and its witnesses say that when Hadnot was approaching, the blacks, having thrown down their arms, started to come out from the burning Court House and were met by a volley of shots which, besides killing many of the colored men, struck down Hadnot and Harris.

Trav lowered the paper again, reflecting, unwilling to believe that while they were streaming out of the Court House with their hands in the air, the Negroes would or could have shot anyone. He read on.

However this may be, a number of unarmed blacks who came out of the Court House were shot dead, and others were wounded. . . . About thirty-seven men were taken prisoners. They were kept under guard until dark. They were then led out, two by two, and shot. Most of them were shot to death; a few were wounded, not mortally, and by pretending to be dead were afterward during the night able to make their escape.

The dead, said the Judge, were left unburied till Tuesday, when a deputy and a militia officer from New Orleans found fifty-nine bodies. "They showed pistol wounds," said Judge Woods. "The great majority in the head, and most of them in the back of the head."

The picture was clear enough; Trav's eyes drifted on to the eventual conclusion, the Judge's final word: "If you are persuaded . . . that the prisoners, or any of them, banded or conspired . . . I trust you will have the courage, I trust there is enough good and lawful manhood among you, to say so by a verdict of guilty."

Trav dropped the paper on the floor beside his chair. Well, he was persuaded; the prisoners, and those others who had not been arrested, and Peter who was not even named, they had certainly conspired together to do that which was done. Bloody murder! But why could not the law put it thus simply; why must the issue be beclouded with so many words?

It occurred to him that the jury must by this time have reached a verdict, and he searched the later papers till he found it. One of the nine men indicted had been acquitted; on the others, the jury disagreed.

He had expected this result, for there were at least five known Democrats on the jury. It might be possible to find one Democrat who would vote to convict another Democrat of killing a Negro, but it would certainly be impossible to find five. Peter's phrases came back to Trav's mind. "A bullet through two or three nigger hearts at once." "They'd hold him and I'd put my pistol in his mouth and his blood would spatter us."

Well, those of Peter's fellow murderers who had been arrested were still unpunished. Acquittal for one; mistrial for the others. But on Peter, judged not by clumsy human courts but by some higher Tribunal, verdict had been rendered. Peter was dead, the Judge's charge his damning epitaph.

For the last ten days of March, there was rain almost every day, and on two days toward month end the showers became a downpour. Rains upriver and in the great watersheds of the Tennessee and the Cumberland brought the level of the flood inches higher day by day. The river threatened not only the plantation, but also the mill in Algiers, and Trav's anxiety and the measures by which he tried to reduce the danger, helped him to put thought of Peter into the background of his mind.

Enid, who had been his first concern, met the tragedy with surprising steadiness. "I suppose it's horrible of me to say so, to feel so, Trav, but we had already lost Peter. He was gone out of our lives before this; he's no more gone now than he was then." And once, lying beside him in the darkness, clinging to his hand, she said: "He inherited all the bad things in me, Trav. I wish I could believe they died with him." And again: "You remember how I cried, two or three weeks ago, whenever it was, when we were talking about him. I think, for us, he died then. That was why I cried."

Peter had told nothing of the manner of his death. His screaming agonies while the surgeon unsuccessfully probed for the bullet had unhinged his mind. But Minnie had named Quinny, and Trav grieved for Cash, and when a few days after Peter's funeral, he proposed that he and Enid drop in on Tony, it was Cash whom he particularly planned to see.

Tony, though his words gave little comfort, was able to talk with them. "The young scoundrel took after me," he commented. "But if he'd lived long enough, he might have settled down—like me!"

He looked across at Sapphira, peace in his eyes, and Enid said lightly: "Oh, you were never such a scamp as you thought yourself, Tony! You're a natural old married man; first Mama, and now!" She spoke to Sapphira: "You're what he had always looked for."

Tony said, with a chuckle: "Peter had some of Papa in him, Trav; the old boy himself. Eh?"

Trav stirred, taken by surprise. Instead of answering Tony, he spoke to Sapphira.

"Is Cash at home, do you think?"

"I expect so. Out with their babies. I'll see." She went through the bedroom to look across the court toward the rear. "Yes, sitting there under the trees."

"I'd like to talk to him." Trav rose. "Can I find my way out?"

"Let 'Phemy bring him in."

"No, I'll go to him." He added in a thoughtful tone: "I expect Peter injured him more than Quinny has injured me."

Enid said: "I'll come with you, Trav."

He nodded, and Sapphira led them downstairs, and along the hall, opening the door into the court. When they started along the path toward Cash, he did not at once notice their approach. His chair was tipped back against a tree, his eyes upon the babies in the dust beside him. Then he saw Trav and Enid, and rose, and after a momentary hesitation he came to meet them. Behind him, the babies watched, wide-eyed.

Trav raised his hand in greeting, and Cash responded, touching his forehead. They met, and the men clasped hands, and Cash said sadly:

"I was going to come tell you my sorrow, soon as it was a fitting time."

"I know how you feel."

"Quinny wanted to run away." Enid remembered an old Negro woman at Chimneys who was a long time dying of cancer, and whose voice held that same hollow sound, like an echo of stale pain. "She was here when I came back upriver," said Cash. "Here wantin' me to carry her away. I made her stay. We just waited, till the Mets came." Enid till now had not been near Cash without a stir and an awakening, frightening yet seductive too. Now, he was a sorrowful and sad and weary man for whom she felt pity, but felt nothing more.

"That was the best thing to do," Trav assented.

"Miss Sapphira got a lawyer for her," Cash explained.

Trav, though he felt little or no curiosity about the reason Peter had to die, asked: "Did Quinny tell you why she killed him?"

Cash wiped his brow. "I don't know as you know about it," he said, hesitating. "It was mostly account of his killing her brother. She told me Bob used to belong to you."

Trav uttered an exclamation of surprise. "Bob? Yes, he was mine. But he was killed in the riot, seven or eight years ago. A policeman shot him. In the Mechanics Institute."

"He was shot, but he was alive for a while after that. Mose Mooney— he used to work for you in the mill, too—he got hurt, that day, and they put him in the dead wagon, and then Mr. Fiddler put Bob in beside him, and Peter came along and shot Bob through the head." He added in an apologetic fashion. "Mose—he's in the Assembly—he says Mr. Fiddler knew Peter did it."

Trav stood like stone; the words were cudgel blows. Enid, at his side, felt the stiffness in him, and she slipped her arm through his. When he tried to speak, the sound had no character; he cleared his throat.

"I never knew it," he said. It did not occur to him to ask how Quinny knew where Peter lived, how she made her way to his room, what weapon she used, where she got it. "Mr. Fiddler should have told me." Cash did not speak, and Trav said: "I hope they don't punish Quinny, Cash." Cash made a grateful sound. "It won't make any difference about your working for me," said Trav, half in reassurance, half in question.

"No sir."

"Maybe I can do something to help her."

"I'd admire to have you, if you could."

Silence bound them; there was no more to say. Enid touched Trav's arm. "Time to go, Trav."

He nodded, and clasped Cash's hand, and they turned away. Sapphira said Tony was asleep. Before they reached home, Trav remembered that he had meant to ask Cash to take down a load of planks, to strengthen the levee at Paradise; but tomorrow would do.

Heavy rains bade farewell to March and welcomed April, while at Paradise Trav and Elon and Don, sometimes afoot and sometimes mounted, put men to drive planks and weave brush through stakes where it was necessary to strengthen the levee, and set others to wade barefoot in the margin of the flood, feeling with their feet for the suction that would betray a crawfish hole which must be stopped. When Trav decided the levee was safe, and returned to New Orleans against the boiling current of the still-rising river, Don and Lucy stayed behind. Trav found the Algiers levee in danger; thus anxiety and strenuous activity deadened grief a while and gave his hurt time to heal. But time would not efface the scar.

Through those months of spring, the political kettle simmered toward a boil, and even at Paradise, white men and Negroes when they met were like strange dogs, walking stiff-legged, a growl in their throats, ready at any provocation—or at none—to spring to battle. Don could not wholly hide from Lucy his awakening anxiety.

"Though I really haven't anything to go on," he admitted. "Mr. Chambers and his friends claim they don't believe a word of the talk, and the people on the place here insist that as far as such matters are concerned, they 'don't pay 'em no mind.' But you can feel the wariness in them, and when you meet a white man nowadays, he doesn't smile. Someone killed a Negro, a mile north of the Four Corners, here one day last week. Nobody knows when, or why—or they don't tell if they know. They just found his body lying there."

"Aren't you ever afraid, Don?"

"I'm afraid for them, yes," he admitted, and he said in a sudden tempestuous resentment: "That's where the trouble starts, in fear. It's because men are afraid—whites afraid of what the Negroes might do, Negroes afraid of what the white men may do—that trouble comes."

"Aren't you afraid for yourself?"

"For myself?" He was honestly astonished, yet he saw that she wished to be reassured, so he chuckled, shook his head. "No, of course not. They all know I'm on their side. They know they don't have to be afraid of me. Don't you worry about me."

And in fact Lucy did not worry about him. The weeks which this winter they had spent at Paradise were the happiest they had ever known. The first intoxicated rapture of their marriage had matured into a profound content. They drew ever closer, each growing into the other, so that even the physical appearance of each was subtly modified, and they looked each day more and more alike. To be together had become their natural state. When they were apart, each was vaguely conscious of some faint discordant note in the symphony of the days; when they were together, the world was all in tune.

Lucy asked one day: "Don, have you noticed something?"

"What?"

"Have you noticed that when we're alone together, we sort of lower our voices, as though we didn't want anyone to hear."

"Do we? I hadn't noticed. Wonder why? We've no secrets from anyone."

"It's like being out at night, in the dark. If there's a crowd of you, you're laughing or singing or carrying on till they can hear you a mile away; but just two people together will always speak softly. You never hear them till they're near."

"I hadn't thought about it," he confessed. "But it's true."

"I just started thinking about how happy we'd been lately, wondering why it was, and I thought of that as part of it."

"You know what I think?" His eyes were smiling.

"What?"

"I think we're getting married."

She shook his hand, nodding gravely. "I think maybe we are," she agreed.

There was a time during the height of the flood when—unless you were willing to swim your horse—it was impossible to get across to

Chambersburg, but with Mr. Tremont as a guide, Don one day rode around the upper end of the swamp to the Four Corners and stopped at the store there before proceeding. It seemed to him that Mr. Brook met them with a cold reserve, nor was Mr. Collins any more cordial. When they rode on, he spoke of this to Mr. Tremont.

The overseer nodded. "Something on their minds," he agreed. "Maybe it's the weather. Rain all the time, it'll get a man down."

Halfway to the school they met Mr. Chambers, and pulled up their horses to pass the time of day. Mr. Chambers had heard of Peter's murder. "By a nigger wench!" he said. "That so?" Don said it was, and Mr. Chambers asked: "Did they hang her yit?"

"She hasn't come to trial."

"Trial? She kilt him, didn't she?"

"I suppose she did."

Mr. Chambers spat. "Trial? Hah! Them city ways." He cocked an eye at Don. "Reminds me, I had to give Pink a larrupin', here a while ago. He come home tellin' his ma and me all about steam engines. Seems like he'd been listenin' to that Cash nigger. I don't aim to have my boys takin' teachin' from no nigger."

Don said at once: "I'm sorry that happened. I know how you must feel." He looked at Mr. Tremont, thinking this had occurred during one of his absences, but the overseer did not speak. Mr. Chambers said in a flat tone:

"You go ahead and teach Pink y'self, if it pleases you. But no niggers."

He rode on toward the Four Corners, and they proceeded to the school. Mr. Tremont said apologetically: "I didn't know about that or I'd have stopped it. That sort of thing gets them up on their ear."

"I suppose Pink just happened by and listened. Maybe Cash didn't even know he was there."

Mr. Tremont shook his head. "Guess he did. Cash is a real good nigra, but he might have wanted to show off. It don't take much to get them feeling big."

A few children saw them pass and followed them to the school house, but neither Pink nor any of the older boys were among them, and Don had not long to stay. School would start up again, he promised, as soon as the flood subsided; but the water was still rising, and when on Saturday Trav and Elon came down on the *Paradise* to see the situation at the plantation, Don and Lucy went back to New Orleans with them to wait for better times.

For weeks the water rose. A break in the levee below Paradise drew the river down and relieved the pressure on them, and there was talk of cutting the Gulf Ship Canal to release some of the flood. A broad but shallow break at the head of St. Ann Street let a stream two hundred yards wide and a foot deep pour down on the French market, but six hours work by a force of a hundred men, who dumped ballast, gravel and earth into the narrowing flow, made the spot secure. Lesser breaks were everywhere, and a high wind that sent waves washing across the top of the levee made each one a potential catastrophe. At the Stanton plantation, fifteen miles below the city and across the river from Paradise, the levee, undermined, caved in, and a gap a hundred and fifty feet wide let the water overflow the fields.

For a fortnight the disaster grew, with a break in the Grand Levee in Iberville as the last and heaviest stroke. Thereafter the waters fell, and the work of repair and relief began.

During and after the flood, the Levee Commissioners, Longstreet and General Thompson, because they were Kellogg appointees, were damned by McEnery Democrats for what they did and for what they did not do. Even Enid thought these criticisms so unjust that she proposed inviting the Longstreets to dinner, but Trav advised her to wait till the pressure upon the General relaxed.

Instead, at Lucy's request, she invited Eleanor and Mr. Cist and Elon. Elon during the winter had several times gone to Paradise with Trav, consulting and advising. "I think he's homesick," Trav told Lucy. "I've half a mind to give it all back to him."

She smiled, knowing he was jesting. "Not the schools," she warned. "Don wouldn't let that go."

"Elon's as much interested in those schools as Don is, by this time," Trav assured her, and she knew this was true, had heard them more than once in long, absorbed discussion.

At supper the night they came, Trav with the utmost gravity produced two clippings. "Clipped them out of the *Picayune* this morning," he explained. "Thought you all might not have noticed them in the paper, might want to fix and go." There was jest in his tone, but Lucy thought the jest was edged with anger.

One clipping was a letter signed by the men indicted for participation in the Colfax massacre. The jury had disagreed, and in May they would again face the court. The letter appealed to the "ladies and gentlemen of New Orleans to aid and assist in defraying the expenses of our trial." The other clipping reported that on reading this letter, twenty New Orleans gentlemen had formed a committee, and had asked Miss Minnie Doyle and the Orleans Dramatic Association to help them in their efforts to raise money for this purpose. The Association had agreed, and accordingly, there would be a benefit performance of Schiller's *The Robbers,* at the Varieties Theatre, Monday night, April 27. Tickets would cost one dollar. Mr. Eugene May was chairman of the committee of twenty-seven New Orleans gentlemen.

Trav watched them while they read, waiting for their comments, and as the clippings went from hand to hand a curious silence fell. Don was the first to speak.

"Well after all," he said, "they haven't been convicted—"

Lucy protested: "Oh, Don, everybody knows they're guilty."

"They're still entitled to a fair trial, by a jury."

Elon said, turning a fork in his hands, his eyes watching his fingers: "I think it's wise to remember the political side of this. The defendants are all Democrats. The nigras who were killed were all Republicans. No fair trial is possible; it's bound to be unfair to one party or the other, to those who were killed, or to those who killed them."

Trav said gravely: "Peter was one of the latter."

Enid pressed her knuckle to her lips, and Lucy looked at Don, and Eleanor uttered a hurt cry, but Elon said gently: "I know he was active in that campaign four years ago. Many people believe that— violence—is necessary." He met Trav's eyes. "Certainly, the situation in Louisiana today is intolerable, sir. I'm ready to lend myself to violence to stop it."

Eleanor protested: "Oh, Elon, you don't mean that!"

"Not to another Colfax," he agreed. "No, I mean organized violence; trained men, marching shoulder to shoulder, acting openly and proudly." He added, meeting Don's eyes and then Trav's. "Not just a dozen men, or a hundred. Thousands." A half smile touched his lips. "Some things are made respectable merely by numbers, Major; don't you agree. As, for instance, war."

Trav said, choosing his words: "An army is certainly more respectable than an assassin; yes, Elon. But there's nothing to be accomplished by an army here; not against the Army of the United States."

Elon, after a moment, smiled and lifted his hand in apology to them all. "We didn't come here for this," he said. He picked up Trav's clippings. "By way of atoning—I'll get tickets for all of us, to the forthcoming entertainment. If I'm ever tried for murder, I hope you'll do the same for me!"

So the tune changed and the evening was a merry one, but Lucy thought her father was unusually silent, and guessed that he was troubled. She had had no chance to talk with him when he returned from the mill today, but tonight when they had seen their guests to the door, she took his arm and shook it, as though to awaken him, and asked:

"Now, Papa, what's the matter?"

"Matter?" he protested.

She nodded. "Something on your mind!" They had all halted, Enid facing him, and he laughed awkwardly.

"Well—" He hesitated, then asked: "Enid, when was it Dolly came to see you?"

"Oh, weeks ago, I guess. Why?"

"Apparently, she's disappeared. One of the General's Metropolitans came to the mill late this evening to find out where she is. They want her and this Indian woman to testify against Quinny, and they're both gone."

"But—gone where?" Enid cried.

"Broderick says they went with Captain Bonaventure, in the *Dragonfly*. Mr. Curtis, Dolly's agent here, says she told him to sell everything she owns and to forward the proceeds to her account at Rothschild's in Paris." He looked from one to the other. "I guess she's gone, for good and all."

Don and Lucy went down to Paradise on a Monday morning, and after dinner Don sent for Mrs. Harper, and Lucy saw them go toward the school, a trail of children following them. The flood had been responsible for a long interruption in the school work, and when Don came to supper, Lucy saw that he was thoughtful. He would tell her, presently, what was in his mind.

Through supper, his abstraction continued, and she did not interrupt his thoughts; but afterward, since the sunset promised to be fine, they walked up to the levee, to the rough-squared log which often served them as a seat. There, as she had expected, he presently began to speak his thoughts.

"I've about decided," he said, without preamble, "that it's not worth while to start up the schools again for the short time we'll be here." And then he added, not looking at her: "Unless we decide to stay all summer."

She waited to be sure she could speak evenly. "Elon says it's terribly hot here, worse than in the city. It would be hard on the children."

"They're certainly thriving now."

She looked at him, her eyes grave. "You know, Don, you'll never accomplish anything with these people; nothing worth the trouble and —well, the love you're putting into it." She added: "But I want you to do what you want to do."

"I know," he agreed. "But Honey, I think you expect too much. Too much and too quickly." He reached across to take her hand and held it while he spoke, but his eyes followed the cloud drift across the sea of sky. "Everything takes time," he reminded her. "Everything worth doing takes time to do. Teaching school takes a long time to show results. You can't take a six-year-old boy and in a year of teaching make him into a man. But maybe you can start him." And after a moment he said: "One day during the flood, I saw where a tree had fallen into the river, and its branches deflected the water, sent a long ripple out into the stream. You know, the river'll never be the same again. The whole flow of its waters was changed by that tree —even though you couldn't prove it with a microscope. Clear across on the other side of the river, the drops of water hurrying by were a little more crowded because the tree shoved a little extra water over that way. All the water in the river would have flowed through different places if it hadn't been for those branches, and that would make different holes in the bottom, and different sand banks out in the middle. A thousand years from now, the whole river bed will be a little bit different because for a day or two that tree lay with its branches in the water."

She watched him, making no sound, and he said in a different tone: "A man must be tremendously conceited to undertake to teach a child. He must be tremendously sure of himself to believe that what he does to the life of that child and to all the other lives which that child's life will affect, in one generation, and the next, and the next, will be good." His eyes widened, looking deep into the sky, and for a time he did not speak, and then suddenly he looked at her, and laughed, and said: "Why, when I think of it, carry it on through to infinity, I wonder how any man ever dares to come into the same room with a child at all! What a responsibility! Think what may happen to all the children and the children's children of a baby to whom someone says 'Boo!'"

She said, smiling: "Now you're making fun of me!"

"I don't mean to." He was grave again. "But Honey, if I knew that because of anything I might do, one of these children—Pink Chambers, any one of them, would turn out to be a better man—" His eyes swung away from her to the sky again, and he spoke so softly she could scarce hear him. "Well, I'd be glad," he said.

Spring days were fine, and it was good to be abroad. Lucy sometimes rode with Don, and she was with him the day he rode around the head of the swamp and stopped at the store at the Four Corners. They went in to pass the time of day with Mr. Brook, and after a word or two, the storekeeper asked Don a surprising question.

"Mr. Page, how come the niggers over at Paradise are buying shotguns?"

There were four men in the store at the time, and at Mr. Brook's question, Don felt silence press like a cold wall all about him.

"Why, to hunt, I suppose," he suggested. "Ducks, or turkeys, or deer. I don't know anything about it, didn't know they'd bought any guns."

"The way we hear it," said Mr. Brook in a guarded tone, "A case of twelve guns came downriver on the *Paradise,* here last week."

"It might have," Don admitted. "We didn't get here till Sunday." He turned to face the other men, smiling as he spoke. "But I haven't heard any shooting, and I never knew a Negro with a new gun that didn't want to shoot it off, did you? It looks as if there'd have been a cannonade by now."

They watched him with level eyes, and Mr. Brook said: "A man was in here the other day, said the Radicals were bringing in guns by the shipload, and he said he saw a box put on the *Paradise* for y'all."

"Friend of yours?" Don asked.

"Seems like I forget his name," Mr. Brook admitted. "But he was a well-spoken young fellow."

"Well, if I hear anything, I'll let you know." Don caught Lucy's eye, and they turned together toward the door. But before they reached it, Mr. Howard said in a derisive tone:

"You ain't likely to hear nothing."

Don looked toward him, smiling. "I can hear a shot a mile, if the wind's right."

"It's the shot a man don't hear that puts his chunk out."

"Well, I suppose that's true. Good evening, gentlemen."

Till they were mounted and away, neither spoke, but when they were out of hearing, Lucy said: "That man hates you, Don. Who is he?"

"He's all right, Hon. He's scared, that's all; he's scared, so he rattles like a scared snake."

"Who is he?"

"Howard's his name. He's always that way. Don't worry about him, please."

They found that Mr. Chambers and others had heard that rumor about the shotguns, and except for the few children they encountered, they saw no friendly faces. Lucy was silent on the homeward ride, and that night she lay in Don's arms, trembling with nameless fears. Saturday, at her suggestion, they took the children up to New Orleans, and on the boat as they backed clear of the landing she seemed to shiver, and hugged herself as though she were cold.

"My," she said. "I'm glad to get away from there." But when on Monday he would have left her in New Orleans, she laughed at him. "I wasn't really scared, Don; just upset for a while. That's all. Besides, I want to be with you." Yet on the way downriver she asked: "Do you really and truly want to stay down here all summer, Don?"

He hesitated a long time before answering. "I'd like to, Lucy, yes," he admitted at last. "You heard that talk about shotguns, about a case with a dozen in it. I asked Cash. One of the hands had saved some money and he had Cash buy a shotgun in town and bring it down, but there've been no others. Someone's circulating those lies to make trouble."

She laughed to hide her terror. "Don Page, if there's going to be any trouble about shotguns, I don't want you having a thing to do with it!"

He chuckled. "I don't expect any," he admitted. "But I wish we could stay. We've lost a lot of time on account of the flood. Oh, I don't mean we've got to make up for that. But Honey, a thing like these schools, you have to keep up their interest. You can't let it die. If I'm here, I can do it. At least, I think I can."

"Mighty hard to keep a nigra interested in anything in hot weather," she reminded him. "But if you really do want to stay—"

So she yielded, and he wrote his father and mother that for this year, at least, they would not make the long journey home. When Elon heard their decision, he called it folly. "Go ahead," he urged. "Maine does Lucy good. She always comes back looking as fresh as spring. And besides," he added, "I'm going to be down at Paradise a lot, this summer. You've a good crop coming, and I want to keep an eye on it. Christian Browning can take care of routine work at the mill." He laughed. "Why, Don, I might even take a turn at teaching school for you. Think I'd make a good substitute?"

But Don clung to his plan, and he and Lucy were at the plantation when late in May a letter came from Pa. Ma was sick. "We hadn't meant to tell you, long as you was coming anyway," Pa wrote. "But long as you ain't, why I guess I'd better. Ma's real sick, and Doc Evans don't look for her to get any better. So I dunno but what you'd best come, if you can fix it so's you can."

Cash brought the letter, and they went upriver with him that evening. They found Enid in distress, for little Travis was ill and the doctor called it cholera morbus. It needed only a glance at his flushed face to tell Lucy she could not leave him.

"Oh, darling," she cried, in Don's arms. "I wish we were two people!" Then she looked up at him and laughed at the absurdity of her own words. "But of course we are, aren't we! Only I always feel as if we were just one. So you take half of us and go to Ma, and I'll keep half of us and stay with Travis, and I'll come as soon as ever I can." And when he wished to stay with her, she would not let him. "No. She'll be happier, having you there, and I'll be all right, darling; I'll be fine."

5

W HEN THE TRAIN drew to a stop at Benton Station, Don saw
his father on the platform with a telegram in his hand, and
he had a moment of shaking terror; but as they met, Pa
reassured him.

"Philbrick says it's good news." Mr. Philbrick was the station agent.
"Come just as I drove up, so he saw me and brought it right out."

Don was already unfolding the message. His heart lifting, he read
it aloud to Pa. " 'Travis better, safe. Will come when he is well. Love
Lucy.' " And he explained: "Little Trav had the cholera morbus when
I left. How's Ma?"

Pa turned toward the buckboard. "Well, some days she's better
and some days she ain't," he said. "Em's with her. Oscar's on one of his
trips." Em was Don's sister, her husband a traveling man selling haber-
dashery for a Portland house. "Doc Evans drops in frequent. She's
got the cancer inside her somewhere. Doc says she won't last the summer." He flicked the horses to a trot. " 'Lowed we'd drive right through,
git home tonight. She's real anxious t'see you."

"Yes, of course," Don agreed. "Yes, we will."

That was a silent drive. They stopped on the way long enough to let
Uncle Josh and Aunt Maisy have a look at Don. She thought he had
fleshed up a bit, but Uncle Josh was not so sure. When they went on,
the horses hit a steady clip till Pa gently pulled them down. "Whoa,
babies. Still some hills ahead, so take your time." Behind them the sun
set and darkness wrapped them around. The night was warm, the smell
of apple blossoms in the air.

At home, a dim lamp shone in the kitchen window, and at the sound
of their wheels, Em opened the kitchen door; but when Don paused to
kiss her, Ma called, her voice thinned to a thread of sound and yet
astonishingly happy and gay.

"Come in, Sonny boy!" she said, and Don strode swiftly to her. In

the dim-lit room her eyes seemed tremendous, and she was wasted
beyond belief, but she could lift her arms around his neck, and she
said: "Take me in your arms, Sonny."

So he held her close. She asked where Lucy was, and he told her why
Lucy could not come. "But Travis is better, and she'll come as soon
as she can," he promised, and she said fondly:

"You tell her there's no hurry. I can wait for her."

Don wrote Lucy that night and sent this message. "But, darling,
don't come. It's a long hard trip for you alone, and Ma's worse off than
she thinks. I don't see how she can live more than a few days. I'd really
rather you didn't see her as she is now."

He knew Lucy would ignore that message, and Ma did wait till Lucy
came; but the wait was a long one, for while Travis was soon out of
danger, Donny and little Sally were each taken ill in turn. Lucy wrote
at least a few lines almost every day, Trav more at length. He expressed
no concern over the children. "Old-fashioned summer complaint, I call
it, but they have a fancy name for it now." He wrote chiefly about
politics.

> The Democrats are organizing. Something called a White League
> is being gotten up, and they say it includes all the best men in the
> state, but I haven't signed up, so they're exaggerating a little, any-
> way. The Crescent City Club has organized itself into the Crescent
> City White League. They're all for white supremacy. They say
> negroes are being given guns all over the state. Speaking of guns,
> they finally found three of the Colfax prisoners guilty and recom-
> mended mercy, let the rest off. Now the ones they convicted want
> a new trial. And speaking of trials, Quinny's been turned loose. Tony
> and Sapphira got a negro lawyer for her—Tony's better all the time,
> looks fine—and he claimed that without Minnie they didn't have
> any witnesses, so they turned her loose. I'm just as well pleased.

At the farm, the quiet days stole by. Pa kept up the work, and Don
sometimes helped him; but unless there was someone to sit with Ma, he
stayed with her. Whenever Em's husband was away, she came to be with
them, and Jonathan and his wife drove over every Sunday from
Fraternity, bringing pies and cakes and bread and biscuits, and perhaps
a pair of dressed chickens, or the leg of a fresh-killed lamb. When Don
and Pa were here alone with Ma, Pa did the cooking, and Ma said over
and over: "Pa's a better cook than I ever was, once he sets his mind
to it."

Don and Em and Jonathan were worried about what would happen
to Pa when Ma was gone, and after some discussion they agreed that the
thing to do was find someone beforehand, have her ready to take charge

when she was needed. But before they began to seek around, they discovered that Pa had already made the necessary arrangements.

"I got Aunt Maisy's sister," he told Don. "She's be'n a widow woman seven years now, had to let their farm go and live around with her children, and she's tired of it and of them. Says she'd like nothing better than to move in with me, and I like her, so she'll come." He added with a growl, clearing his throat. "She'll come soon as Ma goes. Don't want two women in the house!"

It seemed to Don that his mother's voice grew weaker every day; it was no more than a thin, silver thread of sound. Doctor Evans left pills for her. "There's no sense in her suffering when she needn't," he said, but Ma never took the pills, nor did she ever admit to Don that she was in pain. "Perhaps she isn't," Doctor Evans conceded, when Don questioned him. "We can't define pain. The person who has it can't describe it, except in terms of other pains. What would be torture for you or me may not be torment for her."

Whenever Ma asked how soon Lucy would come, Don explained first that Donny was ill, and then that the others had sickened. Trav's letter had treated the matter lightly, but Don worried, till a telegram reassured him. Yet its wording was a puzzle.

Sorry I wrote so. Sally's fine. Starting Sunday. Love. Lucy.

Lucy's letter, reaching him the next day, explained the mystery. Donny was himself again, she said. "But darling, Sally's so weak, I really think she's going to die." Don was glad he had not received that letter before the telegram came.

Ma died in her sleep the second night after Lucy returned to the farm under Frye Mountain. Lucy and Don had been with her almost every hour since Lucy's arrival. They sat late that first night, while Lucy told Ma all about the children and how sick they had been and how fine they were now, and how many messages Donny had sent. "And Travis, too. He talks so much now I can hardly keep up with him, and so plainly." Don questioned that, and they argued it together, and Ma smiled and smiled, and sometimes tried to nod, and sometimes— though they had to lean close to hear—she asked a question.

Next day she slept a great deal, but after supper that last night they were almost merry together, Ma's frail silver thread of a voice making them ache with listening, till she fell asleep and they stole away. Pa nowadays slept on a couch in the kitchen, the head of it pulled near the doorway of her room. When Don came down next morning, Pa was in the barn, and since Ma did not call to him, and without turning up the lamp, he went to help with the milking. Knowing that Pa would have spoken to her, he asked:

"How's Ma, this morning?"

Pa, his head against the cow's flank, grunted. "How is she? Why, she's dead." And while Don stood for a moment, his breath caught, Pa said: "Died seventeen minutes past three. I heard a kind of click, and went in, and she was gone. I dressed and set with her from that on."

"Were you awake?"

"Half awake. She made that little clacking sound they all make." Pa stood up; he blew his nose, nodding toward the cow. "Strip Betsy for me, will you, son? I'm kind of tired."

Don took the stool. "Call Lucy; she'll make you some coffee."

But as he spoke, the barn door opened, and Lucy came in, her lamp held high. "Don!" she whispered. "Pa! She's dead."

Pa strode to her. "Dad rot it!" he protested. "Don't you know enough yit, not to bring a lamp into the barn! Come on and le's us make some coffee."

He strode out, the door crashed shut behind him. Lucy ran to Don, stooped to kiss him. "I'll bring you a cup," she promised, and darted away. Don finished Betsy and moved on to Sue. The warm milk foamed in the pail.

Aunt Maisy's sister proved to be an energetic little woman somewhere near Pa's age, though with never a gray hair, and within the week after the funeral she and Lucy—she was the directing spirit—had cleaned the house till it shone. Lucy liked her from the first.

"And you'll never have to worry about Pa with her taking care of him," she told Don. "She's really a dear woman, and so fond of him." Her name was Mrs. Tate, but Pa called her Maggie, and to Don and Lucy she was "Aunt Maggie" from the first.

Before Trav's next letter came, the routine of the farm had resumed its even pace. Ma was buried in the family burying ground up in the edge of the woods above the orchard, and Pa ordered the stone to mark the grave, and Don and Lucy brought fresh loam and planted wild flowers there. Don showed Lucy his grandfather's grave, and his grandmother's. Four of their children lay beside them, and Lucy read the stones, scraping away the lichens that had filled the carved letters. She found that the children all died in infancy.

"But there were other children, too," Don reminded her. "Three aunts and an uncle, besides Pa and Uncle Don and Uncle Josh. If you lived to be a year old, those days, you usually lived to grow up and be married."

"I was so scared, when our babies were all sick," she confessed. "I want us to have another, right away."

His eyes twinkled. "Well, I don't mind if we do."

She laughed with him. "You know, that's the way graveyards affect me," she said thoughtfully. "Graveyards, and people dying. Now that Ma's dead, I want another baby awfully."

"I suppose it's instinct," he agreed. "To keep up the supply." He showed her where Pa someday would lie. "Here next to Ma. Uncle Don was buried in California, and the others wherever they were when they died. There's Uncle Josh and Pa to go here, and then the rest of us; Em, and Jonathan, and Horace, and their children, and ours." The little burying ground was enclosed by a low stone wall, and he smiled and said: "You know, this place will be crowded by and by. They'll have to move the wall."

She turned to look out across the valley below them. "It will always be beautiful here. And such friendly company." Her shoulders lifted. "Come. I must help Aunt Maggie get supper."

Next day there was a letter from Trav. The Republican State Convention had met on August fifth, the Democrats would meet on the twenty-fourth. "September looks like a big month," he commented, and Lucy looked up and met Don's eyes and knew his thoughts, and she read on.

> Elon tells me the White League is getting more members all the time. He's a sergeant in Captain Pleasants's company. They're raising money, and ordering guns. We hear rumors of threats and murders by the White Leaguers, all over the state. One of their ideas is to compel Radical parish officers to resign. Things will be worse before they're better.
>
> Mama says to tell you the children are all fine. The way Donny and little Enid stick together, you'd think they were old married people. Mighty cute, all of them.

Over Lucy swept a wave of longing. When Don said Pa was comfortable in Aunt Maggie's good hands, and suggested that they might start South, she eagerly agreed.

6

DON AND LUCY reached New Orleans at the end of August, and Donny and Travis swarmed over them in happy welcome; but Sally, though she knew Lucy, was not sure about Don, burying her face under Lucy's ear when he would have taken her in his arms. Lucy said: "Just ignore her for a while, Don. She'll be all right."

Don obeyed, and tumbled Donny and Travis on his knees, giving them each in turn a ride to Banbury Cross, so that they screamed with delight, and Sally watched, and finally held out both arms, saying: "Uh! Uh!" in tones so manifestly peremptory that it was obvious she wished to share the fun. Everyone agreed that was a woman for you!

Over the noise the children made, Lucy told her father and mother about Ma's death, and how well Aunt Maggie would take care of Pa, but at last she and Enid led the youngsters away upstairs. Don and Trav, left alone, looked at each other in an equal relief, and Don said:

"I'm afraid you've had quite a dose of them, Major. Besides having to stay here all summer."

"We were glad to help out," Trav assured him. "That's what grandparents are for." He smiled. "And they kept little Enid happy. She and Donny are a pair."

Inevitably their talk drifted to politics. There had been reports that day of trouble threatening at Coushatta, up the Red River above Colfax. Trav spoke of this, and Don said:

"Coushatta wasn't much of a town when I saw it, five or six years ago."

"I'd never heard of it," Trav admitted. "So I looked it up. The parish was set up in 1871 so Governor Warmoth could appoint a lot of new parish officers: sheriff, judges, clerks of court, prosecuting attorney, recorder, I don't know who all. They had to raise land valuations to forty dollars an acre to pay all those salaries and to build a Court House and a jail. A carpetbagger named Dewees is boss of the parish,

and another named Twitchell is his partner. The Democrats say those
two have made three or four hundred thousand dollars out of the parish
in three years."

"What's happened up there now?"

"Well, the way I get it, here last Wednesday there was some argument
between some nigras and a white man named Williams. He left town,
and nigras broke in and searched his house, so some white men went
after them, and two nigras were killed and a white man wounded. Or
so they say. And now a lot of armed nigras have trooped into town."

"So they're expecting a Negro uprising?"

Trav nodded. "The pattern's always the same."

That was Saturday. The Sunday papers said the danger had subsided, the trouble was over. A number of the ringleaders had been
arrested, said the *Picayune,* and named Sheriff Egerton, Collector
Twitchell, Register Hubbard, Mr. Dewees, Deputy Kane, and W. F.
Howell.

To list the parish officers as "ringleaders" who had summoned an
armed Negro mob seemed to Trav so remarkable that he sent for the
Sunday *Republican,* in order to read the other side. Under the headline
"Still another Parish Captured," the *Republican* reported that White
Leaguers had called upon the parish officers a few days before and
demanded that they resign. When they refused, the Leaguers threatened
to return with a larger force and compel the resignations.

"A large portion of the parish," the *Republican* commented, "is
owned by Northern men, white Republicans; hence it must have been
a special object of hatred of the White League."

Trav read this aloud. "I hadn't heard that the White League did it,"
he commented, and looked at Don. "I judge it's white men they've
arrested. Maybe the pattern's changed."

He learned the sequel next day from General Longstreet. The General
was just back from an inspection trip upriver, and Trav called to pay
his respects. He found Longstreet in ill humor. Had it been an interesting trip? Damnable; wading in mud and water, daylight to dark.
Had they learned anything useful? Discouraging, rather than useful; a
lot to do and no funds to do it. How was the General's health? Bad, all
tied up with rheumatism.

Trav changed the subject. "Anything new from Coushatta?"

The General fixed him with a stern eye. "Major, let me first ask you
a question. Are you a member of the White League?"

"No. No, I never mingle with politics."

The General snorted. "So! And you seem proud of it! Perhaps that's
the trouble with Louisiana; too many fine Southern gentlemen refuse
to mingle—" He almost snarled the word. "To mingle with politics!"

Trav, astonished, came slowly to his feet, his color rising, but the General said quickly: "No, no, sit down! No insult intended! Perhaps you're right! Nobody but a God damned fool would get into politics in Louisiana. Unless it was someone like Warmoth, loving the tricks of the game." Trav, after a moment, resumed his seat, and Longstreet said: "Reason I asked, the White Leaguers took those six Coushatta men, the officers of Red River Parish, and shot them."

"The officers?" Trav was startled.

"Yes, yes! Oh, it wasn't as simple as I've made it. They were sent off under escort, as prisoners, headed for Shreveport. They'd resigned their offices under guarantee of safe conduct, and with a promise on their part to leave the state. A seventeen-man escort. Some of the escort say they were overpowered by superior numbers, and some of them say the murderers chased them and that the prisoners had the better horses and so got too far ahead of their guards, and thus had no one to protect them. Some tell one lie, some another. But the essence of it is simply that duly appointed parish officers have been taken out by the White League and shot."

"And they were white men?"

"Yes, yes, white men. Northern men, if you like, but their homes were in Coushatta, and they were properly appointed officials, and they've been murdered; not assassinated, but calmly and openly murdered, in the light of day."

"That's something new," Trav commented.

"New? What's new about it? There've been killings before!"

"Nigras, yes; but these were white men!"

"Why not? The Democratic papers up in that part of the state have been threatening to hang carpetbaggers. They didn't hang these gentlemen, but men are just as dead when they're shot as if they'd been hung. And they weren't carpetbaggers! They'd settled in Coushatta, built homes, gone into business. They weren't carpetbaggers and they weren't nigras. But white or black, murder is murder." Trav did not speak, and Longstreet said grimly: "And it was the League's work! A thousand white men rode into Coushatta, and a body like that doesn't appear spontaneously out of nowhere. They were summoned, and directed, like a military force."

And after a moment, he said in quiet rage: "Well, if the Governor takes my advice, he'll give them all the military force they want! I'm advising him to declare martial law. The Democrats have been saying for months that they'd rather have martial law than nigra rule. Well, I'd give it to them!"

Trav rose, unwilling to risk discussion in the face of the other's anger. At supper, he reported what Longstreet had said. "And it's the first time carpetbaggers, instead of nigras, have been the victims."

"What about Pope and Chase?" Don suggested.

"That's true, yes. But to take the principal officers in the parish, demand their resignation, make threats, and then put those threats into effect—that's something new."

Enid asked, after a moment's silence held them all: "Trav, do you think they'd dare shoot the General?"

"No, of course not. In spite of his politics, he'll always be beloved for what he did during the War."

"People are saying he disobeyed orders at Gettysburg."

"You never heard anyone say it while Lee was alive."

"I know," Enid agreed. "And never till Longstreet turned Republican. But Trav—well, I'm fond of poor Louisa, and of him too, but he is a scalawag! A lot of people hate him."

"That's just because he was right," Lucy urged. "He was right and they were wrong. That's why they hate him!"

Trav smiled. "You and I have always been on his side, Honey, but I think he was wrong. I told him so then— and I've told him so since."

"You ought to be more loyal to the South, Lucy." Enid spoke gently, and Trav wondered at this new quality in her.

"I'll always love the things that are fine in the South," Lucy agreed. "But we've gone on for ten years—nine, anyway—bragging that we weren't conquered. How much finer and more honest and honorable it would have been if when we were beaten we had admitted it, and accepted it, and tried to be good citizens of the Union."

"But we were right, Lucy," Enid suggested.

"Well if you're just discussing something, it's nice to be right," Lucy admitted. "But when you start fighting to prove it, and one of you wins and the other loses, if you're all going to have to go on living together—" Her eyes met Don's and held them like an embrace. "Well, it's like being married. The South's acted like a spoiled, sulky bride!"

Before Trav or Enid could speak, Don said with a good-humored mirth in his tones: "The bridegroom's acted like a pretty rough husband, Lucy."

She laughed in spite of herself. "All the same, I don't think much of Southerners who brag about being unconquered."

Trav held up his hands. "I don't do that, Honey! I was licked, and I know it! So let's pretend the War's over. Can we, now?"

Next day, and through that week, the papers printed much from Coushatta. The arrest of the parish officers, who were subsequently killed, had followed an incident in which two Negroes fired at pickets who were on patrol under orders from the White League. The Negroes, having admitted that they fired at the pickets, were taken into the woods and hanged. Next day Governor Kellogg issued a proclamation

declaring martial law, and offering five thousand dollars for the arrest
of any person implicated in the Coushatta murders.

Don was anxious to go down to Paradise, but there was something
in the very air in New Orleans which kept him here. Whatever had
happened at Coushatta, the White League was responsible, and Elon
was a member of the League; but for days after their return from Maine
they did not see him. Don was anxious to talk with him, but to go out
of his way to question Elon about the League might be a trespass; so
though he might have gone to the mill to seek the other there, he did
not do so.

He and Lucy had been at home a little more than a week when Don
one day noticed a small, silent group of men gathered around Olivier's
gun store. He went to see what was happening. Some Metropolitan
Police officers had stopped a wagon in front of the store, and now they
carried out four long, unopened wooden boxes marked with a stencil,
and loaded them into the wagon and drove away. Two men stood near
Don and watched them go, and one of them cursed under his breath.
Don spoke to him.

"What was that all about? What's in the boxes?"

The man looked at him with unfriendly eyes. "Well now, Yank, don't
you wish you knew?"

But his companion was more informative. "They were muskets, sir,"
he said politely. "Consigned to Mr. Armand Guyol, Jr." And he added:
"For the White League."

Don thanked him and turned away, but the newspapers reported
the sequel. Mr. Guyol secured from a friendly judge an order on
General Badger of the Metropolitans to surrender the muskets. General
Badger refused to obey, and was cited for contempt and arrested, but
at the jail he produced a pardon already signed by Governor Kellogg
and was at once released.

That was Tuesday. Thursday there was another raid on the Olivier
store, and more muskets were found and seized. This time a considerable crowd gathered, but not all the watchers were of one mind, so that
beyond threats and curses, no one interfered.

But this seizure, like the first, was followed next day by court proceedings, and Don went to watch and listen, and saw Elon among the
spectators gathered there. When they came out, he joined Elon, and
after warm and friendly greetings they turned to the St. Charles for a
julep on the cool veranda.

Inevitably, Don spoke of the White League. "I hear you're a
member?"

"I'm a member, yes," Elon assented. "I'm sorry Major Currain isn't.
Some of the most respected gentlemen in New Orleans are at its head."

"Does it cover the whole state?"

"Not as a single organization, no. In Coushatta, for instance, there are five different societies. The White Man's Club is the biggest, but they all work together under an executive committee, with Mr. Abney as chairman."

Don asked: "Did he order these men shot?"

Elon flushed. "We're not assassins, Don. We're responsible citizens trying to establish an honest state government, and prepared to fight to do so."

"Anti-Kellogg, or anti-Negro?" And Don added in an apologetic tone: "I'm not critical. I'm just asking for information."

Elon said steadily: "There's no secret about it. Our program, our ambition has been published." He smiled faintly: "I can even quote it: 'to resume that just and legitimate superiority in the administration of our state affairs to which we are entitled by superior responsibility, superior numbers, and superior intelligence.'"

Don nodded. "It always comes back to the Negroes. It has to, I suppose. Yet this court affair this morning sounds as though you might be preparing to fight the Metropolitans."

Elon's eyes hardened. "Yes, and I'll welcome the opportunity. They're made up of nigras and beggars and criminals and hired fighters. Besides their own crimes, they too often protect the criminals." And he added: "Last spring while they were in Colfax—this was two or three weeks after the massacre—a band of nigras raped a Mrs. La Coue and her sixteen-year-old daughter. The leader, Hamp Henderson, was caught and hanged, but the Metropolitans up there protected the others." He added, his voice firm: "And now the Mets here in New Orleans are trying to disarm us, seizing every gun they can lay hands on. That we will not tolerate!"

"That's what started the Revolution," Don remembered. "The British attempts to seize powder and shot and muskets collected by the colonists."

"They'll start a revolution here if they keep on doing it," Elon predicted. "There's a mass meeting called for tonight to decide what we'll do. I'll pick you up if you want to come."

Don agreed, and at home he suggested that Trav join them, so the three walked down town together. Don, used as he was to the bitterness of political feeling in Louisiana, thought the speakers that night were the most violent he had ever heard. Elon had business afterward, and Trav and Don walked home in a thoughtful silence. Enid had gone to bed, but Lucy was awake to greet them.

"How was it?" she asked. "Did Elon make a speech?"

"No; no, he stayed with us," Don told her, and he said: "They say they'll get rid of the Kellogg government at any cost. There was some hard talk. They said any white man who wouldn't fight to end Negro rule ought to be driven out of Louisiana, proscribed, ostracized."

Lucy shivered, and Trav said mildly: "If you think that's strong talk, you ought to read some of the papers from upstate. "I've been keeping a scrapbook, lately." He went into his study, returned and spread a wide volume on his knees. "Here's the Alexandria *Democrat*," he said, and read: " 'We fully and cordially approve what the white men of Grant and Rapides did at Colfax; the white man who does not approve is a creature so base that he shames the worst of his species.' " His eyes met Don's, returned to the clippings. "And here's another, from the St. Mary's *Enterprise*. 'If our political prosperity demands it, the Negro population must be thinned down to give place to white labor.' And here's a fellow who says: 'If we can't vote the Negro down, we can knock him down, and the result will be the same.' " He shuffled through the pages. "And this: 'In the impending war of races, it behooves Democrats to protect themselves by any means in their power, and deliver their votes in a new style, without waiting for election day.' " He looked up, spoke to Don. "Want more?" And without waiting for a reply, he went on: "The Shreveport *Times* says it would require an army of twenty thousand men to sustain the Kellogg government, but it also says that if someone doesn't annihilate the Negro power with blood, it means the Africanization of Louisiana. The Natchitoches *Vindicator* says that a war of races is imminent, and that the contest will be quick, sharp and decisive." He read in an affectedly solemn tone: " 'An appeal to arms and the God of Hosts is all that is left to us.' " He closed the scrapbook with a sudden violence. "I tell you, Don, there are mad dogs loose in Louisiana today."

Lucy, as though she had been waiting for a pause, rose. "Don, I'm dreadfully sleepy. Papa, mind if I say good night?"

Don felt the haste in her, and when they were on the stairs, her hand in his arm, he asked softly: "All right?"

She nodded. "But I couldn't bear to listen to any more! He's right; they're just mad dogs! Oh, Don, let's go home to Maine and never come back here again."

He pressed her hand in silence, but when they were in their room, the door closed, he said firmly: "You wouldn't want that! Remember, when the War was over, when the South needed them more than ever, a lot of Southern men ran away—to Mexico, or South America, or Europe. You know, Honey, I don't admire men who run away from a job they ought to do."

"You wouldn't be running away!" she protested. "You're a State-of-Maine man! You've told me so, often enough! You'd just be taking your wife and children home to Maine!"

"Maybe, someday." His eyes shadowed. "Oh, Lucy," he confessed,

"I don't really expect to accomplish anything. I don't even know what I can try to do. But there must be something I can do—and I want, at least, to try."

After supper Saturday night, Trav asked Don: "Care to walk downtown, listen to the talk?" Don agreed, and they strolled down Prytania Street till it lost itself in Camp; but when they came up through Lafayette Square to St. Charles, they recognized a change in the sound of the city. Just as the murmuring hum of a hive of bees takes on, when the bees are angry and disturbed, a different tone, so now the voices of the men they passed had subtly changed. And not only the voices; wrath increased the violence of their gestures, and accented their words.

In the rotunda at the St. Charles, Trav and Don heard the explanation. Not only had the Metropolitans today seized a wagonload of arms on the way to be delivered, but also they had halted a hunter returning to the city and taken his gun. Every man, for some reason, found this more infuriating than the previous seizures. To find and cart away boxes of muskets from a merchant's store was an impersonal proceeding, but to stop an individual and take his gun made every other individual realize what under the same circumstances his own feelings would have been. This was the final outrage. No one seemed to know who it was who had been thus abused, but his name did not matter; he was every man, and every man was he.

So the spark was set; but also, the mine was laid. Monday morning the steamer *Mississippi* would begin to discharge her cargo. It included a large shipment of arms consigned to White Leaguers, and which the League would certainly seek to save from seizure. Among the men with whom Trav and Don talked that night, none knew exactly how that would be accomplished; but every man was sure it would be done.

Walking homeward, they agreed that open violence was just around the corner. "Both sides spoiling for a fight," Trav commented. "Each stalking the other, and these muskets are the chip on someone's shoulder."

Don asked: "Will the Negroes be drawn into this? Another riot?"

"Worse than a riot," Trav predicted. "If the Leaguers are as well armed and disciplined, and as numerous as Elon claims, it will be more like bloody war."

Sunday morning Trav was first down to breakfast, and the papers were ready for him. He glanced at the *Picayune,* eating while he read, and Don joined him, and then Lucy and Enid too, and he said in sudden interest: "Hullo! What's this?" He was at once absorbed, till Enid asked:

"Well, what is it?"

"Proclamation to the Citizens of New Orleans," he said, his eyes running down the column.

"We're all citizens," Enid reminded him. "So it's meant for us. Read it aloud."

Trav's eyes lifted reluctantly to the beginning of the proclamation, and he began to read:

> Citizens of New Orleans. For nearly two years, you have been the silent but indignant sufferers of outrage after outrage, heaped upon you by an usurping government. One by one, your dearest rights have been trampled upon, until . . . this mockery of a republican government has dared even to deny you the right . . . to keep and bear arms.

"We've heard all that before, a hundred times," Enid reminded him.

"I know," Trav agreed, his eyes on the text. "But this time it goes on to say that they want to find out whether they've lost the right to peaceably assemble, and it tells everybody to close his place of business tomorrow morning and meet at the Clay statue." He added: "Fifty or seventy-five business houses have signed it."

"Isn't there ever going to be an end to all this arguing and quarreling?"

Trav said abstractedly: "Have to wait and see." He continued to read, while they talked together of many things. Trav finished the *Picayune,* handing it across to Don. "Nothing much in it, except that," he said, and picked up the *Bulletin.* The two men became equally absorbed, and Enid and Lucy exchanged amused glances. Enid raised her voice a little, and a little more, and so did Lucy, talking deliberate nonsense, waiting to see how long it would take to attract their attention, till Don looked up with suddenly puzzled eyes, and understood, and smiled and looked at Trav. Then Trav began to chuckle as he read, and Enid in amused exasperation reached across and snatched the paper from him.

"Eh, what's the matter?" he protested, startled.

"You're not very polite," Enid told him. "If it's as funny as all that, read it aloud! Let's all laugh!"

Trav grinned. "Oh, all right. It is funny, certainly. Listen!" And he recovered the paper and read, in suddenly plaintive tones:

> Appeal of the Women to the Men of New Orleans

> Out of the depths of our humiliation and despair we call upon you, by all that is dear and sacred to the human heart, to be true to your country, to yourselves, and to us.

All is at stake! The integrity of your race, the preservation of
your free-born heritage, the honor of your wives and daughters!

Trav paused. "It gets pretty highfalutin through here," he warned
them, and he read:

Is there left, in all the length and breadth of our lovely southern
land, "no arm to strike, no soul to dare"?

He paused, eyes on the paper, and said: "Then they remind us of
General Butler, and Order Number Twenty-eight. Then there's this."
And he read:

Our cheeks tingle with shame that, in broad daylight upon our
most frequented thoroughfares, almost within your sight and hearing,
we are subjected to assault and insult. . . . To whom, under high
Heaven, can we look for aid but to you?

"I think that's wonderful," Enid declared. "I don't see anything
funny about it."
"There's a poem, too," Trav assured them. "Several verses. It ends
like this."

> Never let the ruthless spoiler
> Lay his hot insulting hand
> On the sisters of your heroes
> Whilst ye bear a torch or brand.
>
> Oh, if we are doomed to perish,
> Man and maiden let us fall,
> And a common gulf of ruin
> Open wide to 'whelm us all!

Lucy looked at Don, but his eyes were grave, so Lucy did not smile.
Yet Enid felt the amusement in them all. "Well I don't care," she
insisted. "I think it's beautiful!"
Trav said thoughtfully: "We Southerners love the sound of words,
love orations, and elaborate periods—even when we write them ourselves." His eyes were on the *Bulletin.* "Listen. Here's an editorial. It
lists all the things Kellogg and his crowd have done to us, and then goes
on to speak of the 'dastardly minions and obsequious lick-spittles of
Kellogg,' and 'The horde of miscreants, thieves and usurpers' and the
'janizaries and the hirelings.' Some fine, stirring words there!"
"Well, I don't see how anyone could read it and not want to just kill
all those Kellogg people!" Enid's eyes were full of tears.

Lucy spoke wearily. "I'm awfully tired of hearing that the way to win an argument is to go kill somebody."

"Well, they ought to be killed!" Enid insisted.

After a moment's silence, Trav rose. "I expect it will make us all feel better to go to church today," he remarked. "Unless the preacher starts breathing out threatenings and slaughter too."

After dinner, Mr. Cist and Eleanor and Elon came and stayed a while. Elon was in a state of unnatural exhilaration, his voice a little raised, his words tumbling over one another, and when Lucy accused him of this, he laughed and admitted it. "I suppose I am excited," he confessed. "And there's no harm in your knowing what's happened. We got in a big shipment of guns and ammunition, late last night, around midnight. They came by freight over the Jackson railroad, and we unloaded them and distributed them to the companies that didn't have guns, and stored the rest in Mr. Leeds's foundry." The building was at Delord and Constance Streets. "They came packed as machinery, and marked the same. There's a switch track that runs right into the foundry. So we're—"

Don interrupted. "You spoke of companies. Is the League organized like a regiment?"

Elon nodded. "Yes, and then besides the League there's the First Louisiana Regiment, 'Louisiana's Own.' Colonel Angell organized that, all old soldiers, and they'll act with us, whatever happens." And he said, his eyes shadowing with memories: "You people weren't here in sixty-one, when we were all going off to War, and making every day a celebration."

"There wasn't much celebration in Virginia," Trav suggested. "Oh, a little noise on the surface; that's all."

"Why, Papa," Lucy protested. "There was too. I remember taking flowers to soldiers. And Mama, remember after we moved to Richmond? It was like a wonderful party."

Don said: "It was too early for flowers in Maine, when I enlisted. They brought cakes and pies and doughnuts to the train, instead." He looked at Lucy. "I was in college at Waterville for the spring term, took the train there."

"I was in the Washington Artillery," Elon told them, and he said with a chuckle. "We were the pride of New Orleans, or at least we thought we were. The ladies of New Orleans, God bless 'em!" His tone sounded so like his father that they all laughed. "They gave us our flag. There was a big muster at the Fair Grounds, four thousand volunteers under arms, twenty thousand spectators. Judah P. Benjamin made a speech. Everyone said it was wonderful, but the wind was against me. I couldn't hear him." He added soberly: "It's different this time. We meet in Mr. Leeds's foundry—and it's not a celebration. But this time, we know what's coming."

Lucy asked: "What, Elon? What is coming?"

"Well, we're certainly not going to let the Metropolitans seize our guns off the *Mississippi*. She came in yesterday, and we've a shipment on her."

"How can you stop them?"

"Fight!" Elon's voice rang. "Fight them! Beat them!" Then, as though embarrassed by his own vehemence, he said with dramatic gestures that made light of his words: " 'Take arms against a sea of troubles, and by opposing end them!' "

They smiled with him, but Trav, listening, watched Elon with a thoughtful eye. Elon had seen his share of action during the War, yet he seemed to contemplate this possible battle with no qualms. "You sound pretty well organized," Trav remarked. "Who's in charge? Governor McEnery?"

"No sir, he's in Baton Rouge, or maybe Vicksburg now." Elon hesitated. "I don't think he's heart and soul in sympathy with our plans. Lieutenant Governor Penn is in charge." The Lieutenant Governor was a distinguished soldier, a man of proved courage and determination. Elon said now in an excited voice: "Matter of fact, Major, we had another plan for a while. We were going to smuggle a sufficient force into the buildings all around the State House, and there was to be a vessel waiting with steam up. We'd rush the State House, take it by surprise, capture the Governor and the other state officers, and carry them out to sea."

"And execute them?" Trav asked.

"No sir, the idea was we'd just keep them away, or maybe land them in some foreign country, keep them out of the way—and out of touch with Washington—till Governor McEnery could be installed in the gubernatorial chair."

Trav smiled. "Elon, you speak as though that was all that was necessary, to drag Kellogg out of the Governor's chair and put McEnery in it. You make it sound like pussy-wants-a-corner, or one of these games children play where everybody tries to sit down in the empty chair."

Elon's color was high, but he laughed with the others. "Governor Warmoth made it work, against Carter," he retorted. "Possession's nine points of the law." And he added: "Lieutenant Governor Penn went all over the kidnaping scheme, and he was sure it could be done, and he and Colonel Angell and some officers went to see Governor McEnery; but he thought it wouldn't work, thought that to attempt it meant incurring too grave a responsibility." He paused: "General Ogden was willing to try it, and he and Lieutenant Governor Penn decided to go ahead without Governor McEnery, if the chance came."

"But now you're under orders for tomorrow?"

Elon nodded. "Yes sir. Every man is expected to be at his company armory early in the morning."

"Will you all go to the meeting at the Clay statue?"

"I suppose we will, but Mr. Penn will be the one to give the word. He has headquarters in the Howard Association rooms, at Fifty-eight Camp. All of us sergeants will report there in the morning and receive the orders—whatever they are."

"Do you seriously expect a fight?"

"Well, Major, we'll not let them seize those guns. We'll fight any force they send against us." His voice rang. "And if we're brought to it, we'll destroy the Kellogg government, once and for all."

Next morning, Trav decided the mill could do without him, and he and Don walked downtown together. Here and there, tacked to trees or hoardings, they saw placards advertising today's meeting, and at almost every crossing, long, narrow strips of paper on which the time and place of the meeting were printed had been pasted along the curb. In Lafayette Square, a company of Metropolitans were assembled, and Trav wondered where General Longstreet was at this hour, and what his purposes might be. Elon had said that each White League company was under orders to stand to, from early morning, at its accustomed meeting place, ready for any summons, and Trav remarked, looking at the Metropolitans:

"I suppose other detachments like that are waiting at the police stations. And the White Leaguers, too, in their armories. Like armies ready to file into position to receive a charge—or to make one."

Don said ruefully: "It's pitiful that men should be unable to settle such issues without fighting."

"You sound halfway sorry for them. For both sides."

Don met his eyes. "There never was an argument with only one side," he said.

Trav thought of General Longstreet. If this matter came to violence, the General would face today a bitter dilemma. His deepest sympathies must certainly be on the side of the League; but his faith, however mistakenly, was pledged to Kellogg. The General would have no mercy on himself, so it was useless to suppose he might find a way out for his fellows; but Trav wondered what would happen if, for instance, Longstreet led his Metropolitans over to the McEnery side, arrested Kellogg, seated McEnery in the governor's chair?

But the question was folly. Even if Longstreet sought to do this, the

Metropolitans would refuse to obey him, and even if he succeeded in delivering the government of the state into McEnery's hands, President Grant in the White House would take it away again. No, there was no hope in Longstreet, no great deed he could do.

As Trav and Don approached Canal Street, they became part of a mass of men all pressing in the same direction, and heard from around them snatches of conversation. The voice of rumor clamored through the crowd: the Mets had no muskets; muskets were being distributed among them; three thousand White Leaguers were armed and ready; there weren't a thousand Mets in all, they would be overwhelmed; the League would take Kellogg out and hang him and be done with it; this was revolution; well, it was better to be in jail or dead than longer endure injustice and oppression.

When they reached Canal Street, a throng was massed around the entrance to the Crescent Billiard Saloon. In the middle of the street, the statue of Henry Clay towered high atop its pedestal; the great man stood with one hand extended a little lower than his waist, the palm turned upward. He was like an orator expounding some simple point with which he expects his listeners to agree. Below him, groups of men clustered around the base of the statue, standing on the flagstones set two or three treads above the level of the street, or leaning against the iron fence. They ignored the silent orator atop his pinnacle above their heads, while their voices rose and fell in argument or agreement, their hands waved in the air, their clenched fists flung high.

Trav and Don paused at the corner, looking out across this scene. "Mr. Clay seems to be taking it all very calmly," Trav suggested.

"He's above it," Don reminded him. "He wouldn't be so calm, down in the street with the rest of us."

Except that the throng steadily increased, nothing happened till almost half past eleven. Then there was a sudden stir in front of the billiard hall, and the crowd churned and seethed and seemed to bubble yeastily, and a dozen or fifteen men came out on the gallery above the entrance. Cheers saluted them.

In what followed, Trav and Don, though they were near, recognized none of the speakers, and heard no familiar names. Judge Marr acted as chairman, and a gentleman named Musson was introduced as president. After the appointment of various vice-presidents and secretaries, each name being received with cheers, Judge Marr read a series of resolutions. He read them like an orator, in a lofty and sonorous voice, pausing after each phrase. The substance of these resolutions, and sometimes the very words, were strikingly like that appeal in the *Bulletin* yesterday. They denounced Governor Kellogg as a usurper and his acts as tyranny, and demanded his immediate abdication.

During the reading of these resolutions, the crowd had hushed, but on the word "abdication" a great shout rose, and men tossed their arms— and their hats—and roared their approval.

"They're as pleased," Trav suggested, under cover of these cheers, "as though the thing were done, instead of merely asked for."

"Will he quit?"

Trav shook his head, sorrow in his eyes. "With the President behind him, Kellogg won't quit. Nothing can come of this—except perhaps some killing. If the League takes up arms, the United States Army will answer them. No, this sort of thing leads nowhere. Except, perhaps, to relieve the pressure for a while."

The resolutions were adopted with a shout, and a committee was named to present these resolutions to the Governor. Two carriages drew up at the door of the billiard saloon to receive the committeemen. The carriages, the crowd making way and shouting encouragement to the messengers, turned to depart along Royal Street, and Don remarked in surprise: "That's a roundabout way to Mechanics Institute."

"Kellogg has taken over the St. Louis Hotel," Trav explained. "They use that as the State House now."

The crowd began to dissolve, but someone on the gallery came forward with lifted hands. "Wait!" he urged. "Wait for the com- mittee's report!" As those departing checked and returned, he cried: "They have gone unarmed, with empty hands, to present to him your resolutions and your demands. They will tell the usurper, firmly, yet without threats or warnings or promises of violence . . ." His words flowed on, his voice rising to a peak, diminishing again, then beginning a new crescendo, in the pattern set by orators since the beginning of time, beating a slow rhythm like the rhythm of the tides.

Trav and Don listened till it was clear that the orator had nothing to say, that he spoke only to hold the crowd. Their eyes met, and Trav asked: "Shall we wait?"

"We'd better. Enid and Lucy will want to know what happened."

Trav nodded, and a little before one o'clock the carriages returned. The committeemen went directly into the billiard parlor. The crowd had cheered their coming; it stood in a murmuring silence till the committee reappeared upon the gallery, and the chairman, Judge Marr, made his report.

"Gentlemen! Citizens!" In the sudden silence his voice carried well. "The Governor declined to meet us!"

A clamor of anger answered him, and he hushed it with upraised hands while he explained. The committee had been greeted by Colonel Dibble of the Governor's staff. They handed him the resolutions, and he bade them wait, and left them, and presently returned. The Governor, said Mr. Dibble, refused to receive any delegation from the mass meeting, because there were several large bodies of armed men gathered here and there in the city. The Governor, while impervious to threats, would gladly meet any peaceable assembly.

"I assured Mr. Dibble," cried Judge Marr, "that if the Governor abdicated, we would guarantee him against harm to his person or property. But it was useless. Now, citizens of New Orleans, what is your pleasure?"

Someone shouted: "Hang Kellogg!" A score of voices took up the cry, but they were silenced by a greater shout. "Troops!" "Fight!" "The troops!"

Judge Marr held up his hands for silence. "Is it your pleasure that we muster our forces and prepare to fight?" The roar of affirmation was like the clamor of hungry beasts. "Then go to your homes! Go arm yourselves! Prepare yourselves to help hold the city against the usurper and all his hirelings!"

The crowd began to dissolve, but his voice checked them. "Wait! Wait! Go home, but return here at half past two o'clock," he directed. "Bring arms if you have them; but come yourselves, whether armed or not. You will find leaders here who will arrange your movements and provide your weapons. The time for words has passed; the time to act is come."

When Trav and Don moved away, the banquettes along St. Charles Street were already crowded, so they went up a block and turned into Camp Street. Just short of Poydras, Elon overtook them. He had passed before he recognized them, but then he swung to face them.

"Oh, didn't see you! Were you at the meeting?"

Trav nodded. "So the War is on?" he asked.

"We'll act, yes. I'm on my way to Headquarters, just across the street over there." He pointed, then said: "Hello, there's Lieutenant Governor Penn, talking to General Ogden. See them?"

Trav turned to look. The two men were listening to a third. "Who's the other gentleman?"

"Judge Hill, General Ogden's partner." And as a fourth man joined them: "That's Judge Alexander." Elon's voice lifted. "That's a final council of war."

He turned to go, and Don said in a friendly tone: "You know everyone in New Orleans, Elon?"

Elon grinned. "More or less. I grew up here. G'by!"

He hurried away, and Trav and Don went on. Trav said, after a moment: "Hope nothing happens to Elon. Fine young man. Don't know what I'd do without him at Paradise. Or at the mill." He quickened his pace. "Well, I suppose we're late for dinner, son."

7

GENERAL BADGER, who had been a Colonel in the Union army, was now Superintendent of the Metropolitans, but Longstreet, as Adjutant General of Militia, was his commanding officer. Having seen the call for Monday's meeting, he expected a summons from the Governor, but when at supper time on Sunday none had come, he sent for General Badger.

"We'll have to see the Governor," he explained. "See what he wants done about this meeting."

General Badger had under his direction a score of detectives, some of them active members of the League, so he was thoroughly informed of arms received and arms expected, and he told Longstreet now: "The Governor doesn't know what he wants. I reported to him that that shipment of arms was coming into Leeds's foundry last night. I knew several hundred Leaguers would be gathered there, so that it might mean a fight, but I offered to seize the arms, asked for orders."

Longstreet looked at him under heavy brows. "Get any?" Badger shook his head, and Longstreet grunted, but after a moment he rose. "Well, we'll see him," he decided. "See what he wants us to do."

When they came to the Governor's office, General Badger explained their errand. "We've come for your orders about this meeting tomorrow, Governor. And also, as you know, there are several thousand muskets on the *Mississippi* that will be unloaded tomorrow." Kellogg made a fretful sound and Badger said stiffly: "If you wish to seize that shipment, my forces are at your disposal."

Kellogg looked at Longstreet. "What do you suggest?"

Longstreet answered promptly. "Don't forget the mass meeting in the morning. Wait and see what they decide. Let them make the first move. We should be ready to meet them, but should leave to them the initiative: stand on the defensive, receive their assaults and shatter them." He added: "Specifically, I believe we should occupy the Custom

House, keep a strong force there in hand. Also, the Third Precinct station should be strongly held, with men ready at the other stations."

The Governor said, in the eager tone of a child anxious to please: "Two companies of United States troops—D and E of the Sixteenth Infantry—will reach here before daylight, or soon after, and the Third Infantry has been ordered here from Brookhaven."

"With orders to take a hand?"

"No," the Governor admitted. "No, their orders are just to protect Government property. That means, certainly, to guard the Custom House." He rubbed thoughtfully at his knuckles. "I might make my headquarters there."

Longstreet said sternly: "You're the Governor of Louisiana. Your headquarters should be here, in your office; not under the wing of the United States Army."

"Yes, yes, I suppose so." Kellogg looked at Badger. "General, can you protect the capitol?"

"Certainly."

"Well, I wish you would," the Governor said in a plaintive tone. Longstreet watched him with an expressionless eye, and Badger asked: "Is that all? No orders except: protect the capitol?"

Kellogg tugged at his beard as though it irked him. "Well, all right, all right," he said petulantly. "I rely upon you, gentlemen! Good night!"

The two Generals left together, parting at the door, and Longstreet walked home through the empty streets, striding slowly, his head bowed. As he passed Trav's house he hesitated, wishing he might enter; but the house was dark and everyone must be asleep, so he went on. Mrs. Longstreet was still in Lynchburg, the younger children with her and the General wished she were here. But only Garland was here, and when Longstreet reached home, the house was dark, Garland doubtless asleep. Longstreet went quietly to his room.

He undressed and in his night shirt sat for a while on the side of the bed, his elbows on his knees, staring at the clean new flame of the tall candle on the table. This was an hour like the hour of his last conference with General Lee before the surrender; yet there was a difference. Then, even in defeat, his mind was at peace. He had been for four years a soldier, whose only responsibility was to do to the best of his ability the task that was set him, and he had the sense of duty faithfully done. The event could sadden him, yet he felt no sense of guilt or blame.

But tonight his thoughts gave him no easement. For these six or seven years, he had been his own master, free to make his own decisions; it was those decisions which had brought him to this hour tonight. Yet he thought now it was hard to believe he had been wrong. He had chosen, thoughtfully and prayerfully, the course which seemed to him most likely to lead to a settled, strong and united nation. Surely, the fact that others had made a different choice, and blamed him for choosing as he did, was no proof that he had been mistaken.

It was even arguable that they proved he had been right. Suppose his counsels had been followed: suppose the statesmen of the South had allied themselves with the Republican party; suppose there had been in the South a general disposition to accept the verdict of the battlefield. Why then there would certainly have been no massacre at the Mechanics Institute in 1866—nor any others of its pattern—and in all likelihood there would have been no Military Reconstruction. There would never have been the long butchery of the campaign of 1868, nor the massacres of 1872 in Northern Louisiana, nor that Colfax business a year ago last April, nor whatever was to happen tomorrow! Had the South nine years ago admitted defeat, these tragedies would never have occurred.

He could thus persuade himself that he had been right, yet to do so did not bring him happiness. To be happy, clearly, a man must stand with his class; he must either stand with the men who are his friends and neighbors, even at the cost of ignoring his own convictions, or he must accept the pointing finger, the turned shoulder, the resentment which becomes increasingly bitter as others realize that they were wrong.

Tomorrow, as his sworn duty, he must rank himself beside the cowering Kellogg; tomorrow he must lead a half-disciplined force of Negroes and white mercenaries against men who had pressed through rivers of blood and hells of lead and fire—yes, some of them under his command—during four terrible years.

And there was no escape for him. Oath bound and honor bound, he must tomorrow do what Governor Kellogg ordered him to do, and even if there were no orders, he must do his duty; as a sworn officer of the state, he must protect and defend the Governor and his cause. A phrase came to his mind: "A whiff of grape". If that were, tomorrow, the advice he must give, and the order he must give—what then?

How much easier to die!

When at last he rose and walked to the window, there was light in the east. Facing that way, he knelt down, and for a while he prayed. Afterward, he slept an hour or two. When he arose, he went at once to join the Governor.

He spent most of the morning in the Capitol, but after the committee demanding the Governor's abdication had come and gone, Kellogg determined to take refuge in the Custom House.

"That building is as strong as a fortress," he pointed out. "And if the mob attacks it, the United States soldiers there on guard will promptly interfere." He appealed to General Longstreet. "Do you agree that that's the wisest course?"

Longstreet did not reply, but Badger said: "The Third Regiment hasn't arrived. Some trouble with the engine, and they had to wait for a new one. But the two companies from the Sixteenth are there."

Kellogg repeated his question. "General Longstreet, do you agree?"

"What are your orders, Governor?"

"Orders?" The Governor, his voice rising to a shrill pitch, scolded like a fish-wife. "Must you have orders? Your duty is to protect the Government of the State of Louisiana from even the threat of danger! A few disgruntled and rebellious citizens arm themselves, pretend to be an army, and demand the abdication of the Governor, and you ask for orders! Hah! Why do you have muskets, cannon, revolvers? You—"

Longstreet raised his hand. "Say no more, Governor. Your wishes are clear! I will order your carriage, and an escort to see you safely to the Custom House."

The distance was short, a matter of five or six blocks. Longstreet saw the Governor depart, mounted Metropolitans surrounding his carriage; he went then to General Badger's office to hear the latest reports of what the Leaguers were doing.

"This is no longer just the League," Badger told him. "The McEnery party has taken over. Mr. Penn, calling himself Acting Governor, has issued a call to all citizens between eighteen and forty-five—" He glanced at a paper on his desk and quoted: " 'for the purpose of driving the usurpers from power.' " He added: "And he has appointed General Ogden Provisional General of Militia and put him in command."

General Longstreet made a barking sound, half laugh, half oath. "Never mind their words! What have they done?"

"A company of them took possession of the City Hall an hour or so ago. They hold the telegraph there, so our police stations can't communicate with each other."

"Let them keep in contact by messenger. What else?"

"They're throwing up barricades along Poydras Street."

"Barricades? Ha!" Longstreet gnawed his lip. "Expecting our attack. General, what is our force available?"

"About three thousand colored militia here; several hundred Metropolitans at Jackson Square. Our artillery's there, too. About thirty mounted Metropolitans in Orleans Alley." And he added: "Ogden has probably twenty-four hundred Leaguers, and a few thousand unorganized militia."

"Very well. Leave one battalion at Bienville and Chartres, to protect the State House. I'll bring up the Mets from the Cabildo." He leaned over the other's desk, scribbled the order, called for a messenger and sent it off. "We'll form our main force on Canal, near the Custom House, and place the guns to enfilade any advance along the streets from Front to Tchoupitoulas." He considered, nodding. "Good! If they attack the Custom House, we'll smash them, and if they move toward the *Mississippi* steamer we'll concentrate and overwhelm them."

General Badger hesitated. "Won't that leave our flank in the air? To anchor it on the levee might be better."

Longstreet looked at him in open astonishment that anyone should question his judgment on tactical matters, and without replying he said in a tone excessively polite, "May I suggest, General, that you dispose your nigra companies not on Canal Street but in Jackson Square? Sight of them might be a spark to touch off the explosion we hope to avoid. Oh, and ask someone to have a mount for me, at the St. Louis Street entrance, if you please."

Badger departed, and Longstreet strolled around the office with an absent eye, till a message came from General Badger: the Leaguers were in line of battle on Poydras Street, from the levee to Carondelet.

Longstreet grunted an assent. "Hah! If they're wise, they'll stay there!" Poydras Street, almost parallel with Canal, was three or four blocks up town from the Custom House. "Ask General Badger to advise me when he is ready to move."

The messenger returned almost at once to summon him. In the street his horse was ready. He swung into the saddle, and he and General Badger rode side by side along Chartres Street to Canal. Their men, five hundred of them with six guns, advanced in three columns, by Chartres Street and Peters and Decatur. They deployed in Canal Street with the Custom House at their back, their line extending from St. Charles Street to the Free Market. Between the Custom House and the levee lay an open square bounded along Peters Street by a few small scattered buildings, by some business structures on the uptown side.

On Poydras, two blocks beyond Common, the Leaguers were already in position, and while the Metropolitans were moving into Canal Street some firing sounded in St. Charles, and an orderly reported to General Badger:

"Skirmishers working down St. Charles Street, sir."

Longstreet, who for all his deafness heard many things, said over his shoulder: "Have our men draw back out of range. They want to pull us off balance there." They were at the corner of Peters Street, looking up Tchoupitoulas, and Longstreet could see the barricade at the corner of Poydras. He caught General Badger's eye. "A gun here would hold them where they are, yonder," he suggested. A whiff of grape! How the phrase persisted.

General Badger summoned a messenger, and when the gun was in position, he called Sergeant Taylor of the mounted Metropolitans.

"Take eight men, Sergeant," he directed. "Ride down as far as St. Charles Street. Don't draw fire from those fellows in St. Charles Street, but speak to the crowd on the banquettes. Urge them to disperse and go home. Say there will probably be some shooting here."

Sergeant Taylor led his men away, and General Badger and General Longstreet rode as far as Levee Street to watch him. An officer found them there to report that the company on the right flank of the League position along Poydras Street was moving out upon the levee. General Badger looked at Longstreet with an expressionless countenance, but Longstreet knew what he was thinking; this was the danger which Badger had foreseen. Down Canal Street where Sergeant Taylor had gone, a single shot sounded.

"They'll try to cross the end of Canal Street and flank our line," said Longstreet. "Mr. Badger, we'll extend our front. Put Gray's battery on the levee to face them, with Captain Flanagan's men."

General Badger gave the necessary orders and rode toward the levee, and Longstreet's eyes followed him. The levee was littered along its crest with piles of freight; barrels, crates, and bales of cotton or of hay which had been unloaded from steamers but not yet moved to the warehouses. Beyond, three river steamers were tied up, and he saw their decks crowded with passengers, men and women and children. He spoke to an officer beside him.

"What are those steamers? If there's any firing, they'll be pelted with stray bullets."

"There's a regatta up at Carrollton, at the rowing club," the officer explained. "I suppose they planned to go up there, but now they're waiting to see what will happen here."

It was a quarter of a mile, or a little more, from where Longstreet sat his horse to the top of the levee. General Badger paused on the way while the battery limbered up to make its move, then cantered on with the guns. Longstreet kneed his horse and walked him up to the corner of the Custom House at Peters Street. He halted there, watching from this distance while General Badger directed the placing of the guns, scanning the levee and the buildings all around. Sergeant Taylor came to report that the crowd on Canal Street showed no inclination to disperse.

"I heard a shot a while ago?"

"Tore my jacket, that's all." The Sergeant showed Longstreet the hole in his sleeve, and Longstreet glanced at it. As he did so, from the corner of his eye, he saw a movement yonder on the levee. Many men, crouching low, were darting up from the river side of the levee, dodging among the scattered parcels of freight, keeping under cover. They were already on the flank and rear of the battery which General Badger was placing, and Longstreet raised his hands to his mouth to trumpet a warning.

But before he could do so, the Gatling gun there in the hands of the Metropolitans opened steady rapid fire. The game was begun.

The game was begun, but it was badly begun. Under cover of the levee, the Leaguers had established themselves upon the flank of the Metropolitan position. Worse, they were on the flank and rear of Gray's two Napoleons, and of the Gatling gun, even before it began its pom-pom-pom. The gunners were helplessly exposed; the Leaguers, behind cotton bales, and casks, and boxes of freight, were almost completely protected. The position was hopeless.

For an instant that seemed longer, the only sound, the only firing, was the steady pound of the Gatling gun, screening itself in a cloud of smoke as it fired. Then, not as a volley, but in single, aimed shots, the Leaguers swept the battery with a leaden scythe, and men fell like grain to the reaper. The Gatling ceased fire, began again, stopped, coughed twice—and fired no more; the pitiless musketry was a steady rain, and smoke hid all.

As he saw that disaster threatened the forces under his command, and even before the first musket fire, Longstreet had pushed his horse toward the levee. He was at a trot when the Gatling gun opened. The horse gave a violent bound, and Longstreet, his right arm almost useless from his old wound, controlled the animal with some difficulty. The musket fire completed its panic, but the General forced it on toward the smoke-veiled levee. He was not thinking of his horse. General Badger had foreseen this flanking move, but Longstreet had ignored the other's doubts. Feeling now a reluctant gladness at the approaching defeat, at the certainty that the force he commanded would be shattered, he wondered whether he had known that this would happen, whether he had wittingly made it possible.

The Gatling gun was silenced, and the battery, and Longstreet saw through the thinning smoke the gunners, those still on their feet, falter and flee. General Badger tried to rally them, and a musket ball toppled him out of his saddle. The fugitives, the gunners and their infantry support, came toward Longstreet and his frightened horse; they came at a walk and then at a trot and then in headlong flight, and bullets overtook them, and one and then another fell. Behind them the jubilant Leaguers raced through the abandoned guns, lashing at the fugitives with musketry and pistol shots.

Longstreet's horse was frantic, and as the flood of frightened men surrounded him, it fought the reins, rearing, bounding, kicking. The fugitives from the levee threw into disorder the Metropolitans still steady on Canal Street; their pursuers were close upon their heels. At the same time, out of Front Street and Fulton and then out of Tchoupitoulas, companies of Leaguers came full charge against the wavering ranks. Longstreet, in an instant's crystal vision, remembered how his corps had swung against Pope's flank at Second Manassas; the Metropolitans now, like Pope's lines that day, were folding up as easily as a wet box.

The charge was from his left, and as the Leaguers came, they lifted their voices in that shrill harmony of hoots and screams and howls like the cries of excited hunters as they drive the deer through some lowland swamp, blending together the shouts of men, the baying of many hounds, the whining bark of the fox, the screech and hoot of a thousand owls, the rattling challenge of the hawk, which a few years before had resounded across so many contested battlefields. They came not headlong, but at a steady trot, firing and reloading as they came; and that hair-raising cry was for Longstreet like the shrill call of beloved ghosts risen from the dead. His horse had wearied him, his right arm hung limply, and a spent ball thumped his left shoulder so that he dropped the reins. The streaming charge of the Leaguers, racing after the breaking Metropolitans, swept past his terrified horse so that it revolved in the current like a log in the eddy below a cataract, maddened and plunging. Someone caught the bridle and jerked the rein, and the horse fell to its knees, and then on its side. Longstreet cleared himself, but his weight came on his gouty foot, so that he winced and stumbled. Then men beside him caught his arms and set him on his feet, and one of them looked into his face and cried in a great voice:

"By God, it's old Pete!" And, with a loud guffaw: "You old Bull o' the Woods, where'd you learn to ride?"

Longstreet looked around. His Metropolitans were gone, the last of them scudding away along Peters Street like mist before the wind. Around him were the Leaguers, but that man yonder had called him "Pete," had called him "Old Bull of the Woods." He wanted to embrace these men, to clasp their hands!

But they were watching him with puzzled, half-angry eyes. One of them handed him his hat; he tugged it on, remembered that he was their prisoner.

"Your servant, gentlemen," he said, waiting.

Then someone clasped his arm; young Elon Villard. "Hurt, General?" Elon signed to the others to go on.

"Wrenched foot. Nothing," Longstreet told him, and turned; but he limped. "Means a touch of gout," he grumbled.

"Better get indoors," Elon suggested. "If you'll take my arm?"

Thus supported, Longstreet reached the Custom House. On the way, the pain eased and his limp disappeared. At the entrance, he turned.

"Thank you, Elon. I'm still your prisoner."

Elon grinned with embarrassment. "All right now?" Longstreet nodded, and Elon hurried away. Longstreet stood alone there outside the entrance; the battle had receded, dwindled in the distance. Governor Kellogg was here in the Custom House; he might as well report to the Governor. He tugged at the heavy bronze door and opened it and went in and began wearily to climb the endless stairs.

Trav and Don, after dinner that day, were undecided whether or not to go back downtown. A battle in the streets seemed to them both to be inevitable. "And I suppose General Longstreet will be in the thick of it," Trav reflected. "That I certainly do not want to see."

But the act of telling Enid and Lucy about the meeting, about what had happened, awakened their appetite to know what was going to happen. Enid said they would be idiots if they did go back and get themselves shot for their pains, but Lucy watched Don with reassurance in her eyes. Whatever he decided, she would approve. After dinner, still uncertain, they went out upon the gallery; but at length the waiting to hear the sound of distant battle became unbearable.

Trav was the first to surrender. He rose with the briskness of a delayed decision. "I want to see what's going on," he decided, and went toward the stairs. Don looked at Lucy, and had her smile, and followed.

They had come almost to Lafayette Square when they heard ahead and to their right the first shots from the Gatling gun, and then the rattle of musket fire. Don's instinct was to hurry forward, but Trav neither hurried nor slackened pace. They reached the barricades along Poydras Street. Barrels and logs here were neatly piled, and horse cars had been tipped on their sides. As they turned up Poydras Street, the firing reached a higher pitch, and they heard the voices of many men raised in a blood-chilling, ululating cry. Don said soberly:

"I've heard that before! It always did send cold chills up and down my spine."

The firing slackened, the cries receded. When they came to Canal Street, men and women and children were hurrying toward the levee, and the shots and shouts of battle were somewhere off beyond the Custom House, dulled by distance and the intervening buildings. Occasionally a shot sounded near at hand, and Trav saw Metropolitans in uniform at the windows of the Custom House, obviously looking for targets in the street below. But while he watched, these figures disappeared, and except for the shuffle of many moving feet, the cries of newsboys selling their extra editions of the papers, and the roar of many voices all talking at once and on a pitch unnaturally high, there was no sound of the battle so recently begun, so quickly done.

They moved toward the levee, seeing here and there a wounded man surrounded by friends or kindly strangers, or the body of a dead man, sometimes in the Metropolitan uniform and neglected and ignored, sometimes protected by men standing by, and covered with someone's jacket or with a handkerchief laid across the face. Here and there, fresh red blood that had not yet had time to clot and change its hue lay in small puddles. Near the levee they saw a dead horse, and another with a broken leg, and as they approached, a gentleman quieted this horse and drew a pistol from beneath his coat and shot it carefully between the eyes, and it was dead, falling with a clatter of hooves.

"I can never get used to the suddenness, the sudden completeness of death," said Trav, and Don nodded, and Trav paused, watching some men yonder manhandling a cannon. "Why are we here?" he asked. "What is it we're looking for?"

One of the men by the gun hailed them, and they saw Elon Villard's sweat-streaked face and the high triumph in his eyes. He came running toward them.

"There's an end to Kellogg!" he cried, as he reached them, and he grasped their hands, one hand in each of his. "Did you see the scoundrels run?"

"Just got here," Don explained, and Trav asked:

"Was Longstreet here?"

"Yes. His horse fell with him, hurt his foot a little, but he's all right. I helped him over to the Custom House. General Ogden's horse was shot under him." He pointed. "General Badger's over there, on a pile of hay, badly wounded. We're looking after him."

Don said: "We were near enough to hear that yell a while ago. It sent shivers up and down my spine."

"Mine too," Elon agreed. "It always does. We yelled, and hit their flank, and rolled them up. It was just a question who could run the fastest!"

Trav said: "Someone managed your battle first rate."

"General Ogden. There was a council of war at Fifty-eight Camp— but you were there. I saw you. I'd forgotten. Mr. Penn made General Ogden Commander-in-Chief, and they drew up our orders—and here we are."

"Not without loss," Trav commented, and Elon nodded.

"Yes, we had several killed, or hurt, and so did they." Someone called him, and he said: "I'll see you soon."

Trav and Don walked down to the Custom House, but at the door Trav hesitated, shook his head. "The General wouldn't want to see us, even if he's here."

Don agreed, and without discussion they made their way home. Trav reported to Enid and Lucy. "A complete victory for the Leaguers, I should say. Certainly the Metropolitans were routed, and the Leaguers hold the battlefield." He looked at Don. "I saw one or two dead nigras; Metropolitans in uniform."

"So did I," Don agreed. "And there were three wounded, by the market building."

"Was General Longstreet in it?" Lucy asked.

Trav nodded. "He had to be. There was no escape for him." And he said thoughtfully: "This was a bitter waste of powder and ball—and blood. It was successful for the moment, but Grant will still back Kellogg. There's no good done."

Tuesday morning the Leaguers took possession of the State House, and Mr. Penn held a triumphant reception at his home and was then ceremoniously installed as Acting Governor. The newspapers exulted in the final collapse of the Kellogg regime, but President Grant promptly moved to restore Kellogg to his place, ordering troops to the city, and Governor McEnery returned to New Orleans just in time to surrender the Capitol to General Emory.

Governor Kellogg, still clinging to the safety of the Custom House, told a Mississippi reporter: "I did not order the disposition of the Metropolitans yesterday; General Longstreet did. I did not want bloodshed; I wanted this trouble left to the ballot box."

Trav, when he read this, sought out the General. "I saw that statement, yes," Longstreet assented to his question. "But I shall make no denial. Let them believe what they choose."

Trav wondered at the other's apathy. "Who actually started the firing?" he asked.

"We opened fire with the Gatling gun."

Trav waited, but Longstreet added nothing to that statement, and Trav remarked: "I hear General Badger will recover." He smiled. "His wounds have made him a popular hero, yet Monday morning there was no one in New Orleans so detested."

"You forget me."

"You should have got yourself a wound!" Trav said, smiling.

Longstreet nodded. "I managed to get in the way of one bullet, but unfortunately it was spent, only left a bruise."

Trav could find no word; he sat a little longer, but Longstreet offered nothing, and Trav took his leave. The big man's hurts would not easily be healed.

Before the week's end, the toll of casualties was complete. Thirteen Leaguers and eleven of the Metropolitans were dead, and more would die. Saturday morning before the city was astir, Governor Kellogg returned to the capitol to resume his office. United States troops, and half a dozen warships moored along the levee, gave him every possible guarantee of his safety there.

8

A WEEK AFTER the battle of the levee, Don and Lucy took the children down to Paradise. They stayed there through October, Don absorbed in his work in the schools. Once or twice Trav and Elon came downriver, Trav to look at the cane, Elon to make sure the equipment at the sugar mill was in order. Elon was apt to drop in at Mrs. Harper's school for whatever time he had to spare. There was never enough time for him to ride over to Chambersburg, but Don always planned to be at home on the days when they were coming, and at the dinner table, Don and Elon might discuss some teaching problem, some new plan which Don proposed to try, while Lucy and Trav watched and listened, and Lucy thought how alike they were, in so many ways.

Early in October, Don asked Lucy whether Cash and Quinny might come to live at the plantation. Lucy of course agreed, and he explained: "Tony's well enough so he doesn't need Cash, and here the other night, someone shot the lock out of the outside door of their cabin. Cash had a bar over the door, so whoever it was didn't get in, but it scared Quinny."

"Well, I should think it would! What were they after?"

"I've no idea! Cash says he doesn't know either. But at any rate, I told him they could come down here."

After the move was made, Lucy now and then saw Quinny, but always at a distance. One day she said to Cash: "Tell her she needn't hide from me. I'm not her enemy."

"I guess she thinks you might not want to see her around, ma'am. And, she always thinks people are looking at her."

Lucy did not insist. Probably the girl was right to think of herself as an object of curiosity, and if it were known that she was here, the word would spread. Almost every day, Negroes passed the plantation, following the trail along the levee, and there were laughing interchanges when one of the passers threw a greeting to some wench upon whom his eye chanced to fall, or when a woman stopped to gossip. Also, white visitors were not infrequent, for men on horse- or mule-back sometimes used the levee trail, and Pink Chambers occasionally rode over from Chambersburg to spend an hour with Don. Lucy knew enough about life in the country to be sure that if anything of interest happened at Paradise, it was soon reported through the region roundabout.

One day—Don was at the Chambersburg school, Cash and the *Paradise* were upriver, and Mr. Tremont had gone to inspect the cane and decide how soon the harvest should begin—a party of four mounted men, carrying shotguns across their saddles, came down the levee trail. Most of the hands were in the fields, but old Matthew was working on a flower bed by the walk that led from the house to the levee. One of the riders called him and gave him some order, and Matthew's shouted summons brought half a dozen Negroes, men and women, to where the men sat their horses. Lucy, watching from the vine-hung gallery, stayed hidden. If they wished to see her, they would come to the house. She recognized one of them as the unfriendly man whom she and Don had encountered in the store at the Four Corners. Don had said his name was Howard.

After they were gone, and the Negroes had scattered, she called old Matthew and leaned over the balcony rail to question him. "Who was it, Matthew?" she asked. "What did they want?"

"Dat uz Miste' How'd, ma'am," he told her. "An' th'ee gemmen f'om N'w Awl'ns. Dey huntin' hoss thieves."

"Horse thieves? Whose horses have been stolen?"

"Dey di'n't specify, Missy; jes' any ole hoss thief'd do 'em, it looked tuh me." He added vaguely: " 'Nen dey wanted tuh know who we'uns uz going t'vote foh, come Novembeh."

Lucy felt the touch of sudden fear, and she hoped Don would come early home. As the shadows lengthened, she walked a little way to meet him, and when he came toward her at a trail trot her heart swelled with a glad relief. He dismounted and they walked on together, Lucy clinging to his arm.

Inevitably, he felt the tightness in her, and while they talked of little matters he watched her, and watching her thus intently he saw a new thing deep in her eyes, and stopped, and swung her to him.

"Lucy! Honey!" he said softly. "Do I see what I think I see?"

"Oh, you!" she protested. "Why can't I ever keep anything from you?"

He laughed, drawing her close, and he asked: "Why should you want to? Keep anything from me, I mean? When, Lucy?"

"Oh, some day, for a surprise!"

He held her in the circle of his arms, kissed her cheek. "When do you plan to spring this surprise?"

"How do you like May?"

"H-m-m! Well, let me see. December turned out to be all right for Donny and Travis, but Sally, last June, was our prize. Do you think you ought to wait till June?"

She laughed. "Wait? You try waiting, sometime. When I start to do a thing, I like to get it done."

They walked on, happily arm in arm. She wished to tell him of the riders who had stopped here that day, but decided to wait till after supper. Then, sitting before the lightwood fire—for the night was cool—she reported the incident.

"And Matthew said they were more interested in politics than in stolen horses," she concluded.

The smile had long since left his eyes, and he said now, with a nod: "There've been other parties through the Four Corners, and in Chambersburg—anywhere they could find Negroes. They make no threats, except that they wear revolvers, and carry shotguns; but they always ask the Negroes how they'll vote, and the people get the point. I suppose it's happening all over the state."

"Will it ever end, Don?"

He said strongly: "Yes it will. Of course it will." And he said, nodding in the direction of the little school house: "That sort of thing will end it eventually; the school here and the school over at Chambersburg, and all the other schools. While we were in New Orleans, I studied the figures in the last census. According to that, there are almost three hundred thousand children—boys and girls, white and black—under twenty-one years old, in Louisiana, and only about seventy-five thousand of them were in school. That's one in four. Some parishes have no schools at all. One result is that out of eighty-seven thousand Negroes old enough to vote, only nine thousand can read and write. And the percentage of whites isn't much better."

"I wonder whether being able to read or write makes a man a better voter?"

"It's a measure of his character, rather than of his intelligence," Don suggested. "I don't suppose there's a white man in the state, say twenty-one years old or over, who couldn't have learned to read and write long ago if he'd wanted to. Negroes might not have been able to learn, under slavery, but a white man who can't read just simply never had enough curiosity to want to!" And he said sadly: "That's the discouraging thing, that the Negroes are more anxious to learn than the whites. The piney-woods whites—the men over at Chambersburg, for example—boast of their ignorance, as though it were a proof of their superiority. I suppose that's really because they're too shy to admit that they wish they were better than they are." Lucy shivered, and he asked: "Cold? Want a wrap?"

"No. Oh no! I don't know why I shivered." She laughed, not mirth-fully. "I had a sudden feeling of being all alone, with thousands of poor, wretched, shy frightened people all around us with guns in their hands, looking every which way for someone to shoot."

He said reassuringly: "They're all right except when they're fright-ened, Lucy. And they're not afraid of us."

She came beside him, drawing his arm around her shoulder. "Hold me close," she demanded, and a moment later: "Don, when we go home to Maine next spring, let's stay there."

For a while, he did not answer. Then he said gently: "There's a lot to be done, here, Lucy; a long, hard job. It will never be finished, cer-tainly not for generations. But I want to try to make a start." He rose and stood for a moment at the hearth where the fire had burned down till only coals remained, and he went out on the gallery and brought a log and laid it on the coals and watched it burst into flame. Then he sat down again beside her. "The greatest thing General Lee ever did may well have been to become a teacher." He shook his head. "I can't imagine I'll ever be willing to stop trying to help these people here."

Pressed against his shoulder, she heaved a long sigh of pretended resignation. "Well, I suppose that means me too." She nestled closer. "So I might as well enjoy it." They sat for a long time, watching the dancing flames, seeing dream shapes in the fire.

Cinda and Brett arrived in New Orleans for a visit just in time to be at Paradise with the others—Trav and Enid, Eleanor and Mr. Cist and Elon—to watch the sugar making. Cap'n Cash, since now he lived at the plantation instead of in New Orleans, usually came downriver some time after noon, so they arrived while it was still daylight.

"But the time to watch the sugar mill is at night," Elon told them. "So we'll wait for after supper."

Trav saw Elon's happy eagerness, and he guessed how much this homecoming meant to the younger man, so he allowed Elon to plan everything. Lucy took Aunt Cinda and Enid and Eleanor away, and the others had their toddies on the gallery, while Don heard from Trav and Elon some of the incidents of these last weeks of the campaign. There had been no open violence. "Not yet, at least," said Trav. "The Democrats—they call themselves Conservatives, now—they're leaning over backward to avoid antagonizing the nigras. Nobody got hurt, even when the New Orleans nigras held their Convention and decided that since nigras were nine-tenths of the Republican party, they should have nine-tenths of the offices."

Don smiled. "They'd be better than some of the carpetbaggers, at that."

"So would slugs under a flat rock," Trav agreed, and he chuckled. "While we're calling names, one of the up-country papers called the Kellogg crowd a 'hybrid pack of lecherous pimps.' He started with that and worked up to a peak!"

Don asked: "How's the General?"

Trav hesitated. "I think he'll resign, repudiate Kellogg and all his works, as soon as he can do so without seeming to quit under fire. He's pretty despondent, and he's half sick besides; a touch of gout."

Elon said: "He thought he might have one after the fight on the levee. His foot was bruised. He said that usually started it up." And he added: "I'll never forget him that day, the tragedy in his eyes. I hated to leave him—but in his place, I'd have wanted to be alone."

The supper bell brought them to their feet. When afterward they went to see the mill at work, the long rooms were lighted with pine torches, flaring and smoking, revealing the kettles in rows and the bubbling syrup, and at each kettle a Negro peering through the steam, his paddle gently moving and turning. Except for Elon and Eleanor, this was a new experience for all of them; but these two were happy as their guides, Elon in charge, Eleanor supplementing his words when the occasion required.

Elon led them first to the iron rollers which crushed the cane and squeezed out the juice; thence they followed the trough through which the juice reached the receiver beside the kettles. The kettles were set on a platform a little above the floor level, against the flaring chimney, which narrowed toward the roof to create a roaring draft. Elon led them up on the platform to see the boiling syrup.

"Four kettles," he explained, raising his voice above the roar of the flames. "This first one, the biggest, it's the *grande*. That next one's the *flambeau*, then the *sirop*, and finally the *batterie*. They're hung by their rims, to get as much fire around them as we can, make them boil hard. We burn the bagasse, the crushed, dry cane for fuel. It makes a fine hot fire."

"Mercy, I should think so!" Cinda agreed. "I'm boiling as hard as the kettles."

"You and I will get back away from the fires," Eleanor proposed. "Now that you've seen the juice." They stepped down off the platform and watched the others. Elon was explaining everything, moving from one kettle to the next, and Cinda could not hear him, but Eleanor told her: "He's just showing them how the juice is boiled down. Each kettle's smaller than the one before it, so when the juice in one kettle is boiled down enough so it will go into the next smallest, they dip it off. See! That boy's doing it now, emptying the last one, the *batterie*, into the coolers."

"Is that really all there is to it?"

Eleanor laughed. "Heavens, no. When they fill the big kettle this time, you'll see them mix some lime with the juice. It has to be just the right amount. We'll wait and watch."

Cinda puffed. "Whoo! I'd rather wait where it's cooler!"

Eleanor laughed. "Well, come along; these are the coolers over here."

They joined the others there, but Cinda said: "These aren't the kind of cooler I meant." Yet when Eleanor asked quickly whether she would rather go outside, Cinda heard the disappointment in her tones and said: "Nonsense, child. I don't want to miss a bit of it!"

Elon was telling the others: ". . . and when it's down to blood heat, and getting sugary, it goes into the hogsheads." He led them toward the huge casks, resting on stout beams above the molasses wells. "We let it stand, to let the molasses drain off." They saw Trav ask a question, and Elon said: "Full of sugar, about half a ton. About forty-five gallons of molasses will drain out of each hogshead."

Eleanor stepped forward. "Now it's my turn," she said, and showed them how to dip a little of the sugaring juice from the cooler and pull it while it cooled and produced a morsel of *colon* taffy. The Negroes at their work were singing here by the coolers and at the kettles. Sometimes many voices rose together; then abruptly there would be a silence, and then one voice would begin a new song, and one by one the others joined in, till all their voices blended. The fire roared, the pitch-pine torches flared and guttered and lanced out little spurts of smoke and of flame, and the songs began and swelled and came each to an end. For those not interested in the taffy pull, Eleanor provided paddles to dip into the syrup and lick like a confection, or to scrape the crusted sugar off the rim of the kettles.

When they were sated with overmuch sweetness, she led them up to the second floor, where there was more room. "For we have to play pussy-wants-a-corner," she insisted. "We always do!" So they did, racing and laughing and screaming with excitement, and Lucy laughed till she cried to see Aunt Cinda, her skirts collected, running from one vantage to another, red, and panting, and laughing as hard as any one, till at last she had to give over.

"I'm smothering!" she cried. "I feel like a hen under a wagon on a hot day! Brett Dewain, take me out and loosen my stays! I can't breathe!"

Brett, at the moment Pussy, called: "Too busy, ma'am! Wait till I find a corner!" But Enid came to Cinda's rescue, and they departed together, and when Lucy and Eleanor were ready to follow them, the game ended.

Back at the house, since the night was warm, the men sat for a while on the gallery. Brett was interested to hear Mr. Cist's report on the work at the mill, and Trav stayed with them, but Don and Elon drew apart, and Don asked how the election would go. Elon thought the Democrats would poll the most votes.

"But the Returning Board may throw them out," he admitted. "And of course, we may not get the votes, anyway. Marshal Packard is using soldiers as deputies, arresting Democratic leaders all over the state, dragging them to New Orleans, refusing bail, causing them endless expense—and never bringing them to trial. His deputies arrested thirteen men in Coushatta the other day, and since then no white men have registered to vote there for fear of the same thing." He added: "And the Radicals are bringing in nigras by the thousands, from Mississippi and Alabama and Tennessee, registering them as voters." He laughed, threw up his hands. "But I still say we'll win. Had any excitement here?"

Don said casually: "Nothing much. We had some visitors two or three weeks ago." He told about the men Lucy had seen. "And similar groups have visited other plantations, brandishing their guns and talking politics. They're apt to say: 'Up to now, the way I get it, we ain't had to kill off a single niggeh down heah!'"

Elon chuckled. "Sounds like they're working on our side! I expect Marshal Packard would call that kind of talk a threat, too. Did Lucy recognize them?"

"Three of them were strangers, city people, she thought. The other, a man by the name of Howard, lives over at the Four Corners. He's a mean-talking critter, but Mr. Brook says there's no harm in him."

"I remember him," Elon agreed. "He's a plain no-account." He laughed, and rose, and touched Don's arm. "He never had a chance to go to one of your schools, Don," he said. "That's the only trouble with him. If we can keep the schools going, the time will come when there won't be any worthless cusses like Howard around here." He spoke to the others. "I bid you good night, gentlemen all."

Before election day they all went back to New Orleans. The Democrats swept the country, converting a Republican majority of a hundred and ten in the House of Representatives into a Democratic majority of seventy-four, and across the South swept a wave of exultation. In Louisiana, although the Republicans held the Senate, the Democrats carried the House, and for the Saturday night after the election, the *Picayune* summoned every Democratic and Conservative in the city to join a torch-light procession by way of celebration. Fifteen thousand people answered that summons. The various divisions and marching clubs formed at designated places; three rockets fired from the Clay statue set the whole in motion; the bands played the "People's Rights Quickstep," composed for the occasion, and for hours the procession wound through every section of the city from Esplanade to Josephine, from Rampart to the river. Don and Lucy watched the parade crawl along Camp Street and they were infected by the joy of the marchers, laughing and cheering with the passing throng.

The Returning Board—of which General Longstreet was a member—would meet November 12 to begin its canvass of the ballots cast in the election. The Sunday before, Trav called on the General and found him so badly crippled by gout that he could not walk without using two crutches. When he offered sympathy, Longstreet looked at him with a dry smile.

"I count it good fortune," he declared. "It's what I've been hoping for." And seeing that Trav was puzzled; he explained: "Why, sir, here's an obviously honest reason for resigning my public responsibilities."

"You mean the Returning Board. I know it meets Thursday."

Longstreet nodded. "I'll attend the first session," he said. "And possibly the second, to demonstrate my desire to continue. But then I'll present my resignation, on grounds of ill health, with this—" He tapped his bandaged foot lightly with a crutch, and winced. "With this to show I'm telling the truth." He sat for a moment, looking at his foot. "After that, the rest will follow." His eyes met Trav's. "I shall be glad to turn my back on New Orleans, Major. But for you, I'd have known few happy moment here."

On the second Monday after the election, Don went downriver with Cap'n Cash. Only his promise to return Friday evening persuaded Lucy to let him go alone. Tuesday he rode over to keep school in Chambersburg, and he came home at dusk with a feeling of accomplishment, a certainty within himself that as a result of his work that day some great good would one day come. Cash and a crew of hands were loading sugar into the *Paradise*, rolling the huge hogsheads along a plank road to the levee and so aboard ship, and their shouts and cries reached his ears as he ate supper, and reminded him that Cash would go up to New Orleans tomorrow to deliver this cargo. He could take a letter, so that night Don wrote Lucy, trying to tell her about his sudden sense of high achievement.

I think this was, in some mysterious way, the happiest day I've ever known. A strange and sweet experience. I have no idea what caused it. The day was no different from any other. I went over to the Chambersburg school, and Pink was there before me, and had

a fine fire going, and the others were close behind him, and everyone seemed particularly glad to see me. That may have started it.
Looking back, it seems to me I did a lot of talking, and maybe
that's why I had such a good time. You know how I love the sound
of my own voice. But today my thoughts seemed to be clearer, and
I seemed to know just what I wanted to say, and just how to say
it, and along with that went a wonderful feeling that they were
understanding every thing I said, and every thing I meant, too; that
there was somehow a full and complete communication going on between them and me—or between me and them.

I don't remember just what I talked about, just what I said; but
it was something about knowing yourself, and recognizing in yourself all the good instincts and all the bad ones, and knowing which
was which: not judging yourself, no question of praise, or blame, but
just knowing; not fooling yourself about yourself. I remember saying that the way a man turns out depends a lot on his recognizing
his responsibilities, and accepting them, not evading. But it was never
what I said that mattered; it was that feeling that I was getting into
their minds and their hearts.

But why am I writing all this to you? No reason, except that
when I'm happy I think of you, and want to share my happiness
with you. Sharing happiness always doubles it, doesn't it? And I
suppose I really wanted to tell you I thought I'd given them something they'd remember, and maybe get something of it. I wanted to
brag to you, so you could be proud of me. Like little Jack Horner
—was that his name?—who pulled out the plum and said: "What
a good boy am I?" Make Donny recite it to you before he goes to
bed tonight.

Oh, I meant to say, I think Pink Chambers is going to turn out
to be quite a man.

Here I go, rambling on, and really nothing to say. Yet I have
everything to say, but perhaps I've already said it, between the
lines. Even if I haven't said it, you know it. We both know it.

Kiss the babies good night for me, every night. And sleep soundly.
I'll see you Friday. I love you.

DON

Thursday, at the school beyond the swamp, Don found himself once
again filled with that same intoxicating sense that everything was simple
and clear and communicable, that there was no confusion in the thoughts
of men, that men knew the true and knew the false. He remembered
a line in the Bible: wisdom is the principle thing; therefore get wisdom;
and with all thy getting, get understanding. It was not important that
he should teach facts to these children; he must strive to teach them
understanding. It was not enough to know a thing; one must also understand that knowledge. He said this to the children, and had again that

certainty that his thought become theirs; that they received what he strove to give.

It was pleasant, while he spoke, to watch Pink and to see the changes this short time had worked in him, and in all the children. In another year, Pink and the boys his age might decide that they were too old to come to school, but that hurdle could be leaped when the time came. And after all, school was only a beginning; there was here a lifetime's task, for any man willing to undertake it, and Don prayed he might find ways to do what so badly needed doing, in this South which slavery had created.

In the old South were four strata: at the top a small group, immensely wealthy; then a more numerous class of yeomen and small farmers who might own a slave or two; then the rest of the white population—Fifty per cent? Seventy per cent? Ninety per cent? Did anyone know?—disease-ridden, wretchedly impoverished, lost to energy and ambition, proud only of the fact that they were not Negroes, boasting only that any man who offered them an affront put his life in peril.

And below them were the Negroes; the slaves who now were free, and fired by something like ambition and with everything to learn and eager to learn it.

That was the South. Where could a man find a land in greater need?

Don all that day was full of dreams of a friendly life of helpfulness among these people. Riding home through the swamp, smiling at his own thoughts, he once or twice sang a phrase or two of song, outlet for his happiness. Once three deer which had stood motionless while he passed, at the sound of his voice thus suddenly upraised went splashing away through the shallows in great bounds, their white flags flying. He laughed to see them go.

He had supper that night with Mr. and Mrs. Tremont, and afterward he walked up to the crest of the levee to look out across the river. The *Paradise* had returned at dusk. She was tied up just below where he stood, and there was a light in the engine room where Cash worked late. Quinny was with him, and Don heard her light tones and Cash's deep voice as they talked together while he worked, and their occasional laughter. They were a happy pair, but Don thought Quinny probably led Cash a dance; he wondered whether they were still troubled by the shadow which lay across their lives.

He went late to bed and quickly slept, and did not dream, till he was wakened by the sound of running feet and panting breath. When he stepped out on the gallery, the night was full of furtive movement, and he heard a whisper in the archway below where he stood, and leaned over the rail and asked:

"Who's there? What is it?"

A hushed voice answered him: "Please suh, dey's a whole passel o' white men down t'de cabins."

Don stepped back into his room and pulled on trousers over his nightshirt, boots over trousers. When he came out and descended the stairs, the night was still. He started full stride toward the quarter, but a shot sounded there, and a woman screamed, and he began to run.

As he came to the first cabins, somewhere ahead of him a pine torch burst into flame, and then another, and another, filling the night with a smoky glare. Between the double row of cabins ran a cart track which at one point divided to pass on either side of a huge old water oak. Its boughs shaded a circle close to a hundred feet in diameter, and lower branches had been trimmed away so that they would not rub against the cabin roofs on either side. It was under these wide branches that the torches had been lighted, and Don saw there now a loose group of ten or a dozen men. In their midst, two men held a small, white-clad woman who twisted and struggled in a futile, spitting despair. He at first saw only the contorted garment, since in the shadows neither head nor hands were visible; but then a shaft of light struck fair, and he saw Quinny's white teeth and gleaming eyes.

The men were so absorbed that till he was near they had not heard him, but as he came closer one and then another turned to look toward him, and he saw at once Mr. Chambers, and Pink, and Mr. Collins, and others whom he knew. Beyond them at a little distance, four men whose garments had a different cut sat their horses among the shadows which the torches cast; and near them other horses and mules were secured to bushes or to trees. The cabins all around were darkly silent except one, from which came the wails of weeping children, and a woman's sobs.

When Don came near, he had slowed to a walk, to steady his breathing so that he might speak in even tones. He went forward till he stood among them, and he said: "Good evening, gentlemen? Mr. Chambers, Mr. Collins." He spoke to three or four by name. The two who held Quinny he did not recognize. Of those he knew, Mr. Chambers was the most likely leader. "What is it, Mr. Chambers?" he asked, quietly and in a friendly tone. "What's wrong?"

Mr. Chambers said gravely: "You hadn't ought to hide a murderin' niggeh, Cap'n Page."

"Has she done any harm to anyone here?" Don asked. "If she has, I wish you had let me know."

Mr. Chambers faced him firmly. "Some of us will be gettin' out of patience with you, Cap'n. You know what she done. Y'all up no'th see things some different f'om us, but around heah, we think, when someone kills ouah kin, they ought to be kilt themselves." He added simply: "And 'specially when a niggeh kills a white person."

Don looked around the circle of attentive faces. "Do you mind if we discuss it?" he asked. And, in the silence: "By the way, where's Cap'n Cash?"

"He laid hold of some of these gentlemen when they went to fetch her, and they had to shoot him." Mr. Chambers added, in a reasonable tone: "Cash is a pretty good niggeh, as niggehs go, and he was doing no moah than any man would do, to defend his wife, and I hope he don't die of it; but he ought to've had moah sense. So ought you, Cap'n Page."

"Are those his babies, crying?"

Mr. Chambers said, in a faint embarrassment: "His babies and his sister, I believe. What was it you wished to discuss, Cap'n suh? We've done a pile of listenin' to you, so don't be long."

"Why, Quinny, and the death of young Mr. Currain. Do you—"

But then Don paused as from somewhere in the shadows yonder, a man led forth a horse. In his hand he carried a coil of rope. He led the horse under the oak tree, looking at no one and speaking to no one, and he took one end of the rope in his left hand, which held the horse's reins, and with his right hand he threw the coil over the limb above his head.

"One of you come hold this hawse till I git the knot tied," he suggested, and Don recognized the voice as that of Mr. Howard. A man went to stand by the horse's head, and Don remembered that he must speak.

"Do you feel sure she killed Mr. Currain?"

"I do, yes," said Mr. Chambers heavily. "I know she did."

Behind Don, Quinny hiccoughed, and thereafter she continued to do so. The repeated sound was loud in the night. Don remembered that to frighten a person would cure hiccoughs, but he had not known that fright could also cause them.

"Will you tell me why you are sure?"

"The Indian woman saw it done."

"And told you?"

"No, Cap'n Page." Mr. Chambers's tone was one of stony politeness. Quinny's hiccoughs came more quickly.

"The Indian woman must have told someone," Don reflected. "I've heard others say the same thing." His eye touched that group in the background, almost lost among the shadows there. They were doubtless from New Orleans, friends of Peter; he remembered the 1868 campaign, the Innocents and the Infantas who drove Negroes off the New Orleans streets. The Innocents had been to a considerable extent recruited among the Spaniards and Italians between Terre Boeuf and New Orleans, and Peter had been a member. Don wondered whether to call one of them over, to question him; but that would lead nowhere.

"I've wondered why that Indian woman was so eager to accuse Quinny," he remarked. "You know, Quinny was sent down to Mr. Currain's lodging on an errand. Suppose when she got there the Indian woman herself had already killed Peter; she might lie to put the blame on Quinny."

Mr. Chambers said heavily: "She didn't, suh. Talking is no use. I wish yuh'd go back to the big house, Cap'n Page. We'll soon be gone."

There was a small stir and scuffle behind Don, and Mr. Howard said, like a man talking to a fractious horse: "Now, now, girl, let me get this knot on you!"

Quinny, in a desperate silence, dodged and twisted, her struggles dragging the men who held her to and fro, while Mr. Howard, with the noose spread wide, tried to pass it over her head. Don was suddenly terribly afraid that she would scream. Even the imagined sound of that inhuman scream of terror and despair was almost beyond enduring. Mr. Howard made a more vigorous attempt, a bight of the rope dragging Quinny's head sidewise, till she again slipped free. The group of which this struggle was the center shifted and changed, men moving away to give the contestants room, till Mr. Howard lost patience.

"Why, God damn you, you yellow bitch, I'll—" He clubbed his revolver to strike her senseless, but Mr. Chambers said quietly:

"Wait a minute, Mr. Howard."

All movement ceased. Quinny, so absurdly small in her thin nightgown, stood now completely passive between the two men who held her, cowering a little, panting, trembling, hiccoughing through chattering teeth. Mr. Chambers spoke to Don.

"I ask you kindly, Cap'n Page, please suh, go back to the house."

Don wiped his brow, dripping with sweat. He shook his head, and he smiled. "I'm sorry, Mr. Chambers. I can't do that. Whether the girl killed Peter or not—"

Mr. Chambers interrupted him: "We can find out." He spoke to Quinny. "Did you kill him?" he asked her, his word a blow. "Don't lie to us now."

Quinny hiccoughed, she looked desperately all around, she hiccoughed again. "Yas suh, I did," she admitted, bowed and humble; then in sudden pride her head lifted. "He needed killin' too!"

Mr. Chambers looked at Don. "Well, suh?"

Don said: "You've been very courteous, sir. I don't think she was too scared to say she didn't—if she didn't. I'm satisfied she killed him."

Mr. Chambers said urgently: "Why not go back to the house, let on you didn't wake up? Or what about Cash? He's hurt, maybe dying. You go take care of him, make him easy, see what he needs. You could do some good there. You can't, here."

Don wiped his brow again, frowning in some perplexity. "I wish I could explain so you'd all understand," he said, and smiled and said: "We're all of us, all of you, and me, we're caught in a hard pew. You're doing what you think's right. But I've got to do the same. Can't you see, Mr. Chambers, that I can't let you take this girl and hang her? The law freed her. I can't let you do it."

"Please, Cap'n, go on back to the house."

"I could never look anyone in the face again," Don insisted. "Why, I'd rather be dead."

"Glad to oblige," said Mr. Howard, behind him. Upon the one report followed quick another. Don dropped like a poled ox, and so did Mr. Howard; and Pink Chambers, his shotgun in his hand, leaped forward to kneel by Don's side. He saw that Don was dead and came to his feet, his eyes streaming.

"I was too slow!" he sobbed. Howard lay face down, his hands like claws to seize the earth, his revolver lying just beyond them. Pink flung his gun to his shoulder. "God damn you!" he cried. The heavy charge of buckshot pelted Howard's spine. Pink, forgetting that he had already fired one barrel, pulled the other trigger. Then he threw the gun aside and looked around and saw his father and went to him. He clung to his father's sleeve. "Pa?" He sniffled, drew his arm across his eyes. "Oh, Pa, he was a good man!"

Mr. Chambers said: "Pick up your gun, Pink. You'll need to clean it." To the others: "Bring the horses, boys."

One of the men still holding Quinny asked: "What about her?"

Mr. Chambers looked to where Don lay. "Let him have her," he said. "Let her go."

Quinny, free, vanished toward the cabins. Someone brought the horses, and Mr. Chambers mounted. "Sling Howard across his horse," he directed. "I'll lead him home. Pink, you coming?"

Pink shook his head. "I'll stay with him," he said. "I'll help Mr. Tremont carry him in."

Chambers turned, and the horsemen rode away. Pink stood waiting patiently beside his friend, and after a little, Mr. Tremont came out of the darkness to his side.

Trav and Lucy took Don's body the long journey home to Maine, and they laid him with his forebears in the little burying ground above the orchard, and stayed a few days with Pa and Aunt Maggie. When they were on the train, homeward bound, Trav said tenderly:

"I expect it's hard to leave him here."

"Oh, I'll be here with him," said Lucy. "And he'll be at Paradise with me. We'll never be separated now."

"Are you going to—hate everything down home?"

"I hate everything that's bad about it," she assented. "But Don wouldn't want me to come away, when there's so much there to do."

"More than any of us can ever manage, Honey," he warned her.

"Of course. But I've three children—it's really four, Papa, did you know—and all their children after them, and all their children forever, to finish whatever Don and I begin."

Postscript

Postscript

THIS NARRATIVE of corrupt Louisiana politics could be continued into our own time, but the more recent episodes are fresh in our memories. It should be remembered that Louisiana, during the Reconstruction period, was by no means a typical Southern state. As early as 1870, four of the seceding states had escaped the worst evils of carpetbagger rule, and others followed them. Either by taking advantage of a Republican split, or by the "Mississippi Plan," which was in some respects copied by Hampton's Red Shirts in South Carolina, and which involved rather a show of force than actual violence, each in turn achieved victory at the polls. Louisiana, where murder was repeatedly used as a political weapon, was the last Southern state to break free.

Louisiana's bloody record arose in part from the fact that New Orleans, with a population of around a hundred and seventy-five thousand, was not only by all odds the largest city in the South, but also the wickedest. To the early French and Spanish citizenry had been added flatboatmen, river pirates, gamblers, trappers, slave traders, adventurers, new-rich planters, Cajuns, Italians with their Maffia, and—during and after the War—thousands of Northern adventurers greedy for loot. "Free men of color" owned millions of dollars' worth of New Orleans real estate, and lived in a world apart, as did the old Creole aristocracy, and the aristocracy which had been created by ability and intellectual capacity.

Add to this mixture, inside and outside the city, the large number of men living on the starvation edge of miserable poverty, and over such a population set the former slaves as masters, and allow political tricksters, conscienceless adventurers and bigoted abolitionist churchmen to achieve control of these men newly free, and the results were probably inevitable.

A word or two of the years immediately following the period here recorded may be of interest. After the election of 1874, the Returning Board ruled that the Republicans had carried the state. This resulted, when the Legislature met, in a flurry of fisticuffs, and United States soldiers entered the House and forcibly ejected several Democratic members. General Sheridan, in military command of Louisiana, asked permission to treat the leaders of the White League as banditti— presumably intending to hang them. This provoked a storm of protest in North and South, and a Congressional Committee unanimously reported that the Conservative-Democrat party had won not only the 1874 election, but also the election of 1872, and that the Returning Board had distorted the result. They recommended that Democratic members of the Legislature should be seated, but since to rule that Kellogg had never been the legal Governor would inspire countless challenges of the validity of acts done by the Kellogg government, he was maintained in office for another two years.

The Legislature, while still controlled by the Republicans, had re-elected Pinchback to the United States Senate, but on March 8, 1876, he was finally denied a seat and presented with twenty thousand dollars to cover the expenses of his long fight for recognition. He continued active in Louisiana politics, as did Governor Warmoth. In December, 1874, the Governor, as a result of a letter he had written to the *Bulletin,* was attacked on Canal Street by D. C. Byerly, the *Bulletin* manager. Byerly struck the Governor over the head with a cane; they grappled and fell, and Mr. Warmoth drew a pocket knife and stabbed Byerly several times, as a result of which he died. The Governor, having acted in self-defense, was freed of blame. He made New Orleans and his plantation his home till his death in 1931.

The battle of the levee destroyed the Metropolitans as a political weapon. New Orleans was policed for a while by the citizens' soldiery, and during the subsequent siege of the State House and at the time of the capture of the Supreme Court buildings, the Metropolitans attempted no defense. Longstreet resigned as Adjutant General of the militia in December, 1874. He was a Levee Commissioner for another year or two, though seldom in Louisiana, and beginning in the summer of 1875 he made his home in Gainesville, Georgia. In 1878 he was appointed Supervisor of Internal Revenue; the next year he was named Postmaster at Gainesville; a year later he became Minister to Turkey, and during the rest of his life he held numerous appointive offices. Before the turn of the century, except in the Daughters of the Confederacy and other women's organizations, the bitterness against him in the South had largely healed.

Not till 1877 was the Radical hold upon Louisiana ended. The carpetbaggers' last flurry came when an all-Republican Returning

Board decided the election of 1876 in favor of the Republicans, seating Marshal Packard as Governor, and the corrupt and debauched Negro, Antoine, as Lieutenant Governor. But the Democrats refused to accept this decision, so once again Louisiana had two Governors. The White League armed six thousand men, and without bloodshed took possession of the city and of all the government buildings except the State House. But Grant ordered the army to preserve the *status quo,* and for four months Governor Packard with his government was a prisoner in the State House protected by the army but under constant watch by White League sentinels.

During this time the Packard Legislature elected former Governor Kellogg to the United States Senate, and though Grant, in the last days of his term, finally refused recognition to the Packard government, Kellogg after eight months of investigation and debate, was seated and served out his term.

In 1877, as an incident of the Presidential election, when Louisiana's electoral vote was needed to make Hayes President, a bargain was struck. When Hayes became President, United States troops were withdrawn from the Louisiana State House, and the White League promptly ejected Packard and all his adherents. Francis T. Nicholls, a Democrat, took Packard's place as Governor, and the White League, its work done, disbanded. White supremacy had been restored.